Bijoux

Dedicated to four loyal Musketeers -
K. "Lisette" Samuel
N. "Françoise" Haley
J. "Susanne" Murphy
K. "22" McGowan
as well as to -
My parents, Anne & Paul
whose true love gifted life,
and Dominick,
whose life gifts true love.

Copyright © 2002 Bovican Books
All rights reserved.

ISBN 1-58898-613-6

Bijoux

Bovican Books
Salem, Massachusetts

Bijoux

TABLE OF CONTENTS

PROLOGUE
Comaetho's Complaint IX
CHAPTER ONE
Children of the Virgin 1
CHAPTER TWO
Monsieur Noctambule 27
CHAPTER THREE
Division of the Houses 57
CHAPTER FOUR
Many Jewels 83
CHAPTER FIVE
Snake Eyes 109
CHAPTER SIX
Good-For-Nothing Rascals 139
CHAPTER SEVEN
Daughter of Taphos 165
CHAPTER EIGHT
Second Chances 197
CHAPTER NINE
Of Covenants and Kings 225
CHAPTER TEN
Poseidon's Cup 253
CHAPTER ELEVEN
Future Benefics 279
CHAPTER TWELVE
Royal Audience 303
CHAPTER THIRTEEN
Enter Amphitryon 335
CHAPTER FOURTEEN
Underworld 361
CHAPTER FIFTEEN
Electryon's Cattle 387
CHAPTER SIXTEEN
 Isle of Immortality 419

CHAPTER SEVENTEEN	
Secrets	445
CHAPTER EIGHTEEN	
Lost Kings Aplenty	473
CHAPTER NINETEEN	
Deadly Wagers	501
CHAPTER TWENTY	
A Grand Design	529
EPILOGUE	
Pallas Athena	559

PROLOGUE
Comaetho's Complaint

18. November, 1664

La Bastille
Bazinière Tower
Cell No. 12
Paris, France

"Marquise," a solicitation born of alchemy's aether urged, *"marquise, awaken. I have returned as once promised you. Was this moment not foretold? Arise and let us to the Isle of Taphos."*

"What?" I murmured, half-asleep, rubbing at eyelids still swollen from the recent shedding of innumerable tears. "Who goes there?"

No answer, no reply was forthcoming. A bad dream, I deduced. Nothing to fear, merely a phantom of slumber come to plague one being detained within a fortress whose walls had seen countless residents tortured 'ere the arrival of cell number twelve's most recent occupant.

Angry that an annoying fantasy had interrupted much-needed rest, I shifted position on an uncomfortable pallet in an effort to return to sleep. Facing a stony dunjon wall, the carved-out initials of a previous prisoner met with my view.

Tangible proof of another's silent suffering.

The pathetic monogram led me to wonder how my former patron and fellow inmate, Nicolas Fouquet, was faring. Did he pace a gloomy confine, anxiously awaiting to be sentenced by the Parliament? Or did he sit composing letters to friends abroad, confident that the judgment levied would be exile from France? Certainly he was awake, never one to scheme during the hours of daylight.

Poor Nicolas, once powerful Lord of Vaux; poor Bijoux, recently styled Marquise de Cinq-Mars. Each hoping and praying for miracles, neither naïve enough to believe a royal reprieve would be issued. How might proud Louis XIV forgive two subjects who had threatened to impede a crusade launched to claim that precious territory historians dub the Glory of Kings?

What a lamentable thing it is when men should rant against the gods and regard us as the source of their misfortune, when they themselves commit the transgressions which bring them to suffering and a fate unintended.

Springing to attention, I sat upright on the worn mattress that rested atop a solid, wooden slab. The surrounding darkness yielded no clues as to who had whispered in my ear. Yet, the silken tone was no stranger to memory, even if I had first heard it uttered more than sixteen years earlier. The same soft murmur, issuing from the mouth of the tormentor whom I had feared since childhood.

"Go away!" I screamed, frightened by the sound of ringing in my ears and the feel of gooseflesh on my forearms. "Leave me be! Have you not caused me enough pain, foul creature!"

"Prisoner number twelve, be still!" the Musketeer outside the barred door warned. "In the name of the king, I order you to silence, or else suffer the blast of my musket!"

"That matters not to me, sir. Better to perish at your hands than to be haunted by He Who Walks in the Night!"

Those words having scarcely passed from my lips, a most familiar scent permeated the space about the crude bedstead. The sweet smell of peonies mingled with the acrid stench of blood.

Human blood.

Then inexplicably, my hands seemed to become wet and clammy, my body shook from the fiercest of tremors. Wasting no time, I raced across the cold, straw-littered floor and held arms aloft in the direction of a window fashioned from three slits cut through stone some twenty-five French feet in thickness. 'Twas then, in the dim glow of an autumn Moon, I fancied to bear witness to a horrible sight: ten fingers dripping crimson, covered with what I was certain to be gore.

The ensuing shrieks of despair sent the Musketeer running to locate the governor of the Bastille, Monsieur de Besmeaux, the sole person in the world allowed to address me, according to his Majesty's pleasure. Sinking down to the floor while the sentry fled, I cared not what became of my person, so intent was I on wiping supernatural stains onto dirty hay, so close did I come to going mad.

> *The camp was won, and all in blood doth steep,*
> *The blood in rivers streamed from tent to tent,*
> *It soiled, defiled, defaced all the prey,*
> *Shields, helmets, armors, plumes and feathers gay.*

"Stop!" I begged of the mocking chant amidst uncontrollable sobs. "Look upon my disgrace! I have nothing to offer you—no favors, no influence. I have been reduced to the lowest of the low—denied my possessions, my titles, the love of my husband—I have lost everything! Have pity, leave me be!"

> *Thus conquered Godfroi, and as yet the Sun*
> *Dived not in silver waves his golden wain,*
> *The daylight served him to Jerusalem won*
> *With his victorious host to turn again,*
> *His bloody coat he put not off, but run*
> *To the high temple with his noble train...*

"No, you are too cruel, monsieur! Rob me of sweet light if you must, yet do not tease me with barbed rhymes concerning the Secret! I know what former ambition led to my ruin and injured those unfortunate ones known as my allies. I know, too, who you are—Noctambule—yet I shall not be forced to relive my mistakes and feel such great a misery before I should die!"

"If you call on me to aid you, I may be powerless to help."

"Be still! Where are you daemon? Show yourself to me, coward!"

"You will see me soon enough. Pass wisely the time remaining you, prisoner number twelve."

Before I was allowed the opportunity of an answer, the dunjon door swung open onto the near empty keep and a white-haired gentleman ventured to enter with reticence.

Leaving the Guard without, the man of fifty or so years clutched a shining lantern close to his neatly attired person as he glanced furtively about the keep. He stepped forward with vigor, however, when he caught sight of my form lying prostrate atop the floor.

"Bring in the prisoner's effects," he ordered in a no-nonsense tone. "Place the crate over there, by the bed. Good...good. Now leave us."

Two sentries, positioned at either end of an oversized traveling case, dutifully obeyed their commander. The pair was probably the same soldiers who maintained a watch over Monsieur Fouquet, I reasoned, especially since they had been brought in to view yet another who would remain cut off from humanity. I longed to ask them how well the former surintendant fared, but did not bother since such an inquiry would have been met with silence on both their parts.

"Madame, I am Monsieur François de Besmeaux, Governor of the Bastille and your sole contact with the outside world. Owing to the king's gracious pleasure, this portmanteau containing your belongings has been forwarded to my attention since your arrest and arrival here yesterday. The contents of said have been inventoried by me and a record of such goods has been duly entered into the official register of this institution. Should you have the misfortune to expire while a guest within these walls, the aforementioned property will revert to the possession of the State of France."

"More likely to you," I grumbled, having regained a modicum of composure.

"My wife, Madame de Besmeaux, shall attend to your

weekly toilette. You are not allowed to converse with any person here, nor they with you, and any requests shall be written out on parchment rag, provided at your own expense; correspondence which you will address to me and slide under this door here, understood?"

"How do you propose that I pay for my writing stuffs, monsieur, when I possess no coins?"

Besmeaux grimaced as he considered the weighty dilemma of whether or not he should answer my query directly.

"The prisoner will be presented with an accounting of her expenses incurred while at the Bastille when—and if—she is to be discharged from this fortress. Should her untimely demise precede release, any unpaid debt will be deducted from the value of her estate."

"I best not play the prodigal while here then, monsieur, for you are looking at one who finds herself in no better financial circumstances than does a pauper."

Besmeaux turned and pushed the door almost shut, leaving it ajar, instead. Stepping closer towards his charge, he bent over slightly when he was close to where I had propped myself up on an elbow and shined his candle next to my face. The jailer's appraising scrutiny closely examined the court day dress made up of golden lace from the Venetian district of Burano and pumpkin colored silk faille from the studio of the fashionable couturier, Monsieur Gautier.

"You sport a fine wardrobe, madame, clothes fashioned from quality materials costing in excess of twenty *livres* per ell, I wager. That asset alone, not to mention your jewels, of course, make you a valuable prospect. One who should be treated fairly by her keeper, *n'est-ce pas?*"

I stared up at him wide-eyed, shocked by his willingness to break the law if I would pay the price. But then again, to whom could I report his improper conduct? One did not need to possess a burgeoning intellect to ascertain that within the boundaries of the Bastille, M. de Besmeaux was the sole sovereign of its four tall towers and portcullis gates.

"Yes, I do believe that a former soothsayer to the more

privileged members of society might be worth treating with a special leniency, think you not, madame? Why, if you were to gift me one of the pretty stones contained in that box yonder—just one, mind you—I would be inclined to forward a message to one of your boon companions at court."

I remained silent.

"And should I receive a more intimate token, say, the invitation to spend an hour or so alone in the company of your lovely person, perchance," Besmeaux winked, "I guarantee that a representative of that circumspect society, known in former days by its membership as the Company, would be alerted to your whereabouts."

His coercive tactics sickened me, causing me to cringe visibly as a result. Afraid that he might try to take what he wanted by force, I backed away from the corrupt bureaucrat.

"Ah, I see," came the malevolent sneer of the ill-disposed, "my plain leather doublet and brown twill breeches do not appeal to a fine lady accustomed to the sateens and velvets of the popinjays who fancy themselves the king's gentlemen."

The slap that Monsieur François dealt was hard and stung at my cheek after the spittle sent flying in his direction hit a scuffed, silver-buckled shoe.

"Hiss at me, would you, eh? Take that, you uppity pretender, issue of a whore! I am worth over a million *livres*, girl, more than a million made in six years off of the likes of you."

"Then I would say, who is the prostitute, monsieur?" I laughed aloud, picturing Besmeaux dressed as a strumpet; his boudoir a locked room hidden away in the bowels of the prison where the governor took great pleasure in caressing gold pieces paid him by those desperate enough to consider buying a chance at much-longed-for freedom.

He would have struck me again; however, the sight of a crazed woman clawing streaks of blood onto her powdered face checked his wrath. Stunned, Besmeaux stared at me for a long pause, then frantically pulled me up by the elbows, bellowing out to his men for assistance.

"Run, fetch Madame de Besmeaux! Tell her to bring water and bandages...hurry!"

"How could you do this to me?" he lamented, beside himself at the thought of losing an inmate—a potential source of income—to a suicide. "The king will stage an inquiry if any ill befalls you while in my care, madame! His Majesty will place me under the severest scrutiny should you succumb to self-inflicted wounds while detained here...did you cut yourself, show me the spot now!"

"...the blood in rivers streamed from tent to tent," I half-sang, the recital issuing forth in a fit of delirium, "and soiled, defiled, defaced all the prey...shields, helmets, armors, plumes and feathers gay..."

"Do not die on me," he beseeched. "Compose yourself, madame! You are a marquise, for God's sake! Stop this rash display immediately! You are a noblewoman, a Cinq-Mars!"

"No," I cried out, struggling against his grip. "No, you are quite mistaken, monsieur. Have pity on me, for I am beyond redemption. I am Comaetho, daughter of the damned!"

Besmeaux hastily let go of me to make the sign of the clergy.

"The charges against you do include consorting with Satan as well as consulting the stars to plot treachery against our fair land, God have mercy on all our souls! Show me your wrists, heretic."

I was duly checked for injury and when no slashes were found, marched brusquely across the cell to the sole piece of furniture decorating the confine. Pushing me onto the rustic litter, the Governor stood back, regarding his new inmate with caution.

"This evil stigmata which you have conjured will be reported forthwith to the king. I, for one, shall not return to this place to consort with the likes of you in the future, witch. Should any harm befall my wife, who is a good woman and does not dabble in portents..."

"You are a veritable hypocrite," I scoffed. "They say that Monsieur Molière's character, Tartuffe, was modeled on the Prince of Condé's toady, the Abbé Roquette, yet truly, Besmeaux, I do believe you, yourself, to have been the playwright's inspiration!"

"Red-headed succubus," he spat back before leaving, "I should take great pleasure in watching you burn, though your rank and your father's name will merit you the ax, no doubt."

"Go to Hades," I laughed as the portal soon echoed with a solid thud and left me alone with sullied skin and a box full of unwanted souvenirs.

"Give my fondest regards to the Princes of Friendship, Astaroth and Asmodeus," I added as a bitter aside, ever mindful of the circumstances leading to my knowledge of daemonology.

A jumble of memories from long-forgotten days, some concerning that beautiful district where I had grown up in Paris alongside the Place Royale—the Marais—and some concerning a less charming locale located in the same capital, on the Rue St. Denis, caught me by surprise, causing fresh tears to dampen my eyes.

I *was* Comaetho of the bright and burning hair, and as she had suffered death at the hands of her royal lover, I, too, was destined to meet a violent end per my king's edict. Noctambule had been wrong to suggest an outing to the mythical Greek Isle of Taphos, for that same place could undoubtedly be charted as the Kingdom of France.

Such was the peculiar scene enacted last night, an odd tableau providing the sole diversion since being brought to the moat and drawbridge entrance of this old goal two days prior, late on the afternoon of November the sixteenth in the twenty-first year of Louis XIV's reign.

The official prisoner's stationery which receives the record of these incidents is of poor manufacture and difficult to write upon when using a pointed quill and watery ink, although M. de Besmeaux most certainly has charged a goodly tariff for the delivery of the supplies. Since the cost of the materials has no doubt been noted on the ledger page headed by the designation, Number 12, the sheets and the blue dye should not go to waste.

Also, composing a makeshift diary is preferable to contemplating the notion of sleep, for a dread fear of being haunted by a malevolent visitor between dusk and dawn's bleak hours compels me to remain awake and alert. Whether that supernatural power chooses to recite grim rhymes or torment a would-be victim by means of terrifying dreams, I know from personal experience the unforgettable horror either visitation is capable of producing in even the bravest of hearts.

Enough concerning the unfathomable, lest any future reader consider this author as having been better suited for admission to the lunatic asylum at Charenton than incarceration in the southwest tower of the Bastille.

An observation that returns my thoughts to the present moment.

Recent circumstances have moved me to consider that perhaps I should pen a memoir, a final testament to my family's downfall—an uncensored record of the events that led to and enabled the rise of France's latest Bourbon prince. More fascinating tales are oft' contained within the lines of a truthful story than in fantastic legend, and I am privy to an honest adventure in need of telling.

For I have seen the richest men in the world brought to their knees, have known the love of a true and gallant soul, have possessed the regard of the most stalwart friends imaginable and have been set upon by those base characters who would consider me the enemy.

And, lest critics accuse me of having committed the sin of omission, a strange creature has indeed walked in my presence: a man of supposed immortal properties who fancies the title Noctambule.

Not one of these singular things is separate from, or unrelated to, the Secret—that mysterious Philosopher's Stone of the Ages—whose definition has eluded plain language for centuries.

The Secret.

Men have killed in its name; died, too, protecting its safekeeping. Popes and princes have quaked at its mention; sinned greatly at its expense. The world wakes and toils and sleeps without a care for its existence, however the Secret is there, waiting, watching for those who would possess the key to its decipher.

No one dares speak of it outside the circle of Adepts, the Initiated; the masses remain ignorant of its influence in shaping the affairs of nations. Yet, I was rash enough to insist on discovering its guarded meaning, no matter the danger involved, to lift the veil draping its sacred countenance from ordinary view. Because of that relentless quest for knowledge and power, I find myself sequestered in the Bastille and am considered a traitor by the king. Allowed to converse with no one.

Yet, may the written word not speak, I wonder? Have anonymous quills not dared to contradict royal edicts heretofore? If one person would dare to break the Secret's ominous code of silence in the spirit of enlightenment, of reason, another might hear—and a secret is no longer a Secret once the enigma is disclosed.

Yes, I think I have struck upon a plan of action that involves regaining a sense of purpose. A mission offering shape and substance to an otherwise miserable proposition, destined to be lived out in a small room attended to by boredom. Simply put, I shall make a record of those events occurring prior to the confinement I now endure—Louis will not muzzle me in the end—and likewise I shall pray to that wise goddess, Athena, that the text will eventually be delivered into the hands of a receptive posterity.

I could go to my death comforted if I thought that another, unrelated soul might one day peruse the account of my short-lived drama and remark: *Such as she may have been—wicked or virtuous, contemptible or good—she related with veracity the circumstances of her era, concealing no crimes and adding no falsehoods. Such as she was, she declared it herself, and in honestly doing so, inspires forgiveness for her own grievous errors from those who are sincere.*

That task, then, will commence with the dawn of tomorrow's new morn, arriving during the mysterious auspices of the month of the Scorpion. Thus decided, much musing awaits me. Order need be imposed on numerous recollections; memories sifted; sweet and dangerous images made fresh and anew.

Only a physical proof of the king's justice or the return of that murderous revenant to these quarters will hinder completion of the project about to be commenced. Since I am not especially inclined to dwell on either distasteful judgment, I shall spend this evening in preparation, far from the warmth of the grate and in close proximity to the one window allotted me. After inhaling the chilled, November breezes blowing off of the river Seine, the scents carried here on those incoming currents should aid me in remembering the details concerning the history which transpired on the streets, within the habitats and about the environs of this city, my home.

Would that I might gaze out from this vantage point over the landscape of Paris instead of blindly settling for a waft of her perfume; however, the barred opening's height is barely accessible on tiptoe and then only when standing on the portmanteau as one might a stool. No matter. For when Luna has retired her dutiful watch and the Sun's rays appear rosy-fingered to assume their sentry in the sky, I shall reach up and push past the iron balusters a final *billet-doux* to the City of Lilies, a short note that will float slowly downwards to the Rue St. Antoine, a fond farewell to the fellow citizens from whom death or exile will separate me.

> *I am the cast-off astrologer of the King of France,*
> *A prisoner today — a madwoman tomorrow.*
> *French ladies and gentlemen,*
> *Pray to Pallas for the soul and the reason,*
> *Of one who was formerly*
> *The confidante of your master.*

Supposed luminaries of the French court, you, who have shared more with me than whispers, beware my pen, the mightiest of Athena Tritogeneia's swords.

CHAPTER ONE
Children of the Virgin

His father was the dour Louis XIII, King of France; mine, the high-spirited Henri, Marquis de Cinq-Mars, that king's lover.

His mother was the fair Anne, Queen of France; my own, the exquisite Marion Delorme, high priestess of the Parisian courtesans.

He was born in 1638, I in 1640, yet both on the same day, September the fifth. As did he, I came into this world with two teeth, though my gender was female and a forelock tinted ill-omened red.

He was christened Louis and called *le Dieu-Donné*, or God-Given; I, Bijoux, not one but many jewels that name's meaning. When people saw my teeth and hair, they wondered if my creator was a daemon.

The general populace of France in the year 1640 did not need convincing that superstition was to be regarded as Gospel by the Church and that the awesome powers of darkness were definitely to be feared. Marion was teased by her many admirers after my birth, for they were convinced that she had exposed her pregnant body to the Moon in order to produce a daemon child. I sorely wish that those men of rank had not mentioned my distinctive birthmarks to her; the gentlemen callers most probably gave the then devoutly Catholic lady some very dangerous ideas.

Louis, although born with teeth, was heir to the French throne and a much-awaited child. Considering that the royal parents had cohabited for twenty-three years in fruitless union, his arrival was a miracle, a sign that the nation had a future. No courtiers spoke of evil omens in Anne of Austria's presence, for she was convinced that her son had been sent from above to inherit a kingdom below which the Dauphin would one day rule by Divine right and with Divine approval.

I was, on the other hand, pronounced the illegitimate issue of the king's favourite, *Monsieur le Grand*, and of the latter's mistress, *Madame la Grande*, as Marion was dubbed during the course of her liaison with Cinq-Mars. Not that bearing a "love child" was an act of which to be ashamed. On the contrary, many nobles preferred their "natural" children to those born to them in wedlock.

Likewise, then, my fashionable parents saw my birth as living testament to the passion they shared, a passion that had led to my conception while they walked together one day in the peaceful forest at Versailles. The popular Marion did not mind the ensuing changes to her highly praised physique or the imposed confinement to her quarters that mothers-to-be suffered.

And she never once attempted to abort me as she had successfully managed to do with her other unwanted pregnancies in the past.

No, unfortunately for the one who writes this account, she was determined to keep the small life growing inside of her and young Henri proudly agreed. Despite the fact that many eligible ladies of high station were flinging themselves at his feet, Cinq-Mars scorned them all, preferring the company of the courtesan, Madame la Grande, whom he dreamed would soon agree to become his own marquise.

Not long before my birth, the two celebrated lovers secretly pledged their eternal troth to a priest, choosing to elope so that Louis XIII, who was wildly jealous of my mother, would not discover that the vows took place. If the wedding ceremony had been publicly announced, the king would have undoubtedly stripped Cinq-Mars of his exalted position, Master of the Horse.

The forbidden nuptials, therefore, were the irrational, impulsive act of a headstrong, nineteen-year-old boy and a cosseted, twenty-seven-year-old beauty. Why the pair risked the threat of royal displeasure I cannot say, for when Marion was in love she was famed for her fidelity. And one thing that was certain in everyone's mind, especially in the king's own, was that the most desirable woman in the land adored the very pretty Henri more than any other man alive.

Thus, both Louis Bourbon and I, Bijoux Cinq-Mars, were born to parents who longed for our arrivals. While the Dauphin was born into royalty, I was royally born—a great number of men from the king's court descended upon Marion's home located in the fashionable Parisian suburb of the Marais to witness her labor pains. Since most of the distinguished visitors had bedded my mother, thus contributing to her purse in the process, Cinq-Mars thought it only natural for his peers to be present at the laying-in. True, Henri had hoped for a boy, though when I finally appeared shortly after midnight on that September eve, he was so relieved Marion had delivered safely that the youth wept tears of joy before consuming much red wine with his compatriots in celebration of the event.

Of course, word of my birth reached the hunting lodge at Versailles, the monarch's private retreat, sometime near to one in the morning, thanks to the tireless efforts of Louis XIII's diligent spies. The distraught ruler cried out when he heard the bad tidings. A sense of betrayal permeated his very soul. To this day, I am convinced that the king never truly forgave Monsieur le Grand the sin of producing a child. To make love to a tart was one thing, to create a life with an infamous prostitute was quite another.

Perhaps that opinion explains why, just two years later, on the same day that both his son and I were born, Louis the Just chose to abandon Cinq-Mars when he begged for mercy from a prison cell in Lyons, charged with the serious crime of plotting treason.

Despite the marquis' boyish charms, neither Louis XIII nor his all-powerful minister, Cardinal de Richelieu, could overlook the favourite's involvement in a plot to kill the latter. One simply did not conspire with the king's brother and the Spanish ambassador to murder the most indispensable servant of the Crown and, in so doing, to turn the affairs of an entire nation topsy-turvy. One also most definitely did not behead one's own kin, a sibling who was a Prince of the Blood, one punished the other members of the cabal swiftly and mercilessly. Thus spoke the cardinal, true ruler of France, he himself born on September the fifth–yet another child of Virgo the Virgin.

The irony of the situation was that Richelieu had originally advised the king to take Cinq-Mars as a companion; however, once Henri had become accustomed to the sovereign's caresses and had secured a stellar place at court as a direct result of the convincing charade, he chafed at the cardinal's attempts to control his wild, flamboyant nature. Why should Marion Delorme not be his mistress, why should he not furnish his apartments with silver and fine furniture, what was wrong with being the best-dressed man at court or collecting precious stones? He was the Master of the Horse, not to mention a Marquis de France from an old, respected family, and no priest would cheat him of his prize.

Having led the king a merry chase for more than two years, my father began to scheme in 1640 to rid France of the despised Richelieu, the despot who had dragged the country through endless, costly wars and who, on a more personal level, threatened to jeopardize Cinq-Mars' relationship with the king. Henri began to spend less time with Marion and more time with Louis, whispering endearments concerning the untimely end of the Eminence Rouge. When the king feigned horror at such a suggestion, the twenty-year-old went to visit his lover's brother, the notorious troublemaker Gaston d'Orléans, who certainly did not blanche at Henri's perfidious talk.

Gaston was quite interested in seeing Richelieu fall; he was bored with his frivolous life at court and the scheme piqued his imagination. Having shared many confidences in the past with his sister-in-law, Queen Anne, d'Orléans knew that he had nothing to lose by getting involved in yet another dangerous intrigue. If unmasked, he might be reprimanded; if not, the cardinal would be gone for good.

The meddler went directly to his sister-in-law, Anne, beseeching the Spanish princess to help put Cinq-Mar's plan into action, especially since the former Infanta and Richelieu had been enemies for years. The queen agreed to participate, and the three unlikely confederates recruited more distinguished lords and ladies to their secret cause, forming a merry group who connived Richelieu's death cloak-and-dagger style for more than twelve months. Cinq-Mars was the least experienced of the conspirators at the risky strategies of palace intrigue, while his Eminence was a seasoned warrior who might be battle-scarred from previous skirmishes, yet, who emerged from each unpleasant encounter the victor. Blessed with an uncanny sixth sense, Richelieu seemed a priest of Satan, or so my father once declared.

Somehow, the cardinal did intuit that the assassin's blade was near to his heart. The wily campaigner ordered his best agents to suspect every courtier in their search for the traitors, whom he wagered would be found very close to the king's person.

In the end, it was Anne, the neglected wife, who gave-up the Marquis de Cinq-Mars. Considering the intimacy existing between the youth and her husband, a king with whom she had produced yet another son for France, who could blame her? Richelieu was brilliant when convincing the First Lady to cooperate with his investigation: produce the damning letters Anne had received from the other conspirators or be separated from her children forever. Following an agonizing pause, the queen capitulated. Richelieu gathered the information, watched and waited. He did not distress the king by telling him of the favourite's treachery, he did not allow Louis XIII the opportunity to weaken, to stall, to regret a decision which would still the most violent infatuation he had ever felt for another human being. The cardinal had his proof; he now prayed to God he would outlive the moment of its unveiling.

The noblemen were poised to strike, although the cardinal opted to approach the king when he was ready to do so, one month after the confrontation with Anne. Then, pretending sorrow, he showed Louis the missives and a copy of a treaty drawn-up between Spain, Gaston d'Orléans and the Marquis de Cinq-Mars, a treaty known forevermore as the Spanish Plot. Shocked beyond belief, the sovereign read and reread the documents with shaking hands. Made mad by despair, he accused Richelieu of having manufactured the evidence, of forgery, of paying for dubious confessions. Even though he had often quarreled with his love, Louis XIII could not believe Henri capable of such duplicity, so intent on grasping yet more power and prestige. Richelieu stood firm; Cinq-Mars and the other participants must be interrogated and if innocent, they would be released. At last the king relented and signed a warrant for the arrest of the listed accused, excluding, of course, his wife and his brother.

The scarlet robed minister then quit the earthly master's presence, leaving the king alone to ponder his own dismal thoughts. Louis XIII was weak, however, and was already regretting his role as Henri's potential executioner. He wrote his paramour an anonymous note of warning, handing it to a hastily summoned Musketeer with the command, "Find Monsieur le Grand and give him this!"

When the messenger was gone from sight, a saddened, middle-aged man paced his apartments in agony. All he could envision was Cinq-Mars losing his head over what had been conceived, no doubt, as nothing more than a silly prank. Even Anne and Gaston had encouraged the boy to stab Richelieu, according to the cardinal's reports. Yet, although the monarch abhorred his wife and mistrusted his brother, they were of his exalted family circle and he could not imprison either miscreant. And, because of his own relatives' self-serving, ungrateful actions, he would now be reduced to a most miserable humor with the removal of Monsieur le Grand.

The terrified ruler was not certain he could bear living without the demanding, yet scintillating, youth. That admission made, the King of the Franks weighed whether his chief minister was as indispensable as was claimed. But who should go—the cardinal or the confidant? Louis went to his chapel and prayed most heartily that Henri would escape Richelieu's Guard.

Cinq-Mars was dining at the Inn of the Golden Lion when a stranger approached and thrust a piece of crumpled paper into his hand. Perplexed, he opened the message to read: *Your life is in danger*. No signature, no seal. Not waiting for an explanation, the marquis fled to the nearest city gate in Paris, but it was locked, as were all the others. Although he was afraid and fearing the worst, at least the fugitive did not venture to Marion's salon, for Henri knew Richelieu's soldiers most probably awaited him there.

Deciding on the address of an ex-mistress named Madame de Sousac to be the best hiding place, Cinq-Mars cloistered himself with that lady until he was discovered a day later during a house-to-house search. He was duly arrested and conducted to the prison of Montpelier where the once proud Master of the Horse plaintively asked an assembled crowd, "Must a man lose all at twenty-two?"

Marion Delorme heard the devastating news while at home and she laid hold of a large kitchen knife, furiously stabbing an oak dining table. Supposedly she vowed, "If he dies, they die," without uttering one sob, her voice taking on a regal, imperious tone. No one who overheard the threat might have guessed at the serious intent of the courtesan.

Of course I do not remember any of this sad tale, being but two years old in 1642 when the events occurred. Yet, I do recall hearing the story of Cinq-Mars again and again while growing up in Paris not far from the Palais Royal where most of the drama had transpired.

A legend developed around Monsieur le Grand, so cruelly taken while still in his prime, at the apex of his stunning career.

Naturally, Richelieu's judges found the favourite guilty along with the friend, François-Jacques de Thou, a young law student who had been coerced into carrying damning communiqués to the queen against his better judgment. The trial held for the pair managed to drag on for a week, until the morning of September the twelfth, when Cinq-Mars and de Thou were pronounced guilty of conspiring to kill his Eminence, Cardinal de Richelieu, and of treason against the State of France. Both were sentenced to die on the block that very day, for as the cardinal had commented at the trial's onset, "Time is pressing; delays are unacceptable."

The Scarlet One feared, even trembled at the possibility that the sentimental Louis might change his mind and pardon Cinq-Mars at the last moment. Plus, the threat of other nobles taking up arms and rallying to save the Master of the Horse was a consideration to bear in mind. De Thou's brother had already raised a force of thirty horsemen who were lingering near the prison in Lyons where the two unfortunate captives had been transferred. The Bishop of Toulon, as well, a relation of the marquis, was petitioning the king for a royal warrant of remission.

Absolution never came.

Instead, my father was decapitated in Lyons that afternoon on the Place des Terreaux, a large audience in attendance. The chroniclers insist he spoke brave words, impeccably attired in one of his famous dark red suits of Dutch cloth, noble and eloquent to the end. The executioner clipped a lock of his victim's shiny, auburn curls and sent them to Marion via Richelieu's own courier; perhaps as a courteous gesture, perhaps as a warning. Oblivious to the intended message, the unofficial widow cherished the token with as much fervor as that of a holy relic, depositing the strands in a golden box of great value.

Cinq-Mars' family was not accorded the same respect, however; the ancestral estate at Chilly was burned to the ground on the day the heir died, only two once-proud towers left standing. Even the trees were cut down and a strange pillar of brick fashioned in the style of the ancients, decorated with twelve shields boasting mystical images, was defaced. Considering the scale of the destruction, why the cardinal spared me, his enemy's only progeny, is a riddle I have often considered.

Marion realized had she herself not been Richelieu's mistress shortly before she had met her beloved Henri, she too may have been arrested as a conspirator in the Spanish Plot. Yet, that admission, in the face of being left alone with no support for either herself or her small child, did little to cheer Madame la Grande and she begin to hate. She contemplated various ways to avenge her departed lover, including the deaths of Louis XIII and Cardinal de Richelieu. Marion did not fear either, for they were both tired, old men. She had vowed, too, that if Henri were executed, that the two would die.

Thus, the vengeful queen of the courtesans resolved to curse them together, the pair of merciless bastards who had taken away the marquis. A rumor of what words the king had spoken when informed of the traitors' deaths reached her ears, and she screamed that she would murder him with her own hands, if needs be. Evidently, Louis had been playing chess with Richelieu when told that Cinq-Mars was gone, and he nonchalantly remarked to his advisor, "I should like to see Monsieur le Grand's face now!"

Unknowingly, those glib words signed Louis XIII's own death warrant, as far as Mademoiselle Delorme was concerned.

The permanent absence of Marion's spouse caused her to readily understand that a new benefactor, someone able to keep her in the lavish style for which Monsieur le Grand had so generously provided, was needed. In our part of town, the Marais, mother held court at her own elegant, glittering salon, the most fashionable in Paris. Attracting a new suitor would not be difficult for the temptress of men's hearts; a line of hopefuls had formed outside our door on the day Cinq-Mars had died. And the gorgeous creature smiled when she saw them. Because of her seemingly callous attitude, the citizens of Paris thought their notorious queen unmoved by her Henri's fate.

Unseen by others, Marion raged inwardly and the greater her hatred for the two most powerful men in Europe, the more beautiful she became. Her loathing cast a radiance upon her visage that dazzled many. Yet, Marion was not flattered by her admirers' praises, she seldom read the poetry dedicated to her magnificence. No, she was intent on revenge and ignored all those except the few who could be useful to her plan. She turned down vast sums if the gentleman offering was not influential at court or possessed unfettered access to a great fortune. Madame la Grande had lived for love only once and she was not about to make that mistake again. She would not be denied a second time.

A month of careful selections was required for Marion to become the mistress to a very powerful, very devious finance minister named Monsieur d'Emery. Meeting the important man had posed no problem considering mother's popularity. The former provincial had lived in Paris for six years and having known or bedded the more illustrious men of her day, she was not wanting for contacts or connections. Most any desire could simply be had by hinting at, or outright asking for, a particular boon from one of the swains who invaded the salon on a nightly basis. The marquise let her wishes be known to all; whomever delivered the best was accordingly rewarded. Little prompting persuaded a friend to invite a friend named M. d'Emery, who, upon entering the salon for the first time on a crisp, October night, was greeted by general revelry: drinking, dancing to the strains of a lute, fine food laden on side tables. Mademoiselle Delorme's effusive manner attracted his gluttonous spirit—finance ministers were never known to lack for creature comforts.

Marion caught sight of the illustrious, albeit portly, financier, and she flushed with triumph. Her eyes sparkled gaily, she loosened her red-gold tresses so they might spill seductively over her bare white shoulders. Slowly she moved towards her prey, slowly she evaluated the man without his knowing. *Yes*, she thought, *he is the one*. Not hesitating, she touched his shoulder from behind; d'Emery turned to gaze dumbstruck at the incredible beauty.

"Monsieur d'Emery, I am honored to receive you in my humble salon," Marion demurred. "To think you would deign to visit *me!*"

D'Emery was immediately bewitched by his hostess' obvious charms. Words failed him, I am told. He kissed a gloved hand in devout adoration.

"Now I understand, mademoiselle, the story I heard of late," he said upon straightening his posture. "I was informed you recently visited a certain judge, Monsieur de Mesmé, on behalf of your brother who had been imprisoned, I believe, for some small debt."

"Yes, that is so, monsieur."

"And until tonight, I could not understand how esteemed a gentleman could free a man on the pretext that he had gazed upon your form!"

"Truly, monsieur, following our brief interview, his exact words to me were, *Might it be true, mademoiselle, that I have lived to this moment without seeing you?*"

Several eavesdroppers cheered aloud in agreement with the judge's excellent verdict. Marion curtsied to them, displaying a bosom shown off to perfection by a very low-cut, gold colored bodice. The fetching minx turned to d'Emery. He regarded her with longing before replying, "Perhaps mademoiselle would be kind enough to gain my freedom, also?"

"I am not a cruel jailer, monsieur," she laughed. "I do accept bribes."

"Anything. Ask and I shall exert all my powers to please your smallest caprice."

Marion smiled, fingers soon entwined around d'Emery's own. "I would like," she began in a normal tone that finished in a whisper so close to his ear he could smell the scent of her musk perfume, "to make the acquaintance of Monsieur Bouvard."

"The king's physician?" he queried softly, as if speaking to Richelieu himself.

"Yes," she sighed. "My health has been weakened by a certain tragedy just transpired not a month ago and I fear for my heart's sake, monsieur. I may die if I do not see the best doctor in the land."

D'Emery saw the tears forming in Marion's huge, hazel eyes and he was moved.

"Monsieur Bouvard will come here and attend to your lovely person as soon as I may arrange the visit," he promised. "A small request, Mademoiselle Delorme, which is easily accomplished. Do you wish to test me further?"

"You are too kind, monsieur. I would ask you one last favor; however, it concerns a most delicate subject, one I cannot discuss before ears other than your own."

Marion's look was furtive. Deciding to seize the opportunity to be alone, d'Emery motioned to a room adjoining the main salon: Madame la Grande's private chamber, the notorious Sanguine Room, decorated exclusively in blood red tones and the place where lovers were entertained in private.

Not pausing for a moment, the *grande horizontale* swept across the crowded reception hall and entered the dimly lit *sanctum sanctorum* with d'Emery in tow, a locked door separating them from the remaining guests. He stayed with her the entire night until dawn, when, utterly exhausted, a nonetheless jubilant finance minister stumbled out to an awaiting carriage.

Never before had d'Emery known such pleasure and he was not a young man. Likewise, Marion was pleased with her fresh victory, for in her hand she held a card bearing a priceless piece of information: the name and address of the most renowned poisoner in Paris, the Abbé Guibourg.

Three weeks following the conquest of d'Emery, my nursemaid much later confided to her charge that Madame la Grande ventured beyond the lovely Marais district to a somewhat seedy part of Paris located on the Rue St. Denis. She traveled over the slime-covered streets in a brand-new carriage given to her by the grateful financier who had managed to exclude all other rivals by way of the taxpayers' pockets; the monies collected from them were often used by d'Emery to augment his own vast fortune.

Marion received many a gift from the financier, no matter how costly or extravagant the presentation. Jewels, horses, expensive fabrics, a new pair of gloves delivered daily for the spendthrift mistress—all were presented by the lover, although charged to the account of the people. Madame la Grande expected to be pampered and fussed over. She was worshipped, and it was only fitting and proper, considering that she was said to be the greatest beauty in all of France. The courtesan chuckled softly to herself when she reflected on how a handful of gold *louis* could help one assuage many hurts and brighten an otherwise dreary day.

The marquise was especially thrilled on that November afternoon, since the plan for the disposal of her foes was progressing far better than she had originally anticipated. She especially relished the thought of the cardinal gasping for his final breath, imagining a slow, agonizing end for the one whom she was convinced was a vicar of evil. Not to mention that Richelieu had also been terribly stingy when she served as his mistress. "A cardinal, believe me," she once confessed to an inquisitive Cinq-Mars, "is not so grand when he no longer wears his red hat and scarlet robes." Madame la Grande thought herself destined to finish the conspiracy her husband had begun.

A coach attended only by a driver halted before the address d'Emery had dared give Marion in his haste to bed her. The marquise alit gingerly, unassisted, having left her regular lackeys at home. She was somewhat embarrassed to be seen on the Rue St. Denis; thankfully she had been wise enough to don the velvet mask which ladies of quality sported on such excursions, so that the dust from the road would not dirty their perfectly painted faces. Hopefully, no one would recognize the lips that had kissed so many prominent mouths as belonging to such a celebrated visage.

Still on tiptoe in order to spare the soles of her costly slippers from the filthy cobblestones, the determined woman knocked boldly on Guibourg's door. It opened swiftly. A man wearing black, lace-lined robes and red shoes ushered her into a modest, though tidy, room hung with dark tapestries and accentuated by heavy, leather upholstered furnishings. Nine black tapers, lit and displayed courtesy a silver candelabra, graced a nearby side table. One wall was painted with strange-looking celestial symbols. A chalice, a plate holding communion wafers and a small bowl of red wine were set out on the same makeshift altar as the menacing display of dripping, ebony beeswax.

The Abbé Guibourg was dressed in the alb, stole and maniple of a priest. He appeared to be the same age as Marion and was not an unattractive man, though not as finely wrought as had been Cinq-Mars. His dark beard was closely trimmed, his brown eyes intensely bright, his tall frame well kept, his demeanor arresting.

Madame la Grande found herself strangely drawn to the renegade priest, to the outcast of a faith she had once believed in sincerely.

"Mademoiselle, welcome to my temple," Guibourg intoned, breaking through any reverie. "I trust you will be comfortable during your stay, despite the humble surroundings."

The guest waived one hand nervously in the air. "I did not expect the Palais Royal, monsieur. Your lodgings are adequate."

"Did you bring the fee?" His question was abrupt, but not rude. The abbé, like the lady standing before him, was very much sought after. They were, the two of them, akin in many ways.

"Here, monsieur, this should suffice," Marion replied, handing Guibourg a leather pouch containing a veritable treasure of three gold coins. The good-looking abbé grinned.

"Mademoiselle, your generosity overwhelms me," he gushed. "Now, to begin, please sit and tell me your ends so we may progress to the appropriate means."

Marion chose an armchair situated near to the lit and reassuringly warm hearth. Flaunting her calculated skill, she pushed back the cowl of a fine wool cape, exhibiting the famed, copper mane. She then dramatically untied the velvet mask with a flourish, allowing the cover to fall to her lap.

Guibourg, completely disarmed, gasped with delight. The tales were true, for Marion Delorme was certainly the reincarnation of that ancient Assyrian queen, Semiramis, who had not only founded Babylon, but whose pulchritude and carnal appetite were also of mythic proportions.

The abbé fell to his knees, overcome with lust for his customer. Crawling over to where the lady reposed, eyes downcast, he wrapped strong arms around legs hidden by the three skirts women of quality always wore: the *secret*, the *rascal* and the *modest*.

Marion, usually so coy, felt a burning in her cheeks, a desire to lift Guibourg from the floor and acquaint him with the specialties of her profession. Instead, collecting her wits, she reached out and touched the abbé's head, as if bestowing a blessing upon a supplicant. Quietly she commanded, "Monsieur, remember your station."

Guibourg released her reluctantly and, with a shamed look upon his face, stood and made for the ritual table, his back to the beautiful courtesan. Again he asked, "What do you desire from this meeting, Mademoiselle Delorme?"

"First, abbé, be advised that I am the widow of the Marquis de Cinq-Mars; you may address me either as *Madame la Grande* or *marquise*."

"As you wish, madame," he parried.

"Secondly, I understand that you enjoy a certain reputation for casting spells and mixing powders without peer in Paris. I have heard say that for much less than three gold *louis*, monsieur, you have removed disagreeable husbands, rival mistresses, even unwanted children from their mothers' wombs. Since I have been assured that you are a sorcerer *par excellence*, I bring you a request worthy of your talents, abbé."

Marion paused so that the priest might absorb her praise, then added, "I wish the death of Cardinal de Richelieu 'ere the advent of the New Year."

Guibourg spun around, an expression of marked interest infusing his distinctive features. He looked Marion up and down, from head to toe, with an estimated zeal.

"Fine. Please realize, marquise, that such strong magic cannot be accomplished with aids as trifling as petty spells or silly potions. We must conduct a *Messe Noir*."

"Excuse me, abbé, I do not comprehend your meaning."

"A Black Mass, marquise, a direct invocation to Satan for the fulfillment of any request."

"Does your ritual work mischief?"

"Always, madame."

Marion was momentarily silent and shifted her weight in the chair. Her supple curves were not unnoticed by Guibourg who devoured the luxurious sight of her body in a sensuous stare. D'Emery was a foolish man to trust him with so inviting a visitor.

"Marquise, may I know your pleasure?" his voice was low, intoxicating.

Marion liked the priest's sense of presence, his obvious seductive nature. She did not need persuading.

"Do the Mass," she ordered.

Guibourg nodded in assent. Returning to her side, he touched her face gently, in a reassuring way.

"You must not be afraid, marquise. Now, again, repeat your intent to me."

"I ask that the death of Cardinal de Richelieu occur by year's end and also that the king, Louis XIII, may fall ill and be taken to his grave."

"Marquise, that requires a separate Mass. We shall start with the cardinal—you may return for the king if you are pleased. Do we agree?"

The client shrugged her shoulders and looked away from Guibourg

"May I make one additional request?"

Smoldering eyes then locked onto Guibourg's, they pleaded with an urgency he could not mistake.

"If it is not too great. Be careful, though, and think before you ask, because you alone must live with the consequences."

The alluring woman did not look away. "Tell your Lord and Master to send me a man capable of satisfying my longing, which has grown unbearable owing to my husband's recent demise."

"That may be arranged," the abbé promised confidently. "Are you prepared to do as I say?"

"Entirely. I am your servant, monsieur."

"Good. Please disrobe."

Marion turned her back to him, not perturbed by the condition.

"Unlace me."

Silently and with practiced dexterity, Guibourg removed her clothing. He had determined to take her by the end of the ceremony, though the sight of her trembling, naked limbs near convinced him to amend his plans.

The abbé led the charming acolyte to a low pedestal, cushioned in plum brocade, located close to the table displaying the components of the *Messe Noir*. A frightened, yet curious, Madame la Grande could sense that the priest had oft' performed the same rite in the past, no doubt for other quaking women. Partly she hated herself for wanting the stranger of ill repute, but moreover she saw in Guibourg an opportunity to quell her needs without fear of reproach.

She would have to wait before succumbing to wanton lust, however; especially since she was to return for another performance when the king's turn came. Marion did not intend to give the handsome prelate what he wanted until her original aims had been achieved.

The sound of Guibourg's voice interrupted her thoughts.

"Please lay your back on the pillow, marquise. Yes, good; drop your head back like so, allow your legs to fall freely."

Once draped across the pedestal, body stretched taut, certain a still-trim figure inspired visions of conquest in the abbé's mind, Marion closed her eyes tightly. She shook her head to allow her tresses to fall almost to the crude wood floor and was surprised to feel her fingernails digging into the rich material upon which Guibourg had placed her.

"We shall now begin," the priest stated in a serious manner, then commenced in a loud, deep tone, "Astaroth and Asmodeus, Princes of Friendship, accept this sacrifice of human blood. In exchange for this token of respect, grant Marion, Marquise de

Cinq-Mars, a petition: firstly, the continued patronage of M. d'Emery; secondly, a gentleman fit to still her raging passion; thirdly, and most importantly, the death of Armand-Jean du Plessis, named Cardinal de Richelieu, Prime Minister of France. May it please You to take him from our midst before the arrival of the New Year and thus favor Your devotee with a sign of Your omnipotence, mighty Princes of Friendship!"

Guibourg reached for the chalice by the candles, filled it with what Marion had thought was wine and proceeded to rest the vessel alongside her stomach. Taking a wafer, he pressed it to her lips, then added it to the contents of the cup.

"Hear this incantation, take pleasure from Your servant, Marion Delorme, who drinks the blood in obedience to You."

Marion's eyes flew open, too late she realized that Guibourg was raising her head to receive the silver goblet. Revolted, she attempted to turn away from him but the abbé was insistent.

Still-warm liquid passed into her mouth; she tried to swallow, coughing back half onto herself. The taste was foreign, indescribable and definitely not of the vine.

"Astaroth, Asmodeus, our ritual is now complete. True Princes of Friendship, look down upon Your daughter Marion and find her worthy of this feast. Observe Your devoted child and find her pleasing. Watch her lay her body at Your feet, a humble gift intended for the Great Spirits who have no peer."

Holding the chalice aloft, Guibourg dipped two fingers into its mixture and dabbed Marion on the breasts, staining them red. Putting the cup aside, he bowed low to the candles and extinguished them one by one with his breath. Then he rang a tiny bell in closing. The Black Mass was finished.

Marion slid down, stopping when her feet touched the floor and she was able to stand. The abbé noticed that his client was shaking and he covered her with the cape she had earlier discarded.

"That was a vile thing to do," she declared, near to spitting venom. "Fetch me some wine."

"Vile, but effective, marquise." Guibourg located a decanter and cup from a nearby cabinet, poured a drink and handed it to her. "To kill the king, we may need to take stronger measures."

"Such as?"

"A human sacrifice would do nicely, but a dangerous move," he admitted. "Definitely a defilement of some sort will be needed. Be of good cheer, what we did today was strong enough for the cardinal. We shall soon harvest the fruits of our labors."

Guibourg moved closer, parting the cloak so that Marion's breasts jutted beyond the fabric. His gaze was appreciative, almost tender, most certainly respectful.

"The time has come for me to test your resolve, madame. Let us see if I am the gentleman intended to bring you the ecstasy you crave, if my offering might compel you to cry out the name of Baphomet while you surrender yourself wholly to glorious sinning."

Guibourg's hand travel the length of her torso until he heard Marion gasp, for the worldly marquise was unaccustomed to subtle technique. The priest was an expert lover, as well.

Urgency gripped at her, an overwhelming surge that compelled the widow to press against the conjurer's finely woven vestments and fling her arms about his neck.

The sensual scene inspired the abbé to accord his lover great honor, no less than had he been in the presence of Lilith, queen of the daemons. Lifting his robes, he edged up slowly between smooth thighs. Marion urged her paramour to be bold, pulling him closer to his prize. The priest needed no further persuading and flesh soon met with flesh, bringing Guibourg to near abandon.

Yet, before he would succumb, the abbé was determined to break the marquise's haughty spirit, should it take him all the night to claim his conquest. Again and again he advanced his frontline, refusing to retreat as the vanquished screamed a promise to allow the soldier of Ares into her bed forever. Those words renewed Guibourg's vigor and the altar of evil shook with the tremors of a furious passion.

Marion's head arched, causing masses of curls to tumble from the cushion and hips swayed to the rhythm of the abbé's solicitations. Guibourg felt the aftermath in his loins, comparable to no elixir, more powerful certainly than the strongest potions he designed. The inveigler grinned with satisfaction. He decided to take Marion to his bed and held her to him closely.

"Wrap your legs about me," he instructed.

An astonished woman did as she was told, finding herself being carried to a chamber housing a massive four-poster bed draped in black sateen. A small light burned-out in its sconce, but the glow was strong enough to cast a shadow of entwined limbs onto the wall opposite the trysting place. Comfortably situated in his erotic lair, Guibourg's prowess became so defiant that Marion became frightened and considered halting the union. Yet, each time she made an effort to speak, the abbé stifled her words with an insistent, forceful embrace.

The veteran enchantress fell victim to her mage's thrall and allowed him every familiarity, making his exploration of her person complete. Smooth material swirled between her legs. Guibourg's lips mouthed an imprecation against all rivals on her skin. One of his hands toyed with her hair. The other lingered in that region most men ignored. For three hours the pair remained thus occupied. Daylight had departed by the time the priest was finished.

The marquise slept, contented and at peace. She awoke later that same evening to find the abbé lying next to her, intently studying the relaxed expression on his lover's face.

"You are divine," he admitted. "I never thought a woman so capable of perfection."

Marion smiled. She found it refreshing to be the surfeited party in an exchange of intimacies.

Her eyes then rested on Guibourg, for he had disrobed and, like herself, lay exposed on the bed. Muscular legs and a chest covered with fine, dark hairs commanded her attention. The marquise conceded that she would not be quitting the house of daemons before sunrise. Gladly, her chosen work provided funds to maintain a household staff, plus a nurse for the little girl, Bijoux. She was free to remain with the priest for an extended consultation.

Marion was soon astride her satyr, silently entreating her own charms to imbue the virile abbé with the fortitude of a Hercules. Redoubling his efforts, Guibourg reduced his partner to near lunacy. Madame la Grande collapsed, begging for a show of mercy.

The abbé left the room, returning with the elegant velvet mask, a silken cord and a vial filled with red powder. Marion was too spent to move. Yet, she was soon posed in a kneeling position, her two finely-boned wrists lashed together and tied to a carved wooden poster. Eyes covered, the sound of the priest pouring water or wine was all she was able to detect. The woman did not see a potion carefully mixed into burgundy, which Guibourg shared with a bound and alluringly disguised marquise.

"You are very strange, monsieur," she confessed. "Does this practice arouse you?"

Hands firmly planted on her waist from behind, Guibourg replied without speaking. Marion was tingling with fresh anticipation and the wine was rushing hot pulses throughout her body.

"Have you poisoned your captive, monsieur?" she asked with mock alarm.

"Why would I destroy this personification of debauchery?" he quipped. "You are a masterpiece, madame, a joy to behold. I merely added an aphrodisiac to the drink, a powder to increase our stamina and add spice to our couplings."

Marion's ardor was peaked well beyond normal.

"What is in your draught, Guibourg? The sensation is amazing."

The abbé laughed aloud. "Do not tempt me, madame, for the ingredients are well-guarded."

"You may trust me. I promise to tell no one," she vowed. "In fact, I shall send you clients, monsieur, rich men and women who will pay much for your philters."

"Will you return to me, as well, marquise?"

"Will your services be the same, abbé?"

Guibourg bit playfully at the nape of Marion's neck. She marveled at his constant attention.

"Might we never repeat this sweet sorcery?" she mused.

"I have many doses, madame. My recipes are foolproof."

"You will not reveal your powers to me?"

"Do not ask again. Anger not the Princes of Friendship 'ere the cardinal's death."

Marion did not respond. Instead, she yielded to the force of the dose coursing through her veins, for the araroba the abbé had prepared was pure wizardry, and she was glad of it.

Guibourg released a willing slave from the bondage of the tasseled rope when he deemed his new servant conquered. The domino concealing half the prisoner's face was stripped off and she slumped gratefully onto plump pillows spread about the comfortable pallet.

"Rest," he urged. "I have matters to attend to before the cock crows."

"At this hour?" the marquise asked, half-drugged.

"Be still," Guibourg ordered. "I shall wake you at dawn."

The abbé donned another alb and returned to the living area of his quarters, adding a log to the dying flames in the hearth. He relit the ebony colored candles that burned bright blue due to the sulfur used in their crafting, and then made his way to a cupboard located at the far end of the room.

Removing a key from his pocket, the priest opened the storage chest and carefully withdrew a large book bound in leather more reminiscent of an animal's pelt than its hide. He lifted the unusual cover of the text to reveal its title page; in his hands he held a translation of an ancient grimoire known as *The Key of Solomon the King*.

An acquaintance, the Schoolmaster Duprat, had located the rare tract in the library of a patron. After a substantial sum had been exchanged between teacher and scoundrel, the volume miraculously found its way to the Rue St. Denis.

Guibourg consulted the precious manual at length. Incantations, exotic talismans and careful instructions were absorbed by his keen eye until he was near to dozing off. Then the abbé returned *The Key of Solomon* to its hiding place and fastened the latch anew. He collected a clean sheet of vellum, a quill pen and the bowl of blood employed earlier in the *Messe Noir*. Sitting at a desk that he wisely drew closer to the fire, Guibourg took in hand the writing instrument he then dipped into red liquid. Words appeared on the page in a fluid hand.

Soon finished, the abbé read the document with a serious air. He was pleased with his handiwork and at last rested peacefully. The priest stirred, though, when the clock struck four in the morning. Time was passing and he and Marion had business to conduct prior to the Sun's rising.

The convert did not rouse easily. Still tired from the potion and from the events of that afternoon, Marion only listened half-heartedly to Guibourg's coaxing to awake and to dress. She attempted to ignore the pestering accomplice, yet when she grasped the seriousness of his resolve, she obeyed. Soon she would be home where she would not be harried. Guibourg might be an adroit lover, however his social graces decidedly lacked polish.

Because the marquise required more sleep, she was not in a pleasant mood as the abbé assisted her with her toilette. Once properly re-laced, re-coiffed and re-shod, he led her from the bedchamber back to the scene of their introduction. Seating the weary woman at his workstation, Guibourg produced the parchment with its crimson script. She regarded it with disdain; no doubt the heretic was attempting to blackmail or otherwise entrap her.

"What is this?" she questioned, annoyed.

"A contract, madame. You must read it aloud and sign where indicated in order for the powers of darkness to guarantee the cardinal's ruin."

"Be serious, Guibourg. First a Black Mass, then your love potion, now an oath of some kind? Really, you must be mad!"

"Read it and sign, or never see me again."

Marion reluctantly turned her attention to the agreement.

I, Marion Delorme, do this day enter into a pact unto death with the Princes of Friendship, Astaroth and Asmodeus, she began. *I promise my allegiance to the Grand Master of Baphomet, Abbé Guibourg, and also declare my unswerving devotion to the Lord of the World, the one whom we call Lucifer. With this pledge, I forevermore refute the Holy Catholic Church and its agents, I deny the rites of the sacred Mass and I shall recognize neither the Host nor the Blessed Sacrament for as long as I shall live. I also agree to dedicate my children to the glories of Lucifer and to raise my offspring in accordance with Satan's malevolent ways. In exchange for this vow of complete subservience to the Princes of Friendship, all my petitions will be granted and my enemies destroyed. Written and signed on the twenty-second day of November, 1642.*

My mother threw the page onto the desktop, recoiling from Guibourg's conditions in horror.

"No!" she exclaimed. "Are M. d'Emery's coins not good enough for you, abbé? Did my body not bring you pleasure? Take the money and the favors, too; however, my soul will not be bartered on any account. That is too steep a price to ask and I shall not pay it. I must bid you *adieu*."

She rose from the seat to go although Guibourg gripped at her arm hard. The pressure from his fingers made Marion wince in pain. She attempted to pull away, but was held firmly in place.

"How fast you forget," he sneered, "that not long ago your naked body was a living altar dedicated to vile daemons, blood offerings and a desecrated Host. Did you think that a game, marquise? You have already proclaimed yourself a disciple of wickedness and are therefore obliged to seal the declaration with your blood. Give me your hand."

"Stop!" she cried out in fear. "Leave me be, Guibourg!"

The abbé was not to be deterred. Despite Marion's struggle, he managed to pick up a letter opener and to still one of her hands. A well-aimed jab broke the skin of a finger, drawing drops of the life force to its surface.

A not-so-grand madame watched as puncture was pressed to vellum. She saw the dark stain her imprint subsequently made, and quaked.

"Forgive my brusque manner, marquise, but it was essential that you agree to the terms. So," he added as he held her tightly to him, "have you recovered from your fright?"

"Yes, although I think it best if you call my carriage."

"As you wish," he replied. "It would also be best if you were not seen leaving here, of course."

He handed her the traveling mask. Marion was safely incognito before the two went out into the street.

"God bless you, my child."

"And likewise, you, abbé."

They said nothing more. The door to Marion's vehicle shut after full skirts. She rapped on the roof of the coach with her slender walking stick to indicate that the driver could begin the journey back to the Marais. The light of day was filtering over the city of Paris and she wished to be abed.

Although she might have been cheered by the deafening noise a matched team-of-four made as they galloped away from Guibourg's house, a profound sadness invaded the lady's thoughts. Suddenly, compelled to change direction, the marquise leaned out a window and yelled at her coachman to stop.

Pulling up the horses was no mean feat, but the carriage soon came to a standstill. The mistress waited for her driver to shout down from his station.

"Madame?" he asked with tired concern.

"Drive me to Nôtre Dame de Bonne-Nouvelle on the Rue Beaurégard," was her quiet reply.

The destination was not far off. Marion practically raced into the church once her coach was parked, images of a cloven-hoofed fiend pursuing her as she ran. Moving with haste up the aisle of the empty sanctuary, she prostrated herself at the steps leading to the altar, praying aloud as women throughout the centuries have done when beseeching their goddesses.

"Blessed Virgin, forgive me my sins. Dear Lady, aid me in this hour of distress; save me from damnation. Take pity on me, most hallowed of women and hear my plea. I repent my actions, I beg You not to forsake me, although my offense is great. Mary, mother of our Lord Jesus, make me clean, please listen to my humble prayer."

She longed to weep, yet, could not, so Marion lay instead on the cold, stone floor. Unfeeling and uncaring, she knew that she could not stop the infernal need to despise the men who had wronged her. Despite that admission, the proud marquise waited all the same, listening for a noise or half-expecting a sign that might indicate her confession had been acknowledged.

After a spell, Marion concluded that her show of penitence was being ignored by the cathedral's lovely statue since she sensed no relief in her heavy heart. Standing abruptly, she smoothed the folds of her gown, humiliated by the naïve attempt on her part to set things right with heaven.

It is too late, she thought, *I am beyond redemption. I am no child of the Virgin.*

Assuming a superior air, she turned her back on the Blessed Mother, not giving her former benefactress another glance.

Madame la Grande returned through the early morning mists to her salon and her shallow existence. She laughed merrily, danced with verve and generally behaved as though nothing unusual had occurred in her everyday life. However, as the Sun set and dusk descended, the brilliant hostess sent her guests on their way. For the first time in recent memory, Marion seemed to be ill and required rest. "Go to the Blue Room at the Château Rambouillet and be entertained by the society ladies," she suggested as an option to her disappointed callers.

D'Emery was likewise included in the dismissal, although his own unanticipated departure required some persuasion. He offered to remain at his mistress' side, although the gallant gesture prompted Madame la Grande to insist that he seek company elsewhere. "I require absolute quiet—my head aches," was her stubborn explanation. So the finance minister went away, rejected, unable to think of anything other than his lady's unpleasantness.

Marion was not sick at all, of course, and once she was certain that d'Emery was far from her door, she escaped the Marais for Guibourg and the Rue St. Denis.

CHAPTER TWO

Monsieur Noctambule

Cardinal de Richelieu was not a young man, although when one reached age fifty-seven, one was not considered to be an ancient, either. The responsibilities accompanying the title First Servant of France could tire a youth, and the minister was beginning to take notice of the long hours spent working for the good of his country. Reading letters from loyal secretaries, negotiating treaties destined to shape the boundaries of Europe, or closeted for hours advising the king regarding matters of state, required a strong physical, as well as, mental constitution.

In Richelieu's case, the mind was willing but the body was weak. Near November's end in 1642, his temperature began to rise. Taking to bed, the statesman asked for M. Bouvard, Louis XIII's own physician, to treat his malaise. The head surgeon did not appear, however–rather, a replacement.

"Forgive my tardiness, your Eminence," explained the apprentice, who was named Monsieur Cousinot, "since I was detained while searching for M. Bouvard."

"Do you not know where he may be found?" demanded the ailing cardinal.

"Yes, your Grace, my father-in-law, M. Bouvard, is attending a soirée in the Marais district, to which he has been personally invited by M. d'Emery."

"So, he's at Marion Delorme's, having a good time for

himself while I lay dying, eh? Doctors," he mumbled, "all a bunch of charlatans, if you want my opinion."

"If I may suggest, Eminence, a treatment consisting of roasted viper and perhaps some bloodletting, I am most confident that..."

"*I am most confident that*," aped the irritated patient, "*that you will expire before midnight*. No, no, fetch me my niece, the duchess; she will provide far better care than you. And," he added, shaking a finger as he coughed, "ride to the Marais yourself, if needs be, and find that foolish Bouvard. A man of his reputation, consorting with that whore, Marion, imagine..."

The voice trailed off and did not bother to finish. Richelieu's health was sinking fast and he feared that he would be meeting his Maker sooner than he had anticipated.

"Hurry, monsieur, hurry," he urged Cousinot with a wave of a bejeweled hand. "Time is pressing, delays are unacceptable."

Bouvard's underling, and kin by marriage, bowed low and quit the bedchamber. The young healer reminded himself that Marion Delorme's residence was located not far from the cardinal's Palais Royal. Cousinot was glad of the errand; now he would meet fair Helen of Troy's successor face-to-face.

Meanwhile, upstairs in his gilded apartment, Cardinal de Richelieu was seized by an attack of asphyxia and began to spit-up a pool of blood.

Monsieur Cousinot tracked down his wife's father without much trouble; he was indeed being entertained by d'Emery and the gorgeous creature who allowed the rotund minister of finance the pleasure of her company. So bowled over by the sight of the incredible Marion was the apprentice, that he did not notice the disapproving glare his father-in-law cast in his direction.

Monsieur Bouvard, for his part, was bored; he had better things to do with his time than to waste an evening listening to a harlot's idle chatter. The esteemed physician considered himself to be a learned man and the people in attendance to Mademoiselle Delorme were nothing more than a group of dilettantes, individuals whom he sniffed at because their status at court was of a rank inferior to his own.

"Cousinot, here, man. Tell me, pray, what news do you bring?"

"Good evening, mademoiselle," he stammered in acknowledgment to the hostess before continuing, "M. Bouvard, the cardinal urgently requires your attention. He is ill and will see no one but you."

"Come then, come," answered Louis' best surgeon, "excuse my rude leave-taking, d'Emery—duty beckons. France's future may be at stake, you understand."

"Certainly, monsieur, I approve of your obvious concern for the cardinal's welfare," Marion agreed sweetly. "Please give his Eminence my best regards. He should remember me."

The shape and form of the notorious siren made Cousinot forget he was a newlywed and the husband to a girl whom he had previously considered an angel. If his wife was an agent sent from above, then the sorceress before him was the representative of hellfire itself. He sorely wished to reach out and touch that infernal blaze, no matter how dangerous its heat might prove. His father-in-law latched onto him, though, leading Cousinot away from eternal damnation.

The pair sped off in a large carriage bearing the king's coat of arms, a shield emblazoned with a field of *fleur-de-lis*. M. Bouvard was in an agitated state and lost no time venting his anger on his companion.

"I saw you stare at her," he bellowed. "Do not believe for an instant, monsieur, that your desire was concealed from me or the remainder of the room. How dare you consider bedding that strumpet when you are wed to the sweetest, most loving creature alive? Answer me that, Armand! Look me straight in the eye and tell your mentor how you plan to ruin his own daughter's very happiness!"

Bouvard's fist pounded heavily on the seat. Cousinot hung his head in shame. Thinking quickly, he offered, "Mademoiselle Delorme is a legend, monsieur. I am guilty of curiosity, nothing more, I swear. How could you think I would want a woman who has given herself to half of the king's court? Do you forget I have witnessed, with my own eyes, the agonies which may befall a man who lays with a trollop?"

"Be that as it may, touch her and I disown you. She is a disturbed creature, Armand, her thoughts are foul. Do you have any notion, son, what she asked of me earlier?"

"No, father, no idea."

"Mademoiselle hinted that she would consider it a personal favor, mind you, if I, in the course of my practice, would deliver up to her the blood collected from the patients whom I lance. Astonished, I asked the wench why she might require the vital fluids, and she became quite gay, claiming that an admirer, a *scientist* mind you, advised she drink a medicine made from the extract of peony flowers, water angelica and human blood. All so she might correct a pale complexion and restore a natural blush to her cheeks. I find that remark odd, my friend, very odd indeed. What say you?"

"I say," Armand reasoned aloud, "that the tonic you describe has been successfully prescribed by others in the past. Her request is innocent enough, most probably."

"I think not," Bouvard declared emphatically. "She also inquired as to how oft' I bleed the king. Now why does she need to know that? What useless information for a tart to possess!"

Cousinot did not care for Bouvard's name calling; still, he held his tongue. The older gentleman was respected and Armand was wise enough to allow him his opinion. The two doctors fell silent and no conversation was raised before reaching the Palais Royal.

Armand was obsessed with a memory, glad for the quiet afforded by the lack of talk. He knew that he had to speak with the woman, to see her at least once more, and he schemed as to how. Then he remembered Bouvard's words and grinned. Cousinot decided that if Marion needed blood, then he would obtain it for her. Chances were that the cardinal would require a prompt bloodletting in order to release the infection invading his system. Cousinot could secret a vial to Marion as soon as the next day.

For the first time since learning his trade, Armand could truthfully admit that he was looking forward to lancing the vein of one afflicted.

Had Monsieur d'Emery not possessed a healthy purse, Marion would have ended their association the moment that Bouvard answered Richelieu's summons. Naturally she was pleased by the report that Guibourg's Black Mass was working against her enemy with amazing accuracy. She was far from thrilled, however, with the exchange that had transpired between her and the gentleman who cared for the king.

D'Emery had intimated that the doctor would find the coquette irresistible and therefore place his services at Marion's disposal without question. The finance minister obviously had not anticipated Bouvard's observant nature or his profound dislike of immoral people, no matter how attractive and eye-catching they might be in person.

Marion knew too well she could not penetrate armor fashioned from disgust and she was disappointed by her inability to woo Bouvard to her side. She pondered the duality of the dilemma facing her: how to get close to the king, thus enabling an accomplice to help hasten the sovereign's just reward, and how also to gain access to large amounts of human blood, thus providing her priest with the sufficient means needed to celebrate the sacrilegious rites he was so adept at performing.

Ignoring the snoring minister, who slumbered in an accommodating armchair courtesy of a Guibourg concoction, Marion continued to search her mind for a solution to her predicament. D'Emery was not her only contact at court. She was familiar with other men in high places who would help. An introduction to a more accommodating apothecary would fulfill her sacred vow to Henri. "I shall never forget," she whispered as she fondled the dead man's lock of hair, "be certain of it. Your murder will be avenged, husband. First the cardinal, then the king."

Marion glanced about the Sanguine Room as if Cinq-Mars'

ghost might appear. Many said that those who were executed walked again. The corpses of criminals were usually buried under rivers or crossroads to dissuade their spirits from rising.

A knock at the door caused the sorrowful lady to jump with alarm. A visitor at six in the morning was peculiar, indeed. Perhaps the intruder was Guibourg. If so, she would give him a good talking-to for assuming such liberties.

Wearing a transparently thin nightdress made of cambric, Marion added a richly embroidered shawl for cover on her way to the foyer. Madame des Oeillets, the efficient housekeeper, was already questioning a well-dressed gentleman of medium height, who appeared to be of a good family, for the caller immediately removed the wide-brimmed hat he wore when he caught sight of the marquise. The blond youth then stepped past his interrogator, despite her warnings to stay put on the threshold.

"Mademoiselle Delorme," he began, extending his hand gallantly, "we hardly met when last I was here."

"When was that, monsieur? I am sorry, your name?"

Seeing her arched brow, the cue was taken.

"Armand Cousinot, physician-in-training to the king."

"How nice," Marion replied, lowering her gaze so he might not spot the surprise in her eyes. "Would you be the young man sent to collect M. Bouvard this evening past?"

"The same."

"Did the First Surgeon forget his gloves, monsieur? Or something more valuable to bring you running so early this day?"

"I came to apologize for my father-in-law, mademoiselle. May we speak frankly?"

"In here," she answered, showing him to her private place, still occupied by d'Emery. Upon viewing the banker, Armand regarded his competition suspiciously.

"Do not fret about him, M. Cousinot. He suffers a drunken stupor and hears nothing."

"All the better, for what I have come to say must remain confidential, mademoiselle."

"As you wish," she replied, sitting on a bed resplendently decked-out with scarlet moiré curtains. "Go on, do not be shy," the courtesan prompted when Cousinot appeared to be more than a little tongue-tied.

"Mademoiselle, I must beg your pardon for M. Bouvard's attitude. He is a busy man and does not socialize, so being invited to your salon was a strange experience. My father-in-law is a simple man."

"What you mean to say, monsieur, is that the First Surgeon considers me a slattern. So be it. People such as Bouvard are free to think as they like and I take no notice of their opinions. I could care less. Thus, your trip has been wasted."

Cousinot gestured with alarm, not ready to be dismissed that casually.

"Marion, lovely lady," he exclaimed, "I know what favor you asked of Bouvard and I must tell you that while he was unwilling to aid you, I am not. As proof, I have brought you a container filled with Richelieu's blood, freshly drawn, as a poor show of my good intent. Here, for you," he offered, removing the vial from his quilted jacket shot through with gold and silver ribbons.

The marquise reached out and took the porcelain vessel from Armand's trembling hand. Clasping the tribute carefully to her breast, she signaled with a glance that he should approach. Cousinot soon found himself enfolded in a grateful embrace. As if in a dream, he was aware of her soft mouth covering his face with enthusiastic kisses, and nothing more.

"You are brilliant and show great promise for your years, dearest. Such character is rarely displayed in a man and your unselfish act sets me aflame with love for you."

Marion loosened the lace collar encircling his neck, running her experienced fingers over his silky white chest. The wrap slid from her shoulders as she caressed the pale champion, eager for a young body again. Guibourg was undeniably a master at lovemaking, but the boy had spirit. She sensed Cousinot was going to prove an invaluable recruit for numerous, future forays.

"Armand," she murmured, holding him closely as was humanly possible, "come to me now. Take the prize you so rightly deserve."

Cousinot groaned aloud. No wife, no prominent relative, no love of king or country could keep him from that woman, from the embodiment of all fantasy known to man. He was completely enchanted and prayerfully thankful that Marion's gratitude took such tangible form.

Ignoring d'Emery, who was still out cold from the draught, the sensuous woman practiced the art she knew best on Armand. She thrilled with the knowledge that the intensity of purpose her new lover exhibited would also be present when he fulfilled her remaining designs. The abbé's contract had not been so exacting after all, Marion thought with relief.

Especially not when one's wishes were granted in such agreeable and wonderful ways.

The cardinal managed to fight for his life despite a worsening fever and horrible pains in his side making rest impossible. Bouvard was unable to diagnose the strange malady or to explain why his remedy of bloodletting offered Richelieu only temporary relief.

By the third day of December, the cardinal's condition had so worsened that the king arrived from the palace at St. Germain to bid his faithful helpmate *adieu*. The interview was cordial, yet brief. Some rumors claimed that Louis XII could not forgive the cardinal the loss of the royal lover. No deathbed spectacle moved the king to forget that cruel September execution staged by Richelieu. Three months had passed since then and no one in the realm could fill the vacancy left by Cinq-Mars' removal.

The middle-aged monarch paid his respects to the cardinal and listened to Richelieu's advice concerning the governing of France. Louis XIII then left with his entourage, laughing raucously as the group made for the Louvre, another residence of state situated not far from the Palais Royal. The departure of the earthly master caused his Eminence to concede that God must be next addressed. He looked beseechingly at a haggard Bouvard, at all the physician's assistants in their somber, brown gowns and rasped, "How long do I have?"

Bouvard could not lie. "In twenty-four hours you will be cured or you will be dead, your Excellency."

"Well said, how true," chuckled the cardinal. He prepared to receive extreme unction and called for the confessor.

"Sir," the attending Cousinot said in a low tone to his superior, "do you suppose we should bleed Richelieu again? The treatment helped when applied yesterday."

"Be quiet. There is no hope. I must fetch his niece, the duchess, right away. Wait and watch, monsieur; the cardinal is in our Father's hands."

As soon as Bouvard had gone from the room, Cousinot seized the opportunity to bleed Marion's enemy. Employing a band 'round one leg to make the veins swell, the apprentice took up a sharp-bladed lancet and nicked the skin of one foot.

The dark, ruby essence soon appeared and spilled into a dish positioned under the heel. Armand let the basin fill and then stanched the flow; Marion would be ecstatic when presented with the latest, and probably final, draught. He did not fear being caught in the act or the reprimand he would receive if found out. The happiness of his mistress meant more to him than the advancement of his career or the maintenance of peace at home.

None of the observers present in the sickroom thought Cousinot's actions to be out of the ordinary, since bloodletting is one of the most ancient antidotes of man. The official medical opinion holds that if illness is caused by evil humors living in the body, then freeing those spirits in one cleansing rush might precipitate a cure. Another school of thought insists that drinking human blood adds years to a person's lifetime. All the attention given bleedings and lances is the explanation for physicians to be commonly known as *leeches* or *barbers*.

Armand managed to conceal the recently filled vial under a long smock. Certain that the statesman would expire with or without his attendance or unwanted advice, Cousinot made himself scarce. The decision whether to stay with the patient or to call on Mademoiselle Delorme was an easy one to make. His absence would hardly be noticed what with the coming of the throng sure to invade the corridors of the Palais Royal when news of Richelieu's impending death was passed by the court's gossips. Armand was in love and cared naught for responsibilities, be they of the professional or the conjugal variety.

True to Bouvard's word, the cardinal passed into the spiritual world during the early hours of December the fourth. Guibourg brought the news to Marion himself. The salon was filled to capacity, and its queen rejoiced aloud when told the glad tidings, clapping her hands together with joy for all to witness. Only Louis remained, the king to whom she referred as the murdering sodomite.

Exhilarated, Marion kissed her attractive priest full on the mouth; d'Emery and Cousinot could only stare in disbelief at such audacity.

"Madame, contain yourself," demanded the older of the injured parties. "Do not make such a wanton display in public."

Madame la Grande ignored the admonishment and focused on her dashing merchant of death.

"Étienne, let us retire. I do believe we have much to celebrate, do we not?"

He smiled at her affectionately. "How did you learn my given name, sweet Marion?"

"Later. Do you wish to see where I make *my* magic?"

"Please, marquise, 'tis a sin to cast spells," he reminded and the two giggled impulsively on their way to the place Marion had renamed the *Salon de Richelieu*.

"Wait, Mademoiselle Delorme," called out the dejected Armand. "What of your guests who long to share in your apparent happiness?"

"Return on the morrow, my darling, and we shall all be merry together. Tonight, alas for you, is mine alone. The abbé and I have much to discuss."

The door that usually closed behind d'Emery and that had recently admitted the novice, shut in both their faces. Neither was wanted. Marion made her own rules and a victor had been chosen. The losers could remain or they could go home, no doubt, to waiting wives.

After a few stunned moments of silence, poor Cousinot was the first to speak, having grasped the real meaning underlying his fickle lover's message.

"Well, I'll be damned," he observed.

"More likely, us all," muttered the peeved minister, more annoyed with himself for hanging about than he could be at his mistress for straying.

Louis XIII was not destined to enjoy a protracted reign. Never the specimen of a vigorous ruler in his prime, the king had long been ailing. Once Bouvard was finished with him, he was also not long in dying.

Cousinot's teacher fed his royal patient more than one hundred different drugs, administered over two hundred enemas and bled him on fifty separate occasions within the course of one year. The young pupil eagerly related these facts to my mother on a regular basis. She then passed on the insider's revelations to Guibourg, who would in turn conduct a satanic ceremony invoking his Princes of Friendship to direct their unholy energies towards the head of the house of Bourbon.

The king's own blood filled the chalice dedicated to the lords of darkness whenever Cousinot could manage the deed. Ever since the marquise had convinced her adoring doctor that noble nectar contained the special restorative properties she required for her tonic, Louis was promptly tapped. Poor Armand was innocent as to how his gifts were employed; never aware of his complicity in aiding daemonic ritual or his not insignificant services rendered to Guiborg's cause.

A new French king came to the throne on May 14, 1643. The child, Louis XIV, not quite five years old, became ruler on that day—the same date as the thirty-third anniversary of his grandfather Henri IV's assassination. The forty-two-year-old Louis XIII quit the stage reluctantly, accusing Bouvard of having contributed to his untimely end. The old caretaker was crushed and, as a result of his dying monarch's stinging criticism, turned more of his duties over to M. Cousinot.

The increase in responsibilities meant a busier professional schedule and less time for Armand to spend dallying at Marion's house. Yet, he still faithfully attended the salon at least twice every fortnight. His personal star was rising at court and the newly appointed First Surgeon, son-in-law of the ex-chief physician, was careful not to jeopardize his career by staying out late carousing and thus angering his wife.

The Marquise de Cinq-Mars' circle was slipping into an established routine and for a while she was content with her life. An air of domesticity temporarily descended upon her home and my existence was slowly acknowledged. Cousinot, for his part, brought me trinkets when he came to visit, and d'Emery offered to sit with me once while Marion and her maid went shopping for beauty spots at the *Pearl of Patches*. That merchant happened to be conveniently located on the Rue St. Denis.

None of the gentlemen involved seemed to mind such idiosyncrasies; the lady's conduct was unconventional, true, but the three lovers constituted a family of sorts. D'Emery played the dependable father figure, Guibourg, the virile husband and Cousinot, the adoring son. Each recognized his special place in Marion's world, and accepted any consequences of her profession without complaint. To be near her was all that any of them wanted, and she gave her men as much of herself as she was able. The performance of such a juggling act, however, did not allow the marquise much opportunity for child rearing.

Between the ages of three and seven, I became the official pet of Marion's salon. Spoiled and doted upon by the members of mother's entourage, I was raised in an atmosphere of decadence, surrounded by flamboyant libertines. As I grew older, I was flaunted before the guests at every opportunity, introduced to the cream of society as the daughter of the late Monsieur le Grand. Sent to bed much later than most children, I would nod off to sleep quickly, too tired to be bothered by the parties that lasted until daybreak. If not resting, I flitted about the house, copying Marion's example, taught to address the woman who had borne me as *marquise,* and tended to by the real head of the household, Madame des Oeillets. Overly protective, the kindly servant did not allow me out of her sight, forgetting that I should play with others my own age or receive more than a sketchy education. Perhaps my elders simply assumed that a girl did not require tutors or companions, especially when she promised to grow up to be as lovely as was the successful beauty who had produced her.

Thus, with the passing of Louis XIII, my mother led a seemingly respectable existence for more than five years. She continued to ply Guibourg for powders and potions and promoted him amongst her friends as a reliable procurer of illegal goods. Due mainly to Marion's endorsement, the abbé enjoyed a certain reputation in the Marais and could count a few customers among the courtiers of the boy king, Louis XIV. His association with the marquise was not only pleasurable, but profitable, as well. The priest's best interests were served when he wiled away many hours at the salon, playing the devoted lap dog.

I truly believe that mother almost loved Guibourg, while I instinctively hated him, both before and after I came to learn of his second profession. D'Emery was rather round and jolly, Cousinot merely silly, but the polished Abbé Guibourg made me feel uneasy. Whenever he crossed Des Oeillets' path, the pious lady crossed herself swiftly and fearfully. Only Marion found the priest to be a delightful addition to her clique; the other members deemed him arrogant and a man to beware.

On a summer day in August of 1648, when I was nigh eight years of age, the marquise decided that she, Guibourg, Des Oeillets and I should venture outside Paris and visit the forest of Versailles. The trip to the small town, located not far from the city, would require less than an hour's ride by carriage and had been a most popular trek amongst court gentlemen during Louis XIII's day. Yet, with the passing of that king, few nobles continued to travel to the hamlet for sport, due mainly to the widowed Queen Anne's dislike of the place.

The attractive Regent wished to forget the past and her unsavory marriage since finding happy partnership in the person of Richelieu's hand picked successor, Cardinal Jules Mazarin. The talk at court was that the queen and the charming Italian statesman were lovers, perhaps husband and wife—a story that was possible since Mazarin had never taken priestly vows. Either way, an indispensable servant had been eagerly embraced, promoted oddly enough by the one man whom Anne of Austria had detested more than any other.

Versailles had been the hideaway for a sullen monarch and his exclusively male retinue, father being the last favourite to occupy the bedchamber adjoining the king's own suite. Anne, the proud daughter of Spain's Philip III, would not lower herself by giving the wretched spot any notice. Yet, Marion was in a sentimental mood and wished to make a pilgrimage to the locale where she claimed I had been conceived. A sudden whim had overcome her, and the ride would prove a welcome reprieve from the heat and odors of the capital.

Our party was assembled with little preparation, the horses harnessed, the footmen liveried and perched at their posts on the back of the coach. Guibourg and his paramour lounged comfortably on the cushions found inside the spacious vehicle while Des Oeillets and I sat stiffly in a formal posture. The prospect of a day spent in the country filled me with glee, however I contained my excitement since I knew that children did not act-up lest they hankered a whipping.

Just as the team was ready to pull away, the marquise noticed that she had forgotten her fan.

"Bijoux, go fetch the damned thing," she ordered and out I jumped to the ground, unaided. The coachman shook his head and smiled at my deft landing on both feet.

"You are braver than a Musketeer, mademoiselle," he called out as I made my way across the rudely paved expanse.

"I know, I am," I sang back, proud he had noticed my stunt.

Running into the kitchen through a side door, the missing accessory was retrieved straightaway. I always knew where Marion left things since I followed her about in hopes of maybe attracting leftover attention. The marquise often found me underfoot and, to the merriment of her devotees, would turn and ask, "Mademoiselle, what would you charge to haunt a small house?"

Guibourg helped me back to my seat so that the new frock M. d'Emery had given me for my upcoming birthday would not be ruined. The relationship between that gentleman and his mistress of long-standing was starting to sour because of the vast sums she consumed in order to maintain her magnificence. Marion sensed that d'Emery was tiring of her and that an end to their arrangement was fast approaching.

She was not concerned for lack of a wealthy sponsor, however, considering a younger, more distinguished financier was ready to assume her debts. His name was Nicolas Fouquet and, according to all accounts, he would soon possess more gold than Mazarin. Friends christened him the *Future* and the man from Brittany employed more spies at court than had the suspicious Cardinal de Richelieu. Fouquet had recently attended one of Madame la Grande's soirées with his best friend, Madame du Plessis, a cohort reputed to arrange dalliances for the man whose motto was: *To what height will he not attain?* The queen of the courtesans would be a splendid addition to Nicolas' growing collection of beauties, titled and otherwise, who had yielded to his charming manner.

The conversation en route to Versailles centered mainly on Fouquet. Guibourg and my mother did not hesitate discussing potential conquests when together. They were completely at ease plotting and scheming the moment of surrender, scarcely aware that Des Oeillets and I could hear their every word. The lovers also speculated as to when d'Emery would announce his departure; both were of the opinion that Fouquet would prove less tight with the purse strings since he was working closely with Mazarin, who was as rich as the mythical Croesus. Perhaps, prompted the abbé, Marion could pay a call on the dapper cardinal himself, whose perfumed monkeys, embroidered scented gloves and fabulous art collection were the envy of all Paris. That proposition made them very jovial; conversing about money was the couple's second favorite pastime.

Their chatter was repulsive to me. I, for one, was going to miss d'Emery. Glancing at the sour expression on Des Oeillets' face, I was truly anxious to reach Versailles-au-Val-de-Galie, the pretty name of our destination. The actual location, however, turned out to be a major disappointment consisting of peasants' huts, two rude inns, an old church near the town stream and a rickety-looking windmill.

I could not envision Madame la Grande spending much time in such a backward locale since it did not appear anything more than an excellent meeting spot for hunters. My father must have been a lovely boy, indeed, to have lured his mistress to such a rustic retreat, there in the middle of nowhere. Had they truly communed with nature whilst King Louis rode through the woods with his dogs and gentlemen, stalking abundant game, I wondered? I also could not picture Marion Delorme having spent the night in a local tavern, for Louis XIII had forbidden women to be housed at the château. Versailles was originally intended solely for men, and no females had ever been allowed quarters in the lodge.

Our party stepped down to a dirt road once the carriage halted and we were greeted by the curious stares of the inhabitants. Marion commanded an audience wherever she went, although the villagers, dressed in their drab attire, looked upon the woman decked-out in lace and fine cloth as if a deity had descended into their midst. Her well-shod feet were a sure sign of prosperity; only wealthy persons could afford shoes with heels. The poor laborers were dazzled by the marquise. More than one peasant bowed.

"Ah, just as I remembered it!" she exclaimed to no one in particular. "How quaint! Do you not agree, monsieur?"

"Oh, yes," replied the abbé with a hint of disdain creeping into his voice. Obviously he had forgotten the blight from which he hailed, the Rue St. Denis.

"I adore everything here, Étienne. This place holds so many fond reminisces for me, you know. Let us find some food, then we may promenade through the flora and fauna."

Guibourg was not enthused, yet he allowed Marion her diversion. Looking my way, he inquired, "What about the child?"

"Go play," mother directed, then said to Madame des Oeillets, "Watch Bijoux. I do not want her lost when the time comes to depart."

Thus ordered, the servant and I made our way towards the smell of pine needles and assorted wildflowers, whilst the birds sang and a delightful breeze rustled the leaves of the surrounding trees. The movements of the branched clusters allowed some light to break through their cover and paint the path upon which we trod with splashes of colorless brilliance.

As I surveyed the testament to Nature's glory unfolding about me, I changed my view regarding the hamlet of Versailles. To a youngster raised in a dirty, rabble-filled city, the country air seemed quite intoxicating once one adapted to the change. I was beginning to like the idyllic atmosphere, to sense an attachment to the area where my life had commenced. A burst of childish joy caused me to bolt from my keeper and run for the beckoning underbrush, for ferns and countless discoveries awaited.

"Come back!" Des Oeillets cried out as I pushed on through the bushes.

"I won't get lost, I promise," was my response.

"Bijoux, be a good girl and get out of there," she whined in protest. "Do not force me to tell the marquise that you were disobedient."

"The marquise may go to Hades," I answered under my breath. Having journeyed over dusty, bumpy roads most of the morning, I was determined to enjoy the afternoon. Guibourg would occupy Marion for the remainder of the day and my whereabouts would be of little or no consequence to anyone other than the maid. I moved on as briskly as my gangly legs would carry me, ready for adventure.

After walking for near to an hour, I came upon a clearing where I rested against a huge, cool boulder situated on the forest's edge. Unaccustomed to much exercise, the hike had tired me and I considered retracing the route already blazed. My dauntless attitude had waned and I wished that the nurse would emerge from the shadows through which I had come.

Where is she? I wondered, really afraid for myself. *What if Madame des Oeillets wanders across a wild animal and is mauled?*

"Do not fear," a kindly voice reassured. "I shall be your guide, mademoiselle. Versailles is my home, you see."

Startled, I spun around to discover an aged man standing behind me. Not forgetting my manners, I curtsied to the venerable one, too abashed to stare for any length at his person.

"Hello," I stammered, eyes downcast, "my name is..."

"Bijoux," he finished courteously. "I followed after you when I saw you had escaped your nursemaid. Children have been known to lose their lives when left unattended in these woods and I wanted no harm to come to you. The marquise would approve of my concern, be sure."

Dumbfounded, my head lifted until I met with the most proud gaze imaginable, although the man whom I contemplated appeared to be a bit disheveled: gray wig awry, stockings a bit baggy, black coat a size-too-big. A dark mole graced his forehead and he leaned on a cane of gnarled wood clasped with a hand missing two fingers. The stranger's thin frame supported the weight of a sack stuffed with two onyx-colored tablets shaped to resemble shrunken gravestones.

"Who are you?" I queried.

"I am called Noctambule by many, *ma petite*."

"An original name. How did you know mine, monsieur?"

"Come closer child, I wish to ask you something important."

I approached Monsieur Noctambule with an unsure step, transfixed by the otherworldliness of his countenance.

"Sit down, please," he instructed, pointing to a log. I did as he bid and he settled next to me after he had placed his burden on the ground. He then removed the slates, cradling them with care on his lap. Noctambule fumbled in a pocket with his good hand and presently withdrew a piece of chalk.

"Did you know, Bijoux, that you have been chosen to receive a special gift?"

"Like mother's?" I blurted out.

"No," he said slowly. "Something far better than beauty."

"Of what do you speak?"

"If you could have your pick of glory, wealth or days without end, which would you select?"

I shook my head in confusion. "I do not know, monsieur. Are you sporting with me?"

"No. Please choose."

Noctambule was teasing, I could tell that much. All the same, I closed my eyes and thought for a few moments. The elderly guide offered no advice while I pondered over the choices: *fame, riches, immortality.*

"I want to live forever," came my declaration.

"Tell me as to why," he chuckled.

"So I don't have to leave any of this," I explained, waving my arms in an arc above my head. "Yes, today I have decided that I never want to die."

"Fine, first sign your name on my stones to seal the agreement."

"Is that all?"

He nodded his head in assent. With a steady hand I took the piece of white shale and traced my name on one smooth surface: *Bijoux*.

"Write *Cinq-Mars* on the other," he said very seriously.

"Why?"

"That was your father's name, Henri Coiffier de Ruzé, Marquis de Cinq-Mars."

"Is that why my mother is a marquise?" Her title made sense to me at last.

"Yes. Please sign."

I wrote down the two words, whose characters looked strange to me in print. Noctambule placed the contract back inside his burlap bag.

"You may see me again at a later date," he stated, "and if you do, 'twill mean that a circumstance of your own making has placed you in grave danger. If you call on me for aid, I may be powerless to help."

"How so?"

"By then you may deny this encounter and your birthright, *Comaetho*."

"You are very mysterious, Monsieur Noctambule," I giggled. "What a funny name you have given me! Are you a magician?"

"I need no magic," was his retort, "for I am One with the greatest forces in the Universe, with the sea and the stars and the night breezes, with great Poseidon himself! Do not take this pact lightly, daughter of Taphos, for you have asked and thus, you will receive. Now," he declared while he stretched eight fingers out to me, "touch and be whole."

A light emanated from the stranger's being as distinct as any halo artists attribute to their canvas deities. I knelt down in reverence and awe. Noctambule's wrinkles faded, his gray locks became chestnut in shade, his tattered coat disappeared and was replaced by a robe of flowing, cloth of gold. Multi-colored gems studded the rich material and I thought myself to be in the presence of a celestial prince.

"I want to be a good person," I confessed aloud. Then, aware that Noctambule had five digits on each, complete hand, I began to cry with joy. Tears spilled onto the ground; where they fell grew tiny violets. Speech failed. Nothing could have moved me from the position at his feet—not even a familiar voice calling out my name.

"Bijoux, where are you? Bijoux, answer me this instant! When I find you, you will be sorry!"

Des Oeillets stepped into the glade and immediately caught sight of me and also of Noctambule. Her expression was one of horror and disbelief. She did not seem to find my new acquaintance enchanting.

"Bijoux, get away from him!" she screamed. "Come over here!"

"No, no I won't!"

Madame stepped towards me. Noctambule lunged forward, drawing a dagger from beneath his splendid cloak.

"Begone, woman, for thou art an offense to me!" he roared.

The maid became hysterical and raced away. Terror-struck, I swooned, overcome by fear.

The handsome youth was gone when I awoke seconds later; no Noctambule, simply a faint whiff of sulfur tainting the breeze. I continued to lie upon the moss-covered ground, too stunned to move. The Sun was sinking in the sky before I arose. I had never been so afraid in the sum of my days spent on Earth, nor have I been since, for that matter.

Rising up, I roamed through the Versailles forest in a dazed state, not stopping until I collapsed in front of one of the inns when back in the village.

A group had gathered there, in whose midst was Des Oeillets, Marion and Guibourg. Madame was babbling on about seeing Lucifer, the marquise was refuting her claim and the abbé strode over to my limp form, lifting me in his arms with a tenderness never before displayed toward his mistress' daughter. Thinking wisely, he placed me in the coach and motioned for the two women to follow. Not a moment was wasted by Étienne, who realized the sagacity of returning to Paris post haste.

He did not speak at first. The carriage jostled down the country lane and no one said a thing except the much-agitated housekeeper.

"I know I saw him, marquise, abbé. He was right before my eyes, he was." She trembled visibly. "'Twas Lucifer himself, I tell you, and he was talking to Mademoiselle Bijoux."

Guibourg sighed as if bored beyond belief by the ramblings of an obvious simpleton. His voice was very grave when he locked a stern gaze on the handsome woman, pointing a finger at her forcefully.

"Not another word from you, madame. Your talk is

blasphemous and may harm the girl." He clutched me closely to his side. "Do you understand my meaning?"

"Yes," she demurred, looking nervously at mother. the marquise wore a deadpan expression, not wishing to reveal any emotion whatsoever.

"The abbé, being a man of God, is more familiar with such things and lends authority to the matter," Marion offered in an even tone. "You know I trust your word, madame, although I think that perhaps the heat of the day has tired you. Chasing after Bijoux also contributed to your fatigue, causing you to believe you had met with a huntsman."

The marquise patted Des Oeillets on the shoulder to comfort her, the first kindly gesture I had ever seen mother make towards the servant. Madame fell silent. Her place was to obey; any further protestations might lead to a dismissal from her post.

Something told me to say nothing, but I pitied the caretaker's state. "I saw him, too, marquise. His name was Monsieur Noctambule and we talked about..."

"Be quiet," Guibourg insisted. "You have had a busy day, Bijoux, and should not be telling stories to your elders. What a fanciful imagination," he remarked, tugging playfully at a ribbon tied in my red hair. "Take a nap, little one, and dream of pleasant spirits."

I did not argue with him. The memory of Noctambule and our discussion at Versailles was a vivid one. I was not going to forget the enchanter or his promise, no matter what mother and her collaborator said. The wonder instilled in me that afternoon was near to unshakable devotion for another being who seemed to be interested in me and in me alone. I knew that I would return to those woods again someday in hopes of finding the soul who had sought mine with an offer of life everlasting, who had named me *Comaetho*.

Nothing and no one would stop me from going back to that place, for I was his.

Our homecoming could not have been more different than

the quiet ride back to the Marais. Mother rushed Des Oeillets off to the servants' quarters straightway when we returned, while Guibourg escorted me to the Salon de Richelieu. Marion was not long behind us and the lock was securely fastened upon her arrival. The abbé paced the floor, as if contemplating how to best interrogate an eight-year-old. Finally, he said, not too loudly, "Tell me everything that transpired."

Surprised, I gladly recounted the events as they had occurred. When I reached the part in the story dealing with Noctambule's jewel-embellished raiment and flowers springing up from the ground, Étienne's look was one of true amazement.

"Then what?" mother asked impatiently.

"Madame came to fetch me. Noctambule showed her his knife because he didn't want me to leave. He screamed at her to go away and then I fainted, so I don't remember anything else."

"Nothing?" Guibourg pressed.

"No. He was gone when I woke up. I waited to see if he would reappear, but he did not. Then I walked back to where you were and I fell down when I saw the crowd outside the inn. I felt weak and light-headed; dizzy, I suppose."

"Maybe you should go to your bedchamber," mother suggested. "I am pleased that you told the abbé and me everything, Bijoux. Tomorrow I shall buy you a doll, all right?"

"A good reward for a good girl," the priest agreed. "Before Bijoux retires for the evening, allow me to inspect her for any hurts, marquise, which this Noctambule may have inflicted. I shall rest easier if I know that your child went to bed unscathed."

The pair eyed each other in a knowing manner.

"Fine," she consented. "Go ahead."

The touch on my head was cool; Guibourg's fingertips lightly searched my scalp, ears and neck. He ceased his examination, straightened and shrugged his wide shoulders.

"Not a scratch," he announced matter-of-factly.

"Well, that settles the whole affair," Marion pronounced.

"Prepare for bedtime, Bijoux. Madame will check on you shortly."

Dutifully, I turned to leave the scene. The adults believed themselves to be alone, they huddled together at the end of the bed frame, mother's back against one end post. Unbeknownst to either, I was outside the room, ear pressed against the door.

"You know whom she saw, don't you?" Guibourg murmured.

"Please, Étienne, be serious," mother scoffed. "Children tell fibs all the time, you know that."

"Not Bijoux."

"So what are you telling me, dear heart? That my daughter was granted eternal youth by Beelzebub, lord of the daemons?"

"Do not mock the Master, madame. Did He not take the cardinal and Louis six years ago, has He not answered all your petitions?"

"Yes, and I am grateful, Étienne. Remember that it was *I* who had Cousinot procure the sacrifice demanded by your Astaroth and Asmodeus. And remember, too, that he brings you more quite regularly for potions and tonics. Without my efforts, where would you get your blood?"

"The contribution is appreciated, Marion, but you signed an agreement to *dedicate my children to the glories of Lucifer and to raise my offspring in accordance with Satan's malevolent ways.* Perhaps our Master has tired of waiting and has come to take what is rightfully *His*."

"Are you quite mad?" she asked. "Bijoux is a nothing, a nobody! What would Satan want with her? He has me; that should suffice."

"Obviously not, marquise. We must teach Bijoux the forbidden art as soon as possible. She has been set apart and elevated above us."

"Oh, and how do you know that?"

"The punctures on the back of her neck—three tiny marks resembling a triangle. Were they there earlier?"

"I do not know," Marion admitted. "But if you are correct, why that sign?"

"Nine is His number, divisible only by three. The Great One has thus placed His symbol on your child and mingled His soul with hers. He means to have her, I believe, forever."

"That is not possible, Guibourg."

"Not possible?" he snorted, "Not possible? Do you not realize, marquise, that the name *Noctambule* is *He Who Walks in the Night*, or *Stalker of the Night*, or..."

"The King of the Undead?" she gasped.

"Precisely. Bijoux must be tended to properly, watched closely. She will require instruction, no doubt, in order to adapt to the ensuing changes to her composition."

The marquise did not answer.

"You know of what I speak?"

"Yes," was all that she said.

I gulped hard. From my listening post I could not see their faces and was only able to make out their forms by peeking through a crack in one bottom panel of the wooden barrier. I yearned to grasp the meaning of the abbé's veiled reference. No explanation came. Gingerly I touched the nape of my neck and felt a bump. Guibourg continued to speak.

"Will Cousinot supply larger quantities?"

"With some coaxing, yes."

"Good. We cannot afford to let him slip away as d'Emery threatens to do. We, you more specifically, must keep the good-looking doctor happy."

"Fine."

I glimpsed Guibourg clasp Marion to him.

"Let us go to the Rue St. Denis and say a Mass of thanks. The appearance today should be acknowledged and a gift made. Our princes do us great honor," he boasted. "Are you not pleased with your daughter, Marion?"

"I wish they had chosen me," was her dejected reply.

That admission uttered, I fled to safety. The priest's talk of devils and blood had frightened me. His revelations were hardly comforting, despite his convictions to the contrary. Noctambule could not have been a bad man, I argued with myself, once I was hiding under the blankets. The old gentleman had merely liked my manner, so he had pretended to grant my request. At best, he might be a troll or a goblin. Somehow, a god of the Underworld did not seem one to limp about with the aid of a walking stick or to grant young ladies fairy wishes.

I did not wish to reflect on the significance of the science of numbers, especially when sweet slumber beckoned on dusk's heels. Everything would be better on the morrow, I reasoned, feeling again for the mark on my neck. Ceasing to torture my brain with additional worries, I drifted off to sleep, unable to stop the tears from wetting my pillow as I did so.

Unfortunately, the morning did not prove kind. Guibourg and his accomplice roused me quite early, intent on keeping me constantly in their sight. The intrusion reminded me of the previous day's events and I was loath to heed any directives issuing from either daemon worshipper.

"Wake up, darling," the marquise trilled. "The abbé has brought you a new drink to try."

"What is it?" I rubbed the sleepers from the corners of my lids.

"A wonderful concoction, Bijoux, one which will protect you from palsy, gout, rashes and apoleptic fits," the priest lied. "You are to drink the tonic regularly, to improve your general condition."

"When did you ever care how I felt?" I quipped snootily.

Marion wasted no time in delivering a sharp slap to my rude mouth. The punishment hurt, though I hid the pain and refused to cry out, an act of rebellion that irked her greatly.

"Take your medicine and stop being a little tart," she ordered. "Who do you think you are, talking back to the abbé?"

The child of a daemon?" I retorted, laughing aloud. "Comaetho?"

She knows," a shocked Guibourg declared. "Who gave you that name?"

M. Noctambule."

When?"

Yesterday."

Wonderful," mother sighed. "Now what?"

The abbé raised his eyebrows.

"Bijoux, I think you mock us," he said. "You find it amusing to make light of the distinction you have received, but I wonder..." he paused, "would you be so flippant if threatened with burning at the stake?"

"Whatever do you mean?" I was taken aback.

"Witchcraft is not exactly tolerated by the Church or by the judges, my dear comedienne. Continue to laugh about M. Noctambule and sooner or later someone will hear. They will listen and they will talk and you will be labeled a heretic and when the king's Musketeers drag you off to the Bastille, then you'll be sorry. I hearsay that being roasted alive is a most terrible death to endure."

"Stop," I cried, "stop it! I meant no disrespect, monsieur! I overheard you talking to the marquise when we came home last night," I sobbed, "and you scared me."

"There, there," Étienne soothed, enveloping me in his robes, "I only wanted to impress upon you the necessity of keeping your story absolutely secret. Why do you think we refuted Des Oeillets' account? We want to protect you, Bijoux. Your welfare is precious to us. That is why you must take the medicine that I brought for you. Every few days, from now on."

"Just tell me the truth, monsieur. Why must I rely on a potion when I know that I am well?"

"Noctambule marked you, Bijoux, he...changed you. This is a good thing, because now you will never die and may live to carry out His plan."

"What?" I cried anew.

"Must we tell her everything?" mother complained. She was not accustomed to being cast in a secondary role.

Guibourg continued, unfazed. "Having consulted with the Princes of Friendship, it seems our Master has chosen you for a special task, indeed. Last night, Astaroth and Asmodeus spoke to me in a dream, indicating that you, Bijoux, are to bring about the downfall of the family Bourbon."

"No! I am a little girl, monsieur, how could I do such a thing?"

"I truly cannot say. The princes did not favor me with that information. Yet, they did reveal that your mission might take many years to complete."

"Monsieur," I protested, "surely no one lives forever."

"Take this," he proffered the metal cup, "and *you* will."

Wary at best, I did as he bade me do. The mixture was tinted a pale pink. I sipped a small amount; the taste was flowery, perfumed. Deciding it to be not too repugnant, I quaffed the remainder.

"Good, good," Guibourg beamed.

"What was in it?" I wiped the corner of my mouth with the crisp, white bed sheet. A small, rose colored stain remained behind.

"The Elixir of Life—the formula sought after by many, but found by few. Any uncommon sensations?"

"No," I replied. "However, your words have had a strange effect upon me."

"Such as?" the marquise inquired brusquely.

"I do not understand why I should want to hurt the king."

"Listen to me," mother said hotly. "That king for whom you weep had a father who killed your father and he has a mother who betrayed my husband. Their name must be wiped-out, forgotten; their line eradicated. All Bourbons, my girl, are our enemies and all born of their loins are our foes. You are a Cinq-Mars of the family d'Effiat and never forget it. Did old Louis feel pity for the marquis he once loved? Did he not turn Monsieur le Grand's aging mother, your grandmother, out into the cold, destroying her château, burning her forests? Thank God the father was already gone, for the king's vengeance would have killed M. d'Effiat for sure. Those Bourbon bastards must pay for their crimes, Bijoux! Do not feel sorry for that pack of murderers and thieves."

"You said that Louis and I share the same birthday, that we are linked," I argued.

"A sign, no doubt," Marion threatened, "however, not a

sympathetic omen for him. Your father's soul will not rest until all of them are dead and gone. I have done my part to avenge his cruel end and now you will carry on the foul business. *You* will finish it, understand?"

"Yes, we take your point, marquise," Guibourg snapped. He turned his attention to me, saying, "For now, Bijoux, we will endeavor to impart to you the ancient mysteries of our rites and the knowledge passed down by the great sorcerers of old. I shall teach you how to cast spells, dispense poisons and mix powders. These lessons will aid you later when the moment arrives for action to be taken. No need at present suggests rushing matters and you are far too young to influence destiny. Yet, you must realize your importance in the Plan and be prepared to perform your duty in the future."

"It appears I have no choice, monsieur," was the only retort I could manage.

"When you signed the stones, child, you relinquished your free will, gaining in that surrender an ally unlike any other. Could the God mere mortals worship offer you better? No, he promises naught but cold graves and inglorious decay. Our Master, on the other hand, has made you a sacred *vrykolakas* with one touch."

Not impressed, I frowned. "A *vrykolakas*?"

"A Greek term found in *The Key of Solomon*," he explained. "I shall show you the holy work later, when you are older. That aside, you must agree to no mention of these things to anyone save the marquise or myself, *oui*?"

"Yes, abbé."

The blemished apostle stood to indicate the end of our odd discussion. He bowed silently in my direction before serving-up some fatherly advice.

"Try to forget, for now, what has happened."

The admonition was a wise one, yet given too late in view of the judgment passed on me. And no matter how intensely I willed Guibourg's counsel to manifest itself in my life during the years that were to follow, the forgetting never came.

CHAPTER THREE
Division of the Houses

As regards my childhood, three major events must be noted. The first being that August 5, 1648 marked the onset of the Fronde, a French civil war pitting the nobles—led by the persistent trouble maker Gaston d'Orléans—against Queen Anne and Cardinal Mazarin. The conflict was named for those slingshots the Paris mob employed to regularly pelt the foreign scapegoat's house with stones.

Marion, usually politically cautious, joined in the fray, attracted by the rebels and their ridiculous cause to liberate the kingdom from the influence of Anne's chief advisor. Everyone knew Richelieu's successor to be the true power governing France, and consequently, many ignorant citizens became inflamed by the capable Italian's rise to glory. Young hotheads brandished swords and fine ladies encouraged rebellion within the walls of their salons. Mazarin was run out of town on several occasions due to popular pressure, yet he always returned and continued to laugh Exile in the face.

The beleaguered minister simply refused to go on permanent holiday, and the Regent, Anne, obstinately stood by her advisor's decision. What of it if the bards wrote scandalous ditties, the *Mazarinades*, for the masses to sing? The shrewd opportunist merely sent agents out into the Paris streets where they bought all the ribald lyrics and then resold the pamphlets at a profit for their employer. Possessing such a determined spirit, the cardinal was not about to relinquish the control he exerted, and the resolute gentleman forced many improvements on the xenophobic French majority whether they liked him or did not.

A composer of some of the anti-Mazarin propaganda produced during the Fronde was a close friend of my mother's, Paul Scarron. The great wit had sadly become a cripple in 1638, victim of a vile malady that succeeded in twisting his formerly athletic frame into a deformed, twitching mass of flesh. Bound either to his bed or to a specially designed chair, Scarron scratched himself with a stick, entertained his frequent guests and managed to maintain his sense of humor despite the affliction.

As a result of his brave attitude, none of the friends who had gallivanted with Monsieur Paul in the past deserted the unfortunate man in his hour of need. Not even a superficial woman such as was Marion Delorme could ignore such an indomitable character, and we visited Scarron's humble home on many occasions. All the great ones paid him court, laden with food and wine to feed their fallen hero. The paralytic writer attacked the pompous and mocked the hypocrite to the general hilarity of those assembled under his roof. Scarron's rapier-sharp tongue knew no equal and his genius was so apparent in his work that prior to his support of the Fronde, the queen had paid him a pension.

Scarron had been quite the rogue when healthy and very popular with members of the fairer sex when young. My mother had been his lover, as had countless other ladies; however, his Z-shaped figure made relations with women no longer possible. The citizens of Paris were shocked when, in 1652, Monsieur Paul married a penniless girl named Françoise. One day that woman would become a dear, personal friend, although she did not appear on the scene until I was sent to live outside the Marais, to experience a world her husband never ceased to decry.

In fact, had mother not done something stupid prior to seeing her thirty-seventh year arrive on the third day of October, 1650, I might have met Madame Scarron sooner; no doubt Noctambule was watching and kept me from the one person who might possibly have saved me from myself.

Marion Delorme, at age thirty-six, was as celebrated as ever for her feminine attributes. D'Emery was no longer interested in her charms—not as much could be said for Nicolas Fouquet. Guibourg continued to wait on the famed courtesan hand-and-foot while supervising and conducting my introduction to the occult sciences. If Marion was entertaining Mazarin's influential supporter, Monsieur Fouquet, the abbé carted me off to the Rue St. Denis to read from his collection of exotica. My education was conducted in private and no one but the marquise knew the scope of what the priest was teaching me.

While I was initially reluctant to learn the black arts, a love of learning inspired me to listen to Guibourg's instruction with a certain interest. Having received no prior religious training, I was ignorant of the possible consequences. Whereas mother was never totally convinced of magic's powers, the abbé was a true believer, and considered his sorcery a business as legitimate as any other. Guibourg demanded concentrated study from me and the apprenticeship I took on was mentally strenuous. We would pour over his treasured grimoire together and I soaked up the information contained within its pages. There was so much to know and remember that I wondered if I could retain any of the book's secrets, never mind tumble a monarchy.

The abbé, however, was not one to be daunted and he drilled me on the measurements of a wizard's circle, how to trace it in the dirt with a knife, the correct number of kabbalistic talismans to be placed about it, what four of the seventy-two names of God were to be written backwards upon the ground, and the dimensions of the square bordering the display. His old book, *The Key of Solomon*, also described and named fantastic daemons to be called forth: *Vercan, Maymon, Samax, Modiac, Arcan.*

King Vercan was the most powerful, almost human in appearance, with a grotesque, horned face of a man, a body covered with hair, and the feet of a hawk.

Maymon was black as night and rode upon a dragon.

Samax was antlered, his steed a panther.

Modiac, fitted out in red armor, was transported through time on a bear.

Arcan flashed white fangs with relish, his ebony skin a stark contrast in comparison. Flames darted from his ruby eyes and he hunted with bow and quiver from the back of a proud stag. His planetary symbol was said to be the Moon, and I could imagine Arcan chasing prey by its silvery rays.

The tantalizing stories were too irresistible for a ten-year-old to deny. I devoured *The Key* with relish, Guibourg predictable in his reminders that I was a member of that privileged society allowed access to its mystic revelations. He was not pleased, however, when I queried him as to the practice of the ancient and noble art of astrology, a move that was to mark the second, most important, highlight of my early years.

"Explain these strange ciphers," I insisted one bright, May morn. "What do these sigils represent, monsieur?"

Guibourg regarded me with disdain. "Those symbols signify the twelve signs of the Zodiac," he sniffed.

"I have read of the heavenly constellations and their differing mansions," came a proud admission. "The king is a Virgo, as am I, and so was Cardinal de Richelieu, too. Mama was born during the season of the Scales. Listen to this:

> *Our vernal signs the Ram begins,*
> *Then comes the Bull, late May the Twins;*
> *The Crab in June, next Leo shines,*
> *And Virgo ends the northern signs.*
> *The Balance brings autumnal fruits,*
> *The Scorpion stings, the Archer shoots;*
> *December's Goat brings winter's blast,*
> *Aquarius rain, the Fish come last.*

Where is your Sun to be found, monsieur? In Scorpion, perhaps?"

"Enough!" he growled, slamming the text shut, causing

me to start. "Such nonsense is beneath us...the stars do not guide, they deceive! Only a priest of the Princes of Friendship may manipulate matter, understand? All other methods are counterfeit."

"I shall learn to read the portents in the heavens," I argued. "The stars are as precious gems. I am going to become the king's own astrologer, mark my words!"

"Bah!" he laughed with relish. "Women do not calculate nativities or cast measures in the night sky, silly girl. No king would be foolish enough to appoint a lady to such a position, rest assured."

"I shall be the first."

"No, you will not! You will do as the Princes of Friendship decree, Bijoux—do not vex me."

Lips drawn in a pout, I reopened the book, risking a slap.

"If astrology is nonsense, monsieur, how then did Louis XIII's seer, Jean Baptiste Morin, predict Cinq-Mars' death while the marquis was still the king's favourite?"

"Who told you that? Marion?"

"No. M. Cousinot. He is a stargazer as well as a physician."

"Fool," Guibourg muttered, stroking his beard. "What does Cousinot understand? Is he a priest? Is he? No, he is a barber, he dispenses leeches..."

"Is the tale true? Is it?"

"Yes. The tale is true," Étienne fumed. "A twist of fortune, nothing more. We shall never discuss this subject again, hear me?"

The intensity of the priest's expression was such that I fell silent. We did not discuss astrology again, that much is certain. I did ask Cousinot in secret, however, to bring me his star books, compass, set-square and mirror, and he complied, teaching me in the privacy of my own room a language I found more beautiful than even the poetry of the great Ronsard. Houses, planets, goddesses and gods became my friends, and I was enchanted by the legends explained forever in eternal, sparkling splendor, available to all who would but look above their heads.

At a young age, then, I truly found my calling—astrology—a circumstance that did not surprise me, for are the lights not many jewels, as well?

At mother's urging, Étienne took to wearing the attire of a proper gentleman, discarding his priestly garb, thus lecturing me on the history of covert Parisian society while he admired the rosettes embellishing his shoes. Due to the danger associated with his job as a poisoner, the cape he wore was casually draped over one shoulder in order to give his sword easy access.

Along with the change in clothing, Guibourg acquired an affected swagger and became fond of twirling his moustache—a long strand formed from a tendril of his new wig—with a deliberate air of preoccupation. Ribbons cinched his doublet in at the waist, showing-off a trim figure in a flattering manner. Collar and cuffs were matched, both trimmed in lace. His proudest accessory was an enormous, brimmed hat of beaver fur decorated with an extravagant ostrich plume. Marion had made her handsome cleric into a foppish dandy and Étienne adopted the mode eagerly.

Much to mother's chagrin, I, too, desired a wardrobe, yet not the conventional type assigned to women. Tightly laced doublets, three-tiered skirts and tulle-covered headdresses did not pique my interest. Beauty patches were fine to wear since they represented a code language to would-be suitors according to their placement. The spots, also known as *mouches*, were strategically arranged near to the eye to indicate passion, next to the mouth for promised kisses or on the cheek when one was gallantly inclined. A velvet *mouche* on the lip meant a coquettish mood, the nose was employed by brazen ladies, while the ultimate height of flirtation was to adorn the upper mound of one's breast. That tempting location was appropriately labeled the *assassin*. Such a tradition was the one rule of fashion I considered to be amusing.

Mother and I battled daily over the choice of styles of dress and their shades. I thought emerald green a suitable color to wear since my hair was red; Marion preferred pink. I liked the scent of ambergris and mother wore musk exclusively. I was of the opinion that gloves were cumbersome, while the marquise was obsessed with them. Her litany, repeated to me with great reverence, was that the perfect *cheveril* used in glove making was tanned in Spain, cut in France and assembled in England.

I, for one, was not impressed.

A dashing figure, the Countess of Saint-Belmont, who loved to dress as a cavalier, fight duels and ride astride her horse, shunning the sidesaddle, was my idol. The marquise was horrified by my choice, and she forbade me to mention the offensive woman's name.

The heroine worship I had developed for the transvestite countess was not the sole factor contributing to my mother's foul humor in June of 1650. A far greater worry was the arrival of an unwanted pregnancy, one hazard of her profession. Carrying me, the lovechild of Cinq-Mars, had been one thing at the age of twenty-seven; giving birth ten years later was a different prospect, altogether.

Not relishing the prospect of another mouth to feed, Marion resolved to be done with the inconvenience. She confided the problem to Guibourg and he suggested taking a substance called antimony. Of course, mother never did anything in a small way and, zealous to abort, she swallowed an overdose. Watching her writhe, doubled-up in agony, was terrifying, and the salon reverberated with an eerie silence.

Marion Delorme took to her bed and would not be comforted by either Des Oeillets or the remorseful lover who had inadvertently induced the excruciating sufferings of his mistress. Étienne produced an antidote of wolfsbane, but her condition did not improve. Mother, in a panic, insisted on calling for a priest despite Guibourg's optimistic prediction for a full recovery. When no cure came on the third day, Madame des Oeillets finally fetched her personal confessor from the parish church. Then the neighborhood learned that their legendary Marion was dying, and all hell broke loose.

Everyone who lived in the Marais, it seemed, kept a vigil for their best-known resident right outside our house. As each hour of the deathwatch passed, the crowd grew larger. Men prayed on their knees in the street and a delegation of women brought a virgin's wreath of flowers to be hanged above the bed's headboard. Mother seemed heartened by the fervent show of support, but thought it best to confess her sins to the visiting abbé a total of ten times in preparation for the hereafter. She was granted absolution by the priest, after which she indicated that I should approach.

"Bijoux," she smiled, too dazed by her ordeal to hurt anymore, "please swear that you will keep my memory alive, do not forget your poor mother who was taken before her time."

"I promise, mother." My emphasis on the last word caused her to grimace.

"Marquise," she corrected. "Also, you must promise to allow M. Guibourg to continue your lessons after I am gone, do you understand?"

"Yes." I knew exactly what she meant, though could not say, in front of a stranger.

"And, most importantly, never forget your father or the pact we made on that day you first saw Versailles."

I squirmed uneasily.

"Say you will fulfill the curse and thus be sworn to the deed."

"Mademoiselle Delorme, I must protest such behavior." The priest was firm. "Your immortal soul wavers on the brink of the precipice."

"Shut up!" she declared with all the strength remaining her. "Get out before I confess my sins anew!"

Guibourg was moved to tears. Marion was the one person whom he had cared about in his entire, miserable life; the first and the last, to be precise.

Étienne turned to his colleague and implored, "Let her be, father. This lady merely seeks justice for her departed husband, Cinq-Mars. Have pity on the widow, for God's sake. Besides, a word to those outside and a riot could erupt."

"Do not threaten me, monsieur, with your rabble-rousers. They think that mademoiselle is a saint because she has a lovely face. Yet I have heard her admittance of guilt, her testimony before God Almighty. Furthermore, this," he raved, tearing down the virginal coronet, "is an abomination! To think such an infamous strumpet could be compared to an innocent is beyond reason! I cannot be away from this den of iniquity soon enough."

The clergyman's outburst intensified my mother's resolve.

"Bijoux, I am dying. Allow me go to the grave in peace, allow me the satisfaction of knowing you will respect my wishes. Come here," she patted the bed to indicate I should sit.

I responded obediently to the sign. Marion lifted my downcast chin and when my gaze met her determined one, she pleaded, "Say you swear to avenge your father's death. I need to hear it from your lips. Do not disappoint me, Bijoux, please."

Her pitiful expression, the miserable state in which she laid, the priest's antagonism—all those factors, compounded by a newfound sense of filial piety, influenced my answer.

"Yes, I shall do as you ask. I don't know how, but I shall try. Your enemies are now my own."

"Thank-you," she sighed and sank deeper into the feather pillows. "Now I may die. Guibourg," an outstretched hand implored, "hold me, dearest, for my legs feel cold."

I ran from the final scene without prompting. A respectful, somber group of men had gathered in the main salon, some present out of curiosity, others out of love for their fading rose.

Recognizing Cousinot to be among their number, I sought refuge at his side. It seemed a better idea than dealing with the neighbors who jammed the street beyond the walls of the overly warm drawing room. Noticing a tug on his doublet, Armand lifted me up without hesitation.

"How is the marquise? Will she live?"

I shook my head from side to side, indicating all was lost. "The eighth mansion of her destiny says *no*."

Armand's brown eyes became watery, droplets wetting their lashes. The emotional response made me cry, too, and I hugged Cousinot 'round the neck, sobbing uncontrollably.

"Help me," I said into his ear, half-covered by the curls of his brown wig. "I have no one anymore and I fear M. Guibourg. Take me to your house and teach me more myths, please."

The physician tightened his grip on me. He had never liked the abbé, either, and suspected of late that Étienne—not Marion—was the end recipient of the vials which he so oft' delivered. Thinking poorly of his rival and glad to be of final service to his lady, he quickly reassured me.

"Fear not, Bijoux, you will be cared for. I, for one, shall never desert you. Your mother is, was, so dear to me. I shall be honored to find you a new home."

Overcome with worry, I could not respond. Because of Marion's vanity and error, I would soon be forced to leave my home and I hated her for that. Because of Guibourg's miscalculation, I had also joined the ranks of countless orphans who roamed the alleys of Paris. The contempt I felt for him consumed my ransomed soul. Being bequeathed to the priest made me feel mother's desertion all the more acutely.

Monsieur Cousinot's faux locks were very moist when Guibourg appeared in the entryway to the Salon de Richelieu, head bowed. The abbé noticeably lacked the poise he displayed when plying his trade on the Rue St. Denis.

"Gentlemen," he began slowly, deliberately, "the Marquise de Cinq-Mars has been released from her suffering. The Abbé La Chaise administered the Last Rites, granting our dear Marion absolution for her sins. She will lie in state for the next twenty-four hours, after which a funeral procession will conduct her heavenly remains to the cemetery at Nôtre Dame de Bonne-Nouvelle on the Rue Beaurégard."

A murmur of disbelief passed throughout the assemblage.

"Damn it, Guibourg," Cousinot piped, standing me up straight next to his side, "she should be laid to rest here, in the Marais."

"Normally, I would agree, monsieur," Étienne replied, "however Marion made it expressly clear that one of her last wishes was to be interred there. Even I cannot ascertain as to why, but she told it to La Chaise himself."

My protector was not swayed from his opinion.

"Fine," he acquiesced, "although I do not agree with the choice. Who may argue with the dead? Let us, those assembled here, be the first to pay our respects to she whom we loved."

"By all means," Guibourg agreed, gesturing towards the much-vaunted chamber. One by one, past, present and former, hopeful lovers made up a long line filing sadly into the scarlet room. Our turn came to pass through the portal, and Cousinot squeezed my hand, as if having me along gave him the courage to step forward.

"Sir, allow me to relieve you of your charge," Étienne offered, ready to take me from his junior.

"No," I protested. "I hate you. You killed my mother!"

"What?"

"You gave her a poison so she would lose her child and instead, she died. You are a murderer."

Numerous heads turned in Guibourg's direction.

"Give Bijoux to me, monsieur," he stated in a calm voice.

I was angry, resisting any attempt to pry my hold from Armand's. The kind man had to rescue me, he had to. Then I watched Cousinot hand me to the cause of all my misfortune. Guibourg's touch told me that the teacher was not pleased with his student.

"Why did you not send for me when the marquise became ill?" the doctor managed to inquire.

"She did not wish to take you from your more important duties, Monsieur Astrologer. We thought her pains a mere trifle, perhaps caused by too much food or drink. As for talk of poison, well, Bijoux has sustained a great loss this evening; she is troubled."

"Yes, of course." Armand crumbled before Guibourg's direct glare. All his noble intentions to interfere in my future plans had left him. Guibourg's intense persona and sinister good looks made people instinctively fear him.

"You are weak," I remarked, and kicked the king's healer hard against an ankle. "An affliction of your Mars in Pisces," I added for good measure.

Shocked, the chastised instructor bent over to grab at his foot, wincing from the blow.

"God's blood, you are strong! Don't be cross, Bijoux, your mother would want her oldest friend to be your guide now that she is gone. She did entrust her daughter to your care, did she not, sir?"

"Most assuredly. Besides, your schedule does not permit for child rearing, monsieur, and I doubt as to whether your wife would understand your concern for this girl. Especially such a pretty lass so devoted to you and your heretical teachings."

"True enough, true enough," the other reflected.

"However, there is one service you could continue to perform for your dead mistress that would be most appreciated and might quiet my dislike of your preoccupation with astral divination."

"Yes?"

"Should an acquaintance of mine arrange for Bijoux to be placed at court, I would forever be indebted to you if you would watch out for her, occasionally, and check with whatever household she is assigned to, from time to time, to inquire after her."

"That goes without saying, monsieur."

"Thank you. Also, she will require her special tonic, the one you so dutifully supplied the marquise during these eight years past."

"Bijoux, too?" Cousinot looked genuinely surprised by Guibourg's remark.

"Unfortunately she has inherited Marion's pallor and lack of energy. The draught is the only remedy."

"Then you will continue to have your medicine," Armand chuckled, pinching my cheek in the process. "How often does she take the mixture?"

"Once a week, monsieur, that is all."

"Fine. Simply inform me when Bijoux has settled into her new surroundings."

Bows were exchanged and one went to mourn, the other to meddle. I was escorted to my own room where I was told, in no uncertain terms, to behave.

"How dare you attack M. Cousinot?" Guibourg snarled

when we were beyond earshot of the others. "We need him at present, not to mention that he is an important man at court."

"How dare you give me away to strangers?" I retaliated.

"Would you rather become a beggar?"

"The marquise said you were to look after me. I shan't go to court. Everyone there is mean." "Nonsense, girl. If my contact agrees to sponsor you, then you will go and rub elbows with the nobility. I shall keep track of your progress and never be far from the scene. You must become familiar with the king's routine if you expect to influence his reign."

"I have no quarrel with the Bourbons," I informed him. "Mother's curse was stupid."

"Oh really, mademoiselle? Have you learned nothing from your lessons on the Rue St. Denis? Do not deny your destiny, Bijoux, or ignore a Force greater than yourself. Your future course has been charted, like it or not."

"Liar. If I died tomorrow, would you still speak of eternal life and daemons?"

"You won't die; we both know that, don't we? Your fate has been sealed, Bijoux, and the sooner you accept your situation, the better."

To my own amazement, I would not be dissuaded by my elder.

"Abbé," I said matter-of-factly, "at my age I am not nearly as clever as you, so for now I must do as you say. The day will come, though, when you will regret that you know me."

"I doubt that, my dear," he scoffed. "Of course, only the sands running through the hourglass will ultimately reveal the truth. For now, go to sleep. Tomorrow will be a busy day, what with your mother's burial to conduct and guests to entertain."

"Madame des Oeillets will help you. By the way," I added, "do you think that she could come to court with me?"

"We shall see."

Pressing Guibourg for an answer was useless. Perhaps he would try to arrange a position for Des Oeillets, perhaps he would not. A familiar face would surely be more comforting than none at all in the strange world that awaited. I climbed into bed wearing the clothes on my back, not bothering to change out of them.

Guibourg, not wishing to undress me himself, extinguished the candle prior to his leave-taking.

"I am sorry about Marion," he offered as a tardy apology.

"Tell your woes to the Princes of Friendship. Too bad they did not make mother immortal."

The hurt I caused him was intentional. He slammed the door in complete vexation. *Good*, I thought, *good. I hope my words cut deeply into your worthless hide, deeper than if I used the blade of a sorcerer's dagger.*

Taunts could not alter the reality that, no matter my feelings for the fraudulent priest, he was my sole ally. My triumph diminished when I considered that predicament. Mother's death had placed me under Guibourg's control. Having lived ten years beneath the roof of the Marquise de Cinq-Mars, that courtesan's example had taught me one did not discard a benefactor without a more attractive alliance waiting in the wings.

But who could that be? I wondered. The unnamed connection at court? Or a person yet unknown to me?

The question was unanswerable and disturbing. To make matters worse, I felt for the bumps on the back of my neck. The three raised marks had remained with me for two years and had developed into a large wen. Was the growth tangible proof of Noctambule's abilities, of Guibourg's vision predicting my uncommon longevity and ultimate, distasteful objective?

Filled with terror, I began to pray.

Never having been to a church, I turned to my beloved gods and goddesses for aid. "They are all probably listening tonight," I reasoned aloud, so I simply continued with, "Dear glorious Apollo, beautiful Venus, bountiful Jupiter, and Diana of the hunt, hear me now and grant me your blessing. I am afraid because both my parents are dead and I have no one to turn to but You. Noctambule said I was to live forever, which does not seem like such a good idea anymore since the abbé wishes me to go to court and kill the king. I don't want to keep the promise that I gave to my mother tonight. Please show me what to do, if you would all be so kind."

Searching the surrounding darkness for some acknowledgment, I could see nothing, only hear the muffled conversations of the mourners downstairs.

Stubborn determination overcame me. Kneeling down beside the bed, I begged, "I need an answer now, I must know which road to take. If I could meet with Noctambule, then You must be out there, too. Astaroth and Asmodeus and the daemons such as Arcan can't be the only spirits in the world, they can't."

Frustrated, I cried into the coverlet. How could the Immortals ignore a sincere request? Did they hate me because I had been chosen by Noctambule? Was I was marked for eternity? How could I have been so stupid as not to have known that the old man with the limp boded me ill? I hated my mother all over again for taking me to that wicked place called Versailles.

"Bijoux, have hope, for the deities are always with you."

A hand alighted on my shoulder, a soft voice offered a gentle reminder. Someone had heard my distress and had taken pity on Marion's daughter. Daring not to look, my voice squeaked when it inquired, "Who are you?"

"My name is Monsieur Jacques."

I ventured a peek. As the visitor claimed, I beheld a youth clad in the style of a courtier: pale silks, laces, ruffles, ribbons, a cape of shimmering gray-blue cloth falling to the floor. The wig, or *peruke*, which he sported was finely made, for each jet black curl wended its way independently of the others down his back.

"Are you a Prince of Friendship?" The question was asked in sincerity.

"In a sense," he smiled, touching my hair. "I have come to give you guidance, Bijoux, because one should not be lost due to unjust ignorance. Circumstances have not been kind to you and those entrusted with your upbringing have done you a disservice. As of this eve, however, you are responsible for your own actions and my wish for you is that you may make wise decisions."

Jacques' skin was transparently fine, similar to the properties attributed to the best bone china. His eyes were bluer than a heavenly sky and all about him was a glow that was soft, steady, warm. Had I seen him before at the salon? Who was he?

"Are you a god, monsieur? Must I never die? An old man named..."

Jacques held up a slender hand. "I know of whom you speak, child. He is a fine actor, granted, but not worthy of our mention. Be still and listen, learn and act. Do not live in the past. You are an eternal part of the Whole, of the One Power that moves the stars, the clouds and the planets above. A certain Guibourg has taught you until now, am I not correct?'

"Yes," I admitted. "Was that wrong?"

"The practices you have embraced of late are one reason I revealed myself to you, why I answered your honest prayer and came here, to the Marais."

"Guibourg and my mother made me learn spells. They said that I must memorize the ancient rites. It's not my fault that they made me study witchcraft."

Jacques' gaze held no hint of reproach.

"Witches do not hate," he smiled, "or worship devils. They are wise men and women who understand that evil only possesses the strength granted it, Bijoux. Now, to become a wise sorceress yourself, you must stop allowing doubts and fears to rule your existence. Thoughts are things and when people harbor dark images, they shelter the most harmful daemons imaginable."

"Do the gods not punish us when we are bad, are they not sometimes cruel?"

"Allow me to explain an iota of pure knowledge to you, then I must be on my way. Do you agree to this?"

I was pleased that he asked my permission first.

"Yes, but I have so many questions. I could talk to you all through the night."

Jacques motioned for me to get up off the floor and return to the mattress. When I was reinstated, he sat next to me, humble in demeanor despite his corporeal perfection.

"Bijoux," he continued good-naturedly, "remember these tenets, engrave them on your soul: the one Power is creative in nature and alive. This creative pulse lives within you and is represented by your actions and your deeds. Men and women have been gifted free will—dominion—and are able to think any thoughts as they see fit. In this way, a person may shape the existence they wish to experience."

"So, we make our own days without end?"

"Yes, Bijoux, you do."

"I signed Noctambule's stones, I agreed to his pact. Am I doomed?"

Jacques did not waver.

"Seek the good, Bijoux, forget this legacy of blood drinking and incorruptible flesh. Your body may live forever, but your spirit will never be at peace."

"I know that Noctambule is a daemon," I protested, "but I am not a bad person, really."

"Of course not," he soothed. "Hear me when I tell you that, were you never to leave Paris, you would journey on many highways while alive. Some of the routes are rough to traverse and fraught with danger, others smooth and pleasant to travel. Today, you have begun a journey that may change your life for the better; however, the outcome depends solely on the road you alone choose to take."

"Should I go to court? "

"Do you not see that as your path?" he smiled, then said with gravity of purpose, "Be kind to those whom you encounter in the palaces of Louis Bourbon, King of France. Share with them the Truth, Bijoux, for every person is a part of the Plan and is greatly esteemed. Surrender to a Power that wishes you naught but joy when you place your trust in it. The divinities do not will some misery, others happiness. The stars are not glad when one falls and another ascends. The Blessed Ones see naught but each individual's magnificent potential. Life loves all equally and with the same intensity; better and worse are incomprehensible to such majesty."

"Jacques, do not confuse me," I pleaded in earnest. "I do not understand."

"Regain your human soul by taking others, no matter their rank, to your heart. Petition wise Athena to illuminate your way. Eschew the daemon spirits who yearn for your end."

"Should I recite a special incantation when I go before such a Divine One?"

The youth's gaze absorbed my own. I sensed that Jacques was sending me a silent, beatific message, and that communication permeated my very soul, quickening my pulse, depositing every drop of its pure balm into my hollow-feeling shell of self. For the first time in a short life, I felt the grandeur of being loved and adored.

"Devote your days to giving and be released from the black taint upon your blood. Repudiate hate, be a seeker of knowledge. Be happy and regard life as a wonderful paradise rather than a gloomy prison. And beware of that which would fill your mind with a disbelief in the Law of Love."

"I need more help," I admitted. "Might you not stay with me a while?"

"No, dear child, stay I may not do."

"Will I never find a true friend, Jacques?"

"She will come to you in time. A lowly girl, destined for high rank and privilege; yet, who cares not for honors or station, for she looks to enlighten the lost. "

"How will I know her, pray tell me?"

Jacques stood and moved with grace to the doorway, his form becoming fainter the greater the distance he placed between us.

"She will be the widow of one once close to your mother. You will know her, Bijoux," he finished cryptically.

"Wait!" I cried out. "Please return."

Nothing more happened. The messenger was gone. Dazed by the appearance, I reviewed every second that had unfolded while in the visitor's company.

Had Jacques been a man or a dream?

Not certain, I got into bed and closed my eyes. Telling myself that the godlike advisor had been a messenger of the Immortals helped to ease my worries, especially since uncertainty beckoned and I was friendless. His philosophy struck me as difficult to comprehend, although the concept of relying upon a Divine Plan of the Cosmos did seem plausible to one who had already dedicated her days to the reading of Urania's dreamscapes.

The youth had instilled in me a hope that perhaps one face of Eternity could be a loving Omnipresence seeking outlets of expression through those mortals able to experience the beauty of life with a child's sense of wonder. It seemed to me better to beseech that Universal Spirit than to rely on the Princes of Friendship for a show of favor, especially when a man such as Guibourg was doing the asking.

That unexpected, miraculous encounter with Jacques was the final, bright spot of my youth, and served to fuel a desire to break free from the abbé and the Rue St. Denis. Conventional evil may have accepted me with open arms, validating my frailties and extolling my faults, yet I sensed something amiss with a belief that encouraged its adherents to laud death and destruction. My friend had told me to trust in wisdom and that, in turn, help would come; not right away, true, although he had predicted a kind girl's companionship. He had also stated that the guide would be the widow of a man once close to the marquise.

Who from Marion's degenerate group would wed a paragon of virtue? Not Guibourg, for he was a priest. Cousinot appeared too healthy to be on the verge of quitting his wife or practice and M. Fouquet had recently remarried, his constitution brimming with vitality. D'Emery's lady was years my senior and would not make a suitable companion. Therefore, I had to be missing somebody, but who, I calculated, who?

Then it came to me, the person whom I had omitted from the list: Scarron, the poor, deformed poet, most probably beside himself with grief over Marion's death.

How could Jacques have meant him? Despite Paul's great mind, I was old enough to know that no lady would consider sharing a bed with the cripple, his appearance was that hideous. Thus, I was unable to surmise whence the comrade might come or who she might be. My guardian had been as clear in his assurances that I would know her as he had been in his rejection of blood drinking. I had not concluded what he had meant by that reference, either. What the future danger was, I did not know, yet, his warning to me had been unmistakable.

As Jacques had remarked, the decision to change rested solely with me.

The Marquise de Cinq-Mars' funeral was well attended. Six proud gentlemen bore the polished wood coffin donated by M. Fouquet, pushing their way through the crowd-lined streets to the Rue Beaurégard. The abbé was not a pallbearer, and he walked with measured step behind the body, pretending to be the bereaved religious advisor to Paris' most illustrious sinner. I shirked when he took my hand in his, most officiously dressed as he was in the trappings of his Order.

None questioned the blatant show of hypocrisy or mentioned the carnal relationship Guibourg had maintained with the deceased. Since the people had chosen to canonize the exceptional beauty, anyone who had sampled her saintly wares was a better man for it. Marion Delorme, who had played mistress to the likes of Richelieu, Scarron, Cinq-Mars and d'Emery, gained recognition through her association with men whom the average citizen could not approach or dare to address.

Ordinary people could only dream of doing what the Marquise de Cinq-Mars had proudly done, of keeping company with the wealthy and mighty of French society. Against great odds, a simple country girl had risen above a strict class system to become a star in the Parisian firmament. And, in the opinion of her public, she had been an enchantress who gave them hope. For that reason, if no other, tears spilled at her graveside on that day in June. Mother would have been happy with the turnout, I reflected, as Guibourg threw a handful of dirt onto the casket held in its vault. Being celebrated, she had craved attention while alive and, in death, she surpassed any notice she had merited as queen of the courtesans.

Guibourg did not dally when attending to the arrangements concerning his ward's future. Following the formal farewell to the marquise, he sent a courier straightway to the Louvre Palace, one royal residence located on the banks of the Seine. What with the Fronde still raging and Mazarin being threatened with imminent exile, Queen Anne, the young king and court remained in Paris close to the largest concentration of their rebellious subjects. The cardinal harbored no delusions regarding his precarious status with the masses. He also had no intention of giving into the demand of the Parliament that he quit France. The wily Italian had collected an able group of spies to keep him abreast of unpopular sentiment, and escape routes had been mapped should he find it necessary to flee.

The commander of Mazarin's covert operations was a soldier named Charles de Batz Castelmore, or more simply put, Monsieur d'Artagnan, formerly of the Grand Musketeers. The cardinal had disbanded that group in 1646, due to a quarrel with their leader, one of his bitter enemies, Monsieur de Tréville. In fact, the latter gentleman had been exiled from France on December 1, 1642, owing to his involvement in my father's plot to kill Richelieu. Yet, when the cardinal expired three days later, Louis XIII happily recalled his captain to court, for the king enjoyed drilling the Grand Musketeers at Versailles.

Unfortunately for Tréville, the protector died in five months' time, and Mazarin had not forgotten the details of the Spanish Plot. Queen Anne's most trusted helpmate urged the ruin of the commander and, for once, the Regent disobeyed the man whom she adored. The captain was elevated to the rank of Count. Mazarin screamed in protest, he threatened to return to his native land. "Not only France, but the whole of Europe, was persuaded that you had confidence in me," he complained in a letter to Anne, whom he called 22 in their private code, "but it must be little, indeed, since you cannot sustain it against the cunning of the Comte de Tréville."

Faced with a decision between safeguarding her passion or performing her duty, Anne surprisingly called her partner's bluff. The cardinal stayed. Yet, he nagged the poor woman and feuded so openly with Tréville that the queen finally disbanded the company of Musketeers in January of 1646. The common understanding was that the move had been made so Mazarin could reinstate the troop at a later date. Their new commander would prove to be none other than the cardinal's spoiled nephew, Philippe Mancini, later styled the Duc de Nevers. That appointment did not come until 1657, so, for the moment, the king's own Guard was gone.

The Grand Musketeers lost their royal patronage. Dedicated soldiers were sent out into the cold of winter to fend as they may, a casualty of the machinations of personal politics. Two of their number, however, found appointments awaiting them. Mazarin had requested that Tréville nominate a team from his ranks to be detailed to the cardinal's household, perhaps intended as a gracious gesture to the defeated Count. The ex-captain could send any duo he saw fit to nominate, but the men selected would possess only uniforms and swords, making them totally dependent upon their new employer.

Such was the crucial lesson the cardinal was to teach Louis XIV—allow the courtiers the shirts on their backs and nothing more. Mazarin impressed upon the young sovereign that the nobility was to be regarded as being not much better in rank than the two Musketeers sent him by Tréville. Besmeaux and d'Artagnan were both grateful and needy, and both arrived at the Italian's palace without a *sou* to their names.

Thus, at the age of twenty-six, Charles de Batz found himself the aide-de-camp to a controversial figure, a job offering a great deal of danger, glamour and opportunity to prove one's service to the Crown. By the year 1650, the versatile d'Artagnan had adopted the disguise of a Jesuit, a tobacco seller, and a drunken valet in order to gather intelligence for his master.

During one such particular adventure into the underworld of Paris, the agent played spy at the salon of a well-known prostitute and suspected *frondeuse*, Marion Delorme. Posing as an apathetic courtier named d'Éstoiles, he met the reputed priest, Étienne Guibourg, who hinted to d'Artagnan that the saving of souls was neither his true calling nor his practiced profession. Something about the abbé piqued Charles' curiosity. He had come across lowly characters many times in his line of work, although the conjurer who kept company with the courtesan was different; the man from Gascony sensed Guibourg's truly wicked nature.

D'Artagnan showed a genuine interest in the stranger's candid talk concerning the ease with which he dispensed his toxic substances. One never knew when a Musketeer might need to rid his king of foes through more subtle means than force. The Abbé Guibourg could be a useful contact in the future should poisons be required. The incognito operative therefore flattered Étienne, offering him to tell certain colleagues in high places that a trustworthy man existed who, for a price, would deal effectively with distasteful matters. If he could ever be of any service, d'Artagnan insisted, the illicit apothecary was to call on him without fail.

The abbé humbly thanked the courtier d'Éstoiles, unaware that he was being duped. All Étienne saw were gold pieces in his grubby fist; if an individual perished as a direct result of his actions, what the matter? The pox or the plague got most in the end—he was simply another cog in the wheel of his Master.

Guibourg knew full well he must take advantage of the accommodating Monsieur d'Éstoiles' offer when the first opportunity presented itself. If no need reared its head in a timely fashion, he was prepared to invent one. In order to gain access to the elite prospects promised through the connection, the consummate liar would fabricate a most dire situation. Then, Marion died unexpectedly, and a real emergency threatened.

A note full of desperation was hastily penned and conveyed to M. d'Éstoiles, care of the Louvre. The missive, of course, went straight to d'Artagnan, who replied with unexpected alacrity and feigned concern for the plight of his new acquaintance. Of course he would meet the abbé at the

Cours-la-Reine on Sunday at the onset of the canonical hour of Nones, it would be an honor to be introduced to Mademoiselle Bijoux, the only child of Marion Delorme. He existed to serve Guibourg's wishes and no demand on the abbé's part would be considered too great.

In the course of his flowery prose, the courtier inferred he would speak to a gentle lady friend forthwith to suggest raising the orphaned girl as her own. Étienne was not to fret, for d'Éstoiles personally guaranteed a solution to the problem within a day's time. A small token of Guibourg's appreciation was hinted at, too. Perhaps he could bring a few aphrodisiacs to their meeting as a nominal down payment of sorts, the first installment on a debt between gentlemen.

The proposed arrangement made sense to both men, constituting nothing more than a mutually beneficial transaction. Except that d'Artagnan was not a courtier, nor did he intend to place me in any household without some calculated motive. Mazarin's eyes and ears did not want the potions Guibourg would bring, for the agent did not care for mystical concoctions. A certain woman would be tempted, however, to accept responsibility for a child in exchange for drugs. Especially when that lady yearned for a daughter and bore only sons.

Nearing the age of fifty, Jeanne-Olympe de Choisy was the wife of Gaston d'Orléans' ex-chancellor and an intriguer at court. She had given birth to François, the last of four unwanted boys, in 1644. The disappointed lady, refusing to accept her child's gender, openly dressed the six-year-old in girls' clothing, pierced his ears, and delighted in calling her son *Mademoiselle Sancy*. Her palace entanglements were similarly void of logic, and Guibourg's burden—me—was about to be sent to the Choisy domicile where I would reside in order to watch the troublesome schemer.

D'Artagnan did not bother to ask his Eminence to bless the operation. The man of action knew an extraordinary strategy when he saw one, and was confident that his plan would stand on its own merits, with or without the cardinal's approval.

Guibourg had me packing my few belongings the moment he received a reply from the Louvre. The thought that he would soon have an ally at court served to diminish, in part, the sadness the abbé had been experiencing due to Marion's passing.

He barked orders at me to be quick, to not tarry, to take only essentials on the move, for he would send on the remainder of my goods at a later date. To Madame des Oeillets, who was neither happy nor despondent in the face of a probable change of employ, he was respectful, politely asking her to prepare most of mother's possessions for sale. Debts needed to be settled, the house in the Marais emptied for new tenants and I surmised that the dependable maid would be following a familiar overseer to the Rue St. Denis. "Wait until she sees a daemon," I muttered under my breath. "She'll run fast enough, then."

I was trying my best to be brave, reluctant as I was to become dependent on strangers for my daily bread. Still, any living arrangement was preferable to being raised by Guibourg, and I was grateful that he had aimed high when deciding where to place me. Perhaps the change of residence would mean new outfits or, better still, a riding costume with a pony as compliment.

To own a miniature steed of my very own was a fond desire, for then I might become a famous equestrienne, such as the Countess of Saint-Belmont. Once I had an epée and knew how to fence, no one could hurt me, not even Noctambule. If that deceiver showed his ugly, mole infested face near mine anon, I was convinced that an expertly wielded blade would cause him to reconsider his objective. The pretender from Versailles would never touch me again, I vowed silently, for if he did, I had resolved to kill him, no matter what Jacques had said about forgiveness.

Inventing problems and allowing my imagination to run amok did not lend itself to the reality of the situation at hand, which meant I must concentrate on Guibourg's assigned task. Gazing upon drab-colored skirts scattered about the bedchamber floor, the acknowledgment that I ought to confiscate some of the marquise's spectacular wardrobe was not a difficult assessment to make. Her clothing had been fashioned from costly piece goods and could be saved for later use or cut-down to fit her daughter's current needs. Marion's many accessories, such as hair combs, gloves, perfumes and trinkets constituted an abundant cache to be brought along to the elegant world of courtly life.

Feeling heartened by the prospect of looking through mother's things, I traveled with a light step to the Salon de Richelieu. Peering cautiously around the forbidden door, I found no one about, so I sneaked inside and began to rummage through a large cupboard situated in one corner of the suite. Compartments and drawers yielded glorious treasures: a locket containing a miniature of Marion, *les mouches* from the *Pearl of Patches*, lace handkerchiefs, and something more curious: a bundle of shiny, red-brown hair tied with a black, satin bow that lay within a golden coffer.

Lifting up the keepsake, I stared at it, turning the bound strands this way and that, watching afternoon sunrays expose a chestnut, then an auburn shade. Could I be holding one of my father's final remains in my hand? Was the shorn tress proof that the Marquis de Cinq-Mars had trod the Earth?

Melancholy engulfed me, an inexplicable morose mood that compelled me to keep the talisman in my grip. Ready to retreat, I turned and found myself face-to-face with Madame des Oeillets, who wore a quizzical expression. The unexpected encounter caused me to jump, and the *memento mori* fell to the ground, landing at the nursemaid's feet.

CHAPTER FOUR
Many Jewels

"Getting your fair share of the booty?" Madame des Oeillets inquired with a guilty look.

I noted that she sported some of mother's finery; the familiar white cap with its long strings gone, hair done in ringlets to resemble a lady of the court—a very pretty lady, at that. I was not the sole heiress to the marquise's estate, after all.

"You look nice," I observed, meaning the compliment. How could I begrudge the faithful servant a few clothes, she who had not been allowed to adorn herself lest she detract from the mistress' radiance? The gentle housekeeper had helped herself to a plain skirt and laced bodice, and another woman, placed in a similar situation, might have behaved with less restraint.

"I meant no harm, Mademoiselle Bijoux," she explained. "I took but two or three trifles—old garb your mother would not have missed were she still here among us."

"Madame, you are deserving. You worked many a long hour for the marquise. Did Madame la Grande boil my eggs in the morning or tell me stories at night?"

Des Oeillets was touched to learn that I had noticed her dedication, especially at my young age. She hugged me with genuine affection.

"You are a good, sweet child. I am glad you are off to a better situation. Would that I could follow."

"You should, madame. On the night mother died, I asked Guibourg if you might come with me to court and he said, *We shall see.*"

Madame smiled at the mimicry, shaking her head with resignation, all the same.

"He told me, little one, that I was to continue as his housekeeper on the Rue St. Denis."

"That place is terrible," I protested. "You must run away, then, or you will surely be miserable."

Des Oeillets looked dejected and paused before she answered.

"He will pay me a fair wage, Bijoux, and I must consider my keep. Finding a decent household these days is near to impossible. Many would be grateful to be offered the position and not care whom they served."

"I wish I could hire you. Perhaps once I am at court, I shall hear of a lady in need of an attendant. Then we could be together again."

"A wonderful dream, mademoiselle. Yet, I doubt any noblewoman would employ a maid who brings along a baby." Her large, brown eyes filmed-over with unshed tears.

"What?" I demanded. "Are you with child?"

She moved her head in assent, unable to speak.

"Who is the father?" I was livid, angered more by Des Oeillets' confession than by my own change of fortune.

"I am sorry, truly, mademoiselle. I was wrong to tell you. Forgive me."

"Only if you give me the father's name. Was it someone from the salon?"

"Yes," she whimpered.

"Who? The abbé must be informed. He will confront the rogue..."

"Bijoux," she clasped me by the shoulders, "he is aware of my condition! All too aware! Say nothing more, please."

"Guibourg did this thing? How? He and my mother shared a bed, did they not?"

"You are an innocent, I cannot explain," she sobbed. "I betrayed my lady's trust and I deserve this punishment."

"Madame," I replied, pretending to be grown-up, "my mother was the most famous whore in France. Nothing you say will shock me."

"Do not speak ill of the dead," she admonished, making the sign of the cross. "Your mother wasn't all bad."

"Marion was selfish and conceited—she loved only herself."

"Stop it, that's not true," chided the good nurse.

"Yes it is. Are you afraid that you will go to hell if you admit it?" I gibed. "She treated you no better than a dog. The same for me. Don't you remember that day at Versailles, don't you recall how terrible she was to us? She and Guibourg knew we were telling the truth. Did either listen? No, and I shall tell you why, madame. My mother and her priest worshipped Satan. They held Black Masses together. Guibourg was—still is—a sorcerer and a poisoner. If you go to live with him, he will force you to pray at the altar of evil!"

Des Oeillets let out a shriek and crumbled to the floor. Her weeping became more intense and I felt badly about hurting her with my harsh words. I had been too honest.

"What am I to do?" she wailed.

"Come with me. Guibourg is headed for either prison or the stake. Do you want to be there when the cardinal's Guards come for him? What if they arrest you, too? Someday he will injure the wrong person, madame, and you will not want to know the abbé when that happens."

"I have no choice but to serve him, unless I try to lose the child. While I may be desperate, I am also afraid of going that far. After seeing what happened to the marquise, who wouldn't be?"

"Promise me you will not take any of his powders," I urged. "He is a murderer. The only reason he does not kill me is because he thinks I'll recruit him new customers at court. He also believes me favored ever since Versailles."

"What happened that afternoon in the woods?"

Madame had ceased crying and her eyes were opened very wide.

"Nothing," I said, denying any claim I might have cause to regret. "Yet I think I saw a messenger of the deities two nights ago when I went upstairs to bed. His name was Jacques."

She was relieved by the change of subject.

"He was probably an admirer of your late mother, child, who had come to pay his final respects."

"No, I think he came from the gods. No mortal could be as splendid as Jacques. He was wise, too, madame. He knew everything—my name, Guibourg's, mother's—he foretold of a girl who would be my friend in the future. He was very kind and not at all as was Noctambule."

"What did you call the huntsman from Versailles?" Des Oeillets was panic-stricken.

"He said his name was Noctambule."

"*Mon Dieu*! Beware, dear girl, for he is a fiend. Legend claims that his subjects are those souls who find no rest for they are the undead."

"Jacques told me that evil has no power unless we believe that it does. He told me to seek the Truth and to see the good around us. He said that the Dieties love us all, madame, more than we are able to comprehend."

"I wish I had been there, my pet. I could use a dose of sage advice. My past judgment has been poor, I fear, and my sins weigh heavily on my mind."

"Tell me what happened. You will feel better if you do. I shan't repeat your story to anyone. We share the secret of Versailles, do we not?"

"I trust you, Bijoux," she smiled, "but you are a little girl."

"I want to know what you saw while you lived here," I begged. "I need to hear the real story behind this," I retrieved the lock of hair from the floor, holding it aloft. "Don't I deserve to know?"

Des Oeillets studied the knotty swirls inherent to the boards beneath her feet.

"I suppose you do," she admitted. "Do not be shocked by what I say."

We sat on Marion's bed and talked. Madame's retelling of the past was stilted in its beginning, yet gained depth and meaning as she spoke with candor. She omitted few facts, and I listened avidly to the tale she told, eager for enlightenment. One topic was too private, however, and when the recollection reached her seduction by Guibourg, the woman stopped without apology.

"I shall say no more. Not to you, nor to anyone else, for that matter."

"Nothing? Not when it happened?"

The caretaker grimaced. "Two months ago. Your mother was entertaining M. Fouquet in this very bed, I trust, when the abbé came to my quarters. He smelled of drink, but I allowed him past my bolt for some odd reason. Perhaps I was lonely, who can say? I saw him standing in the dark hallway, his face more handsome when lit by the glow of a taper, and I decided to have him, rightly or wrongly. I regret the decision and then again, I don't, God forgive me. One day you will understand my meaning."

I fell silent. Not sure what Des Oeillets was talking about, I did know that men and women often removed their clothing and slept together naked. What actually went on between the couples did not interest me. All I was certain of was that it must be something nice, since mother had been paid thousands of gold *louis* to do it for her lovers.

The only nasty aspect of disrobing appeared to be when the lady involved was left with a growing belly, as had eventually happened to the marquise and apparently to Des Oeillets, too. That result stymied me; why did women sometimes get children and at other times, nothing? Too shy to ask the housekeeper about the mystery, I opted for another question.

"Do you love Guibourg?"

"No, dear. The streets of Paris are a deadly place, rife with beggars and thieves. I could not survive on my own, never mind with a child."

"As soon as I am able, I shall send for you. I know where Guibourg lives. His address is one I shan't forget, madame. Just be cautious and keep to yourself, for the abbé is no gentleman. His fine costume is a cover for his fiendish ways. Never trust him, I beg of you."

"I shan't, on that you may depend. Please forgive me if I my words disturbed you. I was your mother's maid and confidante since the days of Cinq-Mars, you see, but until I heard you speak your mind, I had no cause to give her boasting a second thought."

"You always knew about the Rue St. Denis and the curses, didn't you?"

"Bijoux, I saw much and said very little. My mistress and her priest were too sly in their actions to be up to any good. Now, between your information and my own, we have a good notion of what transpired under our noses, don't we?"

"Yes," I agreed. "Thank you for telling me everything. The not knowing bothered me more than anything else might. Leaving home tomorrow will be much easier, thanks to you."

"I wish you naught but *adieu,* dear Bijoux. We may never see one another again, but I am glad that our paths did cross."

She leaned over and kissed me timidly on the brow. Unexpectedly, my lower lip quivered while my throat constricted with pain. Before that tender overture, no one else had shown me as much affection as Madame des Oeillets had with one, simple gesture.

"Let us find you a jewel from Marion's collection," she suggested, likewise moved. "Should circumstances become unkind, you might sell the stone for a tidy sum. Some of the larger rocks are quite valuable and I, alone, know where she kept the best ones."

"Guibourg has no clue?"

"None whatsoever," she gloated. "Marion Delorme never revealed their hiding place to any man, though I am certain the favourite Étienne would deny it."

"This is perfect!" I exclaimed, hugging her about the waist. "You need not live with him, after all. I know what to do."

"What?" Des Oeillets was dumbfounded.

"We split the treasure in two—half for me, half for you. Then we leave some paste pins and necklaces on the dressing table. Guibourg will mistake the forgeries for mother's real gems, and take everything he finds. He'll never know the difference."

"He would kill for those jewels," she warned. "I can get out of town fast enough, but he will definitely know where to find you."

"He won't harm me. You know why. Besides," I laughed, "if he accuses me of theft, I'll lie. Do you mind taking the blame?"

"Not at all," she beamed. "I'll escape as soon as Guibourg takes you to meet your new keeper. Meanwhile, tonight I'll sew your share into the hem of a traveling cloak and, that way, he will never know what you carry away with you."

"Wonderful! Imagine his face should he confront me some day! By then, who knows, the abbé could be rotting in a cell at the Bastille or sentenced to work on a galley ship."

"I hope you are correct," she chimed. "This is the first, real chance I've had at a better life and I'll risk the danger of getting caught, I don't care. I'd rather be on the run than slave to Guibourg."

"Leave the country," I said. "Go to England."

"I'll think of a safe hiding place, trust me, Bijoux. France is a big country and he will never find me, especially if I make for the mountains in the south."

"Try to contact me from wherever you settle. I plan to watch Guibourg closely—I could send you news of him."

"I'd rather hear about you," she said. "How could I forget my generous benefactress?"

"It's the least I can do, madame. You were honest with me about mother and father. People are bound to ask me questions about my parents—what would I have said before today?"

"Don't remind anyone that Cinq-Mars was your father," Des Oeillets advised. "He died in his shoes, after all."

"True. Who was my father?"

"That's smart. So, from now on, you are Bijoux Delorme. Until you marry, of course."

"I don't like boys."

"Stop it, girl. You are a pretty thing and if you grow up to be half as attractive as was your mother, men will be begging for your hand."

"I have no name, no dowry—who would want me?"

"You will have the gems—as in your name—how strange. Perhaps your parents had a premonition when they called you *Bijoux*."

"A most curious choice," I agreed, hopping off the bed. "Let us collect the bounty."

Des Oeillets followed suit.

"The jewelry is rightfully yours, not his," was her comment, "and after what that swine did to your mother, he doesn't deserve a *sou*, anyway."

"The abbé will get exactly what he deserves, be sure," I laughed.

Glad to be free, I was thrilled by the prospect that on the following dawn, I would be embarking on a new life in a better place. A tremendous burden had been lifted, the association with Marion and Cinq-Mars an unpleasant detail. Their mistakes were not going to stop me from finding happiness; greatness was waiting for me, I knew that it was, for my future had already been written in the stars.

The abbé displayed an excellent spirit as he sat in the departed Marion's valuable coach, being wheeled through Paris in style to the Cours-la-Reine, or Queen's Drive. That promenade, referred to simply as the Cours, consisted of a strip of road running parallel to the river Seine. Five or six carriages could be driven abreast on their way to the circular meeting spot, or Rond-Point, where most romantic business in Paris was conducted. More than one hundred vehicles could be easily maneuvered on the Cours; no mean feat in light of the large crowds jamming the sidewalks, the sedan chairs competing for space, or the riders putting their horses through their paces.

Four impressive rows of elms flanked the entire length of the avenue where serious lovers were expected to be found trysting beneath those tree boughs. The attendant vendors who supposedly sold sweets made more money ferrying perfumed notes between amorous parties than they did hawking candies. Of the six hundred streets located in Paris, the Cours, in its day, was the indisputable venue of Eros, where Cupid held a most visible court.

Guibourg had not informed me as to exactly what arrangements he had concluded with M. d'Éstoiles on my behalf, nor did I ask him for the details. I preferred to catch a glimpse of the sights that one could take in on the rather lengthy trip from the Marais to our intended destination. The route we followed began on the Rue St. Antoine, the second busiest thoroughfare in the city. Filled with pedestrians, carts and animals, most travelers walked close to the buildings to avoid the disgusting stream of filthy water that ran down the street's middle. Those who could not afford a coach or sedan chair carried their good shoes in a bag or were booted to the thigh to prevent contact with what the citizens of Paris called *odure*. Not to mention that relieving oneself in public was not considered an unusual act. If and when Nature called, the summons was duly answered.

The carnival atmosphere of the Rue St. Antoine was further enhanced by the presence of beggars plying their trade, street merchants offering up miracle cures, lurking pickpockets, and clowns juggling brightly colored balls. My favorite performers were the gypsy dancers and their adorable dogs; small creatures that stood straight like humans on their tiny hind legs, yapping ferociously at no one in particular. The rat killers who shouted out their services to those who would listen were less appealing a sight, but a welcomed one if the onlooker's home was vermin infested, a common nuisance. Letter writers penned correspondence for the illiterate, book vendors promoted the latest titles and the attorneys' stalls were filled to capacity with customers. The beguiling street was a showcase for the remedy of unpleasant conditions as well as a stage for the most pleasant of diversions; a multitude of life's facets were exposed in its treading, and the audience swarmed there faithfully to witness the spectacle.

Due to the numbers of people out and about, our journey to the Cours was slowed and required an hour's time. When we reached the vicinity, I mouthed a prayer for Des Oeillets and asked Athena of the bright and flashing eyes to keep Guibourg's hands off my cape.

The wrap sat atop a chest containing my worldly effects, having been dumped on the opposite seat by an unconcerned lackey. Madame had appeared shortly thereafter, poking her head through the carriage window to say her good-byes, giving me a quick wink and a peck on the cheek. The coach, by then, had begun to roll away, and I regretted that I did not know the proper words to utter as a farewell to my partner in crime.

So I leaned outside the door and waved to Des Oeillets, instead. After a few moments of frantic arm motion, the abbé pulled me back inside through the opening into a seated position.

"Stay put," was all he deigned to convey.

"Go to Hades," was what I wished to reply, yet did not have the pluck to say, so I looked down contritely at my lap.

Convinced that I was too filled with dread to misbehave, Guibourg returned to counting and examining the small vials he had brought with him in a leather pouch. More drugs, or worse, poisons, I guessed. No doubt they were intended for whoever was lucky enough to be getting me as their part of the abbé's bribe.

The air was heavy and the weather unseasonably warm, causing nasty smells to circulate through the area. Relief came when we reached the open space constituting the Cours. Everyone in Paris appeared to be enjoying the sultry summer afternoon as they strolled along the walkways in their meticulously selected finery. Everyone who could afford a day of leisure, that is to say.

A sector of the populace seemed unaware that a civil war was being waged, or that the fate of a nation hung in the balance of that struggle. Flirtations and dalliances were more interesting pursuits; rebellion and lofty sentiment the stock and trade of poets who entertained drawing rooms occupied by ne'er-do-wells or the pretentious. A minority of French men and women of means may not have liked Mazarin influencing politics to the extent that he did, yet, they thought him a more tolerant advisor than had been Richelieu. The Italian was not worth dying for, in their opinion. Seize the day, revel in the moment, were all the politics such persons needed to espouse, for all would come right in the end, with or without their involvement.

To a degree, that consensus, in hindsight, was most probably correct. Similar to those ambivalent souls parading to-and-fro between carriages and sedan chairs, stealing kisses from behind drawn curtains, I harbored only a concern for my own well-being and safety.

Would Guibourg's connection at court turn out to be male or female, friend or foe?

Was I destined to become the companion to some well-bred lady or merely a scullery maid relegated to a palace basement?

To confess I was unafraid would be a lie. To admit that fear of the unknown was making my throat dry and stomach queasy, was closer to the truth. Goose flesh covered my arms, sending an occasional shiver through my tiny frame. As a comfort of sorts, I retrieved my cloak and hugged the wrap close to my chest; Guibourg took no notice of my actions.

"Here we are," he announced when our coach halted to one side of the Rond-Point. "Let me seek out M. d'Éstoiles; he should have arrived by now, seeing as though we are late, ourselves. Don't leave the carriage, understand?"

"Yes, monsieur." My reply was automatic. The abbé stared at me hard, as if he would never see me again, then went forth to do his searching. Because I was frightened by the prospect of being adopted by a total stranger, I considered pleading with Guibourg to keep me with him on the Rue St. Denis.

Quite an interlude passed and then the door reopened, in streamed sunlight, and a leg clad in fine footwear appeared. The boot's leather was soft and slouchy around the ankle, a huge top cuff was turned down at the knee. About that juncture was tied a satin trimming that gathered the visitor's full-cut breeches and secured the pants' leg in place. Next came a green silk doublet with small epaulettes, complimented by a shirt of lawn, whose bouffant sleeves were pleated in crisp rows. Two white tassels dangled from a thin cord fastened under the blouson's collar, and together they laid neatly side-by-side on a broad chest.

The first impression I had of the person sitting next to me was that the man was no courtier. Judging from the size of his sword, a soldier, possibly, but not some fop who was fond of gossip and wagering at the card table for hours. Squandering vast sums on the latest Italian gaming rage, *Quantonova*, or playing the court lottery, did not seem to be his true calling.

Close on the heels of d'Éstoiles, and I might add a bit tensely at that, followed Guibourg. Fishing about inside his peacock blue coat that was trimmed in sarcenet, the priest sat and produced the requested lure, handing the bundle over to the fair-haired gentleman. D'Éstoiles nodded in thanks, placed the contraband underneath his doublet and clapped his gloved hands together loudly.

"Good work, monsieur, your thoughtfulness is noted. So," he remarked, fixing his intensely blue gaze in my direction, "are you at the ready, mademoiselle?"

"Whenever you wish, monsieur."

"Well, say your good-byes," he suggested in a brusque tone, "then off we get."

Guibourg bent forwards from the waist and I gave him a perfunctory kiss on the cheek. I had to appear to be obedient. The priest embraced me in return and the hug was not half-hearted.

"*Au revoir, ma petite* Bijoux. You will not be forgotten, nor neglected."

"Do you mean that, abbé?"

"I shall call on you at court. Your mother left you in my care, after all."

"And M. Cousinot? Shall the three of us be friendly still?"

"Of course, " he smiled in a patronizing way. "Why should things change? We are as much a family as any, Bijoux."

D'Éstoiles made a move to depart.

"I swear that M. Guibourg will be kept apprised of your condition on a routine basis."

He stepped down from the velvet-draped enclosure, swinging the door wide open, reaching back for me to follow.

I did as he prompted, a sure hold on the garment concealing my inheritance. Remaining inside the precious transport, Guibourg motioned for a lackey to fetch my trunk and it was duly removed to d'Éstoiles' vehicle. The coach was smaller than mother's, with less gilt trim on its black exterior. One could only speculate as to how Étienne would manage to maintain the expensive tastes to which the marquise had accustomed him.

Guibourg's driver whipped at the team of matched grays as a sign to be off and the abbé disappeared from my day-to-day existence. The end had been so abrupt that I was left dazed, compounded by the reflection as to the number of stones I had carried away. I was certain that Guibourg would not suspect me of their removal when he retraced each step leading to our separation. Yet, Des Oeillets had best be gone, for her remaining behind at the house had afforded the best opportunity to ransack Marion's property. Étienne was not the forgiving type. He would be back to interrogate me concerning the missing gems. How I handled that inevitable meeting might depend a great deal upon the man who was accompanying me to the Louvre, M. d'Éstoiles.

"Pardon me, monsieur," I dared to speak at last, "but am I to be lodged with you or another?"

"You are bold," he smiled. "Do not be concerned, Mademoiselle Bijoux, for I have your best interests at heart. Did M. Guibourg not inform you of your destination, poor child?"

"He told me nothing, M. d'Éstoiles, scoundrel that he is."

"You are well-spoken for a youngster," he noted.

"Thank you, monsieur. Raised as I was in the house of Marion Delorme, conversation comes to me with ease. I had good teachers back in the Marais."

"And Guibourg, is he...?" A raised eyebrow indicated at what he was hinting.

"No," I replied emphatically. "The abbé is not my father. My mother did not know him at the time of my birth. She had famous lovers then, such as the Marquis de Cinq-Mars."

"So I have been told, Bijoux. Still, the priest could be your papa."

"Believe what you like. What the matter?" I shrugged. "Perhaps you are my long-lost father, monsieur. What is your age? Thirty? What season is your Sun to be placed?"

"God in heaven," d'Éstoiles laughed aloud, "but you are amusing! If I were able, I would keep you with me, mademoiselle!"

"And why are you not free to do so?" I shot back. "Could it be because you are no courtier? If I were to judge, I'd say you are a soldier, born in the sign of Leo."

He did not become angry with me. Instead, the gentleman stroked his goatee and pondered the denunciation.

"Astute, too," he finally said. "Mademoiselle, you are correct. My true name is Charles de Batz Castelmore d'Artagnan, a Gascon lion and former member of the Grand Musketeers. I am currently in the employ of his Eminence, Cardinal Mazarin, and my duties have not changed much from when I was a soldier. At present, however, I wear a disguise instead of a uniform in my service to the king."

"Are you truly a spy?" I was intrigued by his dangerous profession and not just a little smitten by his handsome face.

"Yes, for the moment, Bijoux; yet, that secret is for your ears alone. I am entrusting you with very important information because I think that you are a steadfast subject. I also think," he added with a grin, "that you might possibly help me to protect our young Louis from his enemies."

"How? I'll do anything," I offered, excitement in my voice. "I've always wished to follow the Countess of Saint-Belmont and fight duels and ride astride a horse."

"Calm down, calm down, mademoiselle. I am well acquainted with your heroine and you will *not* turn out the same, cursing and drinking and dressing as do cavaliers. You may care to assist me in my espionage, though, by telling me everything that you hear at the apartments of one Madame de Choisy, the lady who is soon to become your guardian. The cardinal and the king would be most impressed if you could remain alert to her schemes and stay abreast of her many plots. Also, I would like you to save any messages Guibourg may send to you."

"That will be simple to do. Is Madame de Choisy an enemy of the Crown?"

"Not exactly, but she knows much concerning the different intrigues at court. She makes it her business, shall we say, to know."

"Is she important?"

"Her husband is a retainer of the late king's brother, Gaston d'Orléans. The couple have produced four sons, yet Madame de Choisy longs for a daughter. Though at her age, fifty, another baby would be a miracle."

"Are you saying she will be kind to me because I am a girl?"

"Use that fact to your advantage," d'Artagnan counseled. "Her youngest is six years of age and is being brought up as a little lady—dresses, dolls, baubles, all the trappings. Madame de Choisy is so involved in the masquerade that she refers to the boy as *Mademoiselle Sancy*."

"How odd! I suppose she does not fancy the Countess of Saint-Belmont?"

"Mademoiselle, I daresay that you are correct."

We passed the Tuileries garden, each immersed in our own reveries; I, for one, mindful that we were nearing the Louvre, where the court was in residence at that particular time. If the king, or rather the queen and Mazarin, decided to occupy another palace such as the Palais Royal in Paris, or St. Germain outside the city, their entire retinue would follow. Each royal establishment had its own staff, stable and caretakers, catering to the whims of France's elite society. Moving house may have been unpleasant for the personal servants attached to the nobility, but the aristocrats rather enjoyed the activity. Boredom was the chief malaise at court and frequent outings, a common antidote.

"Monsieur d'Artagnan?" I asked suddenly.

"Yes?"

"Why did you tell me the truth about yourself?"

"You are inquisitive, I must say. A good sign, I suppose." He paused, then admitted, "Well, for one, I admire your spirit. Two, I share your dislike of the Abbé Guibourg; he is not a man of honor. And lastly, you are bound to discover my real identity at some point, so why make an enemy when you could be a friend, instead?"

His candor made me think of Jacques and I beamed back at him.

"M. d'Artagnan, always count on my help. You took me away from that terrible man, and I am forever in your debt."

"As long as I am alive, you are safe from that wolf in sheep's clothing," he reassured. "You owe me nothing in return, yet the king needs all the support he may muster. Bad people are leading the Fronde, Bijoux; men and women who will stop at nothing, I fear, to see their aims achieved. We must crush the traitors once and for all. You are on the side of the monarchy, are you not, *ma petite?*"

"My mother told me to hate the king, monsieur. Both she and Guibourg said that no Bourbon should rule, though I never had a taste for their hatred." I stopped, cocked my head sideways and remarked, "To prove my sincerity, I shall tell you a secret."

"What is that?" d'Artagnan chuckled, bemused.

"Young King Louis and I were both born on the same day, September the fifth, although he is two years older than me," I boasted, rather proud of the coincidence. "Plus, he arrived with teeth and so did I—a couplet, to be exact."

"That seems more than lucky chance to me, mademoiselle. Not that I am a superstitious fellow or inclined to consult the stars on important matters, but sharing a natal day with his Majesty will not go unnoticed. Be a model of virtue at court and that corresponding date could bring you a pension or honor."

"Do you think so, monsieur? Do you think the king will notice me? I have always felt that Louis and I were linked to one other. My mother, of course, said I was wrong to believe such a thing, yet, I believe the stars do not lie. Do you think me silly?"

"No, not at all. When you are older, I shall arrange an audience between you and the king if you prove to be a good girl," d'Artagnan vowed. "That will give you something to look forward to, won't it?"

"Yes, that would be marvelous, monsieur. You are so kind. May we be friends forever?"

"Somehow, I think that we shall."

D'Artagnan's apparent mirth caused him to pull on a strand of my unruly hair.

"You remind me of a vixen with your red brush and sly tongue—a tiny fox who is about to lead the big hounds a merry chase, no doubt."

"Oh, I am not that clever, monsieur, although I am smart enough to be the nicest girl in the world and then Louis will want to make my acquaintance because he is a good person, too. The king will like me, monsieur, he will."

"If your conviction is that strong, then undoubtedly it will be so," my Musketeer agreed. "All things are possible to those who believe."

"Monsieur, do you know of a Lady Comaetho?"

D'Artagnan eyed me suspiciously. "No, I do not. Why?"

"An old man once gave me that name. No matter," I giggled.

"Most probably a character from Greek myth, dear girl. Madame de Choisy will know of whom you speak, no doubt, since she is well steeped in the Classics!"

I gazed up at him in total adoration. The man who was my deliverer and favorite hero, next to the Countess, was beyond compare. To me, he seemed larger than life, grander than the mightiest conqueror fable could describe. D'Artagnan had saved me from Hades and was escorting me to a paradise, the court of Louis XIV. Madame de Choisy might be a meddler and her offspring an oddity, but I, Bijoux, was determined to bear all hardships and suffer the eccentric woman if my doing so would please Mazarin's right hand.

A sense of duty to the Crown would also see me through the most difficult of trials; on that point my resolve was unshakable, my will, unstoppable. In due course, I reasoned with a child's faith, Louis would recognize my unflagging devotion to his cause and he would regard me with favor. A mental fabrication of a scene from the future played on the stage of my imagination: the previously sworn enemy and I were on intimate terms, sharing surreptitious reports; me, a trusted aide, an agent on a mission for the king and for France. Louis XIV loomed large on a horizon of tantalizing possibilities. His bearing would be majestic and his character poised. The man whom I followed would be every inch a monarch. Our birth dates were one and the same, I told myself, his father had loved my father—were we not meant to work together, was I not meant to become the young king's personal astrologer, had Jacques not encouraged me to follow the path that led to the throne?

While I dreamed of the strategies involved in obtaining a royal nod, d'Artagnan chatted about the modes of acceptable behavior practiced at the palace, better known as *etiquette*. In his opinion, a lady must curtsy properly when presented to a superior. Evidently the queen, herself hailing from Spain, the Land of Ritual, put great store in the correctness of a courtier's form and had decreed that her son would not be surrounded by people with sloppy manners.

Being at ease with my host, I asked d'Artagnan if he would watch my dip and correct any imperfections in its technique.

To stand straight in a swinging carriage was a difficult test; yet, I managed, bending at the knee, skirts fanned, shoulders back. As I moved to complete the practice attempt by rising, however, one of the wheels beneath us hit an obstacle in the road. The subsequent jarring sent me flying across a not overly spacious interior and my body tumbled against one of the wood-paneled doors with a thud.

D'Artagnan immediately stooped and helped me back to the banquette. He had me near to resituated when the driver reined in the galloping team hard, pitching us both towards the rear of the coach. Flung back with force, the rough-and-tumble young man bumped his skull in the ensuing fall and I landed atop him in the fray.

Both embarrassed, we disengaged ourselves when the stop was complete.

"Not too elegant, are we?" he mocked, brushing dust from his sleeve. "I wonder what the commotion is all about—it best be well explained. We've reached the Louvre," he said, glancing out a window. "Ah, yes, the culprit who was the cause of our near-accident has been apprehended!"

The jovial lilt in d'Artagnan's voice compelled me to look outside, too. The impressive courtyard was not teeming with drill soldiers, rather occupied by a handful of stable hands and an irate woman. The older lady, dressed in black, chastised a boy who wore a rather shabby costume.

"Who goes there?" d'Artagnan called forth with as much serious cadence as he could muster.

"'Tis I, the good-for-nothing rascal!" the dark-haired youth answered in return, hands placed on his hips, stance defiant. "I command you to quit your carriage, sir, to attend to your better on the double!"

The order caused my mouth to fall agape.

"Who does he think himself to be?" I asked. "How dare he speak to you in such a fashion? We should have silenced his impertinent mouth with our wheels, I say! Do you know the lad, monsieur?"

"That, Mademoiselle Bijoux, is the *enfant terrible* of the royal family: Philippe Bourbon, the Duc d'Anjou, the king's heir and brother."

"Come out I say," the tiny spitfire insisted, "come out at once or I shall call my men and have you arrested!"

The prince's ridiculous threat caused general hilarity amongst his elders. Then he stamped one of his scuffed shoes impatiently on the gravel drive, and we all roared aloud.

"I come in the name of the king," d'Artagnan managed to shout between belly laughs, "and in the name of Cardinal Mazarin, to boot, your Highness!"

The veteran of many a siege and battle looked at me with

an expression worthy a buffoon. Then the Musketeer exited our vantage point with a dramatic leap; hand at the ready on blade's hilt, lace and linen sent wafting on a light breeze. He cut a most spectacular figure and I fully expected Monsieur Philippe to soil his breeches from terror at the sight of Charles de Batz Castelmore.

No such good fortune attended. The duke, who was my contemporary, strode forward to meet the envoy of the Crown.

"Who is that with you?"

D'Artagnan acknowledged Philippe's presence with a respectful nod, then motioned in my direction. Lowering me from the carriage with a flourish and a spin, his introduction was brief.

"Your Highness, may I present Mademoiselle Bijoux Delorme, soon to be assigned to the Choisy household."

"Bijoux," Philippe repeated, advancing in spite of his governess' instructions to the contrary, "what a fabulous name! I love to collect jewels and when I am a grown-up, I shall have more of them than anybody—especially more than my brother, the king."

D'Artagnan's poke to my back was gentle, yet prodding. His advice drifted back and I made a quick curtsy that was executed with much more style than the former attempt. My preoccupation to be flawless, however, made me forget that I was clutching a cape in one hand and the weighted-down wrap fell at the Duc d'Anjou's feet.

Philippe pounced on the mantle with verve, with more speed than mother had displayed when collecting gold coins. He resembled a guttersnipe or street urchin; desperate and grasping in his actions. As I watched him in amazement, I did not care if he was a prince, no one was going to steal that swathe of gray velvet from me without a fight.

"This is lovely, mademoiselle. Would you care to gift it to me, per chance?"

He fingered the soft nap covetously.

"Never. Give it back this instant!"

"I don't think so," was his snooty reply. He pivoted on heel and walked towards the main gate, dragging the trophy through the dirt.

D'Artagnan ran after Philippe.

"Your Highness, return mademoiselle's property lest I inform the cardinal of your behavior."

"No, *mignon,*" he chortled.

The expression caught my attention. What was a *mignon*? I had kept company with sophisticated gentlemen my entire life and they had not spoken in such a manner. It had to be a bad word, I deduced, given the flush on M. d'Artagnan's cheeks. The king's rotten brother had to be stopped and *I* would be the one to stop him.

"Surrender my cape, thief!" I screamed in frustration. "You not only resemble a peasant, you behave as one, too."

The prince checked his processional retreat. When he faced me, in a few moment's time, Philippe's jaw was taut, his scrutiny piercing.

"If you desire this rag so badly, Mademoiselle Bijoux, take it from me! I dare you!"

I bent over the spot where the hem lay ignobly in a patch of caked mud. Taking the turned-up fabric in hand, I saw the long, running stitches Des Oeillets had sewn in haste and a covered lump rubbed against my fingertips.

The jewels were mine and I was not going to lose them.

Gathering together the remaining material, I moved towards the Duc d'Anjou, who maintained his hold on the purloined article. To emphasize his superior strength, Philippe jerked the garment with a quick snap-of-the-wrist, bringing me closer to him than I cared to be.

"Give it a pull," he jeered. "Go ahead, try harder!"

"Fine," came my answer and I hissed that word at him, spittle spraying the air. I proceeded to tug on the cloth with all my might, stepping several paces backwards as I did.

"You can't do it, can you?" he teased unmercifully.

"You are a brat, a scoundrel," I retorted, vexed beyond belief.

Tears threatened; however, crying would have been a sign

of defeat. Instead, I reached out, clamped onto Philippe's right forearm, drew it to my lowered head and bit into his blouson-covered flesh.

Yelping from the ensuing pain, Philippe shoved me off of him, causing me to fall for the third time in less than an hour. And he maintained his grip on the cape. Before I could stand, the duke took advantage of my spill and kicked me solidly on the rump. He then slapped the rest of me several times for good measure. The boy was bleeding onto his shirtsleeve, yet I ignored his hurt, angry that I had not regained possession of my property.

"Babies fight better than you," I declared while he continued to thrash at me. The observation raised his royal ire to a heightened pitch.

"Cease with this brawling, both of you," d'Artagnan insisted, concerned because Philippe was wounded.

He attempted to pry us apart, and when that effort appeared fruitless, the Gascon grabbed onto a handful of the cloak and wrenched it away into his safekeeping. I heard the sound of threads tearing with his forceful action; too late some of Des Oeillets handiwork was ruined and the Marquise de Cinq-Mars' gem collection tumbled out of hiding before the assemblage.

Sparkling diamonds, rubies, sapphires and emeralds—all set in gold—cascaded to the ground, casting prisms of color everywhere. Terrified I would be forced to forfeit the hoard, I scrambled to retrieve as many rings, bracelets and pendants as I could carry. Philippe joined me in my efforts and confiscated a valuable set of diamond eardrops. He stared at them, enraptured by their dazzling brilliance.

"Mademoiselle Bijoux, it would appear you brought more than clothing on your journey," d'Artagnan remarked with a grin.

"The jewels are rightfully mine, they belonged to my mother. If I hadn't hidden the stones, Guibourg would have taken them for himself. They are all I have left in the world; please monsieur, believe me, I did not steal them."

"There, there, do not fret," the soldier soothed. "I have no intention of taking your inheritance away, mademoiselle. Who am I to make a claim on your possessions?"

"I'm keeping these," Philippe announced. "I'll never return them, never!"

"Your behavior is unbecoming, monsieur. Madame," d'Artagnan turned to address the incompetent nursemaid, "please discipline your charge or else I shall do your job for you."

"Forgo the diamonds," the woman sweetly prompted, "and I shall tell the queen of your chivalrous deed, monsieur. Be a good boy and return the clips to Mademoiselle Bijoux."

Philippe pouted.

"No," was the sole answer he had for the unwanted advice.

"If you were not the king's brother," I snapped, "I would find a sword and run you through. Keep the eardrops if you must, yet be disgraced if you do."

Philippe considered his options. A smile formed at the corners of his mouth, and he attempted to barter with me.

"If you will stand up for me, instead of for Louis..." he dangled the earrings from an outstretched hand, tormenting me further.

"No, never, you...you...*mignon!*"

The slander burst forth from my mouth and the copied insult sounded silly. Rattled by the confrontation, I hardly noticed the bright sunshine stinging my eyes. My legs began to tremble and I felt the urge to vomit. Following the experience with Noctambule, I knew I was about to faint.

"M. d'Artagnan, help me," I asked, leaning against him for support. "Please find M. Cousinot—take me to him. Watch over the jewelry," I added with concern.

D'Artagnan picked me up and whisked me away, well prepared for trouble having been trained to expect the unexpected. He started for the palace without delay, and Philippe trailed behind, jabbering at us as we made our way across the courtyard. I clutched onto the precious cargo I had saved with such intensity, the stones' fittings dug into my skin.

"Are you going to die?" asked the prince, near to weeping with concern.

"No, your Highness," I said weakly. "I must live so I might trounce your backside again."

"I like you," he giggled. "You are funny, mademoiselle."

After that, I do not remember much else; blackness overcame my senses. When I stirred, d'Artagnan was carrying me through a cool, dimly lit hallway inside the immense, old structure of the Louvre.

"Where are we going?" My inquiry was whisper-like.

"To my apartments. Then I shall fetch the doctor for you."

"Thank-you," I managed, glancing down at the marble floor. Philippe tagged along, barely keeping apace. Since I was not paying much attention to where we were headed, I did not expect my bearer to halt suddenly in his tracks.

"Your Majesty, your Eminence," Charles de Batz acknowledged, unable to bow with me in his arms.

"What have we here?"

A scented, red glove grazed my forehead. My heart began to beat faster and I felt dizzy again, for the man expressing an interest in my well-being was none other than Cardinal Mazarin. Close to his side stood a somberly clad, serious-looking boy who was his godson, and also, the ruler of France.

Similar to Jacques, fine black curls framed Louis' regal features. Unlike the other, the king did not wear a peruke.

"Who is she?" Louis queried.

"Mademoiselle Bijoux," Philippe announced. The second son was entitled to a modicum of familiarity when addressing his elder brother. The Duc d'Anjou was not allowed, however, to display his notorious lack of patience when in the sovereign's presence.

It was a mistake, then, when Philippe informed the king, "This lady is not interested in you. Leave her alone for she is my friend, not yours."

I shrank inwardly as Louis drew himself up to full-height and glowered at his impertinent relative. Philippe's sharp tongue was going to ruin any chance I might have had of becoming an important person at court.

"Monsieur," Mazarin warned, "we shall not tolerate boring and vainglorious remarks from you. M. d'Artagnan is our most esteemed emissary; he speaks for himself well enough."

"She is my companion," he whined in return. "Louis always gets everything, it's not fair! She's my friend, she's my friend..."

Philippe jumped up and down on the verge of a temper tantrum, waiving his fists in the air.

Louis exuded disdain, he ignored his brother's embarrassing snit. Looking about him with an imperious air, he sniffed, then sighed to indicate his complete boredom at being detained.

"My brother," the elder Bourbon remarked, "only one fact interests me in this matter. A fact you have obviously neglected."

"What is that?" Philippe sniveled, already beaten.

"No matter who this girl is, or what her connection to you," he paused, "never forget, imbecile, that Mademoiselle Bijoux is *my* subject, not yours."

That pronouncement made, our troupe was allowed to pass. Louis XIV had spoken, he had taken me into the esteemed fold, I was one of his flock. The benediction delivered, he and Mazarin went about their business, and we went about ours.

I was glad of the abrupt dismissal because all I desired was a soft bed and some of Cousinot's tonic to dispel the weakness I was suffering. D'Artagnan would hopefully find the doctor quickly enough, and I was thankful to be in the midst of the powerful.

A pair of heavy eyelids closed, too sapped of strength to remain open. Lost in a dream, I relived the wondrous moment when the king had recognized my existence. Nothing could be more glorious than to belong to him, to be his subject. Allegiance to Louis would be an easy thing to pledge, for I truly could not imagine serving a more perfect sovereign.

That very day in June of 1650 marked the inauguration of my introduction to the potential hazards of a career spent at court. An adventure capable of satisfying several lifetimes had begun, and that personal odyssey, started so long ago in the shadow of the Louvre, was to lead me back to a place I had vowed never to return: a then insignificant hunting lodge nestled in a wood named Versailles.

My parents would have been gladdened by the unexpected development had they survived long enough to see their daughter's triumph; I, on the other hand, would have run back to the meanest street in the city of Paris, had I suspected as a child how this tale would unfold.

CHAPTER FIVE
Snake Eyes

D'Artagnan and Cousinot nursed me back to health following my fainting spell in the courtyard of the king's palace. I wish I could report that a fatigue such as I experienced on that day never returned to render me helpless and vulnerable, but that would be a lie.

The doctor's pink draught, made to Guibourg's earlier specifications, offered the sole relief for my weakness of limb and symptoms of vertigo. Unfortunately, during the week I spent convalescing in M. d'Artagnan's quarters, I required no less than three doses of Cousinot's elixir in order to leave my sickbed. When the concerned soldier asked the dedicated physician what my medicine contained in its mixture, Armand evaded the question with a simple, "Do not pry, monsieur."

The episode left its mark: the First Surgeon was careful to send the tonic during the whole of the Fronde and after. Not a week passed when a member of his personal staff failed to deliver the vial of liquid needed to keep Mademoiselle Bijoux strong.

Seven day's time elapsed before d'Artagnan deemed me well enough to travel the short distance between the Louvre and the Luxembourg Palace where Madame de Choisy was housed. The mischievous lady was seldom found in her apartments, however, so occupied was she with leaving her mark on the various to-dos continuously being hatched at the king's court.

Living under the roof of Gaston d'Orléans, officially known as Monsieur to the court, suited Madame de Choisy's needs to the letter. Who better to lend credence to her scheming than a Prince of the Blood notorious for his past allegiances to no party other than his own? The double-cross had been refined to an art form inside the walls of the Luxembourg; no one quite sure on whose side Gaston would be found when the cock crowed at morning.

Prior to describing the bizarre personality of Jeanne-Olympe de Choisy, it is necessary to explain that she was considered one of the leading *Précieuses*, or *Perfectionists*, of her generation. That honor was given a clique of society women—and a few gentlemen as well—whose literary hysterics and chivalrous behavior, combined with a disdain for physical intercourse in general, made them worthy of worship by the average philistine, or so the members of the group imagined.

One of the leaders of the *Précieuses* was the gorgeous Duchesse de Longueville, who happened to be a cousin of the royal family and whose brothers, the Princes of Condé and Conti, were two of the greatest warriors in the land. Condé, called the Grand Condé, had saved France from a Spanish invasion in 1643 at the Battle of Rocroi, and was adored by the masses. The three siblings were also deeply involved in the politics of the Fronde, and by the time I came to court, Condé, Conti and the Duchesse de Longueville's husband had all been imprisoned five months earlier by their mutual enemy, Queen Anne.

Hiding behind a veil of romantic idealism, the snobbish *Précieuses* championed one of France's first women novelists, Mademoiselle de Scudéry, whose tales of platonic love had attracted an enormous cult following; incredible in light of the fact that her stories, such as *Clélie*, were more than thirteen thousand pages long. Young girls in the provinces read her books and dreamed of coming to Paris where they would be admitted to the ranks of the *Précieuses*; of meeting the gallant knight who would sigh after them, but who would never touch a single hair of their head.

Madame de Choisy's involvement with the group of foppish aristocrats perhaps provided one explanation as to why she clothed her poor little boy, François, in dresses. D'Artagnan had warned me concerning her strange habits, as well as emphasizing that Mazarin would be most interested in any information I gathered while housed at Jeanne-Olympe's apartments. The secret agent also advised being especially kind to *Mademoiselle Sancy*, thus win his doting mother's trust in the process.

A previous lack of playmates caused me to dread the assignment; adults could be conversed with, six-year-olds, another matter altogether. The age difference of four years that existed between me and Choisy's child, seemed an insurmountable obstacle to overcome.

On the appointed day of our interview, d'Artagnan secured a palace serving woman to help me dress, paying careful attention to my appearance when the maid was finished with her task. Knowing how much store Madame de Choisy placed in favorable first impressions, the temporary guardian was insistent that every bow and rose petal be strategically placed on my small person. Jeanne-Olympe was a formidable opponent whose viper eye missed no detail of fashion, and I was fastidiously groomed when the clock struck the hour of two in the afternoon, signaling our departure for the Luxembourg.

Kindly Monsieur de Batz held my small hand in his large one as he led me away from the Louvre. As we walked along together, I realized he was truly protective of me and did not want to see me go, but the reality of a soldier's life did not include children.

We crossed onto the opposite bank of the Seine via the bridge, Pont St. Michel, and the prospect of soon meeting a new mistress made me quake. I looked up at d'Artagnan for some sign of assurance, and he must have felt me staring at him, for the Musketeer returned my uneasy appeal with a wide grin. He stopped our stroll then and there, not far from one of the entrances to Gaston d'Orléans' grand residence.

"Bijoux," he said, bending at the knee to look me straight

in the face, "I am not good at flowery speeches, being a simple man from the countryside, yet I must confess my fondness for you, *ma petite*. I want you to have this," he explained, handing me a package he carried.

"For me!" I exclaimed, inspecting the gift that was shrouded in tissue and decorated with a clumsy bow. It appeared that d'Artagnan had wrapped the offering himself, and I was visibly moved by the sweet gesture. The gentleman cared for me more than I had imagined.

"A mere bagatelle," he replied with a quick wave, mocking the language of a courtier.

Carefully removing the ribbon, the paper fell away on cue, revealing a doll crafted by the premier toy maker in Paris, Madame Aragonais. The pretty thing, whose signature ringlets framed each side of a pale face, was dressed in a lavender creation complete with gold embroideries, lace, and even rosettes attached to fashionable slippers.

"Oh, monsieur, she is lovely, beyond compare! You should not have done this thing, though—the expense..."

"Bijoux," he interrupted, giving me a shy hug, "I care not for savings, my dear girl. In my line of work, I may die tomorrow. To please you pleases me."

I kissed him on a pink cheek in gratitude, not immune to the sensation the rub of whiskers produced against my own soft skin.

"I shall treasure this doll forever, monsieur. What shall we name her, do you think?"

"Mademoiselle Sancy?" d'Artagnan teased.

"No, silly," I giggled. "I think Louise, in honor of the king."

"So be it," he declared. "Now tell me, Bijoux, how exactly did you figure me to be a Gascon lion that day we met?"

"Due to your noble heart and golden mane," I offered, close to tears.

D'Artagnan cleared his throat, looking away, likewise moved. "I must tell you something important, Bijoux, and this is a secret between you, me and one other. I gave your jewels to Monsieur Colbert for safekeeping," he revealed. "That gentleman is one of the cardinal's most trusted servants; should our benefactor be exiled again, Colbert has been instructed to manage and protect Mazarin's fortune. Do you understand what I am saying?"

"Yes," I replied, dragging the tip of one shoe through the dirt.

"Bijoux, attend me," he insisted, serious. "If the cardinal is sent away, I must follow him and you may not see me for some time. Should any misfortune befall me, a receipt for your goods is hidden inside the Bible in my bedchamber. The book is located on a table near to the window. Find the paper and take it to M. Colbert immediately; he will return the gems to you only with that proof."

"Nothing bad is going to happen, is it?" I asked in fear.

"No, of course not," he smiled. "Since I cannot predict the future, it is best that you know the truth. Will you remember what I told you?"

"Yes," I assured him.

"Repeat it to me."

I did. Again and again until d'Artagnan was satisfied I had memorized the hiding place and the name of the stranger who had custody of mother's gems.

Soon we set off to meet Madame de Choisy, entering a very grand abode via a side entrance following our short trek. The interior of the Luxembourg was lighter in feel and in better repair than that of the Louvre; the fact that Louis XIV's uncle had taken a certain Mademoiselle Marie de Montpensier as his first bride accounted for the charming decor. That lady, who unfortunately died in childbirth one year after the marriage, was once the wealthiest heiress in France. The inheritance passed on to her more fortunate newborn who became the richest baby girl in the kingdom. Gaston, being the father of Anne-Marie-Louise and thus the executor of her funds, naturally helped himself to a few coins now and again. And, he married a second time for love.

Much to our mutual annoyance, Madame de Choisy left

d'Artagnan and I awaiting her pleasure in an antechamber outside what I surmised to be a salon. Beyond the door denying us access to the main apartment, could be heard the sounds of irregular laughter and the low drone of a male voice reading aloud.

We were patient guests considering her rude treatment; after an hour had passed on the face of a then-rarely-seen clock displayed on the room's mantelpiece, d'Artagnan was about to go mad with rage.

"Let us be on our way," he ordered, barely checking his temper. "This was a bad notion—I won't be kept cooling my heels, damn her!"

"No, wait," I urged. "Madame is testing us. Either that, or she was born beneath the sign of the Twins, monsieur, for Gemini natives are rarely punctual."

"Fine. Five more minutes, Bijoux, I swear, although that is my absolute limit, not a second longer, Gemini or no!"

As I recall, I held my breath, fearful that Madame de Choisy would continue to ignore her scheduled guests. Immediately following d'Artagnan's concession, however, a handsome, middle-aged woman decked-out in pearls and pale blue brocade practically winged her way into our midst.

The lady's tightly curled, brunette tresses were piled high atop her head, and a wide swath of white streaked backwards from a prominent widow's peak to a mass of haphazardly arranged hair. She was elegant in a quirky, unconventional way; I sensed an independence of spirit lurking beneath the fine trappings and forthcoming apologies.

"Monsieur d'Artagnan, forgive me my most inconsiderate thoughtlessness," she effused. "How could my base manners keep an esteemed warrior such as yourself, comparable only to the ancient Cyrus in valor and deed, standing at attention? Please believe me when I tell you that the sole explanation for my inexcusable conduct lies in the genius of Monsieur Costar's verse. I listen to his melodious rhyme and I quite forget the hour, so captivating are our dear friend's immortal words."

My eyes blinked hard. Who was *the ancient Cyrus*, I

wondered? Or M. Costar, a poet who had never graced Marion's home. What was the learned lady chatting on about? To d'Artagnan's credit, he reacted politely, bowing to signal acceptance of the dubious acknowledgment of guilt.

"Madame de Choisy, may I present Bijoux Delorme, daughter of the late Marion, whose illustrious life was recently cut short, sad to say."

"Marion Delorme, yes, I knew of her," Madame de Choisy said in a condescending manner. She then addressed me with a pointed index finger and a curt, "I shan't abide whoring in this household!"

"No, madame," I replied meekly, dropping to my knees, using the submissive posture for added emphasis. "I would never dishonor your good name or take advantage of your charity. My mother was wicked—I shall never be compared to her."

"I hope not," she sighed, twisting a rope of milky-colored beads as if contemplating a grave matter. "I saw your mother once or twice and you do resemble her, mademoiselle. Perhaps when you are older, if you show promise, you could be of help to me, I suppose. Do you dance or sing pleasantly?"

"No," I answered honestly. My knees were beginning to hurt and I desperately wished to stand.

"Are you familiar with games of chance?"

"No, madame, but might I ask if you were indeed born in the season of Castor and Pollux, the Twins? I could cast your birth chart."

Choisy turned to d'Artagnan, exasperated.

"This girl is a little fool! What good is she to me? Why did you bring her here to waste my time? Really, monsieur, I am a busy woman and cannot afford..."

"*Mama*," a tiny, plaintive voice called out, checking Choisy's verbal assault.

We all stopped to observe a little girl who ran timidly from the salon to Jeanne-Olympe's side, burying her fair head in the mother's voluminous drapery. The child could not be a boy, for I had never seen a better example of juvenile femininity. Cothing, jewelry, even the hairstyle were representative of how a woman of means would outfit a daughter. The doll that d'Artagnan had gifted me resembled the shy creature who cowered in our presence: the essence of fragility, tender and innocent.

Unprompted, I held out a hand and motioned for the small vision to step forward.

"Come here, I shan't hurt you," I cajoled. "Would you like to hold my new lady friend, Louise? She is a spy for the king and her secret name is Comaetho."

A pair of enormous, brown eyes peered out from behind their blue shield. Full of inquisitive reticence, the look inspired in me a desire to protect and nurture a fellow human being. The gentle side of me emerged, one foreign, yet welcome, all the same.

Madame de Choisy regarded us with interest.

"Go ahead," she said softly, "Mademoiselle Bijoux is a good girl. A good, smart girl who knows her Classics, Françoise."

The playmate was soon seated at my side, engrossed with Madame Aragonais' miniature recreation. Mademoiselle Sancy examined the toy from all angles, oblivious to the adults who hovered. I made a point to reveal Louise's pretty shoes and the youngster giggled.

"You are nice," the child whispered, then cuddled closer, leaning against me. Soon a head covered with the silkiest hair imaginable lay in my lap, no doubt tired by all the commotion.

"It would seem that Mademoiselle Bijoux does indeed possesses an excellent talent," d'Artagnan supplied, planting the seed in Choisy's mind that I was a rare find. "Mademoiselle Sancy is at an age where a companion could prove a welcome addition to the nursery. Other children at court have special friends, madame."

"Oh, I know, you are speaking the truth," the adoring mother agreed, "and I deny Mademoiselle Sancy nothing," she beamed. "So, Bijoux, my little Greek scholar, you may stay on!"

"Thank-you," I said, marveling at the smooth skin and cherubic expression of the napping charge. "May I ask, madame, how you would have me address your child?"

"*Françoise*," was my answer, the feminine pronunciation of a boy's Christian name, François. Not about to ask any further questions, I fell silent, stroking Françoise's locks.

"M. d'Artagnan, I believe our business is concluded," Jeanne-Olympe hinted, anxious to return to the poetry reading, "except for one tiny, unimportant detail."

"Quite right, the cosmetics," he grinned, removing Guibourg's pouch. "Take them, madame, and use the mixtures sparingly; your natural radiance requires little embellishment."

"Why, thank you, kind sir," she flirted in return. "For a former soldier, monsieur, you are frightfully suave. Living in close proximity to the cardinal must agree with you, does it not?"

"Oh, yes," Charles agreed, nonplussed. The embarrassed agent, recognizing the futility of any attempt to banter with the likes of Choisy, turned his attention, instead, to saying goodbye. His voice and demeanor pretended that we would not meet again, though we both knew that outcome was unlikely.

"Be a good girl and listen to madame. Remember me as fondly as I shall certainly remember you."

"Yes, monsieur. *Adieu.*"

D'Artagnan scooted down and ceremoniously kissed one of my hands, making me feel very ladylike, indeed. I blushed because I was thinking that, had I not met with the king days before, the man from Gascony would be the stuff that dreams were made of.

The Loyalist departed and Jeanne-Olympe was about to dash from the foyer. Almost as an afterthought, she caught herself, spinning around to give me instructions.

"Should Françoise stir, she will show you to the room the two of you will share. The governess, Madame de Ventadour, will guide you on all matters, unless I decide to the contrary."

"Madame, should I not rouse Mademoiselle Sancy?"

"Do not contradict me, Bijoux, or cause me consternation. Sit where you are until my daughter awakens. When she rises, so may you."

As ridiculous as it sounds, I did her bidding. Not about

to be dismissed from the Luxemboug on my first day, I sat waiting.

Françoise did not stir. She was adorable to behold and I imagined that if I had a sibling, I would want him or her to resemble the blonde bundle. Still, one doubt nagged at me. I had to know for certain whether Mademoiselle Sancy was a boy or a girl.

I lifted the taffeta skirts cautiously, a very sheepish look upon my face, accompanied by many surreptitious peeks sent in the direction of the salon. Rustling silk did not warn the child of what I was up to and the quiet, deliberate breathing continued undisturbed. Only after the last petticoat was suspended above Françoise's face, did I venture to view the lower half of the unveiled torso.

François was most definitely not fashioned as was I, and consumed with shame, I hastily dropped the three veils of disguise.

I was disgusted by Madame de Choisy's deceit. How could she be so cruel to her own child—how could any mother require such a sacrifice of her own issue?

The boy began to move. I helped François to sit and he yawned, his heavy eyelids trimmed with long, pale lashes that blinked close, then open. He seemed well; probably unaware of the distorted circumstances surrounding his dainty wardrobe.

"How did you sleep?" I asked, taking the opportunity to stand and collect Louise. "Do you feel all right?"

"Yes," he smiled. Not staring at him was impossible, for the image I looked upon was difficult to believe counterfeit.

"What name do you use?"

"François-Timoléon. You see," he chirped, "I know I am a boy, but mother likes to dress me as a lady. It makes her happy, so every day we play a game together. She calls me Mademoiselle Sancy, or Françoise, and we pretend that I am her daughter instead of her son. I don't mind—I like pretty things and girls are much nicer than boys, *n'est-ce pas?*"

"I suppose," I confessed. "Why don't you show me to our room and then we'll seek out your governess. What is her name?"

"Madame de Ventadour. She is kinder than any grandmama."

"Good. Lead the way," I suggested and François, as I forevermore would address him, skipped down a hallway. As I tripped after him, I reflected on the odd set of circumstances in which I found myself involved. The boy's lack of concern regarding a most peculiar routine jarred my sensibilities more than anything I had seen on the Rue St. Denis.

Contritely I followed the cross-dressing youngster, swallowing any revulsion. No one had to remind me that I was part of a dark secret, too, although one I was not privy to in its entirety. If the Abbé Guibourg were to make the circumstances surrounding my childhood a public matter, his disclosure would concern a grave evil, whereas François could declare his quirk aloud and elicit no more than a titter at court. The less I said, the better. My own past was hardly taintless and my present security depended greatly on personal discretion.

François-Timoléon possessed such a pure, good nature that I readily overcame the aversion towards his mode of dress and became the boy's friend. Madame de Ventadour, the capable teacher and surrogate mother to the little man, was responsible for his charming personality and the extremely moral woman was to instill a strong sense of right and wrong in us both.

From the beginning of my association with the governess, she accepted me into the nursery with warmth and grace, never complaining about being given an extra pupil to instruct. I learned much from the serene lady; her approach to tutoring was that she explained things, rather than preached or lectured. Our normal studies, such as reading and writing, centered on classes conducted with wit and verve. Playtime was allowed, too, with our mentor often joining in our games. Despite what François had said about Madame de Ventadour being grandmotherly, I regarded the exceptional young woman of the pleasing face and plump figure as I would a big sister or favorite aunt.

Thanks to the stimulating atmosphere, the remaining

months of 1650 passed quickly. I was hardly aware that I rarely saw Madame de Choisy, or that the abbé never tried to contact me, or that d'Artagnan was occupied with missions, or that I rarely dwelled on my former life in the Marais.

Leafing through lovely books about the ancients accounted for most my time spent; either that or trying my hand at mathematical tables, a skill required of any good astrologer. Besides studying star maps, I ached to see the stables and perhaps be given riding lessons, but François was afraid of horses and my dream went unfulfilled. Once, however, while out walking the enormous parameters of the Luxembourg with Madame de V, the pet name I had given our nurse, the sweet smell of hay and the pungent odors of harness leather drew my attention to the buildings that made up the palace stud.

I was tempted to run over and investigate, yet the sight of a tall, regal-looking black man stopped me from venturing further. Madame, noting the stymied look I had assumed, explained that the groom was a Moor named La Rivière, most proficient at performing bareback stunts on Barbary steeds and a regular entertainment at the fêtes given by Gaston d'Orléans. As we went on our way, I could sense his bright, white eyes locking onto me, even though my back was to the dark-skinned servant. La Rivière was to later recall the incident, and he told me that he had been held spellbound by the sight of such flaming, red hair.

The political situation began to boil again near to the time when winter with its icy winds swept over Paris. The stubborn *frondeurs*—still counting the king's uncle their most influential member—decided that, while Mazarin was off traveling in the provinces, suppressing the rebellion and chasing the beautiful Duchesse de Longueville from one safe haven to another, they would petition the Parliament to banish the cardinal. The Duc d'Orléans supported a proposed exile based on an old decree of 1617 prohibiting foreigners from holding office in the French government.

Based on that forgotten law, the cardinal was branded a criminal, unless he agreed to leave the realm, taking along with him his very unpopular relatives who had been imported from Italy to France four years earlier. The king and his court were by then back at the Louvre, being forced earlier by Parisian rioters to flee for their lives to the countryside at Rueil during the latter half of 1650. The Parliament, in issuing its ultimatum concerning Mazarin, was sending a basic message to the returning royal family: discharge the Italian, or else support him and lose the throne.

Madame de Choisy was in jubilant spirits for the next month, wagering like everyone else in Paris as to what date the queen would set for her partner's official dismissal. The fateful evening arrived near to February's close in 1651, when, amidst a throng of curious onlookers, Jules Mazarini came to visit his lovely 22 for what might be the couple's irrevocable parting.

The dependable Jeanne-Olympe ranked among the heartless spectators, and she raced home after the audience, rushing into our room when she arrived at the apartments. She longed to tell someone what had transpired and François and I were the only ones about, already tucked into bed by Madame de V.

"My treasure, are you dreaming?" she sang out, beside herself with happiness, carrying a heavy silver candlestick and its accompanying lit taper for illumination.

"No, not yet," François replied, popping a head covered with lace outside warm blankets.

"Wonderful, for you must hear this," Madame de Choisy maintained, dropping a fur-lined pelisse to the floor, warm from her mad dash. "You may listen, too, Bijoux."

"How grand!" I exulted, hoping she might reveal some news I could give to d'Artagnan—if I could ever locate the secret agent.

"The cardinal, that oily Levantine, is ruined at last! I saw Queen Anne send him off myself, without a tear or fond word for the commoner who shares her bed. What a consummate player she is, that Spanish whore, but the Duc d'Orléans always told me she was a great deceiver."

"What happened, what happened?" François begged.

He didn't care at all, being only seven, but he did enjoy the attention his mother momentarily lavished upon him.

"Everyone was there, sweet children: the king, Gaston, all the courtiers—the only ones missing were the poor Princes Condé and Conti, since they are both locked away in prison. Be that as it may, when all were assembled, the cardinal appeared, not one wrinkle in his opulent robes, reeking of his exclusive perfume," she paused, suspense building, "and what do you think someone did as Mazarin approached the sovereign?"

"I don't know, do tell," François pleaded, titillated by the report.

"An unidentified gentleman flatulated," Choisy answered, shaking with laughter, sitting on her son's bed as she hugged herself about the waist. "The effect was hilarious; the entire court roared at the undignified salute—all except for their Majesties and the target of the jest, of course."

I swallowed hard, bit my tongue, then lied for France, saying, "The cardinal deserves no better."

"I am glad you think so," Jeanne-Olympe said, regaining her composure. "I was suspicious of your loyalties, mademoiselle, because M. d'Artagnan is the cardinal's best agent in the field and he is the one who brought you here."

"My mother was a *frondeuse*, madame. She hated the Italian with a passion. She was friends with the princes, and an honored guest at the Grand Condé's marriage to Richelieu's niece."

"That is correct, she did attend the nuptials. What else might you tell me about Marion Delorme, little Bijoux?"

Then I knew the reason why I had not seen much of Madame de Choisy: she did not trust me. I could be anyone, as far as she was concerned; she had no proof I was Bijoux Delorme. The chance had come for me to prove myself and the opportunity beckoned to win her to my side.

For d'Artagnan's sake, I knew I must become Choisy's ally. The trusted operative would be accompanying Mazarin across the frontier to whatever city would take in the fugitive cardinal and his retinue. Charles de Batz would soon need me as much as I had once relied upon him.

Trembling, I decided to gamble all for my Musketeer and confide in Jeanne-Olympe those things I had been warned never to reveal.

"Marion Delorme's true title was the Marquise de Cinq-Mars. Her husband was Henri Coiffier de Ruzé, my sire. As you know, he was executed for treason two years after my birth for his involvement in the Spanish Plot. Because of my father's crime and the shame attached to the name of Cinq-Mars, I was instructed to hide the facts concerning my birth. When my mother died, her companion, the Abbé Guibourg, gave me over to M. d'Artagnan's care, for Mazarin's spy had once visited Marion's salon disguised as a courtier, d'Estoiles, promising favors in exchange for the priest's powders."

My mind was racing and I was talking much faster than I could think. I had to slow down; I had to say enough to be credible, yet not too much.

"Your story is well-wrought and I would be inclined to believe you," Choisy purred, examining her manicured nails, "however, you have no proof to substantiate your claim."

"Wait, I do," I said, scrambling from a comfortable bed, nightdress well above my knees. In a hasty bid for legitimacy, I made for the chest containing everything I had brought with me from home. Opening it, I rummaged frantically through the contents before finding what I needed.

"See, madame, I have a lock taken from my dead father, sent to his lady straight from the executioner's block by Richelieu himself."

I held the strands before her face. Jeanne-Olympe shuddered and took the evidence tentatively in hand.

"It resembles his hair. Monsieur le Grand was the most gorgeous creature at court, whether the competitor for that honor be man or woman. We all knew that he visited Marion four or five times between sunup and sundown, sporting a new suit for each passionate encounter," she chuckled almost to herself, as if tenderly recalling halcyon days.

"Do you believe me?" I asked impatiently.

Choisy fondled the ribbon that had bound the heirloom

for the past nine years. She was weighing the validity of my case, deciding for or against me in the wary recesses of her mind.

"You have nothing else?"

I hung my head in defeat. What else was in the trunk that might convince the impossibly skeptical woman whose stare was colder than any viper's? I sorted through a mental inventory of my belongings without a glimmer of hope until I thought back on the miniature of Marion, housed in a locket of gold.

Not wasting an instant, mother's clothing, patches and other accessories found themselves thrown on the floor whilst I searched for the necklace. Finally, a shiny orb, suspended from a delicate chain, tumbled from its hiding place, stuck in a finger of one of the marquise's prized gloves.

"Here, look—the locket my father always wore 'round his neck containing a likeness of his wife," I guessed, supposing that Henri could have been attached to the piece

Madame de Choisy's reaction was anything but reserved. She grabbed the adornment from me in a thrice, mouth agape, fingers fiddling with the clasp that, when clicked open, revealed a representation of the familiar visage of Madame la Grande.

"Oh, my Lord!" she gasped. "Henri wore this constantly! When he was arrested, he sent it to Marion as a warning. She was the only person in Creation who could have had the pendant. Good God, you are their daughter!"

François leapt from his cozy cocoon, overcome with glee, hugging me with joy. He had been afraid of our being separated, and was relieved that his mother believed my claim.

The canny lady drew us both to her side. Still clutching the locket, she touched my hair, my face, she gazed into my eyes, poignantly transformed. Then Jeanne-Olympe embraced me, her head at my chest, tears flowing freely.

"I loved your father so, dear Bijoux, he was the brightest beacon in the land. He brought merriment wherever he went—he was an amazing man. Then that bastard killed him, and we thought we would all die from grief. It was a horrendous travesty to snuff out such promise..."

Choisy was crying aloud and François followed suit,

distraught to see his mother upset. All we lacked was Marion uttering curses and Guibourg muttering a Black Mass to complete the scene.

"Forgive me, how silly," she managed to say, regaining a semblance of calm. Jeanne-Olympe released me and sat still, quite dazed.

"You are now one of us," she acknowledged. "I shall arrange a meeting between you and the Duc d'Orléans as soon as possible. Gaston will be most interested to speak to the only child of his former ally."

"Ally? Did he not betray my father?" My tone was incredulous; I did not want to have anything to do with Monsieur.

"No, Bijoux, you do not understand. Gaston and your father were members of a secret society that for many years has concerned itself with matters vital to our country's welfare. We believe—and our number is not insignificant—that a noble family exists whose right to occupy the throne is more valid than that of those hailing from the house of Bourbon. Our group has sworn to work on behalf of this family, to further their ends, so they might regain the power rightfully belonging to them. Your father gave his life for this cause, and he understood all along that Monsieur would never be implicated in the Spanish Plot should its details come to light, owing to Gaston's importance in the grand scheme of our Order."

It was my turn to be amazed. Madame de Choisy's divulgement scared me and I feared for my beloved Louis' life. I had to get word to d'Artagnan immediately about what I had learned. The situation was more serious than I had previously dared to imagine.

"Thank goodness, madame, that I was honest with you and did not heed M. d'Artagnan's advice!"

"What did that weasel say?" she jeered.

"He called you an old hag and a meddler. He told me to write down everything I heard you discuss so I might not forget any details when I reported your conversations to him."

"That vermin-infested piece of refuse!" she cursed. "I'll fix him, that sly boots. Wait and see, children, M. d'Artagnan's days are numbered. If he should try to contact you, Bijoux, come to me right away. We shall work together from now on, *n'est-ce pas?*"

"You honor me, madame," I said, acting bashful. "If M. d'Artagnan sends me a message, you will be the first to know. However, since he leaves soon with Mazarin, for God knows where, I doubt he will bother with me."

"They set out tomorrow for the coast. Rumor has it that Mazarin intends to travel to Le Havre and release the captive princes," Jeanne-Olympe offered. "What he means to gain by that tardy gesture, only a fool could say. He'll be lucky if Condé doesn't cut him into pieces on the spot."

I climbed back into bed and Choisy made the blankets snug. She did the same for François before retrieving her candle and quitting the room.

"This has been an eventful evening, children. Go to sleep because tomorrow will be a busy day. The tide has begun to turn in our favor and I see great things being accomplished. Now, say your prayers, both of you, and don't forget to ask the angels to keep watch over our benefactor, Monsieur Gaston."

The door shut and she was gone. The nursery became darker and the only noise, François' and my measured exhalations.

I waited for the boy to nod-off before arising to dress. I had already decided during the conversation with Madame de Choisy that no alternative existed for me except to warn d'Artagnan about what was afoot and that meant sneaking out of the Luxembourg. Although Paris was a dangerous place to roam about at night, I knew I had to go to him. The perils of the street were not a factor for consideration when my king's future was in jeopardy.

Pulling on heavy, hand-knit stockings, a wool smock over my nightclothes and sturdy, dependable shoes, I finished the dowdy ensemble with the gray velvet cape Des Oeillets had altered on my last night in the Marais. I then checked on my junior, who was sleeping soundly. Satisfied that he would not awaken, I took a pair of mother's too-big gloves with me as protection against the chilly air, and departed.

The escape progressed down passageways I had memorized during the eight-month stay; the front doors were reached without the detection of the snoozing sentry. Stepping outside, the Rue de Vaugirard greeted me, and the newly erected Cathedral de St. Sulpice with its uneven steeples towered across the way. The hour being near to midnight, no signs of life were visible since most were at home and at rest.

The walk to d'Artagnan's apartments involved heading east on the Rue de Vaugirard, crossing a small square onto the wide Rue St. Germain, passing from there over the Rue Mazarine, which in turn led to the Rue Dauphine, and also to the largest bridge in Paris, the Pont Neuf.

Electing to travel on the latter was risky, since the path spanning the river Seine had houses, shops and crowded taverns lining each side of its considerable length. Murderers and thieves could be found lurking in poorly lit doorways, while the inhabitants and visitors to the area were partial to participating in all-night drinking binges where wine flowed like water. Because of its shady reputation, the strip was jammed with bodies round-the-clock and offered diverse entertainment to amuse its revelers. Prostitutes, of course, did not lack for customers there, and were considered another attraction amongst the many one could view on the Pont.

Getting to the other side of the bridge was absolutely crucial since the Louvre was located across the river on the bank opposite of where I stood. I took a deep breath and boldly went forward, despite strong misgivings.

Avoiding the derelicts sprawled outside their favorite watering holes was one hazard I recall; watching women flaunt bared breasts, another surprise. Most of the men loitered about in stained breeches, rumpled blousons, and cock-eyed hats. The degenerates reeked of odors far worse than fermented grape, and the stench floating about on cold gusts of wind was disgusting.

One whiff alone was enough to make me hurry to safer shores, and I did not tarry, keeping to myself as I weaved between the drunkards and the whores who littered the way.

The welcomed sight of a quay, running alongside the western face of the palace, loomed ahead. Stone steps leading to the embankment marked the end of the Pont Neuf, and an arrival at more civilized terrain. The Louvre was not far, and I ran in that building's direction.

Entering the old residence posed no problem since many courtiers were strolling in and out of the building, celebrating Mazarin's defeat. So concerned was I with finding d'Artagnan's apartments, that I scarcely admitted how lucky I had been to traverse the Pont Neuf unscathed.

The door to d'Artagnan's suite was closed, yet unlocked, as I discovered upon turning the knob. A knock had not elicited a response, so I assumed that he was out, attending to plans for the morrow's journey. Knowing he would not mind me waiting in his room, I entered the soon-to-be-vacated apartment without a second thought as to propriety. No intrusion was intended and after what I had experienced, I also needed to rest.

A comfortable chair was situated close to the fireplace; within, the charred remains of a log burned near to extinction. Climbing onto that seat, I huddled against worn upholstery and wondered when d'Artagnan would return. The glow of low flames constituted the sole attempt to lift the cover of the night, so I was unaware that another person was in the room, awaiting Charles de Batz, as well.

The shrouded figure was skulking in a corner across from where I sat, and must have observed my actions for several minutes prior to making his presence known. When he spoke, I nearly leapt out of my body in response.

"Good evening, mademoiselle," the man said with a malignant ring to his tone, "how good it is to see you again."

Gasping aloud, a hand covered my mouth as I watched the Abbé Guibourg step into view.

"What are you doing here?" was the obvious question I heard myself asking.

"How impolite," Étienne remarked. "Have you learned no manners while at court, Bijoux?"

"I have received instructions in etiquette, monsieur," I

sniped. "My guardian is a lady of quality who treats me quite nicely, thank you."

"Marvelous! And how fares M. d'Éstoiles?" he queried, squinting at me hard.

Leery, I repeated, "What are you doing here, abbé? You know who lives in these apartments, do you not?"

"I do now, having personally conducted an inquiry or two. Imagine my dismay when I never heard from you, Bijoux—not one single message. After everything we had been through together, you forgot your old teacher," Guibourg scolded. "I arranged for you to come to court, you know, I'm the one who contacted d'Éstoiles and asked him, no begged him, to give you a chance at a better life. And what thanks do I get? Not only do you ignore me, but to add insult to injury, you steal my property!"

"I did no such thing. Prove it here and now—tell me what I took from you."

"Bijoux, do not toy with my patience. You know of what I speak. Recall, if you will, that day we drove to the Rond-Point and I gave you into d'Éstoiles' care. Once you were on your way, I went back to the Marais to fetch Madame des Oeillets. Picture for yourself *my* amazement when I returned to find Marion's home ransacked of its precious contents and the pretty maid nowhere to be found!"

"How does that concern me, monsieur?"

"Oh, it concerns you, you little brat, and you know right well it does," he fumed. "I say you took the best stuff for yourself without me being aware of it, gave the housekeeper a few coins, and have been hiding at court ever since. As for M. d'Éstoiles, I checked out his background this very evening, only to discover that one M. d'Artagnan employs that alias. Too bad Mazarin got the heave-ho tonight, eh?"

"Monsieur Guibourg," I reasoned, "how would I have known where the marquise stored her valuables? Madame des Oeillets took whatever went missing, I wager."

"You know, my little vixen, I taught you well," he chuckled, coming closer to the chair. "*You* are the consummate liar,

Bijoux, not I. The rebuttal would be a good one, however, I found this," Guibourg waved a folded note in front of me. "The proof of your treachery, made out to one Monsieur Charles de Batz Castelmore d'Artagnan by a certain Jean-Baptiste Colbert, acknowledging the receipt of a gem collection estimated to be worth fifty thousand gold coins. Precious jewels to be held for safekeeping by said Monsieur Colbert until Monsieur d'Artagnan or one Bijoux Delorme should request their return by presenting this very contract."

Étienne was pacing the room, resplendent in his cavalier costume, gesticulating and dramatizing to a fare-thee-well. I had been caught red handed. Alarmed, I offered a lame excuse, although I should have remained mute.

"Abbé, everyone knows that Monsieur Colbert has been entrusted with Mazarin's fortune while the cardinal is in exile. M. d'Artagnan simply took him jewels belonging to his master."

"You don't surrender easily, do you? Explain then, why your name appears on this paper!"

Guibourg was very annoyed. He was ready to forget I was Marion's daughter, he was willing to overlook Noctambule's mark on my neck, he was definitely prepared to wreak vengeance on my person. Nothing I could say was going to stop him from hurting me, so I began to cry.

"I am sorry, monsieur, I shall deceive you no longer. I did take the stones, but they were rightfully mine. Plus, Des Oeillets needed money to care for the child you put in her belly. You are not blameless in this affair, you know—you did poison my mother."

"I did *not* kill Marion," he shouted as he throttled my neck, lifting me up off the chair in his rage. My dirty shoes dangled above the cushioned seat and breathing was becoming increasingly difficult as the abbé squeezed and squeezed with murderous intent.

"When Monsieur Musketeer returns, he'll be greeted by your putrid corpse, you blood-guzzling hellion. And after he gets a good look at you, he and I are going to pay Colbert a call to collect what's *mine*, not yours, understand!"

"Vermin-infested piece of refuse," I swore, aping Jeanne-Olympe, gasping for air as I did. The words came out in a gurgling manner, though, and I clawed at his hands with my nails.

The scratches did not bother Guibourg and he laughed, unmoved by the sight of me dying, no pity in his soul.

"Put her down," a voice boomed from the doorway. *D'Artagnan*! I thought, trying to turn my head to see, praying to Athena that my friend had returned.

The abbé's attention was distracted and he focused on the intruder. He lowered me with deliberation, his fingers cautiously leaving my throat.

"Bijoux, come here," the shadow commanded, sword drawn. Upon reaching the man who was indeed the rugged Gascon, I made a move to hug his frame in a show of relief, although he glowered and ordered, "Stand over there, out of the way."

Confused and hurt, I made no attempt to reply or to disobey. D'Artagnan then left his post, approaching Guibourg unafraid, the tip of his blade twitching as would an angry cat's tail, advancing on the past acquaintance whom he rightly assumed had penetrated his former charade.

"To what may I attribute the dishonor of your presence?" the military man quipped when the steel was an inch away from the priest's nose. "Answer me quickly, scum, or I'll run you through."

The abbé glanced down, too wise to move a single sinew.

"Monsieur d'Éstoiles, or should I say *d'Artagnan*," he mocked, "it would seem you have me at a disadvantage. Lower your epée and I shall be more than happy to discuss the matter with you, sir."

"No!" I warned, but d'Artagnan ignored the caveat, allowing a well-honed point to rest on the floor as a conciliatory sign for the trespasser to speak.

"Go ahead, Guibourg, state your case."

"Out of concern for my ex-ward," the scoundrel began, "I came to the Louvre in search of the courtier whom I had met at

Marion Delorme's. When I arrived here and asked about, no one was familiar with M. d'Éstoiles, except for one of the cardinal's Guards who brought me to this place. I, of course, paid him a few *sou* for his trouble and was assured access to your quarters by a hastily picked lock. When you move to your new home, monsieur, a change of staff might provide better security."

"*Touché*," d'Artagnan bowed in farcical tribute to his adversary. "Any other recommendations on this eve 'ere my departure?"

"Do not leave your private papers in full public view," Guibourg parried. "'Tis quite unnecessary to tempt prowlers to rob you blind; they will do that of their own accord, monsieur."

"What have you of mine, then?"

"This," he exclaimed, flaunting the slip previously stashed-away in the Bible. "As I was explaining to Bijoux, and now to you, the jewels belong to me, not to her. If you possess a shred of honor, monsieur, you will escort me to Colbert this instant and help me to regain my assets."

Charles de Batz stroked his chin hairs and pondered the abbé's demands.

"Correct me if I am wrong, monsieur; however, the true reason for your breaking into my domicile was not to learn of Bijoux's whereabouts, as you formerly stated, was it?"

The sword touched Guibourg's neck.

"No," he stammered, "yet be reasonable, monsieur, and admit that I have been duped by the pair of you. I could not expect a fair accounting had I come forward in an honest manner."

"Give me the deed of ownership," d'Artagnan threatened.

The abbé reluctantly passed the paper to him and the menacing soldier leaned forward a tad to snap the document away from the thief.

"Get out of my house, Guibourg—get out and run back to your stinking Satanists before I have you arrested, here on the spot! Never doubt, sir, that if you dare speak to Bijoux again, I shall kill you—do I make myself clear?"

"Oh, very," the contemptuous reply rang out as the

disgruntled one made a tentative move to leave, reaching inside of his coat as he did so. "Yet, monsieur," he continued, "is there nothing I might say to change your mind about returning my goods?"

"I don't haggle with street slime such as yourself. Get out, lest I rid France of you this minute and save myself the bother of finding Bijoux a bodyguard."

"All because of harmless me? Really, I am honored," Étienne said.

D'Artagnan made a quarter turn to his left, moving Guibourg with short, effective jabs in the same direction. Soon the priest was no longer facing the exit and was gingerly stepping backwards towards the door. The retreat was close to finished, when the abbé made a foolish move. Removing his straying hand from underneath his outerwear, he displayed an opened sack that fit comfortably in a palm.

"Did you think that I would take money? Do you intend to buy me off, you miserable cur? You would vex the likes of St. Anthony, I swear! Leave, begone, don't make me say it again!"

"I'm going, monsieur, believe me," Guibourg said, walking out. Then, looking back over his shoulder in parting, he made a strange remark.

"Never underestimate your opponent, Bijoux."

I cowered near the hearth while I watched in disbelief as Étienne whirled about, flinging a finely ground substance from the pouch at d'Artagnan. What it was made of, I could not tell, but the mixture practically sparkled in the dark and caused my hero great distress, having landed in his eyes and robbed him of his sight.

"Merciful saints!" the Musketeer bellowed. "You've blinded me, you bastard!"

The sound of his obvious torment reverberated down the nearby halls of the palace. The abbé wasted no time and lunged forward, trying to retrieve the receipt. I heard myself yelling, "Help," louder than I had ever managed to call out before.

Somehow, Charles managed to stuff the document inside his doublet lining, keep his weapon at the ready, and fend off the poisoner. Guibourg's taunting laughter, as he danced about his crippled victim, enticed d'Artagnan to only greater rage and the Gascon thrashed about, barely missing his quarry each instance he tried to wound him.

Frustrated, I decided to help, having already put my friend in more peril than my unimportant existence warranted. In a valiant effort, I joined the fray, sneaking around to the abbé's hind qaurter, where he could not spot me, and shoving him with all of my might into the direction of the shiny metal upon which he deserved to be impaled.

Unfortunately, I missed the mark. As Guibourg stumbled, losing his balance, d'Artagnan drove his epée, accompanied by a veritable battle cry, and scored a hit. The defensive tactic grazed the abbé in the right eye, damaging it beyond repair. The roar of excruciating pain emanating from the disabled conjurer made me wince in unexpected sympathy.

"Astaroth, Asmodeus, save me! Princes of Friendship, deliver me from this agony, I cannot bear it!"

Blood was everywhere, running down Étienne's chiseled features, matting the curls of his peruke, staining the front of the jacket my mother had gifted her lover. The sight was gruesome and I was relieved that d'Artagnan could not see what he had done, for it would have sickened his decent spirit.

So much senseless hurt caused by greed: the contested stones would be cursed forevermore. That reality I understood as clearly as I recognized my own name. Another burden to shoulder, another inequity to bear. The chart of my nativity was proving accurate–an Aquarian Mars and Saturn joined in the eighth House was indeed proving malefic. I had been born under the feared September star of the serpent Medusa's gaze, after all. All around me was naught but snake eyes–the Gorgon's curse.

"Bitch," Guibourg shrieked, in tune with my own musings, "this is your doing! A thousand scourges do I wish thee, a multitude of baneful calamities I cast your way. I shall see you dead, *vykrolakas*, you will go the same way as did your arrogant father, to the block! I commend thee to all foul daemons forever and a day. No rest shall ye have, child of He Who Never Sleeps!"

Covering the vacant socket with his hands, the gentleman whose trade had previously prospered due mainly to a combination of good looks and deadly skill fled. D'Artagnan slumped to his knees and groaned and muttered to himself as if praying to the Dieties to restore his vision.

For my part, I went to the door, shut and bolted it, then fumbled about for a wash basin. Eventually one was located on the nightstand. I slid the wooden bowl to the edge of the table and transported it with measured tread to the poor man who had saved me yet again.

"Here, let me," I offered, tearing off a piece of my nightdress at the bottom, dipping the cloth into the water, soaking it, then applying the compress to d'Artagnan's shut lids. His stunning blue eyes had to be cleansed of the powder; I wiped lashes with care, cursing the day the abbé had come to Paris.

"Please forgive me, monsieur, I had no way of knowing Guibourg was here tonight; I came only to see you. Do not hate me, especially when you leave tomorrow to go with the cardinal."

Charles de Batz said nothing. I continued to bathe his face, a knot in my throat, a lump there bigger than the one I had felt when I had said good-bye to Des Oeillets. He despised me, I was certain; nothing I could do would make him like me again.

"Bijoux," d'Artagnan at last remarked, signaling that I should stop tending to him, "this has not been a good day. In case you were not aware, I have more important things to do than to chase thugs about Paris, or in my own home, for that matter."

He rose to his feet, using his sword as a cane.

"Are you still...blinded?" I dared ask.

"No," he said. "Tell me, did I scar the bastard, at least?"

"D'Artagnan," I hesitated, "you robbed the abbé of an eye."

"Good. Serves him right."

He sat on the bed, elbows on knees, head resting in his hands.

"Guibourg certainly fights dirty. Maybe he'll think twice before beating on young ladies again. Don't mind what I said earlier, dear, I'm simply in a bad way."

"Things will get better," I comforted. "Especially when you hear what I have discovered."

"What?" he asked wearily.

"Madame de Choisy came to the nursery tonight from the cardinal's farewell to tell François and I about the naughty trick someone played..."

"A childish prank," he interrupted.

"Yes, of course," I agreed, not pausing for a breath, "and then she questioned me about whose side I was on seeing as though you had brought me to her. Madame was quite suspicious, so I said that my mother had been a *frondeuse* and a friend of the Grand Condé. She then asked for proof that I was Marion Delorme's daughter."

"What did you offer?"

"I told her that mother had secretly married the Marquis de Cinq-Mars and that he was my father; I showed her a lock of his hair. Don't be angry, but I also said that your name was d'Éstoiles when I first met you."

"*Adieu* to that disguise," he sighed.

"I had to be honest or she wouldn't have trusted me," I maintained. "Really, monsieur, I had good reason; be patient and hear me out."

"*Ma petite*, how could I ever be peeved with you?" He lifted me onto the bed where I had convalesced, seating me at his side. "Tell me more — I promise to listen."

"She challenged me again. I began to panic because I couldn't think of anything else to dig out of my trunk from home. Luckily, I remembered a locket of Marion's, found it and gave the necklace to Choisy. You should have seen her expression when she opened it and saw Mademoiselle Delorme."

"Shocked?"

"She was beside herself with joy and said my father never

took the love charm from his neck. Choisy claimed that Cinq-Mars sent it to mother when he was arrested and that I must be their daughter. Madame is very happy to have taken me under her roof. She said that she is going to arrange for the Duc d'Orléans to meet me, because he and my father were friends."

"Friends?"

"I thought that Monsieur had betrayed the marquis, too, but madame said they had more in common than wishing Richelieu dead. Both belonged to a secret society that still exists and is headed by Gaston. Madame said she is a member, too."

"What society?"

"Madame did not tell me. She said it is a group of nobles who think that Louis should not be our ruler because another family has a better claim, no right, to sit on the throne. Those were her words. And she added that everyone who joins the Order must swear to serve this special family."

"Did she divulge any other facts?" Mazarin's agent no longer complained, he was concerned with my story, first and foremost.

"No, nothing. I did confess that you had instructed me to snoop on her and that news made madame angry. She said that I was to let her know if you tried to contact me, and that she and I were going to work together. I think she has faith in me, at last, monsieur."

"Good," he agreed. "Back to this secret society. The cardinal has had his suspicions for a number of years that a clandestine organization is behind the Fronde, stirring up trouble, although he has not been sure as to why or the cabal's true agenda. You were correct in coming here to share what you discovered, Bijoux. I daresay the cardinal will be rallied when he hears this juicy tidbit."

I stretched out on the bed, tired.

"May we go to sleep, monsieur?"

"No, my little friend, I must return you to the Luxembourg. What will madame say if she finds you've gone missing when she checks on the nursery in a few hours time?"

"I don't want to go back there, monsieur. I hate Choisy."

"Bijoux, I need for you to become Madame de Choisy's shadow. You must obtain her total confidence, uncover why these people believe what they do. Determine why they would risk life and limb for the distant descendant of an ancient king. Get me facts and names that will help speed our return. You have accomplished much in eight short months...the cardinal's other agents will be green with envy."

"No," I smiled.

"I speak the truth," he assured me. "Come, let us be off. Hope exists for our cause."

"Yes," I concurred. "Wait and see, monsieur, I shall become a member of madame's Order one day. I shall get you your secret, I promise."

"Somehow, Bijoux, I do not doubt your boast for one instant," d'Artagnan chuckled.

And that, dear reader, marked the eve of my initiation into the clandestine world of espionage.

CHAPTER SIX
Good-For-Nothing Rascals

Madame de V was chipper when she roused François and myself that same morning. Unaware that one of her charges had played at alley cat the night before, she sang gaily while she washed sleepy faces and brushed-out tousled hair. For once, I did not notice her pulling snarls from the mass of red curls she tended. Instead, I concentrated on d'Artagnan's words of parting that repeated over and over again, silently, inside of my heavy head.

The directive he had given me was straightforward enough: never attempt to contact him in writing, expect him to visit the Luxembourg in disguise, look for hidden messages from the Loyalist party under the last pew on the left in the conveniently located church of St. Sulpice. The warning to be careful was implied yet left unsaid; detection would mean being sent away to live in a dreadful convent.

Our governess had finished the task of tying the last bow in François' flaxen tendrils when Madame de Choisy made an entrance. Garbed with exceptional elegance, the white-blazed coiffure was sublime, all adornments flawless. Jeanne-Olympe's demeanor reflected nothing, if not the epitome of *hauteur*.

"Children," she announced, "I am off to call on Monsieur. Try to stay clean and tidy. Ventadour?"

"Yes, madame?"

"Teach them something clever. Perhaps a verse the children could recite for the Duc d'Orléans, should he decide to interview Mademoiselle Bijoux later today."

"Madame, do not fret another moment. All will be prepared when you return."

"It best be," she answered, glancing at me.

"How do you feel this morning, Bijoux?" Choisy inquired.

I froze, amazed. Did she know of my midnight promenade? Then I recalled that my patroness had indeed been born to the sign of the Twins and was ruled by the trickster god, Mercurius.

"Quite well, thank you, madame."

"Hmmm..." she drilled me with her relentless adder's scrutiny. "Well, be on your best behavior should Monsieur come to call. And Ventadour," she addressed our lady companion anew, "dress François in a more masculine fashion. Monsieur is a man's man, you see, and is not fond of frills and flounces."

Madame de V curtsied obediently, grasping her mistress' message. Jeanne-Olympe was gone without another word, off to inspect much grander venues.

"She is chipper," I noted. "*Latet anguis in herba.*"

"Be nice," my elder admonished, knowing better than to criticize, simpering because I had remembered a Latin lesson from Virgil: *A snake is lurking in the grass.* She did manage to roll her eyes in a comical manner, however, to show her agreement with the ancient, Roman poet's estimation. I had to laugh in response, mainly because I thought the entire charade ridiculous.

"Now, François, Bijoux, let us consider the challenge Madame de Choisy has posed. She wishes a rhyme for Monsieur, but which would be appropriate, I wonder? Any preferences, my little ones?"

"I know," François volunteered. "*A lady who is born and bred, will dress her feet before her head.*"

"Good, very witty," Madame de V praised, "although might we lengthen your ditty a bit, perhaps add a pleasing dance as they do at court? The king and his brother perform ballets quite frequently."

"I met Philippe on the day I left home. He's a brat. We got into a big fight because he stole my cape."

François was enthralled. "Did you get it back?"

"Of course, I beat him up," I bragged. "He is a baby."

"Children, you are not attending to your studies," Ventadour warned. "Let us return to composition. Bijoux, please collect paper and ink and we shall write a poem together."

We toiled on the project for what seemed hours. Finally, our governess decided the composition was ready to be rehearsed. Standing us side by side, she stepped back a few paces to survey our act with greater ease and motioned for me to begin.

"Go ahead," she prodded, "don't be shy."

"This is a game for idiots," came my protest.

"No it isn't; stop complaining," François insisted.

"Bijoux, be a good girl and act your age. How old are you now?" Ventadour chided sweetly.

"Almost eleven."

"Be a good example to François and show him how proper young ladies conduct themselves."

I shuffled my feet, uncomfortable.

"Does the king really jump about as would a frog?" I demanded.

"Bijoux! Louis puts great store in artistic endeavors, as does his mother and the cardinal."

If my idol could go on stage and dance before his horrid uncle, so could I. Clearing my throat, I mumbled, "*To live at court you must rely...*"

"Speak louder," the prim lady suggested.

"*To live at court, you must rely, on proverbs till the day you die...*"

"Good, continue," she directed.

"*And one of these we think the best, is wiser beyond all the rest...*"

"Wonderful. Now curtsy and hold the pose."

Down I went on bended knee, shooting a look at François-Timoléon. The recital was a lark for the impostor and he joined in with vigor.

"*A simple verse, yet one so true, a song we beg to sing for you...*"

The lovely child required no cue and bowed with precision.

"Divine!" Madame de V raved. "Stand slowly; that's right, both slowly…"

Once upright, we joined hands, facing each other, arms raised high and sang in unison.

"*A lady who is born and bred, will dress her feet before her head.*"

The patient nursemaid clapped loudly when the final note died out. Much to our combined amazement, someone else applauded, too.

"Bravo, bravisimo!" a deep voice hailed.

Unbeknownst to Madame de V, François or myself, Jeanne-Olympe was present with a fine gentleman at her side, the two newcomers reviewing our production.

I turned a shade of scarlet, while François raced to his mother's side. Our nanny dipped low in the presence of a Bourbon prince, Gaston, Duc d'Orléans who, with Mazarin's departure, was the most powerful man in France.

"Hello, Monsieur," François piped, the only member of the troupe who kept his wits about him when confronted by greatness. "Did you like our poem? Were we pleasing?"

"You were excellent, both of you," he smiled, patting the boy on the cheek. "Dressing you to resemble a lady was an amusing touch, very droll."

"Yes, we thought you'd enjoy that," Madame de Choisy quickly interrupted, sending Madame de V a dagger-look. "Not that I am encouraging François to be an actor, Monsieur."

"No, of course not," he chuckled. "Maybe a priest but not a player! Philippe," he called out over his shoulder, "Philippe, hurry up, you good-for-nothing rascal!"

"Here I come, good-for-nothing rascal," sounded the echo from outside the confines of the room. "Where did you go, uncle?"

"Is that the prince?" François asked, jumping up and down in his excitement.

"Yes, darling," his mother replied. "The king's only brother was kind enough to come and play, isn't that nice?"

I could not imagine how bad my luck was capable of being. The Duc d'Orléans had caught me behaving no better than an ape and, to make matters worse, his horrible nephew was approaching.

Philippe appeared on the scene, huffing and puffing. Gaston mussed his hair with affection and the Duc d'Anjou beamed with happiness. The two could have been father and son, so close was their resemblance. Both possessed dark hair falling in waves to their shoulders, they shared the same olive tone, identical black pupils reflected the other's image. Philippe was the male heir Gaston had not been blessed with; the Duc d'Orléans, a father figure to a lonely, neglected child whose own sire had died when the youth was not quite three years of age.

The ladies curtsied to the heir, as was his due. Looking about, Philippe recognized me and said to Monsieur, "That's Mademoiselle Bijoux. I know her."

"Oh, really?" Gaston replied with an eyebrow raised high. "Why don't you go say hello, then?"

"Good day, your Highness," I said, bowing low.

"Hello," the prince answered, offering me a hand. I noticed his wardrobe consisted of the same shabby clothes he had worn at our first meeting. Placing my fingers in his, I straightened, our mutual apprehension apparent.

"Are you not going to introduce me to your lady?" Gaston inquired of his nephew.

"Monsieur, this is Mademoiselle Bijoux...what is your proper name?" he asked impatiently.

"Cinq-Mars," I stated with pride.

Madame de Choisy smiled, radiant in her discovery. She had scored another coup.

"So, you are the daughter of the late, not-so-great Monsieur le Grand. Welcome to the Luxembourg, child."

"Monsieur is too kind." I choked on the words, bowing to the man who had helped to kill my father.

"Come here," Gaston requested.

I approached and stood before Monsieur; he touched my hair, evaluating my countenance intensely.

"She resembles Marion," he said, addressing Jeanne-Olympe, ignoring my presence.

"Yes, I thought the same when I first saw her. Then, last night, she brought out the locket, and I realized that I must inform you of the incident right away."

Gaston nodded his approval and I stood there before them, silently. Not one to miss an opportunity, Madame de Choisy asked Philippe's permission for François and I to reenact our skit.

"That would be amusing, please do," the prince agreed.

Thus commanded, we obeyed. Much to my chagrin, our second effort was not our best, the three adults bestowing compliments, all the same. Innocent François stared up at Philippe with a timid expression and inquired, "How did you like the poem, Petit Monsieur? Bijoux and I wrote it all by ourselves."

The royal monster knew how to be cruel. Ten years spent playing second fiddle to his brother, Louis, had left him with a number of faults, the chief being his impulsive manner.

"I think," Philippe began casually, "that your composition was..." he paused.

"Yes, yes?" François was expecting praise.

"The most ridiculous thing I have ever heard!" the prince exclaimed, a wicked-sounding snicker accompanying his critique.

Madame de V caught her breath at the bad review, François began to bawl and Madame de Choisy tittered into her fan, not wishing for Gaston to see her disappointment. As far as I was concerned, Philippe had declared war.

"You possess a sharp tongue," I announced, marching over to the boy. "François is my best friend and I demand an apology!"

"Or what? You'll bite me again?"

"Listen, you, I don't care who you are! No one should treat others the way that you do, especially a Prince of France!"

"Remind you of someone?" Jeanne-Olympe cocked her head at Gaston, who immediately began to roar with laughter.

"God's blood! You are the spitting image of Monsieur le Grand! Henri would yell at my brother in the same manner! This scene is uncanny!"

"Tell him to apologize," I persisted.

"Philippe, be a gentleman," d'Orléans said sternly.

"Please forgive me," the nephew said contritely, without a second warning. Gaston was the sole person whom he respected.

"Give Petit Monsieur a kiss and say all is forgotten," hinted the diplomatic Madame de Choisy.

Against my will, I took her advice. Philippe sheepishly mimicked the action, nipping one of my ears in the process.

Peace restored, Monsieur ambled into the nursery, sitting down on François' bed.

"Because we are all friends here," he began, "I am going to tell you children a story. Gather 'round."

We sat at the large man's feet, thrilled by the prospect of hearing an interesting tale. Gaston seemed the type capable of spinning a good yarn and anything was better than listening to people talk about me.

"Once upon a time," the duke began in the traditional style, "three friends lived happily at the court of my brother, Louis XIII. One was named Monsieur, that's me," he explained, tapping Philippe on his button nose, "one was called Jeanne, that's your mama," he tweaked François' chin, "and the last was known as Monsieur le Grand."

The Duc d'Orléans did not look at me or touch me, choosing to continue without mentioning that I was Monsieur le Grand's daughter. I overlooked the slight, concluding he thought boys superior to girls.

"Our trio made merry and we were content with our lot, for we had fine food, fast horses and plenty of gold coins at our disposal. Then, one day, a mean, old man came along who threatened to take all the pretty things away and the friends became sad. Does anyone know who that bad person was?"

"Cardinal de Richelieu," Philippe supplied.

"Precisely! The cardinal was a greedy and cruel man who

treated my brother, the King of France and Navarre, no better than a servant. Not that Louis was to blame," Gaston pointed out hastily, "for he was too nice for his own good. So, as you can see, something had to be done about the cardinal and the king's special companion, Monsieur le Grand, devised a scheme."

"More a palace revolt!" Jeanne-Olympe jested.

"No interruptions from you," he winked. "Monsieur le Grand begged the king to send Richelieu far away so that he might take the cardinal's place and become an important minister of France. Not quite what any of us had intended."

"What?" I asked, appalled.

"Oh, yes, Mademoiselle Bijoux. Monsieur le Grand wanted a powerful position for himself, which was wrong of him because he knew, in all fairness, that any honor belonged to me."

"You did deserve an exalted post," Choisy sighed.

"No, Monsieur, all he intended to do was remove the cardinal because..."

"How would you know?" Gaston cut me off completely. "Unless I am mistaken, you were not one of the three friends."

"Pardon me, Monsieur," I acquiesced. "I was wrong to speak."

"Just like Monsieur le Grand, eh?"

"No, never," I mumbled, ashamed of my heritage: a whore for a mother, a traitor for a father.

Monsieur softened, sensing my embarrassment.

"As I was saying, Monsieur le Grand fancied himself running the whole of France at my brother's side. Louis did not share his lover's vision, for he trusted Richelieu more than anyone else at court. He had banished our own mother when she dared to question the cardinal one too many times."

Madame de Choisy appeared slightly pained by Gaston's lack of sensitivity when describing his brother's liaison with my father. Madame de V was likewise flustered by the pronouncement; the boys remained unmoved.

"Thus, Henri, when denied his entreaty, came to me and we plotted, together with the Spanish ambassador and some others, to assassinate Richelieu. 'Twas a dirty business, yet one that needed to be done. Unfortunately, however, the cardinal had many spies and was soon hot on our heels. I begged Monsieur le Grand to give up the plan, to hide away for a time, but he would have none of my advice. His ambition was greater than any other I have since witnessed. And, because he outgrew his breeches and deserted his companions, guess as to what transpired next."

"My father was arrested on September the fifth, 1642, and executed one week later," I supplied almost with pride, determined to defend the name of Cinq-Mars.

"Do you grasp the moral of my story?" Monsieur asked me directly and no one else.

"I think Monsieur is telling me to know my place." I glared at him.

"And where might that be?" he continued, not through with the lesson.

"Serving you," I replied. "If Cinq-Mars had been half as loyal as I, then he would still be alive and I would not be an orphan, relying on the kindness of strangers."

Gaston's expression was stern, his countenance hardened by numerous disappointments in his own attempts for dominance of a realm which should have been his except for an accident of birth. His experiences had made him shrewder than shrewd, although something about me convinced him I was sincere.

"Your answers impress me, mademoiselle. Perhaps when you are older, you may be of service. In the meantime, prove yourself worthy of such a distinction and I shall be inclined to forget your father's sins."

"I am your servant, Monsieur."

Gaston stood, helping each one of us to our feet in a paternal fashion, making me wait, the last to rise. He was so strong that when he lifted me, I felt as light as eiderdown.

"If you would care to assist me, mademoiselle, I shall make you a proposal."

Choisy nodded at me, though the sign was unnecessary.

"How would you and François like to see my nephew more often?"

I hugged Philippe in order to hide my aversion to the idea. Surprisingly, he clutched me back, as though starved for any demonstration of warmth from a living, breathing person.

"Fine. The Petit Monsieur will arrive here at noon twice a week. Do you agree, madame?"

Jeanne-Olympe blushed with pleasure.

"I am overwhelmed by the gracious favor bestowed on my unworthy household..."

"Yes, quite," he interrupted. Gaston did not harbor any desire to attend a *Précieuse* gathering.

"Ladies, François, the pleasure has been mine. Let us depart, good-for-nothing rascal. You'll see your mademoiselle soon enough."

Philippe kissed me on both cheeks, then regarded me seriously and asked, "I still have the eardrops. Shall I bring them to our next audience?"

"No," I stammered, not wanting the adults to hear. "No, they belong to you, not to me."

Philippe was positively radiant as he tagged along behind Gaston's imposing frame.

"I love you," he declared and I reacted by turning redder than the walls of mother's flame-colored bedchamber.

The royals disappeared from sight. Immediately, François began to tease me concerning Philippe's parting remark.

"Bijoux and Philippe," he sang, "Bijoux and Philippe..."

"Be quiet!" I lashed out. "I hate him!"

Choisy's fan promptly snapped shut and rapped across the back of my head.

"Mind your tongue, silly girl! If the Petit Monsieur says he loves you, then you will most assuredly love him back."

"No, I won't." I defied her vehemently. "I don't love him, nor could I ever!"

"Oh, really? And who might you deign to spend time with, Louis himself?"

She had discovered the secret infatuation and I detested her for penetrating my façade with her finely honed skills.

"Do not forget that if Louis should die, Philippe, the Petit

Monsieur, would be king. His title now should be *Monsieur,* but since the Duc d'Orléans is alive and was always called that while his brother lived, the heir is distinguished from his uncle by the word *Petit.* When Gaston passes away, the king's brother will be known as *Monsieur* and will probably become the next Duc d'Orléans. You could do worse for a friend, or better yet," she paused, a sly grin forming, "a lover."

"Mama, will Philippe and Bijoux get married?" François asked hopefully.

"No, dearest, I don't think so. However, you could both become important to the prince if you make him like you by flattering him a bit. Be kind to Philippe while the two of you are young, and when you grow older, he will shower you with rewards."

Madame de Choisy's logic was sound, whether I liked to admit it or not. My practical Taurus Moon said *submit,* while Mars in the sign of the Water Bearer urged *rebel.* Then, the answer to the dilemma came to me as if by the auspices of prudent Mercury in Libra, a thought causing my spirits to soar: if I became the Petit Monsieur's confidante, the chances of my meeting the king would be greatly improved.

"Madame, please have patience with me. I have much to learn and I must bore you at times with my ignorance. I shall try my best to be pleasing and gracious when with the prince, should you wish it."

"That's much more sensible of you," the lady replied with relief. "Ventadour, see to it that this place is in proper order for the Petit Monsieur's visit and that the children have games with which to amuse themselves."

"Yes, madame."

"I would personally oversee the details if I were not required to appear at the Blue Room this evening. I shall tolerate no mistakes tomorrow—you were fortunate, indeed, that Monsieur was duped by the play and thought that this," she gestured at François, "was a costume. If he suspected, in the least, that you dress my child as a girl, well, Prince Philippe would not be sojourning in this nursery. Remember that, for I should hate to dismiss you, Charlotte-Anne."

"I understand your meaning completely," Madame de V answered, chagrined. "I shall never disappoint you again."

"Never say never," Jeanne-Olympe delivered, never content herself unless she had the final say. The lady then kissed her son, deposited a pat on my crown and glowered at our governess. When satisfied that our small group was sufficiently awed by her supreme authority, she sighed and flitted off.

My sole regret was that I did not have the nerve to poison the impossible woman, for Guibourg's instruction had not left me; I lacked only the powders and the courage.

Madame de V sank down into a high-backed armchair, her face screwed-up in one, great frown. I knelt beside her and in doing so, hid my countenance, mainly so that she would not be further annoyed by the sight of my angry tears.

"You are the nicest teacher anyone could ask for," I whimpered. "How do you abide her; why do you stay here when she treats you so poorly? She is such a charlatan, such a two-faced daughter of Gemini..."

"Shh...sweet thing. I take no notice of her, and nor should you."

Ventadour leaned over and whispered, "She's crazy. Don't get involved in her dirty schemes."

"I should die if she sent you away," I confessed. François dropped the doll he was playing with and crawled on hands and knees to where I sat. Concerned, he wiped away a rivulet threatening to run across the bridge of my nose.

"Don't be sad. Everything will be fine, Bijoux. Mama says bad things sometimes, but she doesn't mean them."

"All the same, it isn't fair. Madame is our friend and we must defend her. Everyone but Monsieur knows that your mother dresses you as a girl, not Madame de V! I swear to Athena that two hearts beat within Jeanne-Olympe's chest!"

"It's not my fault—don't be cross with me," he whined, a child of Cancer through and through.

"Enough, enough already," the nanny cried out, pushing me away none too gently, leaping to her feet. "Leave well enough alone, Bijoux. God knows, I've survived worse scolding."

"When? Such as when?"

"Such as none of your business, young mademoiselle!"

The pain etched across her brow and around her mouth revealed much. I knew she was suffering from a hurt that ran deeper than Choisy's attack, yet I needled her all the same.

"You lecture us on the nobler virtues, madame, but then you, yourself, lack a spine! Perhaps because you, like François, are a child of the Crab and tend to sidestep important issues..."

"How do you know who or what I am?" she yelled. "How dare you sit in judgment of me—you, a mere child who spouts nonsense about sea creatures? Did you ever stop to think that perhaps I am here for a reason, Bijoux, that perhaps this was not always my home? Imagine a beautiful house in the country, built upon the banks of the Loire. Try to see me there, if you will, married to a man hand-picked for me by my parents and the Duc d'Orléans; a man who beat me and scarred me, who would drink and flog me for the sport of it. Relive my horror when I finally defended myself against him, using a fire iron, and nearly broke the bastard's skull wide open. Was it his fault? Oh no, I was sent away to Paris to become naught but a servant, a punishment for my wild and uncontrollable temper."

"I'm...I'm...sorry," I stuttered.

"Think before you speak," she growled. "Madame de Choisy—that conniving bitch—do you not think I perceive her motives? Yet how may I fight back, Bijoux, when my very existence depends upon her changing whims? If she sends me packing, it's back to Blois and a whipping, although that prison, better known as the convent, is another alternative. I'm not *that* old, my dear, and I shan't be locked away to die no better than a spinster."

"By Athena, I am such an idiot, madame. Please discipline me as you see fit," I begged, closing my eyes in preparation for the switch.

"Stop it, girl! Granted, I am cross, but inflicting pain is not an intelligent way to deal with anger."

"Thank you, madame."

She ignored me. "François, time for bed. Bijoux and I have things to discuss."

"I don't want to sleep. The Sun is in the sky, madame."

"Get moving, don't argue with me," she replied, her voice gaining a recalled sense of purpose. Not bothering to undress the boy, she helped him onto the pallet with a shove, landing François on his back wearing a bemused look, unaccustomed as he was to such treatment.

"If your mother wants me to treat you as a little man, it's best you learn to behave as one. No more girl games or skirts, understand? From today forward, you play soldier and you learn how to sit a horse properly."

François hid under the blankets.

"I want to be a great lady, madame."

"Too bad. God made you as you are and I'll be damned if I fight Nature any longer."

She handed me my cape as she took her own from the oversized wardrobe that held our clothing.

"Bijoux and I are going for a walk. Short of a fire, don't leave that bed. Do I make myself clear, François-Timoléon?"

"Yes." I could barely hear his whispered response, my friend was that confounded.

Madame ushered me out of the room and slammed shut the outside door to our apartment. She was in a hurry to get away, for fresh air, as though she might change her mind and return to her former self if allowed a moment to reconsider her actions. The two of us bustled down the east staircase that descended from the third floor, where we lived, to one of the many side exits of the Luxembourg Palace.

Reaching the outside and the subsequent rush of cold, Madame de V gathered some snow found resting on a stone ledge of the building and pressed it gratefully to her forehead.

"Sweet Jesus, I'm burning hot. Merciful heaven, how I despise it in there!"

"You do?"

"No better than a crypt," she maintained, leaning against a wall for support. "To think I would end up in this state makes me want to weep."

"Run away," was my solution, remembering Des Oeillets' plight.

"With what? My family has disowned me, I have nothing save the clothes on my back and Choisy sees to it that no gentleman makes my acquaintance. Who'd want me, anyway?" she despaired, referring to her heavyset figure.

"Don't be an ass. I know of someone; however, he's presently away on the cardinal's business. You could be thinner by the time he returns."

"That might take years, Bijoux."

"He could be away that long," I mused.

Suddenly, Madame de V began to laugh, amused by the wry pursing I gave to my lips.

"You are such a monkey!" she exclaimed. "Would that I could be your age again!"

"Madame, you are very comely lady. Your husband might die and then you would be free. In fact, if you like, I could rid you of him with poison..."

"Be still, child," she gasped, fitting a chubby palm over my mouth. "Don't even think such an evil thought!"

I nodded in assent and she released me.

"No more talk about the past," she ordered.

"Fine, I promise, and I shall mention you to my gentleman friend. What is your given name?"

"How did you know that I am not a Ventadour?"

"I did not, truly. I meant your Christian name."

"Oh, I was christened Charlotte-Anne," she replied. "You may as well know the rest of it. My title is the Dame de St. Croix, or Madame de Chanlecy, take your pick. The false name of Ventadour shields my kin who are living at court from the disgrace of association. The man to whom I belong is quite rich and my own relatives are of the true nobility."

"What mean you by *true*, madame?"

"We did not buy our rank as others do. Nobles such as Monsieur know this and need the support of families such as mine. That is why when he remarried, the king's uncle chose the impoverished Duchesse de Lorraine, for her family tree is stronger than his own."

"Is a bloodline that important? Is a king not a king, a prince not a prince?"

"It depends upon origins, yes, upon descent," Charlotte-Anne offered as explanation. "Enough, though. What you need to understand, Bijoux, is that the less you get involved with the likes of Choisy, the easier you will sleep. She and her kind are ruthless people who would like nothing more than to establish Gaston or Philippe on the throne and depose King Louis in the process."

"Why Philippe? Is he not Louis' brother?"

"Yes, girl, but the Petit Monsieur may be controlled by Monsieur. No Mazarin, no Queen Anne to interfere with Gaston's plans. What do you think the damn Fronde is about? The side that wins the war, takes the throne."

"Tell me the name of Madame de Choisy's secret Order. The one in which Monsieur plays such an important *rôle*, please?"

Charlotte-Anne twitched at the sound of footsteps crunching on a nearby gravel path. She hesitated, weighing whether to tell me what she knew or not.

"Forget I was the one who said it, but the group is the Company of the Blessed Sacrament. Do not repeat that information to anyone. I care for you, Bijoux, and I would hate to see you harmed. Swear to be silent on this matter, for my sake, as well as for yours."

"I swear," I lied, crossing my fingers behind my back as Guibourg had taught me to do.

The Dame de St. Croix invisibly traced the sign I had seen the priest make over mother when she lay dying. Oddly, the ritual repulsed me.

"There, our pact is sealed. Let us return to the nursery. We shouldn't leave François-Timoléon alone for long."

"Quite right, madame," was all I said, my mind intent on keeping and storing the material garnered during the conversation with Charlotte-Anne. *The Company of the Blessed Sacrament, the Company of the Blessed Sacrament,* I repeated silently, over and over to myself. Much work awaited, more facts needed to be had, yet I had made a start, an in-road that could lead me to the Secret the society guarded with their lives.

What I was too young to appreciate was that great mysteries are often truths suppressed for an important reason; be that for the good or be that for the ill of society. The enigma at the heart of the Company of the Blessed Sacrament is just such a secret: an old, delicately balanced conspiracy certain to cause sorrow for some, joy for others, if revealed.

And that is the only reason explaining my reluctance to record this tale. The gist of the matter is, however, that deep down I always knew the Secret should be told.

Yet, I was a coward for many years and, not unlike Madame de V on that dusky March day, I feared the consequences of speaking out, of facing public ridicule. Not until I had lost something I treasure far more than my own life—someone whom I adore completely and unequivocally—did the urge to risk all and speak become manifest within me.

Also, it must be added, lest I appear overly brave, that when one is awaiting death from a prison cell in the Bastille, the difficult things are easier to say.

Madame de Choisy may have been an heartless wretch, though I must concede that her sources and observations concerning life at court were unusually accurate. Having that singular advantage at my disposal, in an age of political upheaval, was worth its weight in golden *louis*. As she had predicted, her suspicion that Mazarin would travel to Le Havre to release the princes was proven correct. So precise that I considered naming her *Madame Nostradame* in light of her supposed prophetic skills.

After being freed from their comfortable dungeons, Condé, Conti and Longueville made straight for Paris without killing their enemy Mazarin, so concerned were they with getting home to clip Gaston's wings. The cardinal and his modest escort moved sadly onwards, and I wondered whether he and d'Artagnan ever discussed the possibility of the *frondeurs* dividing amongst themselves and diminishing the rebel power base in the process. Because that was exactly what happened the moment the malcontent nobles reconvened for a strategy meeting at the Luxembourg.

Meanwhile, situated miles away in a castle at Brühl, the exiles awaited their status reports, the courier d'Artagnan often riding into the night towards his homeland to deliver messages from Mazarin to 22.

Not to diminish the Fronde in and of itself, the struggle that ended in 1652 was won by the Loyalists, aided in their fight by the aforementioned protagonists who could not help but turn on each other in their contest over the throne. I could dwell endlessly on the period in question; however, considering that the Grand Condé, who himself took the whole business rather seriously, dubbed the civil unrest *the war of the chamberpots*, let us dispense with the boring details.

To wit, the rebellion was squashed: Gaston was subsequently disgraced and banished to his estate at Blois; Conti became a recluse and was forced to marry one of Mazarin's nieces; the Grand Condé—a famous general with an illustrious reputation to maintain—elicited Spanish aid in order to stage occasional border skirmishes with the king's forces. The court, having relocated to the Parisian suburb of St. Denis shortly after the princes regained their liberty, returned to the capital city and cheering subjects on October 21, 1652. On February 3, 1653, the cardinal, who had managed to inch his way back onto French soil and repose in a château in the Sedan with six thousand troops at his command, was restored to his jubilant queen by act of general amnesty issued by his godson, King Louis XIV.

Mazarin, to the dismay of those abiding at the Luxembourg, was back for good in 1653, as was my Musketeer, who was sent straightway to England bearing tidings from his Eminence to that country's new Lord Protector, Oliver Cromwell. Other than d'Artagnan's continued absence, things were quite regular in my world, despite Monsieur's enforced retirement. Well, as regular as they could be, sharing quarters with Madame de Choisy.

Jeanne-Olympe and most of the d'Orléans' retinue

remained in their apartments since someone was required to keep an eye on things for Gaston while he was away. Madame believed that the duke would be recalled to court once he had served a short punishment, and she eagerly made plans for that happy day. New frocks were ordered for her intimate circle, including the nine-year-old François, who had resumed his cross-dressing. With the duke on leave, the strange habit became more overt and my friend actually accompanied his mother to the Louvre powdered, perfumed and complete with patches. The odd thing was that no one commented on the practice; none of the other courtiers seemed to mind the peculiar Mademoiselle Sancy.

Philippe had been shuttled off to St. Denis along with the rest of the Louvre's inhabitants in 1651, and the proposed play sessions his uncle had envisioned never come to pass. Having been at Monsieur's side during the Fronde, the Petit Monsieur was grouped with the losers when the war was concluded. Not quite a traitor, yet certainly shunned, the king's brother was sent to reside apart from the family at the Tuileries Palace by order of Mazarin himself. The deserted space belonged to Gaston's eldest, the Grande Mademoiselle, who had been obliged to vacate her lodging, relegated to obscurity in the provinces as had her father.

Definitely Gaston's daughter, Anne-Marie-Louise, still the richest girl in France and unmarried at the age of twenty-five, had taken it upon herself to assist the rebel Grand Condé during a decisive battle of the Fronde being waged outside the gates of Paris. From a not-too-distant hill, her cousin, King Louis, watched as she personally fired the guns of the Bastille on the advancing Loyalist soldiers, turning the tide in favor of the *frondeurs*. The military tactic enabled Condé's men to seek shelter within the walls of the sympathetic capital and to live another day to prolong the fray.

Prior to the incident, Queen Anne had wished her son to marry his wealthy relative; once done, Mazarin had tersely remarked from his outpost, "Mademoiselle de Montpensier, by employing that cannon, has killed her husband."

Louis never forgave Paris its arrogance, the Grande Mademoiselle her stupidity, or Philippe his determination to remain loyal to Uncle Gaston. The king was not amused when the heir pined for the duke, writing him letter after letter, all addressed to *My good-for-nothing rascal* and duly signed by *Your good-for-nothing rascal*. In a pique, the eldest son complained to his mother and she promised to keep her youngest in line. Yet, the offensive behavior continued, and Louis petitioned Mazarin to make things right. The cardinal listened seriously to his protégé, recognizing that Philippe was potentially another Monsieur in the making. But what to do? Short of castrating the prince, how could one control the audacious lad? Mazarin then hit upon a cunning plan. Louis' brother would no longer be schooled in fencing or in the art of war, he would no longer ride with the hounds or learn how to shoot a musket. No, Philippe, Duc d'Anjou, was to attend a classroom of a different bent. And his tutor would bear the name Choisy.

The rumors that the cardinal had heard regarding François-Timoléon's upbringing influenced his decision to favor his former enemy with the distinction of educating the royal nuisance on the finer points of feminine conduct. Jules Mazarin could only hope that Madame de Choisy would transform Philippe as convincingly as she had her own son. Most gratifying of all was that when the Petit Monsieur was summoned to the cardinal's sumptuous palace to be informed by d'Artagnan of the arrangement—the boy did not argue. On the contrary, the Petit Monsieur was glad because, as he told his elder, the change meant he would be reunited with the girl whom he liked more than any other, Mademoiselle Bijoux. I am certain that the avowal made my Musketeer smile, for it mirrored his own sentiment exactly.

D'Artagnan and I had remained *incommunicado* since the evening he had deposited me at the Luxembourg. He never once managed to sneak into Paris when delivering covert messages to the queen at nearby St. Denis, considering it foolish to risk capture. The lack of contact caused me to worry incessantly as to the Gascon's welfare, plus I was driven to distraction by the knowledge that Madame de V's morsel concerning the Company of the Blessed Sacrament was going to waste. Sometimes, after having come home empty handed yet again from the last pew on the left at St. Sulpice, I wondered in despair if my friend was dead. Feeling deserted and alone, it seemed the only rational explanation for d'Artagnan's total disappearance from my existence.

My relief, therefore, was great indeed when, on a crisp morning near to September's close, a most welcome sight was restored to me from a nursery window: the figure of Charles de Batz accompanying a boy my own age through the Luxembourg gardens towards the palace.

Forgetting to ask permission of Madame de V, nor caring if I had it, I lunged out of the nursery, ran down the steep stairs and flew outside into the cool breezes.

The Sun's light was brilliant beyond compare, a few hardy flowers lived on in their well-tended beds and a fountain jettisoned sprays of diamond droplets at any who approached. A perfect setting for a tender reunion, however not the one I expected to make.

Nearing the two at breakneck speed, I halted when I realized that d'Artagnan was strolling with the Petit Monsieur. Confused, the happiness I had felt at seeing the Gascon—ever attractive and ready for an exploit—was diminished by the gnawing sensation in my stomach caused by Philippe's appearance.

Why was the Petit Monsieur accompanying d'Artagnan? Not wanting to know the answer, I flew into my hero's arms, clinging to him, hugging him with all of my might, glad that he was safe.

"You're alive!" I shouted to the world. "Thank the gods, monsieur, for I feared you dead."

"Not yet," he guffawed, putting me down. "I ought to go away more often, mademoiselle; it isn't every day that beautiful ladies throw themselves at my feet."

"She is pretty, isn't she?" a taller and older Philippe asked proudly. "Mademoiselle Bijoux is mine, though, monsieur. For the past two years, I have thought of nothing else than how I shall one day make her my mistress. I should have the loveliest girl at the court by my side, do you not agree?"

"And so you will," d'Artagnan reassured the prince, his avowal a revelation to me. "Yet for now, why don't you run ahead and try to find Mademoiselle Sancy and be the first to give her the good news."

"Right enough, well said," Philippe commended, more grown-up than I remembered him as being. He took one of my hands and kissed it with fervor, lips remaining on my flesh longer than I cared to admit liking. A sensuous stare, engulfing my person from head to toe, came next, 'ere his departure.

As he flitted off, I had to concede that he was awfully nice to look at. Too bad that he annoyed me more than any other person I had ever met, Madame de Choisy included.

"Please don't encourage him, monsieur," I admonished. "I don't wish to be dragged off to prison for killing the king's only brother."

"Still that sharp tongue, eh? You are not only developing into a stunning young woman, but a great wit, also," he teased.

"Stop it," I blushed, accepting d'Artagnan's proffered arm with an air of sophistication. "I have so much to relate. Imagine, I discover the name of your secret society and you make me wait more than two years to tell."

"No," he stopped. "Bijoux, do not jest with me. 'Tis cruel to torment an old man."

"You're not old," I laughed, then added in a quieter tone, "I am not jesting."

"Dearest girl, who are they, then? Good God, what a fool I have been—running here and there on the cardinal's business, too busy to sleep, never mind think about that group of scoundrels! What's their name—I must inform Cardinal Mazarin immediately. This is one of his top priorities, you know, ever since I told him about you."

"You mentioned me to his Eminence?" I swallowed.

"Of course. We passed many a cold evening in Brühl with nothing to do other than reminisce. Thank heaven better days have come. Now, what did you learn? Tell me here, outside, rather than trying to converse inside the palace. The walls in there have ears, they say."

"My governess, Madame de Ventadour, said our enemies call themselves the Company of the Blessed Sacrament."

D'Artagnan became pale, as though he had seen a ghost. I tugged on his doublet, yet he did not flinch.

"Whatever is amiss? Did I say something terrible?" I queried.

"No, no," he said shaking his fair head. "Just something incredible, *ma petite*. If your nursemaid is correct, treachery of the foulest sort is afoot."

"Such as?" I asked as we resumed our stroll.

"Could you arrange for her to meet with me?"

"Who? Madame de V? Why, yes, I suppose so. Actually," I said, remembering the lady's lamentable romantic state for the first time in months, "if you were to woo her, she might tell you much, monsieur."

It was his turn to go scarlet.

"What is her age?" he croaked.

"Very old," I laughed. "And she longs for a swain, Charles; someone handsome and dashing!"

Giggling, I skipped away. I could hardly wait for him to see the Dame de St. Croix, who had slimmed her figure and was drawing appreciative glances from gentleman who espied her during our daily outings.

"Let no man say I do not love my king and country," he sighed aloud. "Get over here, minx. First Guibourg, then this intrigue—you could try the patience of..."

"St. Anthony!" I finished for him and we pealed forth with mutual amusement, although I noticed that the look d'Artagnan cast my way was not the same he had given me in the past. Brotherly love did not simmer in his eyes but rather a stronger emotion, one which I would not have recognized except men had eyed Marion in the same manner.

Pleased and scared, I ran away, wondering if he would follow. He did, beating me to the side door, flush with his triumph as he barred my access to the iron gate.

"Give me a kiss and I shall allow you to pass," he declared, forgetting the twenty years between us.

"Monsieur, really," I protested, "Madame de Choisy would not approve."

"Did you not yearn for me, Bijoux? Not even a little?"

"You have changed, monsieur. Do not meddle with me, for I am no whore! I am not Marion!"

That observation checked his lecherous advances. Ashamed of himself, d'Artagnan allowed me to shimmy past. Once inside the palace, he bowed, obviously contrite.

"Forgive me, Bijoux. I have been a stranger to polite society of late and my manner must seem rude. It's just that..."

"What?" I asked in a curt, impatient tone.

"Well, you are a young lady now. A fine young lady, I might add. Many girls marry when they are not much older than thirteen. Surely you must realize how lovely you are."

"If that is the truth, then no one has said anything to me about it. Furthermore, I hate boys and shall never marry. They are all horrid," I pronounced, though when I saw the hurt expression on his face I adjoined, "except for you, of course, but you're a man, so it doesn't count..."

At that point, I was babbling and never expected what happened next to occur. Drawing me gently to him, Charles de Batz lifted my chin until his clear, blue eyes were all I could focus upon; that and the warm tongue parting my mouth open, his breath mingling with my own.

He was kissing me and, despite the sense I was being wicked, I gave him leave to, his embrace becoming all the more impassioned as my fingers ran through his thick, golden curls. His smell, his touch, every aspect of his person was thoroughly intoxicating. Not for a moment did I hesitate to return his ardor with my own, breaking with him only to gasp for air.

"What of Philippe?"

"Who cares?" he murmured softly, convincingly. "What of us?"

D'Artagnan's use of the word *us* terrified me more than the prospect of a courtier stumbling across our groping on the stairs. More than scandal, I feared the intimacy implied by his low whispers, the unspoken demands his soul would make of mine if I yielded to the force driving our bodies closer together. My heart still yearned for the king and no one else, plus I still had my future as an astrologer to consider.

"Monsieur, you sent the prince running to find François to tell him some good news, did you not? Should I not be privy to your glad tidings, also?"

"I think you are dismissing me, mademoiselle," he correctly observed. "Not all women find me displeasing and now that Mazarin is back in charge, I am considered an eligible bachelor, Bijoux."

"How dare you insult me in such a manner? I kissed you because…"

"Yes?"

"Because I…like you more than anyone I've ever known, d'Artagnan. You are my best friend."

"Then marry me," he suggested matter-of-factly, striking a defensive pose. "I am able to wait a year, that is no great sacrifice. Say you will be mine; give me your word that you will be my wife."

"I cannot. Do not make me say it, please. God knows I owe you my life, yet I cannot pledge myself. I am too young," I argued. "You are a Leo and I am a Virgo—the match is not a good one."

"If you loved me, you would care not for such ridiculous portents!"

"Do not mock astrology, monsieur, or else I shall never speak to you anon!"

"Fine. I am a patient man and I shall respect your concerns because you are that dear to me. However, do not expect me to dally about, waiting forever."

"No, monsieur, I would not wish that," I replied. "May we go upstairs?"

"After you, my sweet," he acquiesced. D'Artagnan then humbled himself as any genuine suitor would, adding, "Perhaps one last kiss?"

"Good try," was my retort as I tripped lightly over the worn, stone steps. D'Artagnan's attentions were flattering, to be sure, and I was no doubt a fool to ignore his proposal, but I could not make a promise of marriage at that moment.

Part of me also could not imagine a man of my Musketeer's caliber finding a pale, skinny thing such as myself desirable. To be blunt, my unmanageable tresses were an unpopular, ugly color and the green-gold eyes inherited from Marion were too big for my face. I was as tall as my mother, the goddess, had been; however, that was where any similarity between us ended. D'Artagnan was merely lonely, I deduced, and marriage was preferable to a celibate existence.

Philippe seemed the best excuse to use against the would-be-husband whose purposeful stride echoed behind me in the hallway. Encouraged by the sound of my pursuer's footsteps, I beat a retreat to the safe company of Madame de V and François.

CHAPTER SEVEN
Daughter of Taphos

"Madame de Ventadour," I called out when I was within earshot, "madame, François!"

The Petit Monsieur, Mademoiselle Sancy and Charlotte-Anne soon appeared on the scene, greeting me with smiles and affectionate pecks on both cheeks. D'Artagnan joined our group momentarily, removing his hat as a sign of respect towards the Dame de St. Croix. Thankfully, she was wearing an embroidered bodice, tightly laced and squarely cut, which showed her ample bosom in its best light.

"Madame de Ventadour, may I present Cardinal Mazarin's trusted ambassador and my friend, Charles de Batz Castelmore, Monsieur d'Artagnan."

"Oh, my," Charlotte-Anne simpered, close to swooning. "What an honor! Bijoux truly is a clever girl to count a courtier such as yourself, monsieur, amongst her acquaintances."

"Bijoux and I are more to each other than mere acquaintances," he corrected, sending Madame de V into a tizzy. She clicked open the fan dangling from a wrist and commenced to flirt shamelessly with the painted accessory.

"Then my young charge is fortunate indeed, monsieur. Would you care to repair to the salon for a refreshment?"

D'Artagnan glanced at me, then stared at the lovely creature who had boldly suggested a private meeting. What he viewed was a flesh-and-blood woman, obviously no stranger to sensual delights, who was offering herself to him in a language only an experienced lover would understand. Watching the pair make eye contact, I was, for a brief flash, consumed by jealousy.

"Madame is too kind," he responded, not about to miss an opportunity to wile away a lust-filled afternoon. "Please be assured it is not my intention to take you from your duties."

"The Petit Monsieur and Bijoux are old enough to watch François-Timoléon," she demurred.

D'Artagnan paused at my side, reflective.

"May I beg your leave?" he asked me in front of everyone. "We shall talk later, you and I."

"By all means, go. Enjoy Madame de Ventadour's hospitality," I blurted out, trying in vain not to sound hurt.

"I'll be back for the prince," he winked, wounded pride restored.

Good, I thought silently, very miffed. I should have been elated by the unexpected cancellation of our lessons and the prospect of a day leisurely spent at play with the heir to the realm; however, I was not.

D'Artagnan had chosen Charlotte-Anne in lieu of myself. Storming off to the room I continued to share with François, a bed soon received me face down, sobbing as I had never sobbed before, not caring who heard or watched me weep.

"Bijoux, what is amiss?"

The Petit Monsieur was at my side, his head leaning against mine, real concern in his voice. When I did not stop crying, he began to coo in my ear, patting down my wild, red hair, kissing me tenderly on the forehead.

"You are making me unhappy," he admitted. "Please don't be sad, my dearest."

Philippe managed to wedge his free arm under me and draw my heaving body close to his solid frame. He really wasn't a bad person, I conceded. Perhaps becoming his mistress wouldn't be so horrid, especially when I considered who he was and how handsome he was turning out to be.

"Tell me what is ailing you, Bijoux."

"No. It is nothing."

"That can't be, or else you wouldn't be wailing like a babe, would you?"

"True," I sniffled, burying my face in his jacket. "Don't laugh at me, *Monsieur*."

The young man squeezed me tightly to him, no doubt thrilled I had addressed him by his rightful title. Later, he would confide in me that I was the first person who had accorded him the honor.

"Bijoux, I adore you, we shall always be together, don't you see? I may be forced to wed another, yet I'll love you forever."

"Don't lie to me," I started to weep anew.

"I am a Prince of the Blood and have my honor to consider."

"Why should I trust you? Your father ordered my father executed, remember?"

"That was between them, not us. We are completely different people, are we not? You don't blame me for what happened, do you?"

His question sent me back to that June eve when Marion had begged me on her deathbed to wipe out the Bourbon name and thus avenge her husband's spirit. That night seemed so far away, as if the oath had never been uttered.

"Say you do not hate me on account of my father's sins."

His plea broke the silence memory demands.

"Monsieur, you are very dear to me. I should like to believe you, but I think it wiser if I ask for a token, a show of your intent."

I heard myself speak and was amazed. What was happening to me? I was turning into Madame la Grande, like it or not.

The prince let go his grip, rolling onto his back.

"That's fair enough," he agreed, feeling charitable. "My brother gives presents to his lady friends—why shouldn't I?"

"The king is enamored?" My heart sank.

"Oh, he is constantly in love with some girl or the other, dear Bijoux. Louis is quite capricious."

Philippe leaned in my direction and I closed my eyes shut,

quite sure that he was about to taste the tears drying on my chin, when François popped out from his hideaway under the bed.

"Aha, I caught you!" he sang as he was wont to do whenever presented with a reason. "Bijoux and Philippe, Bijoux and Philippe..."

"You best take cover, François, because I'm coming after you," I cautioned, boasting for Philippe's sake.

Leaving the royal guest and our cozy love-nest, I jumped down to where François was dancing about in girls' skirts, chanting his infantile taunt. Soon after, we were entwined and rolling about on the floor, not unlike two puppies.

"Pardon the interruption, your Highness. I come with a delivery from M. Cousinot."

We were collectively distracted by the intrusion. Winded from my tussle with François, I stood up, panting, to find a comely messenger in our midst.

"What have you there?" I queried. "Is that my tonic?"

"Are you Mademoiselle Bijoux?"

"Of course, boy. I am the only girl here, aren't I? Or were you tricked by this?" I laughed, giving François a shove with the tip of my shoe.

"No, I mistook *you* for the little man known to all as Mademoiselle Sancy."

What nerve! What cheek! How dare he?

Hands on hips, I stomped up to the page, who appeared to be age fifteen or sixteen, and ripped the package from his safekeeping.

"What is your name? Answer me quickly or M. Cousinot will hear about this."

The courier ignored me. He stared straight ahead, unblinking, as though in a daze.

Studying the young man's interesting countenance—a steel-blue regard, dark hair reaching the nape of his neck—I could not be cross. His looks alone intrigued me and the wit he exhibited was estimable. A more charming tactic was needed to attract his dignified attention.

"Monsieur, I fear my brusque manner has rightly offended this good gentleman, whose bull-headed manner most probably is a consequence of his birth date, and no fault of his own."

Philippe sat upright, legs dangling over the side of the bed.

"Be kind and forgive my angel. What is your name?"

The young man bowed to his superior and replied, "I am César de la Tour of the family d'Auvergne, your Grace, presently attached to the household of Cardinal Mazarin. M. Cousinot was tending to my master when he recalled that Mademoiselle Bijoux's medicine needed delivering and Mazarin, pardon me, his Eminence, insisted on sending me to bring it to her on the double. However, being the plodding son of Taurus that I am," he winked, "I arrived at an inopportune moment."

"No, monsieur, you deserve a reward for a job well done," the prince observed. "Bijoux, give Monsieur César a kiss."

Not one to disobey, I stood on tiptoe and did as instructed, brushing an endearment against the smooth skin of a cheekbone. Monsieur César retained his stoic expression, unmoved by the gesture.

"You may go now," Philippe declared.

"No, please wait," I begged. Rushing over to the desk, nearly tripping over François-Timoléon in my flight, I put down the bundle and wrote Cousinot a short note requesting that he come to visit. A foreboding had been haunting me since the days of Noctambule, a private fear I wished to confide to the physician whom I hoped might possess the knowledge needed to put me at ease.

"Please see that M. Cousinot gets this—I would be indebted to you if he does."

"Anything else?" The timber of his voice was dismissive.

"No, that will do," I returned in the snootiest tone I could muster. Wishing to show M. César that I outranked him, I flounced back to Philippe, recreating the familiar scene we had earlier enjoyed.

Mazarin's retainer was not impressed. With a, "Good day," he was gone. A mere lackey had reduced me to bad behavior and with that realization, mortification set in.

"Disappointed that your handsome heifer did not remain?" the Petit Monsieur gibed, inspired by my sullen pout.

"No, simply annoyed that a stupid bull got the better of me."

"I shall have him reprimanded."

"I'm bored," François interrupted. "Let's play dress-up."

"Go away," I scolded. "Monsieur does *not* wish to play your ridiculous game—he is Prince Philippe!"

"Oh, I don't know. It might be fun. I have a notion," Philippe's smile was crafty. "Why don't we swap outfits? I'll pretend I'm Mademoiselle Bijoux and you can make believe you're me."

"No," I snorted back at him, annoyed. "Your ensemble would never fit me properly."

"Poop!" François jeered. "You never want to do anything fun."

"She'll do it," the good-for-nothing rascal assured him, removing his coat, tossing it to me.

"What?" I asked in utter amazement.

"Why not?" he shrugged. "You are going to see me in the flesh sooner or later."

"Later is better," I quipped. Philippe took no notice. He left me sitting on the mattress, slipping to the floor to stand and remove his trousers.

His breeches, when undone, slumped around his ankles, hobbling him; silk stockings drooped, also, released when the ribbons keeping them in place were untied by an eager François. The remaining blouson of sheerest lawn, stopping at the knees, saved the Petit Monsieur from total exposure.

"I cannot watch this. Stop it!" I asserted.

"Bijoux, I command you!"

Mademoiselle Sancy began twittering uncontrollably.

"Now you have to join in, Bijoux. The Petit Monsieur has spoken!"

While I tossed my head and intoned, "This is unbelievable, I am leaving," Philippe wriggled out of shoes, breeches and socks. François collected the lot, Monsieur's attentive lady-in-waiting. I had slid off of the bed, myself, and was about to depart the nursery in protest, eager to fetch Madame de V.

The playmates had other plans, though. Sneaking up on me from behind, the boys staged an ambush and I found myself being pulled to my knees.

"You brats!" I squealed. "I'm telling Madame de V on you!"

"Go ahead," Philippe answered, pushing me back, pinning me to the carpet by the shoulders. "Who's going to punish me? I am the king's brother."

"Then I'll tell d'Artagnan and he'll report to Mazarin..."

"Be still. You talk too much. François, remove her skirts!"

I commenced kicking and screaming, hoping they would unhand me, however, they did not. In hindsight, the incident loses its import, yet at the time, I was humiliated by them as only a virgin may be.

The young gentlemen did not quit with petticoats and were satisfied only when they had somehow managed to unlace me, securing the remainder of the articles Philippe required for his transformation. The two then scurried away with the stolen goods, uninterested in my nakedness.

I crawled to the spot where Philippe's clothes lay scattered and laid claim to his shirt.

"Your Highness is quite clever, fooling me as you did," I remarked, swallowing my tears. "However, you do understand that once I don your clothing, I am not required to return the prize."

Philippe spun around, half-dressed as a woman and still attended to by his blond minion.

"What do you mean, dearest? You cannot expect me to return to the Tuileries in this costume."

"Why not?" I stretched his hose over a calf. "You obviously take delight in acting like a sissy; why should I deprive you of the pleasure?"

"Don't listen to her," François urged. "I think you look beautiful."

"See? I am beautiful," he declared. "All I need is a wig, white powder and rouge. No one will recognize me, not even Louis."

"Don't forget diamond ear drops," I added, placing a foot in one of his heeled and buckled shoes. "A Princess of France must have her jewels."

"Would you like me to fetch one of mama's hairpieces?" François offered. "She has face paints, as well."

Philippe clapped his hands together gleefully. "Yes, yes, bring it all! Let's show Bijoux how pretty I shall be."

I finished dressing, trying to convince myself I was the Countess of Saint-Belmont, while François and Philippe primped and preened, engrossed as they were in their effort to change the Petit Monsieur into the Petite Mademoiselle. Having had his body dilapidated since he was a toddler—a painful procedure employing crushed eggshells rubbed on arms and legs—the young Choisy was no newcomer to the art of applying cosmetics. He was also skilled at fixing coiffures, having practiced on Jeanne-Olympe daily. It came as no shock, then, when François presented Philippe, looking as lovely as any beauty gracing the court of Louis XIV.

"What do you think, Monsieur?" the prince asked of me, mincing about the bedchamber.

"Pure perfection, I must say. Which is fortunate for you, seeing as though you'll be leaving here dressed as one of Madame Aragonais' dolls."

"Thank you for the compliment, Bijoux. By the way, you are rather dashing yourself," he laughed, thoroughly amused by the switch.

"Let's pretend that you two are getting married," François enthused. "I shall be the priest."

"Gods, little one, aren't you tired, yet? Monsieur is now a proper lady, thanks to you. All that hard work must have left you sleepy, did it not?"

The endearing tike yawned and rubbed his eyes. "Let's nap," he agreed. "All fine ladies rest in the afternoon."

"How true," chimed a voice I knew all too well. Choisy had arrived in the nursery.

"And what do we have here?" she inquired, pointing her closed fan at Philippe.

"That, madame, is one of the Princesses of the Blood, Mademoiselle d'Orléans," I lied.

Madame de Choisy appeared to be puzzled.

"That cannot be," she argued. "Mademoiselle d'Orléans is at home with her parents in Blois. Who is this *thing*? And why are you wearing boys' clothing, Bijoux? What is going on here?"

François' mother grabbed a handful of my hair and yanked on it to emphasize her disapproval.

"Someone give me an answer or Bijoux gets a whipping!"

"Madame, leave her be," Philippe advised, approaching the spot where the lady held me captive. "Mademoiselle Bijoux did nothing wrong, she merely did as I directed."

"Oh, really? Were you never taught to respect your betters, mademoiselle? Did you happen, per chance, to be raised on a farm?"

"Actually," Philippe bantered back, "my mother's country house is at Fontainebleau."

That was when Jeanne-Olympe knew the truth of the matter. Releasing me, she knelt at the feet of Gaston d'Orléans' beloved nephew.

"Forgive me, Petit Monsieur, I had no way of knowing that you were...*you*."

"Then this entertainment was a success," he laughed. "Rise and listen."

The prince had all eyes upon him and he loved the attention. Leading Madame de Choisy to an armchair, he motioned for her to sit—something unheard of at court where few, if any, sat in the presence of a royal.

Honored and overcome, Jeanne-Olympe silently watched Philippe make his way to the center of the room. The Petit Monsieur curtsied in the older courtier's direction and she became his completely, won over by the heir's charm.

"Cardinal Mazarin," he said in way of beginning, "having heard talk of your many talents, decided it would be most pleasing for the king's brother to attend your salon. He instructed M. d'Artagnan to collect me every day and to escort me to the Luxembourg for that purpose."

"The cardinal desires this?" Choisy was unconvinced.

"He recalled M. d'Artagnan from the field," Philippe proudly declared, puffing his chest out. "That is just how serious the cardinal is about the entire business."

Madame was opening her mouth to speak when our Musketeer entered the room, none the worse for his recent adventure. The willing accomplice arrived in tow, correct and dignified in her comportment. Charlotte-Anne would do well as the wife of a secret agent, it seemed.

"The Petit Monsieur speaks honestly," Charles de Batz intoned, confirming the prince's words. "The cardinal and the king wish you to oversee our heir's education insofar as matters of etiquette are concerned. Madame de Ventadour and I were discussing the matter in your absence, gracious lady."

"I am speechless," Choisy replied, fanning herself in earnest. "Especially when I consider that my allegiance will always be with the Duc d'Orléans, and not with...."

"His Eminence is prepared to forgive and forget, madame," d'Artagnan interrupted. "As a man of God, he believes in turning the other cheek."

"Well, the Fronde is done with and finished," she sighed, "and I suppose that the past is the past. The Duc d'Orléans always intended to have his nephew come 'round here to play, thus, I shall fulfill his wishes by doing his enemy's bidding."

She moved as if to wipe away a nonexistent tear.

"Then, with your permission, madame, the Petit Monsieur and I shall be on our way. Your Highness," d'Artagnan beckoned, hand outstretched.

"Are you out of your head, monsieur?" Philippe asked. "You cannot expect me to leave here dressed in such a manner!"

"Why not? I do," François-Timoleon replied.

"Right," d'Artagnan agreed. "Mademoiselle Sancy is famous for her costumes—is she not, Madame de Choisy?"

Jeanne-Olympe's eyes narrowed and she eyed Mazarin's right-hand-man angrily.

"For God's sake, monsieur, allow the Petit Monsieur to resuit! Consider Mademoiselle Bijoux, as well. I cannot have her running about dressed as a boy."

"Mademoiselle is adorable," he maintained, unyielding, "and do not fret, madame, for the cardinal commissions a new wardrobe to be sewn for the children, as we speak. He intends the gift to be a small token of his gratitude for your aid in this undertaking."

"How generous," Choisy sulked, certain she was being hoodwinked. Her outward appearance lost its hard edge, though, when Philippe stepped forward and touched her on the shoulder.

"Until tomorrow, good lady. Your belongings will be returned; I pledge it," he smiled, leaving a red smear on his supporter's cheek during their embrace of parting.

"Hold your head high, Monsieur," she counseled, "for one day you, yourself, will be the Duc d'Orléans — or hold a grander title, who may say?"

"Precisely," the Petit Monsieur revealed, heartened that his uncle's retainer was on his side. "Mademoiselle," he continued, "shall I see you on the morrow? Did my fancy distress you?"

"Not at all," I said with a manly bow, "A lady who is born and bred..."

"...will dress her feet before her head," Philippe giggled, forgetting the odd set of circumstances. Encouraged by the support of his ladies, the Petit Monsieur exited the room, swaying his hips, making light of the farce. D'Artagnan followed his charge, ignoring Madame de V, yet sending a big smile of approval in my direction.

"*Mon Dieu!*" Madame de Choisy exclaimed, slumping deep into a chair. "What a strange day! To come home to find the Petit Monsieur, an honored guest, being encouraged to copy Mademoiselle Sancy's example — I do not know who to blame!"

"What could I say, madame?" Charlotte-Anne asked, defending her actions. "Monsieur d'Artagnan came with orders from the cardinal himself. Should I have defied the Italian?"

"No, of course not, idiot! Stop whining! The sound of your insipid voice makes my head ache!"

That was all the warning I needed. François ran to me, distressed, while his mother sent the governess away to fetch a cool cloth. I hugged the child to me, dreading a scene. Jeanne-Olympe was not angry with us, however, when she chose to speak, moments later.

"Darling treasures, come hither," she invited. "*Mes petites*, ignore my temper, for I am not sore with either of you. That damn d'Artagnan," she muttered. "He is the one behind this."

"Behind what, dearest?" François asked in all innocence. I was inclined to offer my opinion, yet decided to give her no cause for a change in mood.

"The cardinal and the queen are up to something and d'Artagnan is doing their dirty work. I fear for the Petit Monsieur, honestly I do. Gaston would suffer from a fit of apoplexy if he knew what had happened here today."

"Should we send the Duc d'Orléans a message?" I wondered aloud.

"No," Choisy said, pondering her next move. "No, we shall deal with this problem without troubling our benefactor. I know what action Monsieur would take, and that is going to have to do. Are you with me, children?"

"Yes," we replied in unison, though I had no idea what Jeanne-Olympe had in mind.

"Good," she said, standing and pacing about the room. "First, we agree that the prince may attend my salon, but that he is *never* to dress as a girl again. Understood?"

We nodded our assent.

"Françoise, it will be your duty to tell the Petit Monsieur all my beauty secrets and to acquaint him with feminine costume so that the cardinal is convinced of his study. Bijoux, your assignment is more difficult."

"I shall do whatever you say, madame."

"Good," she smiled. "It has always been my intention to promote you to the prince when you were slightly older, however, considering the circumstances, we cannot wait that long."

"Wait for what, madame?"

"Your task will be to win the prince's love, to become his closest confidante, to…"

"He said today he would always love me. Is that your meaning?"

Choisy was overjoyed. "I *knew* he liked you!" she exulted. "Do you understand, sweet Bijoux?"

"I suppose it means that he will do whatever I ask of him. My mother had men at her beck and call."

"Yes, but Marion never won a Prince of the Blood," she retorted. "Madame la Grande could not claim the heir to a throne as one of her conquests. Mademoiselle, you have power at your disposal, great wealth—who knows, if Louis were to die, a chance at playing queen!"

"The king won't die," I protested. "He's young and he's strong."

"Stranger things have happened," she prophesied in her singsong way. "The pox doesn't care if you're a peon or a prince, dear. Actually, it would be better for us if Philippe ruled France. Then Mazarin could be arrested, Anne exiled, and Gaston made a minister!"

Nothing had changed since the Marais. When would I escape the infernal plots of those who wished to harm the king? Mother's curse was alive and well, ready and waiting to be fulfilled by one who had sworn, against her will, to do so.

A wave of despair swept over my senses, driving me to the floor, leaving me helpless. Patches of conversation drifted by, shards of sentences, jumbled words invading dark peace.

"Leave me alone," I yearned to cry out, "let me die, go away."

I heard the word *blue* uttered, then *help*; a damp cloth was applied to my forehead, François was hysterical with fear.

'Twas then that Armand Cousinot arrived in response to my letter, interrupting Madame de V's attempt to make me drink cognac and Madame de Choisy's prayers. Upon viewing the desperate ladies, the First Surgeon went directly to the package he had sent earlier, still awaiting inspection on the writing table. He tore off its cover, removed the vial from its box, and forced the vessel into my mouth.

The released tonic trickled down my throat, its healing

properties halting the seizure. All thrashing ceased and the grateful adults lifted me to my bed.

I had been saved, thanks to the doctor and a messenger named César de la Tour.

François and Charlotte-Anne remained by my side, keeping a watch. Armand and Madame de Choisy exchanged pleasantries and I was able to hear Cousinot relating to her the circumstances surrounding our acquaintance. He then spoke in a more discreet manner and Jeanne-Olympe did not respond. I suppose she was forced to listen, considering that Philippe was rather fond of me and it was to her advantage to keep me alive.

However, what the physician imparted to the lady was most disturbing. So distressing, in fact, that Madame de V later told me the streak in Choisy's mane had matched the color of her face.

"Cousinot," I said, feeling quite out of sorts, "I must speak plainly. Tell the others to leave us be."

Rushing to my side, the healer felt my forehead and scowled.

"You are as hot as Hades," he declared. "Bijoux, you require rest. Try to sleep. I promise we shall talk when you awaken."

"No," I disagreed. Everything around me was hazy. "Now. Send them away."

"Bijoux, you aren't dying."

"Get them out." I was adamant. Choisy was not going to be privy to what I had to say.

"All right, everybody, Mademoiselle Bijoux has spoken," Armand quipped. "Run along, the lot of you. I must consult with my fair patient."

"Bijoux, we shall be right outside the door," the experienced eavesdropper let slip. "Call me if you need anything."

I did not respond to Choisy's offer. Cousinot took a place next to mine on the pallet and stared.

"Are you thinking of Marion?"

Three years and three months had passed since the marquise's death, yet the ex-lover was moved.

"Yes, forgive me. You resemble her."

"Is that why you send the tonic by messenger and never deliver it yourself?" I pried. "Does it hurt you that much to recognize her in me?"

Armand looked the other way. Pity seized me. I had acted thoughtlessly, fever or no.

"Monsieur, it was cruel of me to say such a thing. You are a busy man and I have no right to make demands of the king's physician. Please do not think me horrid. Remember our talks about the stars?"

"You are not feeling well," he managed. "I would not disgrace the love I bore your mother by being wicked to her daughter."

"Tell me what you put into the tonic," I pleaded.

"Nothing special. What does it matter?"

"A great deal. Is the chief ingredient blood?"

"Bijoux, you are overwrought. Close your eyes and dream of pleasant things."

"I am no longer a child." I struggled to rise. "You say that I am sickly. You yourself cast my original natal chart, only you have treated me since the days of the Marais. Tell me, then, what is this strange malaise, what is the cause of my illness? The cure is effective, to be sure, but why?"

"Guibourg informed me that you suffer from pallor. He said it right in front of you, yourself..."

"The night Marion died."

"Yes. He asked that I bring the *special tonic* to you once a week, and I have done so."

"What is in the draught?"

Cousinot did not wish to reply.

"Damn it," he mumbled, "Bouvard told me it was an evil brew eleven years past. And I argued with him as to its properties. How ironic!"

"Do not be mysterious with me, monsieur. What is it that I drink?"

"A mixture commonly prescribed by charlatans. Your mother asked for it because Guibourg claimed the draught would bring a rosy hue to her cheeks. She asked my father-in-law, old King Louis' surgeon Bouvard, for the tonic and he flatly refused. I, on the other hand, proved only too willing to comply."

"Why was that bad?"

"I did not think it evil at the time." He rubbed his forehead wearily. "You tell me if it is a crime to dispense a dose made from angelica water, tincture of peony flower and, yes, human blood."

I fell back onto the pillows. Jacques had known and warned me. Where was Jacques now?

Guibourg's *vrykolakas* was therefore one who consumed the life essence of mankind. The abbé had compared me to a blood-guzzling hellion. Had he not been correct?

The explanation dispensed with all the previous riddles. Noctambule's touch had been poisoned. Small wonder the messenger of the deities had come to my aid, for I was one of the damned.

"No," I groaned miserably, "no! I am Comaetho, a daemon!"

Armand abandoned his melancholy, offended.

"Really, mademoiselle! Dispense with the pagan ritual, please!"

His strident rebuttal flared my ire.

"Of what do you accuse me, monsieur?"

"Of dangerous habits," he hissed in a low voice. "Call on our Lord for guidance; speak not of devils!"

"What Lord? Gaston, Philippe, the king?"

"The King of kings, who else? The Son of God. Our Savior, Jesus Christ."

"Who?"

Cousinot drew a blank.

"Did my lover not instruct you in the principles of the Christian faith?"

"Your beloved provided me with lessons, monsieur, and my teacher was none other than the Abbé Guibourg. You remember our own Étienne, do you not?"

"Bijoux, do not toy with me, I warn you. Did the priest neglect to read to you the Gospels?"

"Despite his vestments and vows, the abbé prefers to worship at the altar of Astaroth and Asmodeus, monsieur. He and mother prayed to daemons, not saints. I was trained in the Black Arts and my Bible was *The Key of Solomon*—my classroom the Rue St. Denis!"

"You lie!"

"To what end? If my report is untrue, explain why mother accepted your vials of blood. Sometimes you brought tonic, but not always, did you? The abbé said many a Black Mass over her naked body and consecrated the perfidy with your tribute."

"No!" he shuddered. "How did I not know?"

"You were young and you loved the most beautiful woman in France. How old were you?"

"Nineteen," he began to sob softly. "Blessed Virgin, forgive me, but Marion was beauteous! Do you think, Bijoux, that your mother cared for me in the least, or were her kisses a deception, also?"

Cousinot would continue to pine over his lost lady, whether she was a tarnished sinner or no. Telling him what he wanted to hear seemed better than sending the man away completely destroyed.

"Guibourg was your only rival for her real affections. Surely you knew that much, monsieur."

Armand smiled for the first time that afternoon. "I am grateful to you for your honesty. Recall the evening when you kicked me in front of the entire salon?" he chuckled.

"Monsieur, yours is my oldest acquaintance—yours and the abbé's, of course. I trust your good heart, you gave me the gift of divination, so please cure me of my ailment, make me well again. Wean me from the medicine, please. The thought of drinking blood is revolting."

Cousinot was pensive.

"For how long have you taken the tonic?"

"The abbé fed it to me when I was nearly eight years old, monsieur."

"Was that when he named you *Comaetho*?"

"No," I fidgeted. "Mother never mentioned an old man we met once, near to Versailles?"

"Not that I recall."

"He named me that."

"How very odd. Was this gentleman a sorcerer such as the abbé?"

"Be serious," I pleaded. "You do not understand. After Versailles, everything changed!"

"Continue the draught," he advised, ignoring my concern. "The tonic calms you."

"Cousinot, no," I lamented. "Help me, please!"

"I shall pray for you, Bijoux. Go to church, girl. Be cleansed of the sin you carry from consorting with unrighteousness. In the meantime, I shall continue your draughts."

"And whose vein did you tap today?" I sniped. "Did I drink of some courtier?"

"To be honest, yes," he replied, rising to leave. "Today it was Cardinal Mazarin who aided you. Go to church and thank God for the blood of his Eminence—its excellent quality no doubt saved your life."

"I'd rather be dead," I replied, sick at heart. "The wise goddess Athena is my only guide."

The First Surgeon departed with not another word of solace, oblivious to my plight.

Truly orphaned, I wept tears of loneliness and bitter regret. I was alone, cut adrift on a sea called the court; a desolate region, dark and always stormy. Monsieur le Grand's vast ambition had initially charted the course I was to sail 'ere I was born, Marion and Guibourg later plotted its wild direction, yet I was determined to navigate a less tempestuous route that would lead my ship through safer waters.

And finding the identity of the true Comaetho, daughter of Taphos, would prove my first guide in that passage.

Everyday life at the Luxembourg continued its hectic pace. The Petit Monsieur came to visit as promised, and while we remained affectionate with one another, he did not speak of love to me again. The prince was disinterested in establishing a physical relationship with a girl, especially after being introduced to the game of dress-up by Mademoiselle Sancy. Soon after, whenever Philippe came by to be entertained, I would stroll in the garden or wander the halls of the enormous palace just to be absent from the company of the boys and Madame de Choisy.

The latter had formed a real attachment to the king's brother and made a point of personally tutoring the heir in all facets of court intrigue. The Petit Monsieur replaced Gaston in Jeanne-Olympe's affections, much the same as Madame de V managed to enthrall my Musketeer, erasing any recollection d'Artagnan may have had of proposing marriage to a long-legged roan filly. Charles de Batz continued to be kind to me, but I could see that Charlotte-Anne had won his heart.

At the risk of displaying ingratitude, the days spent in Gaston d'Orléans' vassalage were some of the worst I was to experience during my association with the court. Ages thirteen and fourteen were quite uneventful; chiefly I recall the onset of my menses, that female development Madame de V coined *the appearance of Monsieur le Cardinal*. While my body may have been changing into that of a young woman, my face was so youthful that people in the palace began to remark that Mademoiselle Bijoux possessed the countenance of an angel, but the personality of a devil. Their observation was not unwarranted—lacking friends or a sympathetic family, my temperament was unpleasant at best.

Why Madame de Choisy kept me about, I shall never begin to fathom. I think she continued to dream that Philippe and I would copy Louis' and Henri's example and fall in love. If I had been born a male, another Monsieur le Grand, she may have lived to see her wish consummated. Yet I was not a boy, and all pretending aside, the Petit Monsieur definitely hankered after his own kind.

By the close of the year 1655, I was fifteen, François eleven, and we were both eager to attend our first, official salon gathering. Jeanne-Olympe agreed that the date was nearing for us both to be introduced into proper society, so she arranged an invitation to be extended by a very learned lady. I understood perfectly well that what she really hoped to achieve was to match me with a wealthy curmudgeon who was in search of a fresh-skinned, unsullied wife. That deception did not sting, because the outing meant leaving the boundaries of the Luxembourg to experience the famed home of the lauded novelist, Mademoiselle de Scudéry.

Jeanne-Olympe ordered lovely clothing to be specially crafted for François and myself by the much-sought-after Monsieur Perdrigeon of Paris. The august tailor and his apprentices spent the better part of one morning fitting us for our fancy costumes, and when I saw the drawing of the gown I was to wear, all nervousness disappeared and my spirits improved quite unexpectedly. Black satin dropped off the shoulders, was cinched in at the waist by a belt made from brilliants and pearls entwined with red, white and jet streamers; sleeves, bodice and hem embroidered in heavy gold and silver thread. A few of mother's diamonds would have completed the ensemble, yet ruefully I knew better than to flaunt the courtesan's treasure at Scudéry's *Samedi* or *Saturday*—nicknamed for that day of the week when the writer always received her guests, rain or shine.

Mademoiselle de Scudéry's hôtel was located on a corner plot where the Rue de Beauce met the Rue des Oiseaux, on the fringe of the Marais. Thus, when François, Madame de Choisy and I piled into one of the magnificent d'Orléans' coaches consigned to transport us to the *Samedi*, plumed and bedazzling in our finery, it struck me that I was going home after a five year hiatus.

The comforting realization stood out as a good omen of sorts, as if benign Athena was keeping watch, urging me on, telling me not to give up hope, that all would be well. Might Jacques also be nearby, I wondered, shining gloriously from the exterior carriage lamp rattling furiously to the beat of the horses' hooves? Or had the marquise found peace in the beyond and returned to the mortal sphere to grant her only child solace? Whatever the case, I was brimming with good cheer as we approached the literary queen's address, expectations high and purpose intact.

Deposited at the front door, we entered *Maison Scudéry* past rows of liveried footmen to be met with an explosion of light. Crystal chandeliers were suspended from the ceiling of the spacious foyer, receptacles for lit tapers whose dripping wax was wiped off the parquet floor at frequent intervals. As our trio stepped lightly over and around the spatters, it did not escape my attention that the house was beautifully appointed and decorated by a person with an eye for grandeur. Paintings in ornate, gilded frames graced the fabric covered walls, intricately carved curio cabinets were jammed with the presents which had been made to the author by her impressive group of patrons. Cardinal Mazarin, Nicolas Fouquet and Queen Christina of Sweden were a small representation of the many notables who showered the gifted wordsmith with material proofs of their esteem. She may have penned her brother's name, George, on the frontispiece of her finished works, but readers as far as to the land of Egypt were aware that the ensuing stories belonged to one named Madeleine.

Taking a deep breath as we advanced on the grand portal and its attendant blackamoor, rumored to have been sent to mademoiselle from an admirer in the East, I steeled myself for a barrage of conversation, color and music such as Marion had provided the Marais during her reign as its Muse. Then the door opened with one push of a white-gloved finger, and the panoply bursting into view was incredible: a spectacular jumble of guests, exotic animals, culinary masterpieces and performing artists. Madeleine's marvelous hospitality made Madame la Grande's seem miserable by compare; I was not about to reveal my identity to anyone lest they connect me with the infamous Sanguine Room.

Too late, for our entourage was met by a figure I recognized instantly. Who could forget those inquisitive, dark eyes, thin moustache, flowing black hair and feathery eyelashes? How could I fail to remember the man who had paid Marion's burial expenses? A paean of welcome was being made by none other than Nicolas Fouquet, *financier extrordinaire*.

Mother's former patron acknowledged my presence with a

sidelong glance while he chatted amiably with Jeanne-Olympe, who insisted on calling him *Cléonime*.

"Monsieur," Choisy inquired, "how fares our dear Madame du Plessis following the unfortunate loss of her poor parrot? I hearsay she was devastated when she discovered him cold and stiff, swinging upside down from his perch."

"Ah, madame, my dearest confidante was so distraught that she withdrew to her hôtel at Charenton to grieve for her comical pet. Being unable to function efficiently without Madame Susanne at my side, I organized a contest whereby all the great wits were invited to submit verses on the subject of the bird's untimely end. An avalanche of poems resulted, all forwarded to Madame du Plessis, intended to amuse the bereaved. The plan was a success and a bad situation was put to right when Mademoiselle de Scudéry generously provided, from her own aviary, a better parrot than the last for her friend's enjoyment."

"How charming, M. Surintendant!" Madame de Choisy gushed, awestruck by the influential man's lordly bearing and confident demeanor. Fouquet made it no secret that he preferred an older woman in his bed to an inexperienced girl; Jeanne-Olympe may have been hoping her night had come to join the ranks of the privileged.

"And how keeps your remarkable mother?" Choisy simpered.

"Madame Fouquet is as busy as ever, devoting many hours to working on behalf of those less fortunate. Her many charities keep her extremely occupied, as does the Company, of course."

I had to speak.

"Do you mean the Company of the Blessed Sacrament, M. Fouquet?"

The Future was intrigued.

"Your attendant's name, madame?" His tone was quizzical.

"I think you know," I smiled. "Shall we play a guessing game, M. Surintendant?"

"Dare you challenge me, mademoiselle?" he asked, a crooked grin emerging on thin lips.

"Bijoux, apologize this moment!" Choisy scolded. "How dare you be so impertinent? You must forgive the girl; she is as precious as a daughter to me, yet..."

"Monsieur and I are old acquaintances," I countered. "I am sure he would recognize me if I gave him a hint. Not many know that our distinguished friend was born beneath the Sun of Capricornus, sign of prestige and wealth."

"Allow me, mademoiselle," Fouquet chuckled, rubbing his pointed chin in amusement. "Hair of a dissembling color, eyes of seafoam beryl, the palest complexion on the planet. Yes...what was your mother's name?"

Had he forgotten?

"When describing that lady's highly praised figure, one admirer simply decreed: *As to the rest, bombs and grenades explode!*"

"I know the answer!" Fouquet exclaimed. "Your mother was..." he paused dramatically, "Marion Delorme!"

"Correct," I curtsied to him. "Now do you remember me?"

"I thought to myself when you walked into the salon *Nicolas, that one is a double for your pretty coquette, Marion, God rest her soul.*"

"Did you, truly?" I was flabbergasted. Fouquet was charm incarnate.

"Absolutely, Mademoiselle Delorme. Our Marion," he sighed, "was a Venus—a creature made for a great man's passionate embraces—taken from us too soon, too soon."

"Bijoux is also the child of the Marquis de Cinq-Mars," Choisy offered, slightly dejected by talk concerning a ravishing ex-mistress. "She was placed in my care five years ago, soon after the famous courtesan died."

"I do remember you! Always hanging about with that nasty priest, what was his name?"

"Abbé Guibourg," I supplied, making a distasteful face. "Monsieur d'Artagnan took me from him, thank Olympus."

"Quite," Fouquet agreed, scanning the room, displaying his famed nervous energy. "So, why are you interested in the Company of the Blessed Sacrament, mademoiselle?"

The question made me go mute. Choisy, the adept interloper, came to the rescue.

"I mentioned Monsieur le Grand's involvement with the Order when I discovered he was Bijoux's father," Jeanne-Olympe confessed, well aware she had never revealed the society's identity to me.

"Bijoux, might you be trusted to keep a secret?"

I nodded my head enthusiastically in the affirmative.

"Consider yourself in possession of one. The name of our Company is not to be bandied about lightly, understand?"

What a coup! Fouquet and his mother were both members of the exclusive organization. More information for d'Artagnan, a valid lead for his ongoing investigation. Unfortunately, neither of us had learned much else concerning the faction.

"Allow me to join your ranks, monsieur. Please. My father gave his life for the cause."

Jeanne-Olympe nearly fainted with horror. Noticing Madame de Choisy's alarm, the Surintendant of Finance held up a hand to signal that he required absolute silence from my guardian. Turning to me, he cleared his throat and I quaked a tad.

"To become a member of the Company, Mademoiselle Bijoux, one must have achieved a certain rank or status within the community; one must be able to contribute something of merit, be that money or talent, to the group. And be of the Catholic faith, of course. Do you attend Mass daily, my dear?"

"No, monsieur, yet, I do believe fervently in the gods and goddesses of ancient days, having once been in the presence of a messenger of the Dieties."

What I did not know was that Monsieur Nicolas' sisters were nuns, a brother an Archbishop and his mother a dear friend of the saintly Vincent de Paul, the respected priest who had founded the renowned *Dames de la Charité*. A Fouquet could not turn away an obvious sinner without denying the fundamental family credo of staunch support for Rome.

Fouquet became animated, snapping his fingers in the air, commanding the attention of the entire salon. He controlled the ledger books of France, the votes in Parliament and his Parisian townhouse was conveniently located on the Rue Croix-des-Petits-Champs that ran behind Mazarin's palace. When the Future spoke, people did his bidding.

"My dear friends," he began in a cultured accent, "I require the presence of Madame Scarron to assist me in an important endeavor. Has anyone seen our lovely Françoise this evening?"

Madame Scarron? Had the poet married? Jacques' prophecy rang in my ears and sent shivers through every muscle in my body. I had waited five years for a sign, five less-than-wonderful years; was an end to the emptiness upon me? Was Athena going to help me, the *vrykolakas*?

"When Lord Cléonime beckons, who may refuse him?" came the tinkle of the clearest, sweetest tone possible. An appreciative murmur passed through the crowd as they made way for the handsome Madame Scarron, who glided effortlessly through its midst to join our circle.

Dressed in a simple black gown with white collar and cuffs, complimeted by a gold cross dangling from a heavy chain of the same metal, the twenty-year-old exuded poise, good taste and a gracious manner. A lack of ruffles and furbelows enhanced her tranquillity; Françoise Scarron, plainly appointed as she was, made her contemporaries look tawdry and no better than the costumed monkeys Mazarin kept about him for amusement's sake.

The minister paid his respects to the exceptional woman from whom I could not wrest my gaze. She was lovely, exquisite, an example of harmony assuming human shape. I wished to assume her serene demeanor, to smile as she was smiling at Fouquet, with a light from within sent beaming through beautiful amber eyes.

Madame Françoise could not be married to the cripple Scarron—her husband was, without question, a great lord and the peerless lady the chatelaine of a château in the provinces.

"*Ma Belle Indienne*, you are acquainted with Madame de Choisy and her son, François-Timoléon, are you not?"

"Of course," Françoise replied, kissing my mistress with

real affection on the neck, as was done on formal occasions to avoid smudging rouge or face paint. Then she turned to François, and Madame Scarron hugged him until the youngster squealed with delight.

"And this girl is Madame de Choisy's ward, Mademoiselle Bijoux Delorme..."

"Cinq-Mars," I corrected. Madame Scarron regarded me straight on, smirking, a mischievous expression surfacing on her placid visage. She extended a bare hand to me and I took it into a gloved one. We stared at one another with mutual admiration; she appeared to be as impressed with me as I was with her. People began to converse, no longer interested in our *tête-à-tête*.

"Are you Marion's daughter?" Françoise inquired.

"Yes," I admitted without pride.

"Do not frown—I was born in a prison!" the honest woman revealed. "We all have our crosses to bear."

"None worse than your husband," Jeanne-Olympe reflected.

"How is Monsieur Scarron?" Fouquet's concern was genuine. "I shall send 'round some cheeses and pâtés on the morrow, madame."

"Thank you," she said with sincerity, unabashedly taking the surintendant's right hand to kiss it with gratitude. "My husband is a brave man, monsieur; however, his infirmities are so cruel I pray God every day to take his tormented soul to heaven. I know that life is a gift," she stopped, "yet I refuse to believe our Father above wishes anyone to suffer the agonies poor Paul endures."

Just as Fouquet declared, *The Lord God moves in mysterious ways*, I burst into tears. Françoise Scarron was indeed wed to the deformed writer, the man who had been close to my mother. According to Jacques, she was also destined to become a widow. That dreadful knowledge overwhelmed and frightened me more than the written word might convey.

"Bijoux, why do you weep?" Madame de Choisy demanded.

"She is sad," *La Belle Indienne* explained. "Come, come," she insisted, wrapping me up in the warmth of her arms, pressing my heaving chest to her own. "With all due respect, madame, it is difficult for you to understand growing up a stranger in someone else's home, unless you have been shipped from pillar to post yourself. There, there," she comforted. "I understand, dear child."

"You are the nicest person in the world," I sobbed anew.

"It would seem the two of you have much to discuss," Fouquet noted. "Madame Scarron, would you help me to save Bijoux's eternal soul, yourself being a recent convert to the true Church?"

"By all means," she enthused, putting some space between us. "Do you wish to become a Catholic, *ma petite?*"

"Do Catholics believe in the deities and in the stars?" I managed.

She hugged me again. "We should go somewhere quiet and speak privately. Monsieur, Madame de Choisy, may we beg your indulgent leave?"

Choisy shrugged her shoulders and Lord Cléonime patted my crown with a patriarchal seal of approval.

"Go, go; use Mademoiselle de Scudéry's study for your discussion," he decided. "She will not mind; I shall inform our hostess as to your whereabouts."

"Come then," Françoise said, "let us repair to the library."

She led me away, and willingly I went. My feet hardly touched the ground as she guided me by the arm to the room where France's greatest storyteller put pen to paper.

"How did you know what I was feeling back there?" I asked, stymied by the lady's perceptiveness.

"My father was a convict, a drunk and an adventurer whom I seldom saw 'ere the age of ten," she confided as she pushed past a rare plant as tall as a small tree and whose waxy green leaves were the size of a bear's paw. "My mother and I were residing with a great aunt when the wastrel next appeared, determined to move his family to the island of Martinique, in the West Indies. He died not long after we were settled, and then it was back to France where I was deposited with

Huguenot relatives. Then another aunt, who is a Catholic, petitioned Queen Anne to be given the responsibility for my religious upbringing. Off to the convent I went and, at fifteen, was converted to Catholicism. It took a long time to convince me, but the Holy sisters wrought a miracle in my case."

"So that is why Fouquet called you *La Belle Indienne*; now I understand. Do you all have secret names, madame?"

"Some of us," she replied, glad I had regained my composure. "Do you realize that when I was first presented to M. Scarron, I did what you did just now—I wept as would a babe? Everyone in the room thought me such a silly cow, but my tears touched the kind man's heart, as yours moved mine."

Françoise allowed a footman to escort us into the impressive den whose walls were lined with shelves bulging with books, sculpture and *objets d' art*. A cream-colored marble hearth, large enough for a man to stand within comfortably, provided a suitably sized hollow for the tree trunks blazing in a pyramid-shaped stack, cradled on a massive wrought-iron grate. Heavy tapestries depicting scenes from Greek mythology covered any empty spaces from ceiling to floor; the size of the room permitted for a dozen or more of the expertly woven hangings.

The woman who had sailed the high seas and lived amongst natives on a faraway shore, sat formally with her back straight against a divan's rigid spine. I copied her example, careful not to crush or wrinkle the satin fabric cascading onto and over the edge of the couch upon which we rested.

Dismissing the servant with a nod, I focused my attention on the companion chosen for me by what, I was becoming convinced, had been a council of the Immortals.

"Madame, may I be direct with you? I do not understand your decision to become Monsieur Paul's wife; your sacrifice is admirable but the wisdom of the choice defies explanation."

"I am devoted to his mind, Bijoux. I consider it an honor to care for a man who, despite his pain, seeks to bring joy into others' lives. When he offered me room and board almost four years ago, so that I might leave the convent, I said *no*; the marriage proposal came next and my response was immediately *yes*. I am his secretary, his nurse and, I hope to God, his best friend. The love I bear my husband transcends the physical—do you understand, dear child?"

"I am fifteen, madame."

"*Mon Dieu*, I thought you younger! Then we do have similar backgrounds, as M. Fouquet remarked. It is high time that you had some religious training, considering you will soon be married yourself. We can't have you going to the altar a heathen!" she giggled.

"If Madame de Choisy has her way, I shan't be getting married, for she wishes me to become the Petit Monsieur's mistress."

"What? How disgraceful of her! What is she, a gentle lady or a procuress?"

"My mother was a whore, remember."

Françoise held me firmly by the shoulders and stared deeply into my eyes. "Bijoux, nonsense. You are a child of God. Remember the message of our Lord."

"And what was that?"

"To love one another, dear. To be instruments of God's healing grace."

"Surely, that is a difficult task, madame."

"Have faith," she advised. "As St. Augustine said: *Faith is to believe what we do not see and the reward of this faith is to see what we believe*."

She was so sage. To be near her was all I desired; that and a tenth of her resolve.

Françoise and I talked into the night. She told me things I found difficult to comprehend; stories from the Bible, tales of hardship from her own life. Her strength was estimable, her commitment to her newfound religion, unquestionable.

A gilded clock positioned on Mademoiselle de Scudéry's writing desk was about to strike twelve when I finally found the courage to ask her another, unrelated question.

"Madame, have you studied the Classics as well as the Scriptures?"

"I have read some Homer, a little Plato," she smiled. "Why?"

"Did either write of a Lady Comaetho, madame? Or of a place called Taphos, per chance?"

"I do not recall," she mused. "Does the subject matter interest you, dear Bijoux?"

"Oh, yes, madame. I would be forever in your debt if you might ask your learned husband as to their meanings...for the old myths are as my Bible."

"Of course, tomorrow," she agreed with a light laugh. "My, such lofty ambitions—Madame de Choisy has influenced you, indeed!"

"Did you hear an odd noise?" I queried, distracted by a faint sound, a rumble not human.

"Most assuredly," she answered, looking about the room.

"Over there, madame," I pointed, whispering. A large, yellow cat walked towards where we sat, too big to be a tabby but not of a size to prove menacing.

"A lion cub, Bijoux! Imagine such a beast prowling about! Mademoiselle de Scudéry has outdone herself this time!"

We both petted the tame feline when it was within arm's length. Its fur was quite soft and the creature's eyes were the same color as my own. When the cub began to gnaw on a finger, however, I pulled my captive hand away fast enough, for its teeth were quite sharp.

"What a little devil," Françoise laughed, but stopped when she saw my reaction.

"What is wrong, dear friend? What did I say?"

"Nothing," I smiled wanly. "Simply an old memory, nothing more."

"Shall we rejoin the others?" Françoise stood, studying me with intent. "Do not fret, Bijoux, all will be put right. I shall see to that promise myself, agreed?"

"Do you fear for my soul, madame?"

"Faith, girl, faith," she counseled, putting an arm around my shoulders, drawing me close. "Have the mettle to believe in what you do not see, and one day you *will* see what you believe."

What Françoise Scarron did not understand was that my visions were often dark ones I knew to be very real, indeed. Her Lord might be forgiving, yet the one who had chosen me was not.

I had to believe, though, that hope existed for me, too, and the frail conviction that Love was the omnipotent power in the universe gave me the desire to go on, despite the disappointment that Madame Scarron seemed to know little concerning the deities. Perhaps that was why Jacques had brought us together, I reasoned, for I was to teach Françoise about glorious Athena.

Little did I know that nothing could be further from the truth, for I was unschooled in the ways of Christendom.

CHAPTER EIGHT
Second Chances

Although Françoise Scarron's waking hours were dedicated to the tending to of her husband's Herculean needs, we maintained a regular correspondence beginning several days following our introduction. *La Belle Indienne,* true to her word, composed a letter to me that, after having read its contents numerous times, filled my soul with foreboding:

> My dear Greek Scholar -
> It is with fond regards and much tenderness that I pen this greeting. Would that I might speak these words to you, in your company, however, my duties here at home leave little time for social calls or participation in the gracious pleasantries of the salon.
> Pursuant to our happy meeting at Maison Scudéry, I most certainly remembered to query Monsieur Paul as to your myth of Comaetho. The tale was not familiar to him, but, considering that you are the daughter of his dearest Marion, he forthwith elicited the noble aid of a most kind gentleman and acquaintance, M. de la Fontaine. The latter is a wordsmith of some acclaim whom my husband presents to all as 'Homer's heir.' Thus, you will recognize in that title some indication as to the estimable intellect possessed by our brilliant friend.
> Imagine our combined surprise when the name Comaetho

did not elicit an immediate spark of recognition from M. de la Fontaine! Intrigued, the learned gentleman traveled forthwith to M. Fouquet's home on the Rue Croix-des-Petits-Champs to search Lord Cléonime's vast library of ancient translations in hopes of solving your riddle.

After many hours spent in relentless inquiry, M. de la Fontaine's efforts were rewarded and the Lady Comaetho was at last discovered in a volume attributed to one Apollodorus, historian of old. The story is a tragic one, and I hesitate to repeat the fable; however, if you must know of it, then hear the sad accounting from one who begs you not to lend it much credence.

The Princess Hippothoe was carried off by the sea god Poseidon, who brought her to the Echinadian islands, and there got her with child, a son, Taphius, who later colonized Taphos and called the people Taphians. And Taphius had a son, Pterelaus, whom Poseidon made immortal by implanting a golden hair in his head. And to Pterelaus were born sons, to wit: Chromius, Tyrannus, Antiochus, Chersidamus, Mestor and Everes.

When Electryon ruled over Mycenae, the sons of Pterelaus came with some Taphians and claimed the kingdom of Mestor, their maternal grandfather. As Electryon paid no heed to their claim, they declared war and when the sons of Electryon stood on their defense, they challenged and slew each other. Of the sons of Pterelaus there survived Everes, who guarded the ships. Those of the Taphians who escaped sailed away, taking with them Electryon's cattle, and these they entrusted to Ployxenus, King of the Eleans. A Prince of Thebes, Amphitryon, ransomed the herd and returned it to Mycenae.

Wishing to avenge his sons' deaths, Electryon purposed to make war on the Taphians but first he committed his kingdom to Prince Amphitryon, along with his daughter Alcmena and as Alcmena said she would marry Amphitryon when he had avenged her brothers, the prince engaged to do so and undertook an expedition against the Taphians.

Whilst Pterelaus of the golden hair lived, and he was

made immortal as long as the lock should remain on his head, Amphitryon could not take Taphos. Yet it came to pass that Comaetho, sole daughter of Pterelaus, saw Amphitryon from afar and fell in love with him. Knowing the secret of her father's long life, she plucked the golden strand from the head of Pterelaus and he died and Amphitryon subjugated the Isle of Taphos. The prince then slew Comaetho on account of her treachery and sailed with the booty to Thebes—among the looted treasure was a famous Carchesian goblet Poseidon had gifted his son Taphius and which Taphius had granted Pterelaus in turn.

Since I have no knowledge of your interest in sad Comaetho, might I respectfully offer that although you share one physical trait with that princess of the bright, burning hair, you are not blessed with six brothers, so all sameness may be discounted. Each one of us is unto ourselves a singular portrait in the vast gallery of God's dominion, a masterwork, and the heavenly Father certainly does not allow for forgeries in his collection.

Monsieur Paul, Monsieur de la Fontaine and I, your devoted Françoise, relay to you our heartfelt salutations and pray that you may be allowed to join with us in conversation 'ere long.

Françoise Scarron

Noctambule had christened me Comaetho, daughter of Taphos. Was he himself an Immortal, as had been Pterelaus? Was I destined to rob the old man of his days without end, or was I merely his heir, princess to a realm of the undead, not unlike a certain isle of yesteryear? The questions nagged at my spirit and I looked about me for additional signs that would tie me to the tragic heroine. Granted, my mother had borne no sons, but François was akin to a brother and I decided he would be Chersidamus. Philippe, my second choice for sibling, was undoubtedly Prince Tyrannus. Four remained: Chromius, Antiochus, Mestor and Everes. Where would they come from and who would they be? Unable to predict the future, I locked the letter away as one would a damning document, more troubled by the knowing than I had been by the mystery.

The special bond existing between the Petit Monsieur and myself was a fragile tie to be sure, however, one that had endured seven years' trial when the king made the mistake of inviting his brother to sup with him at the Louvre. Whereas the nineteen-year-old Louis assumed the two would share a pleasant repast in each other's company, the junior Gaston d'Orléans had a different notion, altogether. Still smarting from numerous royal oversights, the Petit Monsieur flung a bowl of piping-hot soup in the sovereign's face the first opportunity granted him. Louis, humiliated before the court, retained enough composure to snarl that were there not ladies present, he would like nothing better than to kick Philippe in the *derrière*. The king was not amused.

My friend, in a rash display of pique, did not wait for Louis to dismiss him and ran unescorted to his apartment at the Tuileries. Soon ensconced in his bedchamber, door bolted, Philippe fumed and cursed and wished his liege dead. When finished with ranting, Prince Tyrannus sat at his desk, penned a note to Madame de Choisy, and summoned one of his personal lackeys to deliver the missive without delay, despite the late hour. The urgent message was in fact a request to allow Mademoiselle Bijoux the liberty of returning with his envoy to the Petit Monsieur's quarters.

Of course, once summoned, I obeyed. Jeanne-Olympe had waited long to be of service to her prince and the momentous occasion was finally upon her.

"Be yielding. Make him happy," was her advice as she swathed me in her cloak lined with vair and rushed me to an awaiting carriage. "It may hurt, but the pain is temporary, trust me," she added, magnifying my ignorance ten-fold. Choisy might have mentioned what was expected of me that evening, but, my being the daughter of a courtesan, she thought her charge well versed in the Art of Love.

I hesitate to continue at the risk of sounding immodest in print. If that eve had not been the Petit Monsieur's birthday,

September the twenty-first, and had he not been weeping when I arrived on the pitiful scene, nothing more would have occurred other than a game of cards. Yet, we had both recently turned seventeen and the natural desire to experience the physical pleasures burned hot in our bodies the instant an embrace of welcome became a kiss portending more than friendship.

To my astonishment, Philippe was tender and respectful; no bites or cruel remarks, only passionate sighs and flattering endearments crossed his lips. When I dared touch his pretty face, he crushed me to him, joining our mouths, steering me towards the bed onto which we collapsed.

"I adore you, my darling Bijoux," he confessed. "Madame de Choisy said you were the proper girl for me to favor and tonight I realized the wisdom of her remark."

"Why tonight of all nights, Monsieur?"

"I disagreed with Louis," he frowned. "I threw soup at him, dearest, during my birthday banquet, and I fear he will send me away as a result."

"No," I protested, "he wouldn't dare."

"Kiss me again," Philippe whispered. "If I must be exiled, I shall go your swain."

I did not reply, not sure what to say, yet I did savor the romantic declarations and the attentions he bestowed upon me. Soon, our clothing was coming off; the joint disrobing frantic, chaotic, a blur of motion and sound. Our haste resulted in naked limbs entwined, hands exploring unknown territory, my eyes kept tightly shut.

Philippe, in his excitement, was making deep, guttural noises. Wishing to view, he rolled me over, pinning my torso under his, pressing into my private regions with quick, jerking motions. The deflowerment Choisy had alluded to was on the verge of commencing, and I tried my best to remain unafraid.

"Snuff out the candle," I requested when a breath was allowed.

"No, you are beautiful. This moment will be mine, forever."

"Philippe..." I objected, although the siege reconvened and my plea was cut short.

The Petit Monsieur's grunts intensified, my legs were pushed apart by his encroaching knees, and I thought he would choke the life from me as his mouth completely covered my own. I clawed madly at his smooth skin, but the show of fear came across as a sign of intensified lovemaking. The sole option was to lie back and be silent; the faster I succumbed, the quicker he would finish the deed.

The onslaught unexpectedly ceased. Philippe moved off of me abruptly, for apparently no reason, and plopped down at my side. Venturing a glance out of one half-opened lid, I glimpsed a dejected prince, arms straight at his sides, lying supine and staring at the ceiling of the curtained, canopied bed.

Had I survived the ritual of the first night with nary a discomfort?

"It's no use," he complained. "I'll never have a genuine mistress."

"What is amiss? Are we not in bed together, did we not...?"

Prince Tyrannus grit his teeth. "Are you an idiot?" he asked in total exasperation. "Look at me!"

Sitting upright, I glanced at his male appendage, flaccid and small. At last I understood how the act was consummated. Drawing my knees to my chin, I thought about what to do. Choisy would beat me if she discovered the Petit Monsieur had not been serviced properly.

Jumping from the pallet, I flung my clothes at Philippe.

"Get dressed, you little slut," I ordered. "Put these on or I'll give you a flogging."

The command came as quite a shock. He regarded me with disdain, pushing a *pannier* aside.

"And who the devil are you? Really, Bijoux, cease this nonsense."

"Bitch!" I exclaimed, whacking at him with a shoe. "Do as you're told, whore!"

That wicked grin I knew from our first encounter at the Louvre appeared.

"A lady who is born and bred," he quipped, "must dress her feet before her head."

"Get busy, you! No more stupid rhymes."

The Petit Monsieur dressed with relish. The faster I handed him garments, the more speedily he prepared. Availing himself of a large looking glass, he adjusted laces, fanned petticoats and wriggled his toes into my prized heels as far as they would go. The spectacle was quite ridiculous to watch, and I did not, occupied as I was with donning his princely garb.

I was just about to tie my hair back with a black garter to complete the ensemble, when Philippe whirled about and curtsied.

"Do you find me appealing?"

"Perhaps," came my retort. "Advance and be inspected."

He minced convincingly to where I waited, hands on hips, feet askance. After looking him up and down with a critical air, I made a move to walk away. Pausing, I reconsidered and took him roughly, pushing my partner backward with a shove that landed him atop the mattress.

"Should monsieur wish it, his lady awaits him."

"I'll do with you what I please," I replied in a deep voice, surprising myself. "'Tis all a tart deserves."

Reaching down, I lifted his skirts and witnessed the successful result of my strategy. Philippe groaned aloud, and I recalled that when Athena had been pursued by the mighty smith, Vulcan, she had evaded his advances by causing that god's seed to be spilled upon the ground. My fingers began to caress the prince's lower torso; the remainder I shall leave to the reader's own fancy.

Ours was a strange friendship, at best; yet, Philippe cared for me and I knew I was fond of him, as well. No one could possibly fill the special place he occupied in my life. Lying next to him I felt safe and secure, our gentle breathing in unison.

"Bijoux," he murmured.

"Yes, my Prince Tyrannus?"

"I wish everyone at court to know that you, witty girl, are my mistress."

"No," I advised. "I forbid it."

"Why?" Philippe was wide-awake, head propped on a bended arm, reclining on his side.

"I shan't be compared to my mother, Monsieur."

"Fine," he relented, peeved. "Cut your nose to spite your face."

"Don't vex me, Tyrannus, or I shall bite you!"

He kissed me, pleased. "Do you love your prince, Bijoux?"

"You know that I do," I said evasively. "Consider this: our natal charts are near to identical, the one difference being that your royal Moon is positioned in the sign of the Archer."

"Yes, so I might shoot you with Cupid's arrows," he exhaled, tired yet thrilled by the evening's turn of events.

I clutched Philippe tightly and we fell asleep in one another's arms. Would we had maintained that pose, my Petit Monsieur and I; would that the warmth of the encounter had remained glowing within our young bodies as a reminder of a devotion worthy those loyal friends Damon and Pythias. Naturally, we did not and when the flame was extinguished, so died the last embers of sweet innocence in our hearts.

A chronicler must not dwell exclusively on pleasant subjects, thus it is necessary to end this chapter on a somber note. To describe the circumstances leading to the summer of 1658 is not a welcomed task, for the impact of a fateful experience would linger with me nigh into the future, and I may safely say that because of my meddling, the course of several lives was changed as a result.

The trouble began 'round the New Year, December of 1657. Philippe, who had earned the well-deserved reputation of being a talker, told the court of our arrangement. In an effort to impress his brother's clique—chiefly the Marquis de Vardes and the Comte de Saint-Aignan—the Petit Monsieur let it slip at the gaming table that his precious mistress, Bijoux by name, was more accomplished a lover than was his brother's lady, Mazarin's niece, Olympe Mancini. When the king's friends demanded how the prince could make such a bold statement, Tyrannus provided them with the details of our numerous rendezvous, omitting nothing. The irreverent courtiers saw an opportunity to make light of Monsieur Philippe, and rushed off to their leader with the delicious scandal.

The well-bred gentlemen conspired as to what moniker I would be assigned in the verses they wrote about the transvestite prince; some of the party preferred *Madame de la Main* because it resembled my mother's title, Madame la Grande, while the others were partial to *La Reine de la Main* or, quite literally, queen of the hand. The latter was overheard by Jeanne-Olympe, while on her rounds at the Louvre, and, quite naturally, my guardian became distraught.

Racing to the Luxembourg, Madame de Choisy was furious when she burst through the door of the cozy nursery. She accused me of the vilest practices in the presence of her son and Madame de V, asking how many men I serviced per day, how much were they paying me, and why I had not given her any coins. The puzzled expression I wore during the verbal volley inflamed her to the boiling point and the offended lady produced a copy of a cheaply printed leaflet pulled from an amateur press. I stared at the filth, my mind not comprehending the black letters stamped on white paper.

Hurt by the gossip, I collected my cloak and ran away in disgrace. Not knowing where to go when I reached the cold, twilight air, I made for the Pont Neuf, home to those characters worse than myself. The prince was going to pay for his betrayal, I vowed en route, he was going to feel his entrails knot with misery. Salty droplets streamed down my cheeks as I imagined the king and court being entertained at my expense. If I had owned a knife, I probably would have ventured further, to the Tuileries, and cut out Philippe's loathsome tongue.

Eventually, I returned to the Luxembourg where I was forced to endure more questions from Choisy. Convincing her I had not administered my skills to every man at court was not an easy accomplishment. However, once I confided Philippe's delicate problem, she believed me, knowing I lacked the *savoir-faire* necessary to invent an excuse of that sort. Her parting remark to me was, "This is the most perverse thing I have ever been a party to!" and then she stormed off to salvage what she could of Philippe's and my liaison.

She wasted her time, for I wanted nothing more to do

with either her or the prince. Determined to hurt both for the grief they had caused me, I forgot Jacques' ominous charge to be kind to all whom I encountered in the palaces of Louis Bourbon. Retaliation had a better ring to it than forgiveness; somehow, some way, I was going to see the pair crawl.

My chance for revenge came soon enough—within six months' passing. In the interim, Choisy abandoned her tutelage following my adamant refusals to accept any tokens or apologies from Prince Tyrannus. Even d'Artagnan appeared at the Luxembourg to advise me to swallow my stubborn pride and to reconcile with Philippe. Mazarin was pleased with my abilities and wished for me to continue the ruse the cardinal considered worthy of his sanction. I retained my dignity and told the Gascon to inform his Eminence that *La Reine de la Main* was finished. The sous-lieutenant of the reinstated Grand Musketeers scowled—I threatened to enter a convent if the king's brother did not cease his pestering.

Françoise Scarron took my side, and had her husband, Paul, been well, she swore in her letters that she would have come to comfort me in my distress. Her advice was to believe in myself, to stand tall and, above all else, to learn from my mistakes. *Do not lower yourself to their level*, she urged over and over again. *God has forgiven you your transgression, now forgive those who have wronged you. Everyone deserves a second chance*, wrote the one whom I admired, yet could not emulate.

Hatred for Philippe and Jeanne-Olympe consumed my sorry person, and I raged inwardly whenever I heard the prince's name or saw Choisy's face. The latter, in her endless quest for favors and privileges, was preoccupied with finding a replacement for me in the Petit Monsieur's bed and she discovered the perfect friend for her royal pet: the handsome, rogue son of the Marshal of Gramont. The youth, Armand, Comte de Guiche, had been raised with Louis and Philippe; therefore, Jeanne-Olympe's idea to pair him with the Duc d'Anjou was logical, made more insidious due to the fact that Guiche bore a striking resemblance to none other than the king himself.

At long last, in July of 1658, the opportunity presented itself to strike against my enemies. To preface, Louis and Mazarin traveled north to Mardyck late in May of that year to review the troops following a French capture of Dunkirk from the Spanish. Philippe and his mother repaired to the seaside city of Calais, never far from king and army. Anne of Austria's sudden and unexplained departure from Paris was due to concern for her younger son's welfare. Despite her disapproval, the queen knew Choisy was arranging liaisons between Philippe and Armand. Months earlier, Anne had forbidden the two young men to be left alone together in the same room.

Not to be deterred, Jeanne-Olympe defied the ban and invited each censured party to meet at her private *cabinet*. Needless to say, Choisy hid me away in my room whenever the lovebirds came to call; I listened at the walls and could hear the pair fooling about. No longer naïve, I flinched when the Petit Monsieur yelped in pain on more than one occasion — Guiche a more forceful lover than I had proved during my turn as the favourite.

June was near to a close when Louis, still at Mardyck, became ill. Suffering from a chill and headache, the physicians concluded the king had contracted an illness while encamped with his men, exposed to unhealthy conditions. By the first week in July, on the fifth, a raging fever had replaced shivers and the king was in grave danger of dying. Fearing the worst, the patient was moved to Calais to be nearer to his mother. Anne and Mazarin were crazed with despair, and the affairs of the country came to a standstill. Churches across France were filled with praying subjects while ex-*frondeurs* dusted their swords, hopes high that the exiled Gaston would soon return to Paris to see his good-for-nothing rascal crowned king.

During the crisis, I remained alert to danger, intercepting and stealing a number of interesting letters addressed to Madame de Choisy from Philippe, Guiche, and the Queen of Poland's sister, Anne of Gonzaga. The three main conspirators, led by my mistress, outlined in their *communiqués* a coup to be put into action the hour Louis quit breathing.

The cabal, centering on the Petit Monsieur, intended to influence Philippe—when he became the king—to exile Anne to her native Spain and arrest Mazarin to gain access to his enormous wealth. I found the evidence on July the tenth, the general consensus being that Louis XIV was as good as in the tomb. Mazarin, who sensed disorder lurking, ordered Philippe locked in a chamber at Calais. The situation had turned serious, and the capital was buzzing with the anticipation of welcoming home a monarch whom they had adored since his birth.

Something had to be done to thwart Choisy and her friends. D'Artagnan was rumored to have recently returned to Paris from the king's sickbed to aid M. Colbert in fortifying the Bastille, and I needed Charles' advice. For the past four years, the unofficial commander of the king's Grand Musketeers had lived in a miniature château known as La Volière, situated in the gardens of the Tuileries on the Right Bank. Although I had never been invited to his home, I decided to venture forth with the setting Sun to pay the Gascon a visit. Before leaving on that errand, I sat at my desk and composed a note to be read only by M. Cousinot, former First Surgeon to the king.

Charles de Batz was shocked to be greeted by me when his aide-de-camp summoned him to the front parlor. A smile dispersed any bad opinions he may have harbored towards the young lady whom he had befriended at age nine and who would soon see eighteen years; more likely the memory of a kiss continued to haunt him more than a spat. I admit, however, that I was quite surprised when he gathered me to him in a loving embrace and squeezed the air out of my lungs with the force of his clutch.

"Monsieur, please," I coughed, "you are crushing me to death."

"Have you come to demand an apology for my rude behavior of late?" he queried, running a hand from my waist to the nape of my neck. His lips caressed skin exposed by fingers moving curls from the path of advance. I pulled away for fear he would detect the wen Noctambule had given me, and also because I was confused by his lack of fidelity to Charlotte-Anne.

"Did you come here to accept my old proposal of marriage?" he asked bluntly.

D'Artagnan was extremely good-looking and I was tempted to say *yes*.

"I thought you to be in love with Charlotte-Anne, d'Artagnan."

"She has a husband, Bijoux. As soon will you."

"That is unfair, monsieur," I bristled. "I never gave my word."

"You are eighteen years of age, are you not?"

"Seventeen."

"Fine, then, seventeen, damn it! I shall wait no longer, Bijoux! Your dalliance with the prince near broke my heart, I swear it."

"I did nothing with him," I fibbed. "We shared a confidence; no more, no less."

He kissed me long on the mouth; a kiss I enjoyed.

"Let us see if you are telling your old friend the entire story," he remarked when we broke, lifting me up off the ground, carrying me towards the staircase. "I may not become a king, such as your Petit Monsieur, but I happen to love you, Bijoux."

"Wait, d'Artagnan, I nearly forgot. I brought you treasonous letters found in Madame de Choisy's possession."

"Bijoux Cinq-Mars," he interjected sweetly, "if you do not be still, I shall stifle you myself. Do you not fathom the depth of my feeling for you?"

At that moment, looking into his intensely blue gaze, watching him kiss me with tenderness, I decided to surrender to my Musketeer. In the absence of objection, d'Artagnan took the stairs to a large, curtained bed on high legs draped with a yellow, flowery brocade. The well-appointed anteroom was unoccupied and its new furnishings were modestly shielded behind a lovely painted screen, although a staid portrait of Queen Anne caused me to giggle.

"We cannot escape the court," I laughed, "not even in the privacy of the bedchamber."

He grinned and joined me on the richly embossed coverlet.

"Did you plan this sanctuary with us in mind?" I asked.

"No, with you in mind," he confessed. "As of tonight, this room is your own."

"And yours?"

"My room is below. No one has slept here since I bought the house. I wanted this place to remain perfect for someone with beautiful red hair and green eyes."

"And all this time I thought you meant for someone else."

"We shall never be apart again, I promise," he said, drawing me to him; the sound of his heart's pounding beat in my ear, lulling me to sleep.

Slumber was not what Charles desired. Undoing my bodice, he released the *communiqués* I had hidden. The papers spilled onto the bed. Lust was temporarily replaced by curiosity, and he picked up the sheets, leafing through them.

"You were serious," he mused, reading bits and pieces of the letters. "I'll send these off to Mazarin. Let us pray the king survives the night."

"What are the odds of his recovery?"

"A thousand-to-one," d'Artagnan sighed. "What a pity to be taken in one's prime, when such promise awaits one. Both the cardinal and the queen are inconsolable."

"Charles," I ventured, "I asked M. Cousinot to meet me here, later. Do you mind?"

"No, but why him? He relinquished the honor of First Surgeon to M. Vallot on account of his recent love affair with drink. The man is a sot."

"He'll be sober enough to bleed me, no doubt. Stay with me when he does?"

"The sight of blood does not weaken me," he boasted. "Your future husband is no coward."

"Charles, what say you?"

"We shall be married in a fortnight, with the cardinal's approval."

"Madame de V will be desolate," I frowned.

"Charlotte-Anne will be fine," he remarked. "Granted, I did court her, but that was that."

"You did not..."

"No, we did not," he confirmed, reading my thoughts. "Is it then not fitting that we should?"

"We could wait."

"And we could not," was my answer.

D'Artagnan, the soldier who had witnessed the agonies of battle and seen much hardship in the field, stroked my face as though fashioned from delicate porcelain. He kindled true passion in my heart and I am not ashamed to write that he was my first, genuine lover.

However, I would not dull the glow a private recollection still inspires by detailing a very personal act bordering on the mystical. To do that would dishonor my Musketeer, not to mention myself. No, suffice it to say that when a polite cough was heard outside our suite close to one hour later, I lay very still in strong arms, quite content to be alive.

"Who goes there?" my affianced inquired, rearranging the coverlet. A red stain was visible on the lemon hued fabric and Charles, noticing my alarm, put a finger to my lips.

"'Tis I, Monsieur Cousinot."

The doctor peered around the room divider, encouraged to enter by a warm welcome.

"Come in, old friend, come in. Bijoux told me to expect your visit. Take a seat," Charles offered.

"And what is this?" Cousinot smiled, gesturing at the two of us.

"We're getting married," d'Artagnan jubilantly announced. "You are the first to hear, Cousinot."

"Wonderful, good news," he exclaimed. "Marion would be thrilled if she were alive."

"Well, we're not dead and we agree!" the Musketeer chortled, hugging me to him. "Bijoux says she needs a bleeding before our nuptials, to put a spring into her step. Might you do that for my bride?"

Cousinot regarded me with a raised eyebrow. "Feeling peeked?" he asked.

I nodded my head in affirmation.

"Your request baffles me, considering you have not been lanced prior."

"You are correct, yet I have my reasons. Trust me, kind sir."

"Very well. Is there a basin nearby? Good. Shall we?" he asked, raising his hands into the air.

D'Artagnan reached for his breeches and began to dress, accustomed as he was to living amongst Musketeers.

"Do you wish me to drain you from the foot or the arm?" he inquired, opening his kit.

"Luna is where?"

"In Pisces," Cousinot winked.

I blanched. "The foot."

I had to be strong and finish what I had begun. France's future depended on it.

The groom-to-be sat close by, soothing my brow when Cousinot tied a bandage quite tightly below my right knee. My entire person stiffened and I gripped the hand d'Artagnan offered.

"'Tis nothing," Cousinot reassured, nicking the skin of my heel with a lancet. "I was bled sixty-four times in eight months by my father-in-law, M. Bouvard, to cure a violent rheumatism that plagued me."

"Were you cured?" I asked, sensing no pain.

"No," he jested, causing Charles to laugh.

"I've seen a man take a musketball in the chest and live to tell about it. A good purging does no harm, darling."

Bliss overcame me; I felt at peace. Nothing could plague me, I thought in a daze; not Noctambule, not curses, not Choisy nor Prince Tyrannus.

"Bijoux, open your eyes," d'Artagnan coaxed.

"Elation of this sort is common," Cousinot confirmed in an official tone.

"Have you finished?" I murmured.

"Done," Armand pronounced, closing the wound.

Smiling at d'Artagnan through the haze, I asked him to fetch me some wine.

"Monsieur," I said weakly, attempting to sit upright when the other was gone on his errand, "how much blood did you draw?"

"Enough, Bijoux. Now, rest."

"Do you desire to cure the king?"

"Bijoux, go to sleep. If the king is to be restored to health, M. Vallot will see to it."

"No, Cousinot, hear me out. Take my blood and make the tonic. Find the fastest horse in Paris and ride to Calais. Feed Louis Guibourg's potion—please, I know what I say."

"You are mad!"

"The mixture is magical."

"Is it?" he answered, scratching his fair brow. "That very question led me to drink."

"Guibourg told mother I was different from other people, that I required special care. He meant the draught. You know that and so do I."

"Bijoux, be still. That bastard Guibourg should be shot for cramming your head with foolishness. As should I for feeding you blood and consorting with a criminal, damn it! Do you forgive me?"

I was saved an answer by the appearance of d'Artagnan.

"Will you do as I ask? Or must I petition my Musketeer?"

"As you wish," Cusinot growled, too afraid of my tongue to refuse.

"Always scheming, my pretty minx," Charles noted. "What shall I do with you, once we are joined in holy matrimony?"

"Keep her big with child," Cousinot supplied, slapping his friend on the back. "That should leave Mademoiselle Bijoux few hours for intrigue, I daresay."

"Good man, good man," d'Artagnan boomed. "'Tis sage advice, coming from a barber."

"Charles, M. Cousinot travels to Calais tonight—give him the packet for Mazarin," I instructed in a small voice, weak from the bleeding. "Hurry, both of you."

Cousinot took the basin of blood in hand and filled a vial, holding the vessel aloft when he accomplished what years of practice had taught him to do with precision. Aware I was watching him, he pocketed the jar in a cache place inside his gown. D'Artagnan went about the business of collecting evidence, placing the lot inside a leather folio he in turn entrusted to the unlikely messenger. Then I fell asleep, certain all would be well.

Armand returned to the Louvre where he gathered and mixed the ingredients that might save the king and his own career. While a dream of an untamed forest swirled in my mind, the guilt-ridden physician took my advice, along with Choisy's letters, and rode bravely for twelve hours, stopping only twice to change horses, reaching Calais by eight the next morn.

Stumbling into the royal bedchamber, covered with dust, the doctor was greeted by a dismal sight. Louis lay close to death on soaking wet sheets and Anne of Austria prayed aloud at her son's side, choking back sobs of resigned loss. The assembled clergy remained calm, waiting for the exalted soul to leave its temporal home. A doubtful surgeon made the sign of the cross, uncorked his vial and administered a final tonic to the dying King of France and Navarre.

Waking with a start, I viewed my surroundings with apprehension. Where was I? What was going on? In the shadows of reverie, phantoms had revealed themselves to me: shiftless forms that called beseechingly, supplicants imploring me to join their ranks. Yet, nothing could move me from where I stood in the menacing wood, no force could budge my feet planted in moss and fern. Had I not pushed away an elderly gentleman who approached with kindly intent? Did a cane not wobble and fall? How had I traveled from that place of the undead to a room draped in yellow?

Suddenly, a pair of living arms returned me to the present moment.

"D'Artagnan? Is it morning?"
"Yes. We should arise."
We were limb-to-limb, meshed at the hip.
"Louis will live. His fever has broken."
"Good. Miracles are nice things to believe in."

"No," I said pulling back. "This miracle is an act of the goddess Athena, born of Her wisdom."

A great roar resounded through the courtyard beyond La Volière. Charles leapt from the bed, rushing to the window.

"Bijoux, a mob has gathered outside! Sweet Jesus, I must rally and go to Mazarin in Calais. The cardinal's life is in peril."

"No, d'Artagnan. The king lives."

"Philippe? Oh yes, I am certain of his health."

Smiling to myself beneath a raised blanket, I made no retort as d'Artagnan bustled about, donning his gear. *Nothing I say will deter him*, I thought. Then he was gone, a quick kiss on the cheek for me, a sword clanking against his spurs as he quit the house.

After lying awake for hours, thinking of Louis, my lids began to close when darkness fell on a sunny eleventh of July. Sleeping peacefully, I awoke to another dawn away from the Luxembourg, the sound of drums pounding out a military revelry. D'Artagnan stood, in the blue uniform of the Grand Musketeers, at the foot of the bed.

"Bijoux," he proclaimed loudly, "attend me."

"Hello, Charles," I said pleasantly, raising my shoulders. "Home so soon from Calais?"

"I am off to arrest Madame de Choisy and her gang of conspirators. Wait here. I shall return to deal with you."

"What have I done?" I asked, perplexed.

"Dress at once," he decreed. "Our troth is broken. Mazarin forbids us to marry."

He would not look at me, he did not dare.

"Why can't we be wed? Why?"

"Fate is oftentimes cruel. Accept that."

"No!" I yelled at him. "You said we would never part, liar! You promised to make me your wife!"

"The cardinal read the incriminating letters filched from Choisy. When he asked how I came by them, I told him the truth. Mazarin was quite impressed, Bijoux. He has decided to make you his agent. Your benefactress will be sent home to her husband, Guiche exiled, and Philippe punished."

"No, Philippe meant no harm!"

"His Eminence is sending you as a gift to the Surintendant of Finance, M. Fouquet. The cardinal is quite taken with the notion of you spying on that gentleman for the sake of France; he is determined to crush the Company of the Blessed Sacrament."

"I won't go," I cried. "He cannot separate us. Do you not love me?"

No reply came. My Musketeer was weeping, wiping tears from his cheeks.

"None of this would have come to pass if Louis had died," he lamented.

"The king is alive?"

"Yes. The crowd outside, yesterday, had assembled to pray for the king. Imagine their joy when Louis miraculously awoke and church bells pealed out the happy news across the land."

"What saved him?"

"A medicine concocted by M. Cousinot. Our good doctor is the First Surgeon once more, thanks to his cure."

The irony was horrible. "I shall never leave you," I vowed.

"You must. Mazarin has decided. You cannot say no."

"Why did I ever steal those letters? I have ruined not Choisy, but myself!"

Charles softened, kneeling on the mattress.

"My love for you is true," he declared. "Yet the cardinal wishes me to take another as a wife."

"Go to Hades," I raged. "You are weak, Charles! If I were a man, I'd kill the cardinal myself!"

D'Artagnan reached out to me, but I slid to the floor, hobbling over to the armchair where my clothing was laid out. Dressing with speed, I soon limped off towards the stairs.

"Bijoux, stop! Fouquet has not been informed as to your arrival—we have a few day's time."

"Surely you jest!"

"We could meet secretly, then. Please, do not be angry with me."

"Angry? I hate you! Forget you ever knew me!"

He was stunned. Turning my back on him, I made for the downstairs. Quitting the house altogether, I was met by a detachment of the king's Musketeers, awaiting their superior officer.

Held in their midst was a captive, a petulant youth whom I knew very well. His sad expression, dark, brooding eyes and characteristic pout moved me to pity.

"Good-for-nothing rascal," I cried out.

The Petit Monsieur's downcast head lifted, his gaze locked with mine. The old playmate beckoned, I ran to him and we embraced, both afraid to speak.

"Philippe, forgive me, please."

"Oh, Bijoux," he whispered, "it is so very nice to hold you once again."

Then the realization came to me, as I smelled his skin and touched his baby-fine curls, that while I had not always loved the king's brother, I had indeed been in love with him.

"What are you doing here?" I asked, surprised he was not with the remainder of the court in Calais.

"The cardinal is punishing me. He's locking me up in the Tuileries until Louis is better."

"Why is Mazarin angry with you, Monsieur?"

"Because of Choisy. She and her friends wrote me letters asking that I exile mother and arrest the Italian should Louis die. Then my brother recovered, and Mazarin got wind of the plot, and he sent me home with the Guard. Of course, I never would have hurt anyone, but for fun, I sent replies as if I would—Armand and I devised some wonderful schemes."

"Armand?"

"My dear Comte de Guiche, Bijoux," he sighed wistfully, parting from me slightly. "Do you know that the only good deed Madame de Choisy ever performed was to bring us together?"

"Thank you, Monsieur. Shall I meet you at the Tuileries anon?"

Philippe made a funny face, confused by my query.

"I care for you a great deal, Bijoux, yet I was referring to the Comte de Guiche."

"Oh, I see," I replied, my ears hot with embarrassment. "I thought you meant..."

"No," he guffawed. "After Choisy, I shan't trust another woman again. Men are more honest."

I bowed to the heir and took my leave of La Volière. Stumbling away, I forgot my uneven gait, I did not exult over the imminent arrest of Madame de Choisy, the argument with d'Artagnan was unimportant. All that concerned me was Prince Tyrannus.

Having scorned his love in the past, the Petit Monsieur had none left for me. A special trust had been broken by my dual obsession with vengeance and hatred.

Approaching the Rue de Médicis, I soon meandered up the street to St. Sulpice. I hesitated and considered going inside. Not schooled in Catholic ritual, my fear stopped me from entering. Then, Françoise Scarron's words echoed in my memory: *Everyone deserves a second chance.*

Going forward, I walked under a massive arch into the cool, candlelit sanctuary. Shuffling along, the last aisle on the left appeared and I knelt. I begged the goddess Athena to forgive me my sins, I pleaded with Her to spare Choisy, and I gave thanks for Louis' life. Lastly, I promised that if a love, such as the one Philippe and I had shared, came my way again, I would treasure it. Remembering my poor Prince Tyrannus, I wept, swearing never to be bad again.

Considering it safe to return to the Luxembourg, my tired legs carried me to the home I had called my own for eight years. Slinking into the foyer, I listened for footsteps or voices, but the Choisy abode was deserted, by all appearances. As I tiptoed to the bedchamber, Madame de V came from around a bend in the hallway, bumping into me and shrieking with fright.

"Blessed Virgin!" she exclaimed, "I feared you taken with Madame de Choisy and François! D'Artagnan and his Musketeers came and they arrested the pair!"

"I know, I know. Calm down, Charlotte-Anne, we are safe."

"Do you think so? Mazarin could lock me up, too. Guilty

by association. M. d'Artagnan was not himself. I'm so afraid, Bijoux! Where have you been hiding at these two days past?"

"At St. Sulpice, praying for the king," I lied. "I saw your Musketeer on the way home this morning, and he told me everything. He also assured me that you and I are in the clear. However, the cardinal is placing me under M. Fouquet's care. What will you do?"

"I do not know," she sniffled.

"Go to d'Artagnan, tonight. Ask him to take you in, madame."

"Bijoux, how scandalous of you, really!"

"If you love him, go to him. My break with the Petit Monsieur taught me a valuable lesson, madame. Do not allow foolish pride to keep you from your heart's desire."

"You see things so clearly," Charlotte-Anne effused, wrapping me in a warm embrace. "Perhaps one day you and the prince will be reconciled."

Tears threatened to expose my ruse; a false smile held them at bay.

Give me a second chance, Athena, I silently entreated, *and I shall sin no more.*

What I did not take into account when I vowed to be good was my new benefactor: the brilliant and devious Nicolas Fouquet. Any resolve was to be tested by a master intriguer far more adept at cunning than Jeanne-Olympe had proved. I was so young, so inexperienced, so full of hope.

Much the same as Prince Tyrannus.

Had it not been for my break with d'Artagnan, being sentenced to sojourn with the family Fouquet at their country house would not have been a terrible fate to contemplate. The surintendant's mansion was located at Saint-Mandé, bordering the pretty woods of the Parisian suburb Vincennes, and was a hub-bub of social activity. Cardinal Mazarin was indeed entrusting me with a very sensitive assignment and one which I could conduct from a most agreeable posting; however, I was not thinking of personal advancement when a knock sounded at Madame de Choisy's former apartment door.

"Yes, come in," I said impatiently, expecting to see d'Artagnan and an escort of Musketeers.

What, or rather who, appeared next, amazed me to no end. Dressed in the robes of an apprentice physician, entered César de la Tour, Mazarin's page who had delivered my tonic five years earlier and whose prompt return of my message to Cousinot had saved me from death.

"Hello," I heard myself say in a lilting manner. "I was not aware *you* were coming to fetch me for the journey to Saint-Mandé, Monsieur Tauro de la Tour."

"You remember me!" he exclaimed. "What a good memory you possess, Mademoiselle Bijoux."

"Oh, so you do not mistake me for Mademoiselle Sancy," I gibed pleasantly.

"Forgive me and be my friend," he smiled, stepping closer to where I stood near to the clock in the parlor, "now that we are partners, you and I."

"Partners?"

"By orders of his Eminence, himself. You are to gather information regarding the Company of the Blessed Sacrament, pass it on to me, and I shall relay the news to our master."

"Truly, monsieur?"

"Do you doubt me?" His voice was gentle. And his eyes, argent and sappur—I was staring into them, wondering how I had failed to dream of their intensity. Had I been blind?

I flushed as would an innocent when I answered him.

"I trust you. I don't know why, but I do."

"Because I am a de la Tour," he supplied with a laugh, taking my hand. "And you?"

"I am of the house d'Effiat. My father was Henri de Cinq-Mars, Monsieur le Grand, in his day."

César embraced me as he would a long-lost relative.

"Your father and my father were great friends! Both had a great passion for beautiful women and fine horses, did you not know?"

"No, I know of little concerning my late father. I was a child when he died."

"I knew I liked you for a reason," he stated. "I sincerely apologize if I was rude to you that day when you were play-acting in front of the prince..."

"Me? Play-acting?" I interjected with mock disbelief. "Come, let us collect my belongings and be gone from this place—I cannot tolerate being here a moment longer, Prince Chromius!"

"Prince Chromius," he laughed aloud. "I know not the name, though I fancy it, my lady!"

César's enthusiasm was contagious and I sensed excitement brimming up inside of me. Not passion or love, but rather a reawakened interest in living that had been lying dormant in my heart for many a month. The young man was very nice and perhaps the cardinal was not so cruel, after all. The wily old intriguer had to have known that César's father had been acquainted with my own. His Eminence had given me not only an escort, but also an ally to assist and to protect me. Another brother, as had been Chersidamus and Tyrannus.

My helpmate and I were to travel in one of Mazarin's coaches to our destination, all arrangements made by the cardinal during the week elapsed between Choisy's arrest and the departure. After persuading Madame de V to visit d'Artagnan, who took her into his home and arms, I was alone during those seven days for the first time in my life. The experience proved an opportunity for reflection; a time when I wrote Françoise Scarron a lengthy letter of farewell, for it was easier to lie and say I was running away from court than to disclose my intent to spy on her good friend and husband's patron, Fouquet.

César and I conducted a pleasant conversation on our way to Saint-Mandé. Evidently, the physician's gown was no disguise for he truly intended to become a surgeon in the king's service. Fouquet had established an excellent laboratory where many of the greatest scientists in Europe studied; César was particularly eager to meet and work with the renowned Monsieur Pecquet. When I asked what field was his favorite, he stunned me by revealing he intended to learn all he could concerning the circulation of the lymph and blood. My subsequent ashen pallor caused him alarm.

"Does the thought of blood bother you, mademoiselle?"

"No," I replied tersely. "You made me remember I left no instruction for M. Cousinot as to where to locate me for deliveries of my tonic. Recall it; the one you brought me yourself."

"Are you ill?"

"I feel peaked if I do not take the medicine, monsieur. The restorative brings color to my cheeks."

"That is odd," he remarked. "Are you familiar with the elemental properties of the substance you drink? I could mix it for you, no doubt."

"I am not privy to the ingredients. It is pink in color—that is all I know."

"Cousinot probably employs crushed flowers or herbs of some sort. I'll have a messenger go to him with a request for your prescription."

"No, don't do that," I demanded, clutching one of his arms. "Do not bother the First Surgeon, for he is busy tending to the king. I shall get word to him on my own."

"What are you hiding from me? Mazarin said that I was to watch over you, to care for you. Allow me to do my duty, for heaven's sake."

I wanted to tell him about my condition, to share the burden I carried with another person. If I confessed, would he hate me? Would he tell the cardinal that I was a daemon? Was I?

"I am a *vrykolakas*," I blurted out. "Please don't mention it to anyone, please?" I implored.

"A *what*?"

"A *vrykolakas*."

César chuckled aloud. "Pray tell, what is a *vrykola...*?"

"The word is *vrykolakas*," I primly corrected, regaining my composure. "A Greek term found in *The Key of Solomon*, an ancient grimoire..."

"You cannot be seriously inclined!" he expounded. "Magic

books are full of nonsense and cannot be taken seriously. I am a man of science, trust me. What did this book say?"

"My tutor, as a child, was the Abbé Guibourg, a daemon worshipper who claimed that I was a *vrykolakas* and that *The Key of Solomon* referred to such a being. I have not seen the pages in question, to be honest. What I may divulge, with certainty, is that without the tonic I succumb to violent fits. I need to drink human blood or else I shall die. That is what my medicine consists of, that and angelica water and essence of peony."

"Cousinot feeds you blood taken from his patients?"

"Yes. Now two people besides myself know the awful truth."

"Don't look so glum," César admonished, bouncing up and down on the velvet cushions that matched the drapery. "You are a healthy, young woman. I cannot believe that drinking blood keeps you alive and well, but if you do, then you shall have your medicine. We must discover where the real problem lies, if there is one, when I have gained more medical knowledge."

"You will agree to help me?" I was flabbergasted.

"We are associates," he grinned. "Nothing is impossible to figure. Most people would rather remain ignorant when faced with a riddle. Are you one of those? Or are you a child of the Virgin?"

"Absolutely," I replied, kissing him on the cheek with happiness and relief. "Has anyone ever told you that you're wonderful?"

César's cheeks turned as red as two love apples.

"No one as pretty as you," he admitted. "Do you mind the compliment?"

"Not when it comes from Prince Chromius," I flirted.

Evaluating the dark-haired twenty-year-old, I knew I would not be pining after d'Artagnan or Philippe. And I would not be requiring M. Cousinot's services, either, seeing as though the apprentice could manufacture my tonic. It was as if Mazarin knew that my blood offering had saved his godson's life and he was rewarding me with a beautiful hero named César de la Tour.

And as we drove through the stone and iron gates of Saint-Mandé, smiling at one another, I could scarcely comprehend how accurate my premonition would prove.

CHAPTER NINE
Of Covenants and Kings

Daily life improved. Quartered with the Fouquet family at their idyllic estate made living with Choisy at the Luxembourg seem, in comparison, as though I had been dumped on a galley ship for eight years. I did miss poor François-Timoléon and Madame de V; however, I assumed that the would-be priest was better off in the countryside, removed from vicious tongues and potential scandal, and Charlotte-Anne could have been dealt a worse hand than playing the mistress to Charles de Batz.

Nicolas Fouquet, Surintendant of Finance, rarely sojourned at Saint-Mandé, being occupied as he was with calculating his percentage of the tax farmers' collection, raising silver for the king's armies or overseeing the work-in-progress of his vast palace, Vaux-le-Vicomte, thirty miles southeast of Paris. Begun two years earlier in 1656, the architect Louis Le Vau had been hired to draw up the plans and rumor had it that Vaux was going to be the finest house in France when completed.

The façade of the brick building was no less than seventy yards in length, an immense central dome commanded the onlooker's attention and two wings projected off the main edifice. The artistic genius, Monsieur Le Brun, had been contracted to paint the finished ceilings and walls of the château with solar motifs, gods and goddesses, and depictions of the minister performing acts of valor in the Classical style. A special factory had been erected near to Vaux to manufacture tapestries and the other necessities needed to furnish the Future's testament to his own greatness. Fouquet, it seemed, was determined to become a power in his own right, whether Louis XIV was in agreement or not.

The first thing I noticed, upon arrival at Saint-Mandé, was that the huge house was a meeting place for artists, writers and intellectuals. Whether the surintendant was in residence or not, the elite minds of French society gathered under his auspices to discuss, argue and create. Morning, noon and night, carriages were heard pulling up in the huge courtyard sprawling before the front entrance. Servants hardly rested, bustling 'round the clock to accommodate their betters' needs.

The much-lauded people whom I watched come and go at Saint-Mandé set my mind to spinning and I was impressed by the accounts César relayed to me concerning Fouquet's mental prowess. The surintendant wrote treatises in Latin and argued theology with Jesuit priests, counting himself a confidant of the Black Pope, the vicar-general of that order. He suggested verses to his friend, the poet La Fontaine, while another illustrious wordsmith, Paul Pellison, acted as his personal secretary. The man was a legend, a figure larger-than-life, and evidently well deserved of his meteoric rise.

Spying on a person who was as universally admired as was the target of my investigation was a difficult undertaking. No one had a bad remark reserved for the official who tightened or loosened the purse strings. Another fly in the ointment was that neither César nor myself had met with the minister since our installation at Saint-Mandé. The July afternoon that had seen us settle into our respective third floor apartments did not hold much promise of being introduced to any of the host family. Half of the court was on Fouquet's payroll, in one way or another, and two additional mouths to feed did not constitute a matter worthy of the busy man's notice. By September, I was desperate and had considered donning one of mother's old dresses and throwing myself at Lord Cléonime's feet, when Athena seemed to intervene on my behalf.

César and I had misbehaved on the evening prior, celebrating my eighteenth year over more than a glass or two of burgundy by the time the clock chimed midnight. In the course of our merrymaking, we both became quite tipsy and fell asleep, fully clothed, on my bed from the effects of the wine. Waking a few hours later, we sat up in tandem, embarrassed by the compromising position in which we found ourselves. I must admit we were attracted to one another then, each too inexperienced to speak of love.

On the following morning, we met in the lovely garden behind the house that stretched all the way back to the forest of Vincennes. Sitting on a bench fashioned from solid silver, I leaned on my compatriot, placing a heavy head against his shoulder.

"Do you feel as badly as I do, Prince Chromius?"

"Worse," he moaned. "How much did we drink?"

"Two bottles. Or did you forget?"

"All I am able to recall is waking to the sight of your lovely face."

"Stop it," I scolded, nudging him in the side with a jab of an elbow.

"Ah, young love," a voice from behind remarked. "Is it not blissful, Madame du Plessis?"

César and I sprang to our feet to find Nicolas Fouquet and his favourite, arm-in-arm, out for a morning stroll.

"Oh, *mon Dieu!*" I gasped and knelt, flustered by their presence.

"Get up, get up," the lady sighed. "Monsieur is not the Almighty, you know."

"I am not?" he protested, hand at his lace collar, his remark eliciting a nervous, uncomfortable laugh from the group. "Are you the girl sent here by Mazarin?" Fouquet asked abruptly.

"Yes, monsieur. We were introduced three years ago at Mademoiselle de Scudéry's *Samedi*."

"Yes, of course. You are Marion's daughter. And Choisy's ex-ward." He eyed me up and down. "A pity that ill fortune befell our Jeanne-Olympe, don't you agree? Who might have informed the cardinal concerning her numerous correspondences, I wonder?"

"I have oft' times mused on that very question, monsieur," I replied hastily, probably a bit too quickly. "I did hearsay that the cause of my former mistress' troubles may have been Anne of Gonzaga, the Queen of Poland's sister."

"That is possible," Plessis agreed. "Too alike in their habits, I say."

"Oh, I don't know," Fouquet murmured, examining his fingernails with self-absorption."I always thought the two on the best of terms."

"No," I insisted, "they despise one another."

Fouquet glowered at me with a stern countenance, but I stared right back at him. Our eyes locked; a tense silence descended upon the troupe.

"Would you care to attend a soirée this evening?" he queried, still glaring.

"That would be delightful," I accepted, "especially if you are present, monsieur."

"I shall see you and your *beau* in the main salon at seven," he concluded, leading his elegant companion away. "We shall discuss certain matters then."

I bowed, waiting for the couple to be out of earshot before I spoke.

"What do you think, César? Fouquet is wary of my motives, is he not?"

"This is your chance to gain the surintendant's confidence, Bijoux. How far will you go?"

"César, I am hardly Fouquet's type! He is fond of older women, not girls."

"You said he bedded your mother."

"She was thirty-nine, not eighteen. Stop worrying about my honor."

"I'm not worried," he coughed, "merely concerned."

"For what? My soul?" I laughed. I took the young man's warm hands in mine and he looked away, miserable.

"I promise that I shall save myself for you and you alone," I pledged. "Feel better?"

"Do not provoke me," he said, "or the next time you are giddy with wine, I shall take advantage of your vulnerable state."

"Promises, promises," I replied, and ran back to my room to prepare for Fouquet's entertainment. I should have noticed that César seemed to care for me deeply; instead, I was distracted by the prospect of sleuthing for the cardinal. Intent on winning Mazarin's praises, my ambition urged me onward; the resolutions made at St. Sulpice conveniently forgotten.

My father no doubt would have been proud.

Mazarin made certain to send me gold coins as prepayment for my anticipated services, therefore I had access to resources and was able to commission a new wardrobe shortly after arriving at Saint-Mandé. Three of the gowns I had ordered were finished, and they lay spread out upon the bed for inspection when I arrived at my room. Deciding on which to wear was not difficult, for an ornately festooned, green satin skirt with a close-fitting bodice of bronze colored silk was my unreserved first choice. A complimentary stomacher, decorated with intricate stitches, semi-precious stones and an *eschelle*, or placement of ribbons, that flattened my front much as a board would do and would be worn outside, over the gown, accompanied the outfit.

Holding the dress up in front of a large looking glass, I came to the conclusion that some of mother's jewels were needed to complete the ensemble. Writing a note to d'Artagnan, I sped to the courtyard and found a lackey who, for a *louis d'or*—which was, and still is, a sizeable sum—agreed to deliver the message to the Musketeer. My jewels would be collected from M. Colbert and transported to Saint-Mandé before the evening's *fête*. The time had come to be noticed.

The remainder of the day sped by, although I awaited the servant's return with foreboding, hoping he would not be waylaid by highwaymen who would gladly relieve him of his precious cargo. I was kicking myself for having sent for the stones by the stroke of five, at six o'clock I was beside myself with fear. The gems represented all the worth I possessed, and without them, I would be no better off than a pauper. Hands trembled as I fussed with my hair, and I was compelled to ring for aid in completing a simple toilette. A maid who had attended to me before, Lisette, appeared in answer to my summons. She was truly a beautiful young woman—a face born of Luna and hair that was nothing less than a tribute to Sol's magnificence.

"Hello, Lisette," I smiled. "Thank you for being prompt."

"'Tis a pleasure to serve you, mademoiselle," she said respectfully.

"Well, I am a bit jittery this evening, so ignore me if I seem out-of-sorts. I have been waiting to be invited to the main salon for months now."

"Being in the same room as the surintendant would fluster any woman. Is he not handsome?"

"Yes, however, M. Fouquet was intimate with my mother."

"Oh, that's a pity. Flirt with another gentleman this evening."

"You are a coy thing," I replied. "Yet, accurate. So, Lisette, make me beautiful."

The maid was skilled at coiffure, far better than François-Timoléon, and soon an entirely different person reflected back at me from the mirror. Hair pinned up and face framed by ringlets, I looked sophisticated, more mature—a softer version of Marion.

"You are so talented," I declared, impressed by the finished product. "Should I return to the court one day, you must accompany me."

"Truly? Do you mean that, Mademoiselle Bijoux?"

"Why not? Just don't tell anyone else," I added, not wishing idle talk to spread concerning my leaving Saint-Mandé. "The pact will be our secret."

"Fine, I agree," Lisette promised. "Did you hear that?" she asked unexpectedly.

The sound of footsteps, booted and spurred footsteps, could be heard advancing down the corridor. *Mon Dieu*, I thought, *did I do something wrong and the Guard is coming to arrest me?*

That fear was confirmed by a heavy-handed rap at the closed door. Glancing at Lisette, I put a finger to my mouth, and moved noiselessly to the bolt. Too late, for the crystal knob turned, and I was face-to-face with Charles de Batz, my former fiancé. Nearby, three fellow Musketeers stood at the ready.

"Monsieur d'Artagnan, what brings you here?"

"I come at your request, Mademoiselle Bijoux," he answered, acting officious, as though we had never kissed or touched or held one another in an intimate embrace. "Consider your property delivered."

Reaching beneath his blue mantle with its appliquéd silver cross, d'Artagnan untied a bulging sack from his belt. Handing it to me, he turned to leave.

"Wait," I implored. "Allow me thank you properly, monsieur, for your kind act."

"That is not necessary," he snapped. "A Musketeer does not require a lady to reward him."

"Fine, take your foolish pride and be away, then! After everything we have shared, you should be ashamed of yourself!"

The soldiers regarded each other with mute shock. How dare a mere girl chastise their beloved commander? Charles pivoted on heel to confront me; however, my arms were around his neck, and I held him close with affection. The men began to grin.

"Stop hating me," I whispered. "Let us forgive and forget."

"How could I forget you?" he replied aloud. "Leave this place, come home with me."

"You know that is impossible, monsieur. I am needed here." Looking over his shoulder, I saw César approaching, on his way to fetch me for our seven o'clock appointment. I separated from d'Artagnan, regretting that I had resurrected a painful subject by my rash display. César appeared to be annoyed, by the tight purse of his lips, and I wondered if he had heard Charles' request.

"How fares Charlotte-Anne?" came a cover-up inquiry.

"Well," Charles said, adjusting his tunic. "Her husband

has taken ill and may not live out the year. Should he expire, we...plan to marry."

"Wonderful!" I exclaimed. "César, come meet M. d'Artagnan, the unofficial leader of the king's Grand Musketeers."

"An honor," my swain acknowledged, bowing low from the waist. He was decked out in an exquisitely tailored suit; the tourmaline shade of his long jacket, a recent fashion called a *justacorps*, matched my skirt to perfection. The eveningwear accentuated César's well-proportioned physique in a way a physician's smock could not do justice.

The two men exchanged pleasantries; one relieved, the other, sullen. Not good at small talk, Charles excused himself forthwith, kissing my hand in farewell. Striding away with his men at his heels, he did not look at me in parting.

"Tell Charlotte-Anne that I shall come to call on her soon," I yelled after him. D'Artagnan raised a gauntlet into the air, and soon disappeared down the staircase.

"Shall we?" César gestured, implying that we should likewise go.

"No, not yet. Come see this," I replied and we entered the privacy of the bedchamber. Lisette was waiting to be dismissed, and I handed her a gold *louis* on her way out.

"Not a word," I reminded. She was radiant as she stared at the coin and her delight touched me. Showing her out to the hall, I shut and locked the door, then tossed the bag to César.

"Look inside," I nearly sang. "Deposit the contents onto the bed!"

My elegant confederate obeyed. Ruby red light streamed through the windows, dying rays that exploded with color as they were captured on the jewels' tumbling facets. César's mouth opened wide as he gazed upon the array of gems.

"Did M. d'Artagnan gift you this cache?"

"Yes and no. They belonged to my mother and when she died, I entrusted the jewels to the Musketeer for safekeeping. Today, I asked for my inheritance to be returned."

"So that's why he was here. Do you know how much this lot is worth?"

"Fifty thousand."

"Merciful heaven! We have to hide it, Bijoux."

"First, pick out what I should wear tonight."

César pulled me to him. "You are beautiful without gems. Whomever named you, knew that."

"César, be serious. You are a refined gentleman; please choose for me."

He stared at me with those eyes. "I wish we were not required to attend this damn function."

I withdrew from his near embrace and busied myself with sorting bracelets, rings, necklaces and eardrops. Diamonds, emeralds, pearls; gems of every description passed through my fingers. Small wonder Guibourg had wished to kill me for the hoard, for the collection represented a veritable treasure.

"Here, I'll wear this and this and this," I announced, showing César a choker of pearls, an emerald ring and a pair of gold ear baubles set with crystalline sparklers. My friend fastened the strands around my neck whilst I clipped the hefty ornaments to thin earlobes and forced the ring onto a digit.

"Let me see, hurry up," I fussed. Taking a mirror from the commode, I peered into it.

"What do you think? Am I presentable?"

"You resemble every inch a Cinq-Mars of the house d'Effiat," he said breathlessly. "I am proud to be your escort."

"Thank you, César," was my answer as I pecked at his cheek. "Let us be off, or we shall be late."

"I wish to gift you something. Here," he offered, holding out a tiny alabaster box.

I lifted the lid to find what appeared to be an antique brooch, resembling a bee. Removing the pin from its casket, I fastened it to a sleeve.

"How unique, César. Look, it seems to have alighted as if alive."

"Do you like it?"

"Better than all that," I assured him, pointing to the pile. "Those stones are naught but dirty coins."

César looked away. "The emblem is sacred to my family, a

copy of a piece belonging to an ancient king. Few are worthy of displaying it upon their person."

"If I do not merit the keepsake, then please, reclaim your goods," I laughed.

"No, be my wife."

I was not expecting that response. Stepping backwards, it was my turn to feel overwhelmed.

"Why would you want me? You hail from a respectable lineage and your elders would not have you wed the daughter of a traitor and..."

"Stop making excuses. Yes or no, Bijoux. What do you say?"

Sitting on the bed, I replaced the sum of Marion's life work inside the drawstring sack.

"You were truly born on the opening day of Flora's month?"

"Yes, the first of May," he confirmed. "I am a true son of the Minotaur."

"Thus, my Moon does conjunct your Sun, in Taurus. Bull and Virgin also make for a trine."

"So be it," the youth smiled. "These are all goodly aspects. I am acquainted with the study of the stars, as well."

"César...I am not an innocent."

"I saw you together with Philippe, I heard the talk concerning *La Reine de la Main*. I could give a damn because I love you. Is that so difficult to believe, stubborn mule?"

He was adamant. Kneeling down before me, César's usually appealing visage turned hard. I thought I had never looked upon a more honest man and I reached out to him, touching his hair. It was more beautiful than the king's.

"If you truly love me, I shall consider your proposal. Grant me a few hours to think."

"I am not moving from this spot until you say *yes*."

"And I am the stubborn mule? What about you?"

"Do you not love me? Could we not announce our intentions to Fouquet this evening?"

César truly yearned for me to become his wife. Why not

wed him? Why not take a chance on a man whom I knew to be good?

Dropping on my knees to the floor, I joined him, near to tears. Seeing that, César pressed me to him, holding me tighter than I had ever been held.

"I shall honor you and respect you, Bijoux. Never shall I hurt you, never shall I disrespect you as did that son of a harlot."

"I love you," I wept. "We must marry in secret, for I would die if anyone interfered with our plans and I lost you."

"I shall find a priest tonight. Go downstairs without me and conduct our business. Then meet me here, later, and we shall exchange vows."

"This is all so sudden." I wiped away the rivulets moistening my cheeks. "Are you certain, César?"

"There is only one, single thing in this life of which I am more certain," he replied quietly. "When we are one, I shall tell you what that is, agreed?"

My head nodded. "Anything you say."

Then his lips were on mine, those exquisite lips I long for as I write. Our initial kiss grew wild as the passion between us mounted, and César broke away.

"Go. Go now, before..."

"When shall I meet you?" I asked, catching my breath.

"Near to midnight, I should think..."

"No, I shall go and come back quickly. We'll go to the stables and procure a coach. Then we'll drive to Paris and St. Sulpice. I want to do this correctly and I want to be married there."

"Why there?" The question was not meant to be frivolous.

"A week before you came into my life, I prayed under that roof, in the last pew on the left, and asked for a miracle. My gift from Athena was you. Is it wrong to be thankful?"

César lifted my chin.

"This was meant to be. Your choice astounds me. Soon you will understand."

"What?" I was totally perplexed.

"Later, tomorrow. Trust me a while longer, my darling."

I adored him with an intensity that went beyond reason. We kissed again and the encounter was rapturous, incredible. Dusk had fallen, the clock read past seven, yet neither César nor I took note of the time. We were doing something infinitely more important than gathering observations for a Cardinal of Rome—we were falling in love.

Upon viewing the mob assembled in the main salon of Saint-Mandé, a complete stranger could have informed me that anyone and everyone of import was present at Fouquet's gathering, and I would have been a believer. The scene was jarring in its enormity. I recalled the surintendant's motto: *To what height will he not ascend?* As I surveyed the connecting parlors and I knew exactly what Nicolas intended to imply by that device. The Minister of Finance meant to rule.

Stepping forward tentatively, I searched for the host so I might catch his attention and then flee the ocean of tightly packed bodies. Jostled none too nicely by the revelers, I moved in the direction of the crowd's center. Practically stumbling into a cleared space, I was greeted by a boisterous *hello* issuing from a strange man attired in a simple suit, whose dark locks were flowing and a tad disheveled.

"Hello," I managed, taken aback.

"Who are you, sweet thing?" he gurgled.

"Bijoux Cinq-Mars. And you, kind sir?"

"Comaetho! I am your Monsieur Jean de la Fontaine!"

"No, not the same friend of Monsieur and Madame Scarron?"

"The very one," he chuckled. "Who invited you here, may I be so bold to ask?"

"Monsieur Fouquet, my master. Have you seen him?"

"Oh dear, he's shut up in his chamber with a headache, so I shall keep you company."

"Thank you," I smiled unconvincingly, trapped. Why had I pried myself from César?

"I am currently at work on a collection of fables," La

Fontaine chattered, "in imitation of Aesop and Socrates; names no doubt familiar to you my pretty *Précieuse*."

"Monsieur, truly, I am no scholar," I protested.

"Let us escape to the library. Come, my beauty," he insisted, gripping one of my arms for emphasis. He shuffled along, dragging me with him, oblivious to those who blocked the path he was hell-bent on taking. Hitting people playfully with his walking stick, he'd look at me, twitter, then carry on.

We were soon the object of attention; certain gentlemen applauded M. de la Fontaine for having captured my attention, and ladies rushed to the sideboards where they took flowers from their vases, returning to strew them at our feet.

"Are they all mad?" The criticism soured on my tongue as I said it.

"I love them, I love them all!" La Fontaine gushed. "These good people are my public!"

"Better yours than mine, monsieur. Do you always attract such tribute?"

"Yes," he howled. "Fouquet took me on and, *voilà*, I am the heir to Homer. You are again?"

"Bijoux—Comaetho—recall?"

"Yes, yes. Bijoux. Lady of the many jewels. How original. May I use your name in a poem?"

"Certainly, should you not forget by morn."

"Ooh, nasty. I like it. *Touché*, mademoiselle, you warm the cockles of this reprobate's heart."

I followed him into the study. What I saw was far more magnificent than even the library of Mademoiselle de Scudéry's mansion, for it was ten times bigger and more grandiose.

"Nice, eh?"

"Oh, my, nice does not adequately describe such a show of wealth," I replied, walking in circles, staring upwards at books, books, books, right to the top of the vaulted ceiling.

"Thirteen thousand editions, hand bound and embossed in gold. Smell them, drink in the aroma, mademoiselle. The wisdom of the ages, waiting to be cracked. You were not aware of this room?"

"What? No, thank you for the tour."

"Now, my little *Précieuse*..."

"Monsieur, I attended one *Samedi*; I hardly think that qualifies me..."

"Mademoiselle de Scudéry, our dear Sapho, is one of my best friends," he jumped in, excited. "*What* is your name?"

"Bijoux," I sighed.

"Of course. Of course. Forgive me, for I am terribly absent-minded. Sit down, over there near to the fire. It's drafty in here and even at my age of thirty-eight years, which must seem ancient to you, I need warmth. Go ahead, don't be modest."

With a thinly veiled groan of exasperation, I did as he asked.

"You know something you ought to disclose," La Fontaine probed, relaxing very close to me on a love seat. His large hand encircled a smooth, emerald encrusted one. "Nice ring. Did the Duc d'Anjou gift it to you?"

"You bastard!" I burst out into laughter. "Fouquet told you to sniff me out, did he not?"

"I expected no less from the daughter of Marion Delorme," he drawled, faculties intact.

"Let us drink a toast to the surintendant. Have we cognac?"

"But of course," he confirmed. "Housed over there, next to the Arabic texts."

"How helpful," I replied, glancing about. Noticing a shelf crammed full with decanters and silver plate, I hurried across a vast expanse to their lodging.

"Good girl, bring a flask over here," he suggested. "We'll drink a toast to our meeting and then another to M. Fouquet."

Juggling stems and a carafe, I came back to the intimate sofa and served the verse-maker a libation.

"Ambrosia," he testified. "Nothing better than this."

"Quite." I sipped the potent liquor carefully. "Now, tell me a bedtime fable, monsieur."

"Doesn't one need to be tucked in, mademoiselle, for late night ramblings?"

"Are you suggesting..."

"No," he tittered, twirling his sapphire-capped walking stick with a twist of the wrist. "Your mother and I were, shall we say, more than friends back in sixteen thirty-eight."

"No!"

"Ah, *oui*, mademoiselle. Cost me a bundle, but I had her," he drew on the brandy with a slurp. "I was seventeen, your father eighteen; we near fought a duel over lovely Marion!"

"Monsieur, are you testing my resolve?"

Following another gulp, La Fontaine rattled on about sly foxes, rancid grapes, dawdling tortoises and speedy hares. He was boring me. When the bard nodded off in a drunken haze, I took his cup from him and set it on the nearby mantelpiece. Roaming about the enclosure, I stretched my arms.

I had to go; César was waiting.

Then I spied a massive desk, through an archway, practically begging to be inspected. The writing table had to belong to Fouquet or to his secretary. Something told me such was the case.

La Fontaine was snoring. Deciding not to linger, I went to the piece and rummaged through drawer after drawer, searching for what, I had not an inkling.

The last pull on which I tugged, after finding no incriminating evidence behind the others, would not yield. I fumbled, I jiggled, I took a letter opener and pried at a skeleton lock; despite my struggle, the clasp would not yield. Frustrated, I slammed the silver knife on top of the desk with a bang; the wooden sleeve popped open.

Inside were parchment documents. Lifting them out carefully, I scanned their content. What I read, caused me to gasp. For within my grasp, I held the Covenant of the Company of the Blessed Sacrament, dated sixteen hundred and thirty. The articles, numbering thirty-three, were laid out in precise detail; the mission of its membership spelled out for my prying eyes.

Rapidly, I skimmed the papers, replacing them when I had finished reading. Barely touching the drawer, it shut of its own accord, locking once more.

Holding my stomach, I paused, ill at ease. Fouquet was not an honest person, no longer did I think him worthy of respect. Mazarin needed to be informed of the cabal's aims.

Passing through the curved portal, I checked on La Fontaine. He was sleeping soundly. Shaking him awake, I roused the slumbering poet.

"Where am I?" he asked.

"Monsieur Fouquet's library."

"Yes, of course. Pour me another cognac, please."

The chalice was filled before he could regain complete coherency. "To you, heir of Homer, my dear La Fontaine," I saluted, sipping the strong stuff, handing it to the cardinal's unwitting agent.

He drew on the goblet, sucking down half its contents. Before he could finish the remainder, I grabbed the sterling grail away and quaffed the rest myself.

"To us and our good fortune! 'Till later, monsieur."

"Bijoux, attend me," his speech was slurred. "Was my moral clear to you?"

"Yes, monsieur, your stories were most revealing."

La Fontaine twirled his pretentious prop anon. "Go to your lover, mademoiselle. The night is young and so are you."

"Thank you," I said, embracing him in a formal farewell.

"By the way," he added in a faraway tone, a final comment as I was straightening my stomacher prior to departing, "the Company is none of your business. Leave it be, Comaetho. Remember the myth."

"Monsieur you *are* absent-minded," I answered. "Go back to sleep and dream of Marion."

"Yes, quite right," he sighed. "Lovely Marion, a goddess in the flesh."

"Good-bye," I said, for some reason hating his analogy. "We shall meet anon."

Then I was off, sick at the core and longing for César.

All proceeded according to plan and my love and I were married at two in the morning in the chapel of St. Sulpice in

Paris. Saying our vows in the presence of the Eucharist, an addled priest, and a hastily roused seminary student, César and I pronounced the age-old litany with solemnity, not minding the awkward circumstances. The service, pronounced in rapid Latin, concluded in a matter of minutes after its commencing; soon César and I were kissing, man and wife.

The Book of Records was retrieved, our names formally entered and we signed the page Bijoux and César de la Tour d'Auvergne, yet, somehow I felt more a Cinq-Mars than before. Nothing inside of me had changed. Departing the cathedral, I hoped I would make a good wife and be worthy of the noble person hurrying me along to our awaiting vehicle.

Although it was our wedding night, I ached to make a detour via Mazarin's palace on the return route to Saint-Mandé. The incriminating documents I had found in Fouquet's library required the cardinal's immediate consideration.

"César," I purred, "may I beg a favor? Might we pay the cardinal a quick visit?"

"What now? At this hour? Are you mad?"

"No," I bristled. "Would I ask if I did not have an important message to relay to him?"

"What? Tell me, for we should have no secrets, Bijoux. Does your news concern the Company?"

The aristocratic mien, arresting in its chiseled symmetry, drew closer. César would become suspicious if I did not confide in him. However, I was not prepared to divulge the contents of the Covenant to anyone but Mazarin.

"My discovery concerns M. Fouquet's book-keeping methods. The minister is diverting large sums from the royal treasury for his own private use and I have the proof."

"No!" he exclaimed.

"Yes," I replied.

That declaration convinced my husband to escort me to the palace of the man whom I had heard much about, but had seen only once, on my first day at court. The prospect of being properly introduced to the godfather of the king, and power behind the throne, filled me with trepidation. However, that same man had sent me on a mission and it was my duty to report my findings. Especially when the subject matter concerned the inner workings of the Company.

César steered me through the labyrinth of corridors, salons and staircases comprising the Palais Mazarin. Accustomed to large, formal residences, the opulence of the cardinal's home left me unmoved. The paintings I recognized to be the work of a Titian or a Poussin provided the backdrop for plumes arrayed in silver vases, candelabra resting on jasper tables and all manner of bric-a-brac. The display was a jumble of excessive splendor, no different from Fouquet's collection or the rich trappings of the Luxembourg. I was forced to admit, though, that for an immigrant hailing from a family of minor officials, Jules Mazarin had done very well for himself. Very well, indeed.

The immense, gilded doors that sheltered the private side of a highly visible, public figure eventually barricaded our course. Approaching the watchman, who recognized him right away, César gained us admission to the apartments with a nod and a whisper. Ushering me into the study, the man whom I was growing to admire more and more squeezed one of my hands in encouragement.

"His study is in there. Knock and go in. Do not be timid, Bijoux—Mazarin is not fearsome, truly."

"I am not afraid," I lied. "The cardinal is a mortal man like any other, correct?"

"No," he smiled, gathering me to him for another kiss, "for I am married to the woman I love. Hurry now; get this over with so we may go home to bed."

"César," I admonished, as if disappointed, "you do not wish to take me in the carriage?"

"I love you," he laughed, realizing my jest. "Get in there or I'll take you here."

I did as he said, rapping faintly upon lustrous, carved wood. Glancing back at my mate, he urged me on with a wave of a hand. The door was ajar, so I pushed it open to behold, in all his glory, the First Servant of France.

Attired in robes of red, Mazarin was seated within the

confines of an enormous, high-backed armchair, fast asleep. Two tiny, adorable monkeys, decked-out in dolls' clothing, were curled up in his lap, emulating their master.

Stepping inside the room, I cleared my throat. "Your Eminence, excuse me, I bring you a message."

At the sound of my voice, the furry creatures awoke with a chorus of screeching. Mazarin stirred, his eyes fluttered open and he straightened, with some difficulty, from a slumped position.

"Who are you?" he asked, quieting his pets with tiny strokes to their heads. "What brings you here in the dead of the night, impudent girl?"

"The safety of the realm. And a sincere desire to protect you, your Grace."

"So, mademoiselle, who might *you* be?"

"I am Bijoux Cinq-Mars, your agent recruited by M. d'Artagnan. It was I who procured the letters belonging to Madame de Choisy, detailing the plot to remove you and the queen should Prince Philippe come to the throne. You assigned me to watch the Fouquet residence at Saint-Mandé."

"Come closer."

I walked towards his chair, not expecting to be offered a seat since no one, not even the king, sat in Mazarin's presence. The cardinal reeked of a scent made expressly for him, the gloves he wore were so white they would have made mother green with envy. I understood how a queen might fall in love with him, for Mazarin was regal, dignified; his silver hair, moustache and goatee groomed with spiced oils.

The cardinal appraised my form before commenting in an accent not French, yet very melodious all the same, "You will be amused to know, Mademoiselle Bijoux, that I named my pets in honor of the two instigators of the plot you uncovered. Meet Choisy and Gonzaga—fitting, don't you agree?"

He snapped his fingers and the monkeys leapt to their feat, dancing together. Then they stopped, sat upon his knee and chattered at me, miniature hairy hands demanding a reward for their exhibition.

"They like you," he chuckled, bemused. "Now, tell me what you came to say, girl."

"Your Eminence, I know much concerning the Company of the Blessed Sacrament. I read the organization's Covenant, having discovered the document in Fouquet's desk."

"Yes? Yes? Do you have the papers in your possession?"

"No, Eminence, I could not steal them, for Fouquet would have suspected me. Yesterday morning he queried as to my association with you and then later, at a soirée just passed, he instructed Monsieur de la Fontaine to stay close to my side. The minister is wary of me, your Excellency."

"We shall right that wrong," the cardinal grinned, "do not fret. You were correct to leave the evidence. We shall have our proof. Do you remember any of the Covenant's contents?"

"The Company was founded in 1630 by the Duc de Ventadour," I began, "as a clerical and lay society dedicated to charitable works. Meetings are held every Thursday, the day dedicated to the Blessed Sacrament. Gatherings include a prayer hour, a report on activities, a collection of monies for the poor and scripture readings. The Company originated here, in Paris, yet has since spread to more than fifty provincial centers, linked by a strict code of secrecy. Some of the commanderies mentioned were Bourges, Gisors, Mount St. Michel, Paris, and an odd reference to a Château Barberie in Nevers."

"Nothing more?"

"According to the final statute, and I quote: *The cornerstone of the organization, the sacred knowledge which shapes the spirit of the Company of the Blessed Sacrament and is essential to its lifeblood, is the Secret.* That, and the membership wish your removal from France, your Grace."

Choisy and Gonzaga flew from Mazarin's lap, scurrying for refuge. The cardinal had bolted upright, fury enlivening his smooth features.

"Enough!" he bellowed. "Enough! I shall destroy them all should it require every last *sou* I possess! Depose me? How in Hades do they intend to do that?" he screamed.

"I...I don't know," I cowered.

"I shall *not* abide another Fronde!" Mazarin thundered. "Fornicating *zentildonne*! Have you told anyone, and I mean *anyone*, about this paper?" he demanded.

"No, your Grace. I know your intention was for me to send messages via César de la Tour, your page, but I thought this matter too delicate for anyone's ears but your own."

"What page? To whom are you referring?"

"César de la Tour, of the family d'Auvergne. He fetched me from the Luxembourg in July and escorted me to Saint-Mandé. He said he was your emissary. Is he, your Excellency?"

"Oh, him, yes. He asked for the assignment and I granted the request. Confide nothing to the lad, for his father was the late Duc de Bouillon, a leader of the Fronde, whose heirs and relations continue to conspire with that bastard, Gaston d'Orléans. Another whom I'd rather see dead," he paused thoughtfully, catching himself. "Behave as though you are passing this de la Tour fellow information—fool the conspirator. Ply him for tidbits—tease the boy—he most likely holds a morsel or two."

I was staring at the cardinal, transfixed. He had stunned me. I was married to the son of Frédéric-Maurice de la Tour, the duke who had also been involved in my father's Spanish Plot. César was the nephew of the illustrious commander, the Vicomte de Turenne, whose military genius was legendary.

Was my husband a member of the enemy faction, a plant sent to investigate me? Had I wed a man who wished to betray my confidences? If Mazarin discovered I was César's wife, my career would end.

"Why do you gawk at me, child? Do you fancy the lad?"

"No, certainly not, your Grace. Monsieur de la Tour has been kind to me…I did not think him the enemy."

"Perhaps not, yet we should not be too clever, now, should we, Mademoiselle Cinq-Mars?" Mazarin was calm, collected once more. "Keep an eye on him and on Fouquet. And one more thing—I am curious—do you despise me for my decision in the d'Artagnan affair?"

"No, Eminence," I said, hanging my head. "You were correct; the match was inappropriate."

"You are very wise for your years, mademoiselle," he replied. "I shall reward your loyal service, have no fear. I shall hand pick a husband for you myself. Agreed?"

"I do not wish to marry," I answered in a panic. "Please, not that, Monsieur le Cardinal."

"How odd," he observed, clicking his tongue against the roof of his mouth. "Well, perhaps you could keep my godson company someday. He is too attached to my nieces and we cannot have that. The people won't stand for their king consorting with any relation of mine."

He was offering me the ruler of France, just as Richelieu had promoted my father to Louis XIII.

"I would consider that proposition an honor, Eminence."

"Good, smart girl," he praised, talking to me as he did to dancing monkeys. "For now, however, let us concentrate on the Company. Expose their leadership; find the traitors out. Report to me alone, understand?"

"Yes, your Grace. I shan't disappoint you," I promised.

"Marvelous. Then our meeting is concluded," he smiled, offering me his ring to kiss.

I complied with the subjugation, wondering not about the cardinal, but rather about César.

Was I a complete fool? Did my husband love me? Had I made a terrible miscalculation?

"Off with you now," the cardinal sighed, pointing towards the door. "Contact me soon with more information, Mademoiselle *Cinq-Mars*."

"Yes, your Excellency," I assured him before taking my leave, not noticing the emphasis he had placed on my father's title, half-hearing the lock click as the door shut behind me.

César was napping in an upholstered *fauteuil*. His countenance was so peaceful, his demeanor so tranquil, that I was nearly moved to tears. He had to love me, I reasoned, it was not in his loyal, Taurean nature to lie. And he had gazed at me during the ceremony at St. Sulpice so wholeheartedly; no one could manufacture that emotion, no one. A camp had to be chosen. César or Mazarin. The Company or the king.

"Darling," I murmured. "Wake up. We should be on our way."

Having been roused from his slumber, César looked at me, perplexed. "Did the cardinal scream, or was I dreaming?"

"He almost popped a vein," I laughed nervously. "Not that the sight was amusing.."

"I love you," he interrupted, taking my face into his hands. "I have a room upstairs, Bijoux. Let us spend the night here. The coachman has been sent on his way. We are not going back to Saint-Mandé, unless to collect our belongings."

"Why not?"

"I promised to explain and I shall. You cannot spy on the Company because your new family is prominent in the group's leadership," he said softly. "I have sworn on my life to protect my brother, my late father's heir, Godefroy-Maurice, who no doubt would become a target of the cardinal's wrath should the latter pry too deeply into our affairs."

"We should not discuss this matter here. It is too dangerous. Let us away from these quarters."

We made our way to Cesar's room as fast as we were able. The bedchamber was small in size, but tastefully appointed, not a bad place to spend one's wedding night. I was also pleased that my husband had been honest with me, confirming my original impression that he was indeed a good person.

"César, I must confess some things to you," I began as he ran his lips along my neck, "things that perhaps I should not confess."

"Later," he murmured, joining his mouth to mine. Moving us toward the bed, we were soon atop it, César hovering over me.

"I love you," he reiterated, "I love you forever. Say that you love me, too."

"I adore you," I replied, running my fingers through his hair, helping him to remove his lovely jacket. Pulling a blouson out from breeches, my hands were under the material when freed, caressing his chest, his back, savoring the taut, muscular definition of his body.

"I want all of you, Bijoux," he insisted, parting me from my garb, leaving the pearls encircling my throat. "God, you are exquisite. I am the most fortunate man alive."

Hours passed, the Sun rose, and we finally lay quietly, sheets everywhere, hair intermingled on a pillow, fingers entwined. Our passionate coupling had left us consumed, yet, closer than it seemed two people could be. We fit together perfectly, as if divinely fashioned for the other alone.

"We must return to Saint-Mandé," I remarked dreamily. "If not, the cardinal will be on to us."

"So? We shall run away to England. My family has friends there."

"César, you don't understand, we cannot. I did not meet with Mazarin to discuss Fouquet."

"Damn," he cursed, closing his eyes. "Tell me everything."

And I did. I related the story of La Fontaine, the desk, and the Covenant. I told him about the cardinal, my betrayal, and the reaction. He listened intently, drawing me to him when I had finished.

"This is my fault, Bijoux, not yours. I should have confided in you sooner. Will you forgive me?"

"Forgive you? I feel terrible—I have placed your house in danger."

"What should we do?" he asked, trying not to despair in my presence. "Between the two of us, we might set this error aright; we simply must be more devious than the cardinal."

"We shall return to Saint-Mandé and play the besotted lovers, which should not be difficult to do," I said lightly, despite the somber mood. "You will inform your people that Mazarin is aware of the Company's motives, that you overheard him discussing the matter with d'Artagnan, or something similar. I shall go to Fouquet and throw myself at his feet, offering to become his agent, disguised as Mazarin's spy. Then you will give me false information about the Company to pass on to the cardinal; in fact, you should go to him yourself with a few yarns and he will no longer think you allied with Gaston."

"It might be a way to avoid disaster," he agreed. "My family will be livid..."

"Please, spare the Vicomte de Turenne the details. Do not give him cause to hate his nephew's wife."

"You know, then, that I am a Bouillon?"

My head shook in affirmation. "Mazarin told me. I don't care a whit for titles, César. You were sent to me by the wisest goddess above," I admitted, placing my head on his chest.

"St. Sulpice is the Company's headquarters," he said out-of-the-blue. "Did you know that?"

"No. What a strange happenstance we were married there, my dearest."

"Our marriage has nothing to do with chance," he whispered, his lips seeking mine.

"Love me, César," I replied. "Never stop loving me."

"Not until the day I die," he promised. "Even after death, we shall be together for eternity, sweet Bijoux."

I then willingly complied with Venus' amorous terms, covering my true love and myself with a bedcover to muffle the sounds of our fervid desire.

César and I were inseparable during the first six months of our marriage. Returning to Saint-Mandé, we were seen there constantly in one another's company, whether in the salon, gardens or laboratory. Anyone who viewed us would ascertain we were a couple; however, one soul alone knew of our nuptials besides the priest and the witness from St. Sulpice.

That person was César's uncle, Henri de la Tour d'Auvergne, the great Turenne, who was somewhat dismayed to learn his nephew had wed the only child of Monsieur le Grand, that infamous friend of his brother's youth. However, when the elder Bouillon was informed that my dowry consisted of fabulous jewels worth a king's ransom, he reconsidered his defiant stance. And, when he was told of our plans to foil Mazarin, protect the Company from further scrutiny, and to keep a watch on M. Fouquet, he agreed with César to postpone any announcement of our match.

The ruse was successful. César and I soon became the darling cupids of Saint-Mandé, our lovesick antics inspiring verses, songs and gossip. Fouquet embraced us fondly at soirées, his wife, Maria Magdalena of Castille, enviously espied her husband's retainers cavorting amongst the clipped bushes, and La Fontaine pinched my bottom every time he crossed our path, vowing to steal me from César. We symbolized pure, constant devotion to those cynical courtiers and their fascination with our public passion encouraged us to play convincing parts.

On March 5, 1659, Charles de Batz Castelmore and Charlotte-Anne de Chanlecy made their union legal, my former governess having become a widow shortly after César and I wed. The couple signed their marriage contract in the presence of court, cardinal and king at the Louvre, d'Artagnan's relatives conspicuously absent.

As was I.

The bride saw fit to invite members of her own noble family and certain politically advantageous guests, not allowing for any in attendance who might mention her previous life spent as an outcast at the Luxembourg. Or who might prompt a longing sensation within her new husband's heart.

The snub was obvious, but I was glad for the pair despite it. D'Artagnan had been in need of a wife and likewise an income, for it was his duty as acting commander to outfit the Grand Musketeers from his personal war chest. Charlotte-Anne thus provided companionship and security, for her late spouse had willed her the Barony of St. Croix with its hefty revenues and sixty thousand in coin. Monsieur and Madame d'Artagnan would be content and free from financial burdens, living quite comfortably in their recently purchased hôtel on the Rue du Bac.

Mazarin, for his part, did not allow me the opportunity to brood, constantly pestering for information concerning his archenemy. The cardinal's notes begged, pleaded, prodded and demanded; rarely satisfied with the fibs César and I shuttled to various palaces via courier. We thought we were masters of intrigue, of course, befuddling Mazarin with false reports of Company treasure supposedly buried at Château Barberie, or with fantastic claims such as the rebels were plotting to kidnap the king and place their own candidate upon the throne. However, the cardinal's creed was *Time and I,* and when the dispatches stopped coming to Saint-Mandé in April, shortly following Easter Sunday, we should have known something was awry.

By May, rumors were flying that Mazarin had disinherited his nephew, Philippe-Julien, sending the young lieutenant of the Grand Musketeers to a prison in Alsace. D'Artagnan, oddly enough, was chosen to arrest his superior officer, and Charles officially assumed temporary command of the troops. The entire court knew that the youth was intimate with the Petit Monsieur's Guiche, that the two noble rakes had formed a secret society, *The Order of the Sodomites,* whose membership wore a cross under their respective tunics, upon which was engraved the likeness of a man trampling a woman. Yet, was that an offense worthy of severe public rebuke? Evidently, in the cardinal's opinion.

Mazarin remained silent. Then, in June, the king exiled Guiche to his family estate; a certain Duc de Vivonne was placed under house arrest at his château in Roissy; a royal chaplain, Le Camus, was dismissed from his high post; one Roger de Bussy-Rabutin, an intellectual, was served with an order to repair to his ancestral home in Burgundy. The court gristmill exploded, in turn, and the sound of the blast could be heard quite distinctly throughout the environs of Paris.

And the shrapnel found its way to Saint-Mandé.

CHAPTER TEN
Poseidon's Cup

César decided to investigate into the scandal and rode off for Paris and the Hôtel Bouillon to confer with his relations. When he returned to find me in one of Saint-Mandé's many drawing rooms, chatting with the fascinating Madame du Plessis, my husband approached, bowed before Fouquet's favourite, and then led me upstairs in favor of a more intimate venue to discuss the recent goings-on.

Mazarin had gone mute because he was busy squashing a disgraceful incident involving his nephew and the group of reprimanded courtiers. According to César's brother, the Duc de Vivonne had invited the merry band to spend the Easter holiday with him at the Château de Roissy, not too far a distance from Saint-Mandé. Arriving on the eve of Maundy Thursday, the friends enjoyed a sedate dinner and then each went to their chambers to retire, perfectly behaved. However, the priest, Le Camus, became nervous because the debauched Guiche was in residence, packed his bags, and quit the château on Good Friday morn. He sensed a revel was about to take place—one he had no interest in attending.

The chaplain's fears were not unfounded. A friend of Guiche, Bertrand Manicamp, appeared on the scene, woke everyone and although it was the most solemn religious day on the Church's calendar—a day intended for fasting and devotions—the boys decided to celebrate, downing many bottles of wine, telling off-color jokes and planning the evening's repast. Choosing a pig from the estate's livestock pen, they baptized the creature Trout, announced it to be born again as a fish, and had the hog delivered to the butcher so the beast might be prepared for that night's feast.

The problem was, being good Catholics all, they were well aware that meat was not allowed on Friday's table, although the brash gentlemen cared not for canon law as they became more and more inebriated. A hunt was organized, the friends mounted their steeds and together they tore off across the countryside, searching for game.

Guiche and Manicamp, breaking away from the others, located their prey. An old man, riding past the two, en route to the capital, was waylaid by the pair and dragged back to Roissy for a bit of fun. The elderly traveler claimed to be Cardinal Mazarin's lawyer and demanded his captors set him free, yet the daredevils laughed as though the solicitor were mad. Then, their cohorts came home, and the gang of five tied the emissary to a chair, forcing him to imbibe many goblets of drink. When they were convinced that their hostage was quite drunk, they sent him on his way, not caring whether the victim of their cruel prank made it to Paris or not.

While César recounted the tale, I stared at him, amazed. He stopped to take a deep breath and I interrupted, saying, "They are beasts. How dare they be so arrogant? Thank the gods that the Petit Monsieur was not present, for Louis would have flogged his brother, himself!"

"They are worse than beasts," César sighed. "I have not finished the Good Friday saga. After eating 'Trout', the crew took to singing profane songs concerning the female anatomy, drinking more wine and eventually falling into various beds where partners were traded throughout the night."

"Leave it to Guiche."

"Precisely," he grimaced. "On Holy Saturday, the Duc de Vivonne sent for a parish priest of ill repute. According to my brother, little is known of this renegade, except he is said to be a sorcerer. To wit, when arriving at the château, the priest encouraged his hosts to drink several bottles of wine. Setting up a makeshift altar, the abbé then conducted a Black Mass over the naked body of Mazarin's nephew, complete with a desecrated wafer. When finished, the others were instructed by the one-eyed priest to kiss Manzini's proffered buttocks in tribute to certain daemons."

"What? César, this thing cannot be true!" I cried out. "Do you know what you are saying?"

"My brother, Godefroy, gave me the details himself. Why the alarm?"

"The priest, that Satanist, is the Abbé Guibourg. He is the man who performed Black Masses with my mother on the Rue St. Denis, he is the vilest being alive! César, he is searching for me, I know it! He is looking for the jewels—he plans to kill me!"

"Darling, stop," he advised, taking me into his arms. "How could this person know what has become of you? Why would he do you harm if he did? Many priests dabble in the occult, dearest. Your Guibourg is not the abbé whom Vivonne employed."

"Yes he is. His name is Étienne and he was blinded by d'Artagnan on the night before the cardinal went into exile. I was present, César, when he lost his eye—Guibourg vowed to see me die."

"We best discuss this, should we not?"

And we did. For hours. I told him my story, omitting no detail. César heard of curses, Black Masses, the woods of Versailles, daemons, *The Key of Solomon*, failed abortions, transvestites, court intrigues, and a soul who had been miserable before she had found love. True love. A love that had made her feel safe, invincible. That is, until Roissy.

My husband was speechless when I finished, lying atop the bedstead, quiet and pensive.

"Are you peeved?" I ventured, afraid I had said too much. "Do you understand why I am terrified of Guibourg, why I told you that I am a *vrykolakas*?"

"You should have confided in me sooner; I would not have stopped loving you."

I could not speak.

"Come to me," César smiled. Feeling at the back of my neck, he located the wen, pulled my hair aside and inspected the growth.

"This is nothing," he confirmed. "Noctambule was a magician, no doubt, a conjurer who wished to scare a little girl. The same for Guibourg. What you have endured, my poor Bijoux."

Our lips met momentarily, yet I pulled away, suddenly annoyed.

"If Jesus, your Christ, could rise from the dead, if he could bring Lazarus back to life as purported in the Bible, then why does a daemon such as Noctambule not exist?"

"The two are not the same thing," he chuckled.

"Why not?" I countered.

"Do not blaspheme," he warned.

"Does your Church recognize the existence of Satan?"

"Why do you insist on arguing with me, Bijoux?"

"Because I must drink a tonic or else die, remember? A fear you could never understand torments me, haunts me daily. Do you think me crazed?"

"No..."

"Then explain why you doubt me," I demanded angrily. "Tell me why Noctambule is a phantom, but a man named Jesus the Christ has been proclaimed the Son of God! Prove *that* miracle to me, monsieur. I put my trust in a goddess who sent *me* a messenger direct from Olympus above."

"Bijoux, I swear, stop this heresy!" he ordered. "I shan't tolerate such talk from my wife, of all people! Did I wed an ignorant peasant or a learned lady?"

That was when I slapped him across the face with all the strength I possessed.

"Ignorant? Go to Hades!" I shouted. "Or better still, read the story of your Christ's temptation; you may learn something."

His expression was one of rage. "Do you know who I am?" he fumed. "Do you have any notion what you are saying? My ancestor was the crusader Godfroi de Bouillon, King of Jerusalem! And Jesus the Christ..." he stopped.

"Was *who*? Why is the Company concerned with restoring their candidate to the throne? Is he another knight in search of a Jerusalem?"

"*That* does not concern you!" César roared. "Keep your nose out of *my* family's affairs, madame."

"Gladly," I shot back. "My nose and everything else, monsieur."

Running away, I made for the garden in tears. I found myself wishing César had not told me of Roissy or Black Masses, and I was blaming myself for taunting him about Jesus and Godfroi de Bouillon. In hindsight, I did not give a damn about the netherworld or the agenda of the Company of the Blessed Sacrament if it meant losing my true love's respect and trust.

Saint-Mandé's grounds were especially delightful in June, yet I hardly noticed the fragrant orange blossoms overhead or the delicate blooms forming intricate patterns across the rolling lawns. César hated me and the world was black; life meant nothing to me without him in it.

'Twas then a gentle voice greeted my petulant form and I jumped from fright, immersed as I was in my bad humor.

"A lovely day, is it not, Mademoiselle Bijoux?"

The middle-aged man addressing me was a stranger; a commoner, by the look of his plain costume.

"You are correct, monsieur—forgive me, your name?"

"André Le Nôtre, at your service, mademoiselle. I am the gardener who has noticed you and your young man, from time to time, frolicking amongst these bouquets I tend. Everyone at Saint-Mandé knows César and Bijoux," he grinned warmly.

"And everyone knows you, too, monsieur. You are an artist, not a gardener!"

"I do what I love and I love what I do," he replied serenely, "though your praise warms my heart."

"Tell me, Monsieur Le Nôtre, do you employ the study of the stars in your plantings? You must be aware that Luna, positioned in the water signs of the Crab, Scorpion or the Fish, is best suited for the sowing of seeds, while when found in the Bull or Capricornus, produces strong, hardy plants," I advised, tears streaming despite my attempt to maintain a modicum of composure.

He touched my shoulder with compassion. "Is everything as it should be?"

"No, monsieur, it is not. César and I have quarreled and I fear he will never talk to me again—we said such horrible things to one another."

"There, there, Mademoiselle Bijoux. Stroll with me and we shall discuss this grave matter amidst nature's majesty. The fresh air will do your sad heart good."

Offering me his arm, we walked slowly between the low hedges running alongside the gravel path, Monsieur Le Nôtre listening attentively as I spoke of the argument. No doubts checked my confiding in the tall man of aquiline nose, sturdy build and affable disposition; I did not fret that he would think me wicked. Indeed, the wizard with spade and hoe reassuringly patted my hand.

"A Divine Order exists in this Universe and you are a part of it, *ma petite*," he reflected following my confession. "You worry yourself—a waste of time—for the Plan will look after you and you need not look after it. Simply be happy with your lover and be kind to others, if you would receive kindness in return."

"But what about eternal life and…"

"You are eternal, I am eternal, this bloom is eternal. Leave the details to the philosophers such as our late Monsieur Descartes, dear girl. Or to the priests," he chuckled good-naturedly.

"Does evil not exist, monsieur?"

Le Nôtre frowned. "When we do injury to others, we hurt ourselves. The Law sees all."

"What law?"

"Read more concerning your dear goddess Athena, Bijoux. She helped many a hero to understand life's meaning."

"At times I think I shall never understand life's meaning, monsieur."

"Just live and you will," he laughed. "You remind me of my own youth; fortunately, I had a wise friend long ago, one Monsieur Poussin, who taught me many truths."

"Not the painter!"

"The very same, mademoiselle. Too bad he lives in Rome, I miss him greatly." Le Nôtre halted our promenade and shook his head. "Back to work, mademoiselle. I must be off to Vaux."

"Vaux, monsieur? Is the house as beautiful as people report?"

"Bijoux, it is perfection, the greatest private residence in Europe."

"When do the workmen expect to finish, monsieur?"

"In two years time, I should think. Three villages have been demolished to make room for the château's park and their water supply has been sent running into reservoirs chiseled from Italianite marble—Monsieur Le Vau is building grottos, canals, and fountains everywhere. M. Poussin is designing beautiful statues of the gods and goddesses that are so lifelike..."

Le Nôtre's eyes shone, he gazed off into the distance as if viewing the completed edifice in a vision; a glorious, gilded dream dedicated to the Twelve of Olympus.

"*Et in Arcadia ego*," he said softly.

"Monsieur?"

"A quote from the great Virgil, and the subject of a painting by M. Poussin. Do you believe, *ma petite,* that heaven may be found before we die?"

I was considering the question when Le Nôtre nudged me. "I see your César approaching!"

My throat tightened. "Will you excuse me, monsieur?" I pleaded, disentangling my arm from his. "I must be going, although it was a pleasure conversing with you."

"Stay," he smiled. "Granted, Saint-Mandé is a large estate, however, you cannot hide from your sweetheart forever. Nor should you wish to."

His estimation was correct. Bowing in farewell, Le Nôtre then departed, leaving me alone.

"Shall we begin anew?" my husband asked when he was close enough to be heard. "Or shall we continue this present nonsense?"

César was so handsome—hair blowing behind him on a summer's breeze; crisp, white blouson open at the neck, tan cavalier breeches and boots worn earlier for the ride to court—that I trembled to think he was mine, I was awed by the power of his hold over me. We greeted one another in an embrace, the altercation no longer important.

"Forgive me," he begged, "for I am the worst husband in Christendom to ignore your concerns. I pledge to find this Guibourg and to run him through, should you desire it. And, beginning today, no more talk of Mazarin or the Company. Your health—making you well—is my main concern. From this moment onward, I shan't rest until I discover a cure for what ails you."

"Chromius, my true heart, your love is all I need to be well," I assured him in a choked voice. "You are the best tonic for me. Never doubt that."

Looking up, I caught sight of Monsieur Le Nôtre waving good-bye from the far end of the pebble-strewn promenade. Thinking of his words, I held onto César as tightly as I was able. The garden architect knew of what he spoke, I reflected, for life could indeed be a paradise when Love's law prevailed.

The reminder that the Abbé Guibourg was alive and performing his old tricks was not the most pleasant fact to be gleaned from the Easter scandal of Roissy; yet, another sinister force was also put into motion due to those same circumstances. Cardinal Mazarin, annoyed as much by the mistreatment of his advocate as he had been by the details of the Black Mass, realized that punishing the culprits had not sated his need for retribution.

The Italian had tired of being ignored by the nobility, threatened by the caprice of the masses, and overtly mocked by most Frenchmen in general. The time had come for harsh action, to make a show of force worthy a Richelieu, to reclaim the honor and respect due a leader of France. Mazarin had been pushed too far, and he retaliated in kind by attacking that group which had provoked his wrath more than any other: the Company of the Blessed Sacrament.

In a rage unbecoming a servant of the Church, Mazarin reviewed the messages I had sent, consulted his map and considered the various locations mentioned as Company commanderies. Bourges did not interest him, Mont St. Michel was virtually impregnable, and his other spies had been unable to ferret out where the Paris headquarters of the traitors was situated. The placement of Château Barberie, however, intrigued the cardinal, for he would like to add the title of Duc de Nevers to his name, as well as a buried treasure to his personal fortune.

That coup could best be accomplished by razing the castle and intimidating the owners into selling him the scorched land. Thus, on July 11, 1659, the king's troops entered the province of Nivernais, proceeded to Nevers, and completely destroyed Château Barberie and its surrounding village. The cardinal also signed a contract with the lord of that domain, dated on the same day, deeding to him the enemy's decimated property. To Mazarin's dismay, the soldiers found no loot. For my part, a goodly-sized bag of gold *louis* arrived at my door, and I was never contacted by the cardinal again.

The Italian statesman's disappointment did not matter, for Madame du Plessis had approached me in June to work on Fouquet's behalf, and I had accepted, sensing the dismissal in advance.

César was unaware of my arrangement with the older Breton woman to spy for the surintendant, mainly because he studied medicine day and night. Shut away in his room, he would pour over books on loan to him from the laboratory; translations of works by an Englishman named William Harvey, who had discovered that blood circulated throughout the body, and a compilation of Leonardo da Vinci's notes, printed in 1651, with illustrations done by Poussin. Monsieur Pecquet was so impressed with his pupil's quest for knowledge, that he had offered to recommend him to Oxford College in England, where he might be tutored by the most advanced minds of our age; yet, César refused, saying his work could be done just as effectively at Saint-Mandé.

I breathed a sigh of relief when told that we were staying put where we were, for, although my lover and I saw less of one another due to his resolve to heal me, I was having a marvelous time fulfilling my new post as Madame du Plessis' helpmate and companion.

Fouquet's best friend insisted I accompany her to parties, salon gatherings, the theater, and to the Louvre. Her sponsorship was unlike Choisy's, since Madame du Plessis was interested in me for my mind, not in the trade she might conduct with my body. She was a remarkable woman who saw things for what they truly were, and her understanding of business, usually left to gentlemen's devices, was keen. Riding back and forth in her grand carriage from entertainment to entertainment, I listened to and learned from the lady whom I had grown to idolize. People might mumble that Fouquet spoiled the lovely Susanne with extravagant tokens of his esteem, and many speculated as to whether the woman ten years Nicolas' senior was in actuality his mistress, but I knew that those courtiers who slandered her were jealous of an intelligence they themselves did not possess.

Plus, the lady was a Virgo.

Plessis was blond and beautiful, wild in her habits, free to do as she pleased, and I wished to be compared to her more than anyone else in the world.

Returning late one night from a ballet staged at the Tuileries, where I had managed to steal a glimpse of the king, I reeled into César's apartment, heady from the evening's festivities and too many goblets of drink consumed with Fouquet and his shadow. Madame, who liked her spirits as much as any man, had been in a raucous mood, amusing her patron and pupil the entire way home. Unfortunately, I noticed that as we roared with laughter at the bawdy tales of court depravity, a sensual stare directed at me by the surintendant. Then, a bejeweled hand was casually placed underneath the folds of my traveling cloak, granting access to my waist. Lord Cléonime held me close to his side, for I was too timid to pull away from the gentleman who attracted me in a manner I was unable to fathom.

"Aren't we merry," César remarked as I stumbled into the room where he lounged across the bed, studying a picture of the human anatomy with grave intent. Autumn had arrived and a chill pervaded the air. "Did you enjoy the fête?"

"The ballet was lovely, but I would have had a better time if you had come with me," I flirted, aware that I smelled of Fouquet's spicy perfume.

"How could you be lonely when you had Madame du Plessis to keep you occupied?" he asked somewhat dejectedly. Putting his book down on a side table, he stood and approached where I teetered, too unsure on my feet to stand still.

"You best be off to bed," he chided in an inoffensive way. "Whenever you go out-and-about with your mentor, you come home tipsy."

"Don't be churlish," I pouted, untying his shirt. "Do you still love me?"

"Now I *know* that you're in your cups! Why else do I toil, save for your benefit?"

"Well, I would hope you might be learning a few things as well," I replied. "If you don't want to do it anymore, don't."

Without uttering a word, César took hold of my hand and led me to the bed. Feeling romantic, I began to kiss him on the neck, certain a passion-filled evening awaited us. Fouquet had aroused strong sensations within my person, a longing I wished my husband would satisfy.

"Wait," he said unexpectedly. "I have a surprise for you."

"For me?"

César turned, went to the armoire, and produced a package covered in a rough material.

"I was going to show you tomorrow, but the suspense is too great. Open it."

With eager fingers, the string encircling the bundle was untied, the crudely spun cloth fell away to reveal a volume whose cover appeared to be cut from a piece of untanned animal hide. I would have recognized the album had I drunk ten bottles of wine.

"*The Key of Solomon!*" I cried out. "How did you ever get your hands on it?"

"An associate of my uncle stole into Guibourg's house on the Rue St. Denis. A priest should not have such contraband in his keeping."

"Let us see if the reference to the *vrykolakas* is here."

The book's pages went flipping at my touch, yet, César took the tome from me.

"Give it back," I whined. "I want to find the thing now, not later."

"The answer you seek is not there. I already examined the volume."

"What? Guibourg said *vrykolakas* was a Greek term found in *The Key of Solomon*."

"Well, he was mistaken. I read every single, strange entry and no mention of *vrykolakas*. I think that he deceived you."

Not wishing to argue, I bit my tongue and became quiet. Undoing my hair, held in place by combs cut from mother-of-pearl, the strands tumbled almost to my waist. César looked down, defeated.

"Don't be disappointed, Bijoux. We'll look again in the morning. Perhaps I missed it, that's all."

"I shall be busy with Madame du Plessis all the day. Fouquet requires us to help him decide on a wedding presentation for the king."

"What? Louis is to be married? When?"

"Soon, evidently. It appears Mazarin will conclude a peace treaty with the Spanish before year's end and the surintendant expects that the cardinal will arrange a match between his godson and the Infanta of Spain. The queen desires the marriage."

"How does Fouquet always know?" César marveled. "Is he endowed with a second sight?"

"No, many spies and much money to pay them with, dear. Shall we retire?"

When we had undressed and crawled beneath the blankets, César blew out the candle on the night stand next to the less-than-spacious bed upon which we lay.

"Thank you for stealing Guibourg's book," I said, addressing the darkness. "I appreciate the fact that you tried to solve the mystery."

Wrapping his legs around mine, drawing closer, our naked bodies met, one warming the other.

"I'll search the book again. There must be a clue in there somewhere. Damn it!" he muttered.

"Stop, César," I advised, kissing him on the forehead. "The tonic keeps me well enough, forget the rest. I am more concerned with Fouquet's choice of gift—what does one present to a king and queen on their wedding day?"

"I don't know," he snorted. "A dwarf?"

"A dwarf? Why say you that?"

"The Spaniards love them. Come to think of it, even Mary of Guise had her little page, Jarvis. And she became Queen of the Scots."

"A clever notion. You are brilliant, my love."

"Bijoux, promise never to leave me," César suddenly whispered from the shadows, sounding fearful.

"César de la Tour, I vow never to leave your side. Count on it."

A weary head rested against my bosom. Presently I heard heavy breathing, for my husband had surrendered to the lure of slumber.

Annoyed by the unintentional rebuff, my main concern should have been that, unlike my spouse, I could not envision, or worse, consider, an existence that did not include in it the person whom I loved and adored.

Fouquet practically danced a jig when I mentioned César's idea of bestowing a miniature human on the king and his Hispanic bride at the celebration of their marriage, if and when it occurred. The enthusiastic minister hugged me in Madame du Plessis' presence and made it well known how pleased he was with my work, despite the fact I claimed no credit. When I reiterated that a dear friend had made the suggestion, Nicolas shrugged his shoulders and proclaimed that from that day forth, he would call me *La Loy*, or the loyal one, in recognition of my devoted service to him. Much to my chagrin, I had the uneasy feeling the Future wished me to do more than spy on his behalf, although I had no intention of entertaining a man who had known my mother intimately, César or no.

That particular game of cat and mouse began to intensify in November, on the eighteenth to be exact, when I accompanied the surintendant to the opening performance of the play *The Ridiculous Précieuses*, written by the actor and playwright, Monsieur Molière. The production was staged in Paris at the theater christened after the Petit Monsieur, and the drama was a biting satire aimed at that group of which Choisy, Fouquet and Mademoiselle de Scudéry were all a part.

Mazarin, no doubt, had lent a hand in the creation of the farce, for he considered the literary clique to be nothing more than an extension of the Company of the Blessed Sacrament and was determined to make light of its membership. And with Molière's comic genius illuminating the script, the cardinal's revenge was a success. Needless to say, following the final curtain call, the ride to Saint-Mandé was a silent one, Fouquet brooding in a corner seat of his regal coach, quite distraught, ignoring my presence.

"Monsieur," I prompted, "are you ill?"

Fouquet glanced at me as an aside, head barely moving, dark eyes smoldering, a mustached countenance sinister. Holding out a gloved hand, he motioned for me to sit closer.

"I need you here," he explained. "The beautiful La Loy, who makes my heart glad."

"Really, monsieur," I blushed uncomfortably. "Are you not worried that your friends may be harmed by Molière's attack?"

"No," he sighed. "I fear our *Samedis* are a thing of the past. To be a *Précieuse* is to be a fool."

"You would turn your back on them, monsieur? Have you no honor?"

My senior of twenty-five years smiled with a lover's intent. "You are so good, so kind," he whispered, leaning closer. "So unlike Marion."

"Monsieur!" I laughed. "How crass of you to speak of my sainted mother in such a manner! But... you are correct. The marquise was not the nicest person. Why then, were you her lover?"

"I don't recall. Forget the association. Come to me, Bijoux."

"Monsieur...I cannot."

I thought my meaning plain and I meant to put him off with the statement, but Fouquet was having none of it. He kissed my neck softly and I felt tempted to succumb to his amorous advances.

"Please stop. I am pledged to another."

"Ah, yes, the dashing César," he remarked in a nasty tone, sitting up straight, staring out the adjacent carriage window. "I do not suffer rivals gladly, mademoiselle...or should I say... Madame de la Tour?"

My husband would be punished if I continued the charade. Reaching out to the surintendant, I touched the shadow of a beard appearing on his pointed chin.

"Are your feelings for me sincere, monsieur? Or am I mere sport in your eyes?"

The manner in which his mouth devoured mine left me pushing him away for breath. No man had ever kissed me with such abandon—not d'Artagnan, nor César. His passion was all consuming, and as he crushed me to him, the blood raced through my veins in a torrent of wild and uncontrollable heat.

"Do you not like me, La Loy, not even a little?" he demanded, causing me to shiver at the sound of his low-toned, tormented solicitation.

Closing my eyes, I swallowed hard, thinking of César and our love pact. How could I betray him? And yet, the surintendant's hands were upon me, I was not stopping him from tampering with the finery I had donned earlier with his very taste in mind: a sumptuous gown of midnight blue velvet and silver embroidery worked in a celestial motif.

"I refuse to make love to you in a coach, monsieur. Other ladies may find the arrangement convenient; however, I do not."

"Then we shall repair to my Paris hôtel," he offered. "Or anywhere you like. Tonight."

Fouquet was a most adept lover and where his lips journeyed next, made it near impossible to push him away.

"And your duties? Were we not to travel to Le Havre tomorrow to inspect the dwarfs from which you are to select the Infanta's companion? Or had you forgotten?"

"No," he teased, entranced. "In fact, on the advice of an associate, I contacted that premier slave trader, the Company of the Islands of America, and the owner of the firm located a perfect male dwarf, Nabo, to send to us at Saint-Mandé."

Nicolas removed his dress sword and rapped on the carriage roof with its hilt.

"Nabo? What sort of name is that? Babylonian?"

"He is a Moor from North Africa and is but two feet three inches tall. The little fellow is supposedly quite adorable and musically gifted; both should please the princess. No doubt, everyone at court will fancy a blackamoor once they see their new queen with one."

"I do not understand the fashion, yet, to each his own," I remarked, shaking my head. "At least the poor thing will be well cared for."

"Considering that you are going to train him for me, yes."

"What?" I asked, astonished. "Me? Why not Madame du Plessis?"

"I need her to assist me with other matters, dearest. Since Nabo was your idea, I thought you would be pleased to teach him manners and some rhymes."

"As you wish," I acquiesced in a pique. "When does he arrive?"

"Tomorrow. If the king is married in June, that allows you six months to work with the Moor. More than enough time," he grinned, reaching out and pulling me to him again. "You have not asked me why we have stopped, my beauty."

"I think you have begged enough favors for one evening, monsieur. If you are intent on winning my heart, you must earn it as would any other gentleman."

"Would any other gentleman gift you this?"

Fouquet reached inside his *justacorps* and produced a tightly rolled parchment, tied securely with a silver cord.

"A piece of paper, monsieur? A land grant, a title?"

"No, Bijoux," he declared, kissing me again and again, "the Secret."

I blanched, unable to wrest my gaze from his own.

"You understand my meaning? Of what I speak?"

I nodded slowly, my arms wrapping about his neck, my lips joined to his in a sure sign of capitulation. Tossing the bribe aside, he began to unlace and possess that which he craved, leaning me back onto velvet bolsters, pushing into me with delight.

"I'll have all of you yet," he boasted as he completed the conquest. "When you see Vaux, then you will desire me every evening—Monsieur Le Brun must decorate a bedchamber to celebrate our union. Would you care for an erotic mural to gaze at? Mirrors?"

"Whatever pleases you, monsieur, is likewise my joy," I panted in response to his silken caresses.

Fouquet kept me with him in the carriage another hour. He possessed me against my better judgment, yet the Sun and the Moon were both conjunct, languishing in Scorpion, a placement that makes the clandestine exciting.

"You are mine at last," he sighed, holding me against a bared chest, our clothing awry from numerous adventures. "Later, we shall meet again, in a more proper setting."

"What of your wife, monsieur? Must we not display caution?"

"Such as this?" he murmured, fondling a bared bosom. "Or this?" whereupon dark curls traveled the length of my torso, lingering in a region that brought me more pleasure than I thought possible.

"Stop," I protested in vain. "Enough. I am breaking a vow to another, monsieur."

"To whom?" Fouquet asked, returning his lips to my face. "To that boy? Bijoux, listen to me. I intend to shower you with wealth, finery, anything you desire. Will César promise the same? He will not even confide in you a mere secret, now, will he?"

"Monsieur, stop, that is cruel," I began to sob, overcome with guilt.

"When Vaux is complete, I shall make you my queen," he promised. "Bijoux, say you agree to become my favourite. You should not weep. You should be mine. For all of this night and every other...what say you, my angel of love?"

Still thinking of the document, I nodded, sealing the pact with another show of intimate devotion.

"Do you truly love me?" he demanded when we were once more one. "Am I your master—as of this moment and forever?"

"Yes," I heard myself saying, "yes."

"Confess no more or I shall lose control," Nicolas warned, leaving my body abruptly. "Do not entice me further lest I get you with child."

Neither of us spoke again during the return trip, choosing to rearrange our costumes with care. Arriving at the iron gates, the minister stared into my eyes with rapt adoration.

"I shall send for you when Nabo arrives. And we must see to moving your quarters closer to my own, agreed?"

"Yes, monsieur."

"And you will keep me pleasant company as you have this evening, my sweet?"

"I tremble in anticipation of that moment, my love."

"Prove your resolve to me with a kiss."

I coveted the Secret so badly that the surintendant received an embrace that did not end before the team slowed their pace outside the house.

"You have truly impressed me," he smiled, "truly. And because you have pleased me so greatly, take your much deserved reward, lovely Comaetho."

My mouth opened, dumbfounded that he knew of the myth, though no words issued forth. The scroll rested in my opened hands.

"And La Loy," Fouquet added as he stepped down from the vehicle, not waiting for me to follow, "be advised that I plan to care for you far better than a de la Tour ever could. You are a Cinq-Mars, don't forget, remember your father's example."

I undid the cord and unrolled the enticement—the paper was blank.

"How could I possibly forget my parentage?" I pondered aloud, leaning against a padded, leather wall. Realizing I had been made a fool, my fist pounded on the seat in rage and frustration. Fouquet had me where he wanted me and soon he would be in my bed for as long as he deemed necessary.

Unless I devised a way to be rid of Cléonime.

Nabo, the slave boy from North Africa who had been wrested from his home six months prior at an early age, reached Saint-Mandé on the morn following my tryst with Fouquet. The Moor was indeed diminutive in stature and pleasing in appearance, according to Madame du Plessis, who woke me so I might attend to the dwarf's needs immediately. The surintendant was apparently thrilled with his purchase and could hardly wait for me to meet the exotic curiosity, yet, as I confessed to my confidante, I was not happy with the assignment. Madame calmed me by offering her guidance and support in the endeavor, for she could see my hesitation was sincere. One way or another, Nabo would be trained in courtly manners and perfectly turned-out when handed over to the king's bride or else I would be blamed for any failure, that much was certain.

The meeting with the stranger took place as soon as I was able to dress, kiss César good-bye and run downstairs to Fouquet's apartments on the first floor, located above the great salon and reception rooms on the ground level. Madame du Plessis led the way, excited by all the commotion Nabo's arrival had caused in the courtyard. Stable hands and household staff had congregated before the great house when the dark-skinned youth debarked from the carriage that had transported him from Le Havre, a port located on the northern coast, to the outskirts of Vincennes.

Held in the arms of a representative of the Company of the Islands of America, the tiny newcomer waved merrily to the assembled throng when greeted by their stares, which caused the servants to cheer him soundly, captivated by a gigantic smile and bright eyes. The Moor may have been far from his own land and unaccustomed to the ways of Europeans, but in his heart he loved his fellow humans and they, in turn, responded with their own show of affection.

Any apprehension I harbored towards Nabo disappeared the moment we caught sight of one another; he, balanced on Fouquet's knee, I, peaking cautiously around a bedchamber door. When Nicolas saw me, his face brightened appreciatively and he held a hand out in welcome, yet I needed no encouragement. Rushing into the surintendant's private suite, I went directly to the chest at the foot of the four-poster canopy where the two sat, getting acquainted.

"Is he not an adorable creature?" Fouquet asked. "Did any queen in history possess a finer pet than our Nabo?"

"For the gods' sake, monsieur, he is a person, not a pet," I admonished, picking up the small boy. A ring of gold pierced through the lobe of an ear and Nabo's skin was the color of ebony, blue-black and fine. Tightly curled hair the shade of a raven's wing covered his skull and he was precious, unique, with the biggest, brownest gaze that would capture any soul it encountered. And it met with mine. I was immediately won over by his charm.

"Does he speak our language, monsieur?"

"A few words. Better that he learn Spanish, though, for the Infanta's French is limited. I think you should play games with him, accustom the lad to being in a lady's presence, teach him some tricks."

"In the fashion of Mazarin's monkeys, perhaps?"

Fouquet found my observation amusing, although it was not intended to be. Grinning widely, he stood, approached and patted one of my cheeks hard enough to leave the trace of a sting. Perhaps he had recognized my sarcasm, I deduced, wincing from the love tap, disliking him all over again.

"Madame du Plessis, please take our guest to the library. La Loy will be along presently."

Madame attempted to relieve me of my charge, who did not intend to let go of the red hair he held firmly in his grasp. Cajoling Nabo with sweet nothings, we finally persuaded him to be transferred to the older woman's keep. Yet he whimpered plaintively as she led him outside, probably afraid he would be transported to yet another, unfamiliar locale.

"Poor thing; it makes me sad to imagine him being taken from his home by profiteers."

Fouquet was not moved. "Would that you were so concerned with *my* sentiments, mademoiselle. Your sharp retort to a simple request has left me very uneasy *vis-à-vis* our conversation of last night."

"Would you rather an idiot for a mistress, monsieur? I was merely jesting, Lord Cléonime."

"So, you remember my nickname from the *Samedi*, eh? What a good memory you have," Fouquet admitted, impressed. "How old were you when you challenged me at Scudéry's?"

"Fifteen."

"And now? Nineteen, twenty?"

"Nineteen, monsieur."

"I usually am not attracted to girls your age. You know that, don't you?"

I said nothing in response.

"Return this evening, after nine. I shall be here, working. Perhaps, if you like, we may peruse the building plans for Vaux, so you might better acquaint yourself with the palace where you will be installed as unofficial queen."

Shocked, I curtsied and fled. Fouquet was not about to forget the impassioned promises of the carriage. He had no intention of sharing me with anyone. Flying down the grand staircase, I literally ran through the main salon to the library, collapsing against Madame du Plessis, scaring Nabo half out of his wits. By then I was sobbing, sure all hope was lost, and wondering how I would explain the surintendant's attentions to the man with whom I was deeply in love.

"*Bon Dieu*, child, what is wrong?" Plessis insisted, shaking me. "Did Fouquet berate you? You were a bit smart with him, you know. There, there; tell madame."

"You won't be cross with me?" I cried, wiping my nose with the lace-edged handkerchief she offered.

"You may tell me anything, Bijoux. Sit down over here." Madame guided me to the same loveseat I had shared with La Fontaine on the eventful evening of the Covenant discovery, the meeting with Mazarin, and my wedding to César. I began to weep more intensely.

"Monsieur Fouquet wishes for me to become his mistress," I blurted out once seated. "He told me so yesterday, after Molière's play."

"Sush," Susanne soothed. "You had to expect that, dear. Nicolas never could resist a pretty face. Especially one living right under his nose."

"I agreed to spy for him, not to sleep with him," I protested. "He knows of my affection for César. Everyone does. Why is he being so cruel, madame, why?"

"From his viewpoint, he is doing what is best for him and for you," the pragmatic lady sighed. "Life is not all black and white for some people, darling. The Fouquets of the world also see the gray."

"So what are you telling me? To accept my fate? To suffer in silence?"

"In a word, yes."

"César will not stand for this. He will take me away. We shall go to England."

"Think with your head, not with your heart," Plessis advised. "César will not know of the affair because I shall personally speak to M. Fouquet and beg his discretion in this matter. And you, you will obey the surintendant in all things, understand?"

I stood, no longer in danger of shedding any more tears. "Madame! I thought you to be my friend, I thought you different from Choisy!"

"Listen and attend me well, Bijoux Cinq-Mars," she said

in a serious tone. "I am no Madame de Choisy by any stretch of the imagination, nor shall I ever be. You are as much to me the daughter I never had, damn it, and I would never, do you comprehend, never, hurt you. You show great promise and I believe you could rise at court, but first you must grow up and become realistic. You are no longer a child and I shall not treat you as one. Think as an adult and behave as one, accordingly."

Nabo was clinging to my skirts, hiding his countenance in their rather ordinary muslin cloth, his nappy hair barely visible.

"Forgive me, madame. I was wrong to compare you to Jeanne-Olympe. But would it not be wiser for César and I to disappear, to seek shelter across the Channel?"

"Oh, and you think that Fouquet does not have friends in England? Does not Monsieur Hervath supply him with all the lead pipe being used at Vaux—and he is an Englishman, dearest. One of many men hailing from that country who are friends with our Nicolas. You cannot escape him, Bijoux. He is too rich and too influential. Besides, César's family would not be pleased if he angered the surintendant, considering that the Bouillons and M. Fouquet are business associates. A rash action on your part could put that alliance in a compromising position."

"What do you mean? I know they are all members of the Company of the Blessed Sacrament, but what does that have to do with my sleeping with Fouquet? How are the two related?"

"I should not tell you this, yet I trust you. Repeat it to no one; swear it."

"I swear," I vowed, not crossing my fingers behind my back, nor even tempted to.

"Bring Nabo over here and sit back down. I dare not say this too loudly."

Doing as she bid, I settled close to my cohort, the Moor in my lap. The boy seemed to sense that a matter of import was going to be discussed, for he sat very quietly, staring at the emerald ring I had taken to wearing since the occasion of my marriage.

"Godfroi de Bouillon, who captured the city of Jerusalem

in the year 1099, was a famous member of the powerful house of Lorraine. I have been told," she whispered, "that Godfroi was a direct descendant of the Merovigian kings."

"Who were they?" I felt ignorant.

"A noble race that ruled France one thousand years ago. Clovis I, who converted the Franks to Christianity, was a Merovingian. Six years ago the tomb of Childeric I, Clovis' father, was unearthed in the region of the Ardennes. The grave was filled with regal ornaments as well as magical objects—the skull of a horse, a crystal sphere, and hundreds of bees fashioned from pure gold."

A chill ran up and down my backbone as I recalled César's gift to me when he had asked me to become his wife. A bee of gold. Said to be a copy of one belonging to an ancient king and an emblem sacred to his family. I hugged Nabo to me, fearing the worst.

"The families related to Godfroi after the passing of the centuries—the Lorraines, Guises, Bouillons, Gonzagas, and many others—all belong to the Company and believe that the Merovingian claim to the throne is more valid than the Bourbon. Why, I don't know for certain. Perhaps it is, perhaps it is not. Venture a guess as to who is their candidate for king."

"I haven't the vaguest."

"Gaston d'Orléans, Monsieur. That is why he married the Duchesse de Lorraine against his brother's wishes, to establish a connection between himself and the would-be usurpers."

"Not him again!" I exclaimed with exasperation. "Is that why the Fronde started..."

"Absolutely, *chérie*. You did not hear it from me."

"And Fouquet?" I reminded her. "Why has he been allowed to join the ranks of the Merovingians?"

"Simple: the house of Guise and Lorraine has been weakened by a history of violence aimed at the French monarchy. And they suffered setbacks, losses as a result—they do not enjoy the prestige they flaunted in the past. Yet, they have an ally in Fouquet, a man with deep pockets who is willing to back their enterprise with gold coins."

"What does he stand to gain by doing that?"

"Maybe he thinks that when Gaston dies, he will be offered the crown. Or, perhaps, he would be content with a puppet king as head of state whom he could control. He has not confided that particular ambition to me. However, I tell you, Bijoux, that if you vex Nicolas, he will take it out on César's relations and the Bouillon family could lose an important ally."

Quite frankly, I was hardly concerned with the political aspirations of Gaston d'Orléans, the Bouillons or Nicolas Fouquet. I thought them to be a group of greedy, grasping men. All had palaces, wealth and prestige. And they wanted more. They did not accept that Louis was an anointed king; the nobles desired power. I had been wrong to be on the side of the anti-royalists, and I was furious at myself for trying to protect the Company of the Blessed Sacrament from Mazarin.

"Madame, " I ventured carefully, not wishing her to catch the deception I was about to begin, "are you truly of the opinion that I may entertain M. Fouquet without César's knowledge?"

"Leave it to me. I'll take care of everything," Susanne asserted, her face brightening. "Nicolas is so easily distracted that you will scarce realize what has happened when he will be moving on to the next lady whom he fancies. Trust me, dear Bijoux, for I should know."

She smiled winningly, although I knew then that Fouquet had duped Susanne at one point, too, just as he had me the evening prior. The hurt shined through her sad eyes, silently enraging me.

I resolved to bring down the Lord of Vaux. I detested the financier more than any person alive. No one was going to spoil my happiness with César, no one.

"Madame, please be so kind as to inform the surintendant that our arrangement will commence when Vaux has been completed, so there is no need for me to visit him this evening. We discussed the particulars yesterday. He will understand."

"You are a crafty one, aren't you?" Plessis giggled, looking very youthful again. "I'd do the same if I were in your position, Bijoux. You are learning girl, you are learning."

Ah, yes—if only you knew what I was plotting against our Nicolas, I wanted to say, but grinned instead. Standing up, Nabo in my arms, I moved to depart.

"Thank you for your sage counsel, madame. Your advice was what I needed to hear."

"Good luck with our little friend. Take good care of Monsieur Nabo. He is an angel."

"Have no fear, madame, I shall," I said gaily in reply, eager to get back to my room. Heading upstairs, I planted a kiss on the drowsy child's forehead in relief.

I had a plan.

Fouquet would have no idea I was setting a trap for him. All that I required to put the scheme into action was to send word to my Musketeer. The rest would fall into place, after that, with hardly any prompting from me.

This Comaetho planned to smash Poseidon's cup and be avenged.

CHAPTER ELEVEN
Future Benefics

While I awaited a reply from d'Artagnan, following the letter I had sent the Gascon requesting an audience, spending time with Nabo occupied my waking hours. From November through the Christmas holidays, César and I coached, instructed and basically befriended the minute youth whose intelligence was keen.

Fouquet thankfully left me to my own affairs. Often absent from Saint-Mandé, the surintendant distracted himself by traveling to the island of Belle-Isle, purchased in August of 1659, installing in its main harbor, Bangor, twenty-five armed vessels. Six of the fleet were warships bought in Holland and the flagship was christened "The Great Squirrel" in honor of the Fouquet family symbol. Located off the coast of his home province of Brittany, the virtually impregnable Belle-Isle represented a safe haven for the Future. Should Mazarin betray his ally and decide to have him arrested for embezzlement of state funds, or worse, plan an ambush against the surintendant, Nicolas was fully prepared to flee to his island where heavy artillery would protect him from capture or death.

Fouquet was a very suspicious person and he trusted no one completely save Madame du Plessis. Constantly in fear of his enemies' jealousy, he went to great lengths to draw up elaborate escape plans and battle strategies. Compounding the distrustful streak, a brother, the Abbé Basile, had been acting as Mazarin's unofficial head of the secret police since 1653 and the two siblings had recently quarreled intensely. Fouquet was convinced that Basile was filling the cardinal's head with details concerning the surintendant's vast operations, and the worry made Nicolas violently ill.

Succumbing to a fever in December of 1659, Fouquet submitted his resignation to the cardinal and it was summarily rejected. What I was concerned about, besides listening for information concerning the Company and explaining the appearance of snowflakes to Nabo, was that at Vaux the windows and doors of the château were being installed ahead of schedule. Eighteen thousand men toiled on the building at an estimated cost of twenty million *livres* and M. de la Fontaine had begun writing a tribute entitled *The Song of Vaux*. Fouquet made it clear that his masterpiece was to be finished *tout de suite* and *tout de suite* the construction of the château progressed.

With the onset of the Christmas season, Madame Fouquet decided that Nabo should be cast as a wise man of the Nativity in a reenactment of the birth of Jesus to be staged on the Eve of the Three Kings, a production I considered worthy since the latter gentleman had been stargazers, themselves. Sporting a ruby colored turban and satin robes of purple and gold, the Moor proudly took small steps across the stage constructed in the main salon, playing the role of the Magi Balthazar with aplomb. We were communicating with the foreigner quite easily within a month of his arrival at Saint-Mandé, and those words that proved difficult to explain were translated by gestures or drawings. When Nabo grasped an expression's meaning, he would clap his chubby hands together in glee and demand a kiss from Rouge, or the familiar name he had given me in tribute to my red tresses.

When the holidays were finished and life at Saint-Mandé returned to its usual routine, Nabo became melancholy near to the close of January, in the New Year of 1660. Playing sad songs on his custom-made, crafted-to-scale lute, a Christmas present from Fouquet, he refused to speak and was very sad.

Concerned, I begged him for a week to communicate, however, the usually cheerful Moor was stubbornly morose and mute. Then he refused to eat.

Close to my wit's end, I awoke one morning in early February, about ten days into the siege of silence, to find him lying next to me, despondent. Staring into space from the spot César usually occupied, Nabo was dressed in his finest doublet of cinnamon hued silk, baby breeches and soft, sueded boots.

"Good morning, little one," I said, trying to sound merry. "Where is Monsieur César?"

No answer.

"Nabo," I attempted again, "would you like some hot chocolate? I know I would."

Leaving the bed, shivering with cold, I made my way to the hearth and threw a log onto dying embers. César must have risen early to do some work at the laboratory, I reasoned. Returning to the comfort of the blankets, I wrapped them about me, noticing Nabo had not moved.

"Will you stop being such a horrid child!" The words rushed out before I could stop them.

Instantly, tears sprang to his expressive eyes.

"*Mon Dieu*, what have I done?" I groaned, gathering him up, holding him close. "I am sorry, my darling, sweet thing, but you are worrying me terribly. Please tell Bijoux what is wrong."

"Nabo unhappy," he cried into my unbound hair. "Nabo go home and see mother and father."

The plaintive yearning underlying his sorrow ripped at my heart.

"Nabo, you must be a brave boy. You cannot go back to your home again. M. Fouquet takes care of you now—he is your new father," I sighed, wondering how I could tell him the truth. That he was a slave. That he was living in the white man's world, a world that did not give a damn about a blackamoor's feelings.

"Do you have mother or father?" he asked.

Separating from him, my answer was, "No, my mother and father are dead. They went up to the sky, to be with the stars."

"Who the stars?"

"The stars live above us," I explained, pointing towards the ceiling, "where they dance and play with the deities, the greatest powers in the world."

"They nice?"

"The nicest," I confirmed. "The gods and goddesses love us, Nabo, more than we might imagine."

"Nabo love you," he said, embracing me.

"I love you, too. And do you know what?"

"What?" he piped, energetic and full of life again.

"Soon you will have a new home in Paris, in a big city. You are going to live with a beautiful queen and be her best friend. She will love you more than anybody, anywhere."

"Me?"

"Yes, you, Nabo." I had to cheer him. He was so lonely and homesick.

"What her name?"

"Maria-Teresa. She is leaving her family, just like you did, to come and live with us."

"Maria," he repeated after me. "Maria. My Maria."

Then he hopped down from the bed, running about in circles, singing the Infanta's name.

"What's this?" my husband's voice queried. "Feeling better, Nabo?"

"*Très bien, très bien*," he sang in reply. "Nabo go live with beautiful queen. Nabo have lady like Monsieur César. Nabo love goddesses."

"Oh really?" César laughed, lifting our friend by the arms and swinging him in an arc. "What is your lady's name, Nabo?"

"Maria-Beresa," he giggled. "Stop, stop!" he howled. "Nabo get sick!"

Putting him down, César gave him an imaginary boot to the rear.

"Go play while I talk to Bijoux. Find Madame du Plessis and ask her to teach you a card game."

"*Très bien, très bien*," he resumed singing, skipping out the door. Echoing down the hallway I could hear, "Maria-Beresa, Maria-Beresa," until the lad was out of range.

"He's in a good mood," César chuckled, climbing onto the bed. "Will you make me that happy, too?"

"Stop," I smirked. "You are incorrigible. Where were you off to this morning?"

"To visit my mistress," he teased.

"César, be serious. Were you at the laboratory?"

"No. I was meeting with a trusted courier whom I have engaged to take *The Key of Solomon* to England where it will be delivered to a gentleman who is an authority on the occult."

"Who is this man?"

"Robert Boyle. He is the youngest son of the Earl of Cork and he is brilliant. At the age of twelve, he was studying in Florence, and later spent two years in Switzerland researching daemonology."

"No! How did you make this gentleman's acquaintance?" I inquired, excited by the prospect.

"Family connections."

"Through the Company?"

His eyes would not meet mine.

"Oh, César, are we never going to be free of that association?"

"Well, darling, if Boyle might prove helpful where your health is concerned, why should you worry as to his political affiliations?"

"So you admit that the Company's agenda is not purely a spiritual one?"

"Bijoux..."

"Fine, fine, I shan't start," I agreed, holding my hands up in defeat. "I do not wish to argue."

"Good," he murmured, moving closer. Kissing me with passionate intent, we were soon interrupted, however, by a knock at the door.

"Damn," my husband sighed. "Who might that be?"

"Madame du Plessis, who else?" my friend called out, sweeping into the room, looking fresh and beautiful, dressed in a rose colored riding outfit trimmed with marten fur.

"Madame, how lovely you look," César said with sincerity. "To what do we owe the honor?"

"My darlings," she complimented, sitting on the bed, "*Susanne* when we are in private, *n'est-ce pas*? *Madame* makes me feel old and we have been friends for more than six months." She paused, her expression becoming solemn. "I have bad news or else I would not have intruded."

"What?" we asked in unison, holding each other's hand in an attempt to allay our sudden fear.

"Gaston d'Orléans is dead."

"What?" César gasped. "When? How?"

"Three days ago, at Blois. No one is certain what ailed him. The Duchesse de Lorraine is mad with grief. The Grande Mademoiselle, well, she was her father's favorite child and comrade-in-arms, so you may imagine her state. And Philippe, *mon Dieu*, Philippe is locked in his rooms at the Tuileries, refusing to see anyone, not even the Comte de Guiche."

"Monsieur is dead," I whispered, "long live Monsieur."

"I must go to my uncle without delay," César remarked. "Stay close to our Susanne, my love."

"Be careful, César," I replied, in a fog. "When will you return?"

"Don't fret, I shall keep you company," Plessis reminded. "César will be home before you know it. We'll keep busy with Nabo, won't we *chérie*?"

"Yes, yes of course we shall. Good-bye, my Chromius, don't worry about me."

"I shan't. You're in good hands," he observed. "And, dearest marquise, thank you for coming to us right away with the news. I shall always remember your thoughtfulness."

Then he was off, speeding to the stables.

"What a nice, young man," she sighed wistfully. "You would be wise to marry him."

"I did marry him," I confessed, burying my face in a pillow. "Madame, I love him so."

"You are married? To a de la Tour? When did this happen?" she asked, genuinely astonished.

"September of fifty-eight. The day after my birthday. Turenne knows, the priest who married us at St. Sulpice knows, and a witness from the seminary there, but no one else. Please, keep this our secret. I had to tell you; I have wanted to admit the truth for ages."

"Why the silence?"

"Consider this: I was sent on assignment by the cardinal to collect information about the Company. If he had suspected I was married to a Bouillon, he never would have trusted me."

"Your association with the Italian is long past..."

"No, not really, my friend. I have been known to feed the cardinal false information to protect César's family."

"You little vixen, you sly minx! And here I thought I was teaching you a thing or two."

Hugging her, I basked in the praise.

We parted and Susanne was quick to hide any tender emotion. "Time to arise and dress. We're going out to the stables. Once we find Nabo, of course."

"Is that why you sport a riding habit?"

"Yes, and you are about to become an equestrienne as well. Nicolas is of the opinion that you will cut a fine figure on a horse. When he heard of Gaston's death, he sent 'round to the Luxembourg for La Rivière, the Duc d'Orléans' most able groom and the best known riding master in Paris."

"The tall Moor?" I asked excitedly. "The famed daredevil?"

"The very same! You know of him, then?"

"Our paths crossed long ago. He possesses a most regal countenance, madame."

"I hear he is a fine specimen. Some ladies at court have supposedly fancied him and Fouquet deems him to be a handsome fellow, can you believe it? A blackamoor?"

"La Rivière is very good looking," I asserted. "And why can't a dark-skinned person be attractive? Consider Nabo, is he not becoming?"

"Not my type," she replied. "Too short."

We howled with laughter, although I knew it cruel. The action was akin to making light of Monsieur Scarron's condition or poking fun at Mazarin's accent. Why could I not be kind as was Françoise, the poet's unselfish wife, who was pure and giving? Yet, while I considered La Belle Indienne to be the finest, noblest person alive, it was not in my nature to follow her saintly example.

Dressing with speed, Susanne and I gossiped, speculating as to who the next Merovingian contender for the throne would be, what with Gaston's expiration.

"César will be absent a few days," my friend observed as I laced the front of the warmest, woolen dress I owned. "The important members of the Company, the leadership, will convene at St. Sulpice. The Duc de Guise is the logical choice, mark my words."

"They will not pick César's brother, will they?"

Susanne regarded me with a queer expression. "Do you mean Godefroy-Maurice?"

"Of course, who else?"

My friend looked at me strangely again, then said, "I doubt it. The young Bouillon is highly thought of; however, Henri de Guise raised forces in an unsuccessful bid to obtain the crown of Naples for himself back in fifty-four, a sure sign of his royal aspirations. My husband lost his life on that campaign."

"How sad," I replied, thinking that César's family was already too involved in the Company for my liking. Who gave a fig if a distant relation of Clovis I was restored his rightful throne?

"Let us find Nabo and be off to the stables," I then suggested, donning a heavy daytime cloak of Dutch cloth, most probably dyed the same color red as father's famous suits. Susanne took the lead, and we made to depart, coming across our missing person in the corridor outside the room.

"Where you go?" Nabo asked.

"To the stables," Plessis explained, "to meet a man who is from the same place as you. Would you like to tag along, monsieur?"

"He black?"

"Yes, Nabo, he is black and his name is La Rivière. He wants to be your friend, you'll see," I assured the tyke.

Handing him his cape, I helped Nabo prepare to brave the cold outdoors. Once appropriately outfitted, the dwarf was in my arms, for we would make better progress if I carried him to our destination rather than expect his little legs to keep pace with our long limbs.

On the way to where horses and carriages were housed, Susanne explained I would be taught to ride sidesaddle, as befit a proper lady, and not astride, in imitation of the shameless Countess of Saint-Belmont. Only women of ill repute succumbed to such temptation. La Rivière was to school me in the art of dressage from within the stables' indoor arena that I knew to be filled with sawdust, hurdles and potted hedges. Fouquet wished to take me hunting with him in Brittany, and insisted that I be able to join in the chase. Quite adverse to that unlikely expedition, I nonetheless was thrilled at the prospect of finally being given the opportunity to learn the art of equitation.

La Rivière caught sight of us when we were advancing close to the grain barn, picking our way gingerly around the horse droppings constantly being swept into pails by stable hands. Leading a delicate looking dappled gray by a lovely tasseled bridle, the Moor approached our party rapidly, causing his charge to trot alongside.

"Mesdames, welcome. Monsieur Fouquet told me to expect you."

The Moor stopped directly in front of us, petting the beauty whose nostrils flared as it regarded our party. A dainty hoof struck nervously on the cobblestone and large, dark eyes rolled with a toss of the head. The striking La Rivière, who wore an elegant, white silk turban, calmed the skittish creature by merely whispering into one of its ears.

"Do you like her?" he asked with pride, flashing a set of teeth that shone white as alabaster in contrast to his chocolate-brown skin. "Which one of you is Mademoiselle Bijoux?"

"Me, monsieur," I demurred. "When I was a child, I lived with Madame de Choisy at the Luxembourg, and I saw you one day while I was out walking with my governess. I suppose you do not recall seeing me."

"I remember you," he boomed, slapping a thigh. "Of course, the girl with the red hair! I stared at you quite ferociously, did I not?"

"Scared me half to death. You were the first Moor I had seen."

"Not anymore," La Rivière observed, tweaking Nabo's cheek. "Who have we here?"

"Nabo," the boy chirped. "Who you?"

"La Rivière," the groom answered with a bow and a flourish.

"Where you from?" Nabo squeaked in his high-pitched voice.

"The Cape Verde islands. And you, little man?"

"North Africa," I interrupted, more interested in the fine steed La Rivière controlled. "You two may become better acquainted after you answer me a question, monsieur. What breed of horse is this?"

"The mare is from the land of Arabia, she is the fastest thing on four legs. She hails from the desert and once belonged to a great warrior."

"What is her name?" I moved forward slowly, not wishing to frighten the highly-strung animal. Holding out a hand, it was duly sniffed with caution.

"Whatever you should care to choose, my lady. The horse is yours, a gift from M. Fouquet."

"No! She belongs to me? I must choose her name? I have no knowledge of such things!"

"Assiz is a lovely name," La Rivière prompted. "The Arab for *beloved*."

"No, Athena tamed the great steed Pegasus," I remarked, stroking the horse's ivory mane. "And in Her honor I shall name my horse in kind. Do you like it?" I asked Susanne.

"Pegasus is certainly most noble," she agreed.

"Then it is settled," I announced. "When may I ride her, monsieur?"

"When I have taught you the basics and then, only inside, under my watch. This mare is a handful, I warn you, but I think you will be able to handle her one day."

"Look, Nabo, is she not exquisite? Would you like to sit on her?"

"Me go," he replied, squirming in my arms, "me go with monsieur."

"All right, all right," I consented. "Would you mind terribly, sir?"

"Of course not. Put Nabo atop Pegasus, and I'll take him for a tour of the stables. He will spend the day with me. As for you, return tomorrow for your first lesson, early in the morning."

"Thank you," I said, placing Nabo on a coat of silky gray. "Isn't this fun, *mon petit?*"

"Monsieur my friend," Nabo beamed back. "Monsieur like me, *n'est-ce pas?*"

"You will be my little brother," La Rivière grinned. "I'll teach you many things, *ça va?*"

"*Très bien, très bien,*" the boy sang. "This best day, Bijoux."

Why I did not notice that the imp's precocity might become dangerous if not checked, that Nabo's foolish pranks might eventually have serious repercussions for those associated with him, namely me, is a question I now ask myself daily and often. Certainly if someone had told me then that the black boy would bring me trouble in the future, I would have laughed in their face with scorn.

For Nabo was my brother, Prince Antiochus.

César returned from the Company conclave after an absence of two days, and I longed to ply him for the details concerning Gaston's elected successor, yet, I bit my tongue. Instead, I attempted to contact d'Artagnan again, having received no answer to the message I had relayed to the Musketeer in November. Using the recent birth of his and Charlotte-Anne's first child, a son, as a convenient excuse to send the couple a watch as a token of congratulations, I was pleased, no, thrilled, when the Gascon rode out to Saint-Mandé to thank me in person for the thoughtful gesture.

Following a formal embrace, the Musketeer listened to

my report as to the truth behind the Company's desire to replace Louis as King of France and agreed to pass the facts on to Mazarin without informing the cardinal of the source. I also let it be known that Fouquet was the chief financial underwriter of the group, a fact that made my Musketeer scowl with disappointment since he was on good terms with the surintendant and bode him no ill.

Something I learned from the interview with Charles was that his home life was not blissful. Madame d'Artagnan had developed into quite a shrew, evidently, and questioned her husband's every movement, accusing him of being unfaithful to their marriage bed, of feeling more loyalty toward his men than he did for her, and of squandering her money on the Grand Musketeers' equipage. Charles was very concerned about his debts, what with another mouth to feed and his wife refusing to give him access to anymore of the funds she had inherited from her deceased Lord of St. Croix. A Musketeer's pay was thirty-five *sous* per day—not enough to support a family, hôtel and military outfit.

Looking into his watery, blue eyes, I took one of d'Artagnan's hands in mine and held it tightly. Begging him not to fret, I went to the hidden bag of jewels and took two large rocks from the multitude of gems. Offering them to the man who had helped me on so many different occasions, he regarded me with wide-eyed disbelief, taking the loan after much insistence on my part, promising to pay me back as soon as possible.

Having accomplished part of my plan to discredit Fouquet, I took to snooping about Nicolas' rooms when he was away on business, looking for evidence of wrongdoing on the minister's part. Finding no damning documents in two months' investigation and certain that La Fôret, the devoted valet to the Lord of Vaux, had caught on to my subterfuge, I quit sneaking through the house under cover of darkness. Wondering how I could infiltrate the financier's quarters without detection, I hit upon a solution to the predicament: Nabo. He was as dark as night and good at hiding; he could become my agent, no one would suspect an illiterate, foreign dwarf of wishing to steal and read a high-ranking person's correspondence.

The plan was perfect and I set about teaching little Antiochus how to pick locks, steal letters and hopefully avoid exposure. The Moor thought the lessons no more than a game and pursued the activity with vigor, becoming quite an estimable thief. By May of 1660, Nabo hit the lottery. Bringing me a most curious dispatch, taken from the chest located at the foot of our master's bed, I knew from the moment that I began to read the parchment that I held within my grasp the proof I desperately needed to ruin Nicolas Fouquet.

Dated 1656 and written from Rome by the Abbé Louis Fouquet, another of Nicolas' brothers who had joined the priesthood, the epistle was fascinating. Abbé Louis had been sent to the Eternal City to approach M. Poussin about designing the statuary for the gardens at Vaux. While in the great painter's studio, more than mere marbles had been spoken of, as Louis Fouquet noted, writing:

He and I discussed certain things which I shall be able to explain to you in detail—things which will give you, through Monsieur Poussin, advantages which even kings would have great pains to draw from him, and which, according to him, it is possible that nobody else will ever rediscover in the centuries to come. And what is more, these are things so difficult to discover that nothing now can prove of better fortune or be their equal.

Then and there I resolved that, while I intended to hint at the existence of such a letter to Mazarin through the trustworthy d'Artagnan, I would never produce the original, the sheet in my possession. No, I had to hide it away, keep it in a safe place, far from prying eyes. The case against Fouquet was growing and I was certain that once the cardinal and his godson heard of the surintendant's circumspect dealings with M. Poussin, they would view Lord Cléonime in a totally different light.

Thus, following Nabo's find, it was with a light heart and confident spirit that I made my way to the stables each morning. Met there by La Rivière, who said I was making steady progress in the saddle, I concentrated on my form and the Moor's patient training, free at last to stop fretting about Fouquet and his plans to make me his unwilling mistress. Considering my contacts and friends in high places, I was bound to succeed in my mission. Riding around the ring in large circles atop the Arabian mare, I dreamed of a day when the surintendant would be led away to prison by an escort of Musketeers; then I would feel completely safe and at ease. *The sooner the better, the sooner the better* the high-stepping horse's hooves seemed to beat out on dense turf, and in my mind, the Future's arrest was already a *fait accompli*.

On June 9, 1660, Louis Bourbon, King of France and Navarre, wed Maria-Teresa of Spain at the church of St. Jean de Luz, located at the foot of the majestic Pyrenées mountain range. The glittering pageant was witnessed by dignitaries from the French and Spanish courts, among whose number was the illustrious Nicolas Fouquet, accompanied by his wife, servants and an odd-looking blackamoor whose growth was stunted. That dwarf was, of course, Nabo, and my Prince Antiochus awaited being presented to his princess with eager anticipation, having hardly shed a tear when he left Saint-Mandé for the long trip south.

I shall never forget how the little man was seated in a carriage 'ere his departure by the kindly groom who had befriended him and the two embraced, promising to meet again when Nabo returned from the wedding. When César, Susanne and I stepped forward to kiss the charming boy good-bye, he held onto me the longest, causing me to weep. Nabo's eyes became wet when he noticed my tears, yet I sent the coach speeding off with a signal to its driver, rather than endure an embarrassing scene.

Louis XIV presented his awkward, child-like bride to the citizens of Paris on August 26, 1660, parading the petite queen of the silvery blonde hair through the capital's streets, heartened by his subjects' cries of: *Vive le Roi, vive la Reine*. Bolstered by the people's show of support, the ring of their cheers still resounding in his ears, the twenty-one-year-old monarch, handsome and virile with the world at his feet, took the advice of his wise, old mentor, Mazarin, and issued a pronouncement against the elite membership of the Company of the Blessed Sacrament.

Two pamphlets appeared in print soon after, anonymously written, attacking the Company by name as a conspiracy, and inflaming public opinion against the group. Then, in December of 1660, the cardinal persuaded Parliament to forbid all secret societies, and the organization appeared to have suffered a death blow; yet, the clandestine gatherings continued to be held as they had in the past, security measures tightened so that the cardinals' agents would not flush out the lawbreakers.

What with Nabo gone away, the Company operating more covertly than ever, and Fouquet busy with a plan to purchase the island of Ste. Lucie in the West Indies—as well as organizing business ventures in Gaudeloupe and the pirate-infested stronghold of Madagascar—César and I at last found some time to spend together, alone. Susanne understood our need for privacy and gradually returned to her old routine of accompanying our patron everywhere that he went, watching and listening in salons, theaters and cabinet offices. And what she came back to report during the first few weeks of 1661, was worth being awakened at one o'clock in the morning to hear.

"Darlings," she nearly shouted, allowing herself into the bedchamber we occupied that evening, "wake up. I have so much to tell!"

"Who's there?" César awoke with a start. "Oh, madame, it's you!"

"Are you in your cups, Susanne?" I groaned.

"A bit tipsy, but certainly not a sot." Assuming her usual place on my side of the bed, she removed the cloak draped about her shoulders, allowing the garment to slide to the floor. Beneath the blue velvet cape, she wore the most stunning, embroidered dress; silver needlework enhanced by a background of palest blue satin, lace dripping from the elbows in the manner of a melted icicle. The effect was amazing, for Susanne's gown shimmered as would frozen snow touched by moonlight.

"*Mon Dieu*, your ensemble is incredible!"

"Thank you, my love," she preened, patting my cheek. "A gift from our great friend, who else? To think, Mazarin petitioned the Parliament to ban the use of gold and silver thread back in fifty-six—small wonder the people threatened to riot."

"He is crazy," César mumbled. "Look at the example he makes with those damn, perfumed apes; taking them with him wherever he goes."

"Strange, true," Plessis agreed, "however, I did not come to talk about the cardinal, now did I? Let's see, the first thing that I heard of interest this evening was…"

"Where did you go?" I cut in.

"Oh, with Nicolas to the cardinal's palace for a party given in honor of Philippe, the new Duc d'Orléans. It was a grand entertainment: an orchestra imported by Mazarin from Rome, Spanish actors who performed a play for the queen, quite the evening."

"All for Monsieur? What does he have to celebrate?"

"Dearest, he is officially engaged to wed his cousin, Henriette d'Angleterre—you know, that skinny creature who is the daughter of Louis XIII's sister and King Charles of England who lost his head? Well, since the princess' brother, Charles II, regained the English crown last May, the little bag of bones has become quite a desirable lady. The Stuart family has lived here in exile for so many years, they are more French than English, when you think about it."

"And Philippe supports this alliance?"

"Supposedly, he is head-over-heels in love with the girl. Which is the oddest thing; no one can account for the prince's change of heart, to put it delicately. Guiche is beside himself."

"Good, I never liked that cad," I asserted. "When I lived at the Luxembourg, Choisy would lend the prince and his favourite her cabinet to meet in, and I would often hear Philippe crying out in pain because Guiche was hurting him."

"Bijoux, must you?" César winced. "The mere thought…"

"Yes, yes, a point well taken," Susanne hastily added, "although your remark is a lead-in to the second discovery I made this evening. Brace yourself, my dear Bijoux, for Madame de Choisy, that shameless intriguer, has returned to court!"

"No!" I protested. "How?"

"She has been living in Paris for almost a year, having been reinstated at the Luxembourg with the widowed Duchesse de Lorraine shortly after Gaston's death."

"Did she bring François-Timoléon with her?"

"Yes. The boy has taken his vows and is now a priest. His dear mother, it would seem, is up to her old tricks again because she has been promoting a lame girl, Louise de la Vallière, as a possible member of Henriette's future entourage. The child is the stepdaughter of Gaston's Master of the Household and grew up with the Princesses of the Blood at Blois."

"Poor Mademoiselle de la Vallière," I sympathized. "A guileless country dove in the clutches of the court falcon. Choisy has her pegged as somebody's future mistress, you may count on that."

"Stay far away from her. Rumor has it Jeanne-Olympe would love to wring your pretty neck," Susanne warned. Not wishing to dwell on that unpleasant subject, she continued, saying, "Our darling Nabo is well, you will be pleased to hear."

"Does he remain the queen's favourite?" my husband inquired with a yawn, knowing that Maria-Teresa, renamed Marie-Thérèse by the French, had been captivated by the Moor from the moment Fouquet presented the besotted dwarf to her at St. Jean de Luz.

"Nabo adores the queen and she, in turn, lavishes gifts and attentions on him as though he were a Prince of the Realm. The Moor rides in the royal carriage with Marie-Thérèse, he eats with her, he entertains his mistress and her ladies-in-waiting with his guitar playing. The king, unfortunately, is of the opinion that blackamoors bring bad luck to a household and disapproves of his wife's association with our tiny friend. Yet, the new queen will not give up her Nabo, much to M. Fouquet's endless amusement."

"I cannot believe that Louis is afraid of a black boy who is no taller than an andiron!" I chuckled. "How silly. People say the queen is stupid, but perhaps she is smarter than they think. I'm glad she loves Nabo—he is such a sweet thing."

"An absolute treasure," Susanne confirmed. "Now, for some unhappy news. I meant to tell you earlier, I'm ashamed to say, yet forgot the intention altogether. M. Scarron has passed away."

With a shudder, I remembered Jacques' prophecy.

"Oh, no, not Monsieur Paul. When?"

"At the beginning of October, before the holidays. As I said, I was going to mention his death to you, but became distracted with Nicolas' foreign ventures and..."

"How is Madame Scarron—have you heard anything concerning dear Françoise?"

"Scarron left his estate to her, the worth of which did not cover what he owed his creditors. Poor Françoise was forced to borrow money to pay for her husband's funeral expenses. Had it not been for the intervention of an aunt, she would be quite destitute, no better than a beggar."

"Fouquet will not offer her aid?" I probed.

"The offer was made, and rejected. I think you are capable of deducing as to why."

"He did not dare, did he?" I asked in amazement, thankful that César had dozed off.

"Nicolas has had his eye on her for five or so years, although she has always resisted his advances. A bit like you in that regard."

"Susanne, please," I frowned, putting a finger to my lips. "César has no notion."

"Of course," she whispered back, "what an idiot I am! I shall go before I cause you trouble."

"Wait! Not so fast. Do you know where Françoise abides?"

"She is living at the convent of the Hospitalières in the Place Royale. Most people call it the *Petite Charité*. One of the dead poet's well-to-do cousins keeps a room there, intended for occasional retreats, and she has loaned it to our Belle Indienne. Damn, I wish Françoise was more sensible."

"She is proud and she is chaste, madame. She firmly

believes God will provide for her needs and that she need not compromise her principles when faced with adversity. Having corresponded with her for near to three years, I am familiar with her resolute nature."

"I admire such brave souls," Susanne admitted, "although I have never quite understood them. So calm, so serene. Placing their trust in the Almighty, no matter what the situation. Oh, well, I think I shall continue to rely on M. Fouquet's abilities; he has never let me down."

Susanne stood to leave. I was unusually quiet, consumed with thoughts of Françoise, weighing whether I should go to visit her at the convent. I had to marvel at my old friend's resolve to guard her virtue, for given the choice between Fouquet or the nunnery, I knew which I would have chosen.

"Susanne, may I ask you a delicate question?"

"Yes, dearest," she granted, leaning against the door she had opened in parting, eyes half-shut.

"Are you in love with M. Fouquet?"

"Do not be impertinent, Bijoux," she twittered, waving her hand at me nonchalantly.

"No, I need to know, dear friend. Were you ever in love with him?"

"You had to ask, didn't you?" she sighed, looking away as if in a dream. "The honest answer is, I never stopped. Yet our Lord Cléonime did, several years ago."

"Madame, what transpired?"

"Ah, Bijoux, when I gave my heart to Nicolas, I was not much older than you are now, married to the wealthy Marquis du Plessis-Bellière, Jean de Rougé. I was spoiled and adored by my husband, and I ignored him. Did I care that my nobleman would have renounced his title for an hour of my devotion? No. And when the poor man died seven years ago on a foreign battlefield, bitter and consumed with jealousy, I daresay he cursed both Nicolas and me with his final breath. Free at last, I left Limoges to join my true love in Paris, where I was convinced he would greet me with open arms."

"And?" I urged when Susanne paused.

"I was mistaken, Bijoux. Arriving unannounced at the Fouquet manor after sunset, I found my paramour in his bedchamber, rutting about with a lady who will remain nameless. On that night my heart froze and has never thawed. I could not touch him again in an intimate way, nor he me. Yet, for some strange reason, we did share the need to remain close companions. So, now you know the truth. Please do not mention the association again, for it pains me to speak of the past."

"And you would have me go to him?" I asked incredulously.

"'Tis better to accept those things we cannot change, dear. Nicolas is fickle, inconstant. He will never love one woman body and soul, for he is a collector." I watched a tear roll unashamedly across Susanne's cheek to her chin. "Whatever makes him happy, pleases me as well. Would you not do anything for your César?"

Leaving the bed, I went to her and wrapped my arms around my friend.

"Susanne, forget about Nicolas and think of your own happiness. I do not care one whit for Fouquet, I care about you, and because I finally know how you feel about the surintendant, I shan't go to him. It was not my intention to do so, anyway."

"Not ever?" she whimpered.

"Not ever," I confirmed. Taking her face in my hands, I looked deeply into her eyes.

"Go to him yourself, Susanne."

"Do not be ridiculous. I am old..."

"You are a gorgeous woman! I would give a million *livres* to have hair such as yours, grace such as your own, a beauty that transcends time."

"No, Nicolas desires you, Bijoux."

"That is nonsense and you know it. Talk about foolish pride! Go to his room right now and take him back, or I shall drag you to him myself! Is he still awake?"

"He is working," she admitted with a blush. "He enjoys plotting and scheming at night, you know, for he is a firm believer that *daylight furnishes matter for inattention.*"

Susanne's bottom lip began to quiver as she reflected on Fouquet's words. Pushing her out past the door, I took her hand and began to lead her down the hallway to the staircase.

"Bijoux, stop this," she protested. "I shan't go."

"Oh, yes you will, damn it!" I swore. "I don't care if I wake him, you are going to settle this thing tonight. Perhaps then we'll all have some peace and quiet in this household!"

Pulling her down the plush, carpeted staircase, we were soon outside the surintendant's quarters. Despite my mentor's complaints, I ordered her to be still while I pounded a fist against the ornately decorated wood separating us from the Future.

"Yes?" came the eventual response to the summons.

"Bijoux Cinq-Mars to see the surintendant," I announced to the valet La Fôret.

"Wait here and listen," I directed to the captive. "If you leave, I shall never talk to you again. And wipe away those tears, it's unbecoming."

Walking through the opened portal—bare feet, shift and all—I was greeted by the surintendant, dressed in a long, sumptuous robe of heavy, patterned silk.

"What have we here?" he queried in a jaunty manner. "Ready for bed, mademoiselle? Vaux is still under construction, last I inquired."

"I have come to speak with you privately, monsieur," I asserted, glaring at La Fôret.

"Go, go," Fouquet instructed, not unpleasantly, with a nod to his manservant.

"What do you wish to report at two o'clock in the morning?" Nicolas smirked. "That you love me, perhaps? That you yearn to..."

"Stop! This is no laughing matter, you rogue!" I answered, really quite angry. "Do you realize that you have broken my best friend's heart?"

"Whose?"

"Bijoux, you have said enough," a composed, even tone confirmed. "Nicolas, forgive her..."

"Susanne, what is this?" he asked sternly. "Have you been keeping something from me?"

"Yes, I have," she confessed, returning his gaze. "A trifle you do not wish to hear."

"Indulge me."

Clearing my throat, I turned to depart, but Plessis grabbed my arm without moving her eyes.

"Stay and listen to this," she invited. "Watch and learn about men, my dear."

"I demand to know what is going on," Fouquet insisted. "I do not appreciate being interrupted."

"Oh, really?" I asked sarcastically. "Unlike madame, I do not care."

The surintendant regarded me with utter loathing. Slamming the papers he had been reading onto a nearby table, he drew menacingly close, shaking a fist before my face.

"You drive me mad!" he shouted. "Who do you think you are?"

Susanne dove between us, holding onto Fouquet by the shoulders.

"Nicolas, Bijoux is saying these things to make you hate her, don't you see? This scene is my doing; find fault with me, not with the child."

"I would rather stab myself in the chest! Why should I be angry with you when you are blameless?"

Plessis placed her fair head against his dark one and began to sob. Instinctively, Nicolas drew her to him, looking at me with a stymied expression.

"She was in fine form at the cardinal's fête," he observed, calming himself. "Whatever happened?"

"Bijoux, be still," Susanne cried pitifully.

Fouquet was smoothing her blonde tresses, kissing her on the forehead. "Tell me, dearest."

She shook her head, *no*. Seeing pen and paper scattered atop Fouquet's stately bed, I went to where they lay, wrote a few words on an empty sheet of vellum and handed the message to the financier. Reading it, he then allowed the paper to fall to the floor, his eyes becoming moist.

"You may go," he said to me in a voice choked with emotion. "Thank you for your sincerity, La Loy."

"Do not make the same mistake twice," I advised as I left. "Her heart beats alone for you, monsieur."

"As does mine for my beautiful friend," Nicolas replied, overcome, holding Susanne closer. The expression he wore convinced me of his intent and I shut the door on the couple, relieved.

I no longer hated Fouquet. To protect Susanne's lover, the intention formed in my mind to contact d'Artagnan with a false report that the surintendant had fallen out of favor with the Company.

The thought was a generous one, yet, born a bit too late, for in thirty day's time the Prime Minister of France would be dead.

CHAPTER TWELVE
Royal Audience

Everyone except Jules Mazarini was surprised by his sudden physical decline in February of 1661. He knew that when a fire-trailing comet was spotted in the evening winter sky of that year, nothing good would come of the sign. Disheartened, the cardinal was purported to have remarked, "The heavens do me too much honor."

Convinced that the appearance of the celestial body was a portent of his own imminent death, the melancholy old man roamed throughout the impressive rooms of his palace, drinking in the sight of his magnificent possessions, complaining aloud, "I cannot believe I must leave all this!"

By the first of March he had succumbed to a combination of aches, pains and fever and took to his bed; the king sent for M. Cousinot and M. Vallot to attend to his godfather, although the subsequent purgings and bleedings left Mazarin weakened. Fearing the worst, Louis had the cardinal moved to the Château of Vincennes. There, he and the queen-mother, as Anne was styled following her son's marriage, personally cared for their loyal servant, keeping a vigil by his side day and night, away from the wagging tongues of the court.

Lying on a soft mattress and feather pillows, his leg encased in a plaster of horse excrement—a surefire remedy for all manner of ills—Mazarin lectured his beloved pupil on a variety of matters. The most important counsel he offered Louis was: *Rule yourself*. No more prime ministers, the cardinal advised; be wary of Nicolas Fouquet, he was too ambitious; heed not the advice of a mistress or any other woman, save the queen-mother. The two men were closeted together for hours, speaking privately, deciding a nation's fate.

By March the ninth, Mazarin was exhausted, his time to go had come, yet he refused to receive a priest, opting instead to save enough breath for one last comment. "Sire, I owe everything to you," was his closing admission, "however, I consider myself quit in leaving you Monsieur Colbert."

His Eminence shut his eyes and France had a new decision-maker at the helm.

Following Mazarin's death, Louis shut himself up in the study at Vincennes where he remained sequestered for two hours. Emerging from the quiet of the library, the king let it be known that he was summoning his first council meeting immediately, to be held at the château.

Michel Le Tellier, Secretary of War, aged fifty-eight, an unassuming tactician from a solid legal family, was sent for, as well as Hughes de Lionne, Acting Secretary of Foreign Affairs, aged fifty, the ablest diplomat in Europe and Mazarin's right hand. The Comte de Brienne, Official Secretary of Foreign Affairs, aged seventy-two, whose son had grown up with the king and was one of his best friends, was politely asked to attend. And Nicolas Fouquet, Attorney General and Surintendant of Finance, aged forty-six, was ordered to Vincennes post haste to wait upon his master.

Louis XIV's reign had truly begun and as he himself informed the assembled ministers, much to their confoundment, that in all things pertaining to the realm, they were to report to him and to him alone.

Then Jean-Baptiste Colbert arrived, frowning and grumpy, his plain robes of brown and straight, lanky hair lending him an air of incivility. Led straight to the king's rooms, Mazarin's former secretary was greeted warmly by Louis and informed he was being appointed, without delay, to the post of Fouquet's assistant. The frumpy administrator was to keep a watch on the surintendant's ledger books and to assist the king with basic accounting principles. Louis intended that Fouquet would go over the figures with him every afternoon and he also intended that Colbert would translate for him what had transpired during those sessions.

Thoroughly a modest, though unimaginable type, the stocky, bourgeois Colbert knelt at his sovereign's feet, overcome by the honor. Working patiently and diligently for Mazarin over the years had paid off. Then he smiled, remembering why he had come to Vincennes.

Slowly and methodically, as was his way, Jean-Baptiste explained to Louis that the silver haired, stingy man who lay cold upstairs had ferreted away three million *livres* in the walls of various châteaux, unbeknownst to anyone save his secretary. Ready money awaited the godson—not Mazarin's heirs—at the cardinal's properties in Sedan, Brissac, La Fère, and, yes, Vincennes.

Sitting down from the shock, the king looked wide-eyed at the accountant. He asked as to why Mazarin had put the funds aside. "For you and for France," Colbert replied. "He did not wish you dependent on Fouquet for money."

Both men were silent for a prolonged lapse, each pondering Mazarin's foresight, in his own way. At last the king stood and embraced the commoner, who was probably the truest man in his kingdom next to d'Artagnan, the latter who stood watch outside the door. Jean-Baptiste could have had the cash for himself—no one would have been the wiser—as King Louis was well aware.

"Together, we shall bring Fouquet to justice," the monarch pledged, "and you will be the new surintendant."

"Sire," Colbert noted, "it will take time to unravel the jumble Fouquet has helped to create in the state registers, but I shall do it."

Those words sealed a partnership between the king and the bookkeeper, one that was to endure for twenty-two years.

Relieved he was three million richer and satisfied he had

discovered an able man to help him govern, Louis decided to ride in the nearby forest where he might hunt. Escorted by d'Artagnan, eschewing his usual retinue of courtiers, the athletic king made his way to the cardinal's excellent stables, drawing in deep breaths of the invigorating March air. Soon he would be surrounded by nature and the peace afforded by the wooded thicket, if only he possessed a lady with whom he could share his quiet time and life would be perfect, indeed.

Unfortunately, Marie-Thérèse, his pregnant wife, created little stir in Louis' heart or loins, and the dwarf, Nabo, who followed the queen everywhere, caused him to cringe. Personally, the king dreaded the old wives' tale claiming that women with child who were gazed upon by a blackamoor would produce a dark baby, and he often considered how to wrench his spouse from her cherished pet.

Louis Bourbon and I were akin in our thoughts on that blustery, gray afternoon, for I had likewise gone to the stables, intent on exercising Pegasus. Aware that the king was staying not far away at Vincennes, I secretly hoped that as I journeyed past the château on horseback, I would perhaps be afforded a glimpse of the ruler or perhaps be permitted to speak with d'Artagnan, especially in light of the cardinal's passing. Susanne had agreed to accompany me because Nicolas was at Vincennes, too, and the jaunt afforded the first, real chat we had shared since her reconciliation with the surintendant.

"Are you content?" I asked the glowing woman as we headed for the paddock.

"He loves me and I love him. What more might I say?" she simpered.

"Oh, Susanne," I said, squeezing her hand with real joy, "now you may be the Queen of Vaux!"

We were laughing as would naughty children by the time we reached the stalls. Two grooms hurried to prepare our horses, and once we were situated on our sidesaddles, we began to trot off towards Vincennes. Susanne urged her mount into a canter, the plum colored skirt of her riding habit billowed by the rather strong breezes.

"Catch me," Plessis yelled over her shoulder.

"No, wait," I screamed, but too late. Sprinting away, Susanne's steed moved ahead rapidly, causing Pegasus to chafe at the bit. She desperately tried to run faster, and I desperately tried to rein her in.

Suffice it to say I lost the battle. Rearing on her hind legs in an unsuccessful attempt to unseat me, the mare dashed forward. I was bouncing ridiculously against the saddle, convinced I was going to be killed. Pegasus truly took after her winged namesake, and careened down the dirt highway, Madame du Plessis gone from sight.

Leaving the path to Vincennes, the horse crashed through bushes, brambles and overgrowth. I stopped fighting her, preparing myself for a fall. A foot slid out of its stirrup in readiness. The opportunity presented itself when the dappled gray jumped a fallen tree trunk. As she touched in landing, so did I, hitting the ground with a solid thud. Mud splattered on a recently purchased, green damask dress edged in fur. I was wondering whether the garment was beyond repair when the world turned black.

I awoke, unable to breathe. Pegasus nuzzled me with concern. A tassel from her bridle fell into my open mouth and I began to gag.

"My lady, do you live?" a man's voice coming towards me asked. Speechless, I coughed, my chest sore, my breath forming in long, painful draws.

A young man, dressed in somber hunting garb, knelt down beside my still form. Removing his wide-brimmed, plumed beaver hat, he placed it on the ground, lifting me to a sitting position.

"You have lost your wind," he explained, acting very serious and mature. Dark chestnut curls spilled around a lace collar that was exceedingly fine. The thin, upside-down V of a mustache made him appear to be older than his actual age. *By Athena*, I thought to myself, *he looks so familiar—who is he?*

The well-bred knight administered to my condition by delivering a hard slap to the area located between the shoulder blades. I tried in vain to speak.

"Compose yourself," he cautioned. "We shall sit here until your strength returns."

Grateful, I leaned against him, my head on his shoulder. The stranger held me with tenderness, behaved as a gentleman should and did not make me feel uncomfortable to be in his arms. The solicitude was genuine, a show of human kindness.

When I felt somewhat better, I moved away modestly, lest he think me brazen.

"Thank you, sir, for coming to my aid. It seems I am no horsewoman."

"At least you do not cast blame on the animal," he smiled. "The mare is a lovely creature, I must say. Does she belong to your establishment?"

"Yes," I replied standing slowly, taking reins in hand. My backside was very sore. "May I ask your name, perhaps?" I inquired, more out of curiosity than any other motive.

"Tell me yours," he suggested, rising as well. I was wearing a pair of mother's gloves, which fit at last, and he regarded one carefully as he formally bowed, kissing my hand.

"Very nice," he remarked.

"You have an eye for detail, monsieur. Since I like to think I do as well, I must confess I am certain I have seen you before today. Have we met? Or shall I dub you Amphitryon?"

The stranger laughed aloud. "I assure you, my lady, I am no mere Prince of Thebes."

"You know the legend then? You are versed in the Classics? Do you know of Comaetho?"

"Perhaps. Your name first."

"I am Bijoux Cinq-Mars, monsieur. And you?"

His face tensed, then resumed its genial expression. Placing a gem-encircled finger to thin lips, he tilted his head sideways and began to chuckle.

"You have seen me," he confirmed. "Approximately ten years ago, in a hallway at the Louvre. I believe that you were once friendly with my brother, Philippe, were you not?"

"Sweet Athena!" I fell to my knees, trembling, as overwhelmed as I had been on that afternoon when confronted by Noctambule in the woods of Versailles. "Your Majesty! I have been waiting all of my life to make your acquaintance; I cannot believe you stand before me."

"You were not this proper with my brother, were you?" he jested, raising me to my feet. "I appreciate the show of respect, mademoiselle, but do not dirty your pretty dress on my account."

We were staring boldly at one another, tongues tied, not knowing what to say. Then I began to laugh, more at ease with the king than I had ever been with another person, César included.

"What is so amusing?" Louis asked, beginning to guffaw himself.

"I cannot say. You would kill me," was an observation that reduced me to absolute hysterics.

"Do you think me that cruel? Be yourself, mademoiselle. Talk to me as you would to any other—please?"

"Certainly, sire, should you promise not to become cross."

"I give you my royal word."

"I was just thinking, as we gazed into each other's eyes, that your father and my father probably did the same."

"So your father was *that* Cinq-Mars! Then this meeting is rather a strange one, is it not?"

"Not to mention we share the same day of birth, September the fifth, sire."

"No," he said gravely, leading me by the arm to the felled tree, which we sat upon, side-by-side.

"Yes, it is true, sire. I was born with teeth, also, as were you."

"How odd. Are we the same age?"

"No, I am two years younger than is your Majesty."

"Most peculiar," Louis admitted. "Do you think, then, that we might be allies, mademoiselle, considering our parentage?"

"My father was a traitor, my mother a *frondeuse*, yet, I have always defended your name, I have always loved you as my rightful king. When I was little, I dreamt of serving you as a loyal subject should, although my mother, on her deathbed, cursed your family."

"What? How preposterous! Why?"

"The handsome Monsieur le Grand and the exquisite Marion Delorme? Secretly wed, cruelly torn apart by Louis XIII?"

"Oh, now I understand. And you are their daughter."

"Yes, although I am not particularly proud of that heritage."

"Well, we are not allowed by God to choose our parents, mademoiselle."

"Thank you for listening, sire, for I feel relieved having told you of mother's ridiculous hex."

"Why are you so pleasing to me?" Louis asked, taking my hand.

"That I cannot explain, sire," I lied, for I did know the reason.

The king had tasted my blood, we were connected. It was as if Noctambule had sent me to protect the Bourbon, as if the accursed one wished for Louis to reign, despite mother's and Guibourg's fantastic claims to the contrary.

"Talk to me some more," Louis begged. "I find the sound of your voice most soothing."

So I spoke. I told the king that I was well acquainted with d'Artagnan, and that I had lived with Choisy at the Luxembourg and had exposed her scheming to the cardinal while Louis lay dying. Then I spoke of Fouquet, Mazarin and the Company. The king was unaware I had gathered information for his godfather from a tender age; impressed, he kissed me on both cheeks in gratitude.

"Sire," I blushed, "should we not be on our way? Dusk approaches."

"Why should I rush back to Vincennes?" he pouted, shrugging his shoulders. "All that awaits me there is a pious mother in mourning, a wife who hardly speaks my language and ah, yes, a dwarf who follows his mistress about as would a lapdog."

"Nabo! How is he?"

"You know of whom I speak?"

"Certainly, Majesty. M. Fouquet put the Moor in my charge when the boy arrived at Saint-Mandé from North Africa. He is terribly sweet, sire."

"Who? Fouquet or the dwarf?"

"Nabo, of course. Fouquet is, well, how should I put it tactfully? A man to keep an eye on."

"That is what the cardinal said," Louis fumed. "Between us, I hate the surintendant—I loathe him. I know he wants to start another Fronde, I know it."

"Fouquet would require the help of the Company of the Blessed Sacrament to do that and since the group was more or less dissolved by an act of Parliament, its membership is no longer a threat to you."

"Mazarin told me of a letter that Fouquet's brother wrote to the surintendant from Rome. Something concerning M. Poussin and the sharing of a great and powerful secret. Did the Company of the Blessed Sacrament not claim to be privy to hidden knowledge as well?"

"Yes, although I have it on good authority that the Company was concerned with the re-establishment of the Merovingian bloodline upon your throne."

"Who told you that, mademoiselle?"

"I uncovered the Company's agenda and told d'Artagnan, who in turn informed the cardinal."

"You never mentioned the plot to anyone else, did you?"

"Sire, I swear to you I did not."

"Whom do you think the Company picked to be my usurper, after uncle Gaston died?" Louis mused.

"The Duc de Guise," I said without wavering. "What the matter? You are the rightful ruler of France, not a supposed descendant of Clovis I."

"Yes, quite," Louis agreed. "I wonder where d'Artagnan lurks," he muttered, standing.

"He is with you?" I practically jumped from the tree trunk in my excitement, face-to-face with the royal companion. With a graceful motion, the king enclosed me in a strong embrace.

"Stay with me," he whispered. "I need you; return with me to the château."

"Sire, I am honored and might I suggest that since the unfortunate demise of Monsieur Morin in fifty-six, you might avail yourself of my astrological talents. I am most proficient at the casting of astral schemes; however, as for other duties…"

"However?" he teased. "I do not care for that word, mademoiselle, do not utter it again."

"Your Majesty, I had relations with your brother."

"As I recall, those *relations* were limited, were they not?"

Louis was driving me mad with longing and for some reason, César was the furthest thing from my mind. I am not condoning that fact, simply telling the truth.

"Are you an innocent?" he pressed relentlessly, not interested in other portents.

Staring at the man whom I had worshipped since childhood, I decided that if my husband was going to keep secrets from me, I was going to keep one from him as well. Not a good reason to commit adultery; yet, the one I employed to justify pressing my mouth to Louis', to satisfy the craving borne for another to whom I felt inexplicably bound.

Louis' kisses were heated, passionate, and I returned his ardor. Whereas César's lovemaking was gentle and warm, as though a greater, benevolent power enshrouded us in bliss, the feel of the king's body cleaving to my own stirred darker, more violent urges; a compelling lust void of decency.

No doubt in a hurry to return to Vincennes, Louis showed some control when he stilled our lips, lifting me onto Pegasus and leading the mare himself through the darkening wood.

"Where is your mount, sire?" I asked.

"With Monsieur d'Artagnan," he answered. "We must find the sous-lieutenant or else he will return to Vincennes and sound the alarm that I am missing."

"Good thinking. However, once we arrive at the Château, how am I to enter your rooms undetected?"

"Go to the stables with d'Artagnan. I shall return to my quarters and make an appearance. When all has been attended to, a few Musketeers will be sent to act as your escort to the royal apartments. You were Mazarin's agent, so why should I not confer with you now that the cardinal is dead?"

"And the queen?"

"The queen will be in bed, resting. She is with child."

The king's statement caused me no remorse, for I was not concerned with Marie-Thérèse's feelings or how my consorting with the father of her unborn child might affect her were she to discover the scandalous liaison. Instead, I focused on the white feathers adorning Louis' hat, a traditional symbol of mourning amongst the French aristocracy.

"Look, d'Artagnan," the king said with relief, waving to the leader of his personal Guard. Besides the horse that he was riding, my old friend had in his custody the royal stallion, which pranced alongside the Musketeer's, whinnying at the sight of his master.

"Your Majesty, I was most concerned as to your welfare," Charles de Batz admitted when we met, dismounting so he might attend to Louis, offering him a leg up, then handing the king a set of reins, "yet, considering your choice of company, I should not have fretted in the least."

"Hello, Monsieur d'Artagnan. How fare you and your charming wife?"

"I am all the better for seeing you, mademoiselle, and my wife, well, she keeps busy with our son."

"Monsieur," Louis crisply interjected, "Mademoiselle Bijoux is accompanying me to the château where I should like you to entertain her until I send for the lady. We have matters to discuss—sensitive matters which you are privy to, if I understand mademoiselle correctly."

"She is correct," d'Artagnan replied, very official. "Mademoiselle Bijoux was a spy in the cardinal's pay. I was her contact."

"And she will remain an agent in my employ," the king announced. Wheeling his steed around, he was off, heading back to his duties and obligations, leaving d'Artagnan and I alone.

"What in the name of heaven is going on?" he inquired. "You are getting in way over your head, Bijoux. Allow me to talk with Louis and I shall tell him of the information we gathered for Mazarin."

"No, thank you," I flatly refused. "The king wishes a private audience with me, not you. I believe he wishes to consult his stars."

"The king wishes to bed you, my dear," d'Artagnan snorted. "No woman will ever chart a Bourbon's stars. You'll regret that you ignored my advice when you're the laughing stock of the entire court!"

"Jealous?" I quipped, tapping Pegasus lightly with my heels. The Arab mare trotted away, my Musketeer following, bringing up the rear of the troupe.

Most of the way to Vincennes, I relived that night when I had saved Louis' life and made love to Charles de Batz in the lovely, yellow room at La Volière—the incident seemed so long ago, as if it had happened to another, not to me. The only memory that was vivid, that I could remember with clarity, was the sound of the roar issuing from the crowd outside the Louvre when the people had realized their young king would live. That and the sensation of joy I had experienced, knowing instinctively the tonic had been effective.

We were nearing the château, Charles was alongside, and silence engulfed us as we walked our mounts slowly, allowing Louis to approach alone so he might appear to enter the main courtyard unattended. Glancing sideways at my friend, I reached out and put a hand on his, patting it to the rhythm of hoof beats.

"D'Artagnan, do not be vexed with me. I thought any romantic nonsense behind us."

"Nonsense? You consider losing your virginity to be nonsense?"

"Charles, you know I shall always love you differently than I love anyone else in this world, yet the fact is that you are married to Charlotte-Anne."

"Yet another sacrifice made for the great cardinal, may he rest in peace. I should have married you, Bijoux, I admit it. I did ask you to come back to me, remember, on the day I delivered your jewels?"

"Speaking of jewels, did you get a good price for the ones I loaned to you?"

"The coins from their sale are long gone. I had to borrow more money from Colbert."

"D'Artagnan, what are you going to do! You cannot continue to make loans! It's bad business."

"What else do you suggest? The men need uniforms, muskets, saddles—the spending never stops."

"Forget our former commerce. Consider the stones a gift, from me to you."

Raising the hand that rested on his, the golden beard rubbed against mother's glove. Looking at me, d'Artagnan resembled the carefree man he had been in the past, before the demands of matrimony and Musketeers had aged him.

"I shall always love you, Bijoux Cinq-Mars. Take care where the king is concerned."

"What are you referring to, exactly?"

"I am referring to sleeping with the king. Is his Majesty who you really want?" He eyed me intently.

"Yes," was my answer. Through a break in the trees I could see a level plain stretching before the impressive Château of Vincennes. Thinking of Madame du Plessis, I asked d'Artagnan for a favor.

"Would you be kind enough to ask one of your men to deliver a note to Saint-Mandé, to my friend, Susanne du Plessis, informing her that I am here and safe?"

"I shall carry it to her myself," he offered. "I have no desire to stand in wait outside the king's chamber this evening. A man may endure only so much, *ma petite*," he smiled sadly. "Let us be off then, and procure for you some paper and pen."

We cantered the short distance to the stables, serving as a makeshift headquarters for the Grand Musketeers. D'Artagnan's company was installed there, busily cleaning tack, dismantling and rebuilding muskets, or practicing their swordsmanship. More than one of the elite Guard cast an appreciative glance in my direction as I rode through their midst with Charles de Batz; his own eyes glued straight ahead, the sous-lieutenant ignored the stir my presence created amongst his men.

Helping me down from Pegasus, d'Artagnan treated me as

he would have a distinguished guest, offering me an arm as we made our way to the commander's office set up inside the warm, lantern-lit barn. He offered me a bale of hay as a seat cushion and I watched him fumble about his field desk for writing implements.

"Here, use this," he said, handing me an old message, written in what I recognized to be the cardinal's hand. "I think the back is clean."

"Are you certain? The note bears Mazarin's signature."

"He's dead now, go ahead."

Taking the proffered quill from my host, I wrote: *Susanne, I am meeting with the king at Vincennes and all is well. Please inform César that I shall be home before midnight. La Loy.*

"There, that should do. Thank you." Folding the paper, I surrendered it into my friend's keeping, watching him place the reused letter inside a leather doublet that was stretched tight across his husky frame. Too much time spent at court and not enough in the field was the cause, I reckoned.

A Musketeer strode forward with a dispatch, bearing the king's red seal. D'Artagnan took the order, unrolled it, read Louis' command and crumpled the sheet into a ball.

"Ready?"

"Yes, of course, monsieur. Do not sound, though, as if I were going to my execution, if you please."

"Quoting your father again, mademoiselle?"

"I do not consider that remark to be amusing," I answered with mock irritation, placing a good-bye kiss on his cheek. "Will you tend to my horse?"

"Yes, yes, off with you now. One must not keep a king waiting, mademoiselle."

Walking towards the main entrance, flanked by four soldiers, I contemplated d'Artagnan's words. Not for a moment did I think I was making a mistake by going to Louis, nor did I consider what impact the action might have *vis-à-vis* the future of my marriage to César; devoid of sensibility, I was being driven to distraction by a man who was little more than an acquaintance.

Yet how might I have been wary of that other soul who had been touched by Noctambule's power?

Bedding-down with a king is different than sleeping alongside an ordinary man, due mainly to the fact that most everyone at court attempts to couch with him as well, whether literally or figuratively speaking. From the moment I arrived at Louis' suite of rooms, a veritable army of courtiers and servants were chatting in the hallway outside his apartments, loitering about the royal confine in hopes of being needed. When I appeared with the Musketeers and was directly ushered beyond the guarded door that granted or denied access to the person of Louis XIV, a stunned crowd began to whisper, speculating as to whom I might be and why his Majesty was interested.

Inside, I was shown through a reception room, ushered past a study, and marched down a short corridor to a foyer, where I was told to await a summons. Within five minutes, an audience with Louis Bourbon was granted Bijoux Cinq-Mars. Entering a king's most private space is an intimidating prospect and I tried to convince myself that gaining access to that bedchamber was no different than paying a visit to the Sanguine Room in mother's day; yet, the comparison left something to be desired and was not exactly comforting.

Stepping over the threshold, I took a deep breath and ventured forward. I had to be brave. Louis burned for me and I wanted him, as well. That was what I had to remember.

"Your Majesty," I said in a clear tone when I saw the king, who was being waited on by a very formally attired gentleman. Louis was a good actor because he feigned indifference when I curtsied in front of him, refusing to look in my direction.

"Leave me," he instructed to the man who was fussing with cape, boots and spurs. "I shall not require your services this evening. I am not to be disturbed."

Glancing surreptitiously at me, the crestfallen attendant bowed and held the pose as he shuffled backwards out of our vision.

"So," the young man began nervously, assuming a different

demeanor indoors than he had out in the open air, "how fare you this evening, mademoiselle?"

"The same as I did earlier today, thank you, sire."

"Good," he replied, clearing his throat. Turning, Louis neared the deep-set marble fireplace. Two large, white-hot embers had burst forth onto the floor, escaped from a blazing stack of logs, and he kicked them back onto the flames with precision.

"I adore hunting," he confided. "I hate being cooped-up in drafty houses, confined inside a place like this, no better off than a prisoner. Do you fear prisons, Mademoiselle Bijoux?"

"I have never been inside a gaol, Majesty."

"Nor have I."

"Never?"

"Truly. I think that being sentenced to a cell would be the worst fate one could suffer."

His morbid fascination with incarceration was puzzling. Why would a king worry about being sent to jail? Had Mazarin scared him as a youth, during the Fronde, with tales of exile?

"Your Majesty, may I speak openly with you?"

"By all means," he said, straightening to seem taller. "Speak your mind, you have my permission."

Trying to walk as gracefully as I was able, I went to his side. When I was quite close to where my host stood, I stopped, touching his face gently. The man before me, whom most people envied due to his position and noble birth, was desperately lonely.

"You are *le Dieu-Donné*, sire. Who would dare harm you?"

Moved, Louis gathered me into his arms, leaning against me with relief.

"I sense you possess a true and loving heart; a rare thing to find at court."

Kissing each other gingerly, as old lovers might do, we separated a bit to make conversation easier.

"Do you possess a lover, as well?" he asked.

"Yes."

"Who is he?" Louis frowned.

"You," I smiled, feeling no shame. When one is living out a dream in the waking world, one does not trifle with details.

The king was enthralled with what he assumed to be the simplicity of my character, and he toyed with a curling wisp of tendril hanging loose from my forehead, remarking on its vibrant hue.

"People say that those born with teeth and red hair are children of Lucifer," was my reply.

"That name means *morning star*," he murmured, taking the liberty to bite at my neck, placing his hands on a bosom covered with costly fabric, clawing at my gown.

Because I am not proud of this particular chapter in the story of my life, and also because I must purge the awful memory from my mind before I die, I shall continue with a description of the mutual seduction. Yet, heed the warning that should you ever find yourself in a similar situation, patient reader, think of my sad example and walk away.

Morality aside, in the meantime I was moved to sighs by Louis' manipulation of my person. I took to a similar form of enticement, daring to move his fingers to a button concealed under fur trim.

"Shall I?" he hesitated, unaccustomed to such a show of familiarity.

"Please, sire."

Watching him undo each closure with a methodical intent, I breathed easier when the last was freed at the hem of the skirt.

"How novel. Most ladies require laces, stomachers, corsets. What fashion is this?"

"My own. I abhor constraints."

"Not that you need them," he observed, feeling underneath the loosened cloth. What he met with was naught but an embroidered shift and the requisite, outer *modeste* petticoat.

"Dispense with the gown, your Majesty."

"Yes, of course, how practical." I was soon immodestly outfitted.

Not one to wait, I allowed the king to stare at my naked

arms while I hurried to strip off his long jacket, lace jabot and full-cut, sweat-stained shirt of lawn.

"Might you manage with the boots as well?"

"If you position yourself on the bed, I think yes. Let us give it a try."

Kicking off my buckled pumps, I went to our eventual destination, patting the mattress. Pushing aside a weighty beige curtain to create more space, I hardly noticed that gold *fleur-de-lis* ran rampant everywhere over the material, busy as I was with making a comfortable spot for the king to rest.

When Louis was ensconced, I pulled with all my might on the heel of a well-shod foot, removing first the right, then the left, leather covering.

"You amaze me, Bijoux. My valet struggles daily with that chore, and yet, you did it quite easily."

"I am indispensable, then, sire?"

"Quite," he held out a hand. Long, thin fingers, inherited from the queen-mother, beseeched that a subject should attend to her sovereign.

Availing myself of the short, wooden box of steps that made accessing the bed's height simple, Louis and I were soon lolling atop a lovers' paradise within moments, two with a mission to become one. Breeches disappeared, undergarments were relegated to the floor, and bedding was tossed aside in our haste to embrace.

"Do you love me alone?" he insisted, breath hot, tongue tasting the length and breadth of my body.

Colors swirled before my closed eyes, a rainbow of light comparable only to the splendiferous robe a transformed Noctambule had dazzled me with at Versailles long ago.

"I shall never forsake you," he vowed as our shared torment forced us to join with a vengeance. "You are a part of me. We are one, at last."

"At last?" I repeated, my head tossing wildly.

"My other self," Louis intoned, none too quietly. We were entwined as though we could never part, our shared ardency beyond control, an insistent team of runaway Furies that sped flesh and bone to an idyll where thought and sight became blurred, only touch and sound and ecstasy all important.

I opened my eyes when I realized we had ceased moving and that the king had become quite still. The candles in their sconces were burning low, casting undulating shadows on the two walls not hung with tapestries. Pinned to the mattress by Louis' exhausted frame, I glanced about the room. Dazed from the experience, I could not help but start when I perceived a form rustling about a dark corner.

"What is it, my darling?" the king asked, head resting against my own.

"Nothing. I was seeing specters," I explained. "Your embraces made me dizzy."

"I have never experienced the like," he commented. "This very afternoon I was thinking how wonderful it would be to perchance upon a soul mate, to love a lady with whom one could commune, in the flesh and in the mind. I have not had that in my life 'till tonight."

"Do you mean me, sire?"

"Of course. You appeared as would a miracle, thrown across my path, thrust before my eyes. 'Twas no coincidence that we met, my dearest Bijoux; you, born on the same day of September as was I. What are the odds of that happenstance, do you wager, not to mention a king being in the forest at the same time as you, yourself?"

"Not great. I must compare our nativities in detail. Yet birth dates and chance encounters aside, you are correct, for our spirits are in harmony."

"I love you. I shall make you my official mistress, my *maîresse en titre*."

Again sensing another presence nearby, I pulled a luxurious, unseamed sheet over our naked limbs.

"Someone is here, in this room with us," I breathed into Louis' ear. "We are being watched."

Kissing me with real affection, the king dismissed the notion.

"No one would venture here not summoned," he asserted. "Do you forget who I am?"

My chin rested on his shoulder and my hands were rubbing a strong, lean back. I was about to answer when I definitely saw the whites of a pair of eyes peering at me from across the way.

"Your Majesty, over there, look!" I pointed, calling Louis' attention to the intruder.

"Who goes there?" he demanded.

"Nabo," answered the squeaky voice with which I was so familiar. Stepping into the light, I saw my friend move forward.

"Dear Antiochus," I coaxed nicely, well aware of Louis' dislike for the dwarf, "why are you here?"

"Nabo mad at you!" he chastised, pointing an accusing finger at me. "Rouge bad and me tell Maria-Beresa on you."

"What?" The king was incensed. He sat upright, glaring at his wife's pride and joy.

"Who sent you here?" I pried, ruing the day I had taught the youth how to be a spymaster.

"My lady, my queen. She love king and want to be with him, but he with you. He mean and you mean. Nabo hate you both!"

"I hate you, too," Louis snarled. "Begone, creature!"

"Stop!" I pleaded. "Anger will solve nothing. Nabo, attend me."

"No."

"Nabo, present yourself, *now*," I barked.

Hanging his head, the tiny Moor shuffled over to my side of the bed. Although he refused to look at me, I leaned over the side of the pallet and lifted him up, depositing him on the edge of the mattress.

"Nabo," I began slowly, in an attempt at diplomatic speech, "do you love your queen?"

"Yes."

"Do you wish to cause your lady pain?"

"No," he insisted, shaking his head from side to side with such conviction his earring jiggled.

"Then you will not tell her what you saw this evening, understand?"

Nabo regarded me with contempt. "You think you smart, but you stupid. Me not tell Maria-Beresa...me tell César."

"Who is César?" Louis queried, suddenly suspicious.

"One of Fouquet's retainers, Majesty," I supplied, poking my perceptive ex-student in the ribs. "He helped to tutor Nabo."

"Oh, I see," my paramour smiled. "We do not want an irate husband in the picture to disturb our happy arrangement, do we?"

"How droll," I laughed. "Me, married?"

"You in love," Nabo protested. "You kiss Monsieur César. You love him."

The plaintive defense on my husband's behalf made me wince with pain. What had I done? A young foreign lad possessed more sense than did I; me, who had lived with, spied for, and occasionally outfoxed some of the great strategists of the court. Had I been mad? What had I been thinking, play-acting lover to the King of France?

"Your Majesty, I beg your leave," I said hurriedly, moving to depart, not concerned if Nabo saw me as naked as on the day I was born. I dressed with haste and Louis observed my actions with surprise.

"And where do you think you are going?"

"Home. I must return to Saint-Mandé."

"You will stay," he commanded.

"I am leaving," I answered, understanding how my father could have argued with his Louis.

"Because of our uninvited guest?"

"No, because I must. Go to the queen, reassure your wife that you were speaking to me about matters of state, about spying, about anything but love, sire. She carries your child."

"I suppose you are correct," he acquiesced. "If I do not go to her, Marie will complain to my mother and then I shall hear a lecture concerning heaven and hell. All that rubbish," he sighed.

Nabo was helping me to button my dress, glad to see me clothed again.

"Good-bye, your Majesty," I said to the king when I had finished, not knowing how else to dismiss oneself from the royal presence.

"Such formality," he chided, motioning for me to come closer. "Kiss me in parting, at least."

Suddenly revolted by the man, I shut my eyes and let his mouth attach to mine.

"Come back tomorrow," he insisted. "We could meet in the woods again and discuss the planets?"

"No," I begged off, trying to think of a suitable excuse, "I have another obligation."

"What could be more important than satisfying my desire?" he asked in a peeved tone. "Or consulting your king concerning the heavens?"

"I promised to visit a dear friend who is living at a convent in Paris—Paul Scarron's widow."

"You are acquainted with her? My mother recently granted Madame Scarron a pension, you know."

"The queen-mother is a true saint. *Adieu*, your Majesty, until we meet again."

"When?"

"I am not a gypsy woman with a ball of crystal, sire," I snapped, irritated. "Whenever."

"Whenever I say," he chuckled. "Soon. We shall test your skill at predicting my future."

I hated myself. Never again would I spend time in Louis' bed. A fiendish spell had been cast over me, one I was determined to break in that instant.

"Come," I said, tugging on Nabo's short arm, displaying my anger to him. "Let us to the queen."

"I love you," Louis called out merrily. "I return to Paris on the morrow—I shall send for you."

"Wonderful," I grumbled under my breath, harried beyond belief. Reaching the door that led outside to the court, I leaned against the polished wood and began to cry tears of fury and regret.

"Rouge, what wrong? You mad at me?"

"No, no," I said, patting Nabo's hair. "Please, say nothing to César about tonight—I love him, Nabo. This, that," I gestured in the direction of the bedchamber, "was bad."

"Me still love you," he admitted, hugging my knees. "Me sorry."

"No, Nabo, no. You have every right to hate me because I am a horrible person. I am the blood drinking *vrykolakas*," I laughed between sobs, "the doomed Comaetho. Marion, you always knew it! I hope you are finally at peace!"

Opening the door, I ran away down the hallway, sick at heart. I was a wretch and so was Louis; we were two of the same kind. Small wonder I had longed for him, dreamt of him, for he was a reflection of my base nature—since that night in June he had become infected by way of my wicked blood.

How could I have slept with yet another man? The betrayal bore Noctambule's imprint; the damned Immortal had steered me in Louis' direction; he did not wish me aligned with César, but why not?

After arranging for a carriage home, Pegasus tethered to the back of the vehicle so she might follow along behind, I decided the time had come to confront my husband about the Company, to ask him to divulge the carefully guarded Secret concerning the Merovingian dynasty.

Either César would tell me why his family tree was specially favored, as he had promised to do on our wedding night, or I would leave our marriage forever.

The coach bearing the royal crest halted in front of Saint-Mandé, and two grooms bounded up to the impressive vehicle, not expecting me to appear. Asking the disappointed lads to return Pegasus to the stables, I dashed into the house, took the grand staircase to Fouquet's quarters and banged on the door. The surintendant, not La Fôret, answered.

"Is Susanne with you?" I was out of breath from running.

"Yes and she has been worried sick," he said in a rather fatherly manner. "When d'Artagnan came knocking, we were afraid a mishap had occurred. What were you doing speaking to Louis?"

"May I come in? Or must I tell everyone at Saint-Mandé what transpired at Vincennes?"

"Forgive me," he apologized. "*Entrez.*"

Susanne was on her way to the door and she greeted me warmly with open arms.

"*Bon Dieu*, girl," she scolded, "you gave me a fright. How did you manage an audience with the king?"

"Did you tell César where I was?"

My friend rolled her eyes. "Yes and he is not a happy young man at the moment."

"Perhaps if he cared for me, he would trust me with certain confidences and I would not be compelled to look for answers elsewhere, *n'est-ce pas?*"

"What did you discuss with Louis?" Fouquet inquired for the second time.

"Not much. We were too busy occupying ourselves with other matters, if you must know."

"Not?" Susanne was speechless.

"Yes."

"*Touché*, La Loy!" Nicolas grinned. "Bijoux Cinq-Mars, my retainer, the first *maîtresse en titre* of Louis' reign. Do not forget to speak well of me, once you have the king at your beck and call."

"Be still," Susanne ordered, pacing the richly woven carpet. "Do you love the king, Bijoux? Are you prepared to give up César and move to the court?"

"I must answer *no* to both questions, madame," I replied. "The king, however, does not take *no* for an answer, I fear. I have landed myself in a fine mess."

"I do not wish to be a party to this conversation," Fouquet remarked. "At the moment I am attempting to win the king's favor, not his ire."

"A tricky situation," Susanne agreed. "For the time being, if Louis contacts you, rebuff him sweetly—cite an uneasy conscience, anything," she counseled, with a wave of her hand. "You are both married people. Double adultery is double adultery."

"Oh?" the surintendant said, intrigued. "You are married to César? You, the wife of Frédéric-Maurice's..."

"Nicolas!" the marquise commanded, flashing a dagger-look at her lover.

"Susanne," I objected, "how could you divulge that information? Louis has no idea I am married."

"My lips are sealed," Fouquet insisted. "Your secret is safe with me."

With that promise, the door burst open and in strode an agitated César. Costumed as though he himself had been hunting, spurs clanged against the parquet floor as my husband made his way to the spot where our triumvirate stood, mouths agape.

When he was close enough to reach, César grabbed me hard by the arm, wishing to inflict pain. The look in his eyes told me that somehow he was aware of my sin.

"Excuse me for interrupting your conversation, surintendant, madame; however, I have come to collect my wife."

"César, darling," Plessis explained, "we were merely discussing Bijoux's audience with the king."

"I do not doubt your word for an instant, madame," he growled, holding me tighter. "Yet, my wife's obsession with subterfuge makes me wonder as to her real motive for riding to Vincennes. "

"Let go of me," I yelled at him. "You understand nothing, you fool! Release me this instant! The king and I spoke of astrology—nothing more."

"Excuse us," César said loudly, escorting me out of the room, dragging me down the corridor, pushing me up the stairs. He said nothing, raging inwardly, shoving me roughly into the apartment when we arrived.

"So," he bellowed at me, slamming the substantial door shut with such force that I thought it would fall from its hinges, "I did not realize until this evening that I had wed a slut! I should have known better, for the apple does not fall far from the tree, does it?"

"Go to Hades!" I retaliated, outraged he dared to compare me to my mother. "What right have you to say I slept with the king? I have always intended to become the king's astrologer, you know of that ambition."

"More the king's concubine, Bijoux! You have broken my heart, you have destroyed me with this infidelity!"

"What are you ranting on about? Why do you accuse me of adultery?"

César's fists were clenched, he walked away, no doubt counting to ten. After a pause, he continued, "When Susanne informed me of your meeting with the king, I saddled my horse and rode to Vincennes, as would an idiot, to return you safely to Saint-Mandé. I arrived at the château and no sooner was I inside the place when Nabo assailed me, weeping and wailing that his Rouge hated him. Naturally, I asked him why he thought that, and venture a guess as to what he told me?"

"You conversed with Nabo?"

"Yes, Bijoux, I did. And he told me that you were distraught because he had found you abed with the queen's husband! My wife, whoring with Louis Bourbon! Was Nabo lying to me, Bijoux, was he?"

César was shaking me by the shoulders, furious. Although I was in fear for my life, I knew telling tales was useless; he would not have believed me if I had constructed the most elaborate lie.

"Nabo spoke the truth."

César's blow struck me in the face and sent me spinning halfway across the room. Falling to my knees, my initial reaction was to touch my mouth, then stare at my fingers to see if I bled.

I did. A split lip was oozing red and I licked away much of the blood. The taste was strangely comforting; a reminder of the tonic that kept me alive.

"I deserved that," I said quietly, looking up at César, who towered over where I knelt. "Strike me again, though, and I shall kill you, I swear it."

"Not if I do away with you first," he exploded, hauling me

to a standing position by the neck of my gown, tearing at the fur trim. "How could you share your body with Mazarin's bastard, with that excuse for a king! Louis is a nothing, a pretender. How could you?"

"He rules all of France which is more than I can say for the great Merovingians," I taunted.

"Daughter of dirt!" he declared. "A person such as yourself has no right to even utter that name, never mind make light of it."

"Then why did you marry me, César? Why not wed a Lorraine or a Guise? Perhaps one of Gaston's daughters would have been a better choice for you as a wife, considering your hallowed pedigree!"

I thought he would hit me again, yet César managed to check his temper and retreat. Going to his desk, he sat on top of the piece dejectedly, watching me tremble from the attack.

"Do you intend to leave me?" I asked, breaking the silence.

"If I part from you, it will kill me, if I stay with you, I deserve to be miserable. And I truly thought that you loved me," he mumbled, shaking his head.

Not wasting a precious moment, I went to him, wrapping my husband in an embrace he tried to avoid, yet could not, since I clung to him with every ounce of resolve I possessed. Kissing the crown of his head, I spoke as I would were I begging to be spared the ax.

"César, I am not going to ask your forgiveness, for I am in the wrong, completely, yet grant me a hearing, please."

"No. Would you wound me anew?"

"You must listen. Do you not care what becomes of us?"

"Oh, very good, Bijoux. As far as I am concerned, we are finished."

"Fine. Hate me. You have every right. Leave me, marry someone else, do as you please; however, first you are going to hear me out, damn it."

I told César of the chain of events leading to the affair with Louis; I confessed I had felt an intense attraction to the

Bourbon since childhood; I tried to put into words my theory that Noctambule's dark presence hovered close to the French throne, protecting the king from harm. I gave voice to the opinion that a great evil was at work in our lives, a sinister power bent on destruction.

"You are possessed by a satanic force?" César mocked when I ceased speaking. "A daemon led you to Louis?"

"Scoff all you want, the statement sounds far-fetched; yet, something strange influenced me today. There is a reason why Noctambule wants the Bourbons to rule France, there has to be an explanation why you and yours are willing to die for the Merovingian cause. You will not help me to understand, César—you refuse to confide in me regarding the Secret—you know the truth and keep it from me, which is something I would never do to you."

I received no response.

"Please," I begged, beginning to cry, "please tell me what you know."

"You want the truth?" he yelled, grabbing me by the hair, pulling me around the side of his work area and forcing me to sit in the seat he used for study. "Bijoux, enlightenment must be earned. The *Secret* may be learned, although it certainly cannot be taught, according to wiser men than myself. If you desire to know what the mystery is about, look. All that you need to help you is right here, in this room, before your very eyes."

"What do you mean?" I asked whilst I glanced about.

"I am referring to opening a book," he said very loudly. "Did it ever occur to you to read anything besides *The Key of Solomon* or an astrological tract?"

César retrieved a thick volume from the bookcase and placed the work in front of me with a thud.

"Start with this," he ordered, "and when you have finished, I shall have another for you."

"Are you granting me a second chance?" I inquired in a genuinely penitent tone.

"Perhaps," he admitted. "If I do, you are not to leave this room, understand? We shall labor here together—me with my research, and you with yours. I want you in my sight at all times: morning, noon and night. No more gallivanting with Susanne. No more talk of becoming the Bourbon's stargazer. And if you should dare approach the king again..."

"I shan't. I promise. Never. I was not in my right mind, believe me."

"Call Lisette and have her draw a bath for you in the other suite," he instructed, his tone cold. "It disgusts me to think that he had his hands on you, that he dirtied what is mine." César's fingers wrapped around my neck and he jerked my head backwards, so that he might look at me with yet more contempt. I did not say a word, closing my eyes to avoid witnessing more of his pain.

"I could strangle you, yet I think that I shall murder him, instead. Would that hurt you?"

I still said nothing.

"Go get clean," he repeated, letting go. Relieved, I hurried to do my husband's bidding, though he caught me by the wrist, stopping me.

"Make it quick. Louis is not the only man in France who has need of you."

I stared at the floor, dreading what awaited. Later, as I cleansed my sullied body in a tub filled with warm, perfumed water, I wept silently, certain César intended to be harsh when I returned to him. Wanting the inevitable to be over with as soon as possible, I bathed quickly, stepped out of the high-sided, metal basin, donned a robe, and went with resignation to my punishment.

That the lover whom I had wronged would dream of revenge was understandable. However, I did not expect the cuckolded husband to push me face down upon the mattress, and tie my hands firmly to the headboard with a rope that had previously supported a drapery swag. The application of a riding crop to my naked body was also a new experience, as was being taken more roughly than had I been at the mercy of an enemy soldier committing a rape.

I did not stir when the offensive cord was loosened, I was

unaware that an ashamed gentleman took his beloved lady into forgiving arms and cried much as would a small boy. Instead, I dreamed the same dream that had appeared to me on the night Louis lay dying and I slept beside d'Artagnan; that reverie of incredible verisimilitude set in a shadow filled, ghostly region, whose unearthly inhabitants invited me to escape the mortal realm and travel to another, more ambiguous, sphere. A place where no one died, yet where no one was considered human, a foggy wasteland where He Who Walks the Night ruled.

In the midst of that somnolent world, sat the old man I had met at Versailles upon a glorious throne, surrounded by adoring minions who collectively applauded their leader; the louder they hailed him, the younger he became. His gray hair turned dark brown and glossy, his handsome mien was not unlike the one I had kissed earlier in the woods of Vincennes, his clothing was fashioned from cloth of gold. Initially a cautious observer of the majestic display, I soon joined the crowd, pushing and shoving to be near to the seat of power.

Noctambule's elegant hand reached out to me in welcome, his subjects bowed with respect in my direction, I was expected to approach the master. Compelled by an inner weakness to obey the call, I walked towards the throne. Then, an ebony blur appeared before me, blocking the way. Looking down, I saw Nabo, who tugged on the skirt of my green dress.

"No, Rouge, no," the Moor beseeched. "That man bad— stay away!"

"What?" the daemon asked in a maniacal voice. "Who dares to interfere with the Immortal Plan?"

"Me," Nabo answered, unafraid. "You bad. Me hate you."

Antiochus was immediately in the archfiend's clutches.

"Leave him alone," I cried out. "He cannot hurt you. I shall do anything you ask, anything."

"Of course you will. You belong to me," the false god laughed. Raising a kicking Nabo aloft so that the disciples might view the sacrifice, he then brought the dwarf's neck close to quivering lips, drove teeth into flesh, and sucked on his victim's blood, tossing a limp body to the ground when he had drained the Moor's life force dry. The spectators went wild.

"Nabo, don't die," I implored, rushing to where he lay, very still. "Come back."

The vision did not end happily. The Moor was dead and Noctambule, whom I finally realized to be himself a *vrykolakas*, was howling with pleasure, delighted his merciless deed had inspired tormented laments.

Then I awoke from the dreadful phantasm, screaming the scream of the dispossessed; a horrifying sound that reverberated down the corridors of a peaceful Saint-Mandé, waking an entire household from their own, less anguished, slumber. Athena had left me—I was certain—for wisdom had been replaced by fear in my heart.

CHAPTER THIRTEEN
Enter Amphitryon

Hidden away, printed upon a page of one of César's books, The Divine Comedy by the Italian poet Dante, I discovered a line that caused my soul to ache when I absorbed the truth behind its message: *There is no greater sorrow than to mindful of the happy time in misery.*

Those words touched me most deeply because the sentiment accurately mirrored the aftermath of Nabo's admission to César at Vincennes. Although I was truly sorry for what I had done, I could not adequately convey the magnitude of my regret. As a result of my inability to beg forgiveness, both my husband and I suffered, avoiding each other's eyes and sleeping in separate chambers at night. Our marriage was a sham and I had only Bijoux Cinq-Mars to blame.

Uncomfortable as the forced confinement was, I spent my waking hours in César's presence, studying by his side. Neither of us spoke to the other and we hardly communicated for nigh two weeks. Susanne was not allowed to visit during that interlude, I was forbidden any correspondence and the name *Louis* was an anathema to the injured party's ears. Not until a week prior to Philippe's wedding to Henriette d'Angleterre, scheduled for March the thirty-first, did we conduct a normal conversation; a discussion prompted by the fact that I had awoken to a severe bout of vomiting.

"Allow me to go to the laboratory," César offered, moved to pity, "and find M. Pecquet. If he has bled anyone today, I shall mix a tonic for you.."

"No," I protested, heaving again into a chamber pot.

"I am going," he replied. Soon dressed, the physician-in-training departed, leaving me alone at last. Watching out a window, I rang for Lisette once my mate quit the house. The lovely young woman promptly appeared and I near fell into her arms.

"*Mon Dieu*, what is amiss?" she asked, holding me tightly against her small frame.

"Find Madame du Plessis. Be quick, please."

She did as I asked after leading me back to the bed. As I waited for my friend, I tried to remain calm, yet a bothersome worry plagued my mind. What if I was with child?

"Darling, you look horrid!" Susanne remarked with concern when she entered the bedchamber. Sitting next to me, she put a hand to my forehead. "Where is César?"

"He went to the laboratory to make me some medicine. I am not supposed to receive visitors, yet I felt so ill..."

"To hell with that husband of yours! The sole reason for my not coming sooner was that I thought the two of you needed some time to patch things up."

"He is angry about Louis, you know that," I groaned. "May I ask you something?"

"Certainly, dearest."

"If one is with child, how soon does it show?"

"Oh, Jesus! You aren't, are you?"

"I think so."

"Is it César's?"

"I am almost certain that I conceived when I lay with the king."

"Holy Mary! That was when? A fortnight ago?"

"Yes, on the tenth of the month."

"And today is the twenty-fourth. Damn!" she cursed. "Did you retch this morning?"

"Do you not smell the foul stuff?" I answered, holding my nose for added emphasis.

"When was the last time Monsieur le Cardinal showed his red hat?"

"Mazarin is dead."

"Bijoux, be serious. You understand my meaning."

"Forgive me," I apologized. "I would say a month ago, about the time of the last full Moon. We're coming on to another, are we not?"

"Came and went three nights ago. Your menses is late. We must travel to Paris straightway and get rid of the thing," she advised in a hushed tone. "I know the name of a woman on the Rue Beaurégard who has much experience in such matters."

"The Rue Beaurégard?" I asked with trepidation, remembering where Marion was buried.

"Her name is Catherine Montvoisin. *La Voisin*, she is called. All the court ladies go to her to have their fortunes told, to buy cosmetics...and the like."

"Susanne, my mother died while trying to abort. Her death was horrible."

"Do you remember what substance she was given?"

"Antimony."

"She swallowed too much, no doubt. La Voisin's draught is made from many herbs. The distasteful business will seem nothing more than a regular purge. You are not far along, at least."

"Quiet. I hear someone approaching," I warned. Sure enough, César walked into the room in a matter of seconds, vial in hand.

"Good morning, madame," he said formally. "I trust you are well."

"Far better than your wife, monsieur," she began curtly. "Look at her, she is ailing!"

"That is none of your concern," he replied, pouring the concoction into a goblet and then handing the cup to me. "Now, if you would be so kind as to..."

The sight of the pink liquid caused me to vomit anon. Unfortunately, the projectile hit the floor since no receptacle could be produced quickly enough to catch the offensive stream.

"Fetch Lisette," my friend ordered in a bossy tone. "I am conveying Bijoux to Paris."

"Bijoux will stay here, at home," César insisted. "I shall not have her flitting off to the Louvre. Do you think me stupid, madame? I know Louis has been sending messages to my wife; letters Monsieur Fouquet has intercepted. Your great friend showed them to me himself."

"What?" I asked, incredulous. "Does Fouquet have the notes in his possession, madame?"

"Yes," she replied quietly. "The king writes you daily."

"*Mon Dieu*! I think I am going to be ill again."

And I was, except that nothing remained in my stomach to disgorge.

"This is ridiculous!" Susanne exclaimed, stamping a foot. "I shall go to Paris myself and find a cure for you, darling," she soothed, leaning over me and winking. "What is that?" she inquired, straightening and turning to my husband, pointing to the chalice.

"A restorative."

"Truly?" the blonde beauty inquired. Walking to where César stood, she peered into the vessel, sniffing at the liquid it held.

"What is in this *restorative* of yours? It smells of flowers."

"Correct, madame. The potion does contain extract of peony."

"And what else?"

"The properties of the elixir are guarded."

"Nonsense," Susanne replied, taking the beaker from him, ready to taste.

"Madame, stop!" I cried out. "The tonic's chief ingredient is blood."

"Human?" she recoiled, regarding me with disbelief.

"Yes," I admitted. "I have been drinking the mixture since childhood."

"Small wonder you're ill!" Susanne went straight to the window, unlatched it and threw the offensive dose into the cold, morning air. "What charlatan prescribed the tonic?"

"The Abbé Guibourg. One of Marion's many lovers."

"Have the two of you gone mad? How could you drink blood, Bijoux?"

"M. Cousinot, the king's First Physician, advises me to take the medicine, as well."

"We shall discuss this matter later. In the interim, rest. And you," she said, addressing César with authority, "you are not to feed her any more of that...whatever, understand?"

"Yes," was the curt reply he gave, whereupon Susanne set down the empty cup and departed for the Rue Beaurégard.

"You could have told me about the king," I said wearily when we were alone. "I would not have accepted anything from him—you did not need to hide his letters from me."

"How noble of you. I wonder, would you have returned these?"

Reaching into a pocket of his long, woolen *justacorps*, César produced a lovely pair of diamond eardrops that were an exact copy of those stolen from me by Philippe.

"May I have a closer look, please?"

"I thought they might pique your interest. Are you really so mercenary, Bijoux?"

"Marion owned a similar set of stones. I thought them to be the same, that is all," I frowned.

Foiled, César returned the gems to their stash. "They go back to the king today. My uncle will also request a royal audience for the express purpose of informing his Majesty that you and I are married. He will produce a document, complete with Mazarin's forged signature, granting us permission to wed. Louis cannot protest our nuptials when shown that paper."

I stared at him blankly. "I must admit I am shocked by your plan to claim me as your wife. I did think that you might deny our marriage."

"Unlike some people, I do not forget my obligations," he responded, hoping to hurt me.

Then the young de la Tour walked out of the room, leaving me to dwell on my problems, least of which included Louis' reaction to Turenne's announcement.

Exhausted after an hour's fretting, I drifted off to sleep, dozing until Susanne returned much later from her outing. She woke me gently, with concern, handing over a bowl of foul-smelling liquor once she had managed to rouse me from an uneasy slumber.

"Here, take this, all of it," she prodded. "La Voisin guarantees results."

"I don't want to die. I am afraid, Susanne."

"Listen to me, you may not be with child, yet Monsieur le Cardinal is late. If nothing else, this will flush him out," she explained. "You will be fine, I promise."

"Stay with me?" I pleaded. "I really am a coward, you know."

"Take the medicine while hot, darling. 'Tis worse when cold."

"Susanne, did you...ever, yourself?"

The worldly marquise blushed. "Yes, many years ago. Now, do as I say."

The bitter brew tasted foul, but the fear I might be carrying a royal bastard compelled me to gag down the warm broth, coughing when finished.

"That was putrid. Must I take it again?" I handed her the empty piece of crockery.

"Maybe. We shall see," she smiled, covering me with a blanket.

Closing my eyes, I tried not to succumb to the temptation of reliving mother's final hours, of remembering the Madame la Grande's cries of self-induced agony.

"Susanne," I murmured, "do you think daughters oft' times repeat their mothers' mistakes?"

"Do not be a simpleton," she chuckled, "or morbid. Think on me as your mother, not Marion. In fact, when I die, you stand to inherit all my property: the house at Charenton and the Hôtel de Rougé in Nantes. Plus my jewels. Now, that's something to live for."

"What?" I asked in a dreamy fashion.

"I am leaving you my worldly goods, dearest. Considering

I have no heirs and you have no parents, the arrangement suits us both."

Susanne held my hand, sitting close to me on the pallet. How long she maintained a vigil by my side, I cannot say, for La Voisin's drugs began their work, rendering me unconscious. Not until the pains grew unbearable did I open my eyes to find César, Plessis and Lisette watching me intently. The room was quite dark.

"Susanne, is it the drink?" I groaned, curled up in a ball from the severity of the pangs invading the lower half of my body.

"Yes, dearest. The worst will be over soon."

"You cannot imagine the pain," I grimaced, tears forming. Amphitryon would see his Comaetho dead yet, I mused silently.

"The spasms are normal, Bijoux. We shall not leave you," Susanne comforted.

"César," I said, grabbing hold of his blouson sleeve, almost ripping it in my throes, "you must forgive me. I love you more than anything. Believe me, please."

"Susanne told me of your sacrifice. My jealousy made me cruel. Forgive me?"

"Too much excitement is not a good thing at the moment," Plessis reasoned. "Lisette, fetch more hot water from the kitchen. César, find some fresh linens, be useful. Darling, be brave."

She repeated those instructions more than once that eve, directing our party through the tawdry experience. The heavy flow of blood draining from my womb and the razor-sharp contractions made me swear aloud while I clawed at the bed sheets; passing through the most critical stage near to dawn, I collapsed with exhaustion, more dead than alive.

Whether I miscarried or not, Susanne would never say. She was of the opinion that La Voisin had made the mixture too potent in her zeal to please a friend of M. Fouquet, and thus the ingredients of the draught were the cause of the unpleasant ordeal. "Do not torture yourself," she advised, "it was too early on to tell for certain."

In the depths of my soul, I knew otherwise.

All strength abandoned me for three days and it was not until the close of March that I was able to sit up in bed and take nourishment, consisting of a bowl of beef stock and a slice of bread. César personally tended to me, refusing to leave me in anyone else's care, and as he fed me spoonful after spoonful of the hot soup, I knew that he loved me again.

"César," I managed to say between mouthfuls, "I am surprised that you are here."

"You have suffered enough," he replied. "The past is the past. When I almost lost you, I realized how much I loved you, and how empty my life would be without you by my side."

A lump was growing in my throat and I looked away from him, unable to respond.

"Bijoux, talk to me. Confide in your husband."

"I cannot," I said, beginning to weep, face in my hands. "I have been such a fool."

"Come here," César answered. "I have something to tell you."

"What?" I asked while I sobbed, relieved that he was kissing me repeatedly.

"Do you recall when I sent *The Key of Solomon* to the Englishman, Robert Boyle?"

"Yes." I replied, wiping at wet eyes. "That was more than a year ago, was it not?"

"Precisely. Monsieur Boyle uncovered Guibourg's mystery."

"He found the *vrykolakas*?" I could not disguise my excitement.

"Yes, however the reference is written in code. Boyle noticed, as he perused the book, that certain letters were misprinted page after page. Writing down the characters in the order they appeared, he soon had a lengthy description of a *vrykolakas*."

"What am I?" Fear prevented me from asking more than that.

"A mortal, in Boyle's opinion. Noctambule, however, is

another matter. *Vrykolakas* is a term applied to those cursed spirits who return from the dead as damned souls trapped in their human bodies. They prey on mortals for their sustenance and thus are condemned to eternal damnation on Earth. Neither alive, nor at rest, these creatures constitute what the Church has recognized to be the living dead."

"Of what do you speak?"

"Officially, in Latin, a *cadaver sanguisugus*, or bloodsucking corpse."

"*Mon Dieu*, that describes Noctambule! Then I am the same!"

"No, Bijoux, Boyle believes that Noctambule attempted to transform you; however, you escaped the blight of the undead because you did not drink of the daemon's blood."

"Then why the tonic?"

"The change was not completed within you, only begun."

"Will I live forever as the old man promised?"

"Only if you drink of the blood of the *vrykolakas*."

"Do you have faith in your friend's opinion?"

"Yes," César said quietly. "He is an expert on such matters. Boyle cited cases of devils similar to Noctambule being seen in Bohemia, Hungary and Poland. And in France and England. He is certain that you are in grave danger and advises that unless we kill the unholy *vrykolakas*, or *vampyre*, as he referred to the hellish beast, you will not be freed of the affliction."

"What did you say? *Vampyre?*"

"That is what he wrote, yet he also cautioned that we should not repeat the name to anyone."

"Why not?"

"I do not know," César sighed, taking my hand in his. "Boyle did not explain."

"I know why. Should anyone find me out, the Church will burn me at the stake as one possessed."

"This will be our secret," César reassured. "Who else knows of the incident?"

"Guibourg and Cousinot."

"Enough said," my love cautioned. "Let us speak of something else."

"Why did Noctambule appear to me?" I complained. "And the beast seems to favor Louis."

César frowned. "Must we discuss him?"

"He is the king, whether you and yours support the Bourbon or not. What is the fascination the Company has with Louis' throne? You break the law merely by belonging to that group."

César smiled unexpectedly, leaving his post and moving to a stack of books piled high upon his desk. "Some people are above the law," he reflected as he sorted through the various titles.

"Do not provoke me," I declared. "I am too weak to argue. All this mystery when you could simply tell me the Secret."

My husband stared at me intently, standing his ground. "I have given my word not to speak about Company business. Not to anyone. Not even to you."

"César, it pains me to think that you are a party to such nonsense. The Company is in the wrong."

"Trust me when I tell you that you are mistaken."

"I shall leave Saint-Mandé," I threatened. "I shall cast my lot with the king, I swear!"

Shocked by my attempt at blackmail, he could think of no suitable response and was saved by a knock at the door of our suite.

"*Entrez*," César implored.

A messenger, whose garb was speckled with dried mud, walked into the room.

"Bijoux Cinq-Mars," the stranger stated.

"I am she, monsieur."

"Louis Bourbon, King of France and Navarre, sends his greetings, madame," he revealed, stepping forward, removing a package from his traveling cloak. Handing the square envelope to me, I first glanced at César, then broke the wax seal. Inside the paper wrapper I found a note and a ring I had seen at Vincennes — a gold band set with one square-cut ruby.

"His Majesty requires a reply," the courier informed me.

Opening what I supposed to be a letter, I found a poem

dedicated to *Comaetho*. Catching my breath, I closed my eyes, afraid to read on.

"What does the king say, wife?" César demanded

Flippantly, I commenced with the delivery of the royal composition, an ode to forbidden love. No longer brazen, I stopped. How had the Bourbon known I was wed? Had Turenne informed?

"Is there no more?" César asked. "Or is that all of it? Give it to me, for I am not ashamed to read the king's verse!" he thundered.

"Monsieur, please," the unnamed one protested.

"I insist," my Chromius shouted, forgetting his manners:

Oh, that you would love me, as others have done,
Cast off this dark mantle, look straight to the Sun;
For the glow of our oneness forever would be,
As the golden, ground sand—its mistress the sea-
Which greets the clear wave and beckons the foam,
Returning it safely, leading it home.

"Very nice!" César commented. "And your reply, madame?"

Still astounded by the outpouring of Louis' emotion, I hung my head in shame. "Please inform his Majesty," I said, addressing the messenger, "that, having recently suffered the loss of the child I carried, my mind is burdened and I cannot accept his tokens of esteem."

"As you wish, my lady," the courier assured. "Monsieur, please return the king's property."

Without a word, César crumpled the expensive stationary into a ball, threw the paper onto the hearth and quit the premises, slamming the door behind him. Louis' emissary did not wait to dash to the stacked logs and retrieve the poetry, which had missed the flames and was only slightly charred by the heat.

"Good sir, please forgive my husband his behavior."

"I shall say nothing to the king," the servant replied,

smoothing the wrinkles from of his master's handiwork. "But you should, madame."

Although a floppy-brimmed hat hid most of the stranger's countenance and his cape's collar was turned up at the neck, I recognized something familiar about him. Was it his fluid gait? His brunette curls? Or perhaps the well-groomed mustache peeking out from the shadow covering his eyes?

"Please tell Prince Amphitryon that I am his most devoted servant," I said softly.

The son of the Virgin was at my side in a moment, fervently kissing my face, my eyes and finally my mouth. I did not resist him, yet rather removed the headpiece he wore, revealing the one face I had not expected to see. The face of Louis Bourbon.

"Sire, what are you doing here? How..."

"I had to see you, my darling, my angel," he explained. "Why have I heard nothing from you in response to my letters? Was it because of *him*?"

"No, Majesty, César is blameless. It was I who sent your messengers away."

"Fouquet will pay for his indiscretion, believe me."

"Then you know everything."

"Enough. Were you telling the truth earlier, about losing the child?"

"Yes," came the uncomfortable admission.

"Was it mine?"

I could not look the rejected lover in the eye. "Yes."

"And was it a natural accident?"

"No," I replied, covering my face with my hands.

"How could you?" he chided.

"Sire, I am married. What else was I to do?"

"You should have come to me. I would have provided for you."

"How could I be sure of that?" I protested, daring to return his hurt gaze. "Think of the scandal a royal bastard would have caused *you*."

Louis smiled, considering my answer. "When may we be together again?" he murmured, touching my hair. "The waiting is killing me, pretty Comaetho. Must I order you to my side?"

"I am not free to obey and I trust you will not prove cruel, dear Amphitryon."

Louis' response was tinged with displeasure. "You will come to court if I say so."

"Majesty, I made a vow to be faithful to one man, not two."

"Madame," he began stiffly, "in France, all vows belong to me."

"Sire, you must forget Vincennes," I admonished. "What we did there was immoral."

"Dare you defy me, rebuff me? Say that I misunderstand your meaning, madame."

"My meaning is clear, sire."

"You will regret this day," Louis declared, leaving his place on the bed to stand, hands on his hips. "Do not expect any marks of favor for you or yours following this incident."

Before I could answer, the spurned suitor turned and left without another glance in my direction, no doubt plotting César's and my demise.

The moment he was gone from sight, I knew I had erred. One did not offend a Bourbon without punishment being meted out as a result—that much I had learned from Cinq-Mars' example.

Too agitated to rest, I decided to make an attempt to rise, dress and locate my husband. Louis had exiled me from the royal camp and the only people to whom I could turn for protection was the membership of the Company of the Blessed Sacrament.

As I set about collecting clothes, my legs were trembling uncontrollably as much from fear of the new Amphitryon's retribution as from the physical ordeal I had endured.

Louis returned to the Louvre and temporarily forgot our confrontation, distracted by the preparations for his brother's marriage. The court was still in mourning for Mazarin, and the ceremony slated to be held on the last day of March was to be a rather simple affair conducted at the Queen of England's chapel in the Palais Royal. Philippe had wished to rush the nuptials along, despite the lack of extravagance, impatient to be granted the larger income that would come to him once married. Henriette, likewise, desired the prestige and power due her once she was Monsieur's wife and she voiced no complaint concerning the rather lackluster celebration. Thus, the contract between France and England was signed and the young couple returned to the Tuileries on a rainy afternoon to begin their new life together, an alliance that would prove an utter disaster.

From the beginning, on the wedding night, circumstances went awry. Philippe was denied his bride's bed, for, as he later commented, "Monsieur le Cardinal slammed the door in my face." Faced with that obstacle, the dejected prince made for his own apartments where the jilted lover, Guiche, awaited. The count proved far more accommodating than the sixteen-year-old Madame, and the handsome courtier boasted he would organize banquets and theatrical performances in honor of Monsieur's stellar match. Thrilled by his friend's loyalty, Philippe basked in the warmth of reunion and promised Guiche that the special friend would share the stage with the wife, their pact sealed with a passionate kiss.

Louis had no choice but to attend the entertainments staged for his brother, who flitted from guest-to-guest with Henriette and Guiche in tow, showing off his two prized possessions. Madame, who was flirtatious owing to a strict upbringing, chatted graciously and made eyes at her brother-in-law, much to the king's amazement. The sovereign also noted that his sister-in-law had blossomed into a lovely creature overnight, gaining confidence and self-possession in her new royal capacity. Philippe's wife intended to supplant the dull-witted Marie-Thérèse as the most important woman in the kingdom, the one whom all would consult on matters of style and taste. The king knew he lacked a pretty, sophisticated wife and the envious Louis forthwith supplanted me with Henriette.

I was unaware of that development and continued to live in fear of the throne. April turned into May, May into June, Vaux-le-Vicomte was nearly completed and no reprimand came. The waiting was torturous. Then Susanne overheard that Madame and her brother-in-law were conducting a passionate affair and my mind was put at ease. Louis had ceased pining for me; Vincennes was naught but a foolish fling. Yet, I should have realized that the king would never forget our union, nor would he forgive me the crime of purposely losing his child. As had his godfather before him, Louis adhered to the wisdom contained in the motto: *Time and I*. The king would wait, he would watch my actions, and when the opportunity presented itself to attack, he would act accordingly.

Naturally, Philippe ran to his mother when he discovered his bride's affection for his own brother. The good-for-nothing rascal would not be made a fool, not by his sibling, nor by Henriette. As soon as he was able, he intended to get Henriette with child and teach her a lesson. And, he also planned to dust his rouge pots and pay a visit to the seamstress. The monarch who had officially forbidden homosexuality at court was about to be challenged, for Prince Tyrannus planned to openly defy the edict and dare Louis to imprison a corseted and bejeweled Prince of the Blood. The torment would be exquisite—an act of cunning worthy Gaston d'Orléans.

The king and his mistress were crafty, as well. Once scolded by two former queens, the lovers decided to outwit their mothers by appearing to end the affair. As a decoy, the pair devised a ruse: Louis would appear to be in love with Louise de La Vallière, the lame girl brought to Henriette's attention by Jeanne-Olympe de Choisy. The lady-in-waiting from Blois was Madame's first choice, certain that no man would ever fall in love with an artless country maid who walked with a limp. And so Amphitryon began to pay La Vallière court; tipping his hat to her when they passed in the gardens, inviting her to accompany him on the daily hunt. The innocent agreed to the charade for a month, until the beginning of July when she found herself madly in love with her attentive suitor.

'Twas then that a spy in the pay of M. Fouquet, Mademoiselle de Montalais, a troublemaker attached to

Madame's entourage and who was also La Vallière's childhood friend, came to Susanne with piquant information. Louise had confided that she and the pretend lover found themselves in the throes of a genuine passion, despite the girl's attempts to thwart a married man's advances. Even Madame did not know of the arrangement, although the timid girl feared that soon everyone would be privy to the truth. Especially when Louis was pressing her to accept tokens of endearment such as valuable diamond earrings and expensive clothing which a person in her position could not afford.

"Louise de la Vallière is positively guileless," Susanne explained as we strolled through the grounds at Saint-Mandé. "She loves the king with a purity of spirit rarely heard of in this day. Of course, Nicolas intends to approach the child with an offer of coins for favorably promoting him to Louis. I have advised against the scheme, but he will not listen, I fear. As with Vaux," she mumbled.

"Vaux? The château is near completion is it not?"

"Yes and Nicolas still insists on staging a fête there in August, a spectacle of staggering proportions. The entire court is invited, and the extravagance he has planned is incredible, yet darling girl, I tremble for my love. Why must he flaunt his wealth, why?"

"Stop him, Susanne."

"I cannot," she admitted, on the verge of weeping. "The Fouquet family receives no more appointments, Colbert watches our Lord Cléonime's every move, and the king infers that something is amiss concerning the ledger books. How might a Surintendant of Finance admit wrongdoing and thus commit political suicide?"

"No!" I cried aloud. "Louis and Colbert will deduce—once they see Vaux—that something suspicious is afoot, that your lover is dipping his hand into the king's purse."

"Having secured the post of Attorney General in Parliament, Nicolas believes himself invincible, for if Louis attacks him now, he attacks the legal system and risks another Fronde. Yet, be that as it may, Colbert would love nothing more than to see the Future fall."

"How might I aid you?" I offered.

"This thing is beyond our control," she observed, wiping her eyes, forcing a smile. "I had to warn you that I see a tempest about to break."

"What becomes of the Company if Fouquet is disgraced?"

"They will survive, no doubt under a new identity. The Company has been in operation for hundreds of years, dear girl; the fellowship is not an invention of the seventeenth century." "Madame, does César know of these events?" I asked in confusion.

Susanne stopped walking, staring at me intently. "Should Nicolas be forced to retreat to Belle-Isle, I shall follow, Bijoux. Because I know of your great wish to understand your husband's tie to the Company, I made inquiries, I asked Nicolas to tell me the Secret. And he did, dearest, he confided in me the truth. Do you desire the knowledge?"

I held Susanne's arm tight for stability; the sky, the clouds, the flower beds were spinning around me. The taste of bile was in my mouth and my entire person tensed.

The end to the search was upon me.

Oblivious to my state, the lovely marquise continued, whispering in my ear, "The Merovingian kings, through an ancient marriage to the Visigoths, were aligned to the biblical bloodline of David and were the relatives of Jesus Christ. That family has in their safekeeping the Holy Grail, the sacred cup which caught Our Savior's blood at the Crucifixion."

"No!" I screamed. "No! It cannot be! Blessed Athena, no, Susanne!" I cried out, sinking to the ground, tears streaming freely, hands tearing at the hem of her gown. "You lie, please tell me that you are lying!"

"Holy Mary! Control yourself," she ordered in a frightened tone, kneeling beside me. "What have I said? Tell me, Bijoux... talk to me!"

Speech would not come. I was choking to death, gagging, clutching at my throat in despair. Could César, by way of his relation to Godfroi de Bouillon, be a descendant of King

David? Could he also be deeply connected to a tradition I did not embrace or understand?

"Help!" Susanne was shouting at the top of her lungs. "Help, please, help!"

A man clutching a spade in one hand, a white kerchief tied about his neck and shirt partly open due to the heat, leapt over a small row of hedges and ran down the gravel path towards the pitiful scene. Joining us, he shook me hard in an attempt to arrest my wheezing.

"Madame, did she swallow a sweet? Did she inadvertently pluck and eat of a poisoned plant?"

The voice belonged to André Le Nôtre, the genteel soul who had given me wise counsel when César and I first argued the existence of Noctambule and Jesus.

"She ate nothing, she touched nothing," Susanne insisted, weeping. "Save her, monsieur, save my darling Bijoux, please!"

I swallowed at emptiness, my bosom was racked with pain. Yet, the thought of César's love, of his good heart, made me struggle, made me gasp with a determination to keep life within my body.

Le Nôtre reached inside his linen blouson and retrieved a golden star, suspended from a thin chain of the same metal.

"Let us pray, madame," he instructed, kissing the talisman and pressing the object to my forehead, holding me firmly by the hair when I attempted to pull away from his determined grasp.

"I banish this adversity, for it has no power," he said with conviction, "and I affirm the supremacy of the Cosmos."

His words rattled in my brain; where had I heard them before? From Jacques, the courier of the deities who had comforted me on the night of Marion's passing. Closing my eyes, I remembered the beautiful being's radiance, his light-filled presence, and I collapsed against Le Nôtre's sturdy frame.

"Look, her chest moves!" Susanne exclaimed, stroking my hair and then slapping my cheek repeatedly. "Bijoux, *chérie*, come back to us!"

I coughed and drew in sweet breath. The attack had miraculously ceased. "Thank you for saving my life."

"Athena saved you, Bijoux, not I," he smiled, pressing a quick kiss against my forehead. "Thank Her, dear child."

"I was useless," Susanne admitted. "Never do that to me again, girl!"

Leaning against the unlikely hero and aided by Susanne, I was able to stand on unsteady legs and return to the main house. Once inside the front doors, we were met by a frantic César.

"My love, what is amiss? I heard a lady call for aid from the garden—was that you, marquise?"

"Yes," I answered for Susanne. "I suffered from a bout of the old affliction, César. Monsieur Le Nôtre saved me from death."

"Kind sir, many thanks," César said with sincerity. "I am forever in your debt. Tell me," he queried, "how did you know to administer the tonic?"

"Tonic? I know not of what you speak, monsieur. Bijoux was cured by...prayer."

"Our friend is partly correct," Susanne confirmed. "Bijoux had ceased breathing, Monsieur Le Nôtre spoke over her, and the choking ceased. Our friend is a powerful healer."

"I did nothing," the modest gentleman maintained, kissing my hand with humility.

"No, you said or did something," Madame du Plessis argued, intrigued by Le Nôtre's reluctance to accept any praise. "What were your words again, monsieur?"

"Good-bye, Monsieur César, ladies," Le Nôtre said with a quick bow. "Take good care and we shall meet again at Vaux!"

The extraordinary gentleman was gone in a thrice, leaving the astonished gathering to their own devices.

"Let us speak privately," I suggested to César, taking his hand.

Susanne smiled wanly. "I must be off to Fontainebleau...the court and its secrets await!"

"Dearest friend, do not fret. All will be well. *The reward of our Faith is to see what we believe.*"

"Please," she laughed aloud, amused by the show of naïveté, "do not turn into a religious convert, Bijoux! I shan't abide visions and voices from Above."

"Well, I have near seen Hades..." I began in jest, although César stopped me midstream.

"*Au revoir*, Susanne, visit us later this evening, should the hour permit," he invited. "We shall share some supper and a few glasses of wine, *n'est-ce pas?*"

"Lovely!" the marquise exclaimed, her face brightening. "Now, that's something to look forward to," she added and was off to Louis' summer headquarters.

"Are you daft?" my husband inquired, leading me up the remaining stairs to the first floor, pausing in the hallway to allow me a moment's respite. "Talking heresy, even in sport, is dangerous."

Without malice, I looked straight into his gray-blue eyes. "Is that why the Company guards its Secret with such vigor?"

He paused. "The Church would not look kindly on what we know," he admitted. "Louis is supported by the clergy, is he not? Your king is a Catholic, do not forget."

"Yes, of course. And *his* Pope would never allow an heir to Pagan tradition to sit a throne, would he?"

César's mouth fell agape.

"Such as a descendant of the Merovingian kings...I do not believe the current conflict to be based on bloodline, alone. Rome would not fear the family of Jesus that deeply, unless, of course, they were not *Christians*, yet rather, *Pagans*, at heart."

With an air of alarm, he covered my mouth with a hand. "Say nothing more. Promise?"

I shook my head in the affirmative and was released. "I discovered the truth in the pages of your treasured copy of *The Secret Secretorum*," I boasted, not about to implicate Susanne or her lover.

"Come with me," he said in a hushed tone. "This is not the place to discuss the matter."

Making for our rooms, César said not another word until the door to our apartment was bolted.

"Now, what were you babbling on the stairs?"

"Do not mock me, César. I see through the Company's façade."

"Let us dispense with the banter. What compelled you to speak of Pagan ritual?"

"César, Godfroi de Bouillon traced his ancestry back to the Merovingians, did he not?"

"Yes."

"And the Company's candidate for the throne is always connected, either by blood or by marriage, to that illustrious Crusader who captured Jerusalem?"

"I would say yes."

"Thus, would it not be safe to assume that the Secret concerns the Merovingian dynasty, those mysterious rulers who lost their power a century ago?"

César said nothing in response, his eyes very wide.

"Why would a particular bloodline be more revered than any other unless a mystical or holy importance was attached to the race? Why would a far-removed heir to long forgotten legends be the rightful ruler of France unless," I paused for added emphasis, "unless César, that individual was the living embodiment of a sacred trust, of an ancient covenant between man and...the Divine?"

"Say it then, Bijoux. I wish to hear the words from your own lips."

"The Secret concerns a pedigree, a venerable and noble lineage bestowed with an inheritance of knowledge stretching back to the Old Testament Kings of Israel, specifically those issuing from the royal seed of David, who originally received their wisdom from the sages of Egypt, I would daresay. The same blood that begat Jesus the Nazarene, who was a son of this same tradition, as had been Solomon and that king's father before him. I see the matter so clearly now—a once blessed, now heretical, family tree that somehow grew roots in France, perhaps with the arrival of Mary Magdalene, Martha and Lazarus to our shores, under the name Visigoth, then Merovingian."

"I have witnessed a miracle," César burst forth, lifting me up by the waist. "My supplications have been answered! I wished to tell you myself, however, my uncle threatened to disown me if I uttered a single word on the subject. He compelled me to take an oath swearing total allegiance to the Company. You do not know how much it pained me to keep the truth from you, of all people."

"Then you aren't dismayed? You are glad?"

"Never did I intend to keep the Secret from you, Bijoux, yet I had no choice. My word is my bond. A man is nothing if he lacks honor."

"Pray tell, does everyone in the Company know the Secret?"

"No, only a select few. Imagine the discord that would ensue if word of the legacy was leaked. The Church would refute our philosophy, they would attempt to steal and destroy our sacred scrolls and Louis would be compelled to lead forces against the Company to protect his considerable interests. The people would be embroiled in yet another war of religion. Why do you think the Church crusaded against the Cathars and the Knights Templar long ago? 'Tis better to remain underground, promoting our cause through intermarriage, intrigue and infiltration of the government."

"Through allies such as Fouquet?"

"Precisely."

"And painters of the Classics such as M. Poussin?"

"Aha, you do see. Did you know that when Poussin returned to Rome in 1642, he had a ring engraved with the word *Confidentia*, featuring a lady holding aloft a ship?"

"César...that is Athena! She is the goddess of ships and of navigators, she fashioned Jason's boat, the Argo, with no aid or assistance."

"Yes, darling, your beloved goddess of Wisdom is well revered by our Company. Pallas Athena was originally known as Trivia, representing Maiden, Nymph and Crone. She ruled the Sun and the Moon, and Comaetho's story concerns your patroness in her aspect as a death goddess."

"Tell me more," I pleaded. "I must understand."

"Long ago, royal rule was determined by women, not by men. Many ladies of noble descent determined the affairs of nations and were considered by the ancients to be as bee goddesses, or overseers of the hives of humanity."

"Athens was known for its honey," I interrupted, "and...the brooch! From the Merovingian tomb!"

"Yes, Comaetho ruled Taphos, not Pterelaus. And she was a High Priestess of Athena."

"No! Then why the story of her treachery, of her betrayal?"

"Athena's status as Trivia was eventually diminished due to the rise of powerful solar kings, who no longer saw themselves as sons of a goddess, wedded to the Moon, yet rather, conquerors of matriarchal governments. That is why Moses usurped his sister Miriam as spiritual leader of the Israelites. We have the proof in an ancient record, kept safe here in France–the Book of Yasher–written by an influential Hebrew courtier at the time of the Exodus from Egypt. The same account that was a Merovingian prize later acquired by Charlemagne; the reason for the founding of the University of Paris, where the work long reposed."

"So women do guard the Grail–they are the keepers of the flame? The Church fears women?"

César nodded. "Wait until Monsieur Perrault's tales of abandoned princesses are published...more myths about forgotten goddesses waiting in enchanted slumber, or beside dirty hearths, to redeem mankind. A kiss of recognition is all that is usually required. That should please you greatly."

"How clever! Do these ladies have names?"

"The Sleeping Beauty and Lady Cinderella are two."

"Tell me more of the Holy Chalice. Is the Company's use of Christian allegory a ruse to keep Rome at bay? Are the Company's ancient grimoires kept at St. Sulpice? Did fair Esclairmonde of troubador song and legend know the Secret, too? Did she truly live in France long ago?"

"You are so full of questions!" César chuckled. "So

inquisitive. Would that you showed such fervor for your poor, lonely husband," he teased.

"Do respectable wives find time for romance with their husbands while the Sun shines brightly, monsieur? Are such dalliances considered proper for daughters of Luna?"

"I care not a whit for custom at this moment," he replied, tightening his hold on me, fingers unlacing the back of the frock separating him from his desire.

I could refuse César no longer and I pressed closer to the man whom I truly loved, thankful I was forgiven-in-full and grateful for a second chance at happiness.

Much later on that warm afternoon, a cool breeze blew in through an opened window and fanned our glistening flesh. Too lazy to rejoin the household, we did not resist the temptation to lounge about together, eating from a tray of sweets usually reserved for guests and drinking from a fine bottle of white wine I had been saving for a special occasion.

"César," I inquired, savoring a bite of marzipan, "when Gaston died, did the Company's leadership chose the Duc de Guise to be the next candidate for Louis' throne?"

"Why yes, my little sly boots," César laughed aloud, nibbling affectionately on one of my earlobes. "For your information, the representative is referred to as the *Lost King*."

"How old is Guise?" I asked, ignoring the lesson in Company protocol. "He must be nearing fifty, is he not?"

"Forty-seven. Why?"

"And if he were to die, to whom would the honor pass? Your uncle, perhaps?"

"Possibly. Guise has no heirs by his wife, Anne of Gonzaga."

"With the blessing of the Company and Fouquet's financial backing, a de la Tour could rule France one day, once the Duc de Guise passed on, of course."

César fell silent, contemplating my words. Watching his expression intently for a sign, I wondered if he thought me too ambitious, too akin to a man named Cinq-Mars.

"If I were to one day lead a challenge against Louis, would

you back me?" he asked, a serious gaze riveted to my face. "Would you stand by my side, no matter the outcome, whatever the cost?"

"Am I not your wife, a Bouillon? Do I not love you more than life itself?"

"Then your mother's curse may yet be fulfilled," César remarked. "Do you think Marion's spirit would be avenged if her daughter were crowned Queen of France? Would that settle the score?"

Queen of France! I had imagined Turenne in charge, not his nephew.

"We shall cross that bridge when we arrive at it," I smiled, taking César's face in my hands. "Never doubt that, as of today, we are one in body and in deed."

Because hindsight gifts one with perfect vision, I am able to attest that had we never heard or uttered the ill-fated name Merovingian, Bijoux and César de la Tour would have been better off by far.

CHAPTER FOURTEEN
Underworld

Although Susanne was absolutely adamant in her disapproval of Fouquet's scheme to bribe Louise de la Vallière, she did agree to approach the royal mistress with an offer of coin, unable to refuse her lover's request. My friend was to inform Louise, in a subtle fashion, that twenty thousand *louis d'or* would be hers if she would speak well of Fouquet to the king. A simple assignment for the experienced Madame du Plessis; yet, as she rode out from Saint-Mandé for Fontainebleau near to July's close, the perceptive woman sensed the interview would not go smoothly. An ominous feeling nagged at her, leaving the poor messenger uneasy; more than once she was tempted to instruct the driver to turn the carriage around and head back towards the woods of Vincennes.

While Fouquet's emissary was off performing the dreaded errand, César and I were downstairs in Saint-Mandé's main salon, mingling amongst distinguished company. Chatting with a charming, aspiring author, Madame de La Fayette, I was too engrossed in conversation to notice that someone was attempting to attract my attention.

"Mademoiselle Bijoux," my astute companion noted, "are you acquainted with that lady who is waving to you from across the salon?"

"Who?" I asked, craning my neck to get a good look. "Where?"

"Over there," she said, pointing in the direction of the room's main entrance. "The lovely woman with blonde ringlets. Madame du Plessis, I do believe."

Upon careful inspection, I discerned Susanne, a striking vision dressed in the lavish fashion of the court. The expression on her face, however, made my blood freeze.

Due to the light weight of warm weather skirts, I was at my mentor's side as fast as it took to practically race across the reception area.

"Where is Nicolas?" she demanded, her cheeks red, but not from rouge. "Where is Lord Cléonime, Bijoux?"

"Marquise," I replied with formality because people listened, "I haven't the vaguest idea as to M. Fouquet's whereabouts. Why not stroll in the garden with me, for you seem flushed."

Taking her arm, I led her away from the others.

"What transpired at Fontainebleau?" I whispered. "Did you see La Vallière?"

Storming ahead, she did not answer, making straight for the out-of-doors. Upon reaching our destination, and seeing no one else about, Susanne began to scream worse than a harpy.

"That ill-bred strumpet!" she blurted out. "That uppity little whore! When I think of what she did to me, I cannot move, I am so angry!"

"Regain your composure, Susanne. Then speak."

"Yes. You are correct. Oh, Bijoux," she sputtered, then said, "so, to begin, when I arrived at the château, I went directly to Madame's suite and located Mademoiselle de Montalais, for she was my introduction to La Vallière. Together we made for the park where Louise was taking the air with another maid-of-honor, d'Artigny. Joining the pair, surrounded by a multitude of courtiers, the four of us exchanged pleasantries and I complimented the king's mistress on her clothing, her hair, her complexion. The flattery was for naught."

"Did she think you insincere?"

"Evidently, for when I mentioned Fouquet's generous offer of gifting her cash in exchange for a few kind words whispered in Louis' ear, she became quite militant against me, saying that an enticement of two hundred *thousand* would not be capable of causing her to commit such a *faux pas*. And then, she repeated the statement with such fierceness that everyone in the immediate vicinity was made privy to our disagreement! We nearly came to blows, Bijoux."

"Did you attempt to calm her suspicions, Susanne?"

"Of course, yet saintly Louise refused to listen, limping off in haste to report the incident to the king."

"*Bon Dieu*! You should heeded your own counsel."

"I know, I know," she snapped. "Yet 'tis late for regrets. Nicolas requires a defense at the moment, not a scolding; we must think of a strategy to discredit La Vallière in the king's eyes."

"Turn the story about. Fouquet will mention to Colbert that Louise approached him, through you, for a loan. Mention that the surintendant was hesitant to comply with the request until he had secured the king's approval. Such a remark, made in an offhand manner, would render Louise's statement suspect."

"Yes, quite true, good point," Susanne praised. "My rage made me stupid. Let us to Nicolas immediately, lest he hear of the disaster from another. That he would never forgive."

As we made for the Fouquet's lair, I recognized that the Future's stellar rise had taken a downward turn and whereas the meteoric tumble would have previously delighted me, I now feared for the man. Unfortunately for the Company, the Merovingian heirs and, of course, Susanne, the La Vallière incident might prove to be the beginning of the end for the financier from Brittany.

Nicolas was informed of the blunder and he took the bad news calmly, withdrawing to his bedchamber where he remained ensconced for three days, content to shut himself off from the world. Emerging from the sanctuary to return to the court and his duties, he informed his worried confidante that he had decided to confess his fiscal sins on bended knee to the king and beg the sovereign's mercy. Susanne clung to her lover and pleaded with him to reconsider such a rash and dangerous measure; the risk of reprisal was too great. Fouquet would not be swayed and he left Saint-Mandé determined to clear his conscience. If things went awry during the candid discussion with Louis, he would retreat to Belle-Isle and wait for the storm to pass from his fortress; if not, Vaux would blaze with a thousand lights on August the seventeenth in celebration of his successful maneuver.

In the interest of brevity, suffice it to say that Fouquet returned to Vincennes a jubilant man. The king had been gracious to his servant; he agreed that the irregular practices of lending and spending to excess had begun in the opulent era of Mazarin and were no reflection on the surintendant's character. Speaking kind words to the penitent minister, Louis graciously accepted his enemy's promise to faithfully serve the throne and let it be known that the royal family would be attending the fête at Vaux. Half-truth had saved the day, and Nicolas left the audience, not in leg irons, but with a confident step—certain his star was again in ascension, positive that Fate intended for him to triumph.

Busy with plans for the unveiling of Vaux, Fouquet and Susanne took no notice of the rumors circulated by Colbert's clerks claiming that the surintendant's fall was imminent. They did not think it strange that Louis confided to his finance minister, during the first week of August, that he planned to restrict Parliament's powers. As acting Attorney General of the judicial body, Fouquet would have a difficult time attacking his fellow magistrates; however, were he to remove himself from the post and lead the royalist assault, the king would be most grateful. Louis also knew that Lord Cléonime wished to add the appointment of Chancellor of France to his collection of honors, for the minister saw the position as a stepping-stone to higher office. The surintendant was gently reminded of the law that stated one could not be Keeper of the Seals as well Attorney General of Parliament. On the twelfth of August, Fouquet sold the latter title to Monsieur de Harlay for the sum of one million in gold coins—presenting Louis with the proceeds and stripping himself of the last protection he had possessed.

Louis and the court embarked from Fontainebleau at three o'clock on the afternoon of August 17, 1661, bound for the fabled Vaux-le-Vicomte. The king, Marie-Thérèse, the queen-mother and Nabo rode in the royal coach; behind them traveled a truculent Philippe and Henriette. Madame was peeved that Louis had cast her aside for La Vallière and Monsieur was annoyed his brother preferred a gimpy servant girl to his wife, a Princess of England and of France. The one consolation left Monsieur was that, once passed over, Madame had returned to their marriage bed and the traitor was with child by July's close. Privately, he prayed Minette would die while giving birth. His wife deserved to suffer and the vengeful husband dreamed of the day when he would be free.

The king and court reached Vaux in approximately two hours time, driving through the domed mansion's wrought-iron gates near half-past the hour of five. Green lawns, a large stable and beautiful *orangerie* were passed before the cavalcade of vehicles crossed over a bridged moat leading to a spacious courtyard where all were greeted by Monsieur and Madame Fouquet. The remainder of that fateful evening, with its tour of the breathtaking palace and grounds, dinner served on plates of solid silver and gold, an outdoor performance of Molière's farce, *The Bores*, fireworks, fountains and festivities, must remain unrecorded by me. Many contemporary accounts exist of the first and last fête to be staged at Vaux, many historians have recounted in great detail the costumes, the six thousand illustrious personages in attendance, the king's stifled rage at being shown up by a Surintendant of Finance whose spectacular country house made the Louvre look shabby and mean in compare.

For the sake of diplomacy, César and I spent a quiet evening at a deserted Saint-Mandé, gathering together our possessions for the eventual transfer to Fouquet's exceptional new residence.

"I shall miss this place," I admitted. "Granted, our apartments at Vaux will be larger and we shall finally live openly as man and wife, yet, this is the place where we fell in love; these rooms are as much my home as was the Marais."

"Be thankful we were allowed to stay behind tonight," my husband mumbled. "To be spared that spectacle makes my spirit gladder than if I had won one of old Mazarin's lotteries."

"César!" I laughed, "Fouquet is our friend!"

"He will be of no use to us or to the cause if he lands his backside in jail."

"Louis would not dare. Not after tonight's success."

"Especially after tonight's success," César speculated. "When the king lays eyes on Vaux and realizes that his own purse funded the project, he will seethe with anger, for he is prouder than Lucifer, and then the surintendant's days will be numbered, mark my words."

"Not to mention our patron's attempt to compromise Louise de la Vallière."

"Well, yes, though the king is just as immoral in that regard."

I averted my husband's gaze. "Why not stroll in the Moon's light, César? We shall sort through our belongings tomorrow."

"You wish we had gone to Vaux, don't you? You feel abandoned by your friends."

"Why provoke his Majesty's wrath? We must avoid the court."

"That self-imposed exile pleases me greatly," he smiled quickly. "Come, let us bid an official good-bye to Saint-Mandé."

Wending our way downstairs and out into the night, arm-in-arm, we walked towards the stables, remarking how calm Saint-Mandé was when deprived of its frenetic goings on. Whether bustling or asleep, the place would always be as lovely and as romantic for me as it had been when César and I were dubbed the cupids of the Fouquet household.

"Do not be melancholy," César comforted, reading my mind.

"Must we move to Vaux?" I complained.

"We cannot hope to become involved in the Company's agenda and remain here at Saint-Mandé, cloistered away from the world, Bijoux."

"Do you ever consider if we are fools to pursue our present course?"

"My, what a mood you are in, wife! Shall I have a carriage harnessed for Vaux and find a driver to conduct us there straightway? The stables lie before us—yes or no?"

"César, no. Missing the revels does not make my heart heavy, but rather the thought of leaving behind perhaps our last chance at happiness. I fear the outside world with its plotting and wickedness; is toppling a throne that important, in the end?"

"You doubt because you fear change, Bijoux. Should we forget about the Secret, should we ignore the injustice committed against our beliefs by the Church and less-than-noble pretenders?"

"No," I wavered, thinking the principle just, yet concerned at the moment with more personal issues, "it is merely a sense that we forget who we truly are, the Bijoux and César who were content to love one another, to be happy together. Let us not lose sight of that secret, either."

As I mouthed those last words of warning, I noticed a man's figure lurking about a broken coach left in the yard for repairs. Whoever the person was, he was intent on staying out of our view.

"César, some fellow is watching us from over there, by the carriage whose axle snapped yesterday."

"I don't see anyone," he reassured whilst peering into a darkness inadequately lit by torches attached to the outside of the stone barn. "Did you sight a groom, perhaps?"

"No, he wears a peruke and a hat, that much I did discern."

"Who goes there?" César asked aloud. "Come out and show yourself, monsieur."

"We ought to leave. What if the intruder is that swine, Guibourg? Or a horse thief with a very large sword?"

"Be quiet," César whispered. "La Rivière," he called out, knowing the arrival of the tall riding instructor would intimidate almost anyone, "La Rivière, are you about?"

The statuesque Moor strode from inside the outbuilding into the courtyard. Dressed in red livery and sporting his familiar white turban, the black man carried a musket. Despite his recent conversion to Christianity from Islam, orchestrated by Fouquet's mother, La Rivière was armed and prepared to shoot any trespasser.

"Monsieur César," he hailed, approaching where we stood, "may I be of service?"

"I saw a man prowling about, Monsieur La Rivière, over there, by the carriage," I blurted.

"A thief?" he bellowed. "Trying to steal my horses?"

"No, we think a gentleman, by all appearances, though who can be certain?" César said with concern. "I thought it best to alert you."

Just as the Cape Verdean was nodding in agreement, the stranger took a lantern from the exterior of the disabled vehicle and lit the quick with a hand-held tinderbox. Holding the contained glow to his face, he stepped out of hiding for an instant, allowed for my eyes to set upon him, then extinguished the flame and made for the forest with long strides.

"Our thief is making his escape," I noted. "Leave him be, for I swear, he is a double of the king."

"Where did he go?" the two men asked in chorus.

"He heads for the wood. The resemblance to Louis was unmistakable."

"The pretender is at Vaux. He cannot be present here, as well."

César was correct in his assessment. Thinking aloud, I mused, "Who could he be, then? An impostor? Who?"

I was certain I had seen the intruder before, yet where?

"*Bon Dieu*, César, recall the nightmare that left me screaming not long ago?"

"Yes. Why? You look as though you have seen the dead."

"I have," I answered with a shudder. "The undead. Our intruder was Noctambule."

"Who?" queried a puzzled La Rivière.

"Nothing, pay her no heed," César replied.

"Listen well," I argued. "When I dreamt of the daemon five months ago, he turned into Louis while I gazed upon him, he was the King of the Underworld and more bloodthirsty than...than a hungry wolf. I tell you, César, the fiend has returned, he has come to make me one of his own."

La Rivière crossed himself as I spoke, mumbling a prayer. "Do not tarry," the Moor beseeched, "we must seek shelter in the chapel."

As far as I knew, the financier's second wife and her ladies were the only inhabitants of Saint-Mandé known to use the chantry, set off by itself at the rear of the property.

"Monsieur La Rivière," César asked, following alongside a quick step, "are you familiar with the expression, *undead?*"

"Do not say that word again," our protector implored. "In the land of my ancestors dwell many spirits, and the most feared are those who have risen from the dead, as though awake, and who drink the blood of the living."

"*Vrykolakas,*" I prompted. "Noctambule is a *vrykolakas.*"

"We call such a devil *lilitu,*" the Moor explained, gaining speed. "Only Allah may protect us from its horrible spell. Hurry, we must hurry."

Running to keep apace with the terrified servant, we tore through the gloomy ground floor of the vacated mansion, leaving salon doors swinging in our haste. Although scared out of my wits, I had to marvel at Noctambule's tenacious nature and the fact he had chosen to strike when the estate was practically deserted. Perhaps the great *vampyre* was a coward, after all.

Or perhaps I was the mouse. Malicious laughter rang out from behind, and I screamed in response, the first of our party to reach the chapel entrance after racing down a shadow-filled gallery. Fumbling with the doorknob, my terror peaked when the lock jammed, fastened in place to discourage intruders.

"Damn all priests," I muttered, envisioning Guibourg. *This is your fault, yours and mother's*, I thought, throwing the weight of my body against a sturdy plank.

"Move," La Rivière directed, arriving at my side. The groom kicked at the barricade, knocking the door open with a single thrust of a foot.

Not waiting for an invitation to enter the small church, we were soon huddled close together within the consecrated structure; a heavy table placed as blockade against the portal.

"We need light—any candles about this place?" I asked, teeth chattering.

"Perhaps by the altar, in the front," the Moor answered. Treading slowly, our group made its way down the center aisle, feeling for one pew after another, groping along the length of the nave.

"I see a faint glow ahead," César reported over his shoulder, as he was in the lead.

The blackness surrounding us did seem to lift as we neared a pair of steps. At the top of the short stairs stood the altar upon which several prayer candles flickered inside silver receptacles.

"If we use the tiny votives to light the long tapers in the candelabra, we should be safe for a few hours," I said as we approached the station. "Then, at least, our foe cannot creep up on us undetected."

"He would not dare enter Allah's house," La Rivière sighed with relief, reaching out and moving a freestanding crucifix across the ceremonial platform until it rested close to his side. "This is sacred ground. We shall wait here for the dawn; then we may leave in peace."

"What does the Sun's rising have to do with Noctambule, monsieur?" I queried, helping my husband to light the sticks fashioned out of tallow.

"A *lilitu* must sleep in its grave during the day or else perish. Certainly you know this."

"Oh, no, that is a false belief, monsieur. The *vrykolakas* who pursues me walks whenever he wishes. Day and night are the same to him."

"No," La Rivière insisted. "Devils are children of the Moon, they cannot abide the Sun's rays."

"Stop!" César said curtly. "Stop arguing, both of you! How

to kill this thing should be the topic of our discussion. What did Boyle write about destroying the *vampyre*? He was specific."

"You must chop off the creature's head, then drive your sword through its heart," the Moor supplied with an air of authority.

"How vile! Does that advice match Monsieur Boyle's instructions, César?"

"Partly. Our English friend instructed me to behead Noctambule. We must find the creature and destroy him," my love reiterated. "The problem is, where does a *vrykolakas* hide?"

"I wager he returned to Versailles," I reasoned.

"I say, we wait here until the morning, then forget the matter," La Rivière countered. "And we shall promise not to speak to anyone concerning the evil spirit, agreed?"

"Fine, agreed, monsieur. However, do you suggest that I sleep in a church every evening to protect myself from Noctambule?"

"Boyle sent a medallion for you to wear, designed to ward off the *vrykolakas*," César informed me. "An odd metal piece, inscribed with magical signs and the symbols of a man, beast and birds. To be honest, the charm is very strange."

"Have I been reduced to daemon worship?" I groaned, leaning against the altar, the lessons of the Rue St. Denis still fresh in my recollection. *Vercan, Maymon, Samax, Modiac, Arcan.* Would I never escape their images?

"'Tis extremely useful to die in God's grace, but extremely boring to live in it, mademoiselle," a deep voice intoned from the vestry, causing the three of us to start. La Rivière lifted the musket to his shoulder, taking aim in the direction of the side closet that served as a storeroom for robes, vestments and other sacred objects.

"Who speaks thus?" the Moor challenged.

"Noctambule," was the response given, followed by a wicked cackle.

"Then show yourself, fiend," I taunted.

"You are no fun, mademoiselle, although extremely

enjoyable to gaze upon," the unknown presence quipped. "Tell your friend to lay down his weapon and I shall leave my hiding place."

"Go ahead, do as he says," César whispered to the groom. "We cannot harm a *vrykolakas* with that, anyway."

La Rivière carefully placed the gun on the floor, watchful the entire time.

"Are you coming out, whoever you are?" I asked.

"My, mademoiselle, you are braver than a Musketeer," an attractive man proclaimed, stepping from the shadows, repeating the compliment mother's coachman had bestowed upon me thirteen years earlier. The courtier was elegantly attired in black, white and crimson; his dark peruke long and shining.

"*Mon Dieu*, Guiche," César exhaled, "what are you doing here?"

"Guiche? Armand, Comte de Guiche?" came my dumbfounded inquiry.

"The one and the only," he bowed, kissing my hand with panache. "And who might you be, my delectable one?"

"She is Bijoux de la Tour, monsieur, and therefore, my wife. Kindly take note of that fact," César replied. "When did you come upon us, Guiche? Out with it. How much of our conversation did you eavesdrop?"

"Oh, I heard some nonsense, de la Tour, about a fellow named Noctambule and how you plan to separate the unfortunate bastard's head from his shoulders—such lovely chat for a lady's ears."

"No worse than listening to you and Philippe through the walls of the Luxembourg."

The retaliation practically flew from my lips. Ever since the days of Madame de Choisy, followed by the scandal at Roissy, I had not been overly fond of Guiche.

"Of course," he flashed a charming smile, eyes riveted to the cleavage a low cut bodice displayed, "you are *that* Bijoux; Philippe's *special*, little friend."

"I thought that the prince's pet name for *you*, Monsieur le Comte," I parried.

La Rivière and César snickered at the insult, but Guiche continued grinning, undressing me with his intense gaze. He possessed a set of the highest cheekbones imaginable, a strong frame and a *hauteur* that defied description. Had I not been already aware of the count's despicable character, his suggestive overture would have been difficult to repel, he was that physically beautiful.

"What are you doing here at Saint-Mandé?" César questioned Armand. "Why are you not at Vaux, enjoying the festivities with the remainder of the court?"

"Oh, I went, I saw, I left. Too many women in attendance; not enough handsome, strapping lads," he smirked. Revolted by Guiche's arrogance, I looked away, infuriated.

"And how did you find us, monsieur?" La Rivière spoke at last.

"I followed you from the stables. I haven't had so much fun in years," he laughed, throwing his head back with glee, making the same frightening sounds he had produced during the pursuit through the mansion.

No *lilitu*, no *vrykolakas* had threatened our lives—only a depraved count who took delight in tormenting others.

"Go to Hades," I spit. "You are nothing more than a filthy scoundrel and I, for one, detest your loathsome person. Go back to Roissy and play games with blackguards such as the one-eyed priest called Guibourg or your good friend, Manzini. I hear say that you love to kiss the latter's backside, or are my sources incorrect?"

"Bijoux, apologize immediately!" César ordered, more offended by my use of foul language than by the slur I had uttered against an influential courtier.

"I take no umbrage," Guiche insisted, holding up a hand whose wrist was bound with lace and whose fingers were long and slim, "for your wife's conduct is understandable, monsieur, considering she is the daughter of that infamous whore, Marion Delorme."

"You are contemptible!" I countered, flinging myself at the count, beating against the front of his ebony, sateen evening coat. "I curse you forever," was all I could manage while the object of my assault held me by the elbows, amused at the show of rage. Leaning slightly forward, he said softly into an ear covered with flying red hair, "I shall have you soon," before César managed to pull me away.

"I would rather die than touch you!" I screamed at Guiche.

"I think you know full well, madame," he said, pointing an aristocratic digit, "that you belong to me more than you care to admit."

The count pronounced the words with such precision, with such careful attention and emphasis placed on *belong*, that my mind reeled. He resembled Louis Bourbon, he participated in daemon worship, he embodied the spirit of Noctambule in his actions; could Guiche be an agent of the enemy?

"Leave before I demand satisfaction," César threatened.

"You are fortunate that dueling is outlawed, de la Tour, for nothing would please me more than to stab you in your pious heart. Poor Noctambule, whoever he is. I should be living in fear, if I were he."

"Begone, monsieur, or I shall be forced to shoot," La Rivière said fiercely, picking up the musket. "I am not afraid to spill your blood, being the savage that I am."

"Another hero. How comforting to know France is populated by such brave men. Good looking ones, too," he added, casting an appreciative glance in my husband's direction.

"So help me, monsieur, I shall have words with the Duc d'Orléans concerning your conduct," I cautioned. "The king's brother would not be pleased if he knew you had designs on his wife." Or at least, according to Susanne, Armand had taken a fancy to Henriette.

"I am leaving, not to fret," Guiche smiled nervously, trying to fathom how I could have been privy to his innermost feelings. "We shall meet again, wild Bijoux. On that you may depend."

The count exited the chapel through the vestry, no longer in a mood to tarry. I paused, then followed, not surprised to find a side door left open to a summer breeze, the villain having vanished.

"He is a rogue," César commented when I returned to the chapel. "What an insolent..."

"...daemon," I finished, taking a candle for the trip back to our rooms. "Let us put the entire evening out of our minds or else we shall be labeled the *Three Fools of Saint-Mandé* if this story gets out."

"Then we shall swear never to repeat the events of this night to another soul," La Rivière said, holding out a sword for us to touch. Placing palms on the blade, we duly promised before the gods to remain silent on the subject of the *vrykolakas*.

Yet, as César and I went back through the house and upstairs to our rooms, tired from the adventure, I was consumed with thoughts of the Comte de Guiche, whose cold stare had chilled me to the marrow on a lovely August night. The nobleman was a survivor, he was as had been Everes, Comaetho's brother who guarded the ships and survived the slaughter of the Taphian warriors by Electryon's sons.

The fifth sibling had been found. Only Mestor remained.

Fouquet and Susanne were not destined to return to Saint-Mandé, choosing to spend their leisure hours at Vaux. Those who had hither flocked to the surintendant's mansion at Vincennes, descended upon the impressive château and its magnificent gardens to bask in the social success of the Future, who strode confidently from one political victory to another, unstoppable in his quest for power. Thus, when Nicolas was summoned by his sovereign to attend a meeting of a provincial assembly, the Estates of Brittany, scheduled to be held in the city of Nantes on the fifth day of September, the surintendant and Susanne began preparations for the trip back to their home province with nary a concern. Fouquet was convinced he would soon be named Chancellor and, when Louis tired of playing at king, the office of Prime Minister would be his, as well.

Louis left Fontainebleau with the Grand Musketeers and court on August 27, 1661, braving blazing heat and dusty roads during the two-day, uncomfortable journey to Nantes. Reaching the city in good time, the king was informed that M. Fouquet had arrived ahead of schedule and was lodged at the Hôtel de Rougé, an establishment belonging to the financier's mistress, Madame du Plessis. The surintendant, however, was confined to his bed with a fever for which the doctor had prescribed burnt brandy and ass' milk; Louis sent a messenger to the minister, wishing his devoted servant a speedy recovery. A lovely Saturday had dawned, more than a week stretched ahead before the start of the assembly and the energetic ruler decided to focus on hunting and not on his rival. The king would soon turn twenty-three and the allure of the chase was an overwhelming distraction, more heady than attending council meetings or conducting dealings with pompous ministers of state.

On the morning of Thursday, September the first, César and I finished packing our material goods into trunks that soon would be collected by Fouquet's staff for relocation to Vaux. Resigned to the move, I attempted to remain in a good humor by gossiping with dear Chromius, speculating as to Susanne's state of mind having to play hostess to both the Future and his wife at the Hôtel de Rougé. I could only imagine the furtive glances, stolen kisses and covert maneuvers being enacted in order to shield the enormously wealthy Madame Fouquet from the truth that her husband and his confidante were, in fact, more to each other than constant companions.

"Do you think Susanne has lost her mind, being barred from Fouquet's bed?" I asked César. "'Tis doubtful that the Hôtel de Rougé is as accommodating a space for conducting an affair as is Saint-Mandé or Vaux."

"Wherever M. Fouquet abides, he has his own rooms, darling. I doubt that he and Susanne have been inconvenienced in the least by Maria Magdalena's presence. In fact, our two lovebirds are probably spending as much time together as is usual."

"Lucky them," I replied, flopping into an upholstered armchair.

"Are you discontent?" César inquired.

"Only a little. Well, yes, now that you mention it, a lot."

"Would you care to go on a journey with me, then?"

"Where to?"

"It begins with *N* and ends with *S*," he teased. "Guess!"

"Nimes?" I taunted back, giggling. Hugging him about the neck when he bent to kiss me, I whispered in his ear, "Nantes?"

"Yes, a birthday present for my beloved," he smiled. "I deduced you were miserable here, with no one but me to keep you company."

"That's not true," I protested. "You are my favorite person in the world."

"You miss Susanne, admit it."

"We have not seen each other for more than a fortnight, 'tis true. A few letters are not the same as being with her."

"Then let us travel to Nantes today."

"Louis is in residence there," I frowned. "We cannot."

"We shall stay out of sight. Don't worry."

"Thank you; you're wonderful. I love you," I effused. "Should we go on horseback or take a carriage?"

"You choose."

"Horseback. We'll get there faster. We needn't take much. I shall borrow a dress and some accessories from Susanne."

"And we shall lodge overnight in rustic inns," he added with a suggestive tweak of an eyebrow. "This could be quite the experience, my little explorer."

"Bring a sword in case of highwaymen," I suggested, jumping up to unpack a plain, yet cool, linen riding outfit which I planned to change into momentarily. Sorting through a trunk, I located the beige habit with its wrinkled skirts and tailored bodice, lifted it from its box and shook the garment hard.

"More *billet doux*?" César sported, picking up a note that had cascaded to the floor after being freed from folds of airborne fabric.

"Oh, I placed some reports in amongst my clothes for safekeeping. What have you found there?"

"A letter," he replied, opening the folded paper and reading the contents. "From Louis Fouquet to his brother, Nicolas."

"Oh, that. Nabo took the letter from the chest formerly at the end of Fouquet's bed, the one that went with the surintendant to Vaux, along with all his correspondence. Susanne told me he never throws away a single *communiqué*."

César blanched. "Talk of a powder keg waiting to explode! What if something terrible were to befall our patron, and a sensitive message such as this one fell into the wrong hands? Such as Louis'?"

"The king is already aware that Fouquet's brother wrote from Rome concerning Poussin's secret. I passed the contents of the dispatch on to d'Artagnan, who informed Mazarin, who in turn told Louis. That is the original copy. I plan to study a certain painting hinted at to me by Monsieur Le Nôtre, a composition done by his friend Poussin concerning shepherds of Arcadia...do you know of the work? I think it may contain a clue concerning the Secret...to a spot where ancient treasure may be buried. All Fouquet cares for is gold."

"This pertains to the Company, Bijoux," César frowned, gesturing at me with the piece of stationery still in hand.

"I realize that, however all the king has been told is that the Company supports a candidate whom they wish to see sitting on the throne of France because of a connection to the Merovingian kings. He has no notion as to *why*."

"Do not tell me this," César lamented, holding his head with his hands. "How could you speak to d'Artagnan concerning Company business!"

"Because at the time, I meant to ruin Fouquet before he forced me into his bed, monsieur. Please give the damned thing back," I asked, holding out my hand for the letter.

"What is this about Fouquet?" he asked, returning the missive that I then placed inside a deep, outer pocket of the wide-cuffed, button-trimmed hunting jacket accompanying me to Nantes.

"He near ordered me to become his mistress; he kissed me, he touched me, understand? And if I had not reunited him with Susanne, I would have had no choice but to have relations with him, thanks to your family's involvement with the Company of the Blessed Sacrament," I stormed, ripping clothes from my body as I undressed to change for the journey at hand. "Think César, think! At times you truly are naïve."

"Have you been with him, privately?"

"No, absolutely not," I lied. "He near had his way with me, though, and his gift of Pegasus is the proof."

"You are a minx," César commented, good humor returning, his mouth attached to mine in earnest. "People have always said that Fouquet's taste is impeccable and now I, too, may honestly agree with their flattery."

One need not be a scholar of note to deduce that the departure for Nantes was delayed. Collecting our horses from La Rivière, we trotted out of the stable yard close to the noon hour, both thrilled by the prospect of a trip through what could prove to be perilous countryside. César wore a cupped-hilt rapier that had previously belonged to his father and had last been used during a Fronde skirmish. The combination of his sword, hanging from a dress baldric worn between suit and shirt, and my traveling mask, donned to shield my complexion from the dirt of the road, made us quite the dashing couple as we tore off at breakneck speed, eager for an encounter with the unknown.

What we did not anticipate was that the sky would become dark, threatening rain, about two hours into our ride. Slowing his steed, César pointed to the heavens. A storm was advancing which looked to be heading in our direction. By all appearances, we would be drenched in another hour if we did not locate shelter. After a hasty consultation, we decided to stop at the first lodging we could find and failing that, resort to the forest where the trees would afford some cover. Silently I prayed to Athena that an inn would appear on the abandoned road, upon whose path we had not seen a soul since quitting Saint-Mandé. I urged Pegasus onward; racing alongside César, I could feel the wind tangling my hair and whistling past my ears, yet I was unafraid, surer of my seat in the sidesaddle than I had been while out riding at Vincennes.

Sprinkles were dropping from the sky when a tavern

came into view, and while we were dismounting and tying our horses' reins to a hitching post outside that establishment, the downpour began. Thankful I had brought along some of the gold saved from the last payment Mazarin made to me in 1659, we used two of the coins to compensate the gruff landlord, obtaining a room for ourselves and a stable for our animals in the process.

Climbing up a narrow flight of wooden steps whose pitch was incredibly steep, we soon found ourselves inside a simple room complete with exposed beams on the walls, a small hearth and narrow bed. Bolting the door, César and I collapsed onto the hard pallet. Outside the wind howled with vigor and tree branches were beating against a shuttered window when we eventually fell asleep in each other's arms, too tired and sore to care about the inclement weather or to worry about resting in grubby traveling clothes.

We awoke to a violent cloudburst, complete with thunder and lightening, and deduced it was evening due to the absence of light inside or out. César rose, stumbled about the pitch-black chamber until he found the door and went downstairs. He returned straightway with a lantern and a plate of food, although discerning the contents of the dish was difficult to do from a half-reclining position. What he had found smelled delicious, and as César placed the hot server on the end of the bed in order to light a log on the hearth, I had to admit I was famished.

"Do you believe how damp the air is?" I commented, reaching for a blanket. "Good thing we have firewood, *n'est-ce pas?*"

"The proprietor tells me it hails outside. The fierce rains, combined with high winds, could damage the crops. We may be in for a lean winter, he thinks."

"Monsieur Fouquet will always have food on his table, famine or no," I reasoned. "Speaking of which, the aroma coming from that supper is mouth-watering. What did you bring us?"

"Food from the kitchen. Rabbit cooked in burgundy wine,

with wild roots and mushrooms. And a slab of black bread and goose liver pâté, of course," he revealed, brandishing the knife which was the one utensil used for eating; forks not being yet in vogue. "Shall we dine together by the warm fire, madame?"

I shall never forget how savory that simple meal tasted, eaten at a roughly hewn table, seated on wobbly stools, or how charming our humble surroundings appeared to be in the glow cast by burning wood. Our stomachs soon appeased, we turned to the sensual delights. Removing rumpled attire we found pleasure with one another; the beat of the pounding deluge drummed on the roof and drowned out any noise the boisterous patrons made below as they ate and drank their fill, happier to be within than without.

The remainder of the journey to Nantes was commenced the following morning when César and I were fortunate enough to purchase a fare on an empty coach bound for the city of Orléans. The driving rain had not ceased, and enclosed travel was thus preferable to being exposed to the elements on horseback. Leaving our mounts with the innkeeper where we had stayed in Étampes, telling him the horses belonged to Surintendant Fouquet to ensure their return, we departed, reaching our destination near to nightfall after slow going on the muddy road. Cold and exhausted, though dry, I thought it best we rest in Orléans, although César insisted we book passage on a barge that would take us down river past Blois, Tours and Montreau, arriving at Nantes on the fourth, two days hence. Not wishing to argue and curious to experience life aboard ship, I agreed to his plan, eager to arrive at the Hôtel de Rougé and have access to fresh garments.

The climate remained inhospitable during the last leg of our journey; however, the current was swift and the waters carried us to our friends by Sunday morning, as promised, depositing us at the quay of the Breton port before the clock in the town square struck noon. By then the forecast had taken a turn for the better, the day was merely overcast and not wet, and disembarking from the less-than-commodious cabin which had been our home for too long was a greatly anticipated event.

Waiting on a busy street for César as he inquired at an adjacent butcher shop as to the whereabouts of Susanne's residence, I marveled silently at the fortitude of the true explorers, those intrepid men who crossed seas and placed their lives at peril for the sake of booty. I could not comprehend their resolve, for already I was dreading the return to whence we had come, wondering if Nantes might be an agreeable place to live unto the grave.

The meat cutter's directions involved walking past the Château de Nantes, where Louis was holding court. Not pleased with that route, though unfamiliar with the city and its back alleys, I followed César along the well-traveled main street, wishing that I had worn my red traveling cape with its concealing hood. Seeing Louis was the last thing either of us wanted, and I shuffled along behind my husband, head bowed and eyes downcast. When I heard César speak, my heart jumped with fear.

"Look, is that not your dear friend, M. d'Artagnan?"

"Where?" I replied, peeking over his shoulder.

"Walking from the barracks toward the main gate."

"Charles, Charles de Batz," I called to the blond-haired soldier. "Stop, please!"

Immediately I made my way to where he stood looking about for the voice that had summoned him. When he caught sight of me, a nervous smile came to my Musketeer's lips.

"Bijoux, *bon Dieu*, is it you? What are you doing here, in Nantes?"

"I have come with my husband to visit Madame du Plessis at the Hôtel de Rougé. How is Charlotte-Anne?"

"Delivered of a fine son this July," he said with pride, "though annoyed, as is her wont to be, with me and my position in life. Never-the-mind, did I hear you say the word *husband*?"

"I am married to this man," I answered, gesturing towards César who had come forward to say hello. "You remember, César de la Tour?"

"Yes, of course," d'Artagnan winced. "We were introduced to one another at Saint-Mandé, on the day I returned Bijoux's jewels. I remember it well."

"You possess an excellent memory, monsieur," César complimented as he bowed. "To think that a man of your caliber and renown would recall meeting a youth who was naught but a page in Mazarin's service, is most wondrous."

"A page who hails from the family Bouillon is naught a mere page, monsieur."

"Are we keeping you from an appointment, my friend?" I asked in an attempt to change the subject matter.

"I have been summoned by the king to meet in his study so that we might examine the Grand Musketeers' muster role together," the soldier explained. "I should not keep his Majesty waiting."

"No, the king is accustomed to getting what he wants, when he wants it," César remarked wryly, casting d'Artagnan a meaningful look. The man who had been Mazarin's favorite agent ignored the subtle inference, doffing his headpiece with its colored plumes, kissing my hand in farewell.

"Madame, it is my fondest wish that I may see you again during your stay in Nantes. Perhaps you and your husband would sup with me at my quarters later today or one evening this week?"

"That would be delightful," I assured him. "Any night but tonight. Susanne and I have too much catching up to do."

"Good. I shall send an officer by the Hôtel de Rougé with the date and time," he offered, then was off with a swirl of his waist length cape, sword clanking against a spurred boot.

"He is rather fond of you," César noted as we continued walking past the château. "That much is obvious."

"I have known M. d'Artagnan since my mother's death, when he took me away from Guibourg and brought me to court. He is my oldest friend of record. Does that bother you?"

"No. I only wondered if the two of you had once shared stronger feelings; a romance, perhaps?"

"Please, César, he is twenty years my senior. Do not be foolish."

"Sorry," he smiled with relief. "I suppose I am a jealous husband, after all."

"You are forgiven," I said, pecking him on the cheek. "Do not tarry, the Hôtel de Rougé awaits."

Feeling badly because I had told César yet another white lie concerning the past, I hurried along the cobblestones, anxious to be with Susanne. I was looking forward to seeing the expression on her face when I appeared on her doorstep, unexpected, but hopefully not unwanted. We had been separated for too long.

The doorman ushered us formally into the hôtel after responding to César's knock at the front door. Susanne and Madame Fouquet were co-hosting a salon jammed with respectable people watching local girls dressed in Breton costumes performing traditional dances. Clearing my throat rather loudly, Susanne's head whipped about to see who was behaving in such a rude manner, and when her gaze met with my own, she approached the spot where I stood across the room, arms prepared to embrace her pupil.

"Bijoux, darling, how wonderful to see you. And César, likewise. When did you arrive?"

"Marquise, be careful, I am filthy," I warned. "We have been three days on the road. The bad weather slowed our progress considerably, and the two of us smell quite ripe."

"My angel, my sweet," she gushed, "I hardly noticed the vile humours. All the same, let us go upstairs and find you some perfume and proper clothes. Madame Fouquet will be fine without me."

Waving *adieu* to the wife of her distinguished guest, Susanne led César and myself out of the salon back to the foyer where we ascended a curving marble staircase to the first floor.

"So, what do you think of your inheritance, my girl?" she giggled, opening white double-doors decorated with molding and gilt and which provided access to a lovely pastel-colored bedchamber. "Did you come to inspect the goods for yourself?"

"I had forgotten your generous offer," came my embarrassed reply. "You really are too kind."

"Are you bequeathing the hôtel to Bijoux?" César inquired, taken aback.

"This house and the manse at Charenton. A lady needs a proper address, don't you think?"

"I am speechless," he said. "Bijoux never told me."

"Well, she was near to death when I spoke of the matter, so be lenient with your wife, monsieur. Bijoux is not a braggart—are you, my darling?"

"Enough about me," I begged. "What have you been up to, Susanne?"

"Well, following the *fête* at Vaux, recuperating. What an evening that was! A triumph for my darling Nicolas. I was wrong to have advised him against staging the entertainment," she declared as she searched an armoire for a suitable gown to loan. "He is more in favor with the king than ever before."

"Really?" I managed, unable to believe that Louis had appreciated either the pretentious celebration or Fouquet's move to besmirch Louise's honest reputation.

"Oh, yes," Susanne confirmed, laying a yellow silk dress on the canopy bed for my inspection. "The king sent the Comte de Brienne's son here today to inquire after Nicolas' health, and to make certain that he would be well enough to attend the council meeting to be held early tomorrow morning at the château. His Majesty's good friend and secretary returns tonight to speak with my ailing lover."

"What ails M. Fouquet?" César asked.

"He suffers from chills and a fever and has been confined to his bed for nearly a week. Although he is feeling better, last I checked."

"And Madame Fouquet?"

Susanne rolled her eyes. "What a chatter box! She is driving me to distraction with her retelling of the events during the festivities at Vaux—as if I was not present at the gala myself. Or planned most of the program," she mumbled, annoyed.

"You will be rid of her soon," I said cheerfully. "Plus, now that I'm here, you have a good excuse to spend less time with Maria Magdalena."

"Don't even say that name," Susanne groaned, then laughed at the dismal sound of her own voice. "Let me get someone to draw a bath for you and you," she ordered, pointing a finger first at me, then at César, "and then we shall gossip some more, when you are clean and refreshed."

"Madame, you are a wonder," César beamed. "Not to mention a good friend."

"The best," I chimed, "the very best."

"Children, please, the two of you will inspire immodesty in my person," she said merrily, starting to leave so she might attend to our needs. Before departing, she added, "When you move to Vaux, I shall see to it that you have your apartments next to my own, with a lovely view of Monsieur Le Nôtre's gorgeous gardens. We shall be very happy there, I think."

"Paradise, what a lovely thought," was my response, spoken with sincerity.

However, a foul Underworld was where the three of us were headed, and the descent into despair was due to begin at sunset—without warning and with no real chance for escape.

CHAPTER FIFTEEN
Electryon's Cattle

Louis-Henri-Joseph de Brienne, son of the seventy-two-year-old Secretary of Foreign Affairs, appeared at the Hôtel de Rougé close to the hour of seven on the eve of the fourth, his fat body squeezed into formal court attire, determined to speak with Surintendant Fouquet.

Greeted warmly by the finance minister's wife, Brienne was granted an audience with the Lord of Vaux, who dressed and came down from his sickbed to speak with the young courtier. When Fouquet emerged from their meeting, and graced Susanne's crowded salon, he looked worried, although I could not discern if his somber mien was a result of the conference with Brienne or a symptom of ailment.

"I require the Marquise du Plessis and Madame Bijoux in the study at once," Lord Cléonime ordered with a snap of his fingers, paying no notice to Maria Magdalena's quizzical expression. Following in his footsteps, my friend and I were soon conducting a conversation with the surintendant, assured privacy by a twice-locked library door.

"Nicolas, darling, why the foul mood?" Susanne queried, taking an elegant hand with its tapered fingers in her own. "What did roly-poly say to you?"

"The Comte de Brienne's obnoxious son came by to inform me that the council meeting will convene early on the morrow, at precisely seven in the morning, for the king is eager to be over and done with business by the time his birthday hunt is slated to commence, an hour later. When my promise to attend the meeting was secured, Brienne *fils* turned away, as though to leave, then hesitated. I asked him if he had finished delivering his message, and he stammered, 'You should take great care, monsieur,' then hurried away. Now what do you suppose he meant by those words?"

"He is an odd fellow," Susanne soothed, patting her lover's brow reassuringly. "Take no notice of him."

"No," I interjected, my stomach queasy, "we should make inquiries. Is Colbert here at Nantes, monsieur?"

"Yes, he came along with the other ministers, ahead of Louis and the court. Why?"

"I saw M. d'Artagnan at noon today while on his way to meet with the king about muster rolls, or some such matter. I wonder if the sous-lieutenant knows anything? Did you know that the leader of the Grand Musketeers is heavily indebted to Colbert?"

"No, how interesting. I shall send a messenger to the barracks immediately," Fouquet said tensely, "with a personal offer of financial aid for Monsieur d'Artagnan."

"What if I were to go instead?" I suggested. "D'Artagnan and I are old friends, monsieur. We were, how shall I put it delicately, intimately involved."

"Would you do this thing for me?" the surintendant asked with relief. "May I impose upon your generosity with so little notice?"

"Monsieur, you have housed me for the past three years and you love my best friend," I paused. "Could you ever doubt my allegiance?"

"No," he said, coming to my side, pressing me to his lace jaboted chest. "My dearest *La Loy*. You are different from the others—you have a noble heart, not unlike the Marquise du Plessis."

"Bijoux, thank you for coming to our aid," Susanne added. "Thank God you are here."

"Yes, well," I replied, on the verge of becoming emotional. "I best be off to visit our Musketeer. May I take a lackey with me for protection?"

"I shall send for La Fôret to accompany you," Fouquet offered his own valet.

"No, he does not care for me, I fear, plus it may look suspicious if we are seen together, as though on an errand for you. Is there no one else available to escort me?"

"Take d'Anger, the one who works under La Fôret." Susanne suggested.

"Eustache?" Fouquet queried, then added with a shrug, "Why not? He'll do. La Fôret, are you out there?" he called through the door as he approached it, unbolting the lock as he did so.

"At your service," the manservant pronounced with a bow.

"Fetch your underling, d'Anger. I have a task for him."

La Fôret silently took his leave. Returning momentarily with a young man, the officious gentleman of the bedchamber produced his charge.

"D'Anger," Fouquet began, "it would please me if you were to show Madame de la Tour to the Musketeers' headquarters at the king's château. You will follow her instructions as though they were my own, understand?"

The brown-haired youth, who was tall, slim and wore the household livery of silvery-gray linen, nodded his assent.

"Speak up, boy," Fouquet commanded. "Loosen that tongue of yours."

"I understand, monsieur," he mumbled.

"Good. Now, off with you both," Nicolas said in a gentler voice. "God speed, Bijoux."

"I shall report to you immediately upon my return," I assured him. "Please tell César where I am or else he will be anxious. You may trust my husband, monsieur, to be discreet."

"I think that César, Susanne and I shall gamble a bit while you are gone. Take your time—we shall be waiting up for you."

Without a further *adieu*, I glanced at Eustache, who did not appear to be relishing his assignment, and quit the study. Not until we left the building did I address him.

"My name is Bijoux," I offered in an attempt to gain his confidence. "Tonight, out here, you need not address me as Madame de la Tour."

He nodded, no words.

"Are you shy, Eustache d'Anger?"

"No," he blurted out, taking longer strides, "I am angry. I am tired of being ordered about, no better than a dog. This cannot be all there is to life — I might as well pass the years of my miserable existence in a dungeon, for I am no better off than a prisoner!"

His dissatisfaction at being cast as a servant in the Fouquet establishment recalled to mind my mother's shabby treatment of Des Oeillets, Madame de V's hatred of playing subordinate to Choisy, and my own dislike of Fouquet when he had pressed me to become his mistress. Eustache needed cheering, for the mission was far more important than his personal feelings.

"So, you do speak, monsieur. And quite nicely, too. I am sorry to hear that you find my company so distasteful."

"'Tis not you, madame..."

"Bijoux," I corrected.

"Please do not patronize me, madame, for I know that once we are back at the Hôtel de Rougé, I should not utter the name *Bijoux* in your presence."

"Fine," I said firmly, stopping in the street, grabbing the sleeve of his plain *justacorps*, "I am going to amend my earlier proposal. You may call me by my first name whenever you like."

Eustache halted. "You need not show me favor, madame, to insure your safe passage through the streets of Nantes."

"Why are you so obstinate? I swear, you must be a son of the rebel Water Bearer!"

"Perhaps I am," he smirked, "or perhaps I suffer from the sin of pride. Why do I not take comfort in the Bible's promise that the meek shall inherit all?"

"Let us be on our way, monsieur. I do not have all night to waste on a discussion of the Scriptures. We must find Monsieur d'Artagnan."

"Why?" he asked, crossing his arms over his chest as he walked along.

"Because Monsieur Fouquet has ordered it, that is why. His future, my future, your future may depend on this evening's expedition."

"The barracks are up ahead," he pointed with his left hand, dropping the defensive posture. "We shall call on M. d'Artagnan there."

Nearing the Château de Nantes, within whose walls Louis no doubt reposed, we took a sharp turn, entering a courtyard bordered by stables and the stone houses being used to lodge the king's Musketeers. Large elm trees stood vigil near to the buildings, a great number of their wet leaves having fallen during the recent storms, rendering the cobblestones slick to tread upon.

Making our way to an impressive-looking red door boasting a substantial bronze knocker, Eustache took hold of the fixture and banged out our arrival with three resounding summons.

"No one answers. Let us try elsewhere," I said impatiently when our call was not immediately acknowledged. "Perhaps they all stand watch at the château."

"Nonsense," d'Anger disagreed, rapping metal against wood, pounding with all the strength his thin frame would allow. "Someone must be inside."

"By Athena..." I was complaining when we were greeted by a burst of light and the image of a well-groomed gentleman sporting a white blouson, blue Musketeer breeches and thigh-high boots of ink-colored leather. His pointed beard, mustache and natural curly black hair made me start, so closely did he resemble a youthful version of the Abbé Guibourg.

"How may I be of assistance, lovely lady?"

"I seek M. d'Artagnan," I curtsied, extending a hand for him to kiss, which he did with a courtly air.

"And you are?" he cooed.

"My mistress, by rights, is the true Duchesse de Bouillon," Eustache supplied in a belligerent tone, catching me unawares.

"Do not speak, boy, unless I grant you permission," the offended cavalier barked. "How dare you address me?"

"Excuse him, he is an apprentice," I offered sweetly as explanation, recognizing that an ugly scene could develop between the two hotheads if I did not diffuse the tense situation with gentle words. "I am Madame de la Tour, kind sir. However, I did not catch your name."

Flattered, the not unattractive Guibourg look-alike straightened to his full height, then bowed ceremoniously. " I am the Marquis de Maupertuis," he revealed, "although, while serving as Musketeer, I am honored with the rank of corporal in the king's Guard."

"How impressive!" I sighed, feigning excitement at being introduced to an officer. "Would you be kind enough to announce my presence to your leader? I should be forever in your debt."

"'Twould be my fondest desire, madame, if M. d'Artagnan, that most excellent of commanders, were only here. Alas, he is attending to the king's business. However, I could make you comfortable in my quarters until he returns."

I saw d'Anger's jaw tighten beneath his baby-fine skin and I fell against him with all my might to distract him from any notion he may have had of defending my honor. Maupertuis was at my side in a flash, lending support to what he thought was a swooning gentlewoman.

"Oh, my," I play-acted convincingly, languishing against poor Eustache, then leaning on the would-be swain, "I must find Charles de Batz—our king's life is in danger!"

"What?" the corporal stood tall. "What say you, madame?"

"An evil cabal plots against the king this very evening," I lied. "They plan to...I cannot say," I insisted, pretending to be near to fainting away. "My information is for Monsieur d'Artagnan's ears alone."

"He is in the mess hall, drinking with his comrades, waiting to celebrate the king's day of birth at midnight," he admitted, eager to assist a lady whose secret message might earn him a promotion. "If you like, I shall fetch him."

"Take me to him," I begged. "He would prefer it that way.

We should meet openly, under natural circumstances. Your officers entertain courtesans, do they not?"

"Yes," he blushed. "You are of the nobility, madame…"

"To save our dear sovereign's life, I would gladly play the part of prostitute, marquis. Besides," I added, cocking a brow, "my mother was Marion Delorme."

The mixture of shock and admiration that passed across the young men's faces assured me that Madame la Grande's legend was alive and well, more than ten years following her demise. Eustache looked embarrassed, as though the behavior he had displayed on the way to the barracks might lower my estimation of his character. I knew in my heart he felt the fool.

"Do the both of you intend to gawk at me the entire eve? Time is pressing."

"This way," the marquis offered, taking my hand and escorting me into the spacious home of the Musketeers while visiting Nantes. The rooms through which we passed were luxuriously appointed: fine furniture, candelabras and rich drapes graced each suite, while a tantalizing aroma issued forth from where I deduced the kitchen area to be. A Musketeer's life off the battlefield appeared to be quite an accommodating one, and at last I understood why d'Artagnan was forever short of funds.

Approaching the entrance to the banqueting hall, the marquis paused before allowing me access to the revelers, who could be heard laughing and shouting through the thick, paneled walls surrounding them.

"Do you wish to be announced?" the officer queried. "Or should I whisper your arrival to Monsieur d'Artagnan?"

"We shall enter arm-in arm, I think. When my dear friend sees me, he will know what to do."

"Of course. And the page?"

"Please wait for me here. I shan't be a moment," I asked Eustache. "Only Musketeers are granted admission to this place."

"And their ladies," Maupertuis jested with a sly wink, probably thinking me a true slattern masquerading as a married woman of social stature. Ignoring the comment, I marched into the imposing gallery that offered no impediment to anyone's entering except for two armed soldiers posted on either side of an arched opening leading from the hallway into the dining chamber.

Because I was a woman wearing Susanne's gorgeous lemon-hued gown, I flounced past the sentries without them batting an eyelid, not needing the marquis' assistance. Scanning the gallery hung with battle flags and armor of old and crammed full with what could have been the bodies of all one hundred and fifty members of the regiment and their female companions of every description, I eagerly sought d'Artagnan in the crowd. Desperate to locate the man whom I knew would never fail to be my champion, I glanced backwards to see the marquis standing directly behind me, his hot breath warming one of my bared shoulders when he bent down to kiss it.

"Really, monsieur, I must find d'Artagnan."

"Come, come, *chérie*," he said with much too much familiarity, "we both know your tale was concocted to gain you a haven from the slimy customers on the street, do we not? Every whore in France is aware that Musketeers pay well for their pleasures."

"Touch me again and I shall rip out your throat," I threatened in an attempt to repel his odious advances. "I am not for sale."

"I have never kept company with a ginger-haired girl," he countered, "though I imagine that the color of your tresses is, as the old women say, a true sign of your heritage, *n'est-ce pas?*"

Repulsed, I moved away from the marquis, pushing through the throng until I reached a long table where, at the head, a man was seated and slouched forward, golden curls spread out before a plate of food. Sidling down to the spot where the Musketeer was sprawled out, I saw with dismay that the sot was my friend.

"Monsieur, wake up," I demanded, shaking a limp arm. "Please, this is no time to pass out."

"Go 'way," he mumbled, taking a whack at me without

lifting his head from its resting place. "Can't a man get drunk in peace?"

"D'Artagnan, 'tis I, Bijoux. Wake up."

Knocking a full tankard onto the floor, he slurred, "Help me."

Motioning to a nearby Musketeer, we were able, together, to raise Charles upright. Reeking of wine, I turned my head at the smell of d'Artagnan's breath.

"I swear, monsieur, you would try the patience of St...."

"Anthony," he supplied, perfectly sober. Pulling me to him roughly, as if in a bawdy mood, he confided to me, saying, "I am acting the drunkard. Go outside and I shall meet you at the stables."

Pushing the actor off of me hard, I slapped his face as though disgusted with his conduct. "Go to the devil," I yelled, then did not tarry as I hurried from that hot and smelly den of iniquity, more confused than I had ever been by another person's actions.

Finding Eustache where he had been left waiting, I urged him to take the lead.

"Might you find the way back to the courtyard?" I implored. "We must hide in the stables and wait there for Monsieur d'Artagnan."

"What? Is that not bizarre?"

"Do not argue with me, d'Anger. Maupertuis is hot on my heels."

With that admission we were off, running through the house, all previous decorating details a blur, not stopping 'till the bronze knocker clanged as we slammed the red door shut. Catching our breath, we glanced at each other and began to convulse with hilarity.

"Stop it, you rogue," I chastised in fun, "if we stay here, we are sure to be found out."

"I am the Marquis de Maupertuis," Eustache aped, "although, while serving as Musketeer..."

"Please...cease with the comedy. Your imitation of that rascal is highly amusing; however, we should make our way to where d'Artagnan promised to be."

Walking on tiptoe, amongst the shadows, towards where the horses were kept, the two of us were careful to not step in the animals' excrement in the process.

"Not as clean as Saint-Mandé, is it?" he asked, turning his nose up at the smell of hay, leather and stinking manure.

"The Grand Musketeers are not as rich as Fouquet, Eustache. We enjoy many privileges residing under the surintendant's roof."

"Still, Fouquet is arrogant, he acts the aristocrat when he is naught but a *bourgeois*, madame. His ancestors were merchants and magistrates, not nobles."

"And does his success not illustrate that people such as you and me, who enjoy no social standing *per se*, might rise above our station in life, as well?"

"If one decides to become dishonest, it does. The French people know Fouquet is a thief. He is no better than was Mazarin."

"Be still, please," I insisted, rubbing a temple. "I must collect my thoughts for when I speak with d'Artagnan. No more politics for now, agreed?"

"Later?"

"Perhaps. Let us see what d'Artagnan has to say."

"Are you worried, madame?"

"Yes," I whispered, shivering in the cool night air. "Yes, I am."

Concealed behind a bale of hay, Eustache and I waited patiently close to an hour for my loyal friend to appear, which eventually he did. Strolling about the paved yard, smoking a long-stemmed pipe, he moved slowly towards the box stalls, teetering a bit so as to appear intoxicated.

"Monsieur," I directed, "over here."

Charles was at my side in an instant, sure-footed and in complete control of his faculties.

"What is going on, Bijoux. What brings you here?"

"I came to spy on you," I laughed. "Why the drunken charade?"

"Merely a precaution," was the mysterious reply I did not want to hear.

"D'Artagnan, you must be straight with me. Is the king angry with Fouquet? Does Louis bode his minister ill?"

Drawing on barely lit leaf, d'Artagnan's face did not register one iota of emotion. "Why do you ask?"

"Brienne *fils* arrived at the Hôtel de Rougé earlier this evening with a message for Fouquet from the king, and, as he was departing, the royal secretary paused and told the surintendant to watch his back, more or less."

"Who is this?" Charles inquired, motioning with his pipe at Eustache.

"My escort, Eustache d'Anger. He is M. Fouquet's retainer."

"Then we shall promenade alone, my dear. Monsieur, I beg your leave to conduct a conversation with madame?"

"By all means," d'Anger replied with gravity, impressed by d'Artagnan's manners. "I shall be here when you return."

Walking away, I looked up at my friend. "What need you say that cannot be said before a loyal servant, Charles?"

"What I need say I have sworn to the king himself not to reveal to any living soul, understand? I am fond of you, Bijoux, you know that, and I wish no harm to come to you."

"What do you mean, exactly?"

"Get out of France. You and your husband. Tonight."

"I cannot! What of my jewels, my possessions? Everything is packed in crates back at Saint-Mandé! I cannot leave Fouquet and Susanne, they are my friends."

"Bijoux, I shall say nothing further. For the sake of old times, for the sake of the love I still bear you, for the sake of your future happiness—begone."

"Louis is going to arrest Fouquet, isn't he?" I asked, terror in my voice.

"Do not make inquiries I cannot answer."

"He is! We are all doomed! I must warn Nicolas..."

"And if you do such a thing, you sign my death warrant, Bijoux! Colbert, Le Tellier and myself are the only men in the land who know of the plan. Should Fouquet escape apprehension, heads will roll, girl. That is why I appear to be enjoying the festivities back at the mess hall—I must behave as though nothing is happening out of the ordinary."

"When do you take him?" the words tumbled out.

"I am not at liberty to say."

"Then tell me why. What has he done that is so terrible?" I cried in despair. "Why must this happen?"

"Because Louis fears the Company of the Blessed Sacrament more than famine, drought or plague. And because, due in part to your excellent intelligence work, the king also knows the name of that outfit's financial backer: Fouquet."

"So the minister's downfall is my doing? What of his own indiscretion concerning La Vallière? What of the ledger books and the tampering? What of Vaux?"

"Minor compared to his involvement with the Company. Of course, Fouquet will be charged with embezzlement of state funds, yet his true crime, in Louis' mind, is treason. Bijoux," he continued gently, "you know too much concerning the throne's enemies. The king no longer trusts you."

That was when my life effectively ended. All the hopes and dreams that César and I had harbored for a representative of his family to rule were dashed, for without Fouquet, we would be powerless. No glory, no pomp, only the drudgery of a life lived at court in the brilliance of Louis' glow.

I was crying. D'Artagnan held me tenderly, kissing my hair. "I shall miss you Bijoux Cinq-Mars. Try to think of me from wherever you go."

Pulling away, I stared at him, some fight left in me yet. "I go nowhere, monsieur. I have faced worse daemons than Louis Bourbon and lived to tell of it. Your secret is safe with me, however, I shall never submit to the king's will!"

"Forewarned is forearmed, do what you must. However, do not forget that I go the way of your father if Fouquet is not present at that council meeting tomorrow."

D'Artagnan left me to my own devices, returning with a stagger to his men. Stunned, I wondered what to do, how I could save Fouquet, Susanne and myself from disaster. Forewarned *was* forearmed—I could not give up hope.

"Eustache," I summoned, "Eustache!"

"Madame?" he came running at the first sound of my voice.

"Will you help me?"

"With anything. What do you require?"

"To get a letter to Fouquet. The delivery must be executed with great cunning, for he must not suspect you of being the bearer, or me of being the sender. Where might we find paper and ink?"

"I have some in my room," he offered.

"Good, although we cannot be detected entering the hôtel. Where is your chamber situated? Is there access from the rear of the house?"

"Yes, I'll take you there," Eustache said gallantly. "Shall we?"

"We best run," I replied and we were off again, beating a hasty retreat to the residence where half of Nantes' society sat at inlaid gaming tables, praying to Fortuna to smile upon them for a while. Yet, Louis, having been tutored by that consummate gambler, Mazarin, was leaving very little to chance; the wager he was making at that moment would pay handsomely if won, with a minimum of risk involved, if he could keep his cards close to his vest and his enemies at bay.

The anonymous note I wrote to Nicolas advised him to adopt a disguise and leave Nantes at once, escaping to Belle-Isle where he would be assured of safety. In the morning, La Fôret would send his master's sedan chair to the château with its curtains drawn, lacking a passenger; a subtle message for the king. However, when I was forced to report to my benefactor that, in the honest d'Artagnan's opinion, nothing had been said or hinted at concerning the arrest of Louis' private banker, Fouquet ripped up the curious parchment, tossed it onto the hearth and laughed, remarking that one of his foes was no doubt attempting to lead him a merry chase. And that person was probably Colbert, the irritating stickler for detail who coveted the post of surintendant.

Susanne agreed with her lover, confident that all was right with the world. Or, at least, in their world, she jested as the two of them embraced, happy that Maria Magdalena had retired for the evening. If only I could have said something to them that night, if only I had not cared what became of d'Artagnan, the history books might tell a different story. Of course, they do not, and the guilt I suffer at times for my complicity in Fouquet's downfall forces me to think my current misfortune is not punishment enough for the pain I ultimately caused both Nicolas and Susanne.

I cannot honestly say if Louis remembered that his father had sent my father to prison on September the fifth, our shared date of birth, yet that was the day selected for Fouquet's comeuppance. Following a hastily conducted council meeting cut short on the pretense of the king's wish to join a prearranged, celebratory hunt, Fouquet quit the château near to seven-thirty that Monday morning. Exiting with his fellow ministers Colbert, Lionne, Le Tellier and Brienne through the main gateway out onto the street, Nicolas made a sign for his porters to bring round his chair. Once the unlucky man was ensconced in the sedan, curtains closed, a watchful d'Artagnan mounted his steed, motioned silently for fifteen of his Musketeers to follow suit, and the troop rode down the main thoroughfare of Nantes.

Near to the Cathedral de Nantes, the sous-lieutenant halted the Lord of Vaux's progress, drew aside the drapes and conversed pleasantly with the man with whom he had no quarrel. Then the courteous Musketeer showed Fouquet the arrest warrant, signed by Louis Bourbon; the order which would change each of their lives dramatically. Blanching, the surintendant left his transport, d'Artagnan his saddle, and the two made their way to a house across the street, the home of Monsieur Fourché, who was Fouquet's uncle.

The worst aspect of the tragic drama was when Maupertuis arrived at the Hôtel de Rougé with three junior officers in tow to seal off the house. He informed Madame Fouquet that her husband had been taken into custody, and that she and their three sons and daughter would soon be escorted to a family property in Limoges where they would await the king's pleasure, banished from society. Maria Magdalena's wails could be heard throughout the hôtel, causing Susanne to seek sanctuary by locking herself in the suite César and I occupied next to her own.

"All is lost," she sobbed, clinging to me in despair, her hair mussed, and a dressing gown hanging from one shoulder. "The Musketeers have Nicolas and my hôtel is seized by order of the king!"

Having not slept the entire night for fear of waking to what was indeed transpiring, I held my friend tightly, too worn-out to speak.

"Susanne, calm yourself," César advised, looking fearful. "Could you call a valet to prepare my attire, perhaps?"

"César, really," I snapped. "Dress yourself. Susanne is distraught."

Leaving the bed, César hurried to the clothes' form on which his garments were draped. Pulling on stockings and breeches in a mad rush, he barely had blouson tucked into trousers when a loud rap at the entrance to the apartment demanded attention.

"Open in the name of the king!"

"Don't let them take me!" Susanne implored, tears running down her beautiful visage. "I must return to Paris and raise support for Nicolas!"

"Hide in the armoire," I directed in a hushed voice, leaving the bed with my friend attached to my person. "Get in; I shall liberate you when the Musketeers are gone."

Turning the skeleton key in its tumbler, securing the frontispiece of the freestanding closet that sheltered Susanne, I looked at César and nodded for him to greet the unwelcome visitor. Fetching my hunting jacket, I used the long coat to cover the sheer fabric of my nightshirt, placing the wardrobe key in one of the *justacorps'* pockets. As I did so, the letter written by Fouquet's brother rubbed against my knuckles and I remembered I had carried the stolen gem of information with me on the trip to Nantes.

"Good day, sir," César said pleasantly when face-to-face with the same rakish officer whom I had met the eve prior. "What may I do for you on this fine morning?"

"I am the Marquis de Maupertuis and I bear the king's order, monsieur, for the apprehension of one Marquise Susanne du Plessis, who is to be placed in my custody and escorted to Limoges with Madame Fouquet."

"Bijoux," César asked, "have you met with Madame Susanne this morning?"

"No, I have not, though last night she mentioned that she planned to rise early. Did she meet the minister at the château, perhaps?"

"Madame, the Surintendant of Finance was arrested by M. d'Artagnan not an hour ago," Maupertuis boasted, eyeing me suspiciously. "As we speak, Fouquet is traveling with our commander and a compliment of one hundred to the Château d'Angers where the prisoner will await trial for the crimes of embezzlement and plotting insurrection against the king."

"What?" I gasped, truly surprised. César and I were in danger; Louis had decided to ruin his surintendant and crush the Company with one fell swoop.

"My duty forbids me to say another word on the matter," the gentleman soldier replied, "yet be informed, madame, that the king is most pleased that you contacted M. d'Artagnan yesterday when you learned of Fouquet's treachery; he is impressed that you placed your own life in peril for his sake. His Majesty plans to reward you in some way for your devoted service."

"That the king mentioned me by name is reward enough," I protested. "Would that I could find Madame du Plessis for you, my day would be complete."

"I shall locate her, do not fear," the marquis promised with a bow. "In the meantime, no one is to leave the premises, understood?"

"We shall stand watch on the front steps ourselves," César answered with conviction. "My wife and I would be pleased to be of assistance."

"So, the two of you *are* married," Maupertuis smirked, tipping his hat at my husband in approval. "Some men have all the good fortune, do they not?"

"Quite," he agreed, grinning in return until the Musketeer took his leave. When he was certain that the corporal was gone, César then shut the door.

"We must help Susanne escape the hôtel," I noted, going to the armoire to release the fugitive. "How?"

"Did they come for me?" Susanne asked as she stepped out of the huge cabinet, lying down on the bed straightway to calm herself.

"Yes," César said softly, "The corporal has a warrant to detain you. The king has decreed that you be exiled to Limoges with Madame Fouquet."

"How fitting. Our king possesses a cruel streak in his nature, does he not?"

"Susanne, you will be no good to Fouquet if Louis holds you captive, under house arrest."

"If Nicolas did not require my assistance, I should kill myself."

"Such a rash action on your part would solve nothing."

"At least I would be at peace. With my lover taken, what is the point of living?"

"Susanne," César urged, "Bijoux is correct. You must not allow your grief to overwhelm you. We shall devise a disguise for you to wear so you might leave Nantes undetected."

"What a good idea, César! We'll outfit Susanne as a lackey."

"*Mon Dieu*," she moaned, "I am too old for such theatrics! Let the Musketeers take me away."

"Call La Fôret and d'Anger," I instructed, "they will help you with the costume's details."

"Are you going somewhere?" César queried, watching me strip and dress in the riding habit Susanne's washerwoman had cleansed of debris and aired the previous afternoon.

"To see the king. I wager he did not go hunting. And I have a gift to present to him on this, his natal day—a letter which will win me Louis' further gratitude."

"Whatever are you talking about? Have you lost your senses?" César complained.

"Do you recall the *communiqué* you read prior to our leave-taking?"

"You cannot give that letter to Louis, Bijoux! I forbid it!"

"We shall retain the original, giving the king a copy. I shall not tell him the Company's secret, although I shall entice him with innuendo. Louis fears another Fronde, he needs to know his enemies. He is mad for power and control, and once he reads this," I asserted, taking the bait from the jacket pocket and holding it aloft, "he will allow me to travel to Rome in order to query M. Poussin regarding the *certain things* Fouquet's brother alluded to in this report. Then, the three of us shall hire a coach and leave France on the double, on urgent business for the king; however, Louis will wait a very long time before he sees our faces at court again."

"Are you saying we should run away?" Susanne was stymied by the notion.

"Do you have a better solution? Prison, perhaps? We shall muster support for Fouquet from beyond France's borders. The surintendant has many friends abroad."

"Madame Bijoux," a familiar male voice interrupted from the hallway, "open the door!"

"Who is there?" César asked cautiously.

"Eustache d'Anger."

"Eustache, come in, the door is unlocked," I said, drawing tight the cords that joined together either side of a dress bodice. Knotting and tying the strings into a bow, my ensemble was completed when the young man crossed the apartment threshold.

"Madame, you are in danger!" he panted, out of breath, kneeling before Susanne. "The Grand Musketeers are searching for you outside on the streets. Monsieur Fouquet..."

"We know," César said sadly. "We heard."

"La Fôret and I had just left morning Mass and were in the cathedral square when Monsieur d'Artagnan stopped our master's sedan chair. Running to the scene, we saw the orders for the surintendant's arrest and La Fôret began to weep. Monsieur Fouquet touched his shoulder and said: *This is nothing—do not be alarmed, dear man. Please locate the Marquise du Plessis and convey my most loving sentiments to that grand lady; tell her we shall be together soon.* And then he smiled, marquise, and walked away with d'Artagnan and his men."

"May his noble soul be blessed," Susanne wept, overcome by Eustache's account of Fouquet's thoughtful gesture. "Where is La Fôret now? Why is he not with you?"

"The valet ran back to the château, took a horse from the team used to relay the king's own messengers, and was off for Paris, with no concern for his own comfort. He means to be the first back to the city with the news. La Fôret said, in fact: *The Company must be notified*."

"Eustache, forget you heard that," I warned. "These are dangerous times."

"What is the *Company*? What did La Fôret mean by that reference?"

"The Company of the Blessed Sacrament," César explained. "That powerful society may be the surintendant's last hope for freedom."

"Where the Company is concerned, Eustache, remain ignorant," I added. "That advice is based upon my own personal experience."

"No, he should know," César argued, motioning for the young man to rise. "We are all on the same side here, are we not? Eustache would not betray us, would you?"

"Absolutely not, my lord."

"Fine, do what you think best, César. I am off to the château. Good-bye," I said cheerfully, kissing him and Susanne in farewell, "I shall return victorious!"

"Be careful, Bijoux, darling," Susanne reminded me. "Matching wits with Louis is a risky business. Have you not heard the witticism: *When princes play, only princes are amused?* Consider what has happened to our Nicolas and do not force the king's hand, my dear."

"I shan't, Susanne. Have faith."

César walked me to the door. "Don't do this," he muttered. "The king may doubt the sincerity of your motives and be angered by a request for an audience."

"What will Louis do? Behead me for finding a letter?"

"He may punish you out of spite."

"Stop," I admonished, touching his cheek. "When we are crossing the frontier together, you will be glad that I went to see the king."

"Remember Vincennes. Be discreet," he pleaded. "Make a copy of the letter."

"I shall find Fouquet's secretary, Monsieur Pellison, and solicit his aid. I hearsay his penmanship is exemplary."

"Go, my vixen, go before I listen to my better judgment and make you stay. I love you."

"And I you," I assured him, then quit the room, walking away without a second look, afraid of changing my mind or losing my resolve. I had to face the king, I had to convince Louis that I should travel to Rome and approach M. Poussin; the happy outcome of three futures depended on whether I could convince the jilted lover that my intentions were bona fide. *Please help me, Athena*, I prayed silently, *please help me to do this thing right*.

The moment had come for me to pay for the latest folly, to answer for the regrettable betrayal of my benefactor, yet I went forward with confidence, blind to the wrong I had helped to precipitate, certain a home in a more pleasant clime awaited César, Susanne and myself. Louis would listen to me, I reasoned, for the king was above harboring petty grudges if the good of the realm and the destruction of his enemies could be used as justification for hearing the petition of one whom he despised.

However, I had forgotten that my king was named Amphitryon and that he was a conqueror.

Monsieur Paul Pellison was taken into custody by the Musketeers moments after he had finished penning the counterfeit letter I was determined to give to the king. I did not know of the unfortunate turn of events, for I had already sent the original back to César by way of a lackey and had ventured forth, clutching the facsimile in a sweaty palm. Poor Paul most probably followed in my footsteps as he was escorted to a secure cell located in the keep of the Château de Nantes, yet, my attention was directed on the path as I hurried to the unwanted assignment. Hopefully Maupertuis had been correct when he claimed the king was pleased with my conduct of late; d'Artagnan had saved me yet again, lying to his sovereign in order to save my hide. The Gascon's heightened sense of honor continued to amaze me, and I knew I was fortunate to be able to count on Charles de Batz as a loyal and trusted friend.

Upon arrival at the château, I was dismayed to see a hunt indeed being organized, the stable yard teeming with activity. Grooms were fetching bridles, braiding manes into lover's knots and cinching girths whilst the sounds of hooves striking stone, whinnies and human cajoling filled the air. My spirits rose when I saw Louis and a five man retinue stride onto the scene in a burst of colorful costume and obvious good humor. The triumphant king was flushed with pride at having vanquished his greatest foe, and the young men who followed were likewise exultant. Catching sight of the impeccable Bourbon, who nodded politely in my direction when he noticed a lady present, caused me to start with surprise, as though I had failed to recall that Louis was every inch a leader.

The sole person in the party whom I recognized was Brienne *fils*, the other participants were unknown to me. Later, I would be acquainted with them all: the tall, dark and well-built Marquis de Vardes, who was First Gentleman of the Bedchamber and Captain of the Swiss Guard; the elegant, middle-aged Comte de Saint-Aignan, who had contrived with de Vardes to nickname me *La Reine de la Main*; the cynical and suspicious Duc de Roquelaure; the Marquis de Peguilain who was short, mean of spirit, and so ugly that the other courtiers had taken to calling him the *skinned cat* amongst themselves. Such was Louis' male entourage, so it was small wonder that, once mounted, the king guided his honey-colored stallion to where I stood dumbfounded, wondering how best to approach the unapproachable.

"So, it *is* you," he laughed when close enough to get a good look at me, "and dressed for the chase, Madame de la Tour."

"Highness," I said from a kneeling position, "pardon the intrusion. I came here to speak to you concerning a matter of the gravest import..."

"If you come to plead for Fouquet, your entreaties will fall on deaf ears, madame. He is on his way to jail, to answer for crimes with which *you* are all too familiar."

"Majesty, forgive me my many shortcomings," I replied, daring to straighten, look Louis square in the eye and approach his steed. "Please believe I would never question your judgment, sire, nor would I dare interfere in matters of state. My honest motive will be plain enough when you read this," I explained, handing him the letter, "for I wish to provide you with a piece of evidence that will damn the surintendant, not defend him."

"Give me the paper," Louis ordered, signaling for his troupe to hang back. "You best be serious, madame, lest you fancy a prison cell as your new home."

I remained silent. Staring at the ground, I had no idea as to how Louis would react to the information until I heard the creak of leather and saw a boot touch the straw-littered pave.

"Is this the letter we discussed during our *tête-à-tête* in the woods of Vincennes?" he demanded, his tone requiring a truthful response. "The brief which, when he learned of its existence, haunted Mazarin 'till the end of his days?"

"Yes, your Majesty."

"Follow me," he stated, walking away towards the barracks. "We must confer."

"What of the hunt, sire?"

"Go on without me," the king called out to the others.

Running to catch the man who at last ruled with absolute power, I was careful to leave a respectful distance between us once I was close to the royal heels. As we hurried in the direction of the Grand Musketeers' lodging, nothing was said; each no doubt wondering what the outcome of our second chance encounter might be. The king charged onward into the recently abandoned quarters; a convenient setting for private conversation or another, more intimate, act.

"We shall talk in Monsieur d'Artagnan's chamber," Louis informed me as he led the way to Charles' room, familiar with the layout of the building.

"Sire," I ventured as I followed him into the Musketeer's suite, "may I be so bold as to congratulate you on your natal day?"

"Where did you get this?" he railed at me, closing the door with a bang and shaking the note in my face. "From Fouquet? Answer me quickly, madame!"

I was greatly dismayed by the rapid change in the king's attitude. He hated me. The rejection stung at my senses, causing me to tense and recoil from the onslaught.

"Why do you vex me so?" Louis grumbled. "Why does the sight of you cause my chest to ache with such a ferocity that I think I should die from the pain of it? Perhaps I should exile you to a convent and be spared the agony of ever seeing you again."

"No," I pleaded without thinking, "send me away, if you must, but not to a nunnery! Please Majesty," I begged, going to his side and falling to my knees, "have pity on me! I meant no harm. Nabo stole the letter for me from Fouquet before your marriage to the queen, more than a year ago. Question the dwarf if you do not believe my story."

"And why did you wait to bring the information to me directly?"

"I thought Fouquet to be in your good graces, sire, I thought..."

"You thought," Louis interrupted, "that you would use this, if needs be, for your own ends, madame, when the timing suited *you*! Is that the action of a loyal subject? Would Monsieur d'Artagnan withhold a find of such a magnitude from his king?"

"Mazarin was told of the letter's contents through his agent, your sous-lieutenant. I hid nothing from you. We spoke of the matter in the woods of Vincennes. Did I deceive you then?"

"Actually, madame, you did. You led me to believe that your

love for me was genuine when, in fact, it was a false emotion, manufactured at the whim of your damnable ambition!"

"That is not true!" came my protest. "I have loved you for as long as I remember loving anyone. If it were not for me, you would be *dead*!"

"What?" The king was intrigued. Helping me to my feet, he stared intently. "How did you save my life?" he asked in a soft voice.

"That is difficult to explain, sire," I hesitated. "Remember when you were ill with the fever at Calais, during the summer of fifty-eight?"

"Yes, of course. Monsieur Cousinot traveled overnight from Paris with a miraculous tonic that saved me from almost certain death."

"And it was I who suggested to Cousinot that he administer the cure, Majesty. I had been drinking the draught since childhood and was aware of its potency."

"No, it cannot be. *You?*"

"Cousinot was wary, though in the end, I convinced him the potion was your only hope."

"Why did he balk? What was in the drink?"

"My blood."

Louis stepped backwards as though slapped. "Your blood?"

"Cousinot bled me on the night he prepared your medicine. The blood he drew from me was taken for you—I made him lance my vein so that you might live."

"You confuse me, madame. How did drinking your blood save my life?"

"My love for you was as a true love should be, neither selfish nor demanding. That love was transmitted to your person through the fluid and healed you. Majesty, a goddess made you well, and my offering was the conduit through which Her power flowed. Does that mystify you?"

Perhaps because I seemed sincere, Louis considered my statement, stroking his chin. Melding my gaze with his, we stared at each other for what seemed an eternity.

"Now I understand the depth of my feeling for you," he said at last, moved by the confession, "and yours for me. You do love me, do you not?"

"Yes," I admitted, "you know full well I do. Yet, I love my husband as well. How does one reconcile two such emotions, sire?"

"By forgetting one attachment when in the presence of the other," the king advised. "Come here and I shall demonstrate the principle."

That same attraction I had known for Louis while lost in the forest, returned. A dangerous, intense surge that subdued my better self and sent me into his arms.

Our lips met and we kissed, recreating a scene from a shared past. And I wanted him, attracted by the king more than I had been consumed with the Secret, César, or any other single thing until that moment. Denying the infatuation was useless, creating excuses for why we could not be together, futile.

Pausing for a breath, Louis held me closely. "Why were you ever involved with that pack of turncoats, my sweet? For a while, I thought you on their side."

"Cardinal Mazarin sent me to Saint-Mandé to spy on Fouquet, remember, sire? And I did, reporting to your godfather faithfully on the Company of the Blessed Sacrament until the Roissy incident. After that, I sent word concerning the Order to him through M. d'Artagnan. I have always worked for the Crown alone."

"I hear you are Madame du Plessis' boon companion, not to mention wife to one who does not respect me."

"You are correct. I cannot lie to you. Yet both are dearer to me than life itself, sire."

"She must be exiled from court. The marquise is too devoted to Fouquet to be left at liberty. As for the husband, what shall we do with him? What does he know of the plans to usurp me?"

"Nothing. If you decide to punish César, I only ask that I share his fate."

The king smiled. "Well spoken, *La Loy*."

Turning red in the face, I stammered, "I am not fond of that name, Majesty."

"It suits you," Louis said, grazing the skin on my neck with his mouth. "Fouquet simply did not understand where your true loyalties lay, did he?"

"Will you execute him?" I asked with sorrow.

"He will be tried by the judges in Parliament as befits his rank. If found guilty of treason by the lawmakers, I shall see to it that a death sentence awaits the man with no future."

"Remove the opposition before it removes you."

"Exactly!" Louis responded, dark eyes gleaming bright. "You understand completely! Did I not say you were my beauty, my other self? Imagine my relief when d'Artagnan reported that you had come to him with valuable information regarding Fouquet's treachery. When I heard of your concern for my welfare, I instructed the sous-lieutenant to rip up the order he carried for your banishment."

"Banishment?"

"From France, on condition of Fouquet's arrest, although when I issued the command it grieved me intensely to consider losing you forever. You are the woman I truly want; any other is a counterfeit in comparison. In fact," he sighed, untying the front of my dress, "when I saw you lingering near to the château, I thought my chest would burst with joy, not agony."

"Then why were you angry with me when we first came to this room? Why the scene?"

"Prudence, dearest. Would you have not put me to the test were you in my position?"

"Absolutely. Did I pass the royal review?" My fingers were in his hair, his hands were beneath an unlaced bodice.

"One trial remains," Louis flirted. "However, if we proceed with the matter, no tears, agreed? No tormenting me with talk of sin or denying me the pleasure of your company."

"A guilty conscience was not the only reason I sent you away. I was fearful, sire."

"Of what?" he chuckled. "Me?"

"In a sense, yes. I thought a great evil would befall us if we continued our liaison."

"Such as?"

"Do not ask," I murmured, kissing him again and again, "do not ask."

"I must," Louis answered, "and you must likewise be candid with me, Bijoux. How could you think our love cursed? What is there that is evil about two people pleasing one another?"

"I am different than other people, Majesty."

"Of course you are. I love you."

"No. I am cursed in a way you cannot begin to comprehend."

"How so?"

"My mother was a heretic. She and a lover, the Abbé Guibourg, held Black Masses together on the Rue St. Denis during which they prayed to daemons for the deaths of Richelieu and your father. The pair dedicated my life to the study of the occult following an incident which occurred at the village of Versailles, when I was near to eight years old."

The king's frown made me halt. Mention of his father had distressed him.

"Let us repair to the settee. You will wish to sit, no doubt, while telling your interesting story."

"Yes, Majesty," I replied, noticing Louis' discomfort.

Taking a seat, I busied myself with my ensemble. Glancing up at the man whom etiquette decreed was the only person in the room who should repose, our gazes met in mutual uneasiness.

"Continue," Louis directed.

"I must beg your pardon, Majesty, for revealing too many details concerning an unpleasant childhood. It was improper to speak sacrilege in your presence."

"Nonsense. You have my permission to be direct, madame. Your tale is intriguing to me."

"If I tell the rest, sire, you might rightfully send me to the stake, should you be so inclined."

"Do you truly believe I could destroy what I love, Bijoux? That I could live without you?"

"I...I don't know. Perhaps."

"I swear to you on the sacred bones of my ancestors that I shall never forsake you," he said solemnly, kissing my hand with reverence. Then he removed from his person the ruby and gold circlet he had tried to gift me at Saint-Mandé, placing the ring on one of the fingers he continued to hold. The token rested where an absent wedding band should have been worn.

"With this ring, we are bound together for the remainder of our lives, be it for good or be it for bad. We are joined forever, agreed?"

"Yes," I answered with a nod, too overcome to say more. I had a feeling, though, that once Louis heard the account of Noctambule's curse, he would send me as far away as was possible.

"You are at liberty to speak your mind, my love," he repeated.

Clearing my throat, I stared at the red stone. The gem was the color of blood, almost black in its intensity.

"One August afternoon, I traveled to Versailles with my mother, Guibourg and our housekeeper, Madame des Oeillets. Because I was quite young and pined for adventure, I defied my elders and ran off into the woods when we had disembarked from our coach. Des Oeillets followed after me in concern, yet I was fleet of foot and managed to lose her amongst the thicket. However, unbeknownst to me, another had witnessed my flight, as well, and decided to track me into the forest."

"Who? A woodcutter, a charcoal-maker?"

"No, sire, an elderly gentleman by the name of Noctambule. He appeared to me in a clearing where I had stopped to rest. We sat together and he showed me curious tablets which he asked me to inscribe with my name in exchange for granting me what he described as days without end."

"Was he a sorcerer, by chance?"

"No, he was and is a *vrykolakas*," I frowned. "Noctambule is what the Church refers to as the undead. His tortured soul is trapped in a body which cannot rest in its tomb, a body which will never decay so long as he feeds upon the blood of mortals."

"*Mordioux!* This is incredible! One day, while out hunting, d'Artagnan spoke to me of such a creature, he claimed the legends of Gascony abound with accounts of men who become wolves by the light of the Moon, and corpses who rise from their graves to wander the night in search of human prey. At the time, I thought the tales mere flights of fancy and I paid him little heed. I did not know such things were possible."

"Very possible, sire. Noctambule left me with this," I replied, showing him the wen, "and the need to drink a tonic consisting of angelica water, essence of peony and human blood."

"How horrible," Louis remarked, making a sour face. "Tell me, did the predator's mark leave you immortal?"

"According to an English expert consulted on the matter, no one becomes a *vrykolokas* unless they drink of the daemon's tainted cruor. And I did not. Therefore, unless Noctambule returns for me, I shall die as would any other."

"Why did he not transform you at Versailles?"

"Please, do not sound so disappointed, Majesty."

The king sat ruminating while I marveled at the fact that he was the first person, besides Guibourg, who had ever heard my rendering of the encounter and believed the story in its entirety. Marion had scoffed, Cousinot, too; César had doubted my word 'ere to receiving Boyle's confirmation. Even La Rivière had questioned my coming upon a *vampyre* during the hours of daylight. Yet, while I was glad of Louis' acceptance, I found his silence disquieting. Had I known then that the king's paternal grandmother, Marie de Médicis, had hailed from a long tradition of royal necromancers, I never would have discussed the incident at Versailles; however, that realization came too late.

"Would you recognize Noctambule if you were to lay eyes on him again?"

"Certainly."

"Good. We shall return to Fontainebleau as soon as possible. I shall arrange for your inclusion in my brother's household. You will share apartments with Louise de la Vallière."

"Sire, do you expect me to break with my husband only to live with a girl who shares your bed?"

"You do not understand, Bijoux. My mother will not tolerate me taking a married woman as mistress, so Louise will remain in place, appearing to be my favourite as far as the court is concerned. We shall be the only two privy to our arrangement, as it should be."

"Sire, might I not serve you better if I were to journey to Rome and query Monsieur Poussin concerning Abbé Fouquet's letter?"

"You are not traveling to Rome," Louis replied. "Your place is at court. We must begin our search for Monsieur Noctambule immediately."

"What?" I could not comprehend what I was hearing the king say. "Why?"

"Why do you think? To ask him for the gift of immortality," he said wistfully, "for the chance to live forever. Consider the possibilities, Bijoux! We need never part, we need never die."

Louis was holding me by the arms, his eyes were open wide in wonder, his lips slightly parted. He expected an answer from me, yet I could not bear to utter one, so great was my disappointment.

"Why do you say nothing?"

"I am stunned, sire. Noctambule is no power with which to trifle. Besides, he told me I would not see him again for decades."

"I say we shall find the mage, and find him we shall. Versailles will resound with the trill of Bourbon hunting horns, mark my words."

The king stood and motioned for me to do the same. "This has proved an exciting audience, has it not? Does all this talk of dark forces and other-worldliness not stir your passions, my sweet?"

"No," I confessed, "such talk frightens me. Yet, I shall agree to ride at your side, to live with La Vallière, to find Noctambule for you—anything you ask—in return for two small favors."

"Name them," he smiled victoriously. "I shall grant you your fondest desire, my angel."

"Do not arrest Susanne or César. Allow them their personal freedoms, I beg of you."

"Would either be so concerned with your welfare if standing here before me? Petition again—those two do not warrant your solicitude."

"No," I said firmly. "That is what I ask, sire. That and nothing more. Promise me that the two may remain at liberty."

Louis walked over to d'Artagnan's bed and patted its heavy padding. "Join me on the pallet and we shall see," he suggested.

"Not before you give me your word, sire."

The king looked up at the ceiling and sighed audibly. "I swear that your husband will not be questioned or detained concerning the Fouquet affair and that the Marquise du Plessis may...reside on her estate at Charenton under house arrest. That is the best I shall do, Bijoux."

"Fine, then I am satisfied, your Majesty. So long as both may breathe fresh air, I am grateful."

"Now, come to me," he solicited as he removed his coat. "We shall be as Venus and Adonis."

I did his bidding. Miserable because my old wish to be Louis' most esteemed confidante had indeed come true, I hid my face in dark locks as he loosened my attire, his eagerness made more acute by half a year's waiting. Not only had the king trapped Fouquet, he had captured me as well; bitter regret made ruing the decision to travel to Nantes, to speak with d'Artagnan, to come to the château bearing the Poussin letter, an easy thing to do. The only good I had accomplished was to strike a bargain that had saved Susanne and César from complete disgrace.

Though at what cost, I wondered as Louis groaned with pleasure, at what cost?

CHAPTER SIXTEEN
Isle of Immortality

César was disconsolate when I informed him of the forced separation about to commence with the imminent return to Fontainebleau; he raged outwardly, kicking out a panel in one of the white doors leading to our guest chamber, and smashing two porcelain vases against a wall. Deserted by his wife and by reason, he swore to kill the king, he vowed to drive a dagger into the Bourbon's heart, he screamed aloud for revenge. Holding my husband close, I tried my best to quiet him and, eventually, he became still, his head on my shoulder and his arms around my waist.

Explaining that the king had meant to exile me and arrest my spouse had d'Artagnan not spoken on our behalf, César reluctantly accepted that the situation could be worse. Certain that the Duc de Guise would take him into his household, especially considering César was a staunch ally of the Lost King, all hope was not abandoned for his coming to court. Then and there we decided that once established under the same roof, we would meet clandestinely at every opportunity and renewed our joint commitment to advance the aims of the Company of the Blessed Sacrament.

Louis' courtiers were prepared to quit Nantes within a day's time and quit the city we did at eleven on the morning of the sixth. Collected at the Hôtel de Rougé by Maupertuis,

César and I were shown to the carriage that would carry us back to the environs of Paris. Allowing husband and wife to travel together for appearances' sake, Louis nonetheless had ordered the corporal to personally accompany Monsieur and Madame de la Tour on the return trek. Thinking that the king might reconsider our arrangement, my fear was allayed when a royal dispatch was sent, less than an hour into the journey, from the front of the processional to where our vehicle rolled along near to the back.

Holding the letter with an unsteady hand, I read that the Marquise du Plessis had been apprehended while fleeing to Belle-Isle and was being conducted, in her lackey disguise, to Charenton. Requesting quill, ink and paper from the messenger who was riding alongside the opened window, a page soon arrived with Louis' personal stationery box and I used its contents to write the king a note of sincere thanks. Reading over my shoulder as I tried in vain to guide pen neatly over paper while riding down a bumpy road, César guffawed at my efforts, then stopped when he realized the corporal was watching him closely.

The Abbé Guibourg's twin was determined to make the time we spent in one another's company as uncomfortable as was humanly possible. Hardly a word was spoken during the trip, and the tense circumstances accounting for our forced *ménage à trois* did little to contribute to conviviality of any sort. During the first eight hours of confinement, Maupertuis gazed at me lasciviously whenever César's eyelids would lower, licking his lips and raising his eyebrows in a suggestive way, causing me to recall the rude remarks the scoundrel had made at the king's birthday celebration. Stretched out full length on his side of the coach, the marquis stared and stared and stared at the woman across from him until she thought she would go mad with pent-up anger. It was a great relief then, when the silent interrogation ended at twilight outside the city of Amboise, more than one hundred miles east of Nantes. Near to seven o'clock, the king had deemed it time to sup, and the horses were pulled up hard and fast outside a sizable inn where they were watered and cooled-down. Wanting to stretch my legs and walk around a bit, I leaned forward to open the carriage door.

"Halt, madame!" the corporal ordered, placing a hand over my own. "You are not to leave this coach under any circumstances."

"What?" César protested. "We must refresh ourselves and find something to eat, monsieur. Your demand is most unreasonable."

"The king said nothing about restraining you, begone!" Maupertuis scoffed. "This fine lady is to stay put."

Fearing an altercation, the sound of a knock on the outside of the coach caused me to jump.

"Open in the name of the king!" a voice heralded.

The Musketeer did not tarry when summoned by Louis' proxy. Allowed access, a page appeared bearing a crude wooden platter laden with nuts, cheeses, fruits and bread.

"For Madame de la Tour, a gift from the king."

"Thank his Majesty most heartily for me," I replied. "'Tis a generous gesture. Shall we be lodging here for the evening, pray tell?"

"No," the young man informed me. "His Majesty deems it necessary that we press on through the night. We may reach Fontainebleau by daybreak on the morrow, God willing."

"Thank you," I murmured as the king's emissary excused himself and left our midst. The men attacked the food as would ravenous hounds, yet I refrained, assessing the situation at hand.

"César, where is Eustache?"

"He rides with the remaining compliment of the king's Musketeers," he answered, mouth half-full. "I saw him in the saddle before we departed Nantes."

"He follows on horseback, exposed to the elements?" I questioned in a tone indicating disapproval of d'Angers' mode of transport. "Should he not be here, attending to his master?"

"Me?" he queried, choking on the loaf he gnawed.

"Well, he is your valet, is he not?" I argued, acting put out for Maupertuis' benefit. "Your uncle is the great Turenne and we aren't exactly peasants, you know. Go fetch the boy, and Lisette, my maid," I pestered, pushing at him to leave and do my bidding, creating a household for us from Fouquet's uprooted servants. "Be quick, go on."

My husband smiled when he saw me wink at him ever so carefully. He understood.

"Do not allow this animal to devour everything," César grumbled, rising to depart. "I shall return shortly."

When he was gone, I took the tray away from my adversary.

"As you have no doubt noticed, marquis, I enjoy a certain amount of favor with the king."

Maupertuis glared at me, saying nothing.

"And with your sous-lieutenant, Monsieur d'Artagnan. Therefore, I advise you to keep your eyes to yourself for the remainder of this journey, or else you may find yourself blinded, as did someone else who once threatened my happiness. To be honest, you resemble that unfortunate soul, and I hate to think you might follow in his footsteps."

"Strumpet," he spat at me. "Do you think I care if you service the king?"

Taking up the very sharp knife resting on the carving board, I raised the instrument so Maupertuis might see its blade plainly.

"Monsieur, I am quite certain that you do not. However, be advised that the confidence I share with our sovereign has nothing to do whatsoever with what you yourself so beguilingly termed—what was the phrase—*my heritage*? I am of the house d'Effiat, sir; *that* is my heritage!"

The message was not lost on the corporal. He looked away, unable to face me. "Forgive my less than gentlemanly conduct. I was wrong to disrespect your family's honor."

"I accept your apology," I smiled. "May we not begin again with civility? Monsieur d'Artagnan would wish it thus."

"Then I am your devoted servant, madame."

"Come here, embrace me in the spirit of friendship," I urged, trying desperately to overlook his resemblance to

Guibourg. "You will be as a brother to me. I shall name you my Mestor."

"Thank you, madame."

"May we stroll outside if I promise to take your arm and not leave your side?"

"With pleasure," he smiled, anxious for exercise. "I shall be honored, madame."

Maupertuis exited and helped me to alight. Hopping down from the iron step that led from the vehicle to the ground, I looked about and saw Louis, promenading across the road with a tiny woman clad all in black, possessing the whitest-blonde hair I had ever seen. Courtiers milled about the august pair, their servants either fetched food or brought carriage lanterns inside the inn to be lit, and a group of Musketeers quaffed tankards of ale to relieve their parched throats.

"Who is that young woman with the king?" I asked my escort.

"You do not know? That lady is Marie-Thérèse, Queen of France and Navarre."

"She is so petite and fair! One would expect a darker complexion of a Spanish princess."

"No, that tone belongs to her beloved companion. See him following behind? That little man is none other than Monsieur..."

"Nabo!" The name came flying out loud and clear and the dwarf's head shot up. Seeing me, he tugged on Marie-Thérèse's gown, jumping about in a frenzy, pointing in my direction and crying out: "Rouge, Rouge!" The very pregnant queen bent down with considerable difficulty to speak to her darling Moor, and Louis flashed me the warmest look imaginable, lifting his oversized tricorne hat in recognition. Then everyone in the nearby vicinity felt compelled to pay me notice and I blushed as I went down on bended knee in response to the king's salute.

"Here he comes," Maupertuis remarked while I straightened. Nabo raced to where we stood.

"Rouge, Rouge!" he called again, to the general hilarity of those assembled, grabbing me by the knees when he reached his destination. "Where you been? Where Monsieur César?"

"How are you little one?" I asked. "May I have a proper hug?"

He kissed me when I lifted him up and some of the other courtiers began to clap their approval. Turning red again, I noticed the king viewing the tender reunion with particular interest.

"Maria-Beresa have baby soon," Nabo informed me with pride. "Me be its brother."

"Oh really?" the corporal roared, holding his sides while I tried not to laugh at the observation. "What does the king think about that?"

"Who you?" Living at court had made my former student more precocious than ever.

"Me the Marquis de Maupertuis," the Musketeer said with a bow.

"Oh. *Très bien*. You nice. Where Monsieur César, Rouge?"

"Here, Nabo," my husband answered, arriving on the scene with Eustache and Lisette. "Rouge sent me on an errand."

I smiled at the lovely young woman who had served me at Saint-Mandé without fail or complaint. "Ready to make good on the bargain we struck a while back?"

"Oh, yes, madame," she said, breathless. "I still have the coin you gifted me that afternoon."

"Well, you'll have more of those, I daresay, with a pretty face such as yours," I chuckled. "And Eustache, you will continue to serve my husband well?"

"For you, madame, anything. When I pledged my service the other evening..."

D'Anger stopped in mid-sentence and glanced at Maupertuis with apprehension.

"Madame Bijoux and I have made amends," the marquis offered, whacking d'Anger on the back. "With Fouquet's arrest a *fait accompli*, we need no longer be wary of one another, eh?"

"Maria-Beresa!" Nabo yelled with enthusiasm while I watched those around me sink to the ground. Turning, I saw the king and queen approach our circle.

"Athena, guide me," I murmured, gently putting down the imp and assuming the posture etiquette demanded.

"Arise," Louis said to no one in particular.

The little Moor was holding his mistress' hand and gazing up at her in complete adoration. "This Rouge," he told the queen. "She my friend."

Louis began speaking to his wife in Spanish and she nodded, then addressed him in her native tongue when he had finished.

"The queen is glad to make your acquaintance, Madame de la Tour," the king translated, "and wishes me to thank you for caring for her Nabo in days gone by. You may kiss her hand."

Not daring to look at the woman whom I had wronged more than once, I pressed my lips to five stubby fingers. In response, she attempted to speak her adopted language.

"That is nice," she giggled.

"Madame de la Tour will reside with Monsieur and Madame," Louis explained in kind, mouthing each word slowly and carefully.

"That is nice," she repeated.

Looking at the queen's swollen belly, I sensed Louis saw her as nothing more than a brood mare for the French royal family, someone to be brought out and paraded in public during official functions.

I withdrew from the couple, understanding better my position at court.

"To Fontainebleau!" the king announced merrily, offering an arm to his wife. The two departed, chatting to themselves, although Nabo waved good-bye as he trailed along behind his Maria-Beresa.

"May I?" Maupertuis offered a hand to Lisette when we were back at the coach.

"Leave Lisette be, marquis, unless, of course you intend to marry her," I teased, tapping him on the shoulder. "Or do you have a wife?"

"No, I do not, madame. Perhaps I should wed."

"Begging your pardon, madame," Lisette said, flushed from her bosom to her forehead, "a marquis would never take a serving girl as wife; even I know that."

"Get inside and be still," I whispered to her. "Consider the marriage I made—my mother was Marion Delorme. And take off that cap. You remind me of my former nursemaid, Des Oeillets."

Lisette's mouth fell open as she climbed into the vehicle, removing the white bonnet that hid her luxuriant, golden hair. César held me back while Eustache and the Musketeer boarded, kissing me unexpectedly on the mouth when our turn came to take a seat.

"This is where we say *adieu*, Bijoux, unless you swear to me you will never lay with that bastard again. Are you mine or are you not?"

"César, please! This is not the time or the place for a scene."

"If you had relations with him in Nantes, then I forgive you. Yet never again, Bijoux, never again. You must make a choice: the king or your husband."

"You," I said without pause. "I want you."

"Good, that is all I needed to hear. As soon as I may arrange it, we leave France."

"May we arrive at Fontainebleau first? The driver is signaling."

"Be apprised of my plan, that is all."

Then he allowed me entry to the upholstered interior that would serve as the communal bedchamber until we reached civilization. Finding the others situated comfortably enough—Eustache seated next to Maupertuis on one row of cushions and Lisette perched by herself on the other—I rested between my new companion and César, careful to leave more room for my husband than for myself.

"Are you well?" I asked the man next to me when the crunch of dirt under wheels told me we were on our way. "Is everything as it should be?"

"Oh yes," he mumbled as he stared out the window at the shadows of countryside passing before him, "absolutely perfect."

Thinking it best to leave César to his preoccupation and

Eustache and Maupertuis to their boring discussion of muskets, I turned my attention to Lisette.

"Excited about going to court?" I ventured in an attempt to converse.

"Oh, yes, madame."

"Bijoux, please. We are nearly the same age, are we not? I'd rather that we were friends than mistress and maidservant. God knows I have need of a trustworthy companion now that the Marquise du Plessis is gone away."

"My heart aches for her, madame. She is a good woman."

"She will be back at court in six months," I said with determination, already plotting as to how I could persuade Louis to recall Susanne from obscurity at Charenton. Not wishing to discuss court politics further, I returned to the subject of age.

"So, Lisette, how old are you?"

"Twenty-three."

"Twenty-three?" the Musketeer interjected. "I thought you to be younger."

Lisette turned crimson again and I came to her defense. "Pay him no heed," I advised playfully, "for my mother was as famous for her beauty at the age of thirty-nine as she had been in her twenties."

"I know," she replied, staring at her lap.

"Truly, now! Who spoke of my mother to you, then?"

"My own mother. Her name was Madame des Oeillets."

The admission left me speechless. Lisette would not look at me, so I took one of her hands in my own and placed my forehead on her shoulder.

"The same Madame des Oeillets who raised me until Marion's death? The woman of whom I spoke when I mentioned your cap?"

"Yes, madame."

"I...I do not understand how this thing came to pass. Madame des Oeillets was with child when I came to court, not before. You are two years my senior."

"May I speak frankly?"

Lifting my gaze, I could see that Eustache and Maupertuis were intrigued with Lisette's tale; César appeared to be asleep. Turning back to the face that belonged to the child of her whom I had loved as a parent, I nodded my head in approval.

"Your mother came to Paris in 1636, at the age of twenty-five, with a handsome poet named Des Barreaus. She had run away from her home in the country because her father, who was rich and of the lesser nobility, had forbidden his daughter to consort with a man of letters."

"My mother was a noblewoman?"

"Yes, madame, her real name was de Lorme, not Delorme."

"This is too incredible! Then why..."

"She wanted to be free to do as she pleased. And when she arrived at the capital, she did. Des Barreaus did not last long, for he was soon replaced in Marion's bed by men such as Condé and Scarron, even Cardinal de Richelieu. My mother came to serve yours in 1638, a few months before Cinq-Mars attended the most popular salon in the Marais and fell madly in love with its famed hostess."

"And where were you?" Eustache queried.

"Living with my aunt and uncle in Vincennes. I was a newborn, however mother left me with family and went to earn a living in the capital following the death of her husband, my father, from the pox."

"Why did she desert you? You could have come to live with us."

"Your mother was not overly fond of members of her own sex, and my mother knew my presence would prove a problem in later years. 'Twas easier to pay people to care for me than to run a household and look after a child."

"Did you see your mother again?" I asked with concern.

"Oh, yes. She came to visit on holy days with gifts. And she spoke of you and your mother often, for she was proud of her association with Madame la Grande."

"Has she contacted you of late?"

"No," Lisette said, shaking her head sadly, "she has not. She did write to me when I was twelve to say she was leaving Paris to start anew in the south, and that soon I would be blessed with a sister or brother. Then money was forwarded to provide me with a tutor for lessons and my daily keep. After that, I had one more letter from her, announcing the birth of a sister, Justine. She promised to send for me once her business was flourishing, but evidently forgot to or else fell upon hard times. My relatives had children of their own to think about, so, when I was sixteen, they found me a place at Saint-Mandé."

"Do you know where your mother settled?"

"My aunt made me promise never to say, madame."

"Lisette, when Marion died, your mother and I divided the marquise's jewels between us before we parted. I gave her the treasure to escape serving a very evil man, the Abbé Guibourg, who was my mother's lover, your mother's seducer, and also your sister's father. Madame des Oeillets and I swore to get word to one another, but we never did because both neither of us were certain where the other was exactly. I merely wish to help you find your mother, if you so wish it."

"I long for her and my sister, I must admit."

"Then give us the name of her hiding place," Maupertuis urged. "I shall ride to wherever your dear mother resides and personally deliver a message to her from you, mademoiselle."

"Would you, monsieur? I fear the journey is a long one."

"Whisper the name to me if you want no one else to know. I am not exactly a stranger," I said.

Lisette hesitated. "No, I shall trust you all with the secret. My mother lives in Marseilles. She
owns a brothel."

"Smart lady," the corporal laughed.

"Why did she run away?" Eustache probed.

"That is none of your concern," César replied, sitting up and rubbing his eyes. "My wife's past is
not a topic for discussion."

The group fell quiet. Lisette regarded me pitifully. "Do you know the answer, madame?"

"César, allow me to speak," I begged. "What is the harm in

telling this poor girl the truth? I am not ashamed of anything I did in the Marais."

"Come, come, de la Tour, do not spoil the suspense," the marquis said in a fraternal tone.

"Fine," my husband relented. "Guibourg is a dangerous man and I shall not have these women compromised by either of you. Swear to me that Bijoux's tale will not be repeated to anyone."

"I swear on my honor," the Musketeer intoned.

"As do I," Eustache said seriously.

"Satisfied?" I quipped.

"You may not care what happens to you, yet I do," was my husband's reply.

So I told the story of Étienne Guibourg, beginning with his involvement in Marion's death to the priest's appearance at d'Artagnan's apartment on the night of Mazarin's exile. Omitting the mention of satanic rite, I still let it be known that he was a man with a very mean streak, and one who harbored no love

for either Madame des Oeillets or myself.

"When you arrive at court, mademoiselle, I think it prudent to adopt another surname," César

suggested.

"Maupertuis?" the Musketeer teased.

"Take mine," Eustache offered, betraying the fact he found Lisette comely.

"No," she replied, "I do not fear this Guibourg. He knows nothing of me. Besides, I have no

jewels for him to covet."

"Still, you are allied with me, and should he hear our two names mentioned together—Bijoux and

Des Oeillets—he would go mad with rage, he would poison us both," I warned.

"*Mon Dieu*," Lisette shuddered, "to think such people walk the streets! Saint-Mandé was a far

safer haven; we were so sheltered there."

"Those days are finished," I agreed, wrapping an arm about

her shoulders, "and we must take care of one another now. Henceforth, you will be known as my companion, Madame de...Ventadour, in honor of someone who was once very dear to me."

"And your husband is dead, which makes you very eligible to remarry," the corporal supplied.

"Yes, well said. And together, Lisette, we shall discover what has become of your mother," I promised. "To think, we lived in the same household for three years and never realized we were connected by a common thread. You touched my heart from the first, although I did not know why."

"Thank you for helping my mother and now me," she smiled. "I have heard it said that Marion Delorme was sharp-tongued and wicked. You may have her face, yet not her ways."

The carriage proceeded down the highway towards the unknown and I did not respond, ashamed to accept Lisette's praise. No matter how much I yearned to believe her, she was wrong in her comparison of me to the Marquise de Cinq-Mars.

Very mistaken indeed.

My first impression of Fontainebleau, observed from the wrong side of a dust encrusted window, was that the old palace was in need of dire repair. Yet, when the king's cortege halted in the château's freshly scrubbed courtyard and our party disembarked, yawning, to be greeted by a glorious autumn morning, I changed my opinion.

The journey had been tiresome and we had stopped only twice following the brief sojourn at Amboise to relieve ourselves—men to the left of the coach and women to the right—so I was hardly in a mood to be charmed. However, the château Louis liked more than any other had a history of romance attached to its weathered walls and entwined initials were carved everywhere in stone. The enormous royal retreat, surrounded by a shady forest, had been built for pleasure, for respite, and I breathed in the scents of herbs and flowers, glad to be alive.

Taking hold of César's hand, I squeezed it with vigor,

smiling at him happily. Witnessing my contented expression, his face brightened as well, a sight I had not seen since our departure from Nantes.

Accompanied by Eustache, my husband and his recently acquired valet went for a stroll to eavesdrop amongst the flock of courtiers milling about the massive horseshoe shaped staircase leading to the entrance and ground floor apartments of the king and his brother, known as the Pavilion of the Princes. I had no notion at the time, but Fontainebleau was a grand house, filled with gold leaf and sparkling crystal chandeliers, ornately painted walls, tables laden with silver plate and the finest furniture resting atop the costliest carpets in the world. Add to that a fraction of the bounty Louis planned to confiscate from his former Surintendant of Finance and the palace would be a showcase. No doubt the much-lauded *orangerie* at Vaux-le-Vicomte would find itself transported to the king's summer estate, and their roots would tangle with those of the lovely lemon trees that grew in the Garden of Diana. Not unless, of course, Louis decided to keep nearby Vaux for himself.

Waiting patiently for César to return to the spot where I tarried with Maupertuis and Lisette, I watched the crowd who was watching the king. Trained as they were to hang on his every gesture and word, the elite of France hovered close to their master. I, on the other hand, remained apart from the throng, content to maintain a respectable distance. Philippe had appeared on the scene to welcome his brother, and Monsieur was looking as pretty as ever, decked-out in an elaborate peruke, beribboned costume and high-heeled shoes. So entranced was I with admiring his finery, I hardly noticed my truest friend and lover returned to my side.

"Bijoux," César whispered, "the two bastards are discussing you."

"Who? Me?"

"Oh, yes," he continued in a low tone meant for me alone. "Philippe has been informed that you are the latest addition to his establishment. He seems to be taking the news rather well."

"How nice of him," I muttered. "What do I do now?"

"Nothing," César advised. "Someone will be sent to collect you. I must be off to find lodging for Eustache and myself."

"Shall I see you later this evening?"

"Of course. Meet me by the Grand Canal at eleven. Wear a mask."

"All of my finery is at Saint-Mandé," I pouted.

"We shall arrange to have your wardrobe sent on. And the same for the jewels. The king cannot refuse his favourite her personal possessions."

"César, I am not interested in asking Louis for any boon."

"Good," he grinned. "Retrieve our crates from Saint-Mandé, all the same. 'Till eleven."

"I shall be there, my darling."

His kiss on my cheek was warm and I held him to me, not caring who observed our embrace. Perhaps Louis would be jealous if he saw me on good terms with my husband and perhaps I could use his pique to my advantage. Playing coy might keep the king at bay. I needed to confer with someone wiser than myself as to how a great lady would play the cards I had been dealt. Someone who was worldly, yet moral. Someone such as Françoise Scarron.

César released me when a page approached, wearing the gray and yellow livery of Monsieur and Madame's household. Mouthing the words, *good luck*, he was off, accompanied by Eustache, the shadow. Watching the two young men stride away, heads together, I was certain they were up to no good.

"Madame de la Tour?" the servant bowed.

"Yes, I am she."

"The Duc d'Orléans requests your presence, madame. Please follow me."

I motioned for Lisette to walk alongside as Maupertuis and Philippe's envoy escorted us to where the prince stood flirting with Louis' male entourage. Brazen in the wake of the king's departure for the council chamber, the good-for-nothing rascal fluttered his long eyelashes at the very masculine Marquis de Vardes, who probably reminded him of uncle Gaston. The

Captain of the Swiss Guard regarded the prince with contempt, as one would a flea on a dog.

"Monsieur," the page announced, "may I present Madame de la Tour."

"Bijoux!" Philippe squealed with pleasure, crushing me to the rose colored waistcoat he sported beneath an emerald green *justacorps*. "My dearest childhood friend! I have been desolate without you, naughty girl!"

"Heh, Saint-Aignan!" de Vardes yelled aloud, "*La Reine de la Main* has returned!"

"*Formidable!*" the count replied. "Ink the press!"

Hiding my face in Monsieur's wig, my mortification knew no bounds. The younger Bourbon took no notice of the degenerates, however, choosing instead to grab one of my earlobes with his teeth.

"To live at court you must rely," he whispered.

"On proverbs till the day you die," came my natural response.

"And one of these we like the best," he laughed.

"Is wiser beyond all the rest. A simple thought, yet, one so true; a verse I'd like to sing for you," we said in unison. Then I stopped and allowed the prince to finish.

"A lady who is born and bred, will dress her feet before her head!"

We clung to each other, consumed with silliness, unaware that our spontaneous display of amusement raised more than a few eyebrows. After a moment, though, we stopped snickering, both sensing the show of familiarity unseemly.

"So, you are now known as Madame de la Tour," Philippe observed, standing back to inspect me in my plain riding habit.

"Forgive my attire, Monsieur; however, I came here straight from Nantes and all my belongings are at Saint-Mandé."

"Including the jewels?"

"You have a very good memory, your Highness," was my evasive answer.

"Do you still have the stones, Bijoux?" he asked with excitement.

"Yes, though not with me," I admitted. "They must be retrieved from Fouquet's house."

"Do not fear, I shall order your property recovered and delivered here immediately," Philippe announced with an air of authority, offering me his arm. "Until the crates arrive, we must do something about your wardrobe. Shall I make you a loan?"

I laughed, almost tripping on a marble step. "You aren't still dressing the part of a lady, are you?" I asked discreetly.

"Oh, yes," he chirped. "Although less frequently what with Guiche being exiled from court."

"When did that happen?"

"At the beginning of August. He was spending too much time in my wife's company, and I informed him of my displeasure. Then the ingrate upbraided me and addressed me as he would an equal! The Marshal, his father, ordered his son back to Paris when he heard of the insult to my person, although Louis had already banished Armand hours before."

"That explains the count's appearance at Saint-Mandé on the night of the party at Vaux!"

"You saw him? Tell me everything!" Philippe demanded with a hint of longing in his voice.

We had arrived at the first great room and I turned to make certain Lisette was following. When I saw that she was indeed amongst the group of courtiers who had decided to tag along in the prince's wake, I nodded to her reassuringly. Then I focused on Monsieur, who was eager to hear about his former lover's bad behavior.

"As did you, I exchanged harsh words with the dashing count. He is the most arrogant man alive and I hope that I never see him again."

"You always detested Guiche."

"Monsieur, you might find another more worthy of your friendship."

"Yes, but who?" he sighed. "At times I fear I shall never love again."

"Pardon me for asking, Monsieur, have you no feelings for your wife?"

"She is a harlot," he sneered. "The vilest woman alive! I hope she dies in childbirth."

"Monsieur, watch what you say," I advised out of concern for my old friend. "We should discuss this matter behind closed doors, I see."

"You will stay with me, then. All day and all night. My apartments are nearby."

"The king said I was to room with Louise de la Vallière, Monsieur."

"The king said I was to sponsor you in my household; therefore, I shall do with you as I please. You will remain with me for as long as I wish it."

"My companion, Madame de Ventadour, also requires lodging."

"You brought her along? Was that lady not wed to M. d'Artagnan?"

"Yes, indeed. My friend is a...relation of that same family."

"Well..." Philippe mused as he allowed a servant to open the large door to the royal suite, "I have it! We'll send her upstairs to La Vallière's chamber! Louis will have a seizure!"

"Is that sage?"

"Do I appear to be concerned?" he replied as we entered a drawing room. "Do you find my apartments comely?"

"Beauteous," I complimented, awed by the intricately painted murals covering four walls from top to bottom.

"Come, come, I shall show you all of it," my host enthused, pulling me by the arm. "There is so much to see!"

Philippe's living quarters were indeed exceptional and decorated with perfect taste. Everywhere was gilt, pastel silks and brocades, *objets d' art* and flowers from the garden. The effect was stunning, breathtaking, yet when the Duc d'Orléans collapsed on his unusual bed, tucked inside an intimate alcove, he appeared to be quite miserable.

"Monsieur," I ventured, "Whatever is the matter? What ails you?"

"Nothing," he sulked.

"Tell me. Tell your Bijoux," I coaxed.

"Send the servants away."

The two attending valets left without further prompting from me. Locking the door behind them, I then joined Louis' brother on his feather pallet.

"Why are you sad?"

"I miss Guiche. Why did he have to fall in love with Henriette? Why did he cast me aside? I tried to tell him my wife makes love to anyone and everyone—even to his sister, the Princess of Monaco—yet he would not listen to me. He threatened to strike me!"

"Henriette lays with women?" I could not imagine the act.

"Of course, many ladies at court do. If men sleep with men, why not women with women?"

"Why bother?"

"Perhaps you should try a lady yourself, darling Bijoux."

"Monsieur! I love my husband."

"Is he handsome?" Philippe seemed cheered.

"Very," I breathed wistfully, reclining alongside the heir to the realm, playing with an ebony curl from his peruke, wondering whose hair it had once been.

"Is your husband a splendid lover? Does he leave you transported unto the heavens?" he snickered, entertaining me with his juvenile wickedness.

"You are horrid," I decreed. "You should be punished for your saucy manner."

"Shall we play our game? Remember?"

"Monsieur, behave. What of my present attire?"

"Yes. Dress-up. How fun! Who is the fairest in the land?"

"You, Prince Tyrannus." I closed my eyes and stretched out my arms. Being bad was sometimes fun and the king's brother did not have to persuade me on that particular day to be his willing cohort.

"Bijoux," he said in a seductive manner, "shall we?"

"Shall we *what*?" I looked at him for an answer.

"You were always so accommodating," Philippe whispered, guiding my hand to his breeches. "Please say yes."

"Do not be perverse," was the scolding he received. "Let our relationship remain a platonic one."

"Who gifted you this ring?"

The unexpected inquiry rattled my senses. Caught in a quandry, I could not be untruthful with him, so I said nothing. No longer interested in lolling about, I made a move to rise, although my companion thought otherwise.

"Louis gave you the jewel, did he not? And why is he so interested in you, madame?"

"Monsieur, that is a matter best left between the king and myself."

"You went to bed with him, didn't you?" he yelled and I winced visibly. "How could you? First Henriette, then you! *Bon Dieu*, I hate him!"

"I was his mistress long before Henriette."

"How comforting! The great seducer strikes again! Perhaps I should dally about with Marie-Thérèse! *Bon Dieu*, I hate him," he repeated.

"Do not be angry with me, Monsieur. I have suffered greatly for my sin. Because of my inability to twice resist your brother's advances, I have been ordered from my husband's side and face living with a cripple! I am a Cinq-Mars, damn it; *you* contemplate a life of bowing and scraping to the likes of Louise de la Vallière! Do not presume to chastise me, for nothing you say hurts me more than Louis' supposed kindness."

Philippe was staring at me, mouth agape. "He did wound you, did he not?"

"Worse than you might imagine, Monsieur."

"And you do not wish to become his *maîtresse en titre*?"

I shook my head *no*, afraid I might begin to weep if I spoke.

"Then I shall protect you," he offered, his embrace tender. "You will become my favourite—won't that surprise everyone!"

"Especially your wife."

"Yes, quite true. Henriette, of course, will detest you."

"Who is she to talk?"

"She is Madame, that is who. You must learn to tread carefully at court, Bijoux. Mind your tongue. And beware her friends."

"Who makes up the clique?"

"Madame de La Fayette; the English girl, Frances Stewart; a witty young lady known as Athénaïs de Mortemart and Bablon, who is the widowed Duchesse de Châtillon. You will become acquainted with the rest in time."

"And where shall I live? I cannot sleep in your apartments every night."

"We shan't be here much longer," he disclosed. "We'll be off to Saint-Cloud soon. You will have your own apartment there."

"Saint-Cloud?"

"My estate on the Seine, west of Paris. A gift from Mazarin shortly after the Choisy affair. A modest château, although I plan to transform the house into a great palace where I shall showcase my growing art collection."

"I did not know you owned that property, Monsieur. May I bring César when we move?"

"We shall see. Allow things to calm down a bit. What with Fouquet's arrest, everything is topsy-turvy at the moment."

"Yes, forgive me my haste. I wonder how the former surintendant is faring, relegated to a prison cell in Angers."

"I sent the Prince de Chalais to hang about the council room. As soon as he discerns what goings-on are being discussed, he will come to me with a full report. Not that I need be told what the ministers discuss," he muttered, resigned to his overlooked status. "Colbert will be the man of the hour; the one to whom Louis will give the dirty work. No mention will be made of Fouquet, I reckon."

"Poor Lord Cléonime, deserted by all."

"Whom?"

"Nothing," I said with a wave of a hand. "Let us speak of more pleasant matters."

"Such as?"

"Such as making a loan of some clothing, Monsieur."

Scampering off by himself to the adjacent dressing parlor, Philippe soon returned bearing a heap of skirts, stockings and gowns. The raiment, which spilled out of his arms and dragged onto the floor, was fashioned from some of the most exquisite fabrics I had ever seen.

"Oh, Monsieur, such splendid things! I could never wear any of them!"

"You must," he laughed and deposited the pile onto the bed. "Keep it all. What with Guiche gone, I have no use for such trifles. Besides," he sniffed, "I've worn all these frocks in the past and, quite frankly, I am bored by them."

Thus, I was outfitted by a Prince of the Blood, donning fashions finer than those my mother or most princesses, for that matter, had ever worn. Stripped and clothed by Monsieur, who dressed me with attentive care, I submitted to the laces of the corset, a stiff hoop under petticoats and more face paints than I thought proper. When he paraded me to the opposite end of the boudoir to view his handiwork in a full-length looking glass, the lady clad in pink who stared back from the mirror caused me to start.

"Pure perfection!" Philippe observed, clapping his hands. "What say you, my beauty?"

"Words do not suffice, Monsieur," I admitted, "I am overwhelmed. Truly."

"Recall when we were children," he began, kissing my hand, "and I told you I would love you forever, whether I married a princess or no?"

"Yes," I replied, looking away, tears springing forth.

"I never forgot my promise to you, Bijoux. And perhaps I cannot adore you as another man might, with the same intensity of feeling, yet I shall make you the loveliest lady at court and thereby pay tribute to you. You will be my creation, a queen..."

"Highness, really, I am no queen..."

"Look at yourself. You are regal, sublime. Every inch the muse Louis desires, yet does not possess. And he shan't have you," he jeered. "He may content himself with Henriette's gimpy maid-of-honor, La Vallière."

"Monsieur, please, I do not wish to be the cause of discord between your brother and yourself."

"Too late. I have decided. Come, it is nearly noon and the

king and queen will be attending Mass. Wouldn't it be lovely to accidentally cross their path?"

I was about to protest when a scratching noise was heard at the door.

"What is that sound?" I queried.

"Oh, that. No one knocks at court, they scratch with the nail of the little finger instead. Etiquette demands it."

"Shall I fetch your visitor?" I offered.

"Go on, go on," he smiled, eager to see me receiving guests and, hopefully, their compliments. Obeying the prince, I was soon gazing upon an elegant young man, who immediately grasped my hand and lowered his head to Louis' ruby ring.

"Mademoiselle," he gushed, "might it be true I have lived to this moment without seeing you?"

While Philippe clapped his approval, my stomach turned from a strange foreboding. The words of the gentleman paying me tribute were the same once spoken by a certain judge concerning my mother's powerful effect.

"Chalais, enter, good man! Meet Madame de la Tour, the latest addition to my household."

"The Prince de Chalais, at your service, madame."

Realizing the dark-haired courtier was a member of Philippe's crowd, and possibly an intimate, I reflected any attention to the king's brother. "The Duc d'Orléans tells me you have performed an important service for him today, monsieur. I best take my leave and allow you both some privacy."

"Very thoughtful, but not necessary," Philippe announced. "We have no secrets here."

"I have made several discoveries, Monsieur," Chalais admitted. "Should I recount them?"

"Yes, please do. Madame de la Tour and I are most anxious to hear your tidings."

"Monsieur Colbert has been named Minister of Finance and Monsieur Le Tellier's son, Louvois, will succeed his father as Secretary of War when the time comes for the elder gentleman to retire."

"How did you come by this report?" Philippe asked, head cocked to one side.

"Brienne *fils* told me, Monsieur. He is usually reliable."

How true, I thought to myself, remembering the secretary's warning to Fouquet.

"And..." Monsieur paused dramatically. "Is that all, Chalais? I could have told you that myself, hours ago."

"The king has confiscated Monsieur Fouquet's property and Monsieur Colbert will have the prisoner's hôtel in Paris for his own."

"And Vaux? Will Louis keep Vaux?" Philippe asked with concern.

"Yes, however the mansion is to be stripped of its treasures and left unoccupied."

"Louis does not covet Vaux?" I gasped. "He plans to abandon the finest house in France? Why?"

"The king has announced to his ministers that he plans to build a finer palace, a residence worthy of a *Sun King*. Those were his exact words."

"Where?" Philippe inquired, frantic Louis might have a sight in mind that would rival his own vision for Saint-Cloud.

"Versailles! Imagine that, Monsieur!" Chalais scorned, wrinkling his nose in disapproval. "Renovations to the old château are to commence without delay: repairs to the roof, additional kitchens and stables added, a pavilion for the Grand Musketeers, extensive gardens and an *orangerie*. Monsieur Le Nôtre has already been sent to that very village, to survey the area and make a detailed accounting of the park he would create there."

"What a fool my brother is!" Philippe laughed with glee. "Everyone knows that Versailles is a veritable dung heap! Whatever might dear Louis be thinking?"

"No one dares venture a guess, Monsieur. The king, however, is intractable on the point. And his reasoning for the project remains an utter mystery to the entire council which attends him."

I stood quite still, more rigid than the marble statues of the deities that Fouquet had commissioned Monsieur Poussin to carve as ornaments for Vaux. I alone, it seemed, understood

Louis' choice of Versailles as the future home of the French court, I alone comprehended the nefarious power which drew the present day solar king to its verdant hills.

What had I done?

Why had I told him of Noctambule and an eternal life that the king did not see as a curse, yet rather, as a blessing? Mother's hex had been kind in comparison. Immediately I imagined rivers of blood running, spilling everywhere, and I sensed that a horrible future awaited both the Bourbons and the nation of France because of my stupidity.

"Bijoux, dearest, you are quaking," Philippe noted, steadying me with a firm grip. "Please do not faint-away as you did our first afternoon shared at the Louvre. Chalais, go fetch Monsieur Vallot or Monsieur Cousinot. My angel is overwrought."

"No," I said, steeling myself to speak, "no doctors. Especially not Cousinot. I am fine, Monsieur, simply overcome by the memory that I was conceived at Versailles. That is all."

"And your father and my father..."

Monsieur's voice trailed off into nothingness, then he added, "Perhaps the king wishes to reawaken old ties, old passions, *n'est-ce pas*, Bijoux?"

"What his Majesty has awakened is naught but ill," I replied, holding my Tyrannus tightly to my person from fear. "Oh, Monsieur, if I could but tell you the horror of it all! This is the worst day of my miserable life! The worst day, by far!"

I did not make the comment in jest, for the knowledge that Louis intended for me to become his true consort, the daemon bride of he who dreamed of becoming the next *vampyre* of Versailles, caused me the greatest alarm. Amphitryon had spotted Taphos, Comaetho his willing guide.

A black magic was at work, one more dangerous and deadly than any grimoire might provide.

CHAPTER SEVENTEEN
Secrets

Cell number twelve is not the most comfortable place from which to pen one's memoirs, yet, the locale is a more peaceful one than an apartment at court. None bother with me here in my dungeon, and I am quite fortunate to have been allowed a decent bed, writing materials, books and the old chest from the days of the Marais. And my jewels, although the bright stones are going to waste in such a desolate place. No costume balls or ballets await me in the future, although, confinement rather suits me, or else I am simply accustomed to being held captive. Having been Louis' prisoner since Nantes, the setting for the incarceration matters little; Fontainebleau, for all its gilt and rich design was a worse lock-up than the dreaded Bastille.

So, how did this captive arrive in the Bazinière Tower? A very good question, especially when last I scribbled I enjoyed the favor of the king. And while I am weary having written page after page for what has been many months, I am obliged to finish the tale, no matter how much it pains me to do so. Should another chance upon this manuscript, please view these words with compassion and learn from my error. Perhaps then my life will not have been wasted, and my departed spirit might rest easier, knowing I tried to do some good in the end. Considering how badly I have acted on occasion, and the hurt I have caused others, I certainly have much to atone and more to explain.

This is my confession, then, and dear reader, act as would a member of compassionate Athena's jury: grant me absolution and wish me peace. That is all I ask; that, and an *adieu* for César, whose beloved face I may never see again.

The resurrection of Versailles was not received with much enthusiasm from any at court excepting the chief artisans who would be employed to create the showplace: the architect Le Vau, the gardener Le Nôtre, the artist Le Brun. All three had worked in concert at Vaux-le-Vicomte and their combined genius, originally recognized by Fouquet, would be called on again to transform an old hunting lodge into the hub of the universe. The skeptics scoffed, the critics guffawed, Colbert complained concerning the project's estimated cost, yet the king held firm to his decision. Versailles became the royal passion. Le Nôtre drew plans for a fairy-tale landscape upon his return from the hamlet, Le Vau spoke of building a *ménagerie* adjacent to the *orangérie* to house exotic animals, and Le Brun designed what was to become the most famous device in Europe, Louis' blazing orb.

Separation from César was the most difficult adjustment to make during that autumn of upheaval, although the forced move-in with Louise de la Vallière was no less unpleasant. The shy lass of the violet eyes, sweet temperament and devout bent was not at all to my liking. Louise bore the brunt of my bitterness in silence, saying little to me and making certain the king was informed whenever I chose to sleep elsewhere. Which was often. Sharing the evening hours with César, who had obtained a place with the Duc de Guise, or sometimes with Philippe, was how I spent my nights. Oddly enough, Louis ignored my existence, either angered on account of César or by my playing confidante to his brother. Or so I assumed, though that was not the case, as I was soon to learn.

The truth concerning my status at court was revealed at the close of a fortnight. The drama commenced when Philippe confronted his wife concerning her refusal to relocate to Saint-Cloud before September's end. Listening outside the closed door of Madame's drawing room—with Monsieur's permission—I overheard the royal couple's nasty conversation verbatim. For a frail woman, Henriette battled fiercely, and her screams of disapproval were matched only by the Duc d'Orléan's own.

"How dare you suggest we move from Fontainebleau, considering my state?" the duchess argued in a loud voice. "Do you wish me to lose your precious heir, Monsieur?"

"You are careless, Madame, and would do better than to question your husband," he shouted. "Because I have considered your delicate health, I think it best you be close to your mother in Paris."

"You know full well my mother and I are not on the best of terms, Monsieur! Why do you punish me thus?"

"Why?" Philippe yelled. "Why? I have been informed of the letters you receive four times daily from the Comte de Guiche; I am well aware of your continued flirtation!"

"You are insufferable! I have returned all his *communiqués* unopened. Ask any of my ladies and they will vouchsafe for me."

"Madame, you are a liar. Your so-called *ladies* are completely unreliable witnesses. Pine for Guiche all you like—you will not have him, understand?"

Henriette did not answer. She must have regained her composure, for her tone was calm when she asked, "Who is the girl with the hair of a dissembling color who keeps you occupied of late?"

"A loyal retainer."

"I do not ask out of jealousy, Monsieur."

"Who she is does not concern you," he retorted.

"I shall discover her name before the day is out, Philippe," she said matter-of-factly. "Perhaps summon her to an audience. To inform her of my husband's likes and dislikes."

"I am good enough at lovemaking to get you with child."

"If it is yours," she laughed maliciously. "Louis may be the father."

"I swear, I shall kill you," he ranted, out of control. "I shall murder you myself, Madame!"

Not thinking clearly, I interrupted the tirade and entered the salon.

"Madame, my name is Bijoux de la Tour," I announced, "and I have been attached to your establishment by order of the king."

I stared at the brunette as I dipped, my icy gaze frozen with hers.

"Yes, that is true, sister," a deep voice confirmed. "Do you disapprove of my choice?"

Philippe and Henriette made the proper signs of respect and my heart began to pound. Louis was standing behind me. The king had probably been spying on me as I snooped on his family.

"My wife is of the opinion, sire, that Madame Bijoux is my mistress," Philippe offered as an explanation for the strange scene. "Could you perhaps put her mind at ease concerning the matter?"

Still bent in a stooped position, I could see the rosettes covering most of Louis' shoes directly under my nose. Daring to look up, I was greeted by the king's bemused smile. His back was to the warring couple and he winked at me reassuringly as he helped me to rise.

"This lady has been acquainted with my brother for a number of years, Madame. Accept my word that she does you no wrong."

The former lovers were by then face-to-face. Henriette glared at Louis but said nothing.

"Are you satisfied?" Monsieur gloated.

"Perhaps you should rest," the elder Bourbon offered as a sign of dismissal to the haughty woman, "or listen to some soothing music. I shall send for Monsieur Lully and his violinists."

"Wonderful!" Philippe said in reply, not allowing his wife the opportunity to speak. "Will you grace us with your presence, sire?"

"No," the king answered, "I am off to Versailles to hunt and to inspect the work being done at the château. Would you care to join me, Madame de la Tour?"

"Majesty, you honor me; however, I am not dressed for the chase."

Louis eyed my attire, a cerise-hued gown formerly a part of Monsieur's private collection, and said, "Go prepare yourself, madame; the hounds will wait."

The message was clear enough. Making a quick curtsy to the duke and duchess, I raced off for the floor above. Louis soon joined my flight, catching me on a back staircase.

"Slow down; you run faster than a deer bounding through the glade," he laughed.

"And you do so enjoy the pursuit," I quipped.

"So what think you of Henriette?" he asked, drawing me to him until my lower body was pressed suggestively against his own. "Be honest with me, my darling."

"She is a shrew," I said with a toss of my head, "and I find her manner to be common. She is so cruel to Philippe—how does he tolerate her jibes?"

"I think the two of you very much alike."

"Me and Madame?"

"Yes," he grinned and kissed me slowly on the mouth, then continued. "After Vincennes, I took up with her because of you. Proud, refined...a true temptress."

"Thank you for the dubious compliment, sire."

"I have missed you so since Nantes," Louis admitted. "I have had to summon all my self-control not to follow you about the château and pay you court. Unlike my brother."

"Monsieur provides pleasant company, sire. Louise bores me to death."

"Do not blame Louise for your midnight *rendezvous* with your husband."

"Is César not our shield?"

"I am having second thoughts about this marriage of yours. An annulment may be in order."

"On what grounds?"

"That you entered into the contract under false pretenses. That your husband is not who he claims to be."

"What?" I whispered. "He is not a Bouillon?"

"He is a Bouillon," Louis replied. "An illegitimate Bouillon. Did you not know? His father, the late Duc Frédéric, doted on the lad, it is true; however, César may never become a titled gentleman. You will not be styled a duchess, unless, of course, I create that rank for you."

"He lied to me," I said, hurt and stunned. "Why?"

"A man in love will say many things to win a lady's hand. Not that your husband's conduct in this matter is excusable..."

"Stop," I begged, "please. I must suffer this blow in private, sire. What a fool you must think me! Now I understand so much...why Madame du Plessis would look at me strangely whenever I spoke of my husband's *brother*. Small wonder my husband detested the soirées held at Saint-Mandé, for he feared being unmasked. What an idiot I have been!"

"Have you not made the acquaintance of Turenne, or Frédéric's heir, Godefroy-Maurice?"

"No, I have not been introduced to any of César's *family*. Why?"

"Godefroy is César's junior. Then you would have guessed a deception afoot, see?"

"Why did Susanne hide the truth? She had to be aware of the scandal."

"She must no doubt have wished to protect you from shame. I may have misjudged the lady," he said thoughtfully.

"Do you think me naïve, sire?"

"No," he remarked, wiping a tear from the corner of one of my eyes. "Not you, my queen of all mysteries."

Breaking into sobs, I clung to Louis, feeling the fool.

"Is your heart finally mine?" the king inquired as he comforted me.

I searched myself for an answer and found none. "Must we ride to Versailles?" I managed.

"Yes. A token of my esteem awaits you there. I also took the liberty of gifting you a riding habit, already laid out upstairs in Mademoiselle de la Vallière's chamber."

"What of Mademoiselle de la Vallière? If she finds us out..."

"Tell her I sit in council. Tell her you ride with Monsieur. Be nice."

"She hates me, my dearest."

"No, Louise fears you."

"I have given her no cause for that emotion, Majesty."

"Bijoux, how might I kiss her with passion when I do naught but dream of you? Today I could bear the separation no longer and had to seek you out."

"Allow me to prepare for the hunt. The sooner we quit Fontainebleau, the better, my love."

"We shall ride with the winds to Versailles," Louis laughed, holding me close.

"Let us away by coach."

"Why say you that, my beauty?"

"Because," I murmured, my hands moving beneath the weight of a heavy *justacorps*, "I cannot wait another hour to be intimate with you, my true heart."

Louis kissed my lips again and again. "A coach will await you, by the goldfish pond. Wear a traveling mask. We must be discreet."

"I no longer give a whit if the entire world is witness to our love," I boasted.

"Nor do I, yet first you must be divorced. Then your position will be made known to the court, and I shall be the proudest man alive. We must appease my mother 'till that day, Bijoux, for she alone could ruin our happiness."

I remembered that Anne of Austria had indeed betrayed my father. Louis was her life, her *raison d' être*; she would not have her son consorting with the married daughter of a man whom she had help send to the scaffold.

"I shall obey you in all things," I promised.

"You excite me to the point of fever," he said in a low voice, my face in his hands. "Away."

Doing the sovereign's bidding, I quit the scene. Soon outside a closed portal, I hesitated and knocked before entering the room. Hearing no response to the rap on wood, I charged ahead, only to be disappointed by the sight of the girl who irked me with her melancholy ways.

"Good day, mademoiselle," I said stiffly.

Louise was reading and barely glanced up at me. "Good day, madame," she aped.

"How keep you?" I managed to ask.

"Well enough," she replied, not daring to lift her gaze from the book.

"Did I receive a delivery, perchance?"

When no answer came from the young lady, I began to fume. Going to the armchair, I yanked the leather bound volume from her grasp.

"Do not ignore *me*, mademoiselle. How dare you?"

"How dare you entertain the king's affections?" Louise began to weep, genuinely unhappy. She was aware I was privy to her arrangement with Louis, as was the majority of the court.

"Who says such a thing?"

"This speaks volumes, madame!" She made for the armoire, flinging open a door, revealing a long blue skirt and matching *justacorps*; the latter lined with silver cloth, replete with gold braid. An exact copy of the jacket worn by the king when hunting.

"My new ensemble! What a rascal Philippe is, for the coat resembles the king's own!"

"His Majesty did not order this made?" Louise sniveled.

"No, silly. Why would he?"

"I...I know not," she admitted. "He has been distant with me and I feared you the cause."

"His Majesty brought me here, against my will, to entertain Monsieur. And to keep an eye on you. Nothing more. You are most fanciful in your opinions, mademoiselle."

"Forgive me," Louise begged. "I have thought such evil things of you, Madame Bijoux—I am so ashamed. Might you find it in your heart to give me a second chance at friendship?"

The girl's plaintive appeal, coupled with a wide-eyed simplicity, was too much for me to bear. Taking the child from Blois into my arms, I kissed her rapidly on each cheek.

"There, there, let us make amends. If you forgive me my sour temperament, then I shall overlook any fault of yours."

We parted and I attended to my wardrobe. Louise did not wait to help.

"Shall we be true friends?" she prompted, removing the habit from a padded mannequin. "You are so worldly and elegant, madame; would you teach me the graces I lack?"

"Me?" I laughed, thrown off-guard by the compliment. I regarded the girl's milky white complexion and pale gold tendrils. That the king preferred me to her was incomprehensible, for La Vallière was perfection in the flesh, limp or no.

"If you like, we shall see more of one another in the future. Today I must attend to the Duc d'Orléans and I am already tardy. I best hurry or else the prince will be peeved with me."

"Never. Monsieur adores you, madame. My mistress should be grateful that you have distracted her husband, for life here was hellish 'ere you arrived."

"That bad?" I asked, relieved to be discussing the royal hellcats.

Louise rolled her eyes in her head, her defenses lowered.

"Their situation appears to be hopeless."

"Yes, as does that of the king and Marie-Thérèse. Another unhappy couple," she commented.

"I would not know," I smiled as I buttoned the front of the ornately decorated coat constructed to barely fit the torso. "I do take your word, mademoiselle. By the way, may I borrow your tricorne?"

Louise returned to the massive closet and fetched the felt accessory. Handing me the hat, glad to be of service, she began to chatter.

"Your belongings arrived today from Saint-Mandé in three large crates. I told the porters to stash them under the bed. Then M. César came by with his valet, took a box away, and said he would return to speak with you later this evening."

"I may not be available tonight. Philippe and I are going for a jaunt and we may be out late."

"How exciting!" she squealed. "I shan't mention your plans to Madame."

"Good. And not a word to that big mouth, Montalais, either. She is trouble waiting to happen."

"His Majesty says the same thing to me, madame."

"Yes, well, the king and I were both born on the fifth day of September," I said, checking myself in a looking glass for any defect. "Perhaps we are also akin in our thoughts."

"That is why his Majesty summoned you here. He knew we would get on well together."

Louise was, as Susanne had claimed, positively guileless. The memory of my dear friend must have caused me to wince, for the pained look on my face did not go unnoticed by La Vallière.

"Madame, are you well?"

"Oh, yes. Your comment reminded me of the Marquise du Plessis, that is all."

"*Mon Dieu!* Are you a friend of *that* lady?"

"I was, and remain, her truest confidante," was my proud reply.

"Then, you have additional cause to think poorly of me. Your friend and I exchanged cross words prior to M. Fouquet's arrest."

"We shall discuss the matter on the morrow," I promised. "Be comforted, mademoiselle, for I consider your argument with Madame Susanne to be none of my affair."

"Enjoy yourself," she beamed and waived good-bye. "Till later, madame."

I rushed out into the corridor and took a deep breath, thankful to be finished with the ordeal. Turning to leave, I remembered the mask Louis had advised me to wear.

"Damn!" I cursed aloud.

La Vallière came running faster than a lap dog. "Are you missing something, madame?"

"A domino. Philippe insisted I bring one along. Mine is somewhere, packed away..."

"Here," she offered, handing me her own velvet mask.

"Mademoiselle, you...amaze me," I stammered.

"His Majesty claims likewise," she chuckled. "You *are* similar to the king, for I am forever bringing small matters to his attention."

Was Louise sending me a subtle warning? Was she more intelligent than I had previously estimated? Suddenly cautious, I hid any alarm in a wide grin.

"I envy you your sensitivity, mademoiselle."

"And I, your boldness," she replied. "If I were only half as adventurous as you, the king might hold me in higher esteem."

"Be careful of what you covet," I advised while I walked away. "The waking world is not always as pleasant as is the realm of dreams, mademoiselle."

Determined steps resounded against the corridor's parquet floor. I was returning to Versailles despite my hatred of the place. Was I doomed? Or merely my father's daughter, drawn to disaster?

"Noctambule," I said under my breath, "beware, for if you dare cross my path, you are dead."

The words were uttered with resolve, yet, as I left the château's interior to be greeted by warm shafts of sunlight streaming from a cloudless sky, the reflection that the *vampyre* could rob me forever of body and soul caused me to shiver. How might I save Louis and France from disaster, I wondered, how might a Cinq-Mars sacrifice ambition in the spirit of honor and charity?

Help me, Jacques, I prayed, *help me to do this thing right.*

Louis XIII's former château was a far more impressive retreat than mother's stories had conveyed, and father's hideaway appealed greatly to my senses despite the tainted memories I retained of the place. To describe the old Versailles as an insignificant waste of mason's mortar would be an error, although many people these days are wont to overlook the original structure, since rendered minuscule on a draughtman's grid filled with grandiose plans. No, the palace I viewed from a rise in the road was definitely charming; an opinion I did not hide from the present ruler who had urged me to peak out an opened carriage window when we were near to arriving at our destination of rose and gold brick.

"How idyllic! Look at the pretty blue roofs and the magnificent clock set into the façade!"

"Is this spot not grand?" the king sighed, seating me on his lap as the wheels underneath our feet slowed their rapid movement. "Could you be happy with me here, forever?"

"I was reluctant to make this journey; now my fear seems unfounded."

Crossing a lowered drawbridge, the coach braked in the main courtyard. Louis' lips joined with my own and I felt oddly content.

"You are the only one who understands the magic of my Versailles," he admitted when we had ceased kissing, "and the power that draws two such as ourselves to its rustic setting. Paris may be the capital of France, yet I shall rule from here, with you at my side, and the glory of my reign and deeds will dazzle the world!"

His zeal left me uneasy. "And the *vrykolakas*? What of him? Is he a part of your heroic vision, as well? These woods belong to Noctambule, who needs not bow to any."

"We shall see," came my glib answer, "we shall soon see."

Well aware that Louis would not tolerate any further argument from me, I held my tongue and made no reply. Sensing a change in mood, the king made an attempt to be gay, bouncing me on his knee as one would a child.

"I have a surprise for you," he sang happily. "Guess what it is."

"I haven't the vaguest."

"Don't frown," the lover advised. "Come, I shall show you."

Leaving *tricorne* and mask inside the coach, I followed after the king, to be greeted by fresh air, the sound of singing birds, and a veritable crowd of kneeling servants. Doffing his hat to the hastily assembled staff, Louis' displayed his impeccable manners and sense of showmanship.

"To the stables!" he announced, replacing the huge headpiece and offering me his arm. As I accepted the royal sleeve, however, an old woman's voice croaked excitedly, "I know her! She is the girl who saw Satan back in forty-eight, she is!"

The king stiffened and did not move. I was so shocked by the declaration that I leaned against my escort for support.

"Who dares to speak?" Louis' tone was more solemn than a priest's.

"Your Majesty, I meant no harm," the offender admitted, scared witless.

"Sire, please, ignore her," I smiled, regaining my composure. "The unfortunate lady is obviously mistaken or..."

The others looked away, as though in agreement that the crone was insane. The king continued to stare at the laborer, stony-faced. The rigidity of his posture indicated the intensity of his ire.

"Your Majesty," I entreated, "may it please you to recall that the people refer to your late father as *Louis the Just*. Do honor to his beloved memory and spare the idiot the rod."

Louis waited to speak, his gaze fixed on the woman, who hid her face with her hands. Perhaps moved by the pitiful spectacle, or by my speech, he finally passed sentence.

"My father was a great and noble man. Because he loved this place and its inhabitants, I forgive you the remark. Madame," he motioned for the elderly offender to rise, "approach me."

She crawled over to him on her knees, and my heart broke at the unnecessary show of servitude. Not thinking, I bent down and lifted the bony woman up off the ground when she reached where we stood. She smelled terrible and may have been infested with vermin, however, I held on to her fast.

"Do not be afraid. The king has forgiven you. Just no more talk of devils, agreed?"

"I was mistaken," she sobbed, "I was mistaken."

"Take her away," the Bourbon snapped impatiently. "Now."

Two young grooms pried the grateful soul from me, speaking to her as kindly as if she had been their grandmother. Leading the aged one away, her cry: *God bless you, madame!* caused a murmur to circulate amongst her peers.

"As I was saying, before we were so rudely interrupted, let us to the stables, marquise."

"Marquise," I heard the remaining servants whisper. "The king's beautiful lady is a marquise."

"Do you address me, sire?"

"You are the Marquise de Cinq-Mars, are you not?" he asked brusquely, walking away. Overcome by the reference to my parentage, I could not follow.

"Are you lame?" Louis sneered, turning around when he had stepped a few paces to the left.

"No, sire," I mumbled, joining him in haste. Wishing no further comparison to La Vallière, I matched his long stride as best I was able, glad when his gait shortened near to the stable yard.

"Never suppose to influence my decision making again! I am the king in this land, not you! If I want your opinion, I shall ask for it, understand?"

"Yes, your Majesty."

"Prostrate yourself and request my pardon."

"Here? Are you mad?"

"Do not make me say it again," he warned.

Losing my temper, a rebellious Mars as Water Bearer caused me to flash the ruby ring at him. "I would rather throw this into that moat, over there, than allow you to disgrace either of us in such a manner! Love should be stronger than pride, sire, especially the love you bear your subjects who serve you well and true."

"You think me cruel," Louis retorted hotly, "and perhaps I am. I could have flogged both of you after that display of presumptuous behavior."

"You would punish an old woman for speaking the truth?"

"To protect you, yes, I would."

"Then *you* should be ashamed, not I."

Our eyes locked, and still I refused to kneel before him. Versailles was bringing out the beast in the king, and I was experiencing how implacable the young monarch could be. Disillusioned, the band fashioned by the court jeweler, Monsieur Légaré, began to slide from my finger.

"Halt!" Louis yelled at me, as though in a panic. "Halt, Bijoux! Remove the ring and I swear, we are finished!"

"Finished?" I retorted. "Finished, you say? What of your fine words: *I swear to you on the sacred bones of my ancestors that I shall never forsake you?* Or, *With this ring...*"

"*...we are bound together for the remainder of our lives, be it for good or be it for bad,*" he smiled, taking me into his arms, no longer angry. "*We are joined forevermore, agreed?* Did you think I had forgotten my vow to you?"

"Obviously, I have not," I blushed, embarrassed that I had admitted to remembering his exact words from Nantes. Yet Louis was enchanted by the slip, and kissed my face repeatedly.

"Forgive me, my love, forgive me," he sighed. "Why were we arguing?"

"Let us enjoy the remainder of our afternoon together," I replied. "Thus far, this day has proved to be a trying one, our trysting aside."

"We have all the eve to improve upon it."

"How so? We must return..."

"Oh, no, for only Colbert knows I am here and his clerks have been instructed to spread the word that the king is engaged in reviewing the growing evidence against Fouquet, privately, behind locked doors. And that I am not to be disturbed for any reason. For the entire evening."

"Will the ruse work?"

"Half of the court was in Fouquet's pay and now that they know I have seized all his correspondence, the lot of them will be shaking in their shoes, speculating as to how many letters of a compromising nature were found, who might be arrested, which fine gentleman or lady will be disgraced. The nobles will be too concerned with hiding to seek me out."

Continuing our walk, holding hands as any couple might, I glanced at the enigma whose shifts in character fascinated, as well as disturbed, me. "You will return to Fontainebleau, then, alone?"

"Two of my men are in attendance. One will escort me on the return jaunt. The other will see to your safe conduct. The coach is on its way once darkness falls."

"Sire, forgive me, yet my equestrienne skills are not that finely honed, I am sad to say."

"You underestimate your abilities," Louis teased. "The mare that threw you at Vincennes was a testy creature, prone to skittishness."

"No, fair Pegasus was full of fire and spirit and I loved her. Would that I had not left her at an inn, on the road to Nantes; no doubt she has been sold to another."

"No doubt," Louis agreed, waving conspicuously to a nearby groom.

The lad disappeared from sight in response to the king's signal.

"Where did he go?" I asked rather snootily.

"To do my bidding," he answered and stooped down to pat a hound running up to greet him. "You are most inquisitive, marquise."

I was about to ask Louis not to tease me with the title *marquise* when I caught a glimpse of white sheeting out of the corner of one eye.

"La Rivière! Pegasus! Your Majesty, how...when?"

"The riding master came to me with Fouquet's other property and the inn keeper at Étampes wisely returned the horses to his king when he heard I had locked up their thieving owner. The moment the mare was shown to me, I recognized her as yours and had her brought here for this reunion."

"Thank you," I cried, impulsively flinging my arms about his neck. Louis tensed at the unexpected show of affection, then relaxed when he realized I was not about to let him alone.

"Go say hello. Go ahead," he prompted.

Releasing the king, I ran to La Rivière and hugged the tall black man, who did not dare return the embrace for fear of offending the sovereign. Pegasus sniffed at my hair and began to make snorting noises, her warm breath blowing directly against my forehead.

"Madame Bijoux, please..." the Cape Verdean protested with a tinge of humor to his tone.

"I am so glad to see you again! Thank Athena you are well!"

"Is this the place where the *lilitu* abides?" he whispered nervously.

"Yes..."

"So I thought!" he muttered. "The horses have been uneasy. They sense the daemon's presence."

"Not another word, dear friend. If the king hears you speak of such matters, he will exile you or worse." I cast La Rivière a serious look. "Do not displease him; consider Monsieur Fouquet's example."

We separated, and none too soon, for I noticed my host motioning for me to return to his side. Petting the mare's white forelock, I winked at her keeper and promised, "You will leave with me on the morrow. I shall arrange it," and hurried back to the impatient monarch.

"I take it that you and the blackamoor are well acquainted?" Louis queried.

"Before Monsieur la Rivière came to Saint-Mandé, he was employed at the Luxembourg, where I lived with Madame de Choisy when I was a girl. I have known the riding master for many years, sire."

"You should not be so familiar with servants."

"I must beg your pardon, Majesty," I replied with a quick curtsy, "for having twice offended your sensibilities. Do you blame me for losing my head when I am in your presence, drunk with love?"

He made a vain attempt to appear disgruntled, although I could see the traces of a smirk forming where the tips of his mustache met the corners of his mouth. Grabbing the brim of Louis' elaborate hat, I yanked it from its perch, astounding the wearer as I did so.

"Ho, madame, return my property at once!"

"Say *please*," I taunted, walking backwards in the direction of the château.

Louis' hands went to his hips and he stalked after me.

"Do you want it back?"

"If I catch you, you will pay," he threatened, both of us moving faster.

"And if you do not?"

"I shall formally invest you with the title *Marquise de Cinq-Mars*."

"You would not dare."

"You doubt me?"

With that, I fled, darting for the main building, hoping to outrun my pursuer. Yet the king had the

advantage of not being slowed by hobbling swathes of fabric, and he beat me to the entrance. Changing course, I made for the westerly pavilion, where I was promptly captured when I tripped and fell alongside the extension's rough wall. Quick to pounce, Louis straddled my body, holding me prisoner by the wrists, amused to see I had not dropped his plumed coronet during the contest.

"It would seem you are the victor," I conceded when breath returned.

"Fear not, for you have won the day, though it would seem otherwise."

"Why is that?" I laughed.

"Because I have completely lost my heart to you. Who would have thought it? Me, besotted with a Cinq-Mars! What will people say?"

"Should I be so ashamed of my lineage, sire? Tell me truly, for I know little of the events that came before me."

"How little?"

"My father was Henri Coiffier de Ruzé, better known as Monsieur le Grand, and he died on the

block September 12, 1642, for his part in the Spanish Plot."

"Nothing more?"

"Only that he conspired with your uncle, Monsieur de Tréville, and César's father to kill Richelieu

and that he was the one who lost his head. Along with de Thou, the sacrificial lamb, who was quite wrongly accused."

"Then we should talk at greater length," Louis concluded. "Better you hear it from me."

We stood and I placed the purloined hat back upon its

perch. "The notion of possessing a family history is foreign to me, sire. Tell me of your plans for Versailles, or anything else you fancy, yet let us not dwell on the subject of forebears, I beg of you."

"Later," he said softly, touching the side of my face with tenderness, as though he understood the request. "For now, I shall lead you on a tour of the château, starting with the kitchens. My father enjoyed going there late at night, when the rest of his retinue had retired, to cook omelets and eat raw onions. I cannot imagine a king doing such a thing!"

"Kings are men, too," I replied as I followed Louis across the courtyard. "Certainly you, of all people, are aware of that."

"When I see you, I am reminded of my own mortality, yes. That is why we shall reside here and lay a trap for Noctambule, conquering death when we kill the creature and drink of its blood. Why wait for last rites and the frail promise of a life everlasting?"

"No, sire! Stop, please! You do not understand what you are saying!"

The king halted below the clock whose hands had not moved since our arrival. "Look closely, Bijoux," he commanded, pointing at the timepiece. "Do you see the hour on the face of the dial?"

"Yes."

"And is it correct?"

"No, sire, it is not."

"That is because the clock was set to reflect the time of my father's passing and shall not be changed again until I die. The custom is a tradition here at Versailles, begun by Louis XIII to mark the hour of Henri IV's cruel murder. I defy this ritual–the practice ends with me!"

I hung my head, aware that a group of workmen headed in our direction. Their leader was a distinguished looking gentleman, dressed as a courtier, and carrying several rolls of parchment.

"Monsieur le Vau, how fares the First Architect?" Louis inquired with genuine interest

"I am well, sire, as is Monsieur le Nôtre, whose company I left not moments ago."

"Le Nôtre, present as well!" the king enthused. "What a stroke of luck! We three must meet then, in the study, to discuss your joint progress."

"Allow me to fetch my colleague, Highness, and we shall await your pleasure."

Louis beamed with approval and sent the artisan off with the royal blessing. I began to fidget with the braided trim on my jacket when his gaze shifted to me and became intense; staring at the intricate design was easier than bearing the king's scrutiny.

"Do you no longer enjoy the sight of me?" he jested, lifting my chin.

"Is it possible to detest what I love, Louis?"

"Say my name again."

"I love you, Louis."

The avowal caused him to look away quickly and clear his throat. Although the king tried to control his emotions, his eyes watered and his chin quivered slightly. Not wishing him to weep, I assumed a comical expression, tugging at a lock of his hair.

"What shall I do with myself while you meet with your artisans?"

"You will accompany me."

"Sire, I am acquainted with Monsieur le Nôtre from my time at Saint-Mandé and if he sees me in your company, he will guess…"

"Bijoux, we cannot hide forever," Louis said gently. "From this moment forward, you will be known as the Marquise de Cinq-Mars. I restore to you your father's property and reinstate his legacy in your name: the lands at Chilly, the Hôtel de Clèves in Paris, the Palais d'Effiat at Saint-Germain-en-Laye, and the rents received from the County of Dammartin. In return, you will agree to become my companion, my lover and eventually, I pray most fervently, my wife. If you do not wish these things to be, say so now and go back to Fontainebleau and de la Tour."

"I think," I said slowly, my head reeling from the

pronouncement, "that I may deny you nothing. Shall we prepare to meet our guests, your Majesty?"

"You will make the finest queen who ever sat a throne," Louis declared, jubilant. "And you will be mine, in time, I swear it!"

My ensuing silence marked the moment when, as had my mother before me, I turned my back on all I held sacred and made my own pact with the Princes of Friendship.

The impromptu planning session was attended by Le Vau, Le Nôtre, Louis and myself in a dark-paneled council chamber. The mild mannered gardener kissed my hand with relish when he made my acquaintance again, and neither his eyes nor mannerisms displayed the slightest hint of reproach. He may have recalled our conversation about the omnipotent Law that saw all, yet he did not allude to our past chat if he did. What I did not understand then was that the man who tended flowers so fastidiously also treated souls with the same care, and he did not think it his duty to pass judgment on a fellow human being.

Le Nôtre's example, much as Françoise's before him, should have inspired me to rush home and be a better wife to the man whom I had loved enough to marry, bastard or no. Foolishly, however, I remained at Versailles.

Later, when the Sun had retired its watch in the heavens and that fiery globe was replaced by the ominous specter of a crimson hunter's orb, the king's pleasure diverted from walking the grounds of the château to showing me more of its interior. Tripping together up steps of black and red marble, Louis called down to a Musketeer that he would take supper in the royal bedchamber; a departure from the routine of dining before the entire court. Relieved to hear we would not be forced to eat in a stuffy salon for form's sake, I followed my guide to a tapestry-lined room whose walls had been hung with heavy textiles to encourage intimate conversation.

By the looks of the extremely large, drape enshrouded bed dominating center stage of the private apartment, raucous lovemaking had been kept muffled, as well. Taking in every detail, well aware that one of my own had been an occupant of the same space, I barely noticed when a Musketeer appeared in attendance, awaiting his commander's directive. The soldier was told to stand outside and perform his usual duty, then the door shut and the king and I were alone.

"What do you think of your future home?" Louis asked, eager to unbutton the *justacorps* I wore. "Fill in the moat, add a few wings, clear away some trees for gardens. Not impossible."

"The work will take longer than you think and cost more than I care to reflect upon, my dearest."

"Do not remind me of Colbert."

"Consider the millions Fouquet spent on Vaux. Does France require another such project?"

"Versailles will be grander, by far."

"Will you levy new taxes to pay for your palace, perhaps? Are the people not burdened enough?"

"Ah ha! And what would your grandfather have said if he heard you speak such blasphemy?"

"Grandfather?"

"Antoine Coiffier de Ruzé, of course. He was first the Grand Master of Mining of France, then later, the Surintendant of Finance until his death."

"I never knew. You seem determined to educate me regarding my family, sire."

"All in good time. I have much planned for this night of love," he disclosed. "Let us savor every stolen moment, slowly, without haste. Do you realize the torment I have endured, separated from you? Tossing and turning in my sleep, trying to put you out of my mind as I touched..."

"Do not ask me to imagine you lying with another," was my choked reply. "I cannot bear it."

"Nor shall I," Louis echoed, pleased to hear the strain my voice, "nor shall I."

Our shared state led to a pile of clothing left discarded on the Savonnerie carpet. Repairing to the pallet that had served our predecessors, we defied the memory of that doomed union and joined our bodies with purpose. When a Bourbon and a Cinq-Mars were again as one, Louis and I screamed aloud; a single cry meant to rent the heavens and summoned the ghosts of our fathers, yet which probably reached the ears of Noctambule, instead.

"To think your mother encouraged you to hate me," the king later remarked.

"Yes," I murmured, nestled contentedly against my lover's chest, "yet she had her reasons for loathing the Bourbon name, think you not?"

"She should have despised the title of Cinq-Mars more."

"Why say you that?"

Louis paused. "I believe some clean nightshirts are stored in that chest in the corner, over there. Would you be an angel and fetch two?"

"Are you evading my question?" I chuckled.

"We shall talk after we eat. I promise you, my darling."

The use of that particularly fond endearment convinced me to abandon the comfort of our cozy sanctuary and make an effort to please.

"Louis, it is freezing in here!" I complained.

"The fresh air is good for you," was his retort.

Hurrying to the other side of the room, I opened the lid to the wooden storage box and quickly flipped through piles of linen. Two long, white garments were retrieved, trimmed in the finest lace. One bore the initials *L de B*, the other, a serpent crest.

"Look what I found," I said, rushing back to the king, who was sitting upright, cushioned by pillows and a quilted blanket covering him to the shoulders, "relics from the past."

"Well, well," the inquisitive son mused as he carefully inspected the monograms. "It seems father was sentimental, after all. He must have kept this as a memento of...his friend."

"Here, you get the royal one and I'll take my father's, if it was his," I giggled, pulling the shift over my head. "What do you think? Not a bad fit?"

Louis leaned forward and kissed the soft skin on the

nape of my neck. "I find it most interesting that your robe is of a better quality than mine. Do you mean to outshine your sovereign?"

"Pardon me this time, sire, and in the future, I shall wear rags to our *rendezvous*."

"Or nothing at all," he grinned. "This comes off the moment the plates are cleared away."

"Oh, no. Not until you keep your word and explain to me why Marion Delorme would have had just cause to rejoice at her husband's passing."

"Why wait? Let us dispense with idle chatter and cut to the chase. Shall I begin?"

I nodded in the affirmative while I repositioned myself under the coverlet alongside the king.

"Four days after your birth, Bijoux, I was introduced to your father. Of course, I do not remember the occasion, however I did read a detailed description of the event in this report," whereby Louis fished about underneath the bolsters and produced a sheath of paper. "Do you care to peruse its contents?"

"How did that find its way here?"

"When I began my examination of your family's affairs, I did not wish to directly question anyone for fear of causing speculation as to why I was taking an interest in the name Cinq-Mars. Therefore, I studied Mazarin's diaries, searching for any mention of your father. As it was, he had interviewed him, at Richelieu's request, when Monsieur le Grand was in jail awaiting trial in Lyons. Since he had been involved in the proceedings, that made me wonder if my godfather had kept any records."

"And had he?"

"Some. Enough."

"Was my father mentioned?"

"Constantly. Richelieu recognized that the young noble was the sole person who had been able to almost turn my father against him. The cardinal was obsessed with Cinq-Mars and set his spies upon him at every opportunity; those efforts yielded little damaging evidence. This letter, dated September 10, 1640, was sent to the Scarlet One by a Monsieur de Brassac, whose wife was a lady-in-waiting to my mother and an informant. The courtier wrote concerning an encounter at Saint-Germain-en-Laye between the king, queen, Cinq-Mars and myself, to which the Brassac couple were witnesses."

"May I?"

"Yes, however what I show you must remain confidential. That is why, when I came across the material last spring, I brought everything to Versailles, for privacy's sake."

"I shan't mention this to anyone. You may rely on me."

Louis handed over the document. "Allow me to explain one thing. Monsieur de Brassac employed code: *Mark Antony* is Richelieu; *Alexander* refers to my father; *Diana*, my mother; *Scipio* is Cinq-Mars, and I am *Carnation*. The remainder is quite plain enough."

My eyes scanned the cursive. The unofficial dispatch claimed that Alexander and Scipio had arrived at St. Germain to visit Carnation and had found the pregnant Diana doting on her firstborn in the royal nursery. The two men approached the babe; Scipio reached out to the heir, the latter began to bawl, causing Alexander great ire. Blaming Diana for the child's bad mood, the king stormed off, threatening to take the Dauphin to Paris where the youngster would be fed a proper diet. Monsieur de Brassac ended by noting that his wife had advised the frightened Diana not to despair, for certainly the excellent Mark Antony would advise Alexander to leave Carnation with his mother.

"So, you did not find Monsieur le Grand to your liking," I commented.

"Do not take offense; I have always mistrusted those gentlemen who practice the Greek vice."

"You hide your aversion well when in your brother's company."

"For mother's sake, I hold my tongue."

"As my mother held hers? Is that why she should have

rejoiced at Cinq-Mars' death? Well, believe me, she knew Henri led a double life."

"No, not two lives, Bijoux, but three. One of the reasons your father hated Richelieu so fiercely was because the cardinal had refused him the hand of Maria of Gonzaga."

"No, that cannot be. He was already married to mother!"

"Yes, yet your parents wed clandestinely, and only the cardinal and his agents were aware of the nuptials. In the meantime, Marie d'Effiat had broken with her son over his visits to Marion Delorme's salon. Your grandmother forgave Henri his indiscretion when she learned he was affianced to the important noblewoman whom Gaston d'Orléans had courted when in the market for a second wife."

Speech failed me. Maria of Gonzaga! The reigning Queen of Poland and sister to Anne of Gonzaga, wife of the Duc de Guise. One of the elite.

"The churl! He meant to desert us!" For the first time in my life, I pitied Madame la Grande.

"You have a right to be angered," Louis soothed, "as was I when I pieced together all the evidence."

"To think I was wont to boast of being his daughter and, were he still breathing, he would disown me. Perhaps it would be better if I deny his name altogether, too."

"No, take the title to spite his cursed memory," the giver of the gift insisted. "Your grandfather was a good man, and I hate to think of his memory being besmirched by an ingrate son."

"Only if you insist, sire."

"Hold your head high. If César's natural father, the duke, had not been a powerful landowner, as well as a coward, he would have been executed alongside the other two."

"What do you mean to say?"

"Bouillon betrayed your father to save his own head."

"Did not Gaston d'Orléans..."

"A written confession was elicited from my uncle, although he never appeared as a witness at the trial. Frédéric-Maurice, however, was arrested and dragged into court where he gladly implicated his fellow co-conspirator. Your father was defending himself quite well before the appearance of the duke."

"The one thing I wish," I reflected, "is that I could remember my father's face so I might despise him better, forever."

"Do you jest with your king, my sweet?"

Choosing not to answer, I scowled instead. Seeing that no smile was about to transform a sullen expression, the king donned his chemise and made to alight.

"What if I were to tell you that I could raise Henri Coiffier de Ruzé from the dead?"

"Do you jest with your subject, my lord?"

"No. Close your eyes and you will understand my meaning."

Not sure what to think, I did as the king wished. Waiting in darkness as black as pitch, my hands covering my face, I listened for a clue. All I knew for certain was that Louis had left the bed and was somewhere in the room, doing something that would cast additional light on yet more secrets.

CHAPTER EIGHTEEN
Lost Kings Aplenty

"May I look?" I inquired.

"In a moment."

I heard Louis draw aside a curtain, and then a weighty object rested atop my lap.

"Behold, the Marquis de Cinq-Mars!" my companion announced in a most official tone.

Lowered lids lifted to allow sight.

The king was standing quite close, holding steady a large portrait. Studying the details of that canvas, I saw before me a representation of what had been an extremely handsome young man.

The stunning, painted youth regarded me with a haughty air; his dark, almond-shaped eyes invited comment, as if defying anyone to ignore his flawless countenance. He wore a white blouson tied around the neck with tasseled cording, partly covered by a button-festooned doublet cut from that famous brick-red fabric, sashed with a baldric. The full lips, pale skin and long auburn curls could have belonged to Adonis, although the eyes—those exotic, arresting orbs—riveted my gaze and held me spellbound, never wanting to look away.

"He...he was attractive," I managed.

"The artist's inscription told me all I needed to know as to the subject's identity. I came to the conclusion that, following the favourite's death, my father was desperately lonely and he kept the likeness here, in his apartment, for the piece must have afforded him solace."

"And neither Richelieu nor your mother would be likely to stumble across the offensive reminder if it were kept at Versailles. How odd all of this is, sire." I traced the vestiges of a brushstroke lightly with a fingertip. "No wonder he inspired great passions."

"As does his daughter."

"Please, do not compare me to him. Henri de Cinq-Mars had more than most people dare dream of having, and he scorned the lot, all because of greed. Why intrigue when one is showered with abundance?"

"I do not understand what factors led to his involvement in the Spanish Plot. Although Richelieu did, he knew the reason why Cinq-Mars was driven to self destruction."

Louis removed the art to a resting place on the floor. His vague admission concerning a mystery connecting the Scarlet One to the marquis bothered me, causing me to seek some clarification.

"Is there more I should know?" I asked when he had returned to our warm burrow.

"Only that Cinq-Mars and de Thou were sentenced to die on the morning of September the twelfth and that prior to their execution, on the same day, Richelieu ordered your father be taken to the dungeon and tortured in the first and second degrees. The cardinal believed his king involved in the Spanish Plot, as well, and wished to secure a confession from the doomed courtier."

"Richelieu trusted his oldest friend that little?"

"Evidently. Cinq-Mars was placed on the rack, but not tortured, for the prisoner gave up important information in exchange for not being torn to pieces."

When I write that my blood ran cold at that moment, believe me, it did. "What could he reveal that had not already been told to the judges?"

"Precisely the point: no one is certain. Yet, it was no small matter, for the cardinal did not wait to inform my father that he was in possession of certain secrets, taken from Cinq-Mars, which could place the throne in jeopardy should he deign to reveal their content."

"Surely, he could have been bluffing."

"The cardinal went so far as to have his armed Guard surround the favourite on the scaffold in order to prevent the doomed man from shouting what he knew to the crowd. 'Ere to losing his head, it is reported your father said: *The people should know. Am I to die unheard?* Is that not strange?"

"Yes," I mumbled, in shock.

"You are shaking, darling, for no reason. Rest assured I am not intimidated by the heirs of ancient, barbaric kings, no matter what they conceive to plot against me."

"You do not understand, sire. I know what Cinq-Mars meant to say!"

"What? Tell me! How do you know these things?"

I could not incriminate Susanne. Fouquet, already the scapegoat, would have to take the blame.

The king bellowed at the mention of his adversary. "Of course! He was the Company's money man, was he not?"

"Everyone in the Company has heard of the *Secret*, sire, while only the group's leadership is privy to the hidden knowledge. I prodded and pried for many years to find the solution to that dilemma and was disappointed in my pursuit. Then, when Fouquet asked me to become his mistress...."

"What?"

"When he asked me to become his mistress, I said that I would if he could satisfy my curiosity concerning a certain matter. Pertaining to the Merovingian dynasty. After much soul searching, the Future divulged everything to me."

"Do not confess to me that you were his lover."

"No, because Fouquet confided in me only recently, while we were staying at Nantes. The night before his arrest. That is why I went to d'Artagnan at the barracks, why I came to you at the château the next morning. Yet, I found I could say nothing, not to you nor to your sous-lieutenant."

"You could speak to me of Noctambule. Why not this subject?"

"I was afraid! People have been done away with for knowing what I know."

"You must be candid with me, Bijoux, and reveal that which you conceal. I promise to protect you from harm."

I hesitated. Could I put my faith in a Bourbon? Did I dare speak?

"Your enemies consider you to be a fraud. They believe the heirs of Godfroi de Bouillon have a more legitimate right to the French throne because he was a descendant of the Merovingian clan that supposedly died out soon after the Church of Rome assassinated Dagobert II. However, one of Dagobert's sons, Sigisbert, was raised in the south of France, hidden away from the enemy, and he lived."

"So, once again we come back to the Merovingians, which tells me nothing at all."

"Sire, the Merovingians were related to a holy family, to a very holy person in particular."

"Who?" he queried, exasperated. "Who, in the name of Christ, could be so important?"

"I think, sire, that you have answered your own question," came my hesitant reply.

The anointed ruler stared at me, long and hard, his mouth set in a thin line until he spoke. "Do you propose to say that the pretenders believe themselves related to the Son of God?"

"Not only that, they are said to be in possession of the Holy Grail, which is not exactly a cup," I began to divulge, a traitor to my own beliefs.

"*Mon Dieu*," Louis groaned, placing his head in his hands, "what blasphemy! Must I kill them all? Who is involved? The families Bouillon, Guise..."

"Lorraine, Gonzaga, Fouquet...Cinq-Mars," I finished.

"You must *never* repeat this heresy to another, do I make myself clear? *Never*! Such talk could start another Fronde. This is the worst day of my life—does Philippe know?"

"He is ignorant of the faction's purpose."

"And so my brother will remain," Louis snapped, arising to dress. "I must be alone, to think this thing out. You stay here and wait. Do not leave the room."

The king was beyond reassuring. He was frantic, disturbed to utter distraction. The carefree lover had become the stern autocrat, and I sensed rightly that the nature of our arrangement had changed dramatically. If I remained silent and obedient, he might allow me to live.

So I sat in bed, mute, watching Louis fumble with his clothing. When the hasty *toilette* was completed, the king left me without comment, and slammed the door to illustrate his point that I should stay put. Waiting a few moments, I arose and dressed as well. The stables were not far off and La Rivière would be more than happy to escape with me to Paris. Home beckoned and I was going to the capital, royal order or no.

Quitting the château was simple, no staff was in sight and the Musketeers in residence were obliged to guard their commander-in-chief. Once outside the hunting lodge, I ran on tiptoe to the grooms' quarters and found La Rivière eating supper with the other stable hands. Seeing me, he dropped his food and we made for the barn without a word. The foreigner was quick to saddle Pegasus and another steed, while I mentioned that when we arrived in Paris, he would be at liberty to do as he pleased.

La Rivière helped me onto my mount and removed his signature turban with a smile. Inside the pyramid of wound fabric was inserted coin after gold coin; enough money to buy a stable full of horses. And that was exactly what he intended to do—establish a fashionable riding academy in Paris close to the court. Every *louis d' or* in his possession represented a performance where his daredevil stunts had earned him notice and a reward. Saving those tokens had symbolized La Riviere's conviction that eventually he would be a free man. That night had come, and we rode off into it together—he with a plan, and I with none at all.

Galloping through the woods of Versailles, both glancing back to make certain we were not being followed, the land of the undead was soon a cluster of trees viewed from the road. I would never venture there again, yet where would I go, what would I do? Roam about Paris only to return to Fontainebleau, Louis and Louise? To face a husband who had duped me?

My thoughts were clouded and I beseeched the memory of a messenger named Jacques to help me again. Clinging to threads of a silver mane, I closed my eyes and tried to recall the advice he had given on the eve mother died. Then it came to me. I would go to Françoise Scarron, hers would be the wisest counsel.

Urging Pegasus to run faster, the mare soon overtook the competition and sped down the highway towards where I prayed salvation awaited in the form of La Belle Indienne, for someone had to know what life was all about, someone had to give a damn. There had to be more to Existence than a Secret pitting brother against brother and engendering hatred amongst the gods' own creation.

If there was not, then Noctambule could have me, I decided, for the air would not be worth breathing. And tears would not be worth crying anymore.

Guests were not usually allowed at the Paris convent of the Hospitalières past the hour of ten, yet, La Rivière and I managed to persuade a nun, who answered our summons at the door of the *Petite Charité*, that we sought Madame Scarron on order of the king. Doubting our sincerity, the reluctant sister nonetheless let us in off the Rue Royale and granted access to a plain foyer where we were asked to wait quietly while the widow was informed of our presence. Françoise must have been awake and dressed, for she hastily appeared wearing a happy expression and her usual gown of simple black with white collar and cuffs. Embracing each other with real affection, I clasped onto the lovely young woman as one would a long-lost relative, immediately comforted by her gracious and conciliatory air.

"I am so thankful that I remembered the name of the Order where I heard you were staying. Forgive me for not writing since the Choisy affair," I apologized.

"You were busy running away," she chuckled, holding me at arm's length. "Did you find Saint-Mandé to your liking, Bijoux?"

"Who told you?"

"Lord Cléonime, poor man," she replied sadly, shaking her head. "Have you any news of our Nicolas?"

"None. He is being detained at Angers; that is all anyone dares say. The king has confiscated his correspondence and intends to review each letter. The talk is that heads could roll."

Françoise blanched, ignored my remark and extended a hand towards La Rivière.

"Are you not the gentleman renowned for his skill on horseback, monsieur?"

"I am he, La Rivière," he answered, stepping forward to kiss her hand. "And you are the lady renowned for her great kindness, are you not?"

"I merely try to follow our Savior's example, monsieur. His is a simple credo to live by."

"Françoise, I need speak to you on a most urgent matter," I interrupted.

"Go, go," La Rivière said agreeably. "I shall wait here, if the sisters do not mind."

"Shall we?" I begged, an official invitation unimportant. Taking the widow's arm, she did not tarry and led me down a taper-lit, stone vaulted passage to more comfortable quarters.

"Would you care for a libation?" she offered when we were inside the small, but adequately furnished apartment. "Bijoux, please stop pacing and sit down while I get the glasses. I suspect you have another mystery for me to solve, not unlike your myth of Comaetho, recall?"

Doing as she asked, I settled into an upholstered armchair, or *fauteuil*, and wondered how I could explain my past or the Secret to a person who was pious. Taking the goblet handed me, I stared hard at my friend. La Belle Indienne was strong, she had been through much in her life, too, and I knew in that instant I could tell her everything.

"What I have to say will shock you, madame. When I was a

girl, merely ten years of age, a messenger of the deities appeared to me and spoke of your wise council."

"Really, Bijoux," Françoise answered, taking the seat opposite mine. "The deities could not think me that important, as I do not subscribe to their credo."

"The messenger, Jacques, said to me: *She will be the widow of one once close to your mother. A lowly girl, destined for high rank and privilege; yet, who cares not for honor and station but rather who looks to enlighten the lost.* He meant you."

She stared at me, mouth agape. "How did you know? Only yesterday, in my diary, I wrote that I would eschew all the material pleasures of this world if I could be shown God's Will for me, what work I might do in His name. At the end of the page, I recorded: *The lost must be enlightened; would that I could be God's instrument in that endeavor.* How did you know?"

"I did not. I am repeating what Jacques prophesized many years ago."

"God has sent you to me," she remarked softly, taking a sip of the amber liquid. "Who am I to question the will of the Lord?" whereupon she crossed herself and motioned for me to go on.

When I had finished telling Françoise the entire tale, with no omissions, I had been talking for more than an hour. Regarding me with wonder, my companion stood and walked to a window overlooking a lovely rose garden barely lit by the red Moon.

"The presence of evil in our lives," she began slowly, "takes many forms. Your talk of a faction that believes its leadership descended from the family of the Christ leaves me with the thought that no method of corruption is beneath Satan's influence. And our king, who rules by divine right, wishes to become as an immortal...what name did you give the daemon?"

"*Vampyre*. Françoise, advise me, please, for I am at my wits end."

La Belle Indienne placed her forehead against a pane of glass and sighed. "You must pray to our Lord for forgiveness, deliverance and strength. And you must save the king from temptation."

"No, I shall not return to Fontainebleau. May I not remain here, with you?"

"No," she firmly and not without tenderness. "Face your fear, for this is the test prepared for you. If you cannot meet the challenge, give up the sword."

"You liken all of this to a duel? Is that your answer for me?"

Françoise returned to my side. "Reflect, Bijoux, reflect long and hard. Ask for Divine guidance and God will not fail you."

"Did God help my father? Did he ever help your pitiful husband? I believe in the Dieties, madame, don't you understand? Athena exists...the goddess of Wisdom is the Virgin of the night sky who displays her sword and spindle with pride, the oldest Creatrix..."

"There is only one God and one God alone," she retorted quietly. "He has come to my aid on many occasions and I think He has helped you in the past, as well."

"Thank you for listening to me, madame," I replied, standing on unsteady legs. "Please forgive the intrusion."

"Bijoux, do not let the drink make you surly with me. Sleep here for tonight. I shall inform Monsieur la Rivière that he may stay in the convent stable with the horses."

"No, no," I protested, tottering towards the door. "I have inconvenienced you, Françoise. May I ask one last thing of you before I go?"

"Yes," she said, taking one of my hands, "of course. You are my friend, Bijoux, despite your heretical ways."

"If I die or am exiled, please promise to help the king. Go to him, tell him what I confided in you, make him see the error of his ways. Will you agree to do that?"

"Dear girl, why would the king heed my words? However, should the oath ease your mind, I swear to try my best to be granted a royal audience in the event of your demise."

"Show him this," I muttered, removing the ruby ring, "then he will know you speak the truth."

Françoise accepted the token. She stared at the circle of gold and red with a puzzled expression.

"You love him, don't you?" she asked.

"Yes. I doubt that I shall ever stop. However, our mutual adultery must end."

"I shall pray for you, Bijoux."

"Thank you," I answered with little joy. I was more befuddled in leaving than I had been when arriving at the convent. Facing the earnest lady in black, I hesitated. "Do you not think it possible, madame, that the Lost King could be who he claims–a leader who wishes naught but to bring down Rome and *that* heresy?"

"The heavenly King to whom I bow was never lost. We are all heirs to His legacy, dear girl."

Jacques had said the same. Squaring my shoulders, I stood up straight and swallowed the lump in my throat. Hope existed. All was not lost unless I decided to capitulate. People were merely confused, having been lied to for centuries.

"I must go. The ride back to Fontainebleau is a long one."

"I insist you stay until morning. The roads are not safe at night; Paris is not safe at night. Rest here and return to court in the morning."

Her argument was valid. "If I may lodge in the stables with La Rivière, then I shall accept your hospitality, madame. Call it a penance for the transgression committed earlier this evening."

"You are a stubborn one," she smiled in order to stifle a yawn. "Since I am too tired to argue with you, let us collect your friend and make for the shelter in the manger."

Shortly thereafter, while I tossed and turned in a hayloft, wondering why I had left the comforts of Versailles, the just-passed discussion with Françoise turned over and over in my mind. While I knew that I must change my life for the better, I also refused to follow a discipline that demanded prayer and self-denial of its adherents. Gone were the days of listening to La Belle Indienne quote St. Augustine's, *Faith is to believe what we do not see and the reward of this faith is to see what we believe*, and be impressed. *No*, I thought, *I shall make my own way, I shall rely on my own wits to guide me.*

For, as far as I was concerned, wise Athena did not need me to bother Her with more problems. She was busy enough tending to the lives of heroes more deserving of Her attention.

The situation was hardly calm when I arrived at Fontainebleau in the early morning hours directly following the brief sojourn in the straw. Tired and grumpy from a bad night's sleep, I probably would not have returned if the turbaned one had not personally escorted me to the château, insistent that he see me to the front gate. Urging me to dismount and leave Pegasus in his capable hands, we parted with a promise to meet again when the court repaired to the Louvre for the winter months. Then La Rivière put heels to his horse's side and trotted away with the Arab gray, gracefully passing my mare's reins to a groom who was crossing the courtyard on his way to work.

Not exactly thrilled by the prospect of waiting on the grand staircase for Louis to appear, I made for the upstairs floor which had been set aside to accommodate Henriette's ladies. Unfortunately, as I carefully opened the door to La Vallière's chamber, hoping I might sneak back undetected whilst the king's mistress slept, I heard the sound of voices, one of which belonged to a frantic César.

"Do you mean to tell me, mademoiselle, that my wife spent the entire evening with Monsieur, driving about the countryside in a carriage? What a preposterous thing to say!"

"You should not be here, Monsieur de la Tour. If his Majesty returns from the hunt and discovers you in this room, we shall both be punished."

"Did the king lodge here last night?"

"Monsieur! How dare you ask such a question? Have you no manners?"

"Did he?" Cesar was shouting.

"No," Louise admitted, beginning to cry the usual tears she most always shed when confronted with the topic of her lover. "Our Sovereign was with M. Colbert 'till dawn."

"I think not," another man said in a accusatory tone, in a

manner I had once heard a junior valet speak in Nantes. "Do you truly believe that Madame Bijoux was with d'Orléans?"

"Since when is my comportment your business?" I snarled, charging over the threshold into view. Eustache was there, standing close to César. The disappointed look on the servant's face indicated he was jealous of the hold I exerted over his master.

"Where have you been?" César demanded. "Where were you?"

"Perhaps I should ask you the same, husband. I went searching for you late last night and you were nowhere to be found. Could you have been out reveling with your new friend here? And to think, Eustache, I picked you for him myself—however, I thought you fancied Lisette."

"Madame," La Vallière protested, drawing my attention to the girl who was still abed and wearing a nightcap, "I shall not abide such talk. Take your dirty thoughts and these gentlemen, if one might call them that, out into the corridor and bicker there."

"Why are you attacking me thus?" César asked, oblivious to Louise's prissy request. "Did the bastard poison your mind?"

The two comrades-in-arms glared at me: one hurt; the other, enraged.

"You are the only *bastard* whom I know! My other lovers have all been of legitimate issue."

"Who else have you been with besides the usurper? Fouquet?"

"No, M. d'Artagnan. The bravest Musketeer in France took my virginity."

"Get out of here! All of you!" Louise screamed in a high squeal. "Now!"

"You are cruel," the offended gentleman lamented. "I never want to see you again. Ever."

"Do you wager that Godefroy-Maurice will take in his father's illicit firstborn?"

"Leave my father out of this! Who are you to judge him? He was a legend."

"He was the son-of-a-whore who betrayed my father in order to save his own neck. Henri Coiffier de Ruzé would turn in his grave if he knew I married *you*."

"Were you aware that the Duc de Bouillon was forced by Richelieu to cede his titles and lands to France as punishment for his involvement in the Spanish Plot? My father lost everything, the whole of Sedan, the title of *prince*, because of Cinq-Mars. Amongst *my* family, *your* name is an abomination!"

"She understands nothing," Eustache mocked.

"Get out of my sight!" I yelled.

"Come," César said quietly to his companion, "let us depart."

The pair walked towards the door. Watching them retreat, it dawned on me that César was leaving me. Going after him, I grabbed onto the fabric of his full-sleeved shirt.

"What do you think you are doing? You cannot desert me. What of our love?"

"You make a mockery of that emotion," was his disgusted reply. "Leave me be."

"Come back," I screamed after him. "How can you do this to your wife?"

"She did it to herself," were the last words that came from César's mouth. Then the sound of a metal latch clicking shut in its housing, and I sank to the floor, too shocked to weep.

"Madame, oh dear," Louise managed. Arising, she approached in her nightclothes and attempted to lift me when she reached where I sat, lifeless, as would an abandoned marionette.

"Do not touch me."

"Madame, allow me to assist you."

"No," I insisted, the tears rushing forth. "I wish Noctambule would come and take me!"

"What a silly thing to say. Monsieur César will be back, do not worry."

"No, he hates me! And it *is* all my fault, you know. A man will only take so much."

La Vallière was moved by the scene. Kneeling down, the

kind girl drew me to her. "Stop crying. There, there. Everything will be fine."

She held me as a mother would a babe, and I sobbed uncontrollably in her slender arms. If the young lady had not been present, I hate to admit what I might have done, such was my grief.

"Were you with the king last night?" she asked while she rocked me.

"Yes," I wailed, "but not for too long. Forgive me."

"Do you love my Louis?"

"No, it is finished. We were lovers before he met you, mademoiselle. I cannot help that."

"I should hate you, another woman might, however I see that you love your husband. If it was not you, it would have been another. How might I blame you for wanting what I, myself, desire?"

"Louis adores you," I lied, trying to control myself by wiping a wet cheek. "He told me so himself, yesterday, at Versailles."

"Really? The king said that? Are you certain?"

"You are the one whom he wants, no other. I was a passing fancy, a...diversion."

"He loves me! I knew it!" she enthused, transported by the revelation, hugging me anew. "Thank you, madame, thank you for your candor."

We released one another and an uncomfortable silence passed, neither sure what to say.

"One good turn deserves another, Bijoux," the happy favourite said at last with a shy grin. "I must help you to regain your husband's regard. Would you care to know the truth about his parentage?"

"You know?" I was flabbergasted.

"I grew up on Gaston's estate at Blois. I heard much about the Bouillons while living there."

"Really? Such as?"

"That they are Huguenots, to begin."

"What? Protestants! That cannot be! César is a Catholic; we were married at St. Sulpice."

"Which is an important detail to keep in mind. Listen and understand. When César's father was a young man, he visited the Low Countries where he met the charming Princess de Brussels with whom he fell in love and wished to marry. The trouble was, however, that the Huguenot Bouillons forbid the match because the lady was a Roman Catholic. Frédéric-Maurice was afraid to anger his family by converting, and the princess insisted that he do so before she would wed him, so the couple did not join in matrimony. Being in the thrall of a great passion, the two, well, they..."

"...were intimate," I provided.

"Yes, thank-you," she blushed, "and the result of their union was César."

"And Frédéric-Maurice still would not convert and marry his love after she had given him a son and heir? What a cur!"

Louise looked away. "The princess died while giving birth to your husband. Her last act was to make her lover promise to raise their son in the true Church. Frédéric-Maurice swore that he would honor her memory by becoming a Roman Catholic himself, which he did the day after she was gone."

"So, if César's mother had survived, he would not be a bastard and Godefroy-Maurice would not be here today."

"Yes," was her simple response. "Your husband should, by rights, be the Duc de Bouillon."

"Why, then, does he not take a stand for himself? Why..."

"Bijoux," Louise interrupted, "not only did the princess ask that her son be baptized a Catholic, she beseeched the penitent Frédéric to marry her much younger sister, whom she trusted would raise César better than would a stranger. As a matter of honor, the bereaved lover took the girl as his wife. Since the bride grew to become the mirror image of her elder sibling, the match was an eventual success. Godefroy-Maurice came four years after his half-brother, then another son, Emmanuel. The duke raised his three boys together, in harmony, and none of them would think to raise a hand against the other."

"I should have talked to César in private. I am such a fool..."

A knock sounded from outside and my heart raced with anticipation. Thinking my husband might have returned, I started, calling out, "Come in."

Lisette appeared instead and I knew the meaning of pain. Real anguish. As though my chest had been pierced by a musket ball.

"Madame, I came across your husband and his valet, heading for the stables. He says he is off to Paris! If you hurry, you may still catch him before he makes the mistake of leaving without you."

"No, he no longer desires me."

"What? Are you crazy in the head? He adores you, madame. Go, stop him."

"Yes," Louise agreed. "Hurry downstairs and beg him to stay."

"He won't."

"Go," they urged, two voices joined as one. "What do you have to lose?" Lisette added.

"My pride."

"Pride is a deadly sin, Bijoux. If you love him, go to him," Louise advised.

Encouraged by their joint recommendations, I ran after César. Not caring who saw my haste, I flew past the courtiers and servants who were flitting about the hallway, bolted down the marble staircase and practically winged my way out into the front yard. Across the expanse I could see two men quitting the stables on horseback, and I tore after the figures, determined to stall their progress.

"César," I called out as loudly as I was able, "César, wait!"

Turning in his saddle, the eldest son of Frédéric-Maurice reined in his horse and dismissed Eustache. Nearing where he tarried, I caught my breath as I took in the sight of the man who was my husband: long, dark hair blowing about wide shoulders, strong hands with a firm grip on the leather straps laced around them, a classical visage marred only by an expression of sad resignation. A handsome, decent soul whom I had ludicrously scorned.

"Please, do not go," I said breathlessly, clasping onto a stirrup iron and pressing César's foot against my bosom. "I love you so much; you can't go. I shall die without you."

"The king can have you all to himself now, Bijoux."

"I want you," I began to cry, "and no one else. I am sorry about your mother—I was wrong to insult her memory. May we not start anew? Will you not grant me a second chance?"

"And a third, and a fourth and a fifth? No, let us part today and leave it at that."

"Forgive me, please," I wept shamelessly.

"Bijoux, dispense with the histrionics. You are making a scene."

"What would Jesus do if he were here?" I asked, clinging to César's boot for dear life. "Would he not forgive me? Did he not preach a message of love, that ancestor of yours? If you are so proud to be related to that man, to a mighty son of Wisdom, then why will you not be more like him? You and yours should be called the Company of the Blessed Hypocrites, I swear!"

Perhaps it was that final commentary which made César reconsider his stance. Or perhaps he realized he was going to have to drag me to Paris with him before I would release his person. Whatever the reason, he swung his free leg over the back of his steed and I allowed him to dismount.

"We cannot go on like this," he observed.

"No," I said, hanging my head. "No."

"Then what do we do, Bijoux?"

"Leave France. This place, him, none of it matters to me anymore. Yesterday, I saw my father's portrait at Versailles, César, I looked upon his features, and a sensation stirred within me. Not the loathing I should have felt for a man who planned to leave his wife and child for the sake of his own personal ambition, yet something more akin to admiration. And do you know why? Because in his eyes I saw *myself*. That thought sickens me, although it is the truth. I am my father's daughter, I am a Cinq-Mars through and through. If I do not leave this wretched land, I shudder to think what fate awaits me."

"Are you seriously inclined? Do you mean what you say?"

"César, my father died when he was one year older than I am now. Two years younger than are you. Imagine kneeling before an executioner, waiting for the ax to drop!"

"Eustache! Over here," my husband directed, whereupon d'Anger approached.

"Let us prepare for a long journey. Please, ready my belongings."

"Yes, monsieur," he grumbled, riding away without further instructions.

"Go gather our valuables," César directed. "Make certain you bring the jewels, for they may be our only source of income for a time."

"Let us hire a coach and load the crates from Saint-Mandé as they are, unopened."

"Traveling by carriage may slow us. Surely, the king will send his men out after you when he discovers your quarters abandoned."

"No, I do not think so, César. Where I am concerned, I do believe his Majesty has experienced a change of heart."

A smile of relief was my reward. And a kiss; the sweetest, loveliest embrace imaginable. Worth more to me than a kingdom, a crown, or all of the jewels in the world.

How long we stood there, lovers on the landscape of Fontainebleau, I truly do not recall. The sound of hoof beats interrupted our tender reunion. Breaking abruptly from César's warm mouth, I spun about to see Louis bearing down upon us astride a huge, roan stallion, the two Musketeers from Versailles in tow.

"Damn him to Hades," I muttered, bowing low before the onslaught.

The king pulled his steed up short, causing the charger to rear on its hind legs and crash back down with a thud directly in front of my kneeling figure.

"Rise, madame. Look at me," he commanded.

"Yes, sire."

"Take him into custody," Louis ordered the royal escort, pointing his crop in lieu of a scepter at César. "Remove

Monsieur de la Tour to the Hôtel Bouillon in Paris where he will remain, exiled from the court, until my pleasure dictates otherwise."

"She loves me," was César's defiant reply as the soldiers laid hands on him. "Lock me in a prison cell and throw away the key, if you like—Bijoux will always be mine."

"Punish me, sire, not him! I am the disobedient one."

"Yes, you are, aren't you?" Louis mocked. Joining his subjects on the ground, the disgruntled monarch stared at me all the while with an icy fix. A gauntlet came off slowly; the king was close enough for me to feel the heat of his breath.

"You traitor!" he exclaimed, striking me across the face with the glove. César struggled against his captors, to no avail, as I received the blow that sent me staggering backwards. Standing straight when I had recovered my senses, I made no show of weakness; rather I tossed my head and struck a pose of complete disdain.

"Get to your apartment, marquise," the wounded lover commanded. "Take him away," was the Musketeers' directive.

I refused to move. César and I said nothing to one another as the threesome made to depart, for we were wise enough to keep our mouths closed, our eyes saying good-bye.

"Where did you hide last night? Answer me at once!"

"I went to the convent of the Hospitalières in Paris to pray for guidance, sire. I was confused."

"And while you were seeking peace, I was mad with worry. Never do that to me again."

"I shan't, your Majesty, since the occasion for me to cause you distress will never again arise."

"Are you peeved because I hit you? I was within my rights. Or could it be, marquise, that you have found God, perhaps, since last we spoke?"

"No, sire," I replied in a calm voice, "simply *myself*."

Louis leaned forward to kiss me and I did not respond. Grabbing a handful of red hair, he pulled me forward, forcing his lips onto mine. When I failed to return his ardor, he pushed me away with a rough shove.

"Go to your room. Immediately. I shall send for you later."

With a curtsy, I fled. The battle line had been drawn at last. Louis and I were about to engage in combat, a contest that, by its very nature, demanded a sole victor. Which one of us would prove the stronger opponent, I had no notion; the fight had yet to be fought.

Yet, in my heart and soul, I knew that as long as Noctambule roamed through the shadows of Versailles and the threat of a Lost King loomed on the horizon, Louis would never sue for peace.

Despite, and more likely because of, his wife's protestations, the Duc d'Orléans announced on the afternoon of my reappearance at Fontainebleau that his establishment would be moving to Saint-Cloud as soon as the journey could be arranged to his satisfaction. Not that Monsieur knew anything of the recent goings-on at Versailles, nor had he heard talk of César's forced removal from the château to Paris, he simply wished to irk Henriette. What Philippe also managed to do was to send his sovereign into a rage, for not only would the relocation mean the king would be separated from Louise, he would likewise be forced to allow me leave to follow the prince's retinue. When a crestfallen La Vallière told me the happy news, I went straightway to my good-for-nothing rascal's apartments, located the royal sibling and personally expressed my thanks to him.

Louis maintained an ominous silence while the harem prepared to quit the sultan's palace, plotting as to how he could thwart Philippe's plans. Even now, sitting here in my cell, I am compelled to admit that the third Bourbon to sit a throne is a cunning adversary and a brilliant judge of character. Some may argue with my assessment—I know of what I speak. It took being rudely booted from a carriage, as would a scullery maid who had forgotten her station, to realize with whom I was dealing; yet, the king kept me with him at Fontainebleau whilst a put-out Monsieur and his household departed through the early Sunday mists for Saint-Cloud.

The order of detainment stated that the Marquise de Cinq-Mars was required at court—that lady having been appointed the Royal Astrologer—and at court she would remain. After delivering the unexpected certification, Maupertuis wasted no time in showing me to my own private suite conveniently situated directly above the royal bedchamber. There I was informed that his Majesty would honor me with an audience later in the evening, after eleven, and that I was to prepare myself for his visit. Although he was a witness to my ensuing distress, the rakish officer could offer me no solace for he was the king's man, whether he felt sorry for my situation or not.

Common sense was not a much-lauded virtue amongst the aristocrats with whom I cohabitated, however, the Musketeer marquis possessed enough of it to send for Lisette when I drenched the blue mantle covering his chest. The dependable daughter of Des Oeillets came to the rescue and, like her mother before her, provided the tender care I so desperately craved. Sending me straight to bed, she sat with me, stroking my wrinkled brow until I fell asleep. When I awoke in the late afternoon, she led me to the new bathing basin I had inherited, filled close to the rim with hot, petal-strewn water and made me submerge, naked, so that the flowers might better soothe my person.

After a good soak, I was dried off and rubbed with a scented cream that produced a pleasant, tingling sensation on the skin. Unaccustomed to such sensual delights, I closed my eyes and wondered if Lisette's diligent kneading was proper to enjoy.

"Have many ladies employed you in this fashion?" I asked in what I hoped was a natural tone.

"Oh, yes, madame. The surintendant's wife received her treatment daily at Saint-Mandé."

"And Madame du Plessis, too?"

"Yes," she laughed. "Don't be silly. Is this your first time? Relax your body and think happy thoughts. You needn't worry about me. I have no designs on you. If anything, I am dreaming about a dashing officer, a fine marquis who says he loves me."

"Maupertuis?" I teased.

"Of course. *Voilà*, you are done. Cover up."

"Have you been staying with him?" was the next inquiry.

"Yes," she grinned, helping me don a dressing gown of claret colored velveteen found amongst the contents of the two crates. "This is beautiful material, madame."

"Red is not my color, although when I saw the fabric, I had to have something made from it."

"No, you may wear the hue," Lisette announced, stepping back and staring at me as one would an oil hanging in a gallery. "Your skin is so white that it works, believe it or not. If we put your hair up..."

"With some of mother's jewels..."

"Yes, lots of jewelry," she agreed with a nod. "The king will be dazzled."

I looked away, no longer chipper. "I swore to myself that I would not lay with the king again and look at what has happened. Here I am, ensconced above his chamber, named the king's astrologer, which we both know is another title for concubine. Yet, whenever Louis and I are alone together, I become weak, I do whatever he wants, I cannot control my desires. How do I resist him tonight when he comes to me? What should I say to put him off?"

"Do what I do when I am alone with my marquis."

"Lisette! You have been with Maupertuis?"

"Near to him. Nothing more. If I succumbed to his passionate kisses and sweet, false promises, do you really think that he would marry me? Never. Yet, if I play coy, he will go mad with longing and take me as his wife sooner than later. Every man wants what he cannot have. Louis Bourbon is no different."

"Are you suggesting I play the coquette?"

"Have you never led a man a merry dance, Bijoux? You, the daughter of Marion Delorme!"

I reviewed the list in my mind: Philippe, d'Artagnan, Fouquet, César, Louis. "No, not really."

"Then begin tonight. Torture him," she grimaced and began to play with the tresses she was deciding on how to style.

I considered Lisette's advice. "Does Maupertuis not become…impatient?"

"So?" she shrugged her shoulders. "Too bad for him."

"You are such a firebrand!"

"I best confess to you that I was born in the spring…"

"…beneath the sign of the Ram!" I laughed, guessing at the truth. "Yet, bold Lisette, men have urges, needs."

"No gentleman would force himself upon a woman. Not Maupertuis and not the king. If you say, *no*, Louis must respect your wishes. We live in France, we are the most civilized people in the world, *n'est-ce pas?*"

"So, when the king arrives here tonight, I should be indisposed?"

"Say that you feel ill, that it is the wrong time of the month for intimacy. Anything."

"Yes," I said slowly as the wise girl fastened my hair high up on my head with decorative combs, "yes, I think I shall follow your counsel. We shall discuss the stars, the king and I."

Thus when Louis XIV deigned to call upon the Marquise de Cinq-Mars in her small salon following his ritual ten o'clock supper, the reluctant astrologer greeted her master graciously, offering him refreshment, good company and an astral scheme. Dressed in the flowing crimson robe—neck, ears and fingers ablaze with fiery gems, coiffure alluringly loose—the king was entranced with his official stargazer. Decked out himself in an impressive justacorps of carmine brocade glittering with gold needlework, a patterned waistcoat of black flock, and more lace about the throat than I had ever seen a person sport, the one who thought himself Apollo reborn gestured for me to approach where he stood, unattended, once decorum demanded a sign.

"Majesty, may I dare to commend you on your magnificent appearance." From the servile vantage point, which afforded me a close look at a silk-stockinged calf and satin-clad thigh, I recalled Lisette's warning to be on my guard.

"And may I commend you, madame, on your display of tact these three days past."

"I exist to serve you," I replied very softly, head bowed. "You have shown me much honor."

"Yes, so I have. Arise and embrace your king."

Louis received a formal kiss on the neck. More than that, I could not manage.

Clearing his throat, the king reached into an outside pocket of his jacket and produced a flat, square box. The leather case was duly offered to me with a staid, "For you, marquise."

Inside were found the diamond eardrops César had confronted me with at Saint-Mandé as a test of loyalty. Surprised, because I had assumed that Louise de la Vallière had been the eventual recipient of the rejected pendants, I laughed, lifting one off its backdrop of white silk.

"Such lovely stones, sire. Monsieur Légaré's handiwork?"

"No, a find originally intended for and sent to the most stunning of women, although a rude gentleman intercepted the gift and returned the love token before it reached its destination."

"And would that rude gentleman have been my husband, César de la Tour?"

"Not for much longer."

Fluttering my eyelashes, I registered no sign of emotion at the mention of divorce. "Thank you, sire, and be certain that I shall cherish the memento of your affection always. However, to repeat my question to you, from where did these stones come? The Duc d'Orléans, perhaps?"

"How did you know that? Who told you? Or did you divine the gift from that chart, there on the table?"

"Would you care to rest on the divan and allow me the pleasure of entertaining you with what I consider to be an amusing story?"

"Certainly," he obeyed. "Your tales are the most fascinating I have been fortunate to hear."

Louis was comfortably situated on the upholstered lounge, sipping from a glass of burgundy—the only spirit he was known to partake—as he listened to the anecdote concerning the skirmish for possession of the cape I had carried to the

Louvre. He roared merrily when I admitted to biting the Petit Monsieur on the arm; his eyebrows shot up when I described how d'Artagnan had ended our fight by ripping the cloak away from two ill-behaved children. The confession, however, that his brother had stolen some of mother's property when the jewels had been exposed caused him to frown, bothered that a prince would act in such a common manner.

"Monsieur is a thief. I shall retrieve whatever he took from you forthwith."

"Too late, for these sparklers, sire, are the same which the then Duc d'Anjou confiscated!"

The king regarded the diamonds, then looked up at me with a dumbfounded expression. "The Duc d'Orléans sold me stones for which he never paid a *sou*? I spent good money to buy you the rarest rocks, only to be told that they were yours all along?"

"Do not be peeved," I said quickly. "I am glad to have them back. Truly."

Louis made a move as though he were about to toss the treasure away, then caught my wrist instead and sent me flying onto his lap. Kiss upon kiss was placed on my astonished face, in between spasms of hilarity, for the king was thoroughly convulsed with mirth.

"You should have seen your face! *Mon Dieu*, how I adore you!"

"You are not displeased?"

"No, charmed, my darling. What a woman you are! Spirited, witty, beautiful," he paused to remove the clusters of rubies attached to my lobes in order to replace them with the heavy, crystalline clips, "not to mention as enticing as a warm-blooded Venus. Feel what you do to me?"

"Yes, sire."

"Let me see you in the flesh," he insisted. Experienced fingers loosened the bow securing the front of the less-than-confining outfit chosen for its seductive qualities.

"Majesty," I said sternly, "do not proceed. That special time of the month has arrived."

"Oh, I had not a clue," he admitted, flustered, drawing away from me at once. "Forgive me."

"You are forgiven," I said lightly. "At least I am not with child."

"True, for I would have wondered if it was his. When you are finished with...this business, we shall start our own family."

"Sire, soon the queen will be delivered of your heir, let us pray. Why speak to me of children?"

"Because I fully expect that both you and I shall outlive my wife, and when that happens, we shall be married and you will be my consort, that is why."

"Correct me if I am mistaken, sire. You wish me to dissolve my present marital obligation due to my husband being born a bastard, yet, you would have me bring more illegitimate souls into the world?"

"I, Louis Bourbon, will be their father, madame, that is the difference! Do not dare to compare me to any member of that stinking tribe of Bouillons! If you loved me, you would be thrilled at the prospect of carrying my issue."

Standing, I walked off in the direction of the enclave where virtuous ladies entertained no men other than their husbands. My mind was in a state. Louis wanted babies from me and was not going to tolerate days of my saying no to his advances.

"Let us consult the stars, perhaps? Shall I prove my prowess in matters of divination?"

"Yes, that would please me greatly, marquise. What say the planets as to my reign?"

"Having consulted the work of the great astrologer, Monsieur Morin, in his influential book *Astrologia Gallica*, allow me to explain the chart of your nativity, represented on this paper you remarked upon earlier. We shall begin with your Sun, placed in the sign of the Virgin and found in your tenth temple, the position of the mid-heaven. This mansion governs your kingship and the signs are very remarkable, sire, for the spot is shared by Helios and Mercury, indicating a long and successful reign—albeit tempestuous in its final years."

"How so?"

"Mars, here, in the second temple, ruled by Capricorn, promises a martial and wealthy rule. Yet, the Hermes-Apollo connection is considered a malefic when so placed, according to several texts I consulted. Therefore, while I might be inclined to advise caution in your later years, I also believe the coupling of the messenger and the soul to provide sound judgment and a strong temperament. The planet of love, Venus, and your Moon are here, in Leo—a ninth temple placement—and a goodly one for a Sun King. Saturn in the third house is overseen by Aquarius, and in this instance, I predict family difficulties, perhaps with your brother," I ventured. "And look see, your eleventh temple, the part of fortune, promises wise ministers and loyal counselors."

"Are we...destined to love forever?"

"No, sire, we are not," I said quietly, hanging my head. "Our Suns aside, we are as different as are night and day."

"I appreciate your calculations, madame, yet I must refute your claim counter our association."

"The stars do not lie, sire, nor does your astrologer."

"You are a woman, madame. What do you know of the heavens, truly?" he chuckled.

"Athena rules the sky and She is a woman," I spat back. "She is the celestial Virgin, your Sun," I growled. "You would do well to pay Her heed and be proud of me and my work, not ashamed."

"I shall build her a statue at Versailles," Louis mocked. "She and all the other Olympians. Perhaps, should you continue to behave yourself, marquise, I shall be inclined to construct an observatory at the palace, a place that will rival the famed Uraniborg of that former noble Dane, Tycho Brahe. I hearsay some of the dead stargazer's instruments are still available, though guarded jealously by his heirs."

"Majesty, you show me too much honor. With your permission, I should like to retire."

"By all means, rest. I may call again in two days, three days time?"

"In five, sire, on Friday," I curtsied. Disappearing behind a curtain, I went to the dressing table and removed the baubles Lisette had piled upon me in order to impress. Holding the gift of eardrops last in the palm of one hand, I stared at them and wondered who had given the diamonds to Marion. Cinq-Mars, perhaps? D'Emery?

Searching the reflection in the looking glass before me, I saw someone who looked sad, not arrogant or confidant as had mother's miniature or father's portrait at Versailles. A woman who was afraid, not knowing in which direction to turn. No daughter of Athena, certainly not.

"I shan't behave like either of you," I swore to the image in the mirror, thinking of my parents. "Gods help me, I shan't. You both may have started this damnable farce—I swear, it ends with me. César, where are you?" I whispered. "Come to me, please."

Holding the pale symbols of eternal troth up to the light of the chandelier, I watched a myriad of colors spin and turn before my thoughtful gaze. Somehow I sensed that Louis and I would be linked forever by our tie to Noctambule—an undeniable bond existed between us—however, I was also aware that I had to escape the court. How, I wondered, how could I break free, short of ending my own life? How might I escape the false tale of Comaetho's ruin?

Oh, wise Athena, I murmured, *when shall we women regain our might?*

CHAPTER NINETEEN
Deadly Wagers

As I was considering whether I should call on M. Cousinot and ask him to drain me permanently dry, the answer to the dilemma came to me: *Death*. Stage an elaborate deception whereby the king would believe that if I became a chaste disciple of Noctambule, the old man of legend would reward my loyalty with a potion containing the Immortal Elixir.

Had Guibourg not trained me to do as much? A vision came to me of a house on the Rue St. Denis, of a room draped in ebony where sulfur candles spit blue flames. Yes, I could do it, I could become a devout practitioner of the Black Mass, I could convince the superstitious king of anything concerning the *vrykolakas* and its dark powers. I would wear only red, a powerful color that would remind Louis of that other great influence in his life, Mazarin. I would appear amongst the other courtiers only at night. I would refuse to look at the Sun. And I would drink the vile tonic, the mixture that had not touched my lips since Le Nôtre's healing had cured me of the dependency.

The Bourbon would have his transformation, yet it would cost him, for in the end the Vampyre of Versailles would demand that I leave the palaces of the Sun King to become a daemon bride, or else, no gift of eternity would be granted.

Thinking myself to be quite clever, I went to bed, eager for morning. I concocted a new name for myself while I reclined, wide-awake; one that I had to be sure to get to de Vardes and Saint-Aignan: *la Marquise de Sang-Mars.*

The bloody marquise.

The veiled reference would be lost on those who would think it a comment on an eccentric taste in fashion, though Louis would understand its true meaning well enough.

Yet, what I did not consider was that to deny the adverse its power was one thing, but to give it form and substance, quite another.

Needless to say, when Lisette woke me to begin another week, she did not expect to find her mistress much happier than when she had left her on the previous eve. A request from me for writing materials, though, changed her mind. Workmen were then summoned to hang inky satin wall coverings over the existing tableaux gracing the main salon, artisans to apply their hand to the creation of silver stars hanging from shiny swags, and boxes of candles and incense ordered up from Paris, all charged to the royal account.

César was alerted to the sudden change in his wife's character by the messenger Maupertuis, who graciously agreed to ferry a letter before court gossip could reach my husband's ears. In it, I outlined the plan of action I had chosen, sparing the addressee no details, closing with the words *Et in Arcadia Ego*, a code phrase intended for either to send when the timing was propitious to flee France.

The ensuing answer from the Hôtel Bouillon read: *Patience. The Order of St. Sulpice offers me solace and comfort in the wake of recent disaster. The hour is near when our king will reign triumphant. Arcadia will be ours.*

The spectacle I devised for Louis XIV was too perfectly executed not to describe at least briefly; a performance worthy of Monsieur Molière's acclaimed acting troupe, if I may say so with conceit. Each element of the carefully thought-out drama added to the supernatural atmosphere permeating the apartment: two hundred black tapers burning in silver candelabrums set-up about the drawing room; puffs of smoke rising into the air as they escaped the censers housing jasmine pastilles; two lute players hired to provide somber accompaniment from the adjoining cabinet.

Center stage stood an altar, upon which the requisite chalice, bell and wafers were placed. Lisette knelt before the shrine dedicated to Noctambule as would an eager proselyte, although she was masked to hide her identity. As for my role in the production, I was cast as an apostle of Astaroth and Asmodeus; a most fantastic costume of flame taffeta whose square-cut bodice had been stitched with black and gold pentacles my prop. Observed as a whole, the *tableau* would have convinced Guibourg he had stepped into Satan's lair. When the velvet and lace clad Louis arrived on the scene, his initial reaction was the very one I had expected a good Catholic to make.

"What is this nonsense!" a concerned king demanded.

"A very good evening to you, your Majesty. Welcome to my humble sanctuary."

"Sanctuary? Whatever are you talking about, marquise?"

"Sire," I said in the lowest tone I could muster, "Noctambule commands and I obey."

"What? You saw him again? Here?"

"In a dream. The Master has come to me but twice in such form, once while you were being cured of the fever in Calais."

"No, truly? When was the other occasion?"

"Following our assignation at Vincennes."

"*Mon Dieu*," Louis whispered. "Why this display?"

"Homage, sire. The *vrykolakas* demands it."

"Who is that?" he asked, pointing at Lisette.

"A handmaiden, one of His minions."

"I order you to approach and bow before your king!" Louis erupted.

Well-rehearsed and aware of her cue, Lisette rose slowly and pivoted about on the spot where she had previously kept a silent vigil. Her skin had been covered earlier with the white makeup known as *Aqua Toffana*, her mouth brushed with the deepest shade of burgundy lip rouge, and her eyes rimmed with smudged coal visible through the slits of a vizard.

"My liege is Noctambule, ruler of the Underworld. No other Master do I recognize."

"Is *she* an Immortal?" the king grimaced.

"No, she was touched by the *vrykolokas*, as was I, though not allowed the gift of His blood."

"The ritual is required should you be redeemed, madame," my confederate intoned.

"Redeemed?" Louis spat, "Redeemed? Who are you, succubus? How dare you speak such words under my roof? I am Louis Bourbon, King of France and Navarre and I say you are a fraud!"

"Do you wish to exist in your body throughout eternity, mere mortal? Do you?"

Her query jarred the king's senses. Completely taken aback, he could only nod in reply.

"Then pay me heed," the golden beauty warned. "You have defiled my Master's property!"

"Versailles?" he croaked.

"No, Madame Bijoux! She belongs to Noctambule and to no other. Leave her in peace and the Master may still favor you with the gift of incorruptible flesh and days without end; keep her as your mistress, and you surely die an inglorious death."

"Take her back," Louis pleaded while he knelt, moved by the maid's convincing act. "I beg forgiveness. Do not forsake me!"

To prevent an embarrassing scene, I prostrated myself at Lisette's feet. "If the Master calls, I answer. My soul belongs to Him alone."

"You must repent. When He Who Walks the Night deems you to be worthy, He will come for His bride. And you," she admonished, crouching low so her gaze met Louis' pained one, "go back to La Vallière for your pleasure, and Noctambule may yet reward the King of France."

Tears ran down Louis' cheeks. Whether they were shed for my sake or not, he did not say.

The consummate actor motioned for me to stand. Enjoying herself, Lisette grinned with unrestrained wickedness.

During the few days allowed us to prepare, my friend and I had practiced the same scene amidst hails of laughter; however, when the moment came for me to strip naked, I trembled.

"Astaroth and Asmodeus, I greet thee! Accept this, your humble servant, the Marquise de Cinq-Mars, who petitions the Princes of Friendship for absolution of her sins against the Great One."

Louis crossed himself and appeared to be praying. His devotions gave me the courage to see the Mass through. The gown presently lay rumpled on the floor and the pedestal awaited. Climbing atop the flat surface, I stretched out upon it, wearing nothing except for stockings and high-heeled pumps crafted from silk, crimson in hue.

"Astaroth and Asmodeus, Princes of Friendship, accept this sacrifice of human blood. Grant Bijoux, Marquise de Cinq-Mars, favor in the eyes of the Master, to be accepted back into His flock and to receive the kiss of Noctambule, the mark that would make her the most esteemed amongst women. May it please you to lead her with haste to her omnipotent bridegroom, sweet Princes of Friendship."

Whereas Guibourg had filled his chalice with blood, ours was brimming with wine. The desecrated wafers were naught but slices of stale bread, but the effect was the same.

"Hear this incantation, take delight in your servant, Bijoux Cinq-Mars, who drinks of the cruor in obedience to you."

Raising my head, I gulped hard. Lisette took the silver goblet away with great ceremony, placed the supposed sacrilege between my breasts and proceeded to pour the remaining claret on white skin. I could hear Louis gasp, although I did not look at the king.

"Astaroth and Asmodeus, your sacrament is now complete. True Princes of Friendship, look down upon your daughter, Bijoux, and find her worthy of this feast. Observe your handmaiden and find her pleasing. Accept her humble gift intended for the Great Spirits who have no peer."

The bell tinkled in closing.

Into the makeshift temple strode a well-built man, tall

and muscular, sporting little else besides a plumed headdress covering eyes and nose. Around his waist was cinched a wide leather belt supporting a large codpiece; otherwise the actor was naked. A gigantic peruke sent curls falling down a strong back, and large feet were bound with leather sandals of the ancient Roman variety. The intruder was a sight to behold, the personification of a fertility god of old.

"Lord Priapus, be praised!" Lisette intoned respectfully.

"I come with greetings from the Princes of Friendship."

"We are not worthy!" she fawned.

"I have been sent to ready the Chosen One. Lord Noctambule demands it."

"We are your obedient slaves," I recited along with the other woman. "Do what you will."

"Kneel, daemon brides!"

Doing as he ordered, I left the uncomfortable bed and joined Lisette on the floor.

"You do us honor," Des Oeillets encouraged, struggling with the buckle of Lord Priapus' harness. For effect, I reached out to aid her with the task.

"Do not touch me," the gentleman roared. "You are to remain virginal and incorrupt according to the Master's wishes. You," he snickered, grabbing Lisette's wild mane and bringing her mouth to within a hair's breadth of his private parts, "you will taste the nectar of the gods 'ere long!"

"Holy Jesu!" Louis moaned, "I cannot watch this!" Shielding his eyes, the king leapt to his feat and ran from the chamber of horrors, convinced, no doubt, that he was going straight to Hades.

The plan had worked. I should have been ecstatic. Instead, I was saddened.

"Madame, put this back on or else you will freeze to death."

"Thank you," I murmured, thoroughly detached as yards of taffeta slid over my head and the maid laced me into the outrageous mode. Half-dazed, I managed to say, "Lisette, you were magnificent. And you, too, Maupertuis. Thank you, both, for your assistance."

"Let us snuff out the candles and be gone," the marquis advised. "I fear the king's return."

"Take Madame Bijoux and go. Quickly, the lady is not herself."

Lisette was correct. The Mass, for all its theatrics, had left me strangely affected.

Lord Priapus took my hand, found a candle and made for the nearby cabinet in haste. The pair of lute players fled at the sight of the intimidating marquis. Paying them no heed, he leaned with force against a panel and that portion of the wall swung open as though on hinges. A steep and dark, hidden passageway led downwards; to where, my guide did not provide.

Treading with the stealth of Mademoiselle de Scudéry's lion cub, the noble porter walked down dangerous steps and presently fiddled with a latch that moved another section of wall located at the end of a short, narrow corridor. When we entered a brightly-lit room, I covered my eyes without thinking, almost blinded by the marked contrast from whence we had come.

"How did you find that route, dear Mestor?"

"Many of the rooms in the palace open onto similar galleries," he smiled at my use of his pet name. "Few people are aware of the fact, that is all. So here we are, safe and sound."

Maupertuis motioned towards a bedcover of white worked all over with silver thread, and I took his suggestion and sat. The hideous disguise came off and was thrown halfway across the room onto a blazing hearth, landing atop the logs with a spray of sparks.

"Would you care for a libation? he inquired, fetching a robe. "I plan to partake of one."

"Only one?" I quipped, beginning to feel at ease.

"Here is a unopened bottle of cognac, sweet Bijoux..."

"Marquise, " I corrected. "I am now your equal in rank."

"Forgive me, marquise. Shall we drink to your new station in life?"

"Let us be merry. Tonight we have much to celebrate."

The obliging host complied with alacrity. Bolting the door, he joined me on the pallet in no time, goblets and liquor in hand. What the marquis was doing was obvious: he meant to seduce me.

"You are subtle, monsieur."

"Call me Étienne, little sister."

"What?" I answered, coughing up a goodly portion of the golden liquid I had begun to swallow. "Tell me that is not your Christian name."

"Most assuredly, *chérie*. Does Priapus please you more, perhaps? I shall answer to either."

I laughed aloud, drinking quickly from the bulbous, metal cup. "Do you plan to be this charming when Lisette arrives, Étienne?"

"Ah, marquise, that impediment has been anticipated and attended to."

"Whatever do you mean?" The spirits tasted good, too good, and I found myself allowing Maupertuis the liberty of leaning his head against my own.

"Two of my associates have been engaged to collect Lisette, take her to the barracks and detain her there until I am able to liberate the poor child in the morning."

"You rogue! How did you know she would stay behind, to begin with?"

"She is a servant, is she not? It is in her nature, therefore, to serve."

I pulled away and reflected on his words while I reached for a refill.

"Slow down, marquise. You drink faster than a Templar!"

"Very funny. Do you love me, Mestor?" I teased.

"Shall I confess to wanting you, instead? What with your husband gone to Paris, and the king's advances no longer an issue, I deduce that you are open, to say, a mutually agreeable arrangement?"

His kiss of enticement was warm and inviting. The recent loss of Louis' love and César's banishment rendered the romantic overture more enticing. As did the dry brandy.

"If I were to entertain your suggestion, marquis, you would agree to my terms?"

"Anything, ask me anything."

"I shall grant you one night of happiness, no more. If you speak of our tryst to anyone at court, I shall deny it with my dying breath. And tomorrow, not only will you free Lisette, you will marry her."

"Wait," he recoiled. "I enjoy being a bachelor. Your demand is a cruel one."

"I am the Marquise de Sang-Mars, they say. I am a cruel woman." The second helping was near to gone. My head was heavy from the potent beverage; however, I was still able to speak effectively.

"God's blood, you are exasperating!" Maupertuis expounded. "The king will not allow a member of the nobility to wed a peasant…"

"Your title was purchased, no doubt, and Louis will grant his approval if I ask it of him. Certainly you must realize that. Besides, I wonder what other antics the king does not approve of?"

"You would not inform on me. I did you a service."

"*Moi?*" I laughed, quite out of my head. "Did I ask you to help me?"

"No, she did."

"Will Lisette make such a bad wife, Mestor?"

"No," he admitted, shaking his head. "No, she will not."

"Then come here," I smiled, responding to my baser instincts. "You know that you want to."

We gave each other pleasure, indulging in two additional bottles of wine during the course of that evening, our couplings frequent and furious. Both behaving with reckless abandon, inhibitions completely forgotten, our fervor was matched only by our daring. The physical exchange was that of two seasoned lovers who were ready to test the boundaries of convention, and who knew full well they would never touch again. Perhaps it was that fact or the fermented grape that inspired us, perhaps it was the Black Mass. Whatever the cause, the sky was turning from dark to light when we passed out in each other's arms, too weak to move, too drunk to care about anything other than sleep.

Maupertuis was roused near to noon when his faithful valet knocked from the outside world, politely suggesting that his master rise and unbolt the door. Sending the man away with a gruff refusal, he reached out for me instead, hauling my aching limbs atop his own.

"I should go," I offered, somewhat nonplussed by the intimate posture.

"No, not yet," was the answer I received. "Stay with me one more night. Just one."

"What of Lisette, what of our agreement…"

"You worry too much," the corporal noted before sliding his tongue into my mouth. Groping fingers squeezed at soft flesh and an insistent probing was completed, causing me to draw in a sharp breath prompted more out of relish than shock.

"Now, will you remain?" the marquis grinned as we began to move as one. "Do you truly wish this sultry interlude to end so abruptly?"

"One more night," I agreed, hating myself for giving in. "Then it must end."

The debauch was far from being finished; rather, my decline into depravity had merely begun.

Sunday, the second day of October, 1661, arrived and my apartment, with all its arcane trappings, beckoned. Leaving Maupertuis was not easy, for he was a most agreeable and exciting companion; yet, I could not be romantically linked to any gentleman following the drama enacted two nights prior. A self-imposed celibacy awaited me and I was glad of it; no more liaisons or affairs to clutter my mind and heart. All my energies were to be focused on being reunited with my husband and securing us a safe passage to our own personal Arcadia. Wherever that place existed, I was not able to say, though I imagined it to be out there, somewhere; a lovely promised land where César and I could live out our lives in peace, far from the intrigues of others.

The first test of my newfound conviction came sooner than expected. On the same afternoon, I sat at a desk decorated with pretty wood marquetry, writing Louis a petition concerning Maupertuis' marriage to my beloved Lisette, when a light rap sounded from the hallway beyond. Jumping a little in my seat, the unexpected announcement made me start. Could it be the king? Was Philippe home?

"*Entrez*," I said coolly, fanning the skirt of a scarlet gown about the legs of the *fauteuil* that supported my weight.

In stepped none other than the Comte Armand de Guiche. Dropping the pen I had been using, I stared at him, unable to imagine that the man who had insulted me at Saint-Mandé possessed the effrontery to seek an audience with his enemy.

"*Bonjour*," the snake hissed with practiced aplomb, silky smooth in his delivery. "You look lovelier than ever, gorgeous creature. Do I detect the bloom of indiscretion on your cheeks?"

"What do you want?" I asked abruptly, placing my elbows on the polished surface of inlay. Picking up the quill, I twirled the blunt end against two pursed lips.

"Why, nothing more than to bask in your pulchritude, marquise. It is marquise...is it not?"

"The Marquise de Sang-Mars," I quipped, dipping a sharpened tip into ink so I might finish the letter. Guiche was not there to exchange *bon mots*, so I was in no mood to be interrupted.

"Your humor is refreshing," Armand laughed with gusto. "Quite macabre. Yet, not quite as distorted as the command performance with which you entertained our king recently, I daresay."

"You are speaking out your backside," I said sweetly, paying him no heed whatsoever. "Your sources are quite misinformed. Besides, last I heard, *you* had been banished from court."

"Oh really? I have been recalled. Does the name Montalais ring a bell?"

"As far as I know, monsieur, that girl will say anything for a coin or two."

"Louise de la Vallière confides in her."

"Quite true. What of it? Both ladies are at Saint-Cloud with their mistress."

"Ah, then you did not hear tell of the king's unexpected journey yesterday to Vincennes and Paris, to inspect construction being done on his palaces, or his subsequent trip to Saint-Cloud where he supped in the evening with our darling Monsieur? He spoke with Mademoiselle Louise but briefly, yet converse the lovebirds did."

"The king traveled far in one day."

"I was at Saint-Cloud myself, making amends, you might say. Walking through the gardens with Madame, we spied, despite the shelter afforded by a secluded grotto, the king at the favourite's feet, begging her to forgive him for some offense. Naturally, we had to know what was going on, so Anne-Constance was consulted this morning and *voilà*! The truth is out! You are a very naughty marquise," he mocked, stepping closer.

"What did that intriguer tell you? I warned Louise to keep her own counsel!"

"Your secret is safe with me, lovely Bijoux. I did the same at Roissy."

"Did what, monsieur?"

"Dabbled in black magic."

"I want to know what was said. All of it, please."

Armand was pensive. "What do I get in the bargain?"

"Anything but my body."

"Your constant devotion?"

"If that is what you truly desire, yes."

"You would make an handsome accessory," he mused. "And no more pesky husband to get in the way, I hear. Relegated to bastard's exile, unfortunate fellow."

Silence was the most effective weapon I could muster against his taunts and slurs. To protest would be unseemly. I was no longer ashamed of César's background.

"The dutiful wife. Satanist and loving spouse. Is that not a contradiction in terms?"

Still no reply would I give the tormentor.

"Fine. I grant you the victory, marquise. You are much changed from the girl I met at Saint-Mandé." He stopped, considered his presentation for a moment, then continued. "Mademoiselle Montalais said that the king came to Saint-Cloud to assure La Vallière of his great passion for her and that he would gladly die rather than be parted from his mistress in the future. When the overjoyed girl pressed her liege as to what was the cause of the sudden and unexpected avowal, she was advised not to ask questions. Determined to win her admirer's confidence, Louise demanded an answer. An agitated confession revealed that the Marquise de Cinq-Mars, adept in matters of occult astrology, had consulted certain spirits during an elaborate casting of an astral scheme conducted on behalf of the throne. The phantoms from beyond predicted that France's present ruler would enjoy eternal glory should he align himself with the one woman in his realm who could be compared to the goddess Diana."

"Nothing else?"

"Is that not enough?" Guiche scoffed. "You, in league with the supernatural? Using sorcery and the stars to influence the course of our sovereign's affections? I must say, I am impressed with your methods, Madame Astrologer."

"My dear count, do I detect a hint of envy in your tone? Do not be jealous of my alleged powers, for I do not understand your meaning in the least."

"What say you?"

"First, the drivel concerning the goddess Diana. Is that meant to be a reference to Louise?"

"Of course. The king commissioned Monsieur le Febvre to paint La Vallière as the divine Mistress of the Hunt—everyone gossiped about the incident when it occurred."

"Before I came to court."

"True," he admitted, rubbing his chin. "You are correct."

"Would you like to know the truth, Guiche?" I inquired, standing up so abruptly that the chair I had been using fell over backwards onto the floor.

"The real story, Bijoux?"

"The real story, Armand."

Because Guiche had previously heard the name *Noctambule*, and had observed first hand the fear its mention had inspired, relating the tale of the *vrykolakas* was an easy thing to do. By the time the monologue was finished, the count stood wiping tears from my cheeks, fussing over me as he would his sister, the Princess of Monaco. Although I had been hitherto ignorant of Armand's gallant nature, the usually cynical courtier became as a chivalrous knight of old, honor-bound to defend a lady against the combined horrors of Louis' mission to become immortal paired with the *vampyre's* threat to make me his bride.

"My sensitive beauty," he sighed, holding me against a brocade lapel, "what you require is a friend, a champion. A man of experience, such as myself, to rely upon."

"I have no one," I admitted between sobs. "No one to help me. Perhaps M. d'Artagnan, yet he is off in Angers guarding Fouquet, the only other person who could have come to my aid."

"D'Artagnan and I are the greatest of friends. If you are dear to him, then accordingly, you are dearer to me for it. Come, stop crying. I shall protect you—I want to—do you doubt me?"

"*You?*" I looked up at him, not believing my ears.

"*Moi*," Guiche confirmed. "You must be introduced to my other friends here at court. Whom do you know?"

"Monsieur, Louise, Maupertuis; that is all."

"Monsieur is a valuable ally. The other two, please..." he drawled with an exaggerated flourish of one hand. "Louise was stupid enough to reject *me* and Maupertuis is beneath you."

"You think so? Truly?" I giggled, a sordid image coming to mind.

"Yes," he said, convinced. "You are regal, close to Minette in bearing. She is as ice, you are as fire; did I not say you belonged to me more than you cared to admit?"

Armand was, and still is, an extremely persuasive gentleman. When his thin, pretty lips alighted on those he wished to taste, it took all my determination to withdraw from him rapidly, else I would have been in trouble. The bedchamber was too close by for flirtation.

"I cannot be your lover," was the apology I offered. "Louis cannot suspect me of misconduct with any man, or else the Mass was a waste. This is not a game, Armand. It is a serious business."

"True, we cannot have you going the way of your father," he smiled, showing off his high cheekbones to perfection. "Later, when night falls, I shall escort you to the gaming salon and teach you to play *hoca*. I have a feeling that your bad luck at love, Bijoux, may make you fortunate at the tables."

"My wagers, to date have not been especially successful."

"No matter! I predict that you will become a fantastic gambler. Perhaps we could devise a system whereby we could assist one another in winning enormous sums. Perhaps..."

"Do you always scheme and wheedle with such fervor?" I chuckled, amused by Guiche.

"Only when inspired. And I do thank you for that," he replied, kissing my hand with respect. "We shall make a great team, you and I. Bloody marquise and corrupt count. How droll!"

"I look forward to a long and fruitful association, *chér* Armand," came a returned compliment and a curtsey. "Never did I expect to find a friend in you."

"And I did not expect to find a devil in you. Tell me, your engaging tale of Noctambule, it is a contrivance, is it not?" he concluded with a knowing wink.

"Go to Versailles and discover the answer for yourself."

The challenge appealed to the count. Departing with a swagger and a grin, his farewell consisted of three simple words, a trio which caused me the gravest foreboding: "Marquise, *j'accepte*."

Marquise, I accept.

What I truly feared was that if any one person might locate the King of the Undead, that person would be the intrepid and dissolute Guiche.

Although Louis refused to speak to me and would barely look my way when he was forced, on occasion, to doff his hat when our paths sometimes crossed, I became the latest sensation at court. Amongst an idle group of boring noblepersons, the Marquise de Sang-Mars stood out in sharp contrast; red skirts and hair seen flying in the glow of torch and candlelight, a reputation for hosting late night revelries in her peculiar salon, and a taste for flirting with the more dangerous elements of life.

That I had found a constant companion in Guiche did not hurt my popularity, either, for the count was much sought after by his fellow peers and through him, I was introduced to those who constituted the smart set in France. Courted and pursued by important men and women alike, I maintained an air of disdain for all except Armand, who was becoming dearer to me than I cared to admit; the one who brought out the wildest side of my character. Staying up until three or four in the morning, we would drink and carouse until the Sun appeared, which was the warning signal to retire. More often than not, Guiche accompanied me to my bed and would sleep at my side, content to be near to his evil shadow, more comfortable in my company than he was when alone.

The king may not have said much concerning my daring new lifestyle, yet he was thinking plenty. By the close of the third week in October, a letter was delivered to my quarters; an urgent plea from a desperate lover that did not leave me unaffected:

Madame - A misery has taken hold of my spirit since we last parted, a great sadness which has not gone unnoticed by my friends, whose ceaseless inquiries drive me mad! These same gentleman say that you, marquise, are a pitiless woman who cares for naught but gaming, drink and augury, yet I know differently, for I alone know how you love when so disposed. That memory of our shared passion is killing me. Stop this cruel mockery and come to me this night. I beseech you in the name of all that is Holy to relent or else deny him whose heart breaks for you alone. L B.

Not sure how to reply, I presented the note to Guiche. Naturally, he mocked the contents of the *billet doux*, unimpressed with Louis' paean to amour.

"He writes no better than would a peasant!" the suave courtier commented. "Certainly you are not considering the proposal, are you?"

"Perhaps. What would you do, brother Everes?" I asked him by his Greek name of legend.

"Well, to begin, I would pull down the king's breeches, Princess Comaetho!"

"Armand! I need your advice. Louis is not accustomed to rejection."

"We must frighten him, darling, or else he will persist in thinking that he is outfoxing Noctambule. What an insolent young man our king is," he said with sarcasm, using the identical voice assumed at Saint-Mandé when pretending to be the *vrykolakas*.

"You do not have that much nerve!"

"Watch. Go to Louis' quarters near to the hour of midnight. I shall lie in wait, on a ledge outside one of the bedchamber windows. When his Majesty begins to make love to you, I shall appear, dressed as your daemon, stinking of sulfur and uttering curses. He will not bother you again."

"Thank you, Armand."

"All that I demand is a kiss for my services, marquise."

We were lounging side-by-side on a settee watching the bright, afternoon light pale and turn into dusk. Resting my head on Guiche's shoulder, I tried to look gay, though the posture was unconvincing.

"Why the melancholy, sweet thing?"

"I cannot say," I answered, shrugging my shoulders. "Ennui, I suppose. Or perhaps the knowledge that our stars say we are unsuited to be true companions, for you are a son of the Scales and I am a child of the Virgin."

"No, you miscalculate. Recast the scopes!" the count expounded. Standing, he scooped me up and twirled around the room in circles while he held me, causing me to squeal for him to stop. 'Round and 'round we went, eventually entering the boudoir where we landed on the mattress meant to cushion a king.

"Say you belong to me, wild Comaetho. Say it," he insisted.

"Armand, you are my friend. Madame returns tomorrow, chase after her."

"You are the one for whom I long," he said unexpectedly. "Not Minette and not Philippe."

"Do not speak of your relationship with Monsieur. How unseemly in my presence."

"I wish we could marry," he sighed. "We are so alike, so perfect for one another."

"Everes, you are becoming sentimental," I warned. Leaping to my feet, I fetched our matching silver cups, filled them with wine and gave one of the drinking vessels to the count.

"Let us propose a toast to our nocturnal friend. I cannot wait to see the look on Louis' face when Noctambule shows up, my handsome devil. The king should be terrified."

"You will come to my apartments when the deed is done. We shall sup late, then go throw the dice. If we win, you stay with me, if we loose, I stay with you."

"No, I sleep here. Always."

"Not tonight," he grinned. "Not tonight."

And then he kissed me and kissed me until I thought I would swoon from lust for him.

Thus we tarried until eleven. Brazen from the fair amount of spirits I had consumed, the march to Louis' pavilion was an easy accomplishment, although I bounced off the walls more than once on the way. Ushered in past the Guard by a Gentleman of the Chamber, Monsieur de Mesves, I was led by the important courtier into a vast salon that served as the king's official place of rest. Left there by myself, my gaze rested on the drapes of the canopy enclosing the colossal bed. They were of such ornate beauty that the heavy folds of fabric, combined with the overall splendor of the residence, caused me to lose confidence in the presence of such grandeur and majesty.

"Bijoux," a male voice called out and I started, for I knew that it belonged to Louis.

"Sire," I said as I knelt, afraid to look at him.

"Good God, how I have yearned for you." Dropping to his knees beside me, I was embraced by the young man who continued to move me, no matter how fervently I denied the fact. Unable to control my emotions, I clutched at the one who would be a part of me forever, and was shocked to hear real, unrehearsed sobs escape.

"There, there, all is not lost," Louis soothed, kissing my brow. "I have devised a plan to silence Monsieur Noctambule. He will not have you, do not fear."

"I am damned, cursed, sire. Forget me."

"If you are part monster, then so am I. Your tainted blood saved my life, remember? No more talk of such things, though; say that you love me."

"I adore you," I said, kissing him deeply, as if in parting. "For all eternity."

"And Guiche?" he murmured, caressing my body with impatience.

"We are allies, nothing more. You know I give myself to no one."

"You are mine," Louis insisted. "You will give yourself to me. Enough concerning Noctambule! I defy his hellish edict!"

I was pushed backwards, none too gently, onto the shiny, wood floor. The king climbed atop my prone figure, pushing layer upon layer of gossamer towards the sky. The skirts piled higher and higher; soon I could barely see my lover's dark curls.

"Stop wearing these damnable red dresses," he groaned. "God, I hate the sight of them."

"Sire, our coupling is forbidden."

Louis' answer to that admonition was to enter me with a vengeance, fully clothed in his regalia, lace, hair and waistcoated torso landing atop my own, crushing me beneath the substantial weight of his fit body. *Where is Guiche?* I wondered frantically to myself. Was he passed out, drunk, upstairs?

"I want to get you with child tonight," the king declared and pushed with increased force. "You will bear my sons."

To protest was futile; however, no comment was necessary. From a nearby bay of balcony windows, I heard a rustle, then a smashing noise—Guiche had arrived.

"Unhand my queen!" the sound of a booming rage insisted. "Did I not warn you, pompous mortal!"

There stood Armand, having entered the room through a large, glass-paned door. Hunched over, dressed as an old man, his yellow-white wig, strategically placed mole on the forehead, and sack containing tablets on his back was very convincing: Noctambule lived.

"Are you deaf, as well as dumb?" Guiche thundered, then limped forward two steps, shaking a gnarly stick in the air. "Unhand my bride or you die a pained and horrific death!"

Louis inched off my person very slowly, unable take his astonished gaze from the apparition for a moment. Adjusting his breeches, he moved to stand, but the king was checked in his action by the furious *vrykolakas*.

"Kneel before your better, impertinent one! You are not fit to kiss my feet."

The daemonic laughter began. Neither I, nor my companion, said a word. Guiche's copy was too good, too ethereal for comfort. When I reached out for Louis' hand, he pulled from my touch.

"Much better. You are learning. I see all, remember *that*, King of the Franks!"

A miniature explosion then occurred, sending puffs of smoke and a foul-smelling stench into the air. The clouds eventually settled and Noctambule had vanished. Louis and I were alone.

"Do you finally believe?" I whispered.

The king stared at the strips of parquet joined to form a pattern beneath us. "I must think, marquise. Leave me be. Return to your apartment."

"Please, Majesty, do not forsake me! I have need of you."

"Find Guiche. Gamble away some more of my money. Leave me in peace."

"Give my regards to Mademoiselle de la Vallière on the morrow," I hissed. "Should you decide to move her into my apartments, I shall be more than happy to prove accommodating, sire."

"Get out," Louis snapped. He stood up and pulled me roughly to my feet. "Now, madame."

"Good-bye. For all time, then."

He turned his back to me, most probably because he feared showing his hurt in my presence. "We are one," he managed to say, at last. "Nothing in the universe will change that, for all time."

I ran out, heels barely clicking against the smooth surface upon which they tread. Guiche's suite of rooms was not far. There I would find good food, hospitality and wine. The anticipation of more forbidden kisses was especially appealing.

Later, the dice fell. The *hoca* board with its thirty numbered squares was half filled by Guiche's and my joint markers. We won the roll and the rules of the game demanded we be paid twenty-eight times the amount of our stake of three gold *louis d'or*. The count graciously accepted the payment, then led me away, quite tipsy, to his apartments. Gambling was no longer on his mind, for he had proved the victor, winning more than a tilt with Fate. He had beaten the social odds, humiliating a king and gaining a mistress; the money did not matter to Armand, the feeling of superiority all important.

Lying naked together on sheets of silk, abandoning my senses to Armand's expert lovemaking, I surrendered to vice and lost any dignity I still possessed. Drunk and in love with the count's devious character, I gave my body to a partner who was only too delighted to aid in the final corruption. I was an adulteress and he did not care; a sot and he was enchanted; a wicked person and he loved me all the more for it. Evil did not repel Guiche—he embraced debauchery gladly—had he not come to me, seeking me out, eager to promote a fellow sinner?

The days of the Luxembourg and playing spy outside Choisy's cabinet seemed far away indeed, too far, in fact, as Guiche bit me on a shoulder. Breaking the skin, drawing blood to the surface, he licked at it with relish, commenting, "Our covenant is ratified. You belong to me."

"I must taste of your life force as well, my love. Then the pact will be sealed."

"Soon," he said, clenching his teeth together, usually smooth features contorted. "The offering which I give you must be hallowed…Bijoux…"

"I love you, Armand. More than life."

"We shall both be reborn," he vowed aloud. "You and I, together."

Awakening later in a shadow-filled chamber, I gazed upon the count's sleeping form. Because neither of us wore bedclothes and the blankets were strewn about, I collected a coverlet and placed it over our bodies for warmth. Opening his eyes, Guiche regarded me with a blank stare, reaching out when he was certain who was lying next to him.

"Come closer," he said dreamily. "Tell me more about that day at Versailles."

Curling up to Armand, I noticed that a corner of his mouth was caked with a smattering of dried blood. Mine. Rather than become ill at the sight, I licked at his lips, removing the spot.

"You are a sorceress," he declared. "And your spell is powerful, marquise."

He was my Guibourg; I, his Marion. How else am I able to sit here, from this confine, and explain our shared attraction otherwise?

Poor Guiche, know that I pray for you often, should you happen to care, for I do believe that some goodness resides in your being.

That is all I shall write at present, sorrowful as I am.

This day marks my three hundred and thirty-third spent in the Bastille.

Less than a year, greater than ten months. I have maintained a count of the passage of time since I was arrested, scratching a tiny line with a diamond on my looking glass every morning I awake in prison. Any hope I may have had of Louis releasing me in the near future has been forsaken. He will keep me in prison for life or else send me to the block. Too much ill will has transpired between us and our families to consider the possibility of a pardon.

Because I do not know how much longer I shall be left in jail, or alive for that matter, and having received no communication from anyone with whom I was well acquainted—César, d'Artagnan, Guiche and the lot—I am compelled to finish this personal history with some haste. To whom I shall will the text, I have no notion, although should I be moved without warning, then the manuscript will most probably fall into the hands of greedy Monsieur Besmeaux, d'Artagnan's friend and aforementioned governor of this stone fortress which also holds Fouquet. Considering what woe has befallen the latter gentleman, I should be grateful to Louis for keeping me holed-up in Paris. The circumstances could be worse.

To continue the narrative, Philippe and his company returned to Fontainebleau, and the prince was transported with glee to find that he, Guiche and the marquise might all become friends. Louise was courted by the king and given the name *Clarice* by the poets, Henriette complained of her difficult pregnancy whenever a pang inspired a swoon, and my husband continued in his state of banishment, writing me strange and mysterious messages.

Madly in love with the virile Guiche, I tried not to remember César, and drank more wine. Often greeting the morn with my head in a chamber pot, neither Monsieur nor the count seemed to mind, escorting me to whatever bed was available, their sole concern being that the marquise might prove too ill to romp again at sunset. However, I did not disappoint and would rally consistently with the twinkling of the stars, especially energetic if Armand had paid me a private visit in order to bolster my spirits. We could not get enough of one another, he and I; constantly heated when together, it took everything in our power not to betray our feelings to a watchful court. Cunning eyes constantly scrutinized, yet we were so brazen that most thought us to be merely fellow libertines, not lovers.

The Sun was at its apex in the sky on Tuesday, November 1, 1661, when Marie-Thérèse gave birth to a son, the Dauphin Louis Toussaint, and France erupted into a wild burst of celebration. The king was the proudest father alive, showing off the newborn to a cheering multitude gathered in the great courtyard of Fontainebleau, holding the baby aloft for all to see. Louis had his heir and the Spanish Infanta was truly queen of her adopted land, having provided her husband with the precious gift of life. Relieved that the royal spouse was alive and safely delivered, I sought out Nabo and kept him company, glad to be there when he asked me why Maria Beresa no longer loved him.

Explaining to my little Antiochus that his lady had been near to death and could see no one, I failed to mention that the king had decreed the blackamoor not be allowed in his son's company, for Louis was convinced that the dark foreigner would place a cast upon the babe. Between cheering Nabo and drying a sensitive Louise de la Vallière's pitiful tears, I was quite exhausted by the end of the three day jubilation, falling onto my mattress clothed, desirous only of a full night's sleep. When I was snatched from the arms of Morpheus one hour later by my smiling fiend, who was feeling quite neglected by his mistress, I could barely wrap my arms about Guiche's neck, I was that spent.

The Marquis de Maupertuis and Mademoiselle des Oeillets were wed at the Tuileries on the twenty-third day of the eleventh month, 1661. Louis XIV had granted the pair permission to marry in light of my request as well as in observance of his namesake's arrival. Feeling magnanimous, the sovereign had approved many such petitions; however, one name received no conciliatory sign from the throne: Fouquet. The newlyweds, Etienne and Lisette, were given little opportunity to enjoy the pleasures of the marriage bed due to the king's hatred of that particular prisoner; not a week had gone by and the couple were parted, Maupertuis sent to Anger to assist d'Artagnan with the transfer of the celebrated financier from a run-down château to a cell in Amboise.

Back with the court in Paris for the winter, I listened to the happy bride chatter and thought of my own husband. Because the king and his wife were off, traveling to Chartres on a pilgrimage of thanksgiving for the heir, I contacted César by messenger and we were at last able to meet clandestinely at St. Sulpice. Unsure of what I was going to say to my husband, the close of November found Guiche and myself riding in the count's carriage to the church, more solemn than if we had been on our way to attending a funeral mass.

"You need not feel honor-bound to do this thing," Armand commented as our transport parked on the Rue de Vaugirard. "Let us return to the Tuileries, Bijoux."

"I must tell him good-bye. César should know I am not worthy to be called his wife."

"Darling, halt there. You are wonderful, magnificent..."

"No, Guiche, you desist. I am naught but a drunkard and little better than a whore. That I am your wastrel makes no difference. I am what I am: a wanton Cinq-Mars."

"Should I accompany you inside?"

"This won't take long. Please wait here for my return."

Outside, the cold preview of a December wind whipped down the street, dramatically blowing a black velvet cloak and scads of rosy Venetian damask up into the air. Guiche leaned out of the coach and caught me by the arm, holding me back, although I was ready to go forward.

"Without you, I am nothing. Do not forget that you are coming back to me."

"We are two of a kind, insofar as my Mercury in Libra conjucts your Sun. My mind matches your exterior form. I need no reminding of that."

"Good. Be quick. I shall be here, anxiously awaiting the woman I love."

I froze, rooted to the cobblestones. The count loved me! Or was he playing the cad?

Making for the headquarters of the Company that had been built atop a goddess' ancient shrine, it hurt deeply to admit that all my lofty resolutions had fallen by the wayside and that I must bid César *adieu*. Whether Guiche wanted me or not, whether I could depend on the king's continued interest in his unruly marquise, whether any man in the world desired me did not matter, for I had failed him who had placed his entire trust in my hands. My husband was going to be better off without me, I told myself as I approached the last pew on the left, far better off indeed.

César was seated, waiting patiently, wearing the same outfit he had worn to our wedding more than three years earlier. He had not seen me approach him from behind, so when he heard a footstep, he jumped up from the bench and went straight for the sword hanging at his hip. Spinning about as if to defend his person against possible attack, he saw me and exhaled with relief.

"Hello," he said as he walked with arms outstretched, too comely to describe. "Will the Marquise de Sang-Mars not embrace her ardent suitor?"

Ashamed, I could not behold him. Staring instead at my gloved hands, speech failed me.

"Bijoux, what ails you?" César chuckled. "Do you not wish to hold me?"

"No," I replied. "Your absence from court has allowed me the leisure to meditate on the state of our marriage. If you were wise, you would renounce the communality of possessions between us and seek a legal separation. Your brother should be able to buy you a papal dispensation."

"What has happened? Have you gone mad?"

"I could ask the same of you, monsieur. Strange letters, cryptic messages; what say you to that?"

"I say this: I love you. What of our plans, our dreams for the future? You know what was being said in those notes I had smuggled to you. Do not play games with me."

"César, I have a new life, new friends at court. The Company no longer interests me."

"You cannot stop being a Bouillon merely because you wish it! Have you abandoned your goddess Athena, too?"

"I am a Cinq-Mars. The Marquise de Cinq-Mars."

"You, madame, are Bijoux de la Tour d'Auvergne, my wife! You are a learned lady! Marquise," he spit on the floor, "what is a marquise other than some borrowed title the bastard gave you! My mother was a princess!"

"Yes, a princess who did not marry her lover and whose son, as a consequence, is no prince or duke yet as much a bastard as the one he delights in calling the same and who probably is not!"

"Why do you defend the king?" César laid hold of an exposed elbow and marched me down the center aisle towards the cathedral altar, pausing at the steps leading to the latter. "We were married here, recall? In Athena's sight. Does that mean nothing to you?"

"If I believed it would. What is the point?"

"This." Taking my face in his hands, not allowing me to avoid his heavenly gaze, the sincere man kissed me lightly on the lips. "Love, Bijoux. Or have you truly gone over to the dark side?"

"I am not a good person, César. And you are. Find a wife more suited to your nature. You have heard the rumors about me since you have been away."

"Yes, what of them? You wrote and warned me in advance, you said to ignore the lies..."

"The lies are true. The daemon worship, the drinking, the gambling."

"I also hear that for all your unscrupulous behavior, you refuse to take a lover. Some say that you are saving yourself for Lucifer himself."

"The court gossips flatter me," a male voice, Guiche's voice, proclaimed. Armand was striding towards us, *epée* drawn, a sacrilege to commit within the hallowed walls of worship. César reached for his blade; however, his virtuous spirit would not allow him to remove steel from its scabbard.

"What is he doing here?" César asked me.

"Bijoux, go back to the coach. Now," Guiche ordered.

"Is he the cause of your confusion? Him?"

"No. We are confidants, Guiche and I."

"She is mine, de la Tour," the count declared, taking me away from his competitor, "leave her be. A bastard Bouillon has no right to touch a woman as noble as my beautiful marquise."

That remark pushed César over the edge. Frédéric-Maurice's rapier flashed into sight. "Bijoux is my wife and *you*, Guiche, are the bastard. Being a man of principle, I say we allow the lady to decide. Is that agreeable to you, monsieur?"

"Most agreeable, de la Tour."

"Bijoux, the choice is yours. Is it the Hôtel Bouillon or the Tuileries?"

Going to my husband's side, I kissed him with tenderness. "I love you with all the integrity remaining in my tainted heart," I whispered, "yet I must return to court. You have been more than forbearing with this wayward wife and she thanks you, kind and gentle sir."

Without waiting for a reply, I ran from the sanctuary and did not stop until I was back at the carriage door. Helped inside the vehicle by one of the attendant lackeys, I threw myself up against Armand when he entered moments later.

"Hold me," I begged, "please."

"I must be rid of that man," Guiche remarked quietly, as though to himself. "He is a nuisance."

I made no comment. However, I did decide, then and there, that no harm would come to my spouse because of my actions. The count was not more precious to me than was César. I was convinced that the dashing nobleman would not lay a finger on the man whom I had married because I knew that, if he tried, I definitely possessed the resolve to poison Guiche myself.

CHAPTER TWENTY
A Grand Design

Too much drink is capable of doing terrible things to a person; perhaps that is why the first three months of the year 1662 are a blur in retrospect. Kept at a safe distance by the king, adored privately by either Guiche or Monsieur, and disliked publicly by most of polite society, wine became my refuge from the performing of life's responsibilities.

How I managed to survive the endless bouts of merriment I cannot say. What I have retained from that period, however, are these few highlights: Philippe and his household moving to the Palais Royal in January when Louis gifted the residence to his brother; La Vallière running away in February to a convent from which she was personally retrieved by the king; Madame producing a daughter in March and Guiche receiving a military appointment soon after which sent him to Lorraine; Godefroy-Maurice's arranged marriage to Mazarin's niece and Susanne du Plessis' return to court, both in early April.

The winter of sixty-two had been extremely harsh and spring was on its way, personified by the brilliant smile of my friend when she appeared unexpectedly on the threshold of the new salon Philippe had assigned me in Richelieu's old home. In fact, the workmen were so busy tacking yards of black sateen to the walls, I did not hear the marquise call my name; the din of their hammers was that loud.

"Quite dramatic, madame. Your decoration is elegant, although a tad bizarre for my taste."

I glanced casually over one shoulder to see who had come to call. Absorbed with the carpenters' progress, the intrusion of some court busybody was annoying.

"When discussing matters of taste, surely, who should comment?" I shifted my gaze for a moment. "*Mon Dieu!*" I exclaimed when I saw who had been so bold as to question the décor.

"Hello, my darling girl," Susanne replied with a grin and walked back into my life.

We melded for a long pause, laughing and crying all at once. Fouquet's brilliant mistress had been recalled to Paris from Charenton, yet, I had been given no advance notice.

"How did this happen? When? Did Louis set you free?"

"Drag yourself away from this commotion and let us speak candidly," she advised and led me from the noisy scene. We strolled arm-in-arm to the downstairs courtyard of the Palais Royal; a huge, rectangle of a garden and a busy center of activity in the capital.

"Have you any word of Nicolas," Susanne ventured as we stepped outside, "anything?"

"He was taken from Amboise to Vincennes last December and only d'Artagnan may converse with the prisoner."

"Yes, I heard as much. Did you know that my love's hair has turned completely white? Do you believe it?" she sighed. "The commissaries may be interrogating him now, as we speak; I shudder to think. But he will fight back, Bijoux. The Company is working on his defense and have begun a campaign to rally the people to Nicolas' side."

"Public opinion is not exactly running in Lord Cléonime's favor, Susanne. The people love the king and hate Fouquet— many wish to see him die for his offenses to the Crown."

"The masses are a fickle lot," the worldly woman replied. "Wait and see."

Many of Monsieur's retainers were outside promenading in the vast courtyard, enjoying the warm zephyrs, so we walked on in silence for propriety's sake. Not until we were afforded some privacy by stepping behind a pillar, one of the many supporting the roofed corridors running alongside the parameters of the park, did the Marquise du Plessis explain her unexpected appearance.

"Bijoux," she began, "the king is concerned for your welfare. He sent for me personally so I might talk some sense into you. You are very dear to him, you know."

"Oh, so you are here doing Louis' bidding? That must be a bitter medicine to swallow."

"Do not be cross with me, darling. Our sovereign loves you. Desperately. For me, for Nicolas, give up your bad habits and please his Majesty. Eschew your obsession with the occult and the carousing with Monsieur and his friends. You are too intelligent to act so stupidly."

"Did you ever stop to consider," I countered, "that a method may underlie my madness? That being named a woman of ill repute is no great disgrace if that label saves me from a worse fate?"

"Bijoux, what? What could be so terrible?"

"Leave me alone! Just leave me alone!"

"No," she insisted, "no." A finger was shaking in my face and I turned my head away. "I love you like a daughter, damn it! And look at you. Wine on your breath, hair loose, hanging about with that reprobate, Guiche! Did he and those other sodomites do this to you? Have you no pride?"

"I love Armand and he loves me! What do you know? Keep to your own affairs, traitor!"

And with that heated remark, Susanne, the Marquise du Plessis, hit her closest confidante Bijoux, the Marquise de Cinq-Mars, with such a blow to the jaw that the younger noblewoman's head slammed solidly against the marble column against which she had been leaning her sanguine self.

She had struck me! Before an audience! Such were my initial thoughts as I teetered on high heels, trying to catch my balance.

"You are not too big for a thrashing, young lady," Susanne began to holler.

"The king wishes to make me his *maîtresse déclarée*, he wishes for me to bear his bastards. He dreams that we shall live happily together at Versailles...and...Susanne...I cannot," I began to gasp, "I cannot do that, neither for my sake nor for the sake of France. Fouquet will not be saved, no matter what I decide; tell the Company *that* on my behalf."

"What do you mean?"

"Louis knows the *Secret*!" I said under my breath, loudly enough for her alone to hear. "He knows everything. Fouquet will never leave prison after having financed the usurpers for years."

"And how did the Bourbon discover the truth, Bijoux?"

"Through my father's indiscretion. On his way to the block, Monsieur le Grand was shown the torture chamber and he told Richelieu's agents the story of the Lost King in order to be spared mutilation. Mazarin wrote of the incident in his diaries," I lied, "and the king found the entry while searching for information concerning Cinq-Mars' guilt."

"Damn! Guise and the others must be alerted. Does César know the truth?"

"No," I shook my head. "No one but you."

"Keep those conspicuous dresses of yours for a while longer, my dear. The streets of Paris may yet run red with blood."

What filled me with dread, more than the implied threat, was the knowledge that often words inspire deeds and that soon we might all be placed in peril. Another civil war, another Fronde, was close to erupting and I was powerless to stop the madness. More killing, more violence—would we never learn from the past—I wondered sadly? Was gaining a throne worth the deaths it would cost? Leaning on my friend, I could say nothing.

For I had invited Amphitryon to Taphos, and any ensuing carnage would be upon my head.

Susanne stayed on at court and for her sake, I did mend my ways. With Guiche gone away, the urge to behave badly gradually dissipated and the king noticed the change in my person with unreserved delight. Louis paid me court on several occasions in the form of notes and trinkets, but always the reply he received was the same: no. I may have redecorated my salon in pastel shades and forgone the vivid Sang-Mars skirts, however, the transformation did not include my becoming the royal mistress and Noctambule was cited as the cause.

That reminder appeared to be effective, for although Louis continued to flirt shamelessly with his marquise when we were thrown together during informal functions, he did not demand more than polite banter from our relationship. Which was a good thing because I was acutely lonely and may have succumbed to stronger language. César was unapproachable and Guiche had forgotten about me altogether. The latter gentleman had taken to worshipping Henriette from afar and I must admit that, when I heard the avowal from Louise de la Vallière's innocent lips, the news made me rage with jealousy. Armand had tired of me and that betrayal hurt. Yet, considering the pain I had caused César, the repayment was just.

Left to socializing with my good-for-nothing rascal, Philippe, I made the acquaintance of Athénaïs de Mortemart, who was Prince Tyrannus' favorite partner at cards and a lady of scathing wit. Since we were destined to meet sooner or later, I introduced myself to she who was rumored to have her sights set on becoming the king's next mistress. Athénaïs was more than happy to chitchat with the Marquise de Cinq-Mars, especially since she wished to ask my advice on winning Louis' heart. When I feigned ignorance on that topic, she displayed scorn; I jested that a love potion might do the trick. She eyed me with suspicion, then asked if I was familiar with the name La Voisin. Unable to hide my surprise, I admitted that I was.

"Well," de Mortemart confided, "her powders may be strong and highly effective, although Olympe de Soissons swears by the *Messe Noir* for the granting of favors. The comtesse claims that a certain Guibourg, an associate of La Voisin's, will perform the rite for a goodly sum. Would you know this priest from the priory of Bois-Courtilz, marquise?"

Athénaïs' unintentional disclosure haunted me for many

uneasy nights thereafter. Guibourg, in league with La Voisin! I did possess the good sense to immediately seek out Lisette and inform her of the abbé's whereabouts. Maupertuis decided to ride off to Marseilles in search of his mother-in-law. Yet what the marquis discovered in that southern port was not Madame des Oeillets' person; rather, her grave. According to those who lived next door to the deceased's successful brothel, the enterprising woman had died unexpectedly one evening while drinking with her patrons to the Dauphin's health. In the midst of the revels, the usually healthy lady crashed to the floor and expired instantly, no doubt the victim of apoplexy.

Unsure of what to do with madame's eleven-year-old daughter, Justine, the neighbors were thrilled when a kindly, one-eyed priest appeared on the morn following the tragedy, offering to care for the child. A miracle had arrived in the form of the abbé, whose name no informant could recall, but who was of such good character that he could be trusted with an orphan's upbringing. The little ward and her guardian had set out for Paris several days and many trunks later, singing songs and playing the Noble Game of the Goose.

Guibourg obviously had plans for his illegitimate offspring, and he had undoubtedly collected what jewels, if any, remained in his victim's house. Lisette and I were determined to find her sister and forcibly remove her from the abbé's care; however, when Maupertuis and a band of his fellow Musketeers ventured to the Rue St. Denis to rescue Justine, the house had been deserted by the renegade priest. No one at the priory of Bois-Courtilz knew what had become of Guibourg, either, for he had disappeared six months earlier for parts unknown.

La Voisin, when questioned by Lisette and myself, swore she had never met a one-eyed cleric in her life. My friend's frustration and grief at loosing both her mother and the sibling was vented in angry tears while we stood on the sorceress' steps at twenty-five Rue Beaurégard. Vowing revenge, I shook my fist at the daemon worshipper and swore I would see both she and Guibourg hang. Catherine Montvoisin, secure in her powerful connections at court, slammed the door in my face. Yet before she did, the fraudulent fortune-teller touched my hair and smirked in an odd way. "You must be the one of whom I have heard many tales, the stargazer whom the ladies call Sang-Mars. I see Satan's mark on you," she howled with malicious intent and went inside, unafraid of Noctambule's bride.

The arrival of summer prompted Olympe de Soissons to sponsor one of Marie-Thérèse's ladies-in-waiting, Anne-Lucie de la Mothe-Houdancourt, as her personal entry in the ongoing court contest of choosing the king's next mistress. The moment Monsieur, Madame and Louise de la Vallière left Paris for Saint-Cloud in July, Louis repaired to St. Germain and accepted the comtesse's challenge with relish. Anne-Lucie was written impassioned letters, sent expensive gifts, and chased about the palace flower beds. I merely heard of the escapade, since the Marquise du Plessis and I had been ordered to Charenton for a rest. The sight of me made the Sun King uneasy, and since my body was off-limits to the sovereign, my continued presence in the halls of power was deemed highly unnecessary since stars paled in the light of solar rays.

Which was not an unwelcome development. Susanne's hôtel was lovely and the break from formality was welcomed. Encouraged by my friend, I developed an interest in Fouquet's impending trial and she and I would sit in her stately library for hours together, discussing what defense Nicolas should pursue. The once powerful surintendant was allowed a lawyer in September of 1662 when the formal charges of usury, embezzlement, fraud and plotting insurrection were finally drawn-up against him one year following the arrest at Nantes. D'Artagnan remained the sole jailer and communicant, although the sous-lieutenant did arrange for two confessors to administer to the number-one-prisoner-of-state and most dangerous man in the realm.

Louis may have thought himself in control of destiny following his rejection of Anne-Lucie and a reconciliation with La Vallière, whereupon the reunited pair made frequent jaunts to Versailles to hunt and inspect the work being done to the château, yet all was not well. Popular sentiment had begun to turn in Fouquet's favor, and Susanne took to hosting secret meetings at Charenton where high-ranking officials of the Company would convene to discuss the Future's dilemma. César and his half-brother were not included in that group—much to my chagrin—although an anonymous Englishman, a close friend of Robert Boyle, was. The mention of that name caused me to start, stop and wonder. The covert faction was gaining strength, and its membership was plotting a coup against the throne.

Susanne held an intimate salon gathering during the 1663 Carnival season, a small social for her closest friends. Afraid to attract too much attention to her actions, the marquise was all the same starved for some gaiety, unlike her companion, Bijoux. The profound disappointments of the past year had not left me with much hope for the future or in a mood to make merry. In an effort to cheer me, the kind lady had sent César an invitation to her *soirée*, although the du Plessis footman was turned away from the Hôtel Bouillon with a polite refusal. Relieved when I overheard the truth from that faithful servant as he reported the incident to his mistress, tears nonetheless swam in my eyes uncontrollably.

No lavish gown or flashing jewels relieved my sorrow, nor did La Fontaine's charming rhymes lift me from the depths of melancholy when he arrived later that evening, for I was consumed with bitterness. The drawing room spun around me, a whirl of flickering candlelight and pomaded *perukes*, bits and pieces of gossip reaching, then leaving, my ears.

"Did you hear, madame, that Athénaïs de Mortemart married the Marquis de Montespan at the close of January? A more luscious bride never existed..."

"The queen knows of La Vallière at last! Poor Marie-Thérèse, so witless..."

"...Guiche? By all accounts, he communicates with Madame daily. How, heaven knows, since their go-between, Montalais, was sent packing to the convent last April, sneaky girl..."

"Fouquet will win the day. The charges against him are severe, true, however, the prosecution's case was prepared by that oaf, Colbert. A more unimaginative gentleman never existed..."

Enough! All of you! I yearned to scream out. There I stood, jaded and worn ragged at age twenty-three. I would have made for my rooms, had a familiar tone not checked a departure. Who that voice belonged to, I could not say, for the well-dressed gentleman was disguised by a domino and wig.

"Marquise," he began, bending low to kiss my hand, then standing tall, "you have denied me the pleasure of your company since the court was last officially at Fontainebleau."

"What, monsieur? Do you mean to say in the autumn of sixty-one?"

"You remember me? What a good memory you possess, Mademoiselle Bijoux!"

"César!" I whispered, beside myself with joy.

"Come follow me up the stairs," he smiled, "for I have sorely missed you."

Following that blessed evening of unrequited love made right, my husband and I were inseparable. Moving his belongings to Charenton the very next day, César took up residence at the hôtel with Susanne's blessing. The past was not discussed for the present was ours again to share. Arcadia was forgotten and our marriage was embraced. Every hour I thanked the gods and especially Athena for my true love, and I promised them we would not be parted again. And that would have proved the case, had a certain group not involved my husband in a dangerous plot I shall refer to as the *Grand Design*.

Troubling signs that something was amiss came on the twenty-ninth of May of that same year. Four months of bliss had passed and no word had been sent me from the king regarding my status at court. Thinking myself forgotten by Louis, I was shocked when a royal messenger, accompanied by M. Cousinot, arrived at Charenton during the early hours of the aforementioned date. Roused by the two emissaries, the doctor informed me that the king had been taken ill at Versailles on the previous morn and lay dying, having contracted measles. I did not need to hear more. "Bleed me," I told the man who understood what was required to save Louis' life. César protested vehemently, taking me aside for a private conference.

"Let the bastard die. He does not deserve to be snapped from death's grip a second time."

"César," I implored in a hushed manner, "everyone deserves a second chance. Everyone."

"No. Leave it be. You cannot control Fate. The Dauphin is a babe, Philippe an idiot. With Louis gone, we shall put Guise on the throne without delay. France will be restored its Lost King, Knowledge will flourish, and your friend will regain her lover."

I walked away from him in disgust. How could a good person be so cold to another's plight? Locking my gaze with Cousinot's, I nodded. "Let us be done with this thing. Quickly."

My mother's champion collected a great amount of the life force from my lanced vein, so much that I became ill and feverish for a day, hovering on the edge of delirium. The thirtieth came, then the thirty-first and I recovered, as did Louis, the kingdom rejoicing that *le Dieu-Donné* had been touched by God yet again. Susanne and César were disappointed with me, of course, though relieved I had survived the ordeal. And, once lucid, the king ordered that the Court of Justice trying Fouquet be transferred from Vincennes to the Arsenal in Paris. The prisoner, along with his defense filling fifteen volumes, was moved to the Bastille on June the twentieth, his carriage surrounded by d'Artagnan's one hundred and fifty Musketeers, plus an added compliment of the same number. Three hundred soldiers to guard one man; a show of strength for those who would rescue the Lord of Vaux.

Louis, grateful for his cure, recalled Susanne and I to a court remaining in Paris for the summer due to the queen-mother's ill health. César returned to the Hôtel Bouillon; however, we agreed to meet daily, since I would be residing at the Palais Royal, not far from his family's home. The parting was terrible, true, yet we were strong in our mutual devotion and committed to one another alone. Convinced I would never be tempted to commit adultery in the future, I went to the Louvre for a private, royal audience with head held high. A nervous gentleman awaited who would not allow me to curtsey and who gathered me in his arms and held me with such tender respect that I could do naught but return the show of affection. Louis and I were bound in spirit for life, until the instant death would part us, and we both knew in that moment the burdensome nature of such a link. The words: *Bijoux, never leave me*, were enough to near rip my heart in twain; the only response I could make was to hold Louis tighter, as if to reassure he who had everything.

Guiche had been sent to the city of Nancy in order to check the aspirations of Charles IV, Duc de Lorraine, who was determined to rule his land single-handedly, without Louis' help. The old duke posed a threat to France in more ways than one, considering he was a descendant of Godfroi de Bouillon. And the Merovingians. Louis had no choice other than to crush Charles, so he went to war in August, joining the siege of the city of Marsal. Making peace with the rogue count, his Majesty watched approvingly as Armand proved himself on the battlefield, earning the reputation of a glamorous hero. When Marsal fell in mid-October, Madame fainted with relief, and the inhabitants of Paris built bonfires in the streets to celebrate the victory.

Louis came home triumphant to his people and the seven-month-pregnant Louise de la Vallière, while Guiche journeyed with his king's permission to Poland where he would nobly fight the Russians. 'Round the count's neck was said to be a locket safeguarding Henriette's miniature; never removed and left dangling close to the heart. When Monsieur's desirable wife heard of Guiche's tribute, she blushed and admitted, "He is dearer to me than I care to disclose." As did everyone, I believed the star-crossed couple to be hopelessly in love.

Perhaps because she was the subject of the court gossips, the Duchesse d'Orléans went to her husband's bed shortly after the fall of Marsal and conceived. The proud father-to-be announced the good tidings to his brother on December the eighteenth, whilst La Vallière lay abed at her new home, the

Pavillon Brion, suffering from the pangs of childbirth. No one was to know of the arrival of Louis' second male offspring, the Colbert couple had been enlisted to find a respectable family to raise the baby as their own, and poor Louise was barely allowed a look at her child following the difficult delivery. Such a secret was not easy to keep under wraps, and soon everyone was whispering about the little boy, Charles—the child that might have been mine had I remained Louis' mistress.

Relieved I had been spared the rigors of motherhood, I attended Mass with Louise at the Louvre on Christmas Day to offer formal thanks to my queen, Athena. The king's mistress was very pale and not well, but since maintaining appearances was all-important, La Vallière bravely endured the ritual. Holding her hand and ignoring the other Christian souls who chatted casually during the service about what nerve the girl from Blois had in coming to church, I saw the tears roll down her cheeks when the priest made mention of a babe in a manger. I could not understand what *Clarice* was suffering, denied her own son, yet I ached for her then—truly, I did.

Bright light reflected in glaring brilliance off a dusting of fresh-fallen snow is how I remember the advent of the year 1664. The year of my undoing. The end of this story. Where does one begin when describing one's own demise? Amusingly enough, the events precipitating my ruin were circumstances in which I had no active part; yet, the Past caught up with me, you might say, caught up with and grappled me with a vengeance. In all honesty, I am not surprised. Or sorry. What good are regrets? A waste of thought and nothing more.

No, I have made my peace with Athena and am prepared for what will come. The words of the ancient astrologer, Manilius, are constantly with me of late: *We begin to die as soon as we are born, and the end is linked to the beginning.* I pray the sage was correct, for death is all I may be certain of from this place of doomed souls. Faith is a difficult concept to grasp when one is accustomed to dealing in absolutes—Noctambule and his Immortality, the Company and its Lost King—yet I have learned to hold fast those things I cannot see, trusting that the reward will be to be held fast by the Universe, in return.

Monsieur Benserade's ballets, Molière's comedies, billiards, card games, pretty clothes—that was the sum of a life spent at court. The community of the privileged stayed on at the Louvre and the Palais Royal from January through March of 1664, then on to St. Germain and Fontainebleau for the spring. On May the fifth, Louis staged the grandiose, week-long entertainment for Louise at Versailles, recorded as the magnificent *Pleasures of the Enchanted Isle*. Excused from attending the unveiling of Paradise, the tales Susanne brought away from the event were wondrous. Most fascinating was the opening pageant in which Louis played the role of the knight Ruggiero, held prisoner on a magical island by the mystical lures of the sorceress, Alcine.

The Game of Princes was fast coming to a close and had I been more perceptive, I would have seen the finale commencing and run. However, blinded by the desire to remain ignorant of what was transpiring around me, the clues went unnoticed. While the court feasted and danced at Versailles, I met César in Paris and my husband's tense, quiet air should have warned me something was afoot. I chose to overlook his serious mien and ask no questions. A stupid thing to do because during the early hours of June the twenty-first, I woke to a frantic youth and his equally disconcerted valet. That the two had dared to venture to the château from which César had been exiled amazed me, not to mention the late hour of their arrival, close to the hour of two in the morning.

"Bijoux, arise. Time is of the essence."

"What? *Mon Dieu*, what has happened?" I queried, rubbing my eyes.

"We must travel to England tonight..."

"You and I, César? Why?"

"No," he said, "Eustache and myself. We witnessed a terrible thing, Bijoux," he started, then could not finish, clearing his throat in an attempt not to weep.

"What? I do not comprehend."

"Fouquet's trial ended yesterday," d'Anger supplied, "and my former master was immediately taken from the Bastille to a remote dungeon near to here, at Moret, by a force of two hundred and fifty."

"No! Why the sudden transfer from the capital? What is going on?"

"The Company has been planning to assassinate Louis for months," César confessed, regaining his composure. "Eustache and I volunteered our services for the job, and we were set to strike, then Fouquet was moved. Not wishing to place our friend in danger, we came here, near to midnight, to confer with the Duc de Guise. The three of us were meeting in an antechamber, when d'Artagnan and a dozen Musketeers strode into the apartment, swords drawn, with orders to apprehend our leader."

"What? They took Guise?"

"Bound and gagged him and placed a velvet hood over his head," Eustache answered.

"We were as good as dead," César continued, "when then the sous-lieutenant recognized my face. He ordered us to surrender our weapons or else Guise would perish. Since we have both sworn to give our lives for the Lost King, the decision to throw down our rapiers was not a difficult one to make. Then d'Artagnan sent his men on ahead with their prisoner, who made not one sound or cry for help."

"Louis kidnapped his enemy! We must all flee."

"No, darling, you must stay. Remain behind and search for me once my disappearance becomes apparent, then have me declared dead when I do not surface. Go to my brother, Godefroy, and tell him everything. Do you understand? I shall send for you later, when your safe passage may be assured."

"César, you confuse me! How did you escape d'Artagnan?"

"His words were: *Because you are the beloved of she whom I love, I shall spare you on two conditions. Leave France immediately, never to return, and speak of this night to no living soul. The Duc de Guise will not be harmed, though his death will be announced and mourned throughout the land. Your Lost King is finished.* Then he marched us to the edge of the forest, blade at our backs, and declared that he would personally run us through if we were ever seen in the kingdom again."

"Promise to send for me. Do not forget your wife," I begged, rising to say farewell, too stunned to protest. Eustache looked away in disapproval when my mouth met with his friend's in a deep kiss, and I did not care. To lose a great love and regain it had sent me to my knees in gratitude at Charenton; then to lose that lover again was cruel, too cruel.

"Good-bye, my darling," I heard someone say to me as if in a dream, "we shall be reunited."

"Go, away. You were fools to come back. Go before you are found out."

"I shall never consider it foolhardy to love you. And Bijoux, Arcadia will be ours."

"Not if you are dead," I replied, biting my lip, doing everything in my power not to scream, not to rant, not to curse the parents who had borne him and me. "Hurry or I shall be made a widow for sure."

He kissed me again in parting and was gone, although not before I gave him half of mother's jewels. The rocks were the sole valuables I could gift César; that and a pledge of love.

Later, sobbing into a pillow for fear of being overheard, I realized that not only Henri de Guise, yet all of us, were lost; another generation adding to the lies of history, distorting the truth. Louis would announce his rival's death, another corpse would be found to lie in a noble crypt, and the Company would be put to rest.

And that is why I have decided to write this confession, for I have signed a contact with my conscience, nothing more.

The Duc de Guise died in his sleep at the age of fifty on June 20, 1664. Or, that was the official version. His coffin went to the tomb closed and many at court remained stony-faced during the funeral procession. The Company's leaders were informed, through unofficial channels, that their Lost King had become a hostage and that any attempt to harm Louis Bourbon would result in the prisoner's death. Having pledged their allegiance to Guise for as long as he was alive, no other candidate for the throne could be put forward and nothing would be done to endanger the duke's safety. Susanne got word to the proper people that César had witnessed the abduction and fled France; later she was told by those same contacts that he and Eustache had escaped and were living in London with a sympathetic gentleman. My husband would contact me when he was granted permission from his elders to do so and not sooner. Had I not feared Louis' spies, I would have gone to England myself. Which is exactly what I should have done, for Guiche had come home to Paris.

The count returned from his exploits, although not to be seen at court unless he behaved, according to the king. The ladies and gentlemen alike were eager to be reacquainted with their darling Armand and hear from his own lips how the cherished locket had saved him from death when a musket ball had glanced off the gold bauble during battle. Henriette, nine months pregnant, said nothing concerning her beau's narrow escape. Nor did I.

Officially a widow by July, I was happy that my former friend had not been allowed at Fontainebleau, and would be cooling his heels in the capital until the duchess delivered. Philippe's heir came two weeks later and Monsieur was thrilled that his son, the new Duc de Valois, was healthier than Louis' Dauphin had been when born. The Company must have been pleased with the birth, as well; a descendant of the house of Guise might possibly inherit the French throne. Should any ill befall the imprisoned Lost King, another candidate existed in the form of Monsieur's male progeny by way of Henriette.

Summer dragged on, d'Artagnan granted a short leave from his duties to rejoin the court, and because I did not wish my Musketeer to know I believed César alive, Susanne and I journeyed to Charenton. How Guiche found out about our move, I cannot say, yet he came calling. Not allowed inside the hôtel on Susanne's expressed orders, the count took to throwing pebbles at the upstairs windows in an attempt to attract my attention. When that strategy failed, Armand resorted to musket shot and ruined several expensive panes of glass. Furious, Susanne found an old saber and went outside swinging the sword with gusto, fully prepared to cut Guiche in two. Forced to laugh at my friends' antics, I negotiated a truce and agreed to meet Guiche at St. Sulpice if Susanne might accompany me as chaperone. Amenable to those terms, the count wore an impeccable suit of white sateen overlaid in ebony thread to the appointment; that and a winning smile reminding me of our many shared escapades.

"Marquise! Free at last!" he laughed, head thrown back. "Are you no longer in mourning? I had this outfit designed when I heard de la Tour was dead. Rather virginal, is it not?"

"Naughty Armand," I snickered, pressing my lips to an angular cheekbone in greeting. "Could you show some respect for the deceased, at least?"

"Come here," he ordered, taking my face in his hands and kissing me with real ardor. "God in heaven, how I have missed you these past two years, my darling Bijoux."

"You have been gone for twenty-nine months to be exact, monsieur, and during that absence, I have not heard reports of your infatuation with the Marquise de Cinq-Mars," came my cool retort. "All tongues at court report you in love with Madame—you wear her image about your neck."

"You mean this? Yes, you are correct, the locket does contain the portrait of that lady whom I completely adore."

"Have you no heart? Why did you ask me to meet you if you meant only to abuse my feelings?" I asked, pulling away from his touch. "This was a mistake."

"Get back here, hellcat. Open the case for yourself; look inside."

"No," I answered, struggling against the grip holding me in place. "Let go of me or else I shall call out to Susanne for assistance."

"Do not be foolish," he grinned. "Take a peek. What do you have to loose?"

"My dignity."

"Fine. I shall do the honors, then. Here," Guiche offered, holding up the talisman with his free hand, "know the truth."

What I saw did not register clearly in my mind. A white face, bared shoulders, red curls wisping about a long, graceful neck. "Marion?" I said in utter stupefaction.

"No, not that Marquise de Cinq-Mars; rather, her daughter."

"You...you took my image into battle?"

"Yes," he confessed and gathered me to his lean frame. "And you saved my life. Did you hear?"

"Of course, who did not? Then why the story concerning Henriette?"

"To protect the lie Louis believes to be true concerning your celibacy. Speaking of which, you have been with no one since I left?"

"No one," I answered falsely, physically drawn to Armand despite my better judgment to stay away from his person. "You have been in my thoughts constantly."

"Where awaits the Marquise du Plessis?"

"Outside, in her carriage. Why?"

The count surveyed our surroundings. "This place will do," he murmured, moving me back towards a stony wall. "Say that you will agree to my terms."

"What terms?"

Guiche lifted me with little effort, pinning my upper torso to the rough surface behind me, pushing up my skirts. "We have been parted for too long, Bijoux. Have you not longed for my touch?"

Before I could answer him, he managed to undo his breeches and produce a very firm testament to desire. Crushing me against the wall, I cried out when the count took possession of me, so strong was his passion.

"You are amazing," he praised while I tried not to writhe beneath him. "Utterly amazing."

"Armand, this is sacrilege. Stop..."

"You love me. Do not deny yourself pleasure."

"What if one of the priests finds us out?" I whispered, digging my nails into his back.

"Let him learn something," was the comment I received, along with a physical experience that left me dazed, lowered to the floor onto trembling legs.

"Athena forgive me," I said, crossing myself for the first

time in my life, sinking to my knees. "That was a terrible thing to do, here, of all places."

"Why?" Armand replied, kneeling down to join me when he had adjusted his suit. "Why is such an act sinful when I love you more than life?"

"You are so corrupt," I answered with real despair, "yet I cannot resist you. Louis I could turn away from—you, I cannot. What do you do to me? How might this be?"

"Here, I brought you a gift from Poland," he offered, reaching inside of the embroidered *justacorps*. "I was going to wait and present it to you later; however, I think now the appropriate time."

"What is this?" I asked, examining the vial he held. "Spirits of some sort?"

"No," he said slowly, uncorking the porcelain container carefully. "A rare elixir. Drink half, then return the remainder."

Taking the proffered reliquary from the count, I sniffed at its valued contents. "How odd. Your potion smells of blood."

"The essence of the Father offered for the forgiveness of sins, Bijoux."

As Guiche spoke those words, I knew their meaning without further explanation. The liquid smelled foul, putrid—the red cruor reeked of death—of Noctambule.

"How did you get this? When?"

"Drink," he urged, "drink."

Armand's hand guided mine to my lips, his eyes became glazed and focused on some distant object, his lips curled in a beatific way. Gazing at the one who would take me into eternity, who truly loved me more than living itself, I instantly knew that if I did taste of the *vampyre's* fluid that I would be lost. Forever. The realization that leading a good life was not so much about making choices, yet rather about doing the right thing for the right reason without reflection, flashed into my head.

"No, Armand, no," I said firmly, lowering the small container. "This is absolutely wrong."

"Bijoux, come be an Immortal with me. We shall be together for all time."

"Do you know what this is?" I yelled as I stood. "This is poisoned filth, Armand—this is not a gift! This is a curse that will *damn* you for all time. Your spirit is already eternal; more wonderful and brilliant than you are capable of imagining. You are a part of the Whole, of a magnificent creation. Armand, listen to me, please! Noctambule is a false prophet."

"Give it back," he menaced, rising as well. "If you will not partake of the blessed stuff, I shall."

"You are *sick*! Take the evil brew," I screamed, flinging the slender vessel in his direction. "Wear it with pride, Guiche."

The front of the white satin coat became splattered with black, handiwork dissolving in the acrid stain. Armand gazed down at his chest in shock, ripping the jacket from his body and placing the soiled fabric in his mouth, devouring the material as would one possessed of a fever.

"I shall be like him," he cried out, eyes wild. "And so will you."

"*Never*. You are damned!" I raved, thoroughly beside myself. "You were so dear to me. How could you do this thing? How?"

"We are two of a kind, Bijoux. Ask yourself that same question when I am gone."

I then fled St. Sulpice, never to enter the Company's headquarters again. The place is as horrible as Versailles, believe me, as wicked as the lair of the *vrykolakas*, both drenched in blood and falsehood, both inhabited by their own daemons of conceit and hypocrisy.

What became of Guiche, I do not know. We did not communicate after the incident, and although I returned to the court housed at Vincennes in September, for d'Artagnan was gone to guard Fouquet at the Bastille, the name of the handsome count was not mentioned. Sick at heart over what had transpired between us, I kept to myself, concerned that Armand may have been transformed into a *vampyre*.

Considering my melancholy mood, I spent much time with Nabo, who was also sad. Louise de la Vallière was pregnant again, but so too Marie-Thérèse, which seemed strange since

Louis was rumored to no longer visit the queen at night. The king's indifference concerning his conjugal duties had left his wife desperate and as a consequence, her constant companion became morose as well. The black boy, or youth, I should say, came to me for advice, though I could comfort him little. For, what I did not understand was that Nabo loved Marie-Thérèse not as a mother or sister, yet rather as a woman. That fact became very apparent on November the sixteenth, 1664, when the queen began a premature labor. Her screams of pain were horrendous and could be heard throughout the château; Philippe came scurrying into my room, his face was as white as a winding sheet.

"Louis is mad with rage, he says he is going to kill you...."

"What?" I inquired, setting down the book of La Fontaine's verse I had been reading and rising from the chair near to the fire. "Your commentary is not amusing, Monsieur."

"The queen has given birth to a black baby girl, all hairy and monstrous. Marie-Thérèse is dying, Bijoux, and the king blames you!"

"Me? Why? He should probably look to Nabo for an explanation if what you say is true."

"You know that and I know that—will my great brother admit his wife's adultery?"

"Might the child live?"

"Perhaps. If she does, she will be sent to the convent of Moret and be hidden away for life. Louis believes you cursed the child, that you put a spell on his wife during a Black Mass..."

"Get out!" a voice boomed as the king entered the apartment. "Leave now, Monsieur, or you will live to regret your lack of action."

Philippe obeyed. As he exited the room, my old friend gazed at me for as long as he dared, as though he knew we would never meet again.

"You damnable strumpet! You haughty slattern!" the king fumed. Using his walking stick, Louis struck me hard on a forearm in a fit of anger. I shrank back, not believing what I was a witness to.

"Majesty, you cannot think I would harm your wife or any child. Why?"

"Because your master told you to turn my issue into a Moor," he spit back at me. "Because Noctambule wished to punish me! Well, I shall put you in a place where no one may get to you, madame, a place with high walls and barred windows. Where you will be watched, witch!"

"I am innocent, sire. Louis, your Majesty, please, stop...."

"You are of Lucifer! If either my wife or the infant die, you go to the stake!"

"You cannot be serious, we are bound together for the remainder of our lives; I saved you twice from death, recall? You know better than to accuse me of this thing."

"I was going to take you back. Once Noctambule was dead and I had tasted the blood of his veins! You could not wait for me, and rather chose *his* side. You said that you loved me, *recall?*"

"I do, in my own way, I do."

"You are a liar, madame. And I have tolerated your inconsistencies for the last time! You should have been locked away long ago."

"As was *Guise*, Majesty?"

I could not resist the temptation to have the final word. Louis' mouth opened slightly and he stared at me. Then the thin lips pursed and he shook his ornamental cane.

"Who told you that? Answer me!"

"I am a witch, *recall?* Certainly, sire, you show me more honor with that title than had you elevated me to the rank of duchess."

"Guards," the king yelled. "Guards, in here at once."

Two Musketeers appeared. Louis regarded me with real contempt, then announced, "Conduct the Marquise de Cinq-Mars to the Bastille. Place her in a cell far from Monsieur Fouquet. She is to speak to no one, allowed no liberties or correspondence and above all, no confessors. From this day forward," he said, shaking a finger at me, "you cease to *exist*."

"More honors, sire," I mocked. "I receive the same treatment as does a lost king."

Louis XIV wished to murder me, yet he walked away instead. Back to his ill wife and Nabo's black daughter, back to the duties of leading a nation. The soldiers escorted me from the château to a carriage and here I sit, in the Bastille, not far from my old neighborhood of the Marais.

I was allowed clothing, mother's jewels and a few books after some time. Madame de Besmeaux, wife to the prison's governor, attends to me herself, although she is allowed to feed me, bathe and clothe me, and nothing more. If I talk to the woman, she does not reply. No communication has transpired between me and another person for three hundred and fifty-three days. Naught but one visitor, although he may not be counted in the scheme of things, for a *vampyre* is supposedly not human.

Luna was high in the sky three nights past and I was watching its transit through the heavens, peering out the slits in rock that are my windows out onto the world. Lonely, I thought of César, contemplating a sweet dream of rescue, yet knowing full well the futility of dreaming such a dream. Going to bed, I closed my eyes, yet sleep would not come. Too tired to write and not inclined to read by candlelight, I arose and paced, listening to the clanking of the sentries' armor when the Guard changed at what I reasoned to be the hour of midnight.

Then, a strange thing occurred. A key turned in the tumbler of the lock to my donjon and a man entered, dressed as a courtier and dragging a soldier's lifeless body behind him. Thinking someone from the Company had come to liberate me, I reached for my cloak, ready to depart into the October blackness.

"Who are you?" I asked the gentleman, drawing close to him with a lit taper, so I might better see his features. "Did the Company send you here? Did you kill the sentry?"

The stranger raised his head and I beheld a striking face, more ashen than any I had ever looked upon, disturbingly familiar. A somewhat older version of a visage I had gazed at, on canvas, in the company of a king.

"*Father?*" My free hand flew to my mouth and I drew a deep, sharp breath of cold air.

The apparition made no reply.

"Are you a *vrykolakas*?"

"You owe me the explanation," was his answer. "Why do you deny me?"

"Surely, monsieur, you are mistaken. I hardly knew you while you lived...yet, that voice...you are the same entity who spoke to me upon my arrival in this wretched place!"

"Yes, I live, Bijoux Cinq-Mars, and my name is Noctambule, He Who Walks in the Night."

"Surely you are not the old man whom I met in the woods years ago?"

"The same."

"You are also my father? You are Monsieur le Grand? How?"

"Why not?" the uninvited guest laughed aloud.

"Tell me," I challenged. "If you were beheaded, then how did you become a *vampyre*?"

"Who said I was beheaded? Do I resemble a corpse? Your mother filled your head with much nonsense, my girl. Did you light candles on my natal day, March the twenty-seventh, too?"

"How did you escape the henchman?" I asked hesitantly, giving no heed to his acrid tongue.

"A long story," the man sighed, taking a seat on the mattress. "Let us say a certain benefactor, a Monsieur Roger, secured my release, and another's head took the place of mine on the block."

"Liar! Who are you? And why do you speak of a Monsieur Roger? I have never heard that family name at court."

"Perhaps because Monsieur Roger needs no introduction at court, needs bend no knee to any Bourbon...he is an Immortal, the greatest gentleman of science ever born, my Savior, my God! One who also supposedly died, in the year 1580."

"Another *vrykolokas*?"

"Hardly," he scoffed. "A most august man of learning who discovered the Philosopher's Stone, my dear. An ebony powder taken from the dross of electrum which, when mixed with blood, renders one deathless."

"Not possible. And how did you escape the Guard at Lyons? Richelieu's own soldiers escorted you to the block! This is too fantastic a tale, " I moaned, sitting next to the mysterious caller on the pallet, head in my hands. "Why do you torment me so, monsieur? Have you no pity?"

"Your unfortunate, crazed uncle, Martin, made the same query of me," the man sighed. "He would take such a beating whenever I cut the tapestries at Chilly to resemble shoes; only a simpleton would do such a thing. Oh well, Martin is now dead, *truly* dead," he chuckled, paused and then remarked, "Why do you think I spoke of Taphos, all those years ago in the woods of Versailles? Is it not a myth of eternal life, of a father betrayed by his daughter for love of a prince? Do you not see, my Bijoux, that one may have days without end, that the Greeks told no children's story, no false promise of a life *after* death?"

"Yes, you know of the myth of Taphos, yet you do not understand its meaning, imposter. Comaetho was a queen, the ruler of a glorious isle devoted to charting the seas by the stars!"

"So, you have read the Classics, child?"

"The noble Homer wrote: *The return of my sire is past all hope; and should rude Fame inspire from any place a flattering messenger with news of his survival, he should bear no least belief from my desperate love*," I answered. "He also disguised Athena as Mentes, King of all the Taphians studious of navigation. Yes, I know of Homer and Apollodorus, too. Enough to know of the Taphians. Enough to know that your rendering of the tale of Comaetho is a false one."

"The Black Powder enables me to see beyond the crack in the mirror of this world's illusion and myth. A trait of... immortality? No, of your *vampyre*? A fitting title; perhaps I shall adopt it, with your approval, marquise."

I stared at the lifeless soldier and grimaced. "I do not wish to become a *vrykolakas*. Do not force this legacy of blood-drinking and black powder upon me, I beg of you."

"You will do as I say."

"As does Guiche?"

"He is better suited to you than is that de la Tour, whose father was a greater fiend than was Richelieu. Let us say that I did not mourn the Duc de Bouillon's death."

"Guiche put you up to this," I reasoned. "Incorruptible flesh is nothing save a soul to go with it and yours, sadly, monsieur, is lost."

"Do not lecture me, Bijoux," the agent directed as he stood, the same arrogant expression I had seen in a painting enlivening his pasty features. "Let us be gone from this place and I shall escort you to where you will be a true queen, to the woods of Versailles."

"And you will act as consort?" I snorted.

"No, the one who saved me from rot and decay wishes you to rule by his side. Forever."

"You are serious? Get out!" I shouted. "Get out of here at once! I would rather die a thousand, painful deaths than swallow one drop of your wretched concoction. You are nothing to me! If you are my sire, then I say this in spite: poor de Thou...poor François-Jacques de Thou!" I began to sob, then cried out, "By Athena...*Jacques*!"

For that wronged youth of Cinq-Mars' conspiracy had been the same Jacques who had come back to me in the Marais as a messenger of the deities.

The true or false Cinq-Mars' eyes, still almond-shaped and exquisite, stared into my own. I could not look away. A scene, or vision, came to me of being led up steep, wooden steps to a scaffold. A stump of wood and an executioner were in attendance. And so was a man, watching from a courtyard alcove.

"*No!*" I cried out. "*No. Stop!*"

"You saw Jacques' end? Do not despair, for you might avoid all that and leave with me. Now."

"Never," was my tearful response. "Never. Only love is forever."

"What?" the courtier growled. "What is this heresy you speak? Love has no might."

"Athena comforts and protects me for I am Her daughter. Athena comforts and protects me..."

"Be still!" he demanded.

Strength began to surge through my being and I felt alive. And certain. Certain that if I did go to the block, Pallas would not forsake me. I would not take my father's path, even were the story true and Cinq-Mars alive. I could not. And the reward of *that* faith would come, I knew.

"I deny you..."

"You are doomed," he warned. "Doomed for the grave."

"I believe in the omnipotence of Athena Tritogeneia."

"Stay here, then, with that foul corpse to keep you company. You had your chance. Die."

"You may walk, yet you are dead in spirit. I deny your worthless powder, your damned days without end. My spirit will live forever, *Monsieur le Grand,* whoever you may be."

"Fool. Stupid, miserable fool. You are not of the house d'Effiat, surely."

"No, I am not."

Henri Coiffier de Ruzé, or his proxy, threw five *sous* at my feet, walked out of the cell, slammed the door and turned the key.

Father? Could my father be a full-fledged *vampyre,* more hideous than any daemon of legend? That was the thought occupying my mind while I felt for a sign of life, pushing back the sentry's helmet.

"Maupertuis!" I cried. He was barely alive. Unbuckling a metal breastplate, I removed the protective covering and loosened the Musketeer's tunic. Then a plain underskirt was ripped along the hemline and that cloth was used to staunch the wound bleeding on the marquis' neck. Cradling the dark head in my lap, I begged Lisette's husband to live.

"Étienne, awaken! Please, Athena, help him."

The corporal was dying and nothing could be done. Or so I deduced until I spied the dagger hanging from the leather strap around his waist. Without stopping to weigh the consequences, I took the knife, sliced open one of my fingers and placed the cut in the marquis' mouth. The pain was intense, although I did not care, for reviving him was more important.

"Take me," I prayed. "Take me in exchange for Maupertuis."

I raised my head and 'twas in that very moment of despairing that I saw the goddess Athena. Standing before me in the rude keep of the Bastille prison, long golden locks streaming over the famed goatskin aegis, shield and spear in one hand, a spindle of silver in the other. Her eyes were a most glorious tint of blue, robes soft shades of saffron and indigo. Trapped in a stupor, I stared, mouth agape, not knowing what to say. Slowly, I began to stand, wounded hand outstretched, then a noise caused me to look away from the vision of smiling loveliness.

A cough erupted from the Musketeer's chest. Followed by another and another, then a long gasp. Kissing the corporal's forehead, I actually laughed when he bit down hard on the foreign object that was jammed between his teeth.

"Étienne, 'tis I, Bijoux. Look at me. Do you see Pallas?"

"What...am I doing here? I was attacked outside, in the corridor. A man, or beast, stuck his dagger into my neck..." he reached for the makeshift bandage.

"Be still. You will live, I promise, by the sword and spindle of..."

She was gone. Completely vanished. Although I cared not a whit, for one sighting of Wisdom is all a mortal needs to feel complete. All the years of suffering and injustice were swept away by one divine nod. I had been blessed, indeed, by the Queen of Heaven.

Fortunately for me, and also for Maupertuis, the Musketeer carried two sets of keys, which meant he could resume his post and not explain what he was doing paying me a forbidden call. While he was reluctant to lock me back up, I assured my jailer he had no choice, for if I were to go missing, the soldier who was on duty would be the individual to suffer the consequences.

"I took you from Lisette once in the past, and that was one time too many," I explained. "Allow me to make amends to my friend in this way."

"You are too good," was his reply as he touched my cheek in fond remembrance. "I plan to speak to d'Artagnan concerning your plight; no Musketeer knew whom we guarded."

"Be wise and remain ignorant, my friend. Nothing may be done to save me."

The marquis took my advice, it seems, for Madame de Besmeaux has not been strange with me since the incident, nor have I heard from Charles de Batz. I have ceased to breathe as far as anyone but the governor and his wife are concerned. So be it. César will find himself a new wife in England or perhaps turn to a life of debauchery. Anything is possible, I suppose, considering what I have seen and done in this short lifetime.

Anything.

To reflect further, however, is a waste of ink, for what will be, will be. My final testament I have scratched onto a stone found here within my keep, a copy of a lament once written to Louis' grandfather, Henri IV, by the beautiful Queen Margot, born a Twin and a captive of her tumultuous passions: *Is it a crime to love? Is it right to punish me for it? There are no ugly loves, no more than there are beautiful prisons!*

I have recorded nothing for several days. This scribble is to say someone is outside my keep, unlocking the door. A man in a brown, hooded robe is entering the room. A monk or confessor, no doubt. The inevitable has arrived in the dead of the night.

Louis need not keep me alive as he does the Duc de Guise. And he has decided to end my life on what I believe to be Martinmas, if I have calculated correctly. I am reminded of the old maxim: *His Martinmas will come, as it does to every hog*, or, put more bluntly: *All must die*. Louis does indeed possess a dry wit, especially when I consider that St. Martin's scribe was none other than St. Sulpice.

And my tormented father's brother evidently a Martin, too.

Prayerfully the shade of Cinq-Mars was correct when he claimed the pain of the ax need not be feared.

My dearest César, I regret we did not reach Arcadia, unless that is the place where our spirits will meet again. If not, I shall wait for you forever from the Shades.

In the supposed last words of another member of my

accursed house, "*Adieu* till then—forever awaits—and forever again, *adieu*."

Sworn this eleventh day of the eleventh month, sixteen hundred and sixty-five, by Bijoux de la Tour d'Auvergne, a humble astrologer who was privy to the Grand Design of more than one Lost King—and a proud daughter of the true Virgin, Pallas Athena.

EPILOGUE
Pallas Athena

Bijoux did not face the executioner on that cold, November eve, nor did she remain a prisoner of Louis XIV for the remainder of her life. I know of what I speak, for I am she, the same woman who wrote that memoir fifty years prior. Soon to be age seventy-five in this year, seventeen hundred and fifteen, currently residing in an Italian village with an old man as my companion, one César de la Tour.

Twelve months ago, while sorting through personal papers, diaries and the like, I came across the manuscript that had come with me to a foreign land from the Bastille. Flipping through the yellowed pages, I remembered long forgotten days, bittersweet recollections of the strange events which had shaped my youth, stories I had so wanted to share, yet could not until now. So, in the interest of bringing truth to light, I am composing this afterward and sending the entire work to a publisher in Amsterdam that prints such clandestine publications under the traditional pseudonym of Pierre Rouge.

Thus, when you arrive at this juncture, please allow an elderly lady the courtesy of finishing her tale. You may be interested to read what became of the main characters involved in this accounting; their individual histories have proved to be most amazing.

To begin, the brown-robed friar of the Bastille was none other than the courageous d'Artagnan. Alerted to my dilemma by the sympathetic Maupertuis, the sous-lieutenant planned not only an escape route, he also donned a disguise after relieving his drunken friend, Monsieur Besmeaux, of the goaler's keys and making for where I was hidden away. After donning a habit similar to my friend's, I collected Marion's jewels along with the damning memoir, and the two of us fled the fortress to a carriage awaiting our arrival on the Rue St. Antoine.

Once inside the coach and temporarily safe, d'Artagnan breathed an audible sigh of relief.

"We are heading for the Pont Neuf. From there you will travel by barge up the Seine to Normandy and the coast. One of my own men will escort you to a ship bound for Portsmouth, England. Upon your docking at that port, another agent will meet and travel with you to London where you may rejoin your husband, whom you and I both know is certainly not dead. I have arranged a false identity for you and this matter will be discussed with absolutely no one."

"You located César!" I cried with joy.

"I have kept my eye on de la Tour and the valet, be sure, ever since Fontainebleau. Understand that the three of you are *persona non grata* in France. Never return. If you do, you will share Monsieur Fouquet's fate for certain."

"I never wish to see France again, monsieur. Believe me. Do tell, what finally became of the Future?"

Charles frowned. "The judges deliberated for six months following the trial's close. Then, on the twenty-second of December, 1664, Fouquet was found guilty by a jury of twenty-two peers. Nine voted for death, the remainder banishment. The king decided that imprisonment for life was better justice, so Louis transmuted the sentence and Fouquet was taken from the Bastille that very day, bound for Pignerol. My men and I took him there, Bijoux, and the terrible journey ended on January the seventeenth, the day that we arrived at the prison. Nicolas near died from the cold weather and his own despair. 'Twould have been kinder if he had, I think."

"Is that why you freed me?"

"Go to England. Be happier than your friend, Charles de Batz."

"Charlotte-Anne?"

"We have separated. My wife has taken to convent life, leaving me with the boys."

"And I am sure that you are short for coins. Here, take these," I insisted, dumping half of the jewels onto his lap. "'Tis the least I might do to repay your brave deed."

"Bijoux, no, you will have need of money abroad."

"I shall be fine. May we stop at the convent of the Hospitalières before I leave? I must say good-bye to someone."

"Have you lost your senses? No."

"D'Artagnan, please..."

"Bijoux Cinq-Mars," he smiled, "you would try the patience of St. Anthony."

We drove on to the Place Royale and gained access to the convent due to the religious vestments we wore. Françoise was hastily brought out and I made the sign of the cross before her. Handing La Belle Indienne the remaining jewelry, all but for the bee César had gifted me, and the emerald ring I had worn on our wedding night, I winked at the widow.

"For your lost souls, Madame Scarron. Remember our pact and speak to the king. Much hangs in the balance."

"Bijoux," she whispered, staring at me and then at the treasure. "*Mon Dieu*, where did you get these stones? They are priceless..."

"Be still," I cautioned with a finger to my lips. "In your hands, Françoise, the gems will do much good. In mine, they were useless. Return the jewels to the people of France—they are the ones who paid for them."

"I shall," she promised, tears coming to her lovely, serene eyes. "Count on it. Where are you going? Stay here with me for a spell."

"That is not possible. Forget my name. Remember the ruby ring and show it to Louis. He will understand the meaning."

"What if the king will not see me?"

"Françoise," I said, hugging her good-bye, "save dear Louis from Noctambule's lies. Help him to rule wisely and justly."

D'Artagnan and I left the good women absorbed in her

own thoughts, too overcome by the unexpected visit to wish us *adieu*. I was convinced in my heart, however, that Françoise would not disappoint me in regards to the rather odd request I had made of her and, true to her word, she did not.

As Jacques did prophesize, Madame Scarron eventually came to court, sponsored by Athénaïs de Montespan, the woman who had supplanted Louise de la Vallière in 1667 as the king's *maîtresse en titre*. The brazen Montespan's wanton behavior made my mother's own sordid life resemble a saint's in compare. *Quanto*, as she was called, reigned as the uncrowned Queen of France for near thirteen years, bearing Louis seven bastard children who were legitimized prior to her fall from favor. Françoise Scarron was appointed nursemaid to the brood, and thus came into direct contact with the king on a regular basis. His Majesty, however, did not care for the widow, thinking her too pious and learned for his royal company.

Yet, when Athénaïs and her maid, Justine des Oeillets, were rightfully accused in 1680 of suspicious dealings with La Voisin and the Abbé Guibourg, of participating in Black Masses where infants were offered up as human sacrifices to the Princes of Friendship, Louis turned to the steadfast, sensible governess for solace and guidance. Montespan lived in disgrace with her contemporaries at the court's permanent home, Versailles, while La Voisin was burned at the stake and Guibourg sent away to an undisclosed prison, sentenced to remain chained to a wall until the end of his miserable life.

Françoise must indeed have shown Louis the ruby ring, for when Marie-Thérèse died in July of 1683, the King of France married the widow Scarron in a secret ceremony held at Versailles shortly after his first wife's death. The *Roi Soleil* has since become a model of Christian piety, and a solemn and dignified atmosphere has descended upon his court. Françoise, for her part, has used a certain inheritance to establish a school for poor girls of good birth, an academy of feminine learning named Saint-Cyr. Many in France may detest the lowly born woman who has indeed been raised high; however I, better than anyone, realize the debt owed that lady. Because of one person's unfailing belief in goodness, a king and a country have been spared an evil charade, and the lair of the *vrykolakas* has been transformed into the most beautiful palace that man might construct.

I safely reached the shores of England and later the arms of my husband; the joy we shared at our reunion defies description. Suffice it to say that I conceived on my first night spent in London, a son of the Virgin born in September of 1666, duly christened Godfroi. I protested the choice of name, yet considering César's pride in his son, not to mention the pain I had caused my poor husband over the years, I consented to allow our child to bear the intended honor. Robert Boyle sent a note of congratulations to mark the arrival of our son, as did several other influential English citizens.

That same gentleman who had decoded *The Key of Solomon* was in fact a leader of the Company of the Blessed Sacrament. The latter group announced its disbanding in 1665, stating that their membership could no longer operate in its present form. The declaration was made in an attempt to protect the Duc de Guise from death and to provide a cover of anonymity for others. Boyle died in 1691, yet the Company lives on, led by the distinguished English intellectual, Isaac Newton. Because of César's continued association with the Order, I have been kept abreast of happenings in France and the reports have not all been pleasant ones.

Anne of Austria and Madame de Choisy both died of vile breast tumors in the year 1666. Deeply affected by his mother's passing, François-Timoléon, the Abbé Choisy, transformed himself into a young noblewoman, lived in Paris as Mademoiselle Sancy, and received a proposal of marriage from a chevalier. When his relatives complained of his strange comportment, the twenty-two-year-old transvestite fled to Italy where he spent his entire inheritance at the gaming tables. Returning to France in financial disarray, François settled in Bordeaux where he made a name for himself as an actress of some renown. His career on the stage ended when he impregnated a fellow thespian. The abbé has had many adventures, catalogued in a memoir. At present, Mademoiselle Sancy lives at the abbey of Saint-Seine, not far from the city of Dijon, where he entertains his fellow clergymen by dressing up in Jeanne-Olympe's old gowns, antiquated fashions he does not have the heart to discard.

Philippe and Henriette were not destined to enjoy a long or fruitful union. The reason for the ever-widening schism between the couple was a courtier by the name of Philippe, the Chevalier de Lorraine, with whom my Petit Monsieur developed a fascination that would prove life-long. Following the death of his heir in 1666 and the loss of his mother in that same year, Prince Tyrannus became quite debauched. The Palais Royal was the scene of many a heated battle between Henriette and her husband, for the proud wife was infuriated by the manner in which Philippe's lover ruled in her own establishment. Lorraine was given lavish apartments, gifts and his own retinue; Minette, ignored.

Then the king decided to favor his sister-in-law with a delicate mission: act as liaison between France and England, approach Charles II with proposals from Louis to dissolve the Anglo-Dutch alliance created to thwart the militant, French neighbor who had invaded the Spanish Netherlands in 1667. Philippe was jealous of his wife's diplomatic appointment and demanded of his brother that he be entrusted with government secrets, as well. Louis laughed and Henriette ventured to the court of England on May 26, 1670. She returned from the assignment to be greeted by political triumph and death: an end rumored to have been hinted at by her husband and engineered by Lorraine.

Henriette expired at Saint-Cloud in the early morning hours of June 30, 1670, aged twenty-six, and gossip was rife that someone had poisoned a glass of chicory water that the Duchesse d'Orléans drank daily. Her cruel malady had been too sudden for another cause. The doctors declared a colic had done-in the young Madame; the courtiers claimed otherwise. Back in England, Charles II was inconsolable at the loss of his sister, and many on both sides of the Channel feared a war erupting as a consequence. Louis hastily ordered an autopsy and the most renowned physicians agreed, including Vallot and Cousinot, that Henriette had suffered from *choleramorbus* and not from poison. Their findings were duly reported in the *Gazette de France*. Yet, the whispers spread that Madame's own steward had confessed to the king that he had seen Lorraine's agent treat Henriette's glass, not water, with white powder and that the duchess had tasted of poison when her lips touched on the crystal.

Neither Lorraine nor his accomplices were punished, and Monsieur was freed from a wife whom he had found most irritating. When forced by his brother to remarry the rather masculine Princess Palatine in 1671, a stipulation of the wedding contract stated that only Monsieur, not the second Madame, would be allowed to wear the deceased Henriette's jewels.

To think that Fouquet, d'Anger, La Rivière and Nabo would share the same prison continues to astonish me, even now that the four are dead—a complicated tale at best. Six months following his imprisonment at Pignerol, in June of 1665, the Angle Tower housing Fouquet was damaged by a large explosion when lightning struck a nearby powder magazine. The governor of the fortress, Monsieur Saint-Mars, transferred the important convict to La Pérouse while repairs were made. Fouquet did not return to Pignerol until August of 1666, and with him came two valet-prisoners, one being a certain Moor named La Rivière. Both Marie-Thérèse and the official mistress were again with child and Louis was taking no chances of another black baby appearing in the royal nursery. Nabo was shipped to Dunkirk, returned to an officer of the Company of the Islands of America. La Rivière, who had been providing Louise de la Vallière with riding lessons, was thrown into chains and sent away to serve the man who was allowed to speak to none but Saint-Mars.

Eustache d'Anger remained in London until the year 1669, when in June, he devised a plan to return to France and work for the Company as a spymaster. My husband begged his friend not to venture back onto dangerous territory; d'Anger would not listen. To free the Lost King was what the youth desired, and he would not be swayed from the perilous delusion.

By August of that same year, Eustache was lodged in Pignerol, no doubt flushed out by d'Artagnan; the warrant for the valet's arrest had come from the king himself. Saint-Mars was instructed that no one, not one single person, was to speak to d'Anger, and a special cell was constructed for the newest jailbird. Then, in December, the governor of the outpost uncovered a plot to free Fouquet: two men had penetrated the walls of the city, entered the prison by offering bribes and had spoken to Nicolas directly. The leader of the operation was found to be the faithful La Fôret, the ex-gentleman of the chamber, who was promptly captured in Switzerland, returned to Pignerol and hanged in full view of Fouquet's window. The advent of April 1670 found Eustache kept in a high-security cell, Guise holed away on the Isle of Sainte-Margeurite and Fouquet without any hope of release. However, the intrigue was not finished, as the Future was to unfortunately discover.

Nabo arrived at Pignerol sometime prior to May of 1670, the month and year that Henriette journeyed to England from Dunkirk, the court following to celebrate her departure. Preparations for the royal visit had been made months in advance of Madame's arrival and a coordinator had espied the queen's onetime companion in the care of the town's mayor. Knowing full well that Marie-Thérèse would become distraught if she glimpsed the Moor, the agent informed Louvois, Minister of War, of the dwarf's presence. Nabo was arrested and sent to Pignerol. The son of Le Tellier—François, Marquis de Louvois—was a cruel and sadistic man whose death in 1691 was not universally mourned. That minister had been entrusted with certain details concerning the Secret by Louis XIV and was frantic that Fouquet or d'Anger might get word to the outside world concerning the Company and its aims.

So, Louvois most decidedly did not desire that Eustache should speak to Nicolas, for then the truth concerning Guise's fate might leak out. The king had entrusted him with the most delicate of missions, and Louvois corresponded constantly with Saint-Mars regarding the very important prisoners in his charge, stressing repeatedly that neither Fouquet nor d'Anger be given the opportunity to tell the world a single utterance.

September of 1674 marked the death of one of Fouquet's two valets, a man named Champagne. Saint-Mars had previously requested that d' Anger be allowed to attend to Nicolas, and Louvois had flatly refused. In January of 1675, however, the war minister relented, aware that another suitable prisoner-valet was near impossible to secure, and Eustache was allowed to serve Fouquet, yet only when La Rivière was not in attendance. Eventually, that edict was revoked and the tall Moor met the sullen youth; one may only imagine what the two discussed. And I know these events to be true for M. Fouquet's own son was allowed his father's papers upon the Future's death, diaries which contained much information concerning the unfortunate man's daily routine.

Many interesting developments concerning the last five years of Nicolas' life have since come to light, although in the interest of brevity, I shall disclose naught but this: on March 23, 1680, on a false promise of freedom from Louvois, one of Fouquet's valets poisoned his former employer while attending to him in his cell at Pignerol. The act of betrayal was to damn the turncoat for life and to transform my husband's former friend, Eustache, into a convict that the world will know many years from now as The Man in the Iron Mask. A young man named François-Marie d'Arouet has been selected and is being groomed by the Company to write this story at a later date.

Do not scoff. The temptation to doubt my word is great, though I ask that you follow the details with a spirit of acceptance. Remove the mystery from history and view the world and people for what they truly are, not for what others, who wish to deceive you or to keep their secrets to themselves, would have them seem to be. Rest assured I would not lie to you concerning these matters, for I have nothing to gain in their telling. Just as I gave a bag of jewels to Françoise gladly and of my own volition, I give you, the reader, this: knowledge. And such information is a powerful tool when used wisely and well.

For Henri, the fifth Duc de Guise, did not die on July 20, 1664, as is carved on his tomb. Rather, he expired in the year 1694, aged eighty, locked away on the Isle of Sainte-Marguerite. Who succeeded him as Lost King I do not know; however, Eustache d'Anger took Guise's place in the vacated cell, a mask of metal covering the valet's features so that the membership of the Company would not discover that their candidate was dead.

Following Fouquet's murder in 1680, Louvois instructed Saint-Mars that the goaler should let it be known that the dead man's servants, La Rivière and d'Anger, were being released. The two were then to be treated as corpses themselves, relegated to the furthest reaches of the citadel: a keep in what was known as the Lower Tower. Kept hidden until September of 1681, Eustache and his cellmate were then transferred with their warden, Saint-Mars, to a place known as Exiles, and great pains were taken that none should be privy to their removal from Pignerol. Once settled in their new home, the pair lived in complete seclusion, alone with each other and their terrible, shared secret.

January of 1687 saw the proud, once handsome La Rivière succumb to dropsy. Immediately, Saint-Mars was informed that he would be moving with d'Anger to the Isle of Sainte-Margeurite in May of that same year. And move they did, the face of Eustache covered with what will be later known as the infamous iron mask. When the Duc de Guise expired in that place, d'Anger, the valet who had witnessed his kidnapping, took the place of the Lost King. Saint-Mars and "Guise" moved to the Bastille in 1698, the unfortunate one wearing a hood of velvet and there, Eustache died on the nineteenth of November, 1703.

Louis XIV has seemingly survived his tormentors, it is true, although I wonder, does he ever consider if Bijoux Cinq-Mars still lives? Or did he give up on finding me once d'Artagnan fell in battle in 1673? Certainly the royal edict banning astrology from the French Academy of Science in 1666 was a sure sign of royal disfavor, although work progressed on the Paris Observatory and the brilliant Italian astronomers, Cassini and Coronelli, were lured from their homes abroad to conduct research for the King of France, thus continuing the noble study of the stars in the land of my birth.

Without a doubt, d'Artagnan protected me from Louis' wrath. I was not to hear from my Musketeer again, though I did have the sense that I was being watched, in a kindly fashion, from the moment I set foot on English soil. The sous-lieutenant, of course, blamed the Company for my escape, and Louis, of course, believed the trustworthy Charles de Batz. That much I heard from César's connections and my worries were slightly dispelled, yet where the Gascon had said I might be hiding was not disclosed. Not that the ruler who had sent me to the Bastille probably cared, for affairs of state, Montespan and plans for war occupied his hours. Because of France's invasion of Holland in 1672, leading to the long, drawn-out battle of Maëstricht during the following summer, d'Artagnan was kept busy, too, playing soldier and conquering hero.

Thus, when I heard the report that Charles had been taken from the world on June 25, 1673 in the Spanish Netherlands, during the aforementioned siege, I cried for days and could not be comforted. Leading his troops into battle, the man to whom I had first given my heart was struck in the throat by a musket ball and mortally wounded. Every year since, I light a candle for my protector on that day and shed many a tear for the most valiant member of the Grand Musketeers.

As if d'Artagnan's death was not a cruel enough blow, Guiche was taken five months later, on November the twenty-ninth, at Kreutznach, dead at the age of thirty-five. Henriette's passing inspired the count to lose any good sense he may have possessed and to become more and more reckless in combat, his feats of daring the talk of the Continent. I confess that, despite his faults, I certainly adored Armand and miss him more with the passing of time rather than less.

And what became of Susanne, the Marquise du Plessis, you may ask? I have outlived her, poor lady, for she met her end in 1705, near to ninety-five years of age, a permanent fixture at Louis' court, reconciled with a formerly estranged daughter from her unhappy marriage. Like Susanne, I, too, was reunited with a relation and in the process, solved the mystery of Noctambule's identity.

Jean d'Effiat, an older brother of my father, had evidently become bitter when Monsieur le Grand's disgrace meant he was to lose the rich revenues provided by the prosperous monastery of Mont St.-Michel, a gift from Louis XIII in the days when Henri was the favourite at court. Turned to a life of depravity by his family's sudden reversal of fortune, the priest Jean decided to keep company with a fringe element of society; in so doing, he devised a scheme involving a character of legend said to bestow immortality to ladies famed for their beauty, notably courtesans.

When I was informed in a roundabout fashion, by a friend who was to follow me from France, that a paternal uncle existed whom I had not supposedly met, I decided to test the theorem that perhaps two brothers might share one likeness. I had recently moved to Italy and, despite the fact that Monsieur Poussin sadly passed away in 1665 while living in his comfortable villa outside the city of Rome, I managed to make the acquaintance of the painter's daughter, who was kind enough to show me his sketches for the famed painting, *The Shepherds of Arcadia*. The lady explained that the artist's intent had indeed been to portray the goddess Athena, standing with her traditional shepherd priests before an inscribed tomb that made mention of Arcadia, the land of that goddess' birth. *Et in Arcadia Ego* was not only Virgil's wording, the poet's own grave could be found in the same spot dedicated to the maiden Tritogeneia.

Poussin, by way of Virgil and Athena, had encoded a valuable piece of information into the tableau: a clue as to the spot where a valuable treasure of antiquity might one day be found—Naples—formerly known as *Parthenope*—quite literally, the town of the Virgin, the celestial Virgo Athena, whose own temple in Athens was named the Parthenon. Perhaps another reason why a Duc de Guise fancied the title King of Naples as his own. Be that as it may, I took a fragment of the information and had it relayed to uncle Jean in the form of an anonymous note, inviting him to the Vatican to discuss the matter with a certain Cardinal Cesare Bologna. The bait was successful and as I had suspected, Monsieur Noctambule's ruse destroyed. Interestingly enough, the five *sous* deposited with me in the Bastille was the reenactment of a Cinq-Mars tradition at Chilly, whereby the master of the house gifted servants that said same amount when a relation died—my coins would later pay for a messenger's time.

Have I neglected to make mention of anyone who figured prominently in the tale of the *vampyre*? Ah, yes, one person in particular comes to mind. Dear, gentle André Le Nôtre. A shining example I have held before me as proof that being a good person is, in and of itself, its own reward. The exceptional man lived to the old age of eighty-seven, leaving this world on the fifteenth of September, 1700, dying peacefully in his sleep at the small house located in the gardens of the Louvre where he had spent the majority of his days.

Famed for his skill as a gardener, beloved by all for his humble and kind nature, Le Nôtre became a boon companion of Louis XIV, inspiring the usually vain and pompous king to don red clogs and join him, on occasion, in the tending of the beautiful flowers at Versailles. Refusing to utter one bad word concerning any, Le Nôtre was to meet and embrace the Pope as he would a brother, with a joy that moved the Pontiff to happy tears. André's home was always left unlocked, for he wished any, who were so inclined, to view his magnificent coin collection whether he was about or not. Many were the visitors and never did a gold piece go missing. Such was Le Nôtre's reputation and such was the respect he was accorded without prompting; a truly remarkable human being. When he was gone, leaving the king his paintings by Poussin, Louis XIV wept bitter tears, saddened by the loss of the most honest gentleman he had ever had the honor of calling a friend.

Now, you may ask, have I been content during the last half century spent in exile? For the most part, yes. Adjusting to new lands and foreign tongues was difficult, assuming a false identity, worse. For the sake of my children and grandchildren, the name our family employs at present will remain a mystery, although it is my sincere wish that one day a relative of mine will return to France. We shall see. When Louis dies, the general consensus maintains that Philippe's son by the Princess Palatine, the current Duc d' Orléans, will rule as Regent until the king's heir and great-grandson comes of age.

As for César's brothers, Emmanuel was made Cardinal Bouillon and in 1685 was involved in a great scandal, along with his brother's wife, Mazarin's niece. Told to go to Rome on account of the disgrace, the youngest Bouillon died there this year. Godefroy, who separated from the poison-peddling Marie-Anne in 1690, lives a life of retirement in Navarre. The duke and my husband do not communicate and the Hôtel Bouillon has been practically deserted. Perhaps the time will come when the old palace will be occupied by the rightful Duc de Bouillon's heirs, and César's mother may rest easier.

Does it matter, in the end, though, all the titles and the *gloire*? I think not when I consider what I have experienced; I think not, indeed.

Which brings me to the final passages of this memoir. A last comment on that which I have learned on the journey Jacques promised I would take down different roads. I have traveled a few dangerous paths and made many mistakes, yet in the name of that great goddess, Pallas Athena, who once wandered disguised as a ruler of Taphos, I would only recommend this: be more tolerant of one another. Through my work with César in the laboratory, I have learned the language of alchemy and now understand Athena's ancient declaration, recorded by the poet Homer: *I am Mentes. King of the Taphians, coming with ship and crew on a voyage to foreign men, being bound for Temesa with cargo of iron, I shall bring back copper.* Yes, iron is the metal of the planet Mars and is associated with war and bloodshed; copper the metal of Venus and love. On my own personal odyssey, I have most definitely experienced the truth back sage Athena's words.

Previously I believed that forgiveness was an overrated virtue, for I cannot imagine absolving a Guibourg who slit babies' throats or a Louis who locked innocents away for life because of the color of their skin. Certain conduct should not be forgotten. However, I have discovered that forgiving slights and purging oneself of hatred is to be recommended. To illustrate my point, I shall share with you a personal anecdote and then be done.

Godfroi was four years of age when I took him to play one summer's afternoon in a field beyond the modest villa of our new home in Italy, a move made necessary by d'Anger's arrest months earlier. Because I was carrying a second child, I rested comfortably under a shade tree with my friend, Lisette, discussing with her what my husband and her husband, one Étienne, might be doing whilst in Rome, meeting with the business colleague of a certain Monsieur d' Éstoiles. We began to speak of times past, of the nurse Des Oeillets and Madame la Grande, of that day when we realized on the road from Nantes to Fontainebleau that we were connected in an unexpected way.

Glancing up at my son, who was pretending to fight a stick duel with an imagined opponent, I thought of Marion and an incredible sadness overtook me. I could not hear Lisette's words as I reflected on how mother had never seen me cavort amongst wildflowers, how she had never known the joy of loving another soul completely and unselfishly. She had been so pitiful a parent that I felt genuine sorrow for her loss and guilt that I had truly hated her for so many years. Breaking into deep sobs, the realization came upon me that I had to make amends to Madame la Grande in my heart, or else I would never be free of the horrors I carried from childhood. I wanted to fondly remember some aspect of the woman who had borne me, yet how, I asked the bright Sun and the blue sky above, how was I to perform the miraculous?

The opportunity arrived on the eve of the feast of All Souls, 1670. The fifth year anniversary of my liberation from the Bastille was ten days in the offing when the pangs of childbirth began. The baby that I carried on the afternoon of my epiphany concerning Marion was ready to appear on that night when the veil between the spirit and the waking worlds is said to be the thinnest—I was to bear a child born beneath the sign of death and rebirth, imprinted with the mark of the Scorpion.

Any mother reading this account need not be reminded as to the very forgettable pain accompanying the birthing process; no man may be apprised of the arduous labors mothers everywhere face in order to create flesh and bone. Within three hours' time of the onset of my ordeal on that memorable eve, Lisette was holding my hand tightly while the men waited outside the bedchamber, soothing her sweat-drenched friend as best she could.

"Where is the damnable midwife?" I swore, in a panic. "Why has she not yet arrived?"

"There, there," the fair one smiled reassuringly, "the lady comes highly esteemed. She will appear shortly."

"If not, I swear, I shall curse the wretch a thousand times..."

"No need," a clear voice responded and a very tall lady then entered the room. Removing her shawl, the nurse turned so all I might view was a long, blonde plait snaking down a plainly attired back. Water splashed in a basin, a spasm came and went, and I beseeched Lisette for a piece of tanned hide to bite on, such was the agony.

Lying prone on at least a comfortable pallet, my watery eyes attempted to focus on the aid who had only moments before arrived. In and out of waking and dreaming, a pair of piercing blue eyes came into view; later, a pale, noble forehead; then, a face in its entirety.

"Blessed Athena!" I screamed out, more in disbelief from the realization that the goddess had returned to me and was standing a stone's throw away, than from any discomfort.

"Breathe," both stalwart ladies—the mortal and the Immortal—coached. "Again."

By all the gods, I swear this accounting to be true. So true that when a shrill cry was heard, I did not mind the intrusion of a very concerned César, accompanied by our son and Lisette's mate, such was my bewilderment.

"Darling," my husband began.

"A name," interrupted a regal, imperious tone. "A name for your daughter, madame."

Trembling, I looked away. A name. For a lifetime. Worthy a goddess.

"Madame?" She insisted.

"Marion de Lorme Cinq-Mars de la Tour," I whispered in a barely audible voice, much to the combined amazement of the assemblage, Athena excluded. César's expression of profound surprise caused me to repeat, more loudly, "Marion de Lorme..."

Monsieur Maupertuis began to clap and whistle with approval, while my husband's laughter resounded through the simple, stone house. Lisette held little Godfroi's hand, tears running down her beautiful countenance, for she truly understood the emptiness of never having had a mother to love.

Pallas grinned, turned and made haste before I could speak. Marion and I were at long last reconciled—a babe began to wail, tiny fingers reaching skyward to touch the Queen of Heaven's many jewels.

For, in the end, we are all Wisdom's children, do you not agree?